THE
VAMPIRE
GENEVIEVE

WARHAMMER™
HORROR

• THE VAMPIRE GENEVIÈVE •
by Kim Newman

DRACHENFELS
GENEVIEVE UNDEAD
BEASTS IN VELVET
SILVER NAILS

THE WICKED AND THE DAMNED
A portmanteau novel by Josh Reynolds, Phil Kelly and David Annandale

MALEDICTIONS
An anthology by various authors

INVOCATIONS
An anthology by various authors

ANATHEMAS
An anthology by various authors

THE HARROWED PATHS
An anthology by various authors

THE HOUSE OF NIGHT AND CHAIN
A novel by David Annandale

CASTLE OF BLOOD
A novel by C L Werner

DARK HARVEST
A novel by Josh Reynolds

THE OUBLIETTE
A novel by J C Stearns

SEPULTURUM
A novel by Nick Kyme

THE REVERIE
A novel by Peter Fehervari

THE DEACON OF WOUNDS
A novel by David Annandale

PERDITION'S FLAME
An audio drama by Alec Worley

THE WAY OUT
An audio drama by Rachel Harrison

WARHAMMER™
HORROR

THE
VAMPIRE
GENEVIEVE

A WARHAMMER HORROR OMNIBUS

KIM NEWMAN

WRITING AS JACK YEOVIL

WARHAMMER HORROR
A BLACK LIBRARY IMPRINT

Drachenfels first published in 1989.
Genevieve Undead first published in 1993.
Beasts in Velvet first published in 1993.
Silver Nails first published in 2002.
This edition published in Great Britain in 2021 by
Black Library,
Games Workshop Ltd.,
Willow Road,
Nottingham, NG7 2WS, UK.

10 9 8 7 6 5 4 3 2 1

Produced by Games Workshop in Nottingham.
Cover illustration by Toni Deu.

See Warhammer Horror on the internet at

blacklibrary.com

Find out more about Games Workshop
and the worlds of Warhammer at

games-workshop.com

Printed and bound by CPI Group (UK) Ltd, Croydon, CR0 4YY

WARHAMMER™
HORROR

A dark bell tolls in the abyss.

It echoes across cold and unforgiving worlds, mourning
the fate of humanity. Terror has been unleashed, and
every foul creature of the night haunts the shadows.
There is naught but evil here. Alien monstrosities drift
in tomblike vessels. Watching. Waiting. Ravenous.
Baleful magicks whisper in gloom-shrouded forests,
spectres scuttle across disquiet minds. From the depths
of the void to the blood-soaked earth, diabolic horrors
stalk the endless night to feast upon unworthy souls.

Abandon hope. Do not trust to faith. Sacrifices burn
on pyres of madness, rotting corpses stir in unquiet
graves. Daemonic abominations leer with rictus
grins and stare into the eyes of the accursed. And the
Ruinous Gods, with indifference, look on.

This is a time of reckoning, where every mortal soul
is at the mercy of the things that lurk in the dark.
This is the night eternal, the province of monsters
and daemons. This is Warhammer Horror. None shall
escape damnation.

And so, the bell tolls on.

CONTENTS

Drachenfels 9

Genevieve Undead 193

Beasts in Velvet 403

Silver Nails 613

    Red Thirst 615

    No Gold in the Grey Mountains 657

    The Ignorant Armies 675

    The Warhawk 709

    The Ibby the Fish Factor 767

Drachenfels

I

The first Genevieve Dieudonné knew of the treachery of Ueli the dwarf was the prod of a blade-end in her right side, just above the hip. Cloth and skin dimpled, and she felt a wasp-like sting. There was something about the knife. It slipped under the flaps of her padded leather jerkin and into her flesh.

Silver. The knife was edged with silver.

Her body took fire at the touch of the charmed metal. She felt the weapon withdrawn and half-turned, ready for the killing thrust, for the heart-strike. She heard herself hissing and knew that her face – the face she had not seen for six centuries – was twisted, eyes reddening, sharp corner-teeth bared. The wet hole in her side closed, tingling. Blood trickled down the inside of her britches.

Somewhere, on one of the nearby crags, an unclean bird was squawking as it devoured the weakest of its young. Rudi Wegener was on his knees, trying to wrestle Sieur Jehan down, a hand pressed to the spewing hole in the scholar's throat.

This pass they had come to, this stony and unfruitful spot high in the Grey Mountains, was a filthy place. It was late afternoon and she was still slowed by the sun; otherwise, Ueli would never have dared strike at her.

She brought her ungauntleted hand up, palm out, and placed it beneath her breast, shielding her heart. The knife leaped forward and she saw Ueli's face contorted in a feral snarl. His thumb-size teeth were bloodied from Sieur Jehan's neck and she could see torn fragments of skin caught between them.

She pushed outwards and caught the knifepoint with the centre of her hand. The pain was sharper this time, as the bones were displaced. She saw the point pricking outwards from the back of her hand. Flesh parted and the red metal emerged from between her middle knuckles.

Even through her slow-flowing blood, the silver caught the last of the sunlight. Ueli swore and spat red foam. He put his shoulders into the attack and tried to push her arm back, to staple her hand to her chest. If the silver so much as scraped her heart, there would be no more centuries for poor Genevieve.

She could ignore the pain of the sundering of her flesh – by tomorrow, there wouldn't even be the slightest scar – but the silver burned

inside her. She shoved the dwarf back, the blade sliding through her
hand by agonizing inches. She felt the hilt against her palm and made
a fist, gripping the dwarf's weapon with still-strong fingers.

With his free hand he punched her in the kidneys, twice. She was
ready for that; the blows didn't bother her. She kicked him square in the
chest and he backed away from her, leaving his knife in her blood-slick
grasp. He reached for the curved dagger in his boot and she backhanded
him. The blade that stuck out like a spiked extra finger from her fist
carved a deep rut across his forehead. Her hand hurt as the knife jarred
against Ueli's skull.

The dwarf fell back, blood in his eyes, and three darts appeared in
a diagonal line across his chest, sunk to the feathers in his ribs. Anton
Veidt had used his trifurcate crossbow well. Genevieve pulled the knife
out of her hand and threw it away. She made and unmade her fist as
the stinging wound closed. Ueli still staggered as Veidt's venom shocked
his body, the little smears of death coursing through his veins, reaching for his brain. The bounty hunter mixed his poisons with unrivalled
skill. Stiffening, the dwarf fell.

Erzbet, the dancer-assassin, looped her wire noose around Ueli's neck.
She pulled it tight, cinching until she was satisfied of his death. Genevieve held out her bloodied hand. Oswald von Konigswald was there with
a kerchief, which she took from him. She licked the slit clean, savouring the tang of her own blood. Then, she wrapped the kerchief tightly
about her hand, pressing shut the already-healing wound.

'Dwarf bastard,' said Veidt, hawking phlegm at Ueli's dead face. 'You
never know when one's going to turn.'

'Less of the dwarfish bastardy, bounty hunter,' said Menesh, who had
joined them with Ueli. Genevieve had always supposed they were related.
'Look.'

The traitor was growing in death. At least, his skeleton and insides
were expanding. His dwarf shell and clothes split, and showed raw
pink and purple through great tears. Human-sized bones twisted on the
ground, their wet contents pouring through the remaining, ragged strips
of Ueli's skin.

Oswald stepped back, leery of getting his fine Tilean leather boots in
the mess. Ueli's still-glaring eyes popped and maggots writhed in their
sockets, spilling over stretched-tight cheeks and into his beard. His tongue
slithered out of his mouth like a strangling snake, twisted down impossibly long towards his chest and then died. Erzbet voiced her disgust
loudly as she pulled her noose free.

'He was no true dwarf,' said Menesh.

'That's certain,' said Rudi Wegener, who had given up stanching Sieur
Jehan's wounds, leaving the doctoring to his tame warlock, 'but what
was he?'

Menesh shrugged, his harnessed weapons rattling, and touched the
still-spreading body with his boot-toe. 'A daemon, perhaps. Some creature of Drachenfels.'

The dwarf kicked Ueli's swollen helmet off the wide ledge. It fell, striking the ground long after they had forgotten it.

The stink of the grave wafted away from the remains of the dwarf-seeming thing who had ridden with them for three months. Ueli had shared quarters with them and broken bread with them. He had never spared himself in their fights and Genevieve knew that without his deftly-thrown knives she would have been orc-meat several times over. Had Ueli always been a traitor to them? Always in the service of Drachenfels? Or did his treachery begin a few moments ago, when the shadow of the Fortress fell upon him? How little she really knew about any of her companions in this adventure.

An adventure! That is what it had seemed when Oswald von Konigswald, eyes ablaze, had recruited her in the Crescent Moon. She had been working in the tavern at Altdorf, trading one drink for another, for a hundred years or so. Longevity brings a heavy burden of tedium. Genevieve, suspended eternally between life and death since the Dark Kiss, had been willing to do almost anything to relieve her boredom. Just as Anton Veidt was willing to do almost anything for gold crowns, or Sieur Jehan for a chance to increase his learning, Rudi Wegener to expand his glory, or weeks-dead Heinroth to achieve his cherished revenge. And Oswald? What was Oswald – Crown Prince Oswald, Genevieve reminded herself – willing to do almost anything for?

An adventure! A quest! The stuff of ballads and chap-books, of legends and tavern tales. Now, with so many dead behind them and two more dying in her eyesight, Genevieve was less certain. Now, their business here seemed just a nasty, messy job of murder. A nasty, messy life had to be ended, but murder it still was.

'Sieur Jehan?' Oswald asked.

Rudi, the ruddy cheeriness gone from his bluff bandit's face, shook his head. The scholar was still bleeding, but his eyes showed only white. He had stopped kicking. Stellan the Warlock looked up from the corpse.

'He had no chance. The dwarf bit clean through his throat to the bone. He'd have bled to death if he hadn't been strangling for lack of air. Or the other way round. Either would have done for him.'

'Enough,' said Oswald, 'we must go on. It's nearly nightfall. Things will be more difficult after dark.'

Difficult for the others; better for her. The sun dipped below the horizon and Genevieve felt her night-senses come back. She could ignore the echoes of pain in her hand and side. Above them all, the fortress of Drachenfels stood against the crimson sky, its seven turrets thrust skywards like the taloned fingers of a deformed hand. The clifftop gates were, as ever, open, a maw in the side of the stone. Genevieve saw the eyes in the darkness beyond the gates, half-imagined unwelcoming shapes flitting past innumerable windows themselves shaped like eyes.

This was where their adventure would end. In a castle as grey and jagged as the mountains around it. A fortress older than the Empire and darker than death. The lair of the Great Enchanter.

Drachenfels.

II

Constant Drachenfels, the Great Enchanter, had been old, had been ancient, long before the first birth of Genevieve Sandrine du Pointe du Lac Dieudonné. And that, she never allowed herself to forget, had been six hundred and thirty-eight years ago.

In true life, Genevieve's home had been the city of Parravon, in the east of Bretonnia, where her father was minister to the First Family and her sisters were counted among the greatest beauties of a court renowned throughout the Known World for its great beauties. Drachenfels had been more often abroad among men in those days and wont to show his metal-masked face in the courts and palaces of Bretonnia and the Empire.

The stories were fresher then. Tales were told in a whisper of his vast debauches, of his inconceivable crimes, of his devastating rages, of his titanic sorceries, of his terrible revenges and of his single defeat. Drachenfels had been one of the powers of the world. She supposed, though half-forgotten, he still was. He had only been bested once, at the hands of Sigmar Heldenhammer. Strange to think that Sigmar had been deemed a man then. A hero, but still a man. Now, the priests called him the patron deity of the Empire. Sigmar was gone, no one knew where, but the monster he had once humbled was still here. The evil of Drachenfels was still very much with the world.

As a girl of twelve, four years before the Dark Kiss, Genevieve had seen Drachenfels in person. He rode through Parravon with his army of the dead, bedecked in gorgeous silks, wearing his mask of gold. The heads of the First Family's militia captains bobbed open-mouthed on pikes. An assassin dashed from the crowds and was torn to pieces by Drachenfels's rotting lieutenants. Daemons danced in the air, bearing away pieces of the martyred daggerman. Genevieve hid behind her sisters' skirts, but got a good look all the same.

Her father's friends had discussed Drachenfels in her presence. His origins were unknown, his weaknesses unknown, his powers unlimited, his evil depthless. Even his face had not been seen by living man. She had tried to conceive of a hideousness under the mask, a hideousness so dreadful that it would make the skull-and-meat faces of Drachenfels's armies seem attractive. Or, as her sister Cirielle suggested,

14

a handsomeness so awesome that all who gazed upon it were struck dead in an instant. Cirielle was always the silly one. She had died of the plague some fifty years – a heart's beat, really – later.

Drachenfels had his tribute from Parravon, but slew the First Family nevertheless. As an example. Genevieve's father also perished, served with other public officials as a meal for one of the Enchanter's attendant daemons. Six hundred years later, Genevieve could summon little thirst for vengeance. Her father would have lived another twenty, thirty years – thirty-five at the most – and would still be lost to her memory. It's hard to think the premature death of a mayfly any great tragedy. She sometimes found the faces of her parents, her sisters, her friends at court, popping into her mind. But mostly those were lost times, a life that had happened to someone else.

A few years later, years that were now minutes to her memory, Chandagnac came to her uncle's house. Chandagnac with his dark eyes and plaited beard, his needle-like teeth and tales of the world's youth. She received the Dark Kiss, and was born a second time, born into this half-life.

Chandagnac was dead, too. He had always been too flamboyant for their kind and made too many important enemies. Finally, the priests of Ulric hunted him down and pinned him to the ground with a length of hawthorn while they sawed off his head with a silver scimitar. That was three hundred years ago. She was the last of his get that she knew of. There were many others older than she, but they lived far to the east, on the borders of Kislev, and kept to themselves. Occasionally, mindless dead things would come to the Crescent Moon, drawn by her presence, and she would turn them out, or put an end to them, depending on how she felt. Sometimes, they could be a nuisance.

Centuries had passed and everything had changed many times. Empires, dynasties, wars, alliances, cities, a few great men, numberless little ones, monsters, arts and sciences, forests; all had come and gone like the seasons of the year.

Genevieve was still walking the earth. And so was Drachenfels.

She wondered if he felt the same suppressed kinship for her that she felt for him. There were songs that they alone of all the world would recognize, once-famous names that they alone knew, extinct animals the taste of whose meat they alone could recall. Probably, he did not feel for her. Probably, he was only dimly aware of her. She was what she was, at best the cousin of humanity, but Drachenfels was beyond even that. He had ceased to be any kind of a man long before he rode into Parravon. The face he kept beneath his bland collection of metalwork masks would not remotely resemble anything else that drew breath.

Tonight, one way or another, she would look upon that face. Perhaps long-dead-and-dust Cirielle was right after all. Perhaps she would not survive the sight. And perhaps, after six and a half centuries, she would not mind dying all that much.

She had followed Drachenfels's career down through the ages, kept a mental note of the kingdoms sacked and bled dry, the plagues unleashed, the tributes exacted, the daemons set free. He had been quiet for a few centuries now, quiet in his impregnable fortress in the Grey Mountains. Some believed Drachenfels dead, but there were too many evidences of his continued handiwork throughout the Old World. The wizards who frequented the Crescent Moon would talk about him sometimes, about the disturbances he was making in that sphere beyond time and space where the greatest of enchanters venture in search of the vast principal beings of the universe. They knew enough not to sign up with Oswald's expedition. Some said he was too old to be the monster he once was, but Genevieve knew that immortals grow rather than diminish in strength as they put years behind them. Some ventured that the Great Enchanter was voyaging within himself, trying to plumb the depths of his own darkness, to summon the worst of his personal daemons. One song, sung only by a strange-visaged Bretonnian minstrel, suggested Drachenfels was meditating his many sins, finding the strength to battle again with Sigmar and that this time he would vanquish the wielder of the warhammer forever, bringing about the end of all things.

She had heard all manner of rumours, but none had touched her more than any other tavern gossip until Prince Oswald von Konigswald, son of the elector of Ostland, walked into the Crescent Moon. He told her that Constant Drachenfels was preparing to return to the world and take over the Empire, and that the Great Enchanter would have to be stopped before he could bring down fiery doom upon an entire continent.

That had been three months ago. Oswald was a year or two older than she had been when Chandagnac had kissed her. She supposed him a handsome youth and could see around him the aura of the great and noble man he would grow into. He would be elector after his father, of course. The elector of Ostland could sometimes sway the others completely and hold the course of the Empire in his hands. Never had a candidate opposed by Ostland succeeded. Never. Oswald's father lived in a comparatively modest palace, but upon occasion Luitpold himself came to his court as if the elector were Emperor and he the supplicant. If Luitpold's son, Karl-Franz, were to succeed him on the throne, he would need the support of Oswald's father. Indeed, since the elector had married late and was now nearing the end of his middle years, the Emperor would soon need the support of Prince Oswald.

Genevieve had heard that the prince was a serious youth, a young man capable of outstripping all his tutors in everything from gastronomy to philosophy, and who was as skilled with the Estalian guitar as with the longbow of Albion. The tavern jesters told jokes about the grave-faced boy who had, it was rumoured, once shamed Luitpold into withdrawing a proposed edict against harlotry by asking if the Emperor intended to set an example by burning at the stake a certain substantial Tilean fortune teller much in evidence at court functions since the demise of the lady empress. And Genevieve had read, with interest, a slender but acclaimed volume of verse in the classical style, published anonymously but later revealed, through a careless boast on the part of the elector's tutor-in-residence Sieur Jehan, to be the work of Oswald von Konigswald. Nevertheless, she had been unprepared for his ice-clear eyes, the strength of his handshake and the directness of his speech.

In the back room of her tavern, Oswald had offered her his wrist. She had declined. Aristocratic blood was too rich for her. She depended upon the friendless, the unmourned. In Altdorf, there were many without whom the Empire, indeed the world, would be much improved. And they had been her meat and drink since she had decided to settle down.

Sieur Jehan was with the prince, a bagful of scrolls and bound books with him. And Anton Veidt, the bounty hunter who cared for his weapons as others care for their women. Oswald knew about her father. Oswald knew things about her that she had herself forgotten. He offered her a chance for revenge and, when that hadn't been a temptation, appealed to her need for variety, for change. The young Sigmar must have been like this, she thought, as she sensed the excitement Oswald was suppressing. All heroes must have been like this. Suddenly, rashly, she longed for a taste of him, a flavour of the pepper in his blood. She didn't mention her rush of lust, but somehow she knew that he had seen the desire in her, and answered her longing with a need of his own, a need that would have to be postponed until after the accomplishment of his current mission. She looked into his eyes, into the eyes in which her face was not reflected and, for the first time in centuries, felt alive again.

Sieur Jehan laid out the proofs of Drachenfels's recent doings. He read aloud the testament, obtained through a medium, of a wizard who had lately been found flayed and boneless in his chambers. The dead sorcerer alleged that all manner of magical and daemoniacal forces were converging on the fortress of Drachenfels, and that the Great Enchanter was reaching new levels of power. Then the scholar talked of a plague of dreams and visions that had been reported by the priests of all the gods. A masked man was seen striding over a blasted land, between the fires that had been cities and the deserts that had been forests. The dead were piled high as mountains and the rivers were nine-parts blood to one-part water. The forces of evil were gathering and Drachenfels was at their heart. Oswald intended to face the monster in his lair and vanquish him forever. Again, he offered her the chance to join the party and this time she relented. Only then did he reveal that his father, and presumably Emperor Luitpold himself, had refused to believe Sieur Jehan's evidence and that he was pursuing this venture unsupported by any Imperial forces.

They set out from Altdorf for the Grey Mountains the next day.

Later, others joined. Rudi Wegener, the bandit king of the Reikwald Forest, threw in his lot with them and helped fight off the possessed remnants of his own comrades during one long, dark night in the thick of the woods. Along with Rudi came Stellan the Warlock, who had lived with the bandits and was determined to pit his magics against those of the Great Enchanter, and Erzbet, the dancer-assassin from the World's

Edge who recited every night like a prayer the names of those she had killed. Ueli and Menesh had been recruited at Axe Bite Pass, where an entire community of peaceful peasants had turned out to be daemons in disguise, and where young Conradin, Oswald's squire, was spitted and eaten by an altered ogre. The dwarfs had been travelling south, but were willing to pledge their swords for gold and glory. Heinroth, whose soul was eaten away by the murder of his children, joined them soon after. A raiding party of orcs from the fortress had made sport with his two little sons and killed them afterwards. He had vowed to scar himself with his serrated blade every day he let Drachenfels live, and grimly sliced at himself every morning. One day, they woke up to find Heinroth turned inside out, with words carved into his bones.

GO BACK NOW.

None of them had heard a thing, and the sharp-witted Veidt had been standing guard.

Through it all, Oswald had been at their head, undaunted by each new horror, keeping his followers together – which in the case of Veidt and the dwarfs or the licentious Erzbet and the fanatically ascetic Heinroth hadn't been easy – and forever confident of the eventual outcome. Sieur Jehan told her that he had been like this since childhood. The scholar evidently loved the boy as a son and chose to follow Oswald when the prince's real father had refused to listen. These were the last great days, Genevieve had thought, and their names would live in ballads forever.

Now, Conradin was dead. Sieur Jehan was dead. Heinroth was dead. Ueli was dead. And before the night was over, others – maybe all of the party – would be joining them. She hadn't thought about dying for a long time. Perhaps tonight Drachenfels would finish Chandagnac's Dark Kiss, and push her at last over the border between life and death.

Oswald walked straight up to the open gates of the fortress, looked casually about and signalled to them. He stepped into the dark. Genevieve followed him. And the others came after her.

III

As they ventured further, Stellan the Warlock began chanting in a language Genevieve didn't recognize. He glowed slightly and she fancied she saw his attendant spirits dancing around him. Sometimes, she could see things the others couldn't. Stellan's voice grew louder as they advanced down the stone corridor and his gestures more extravagant. Firefly entities spiralled around him, clustering to his amulets, stirring his long, womanish hair. Evidently, he was invoking great powers. He had done so before other battles and claimed credit for their victories.

At the end of the passage was an aged wooden door, with inset copper designs. It was too easy to see a face in the abstract curlicues. Genevieve knew the effect was deliberate. Nothing in this place happened unless it was by design. Drachenfels's design. The face she saw was that of the impassive mask the Great Enchanter had worn in Parravon. Maybe there were other faces for the others: a cruel parent, an implacable foe, an unbanished daemon.

Erzbet was badly affected. Genevieve could hear the dancer-assassin's blood quickening. Even Veidt and Rudi were tense. Only Oswald kept his chilly calm, his princely composure.

Oswald went ahead, a torch held high in one hand, sword out like a blind man's cane. Stellan followed close behind, feeling the way with his magics. Genevieve heard rhythms and repetitions in his chanting now, and noticed Rudi praying in unison with the warlock, his thick lips mouthing silently Stellan's words. The warlock's spirits were around him like a protective garment. They all must be praying to their gods now. All who had gods.

In this heart of Drachenfels, Genevieve's night-senses told her things she wished not to know. It was as if a million insects crawled upon her skin, biting with silvered mandibles, shrieking in a cacophony. There was great danger nearby, great evil. But you didn't have to have the heightened perception of vampirekind to know that. Even poor, half-witted Erzbet could tell they were walking into a great and dreadful darkness. Their guttering torches were pitiful against the blackness of the interior of the Fortress.

'The door,' said Stellan in Reikspiel. 'It's guarded by spells.'

Oswald paused and extended his sword. He touched the metal and sparks

19

flew. The inlay grew white hot and foul smoke curled out as the wood
burned. The imagined face looked angered now and glared hatred at them.

'Can you open it, warlock?' asked the prince.

Stellan smiled his confident one-sided smile. 'Of course, highness. A
mere conjurer could penetrate these petty charms. I'm surprised that an
enchanter of Drachenfels's standing would stoop to such things.'

The warlock reached into a pouch and, with a flourish, threw a handful of sweet-smelling dust at the door. The face went dark again and
Stellan reached for the doorknob. He twisted it and pushed the door
open, standing aside to let the Prince through before him. With a mocking grin, he bowed.

'See,' he said, 'it was simple.'

Then, Stellan the Warlock simply exploded.

They were drenched in gore. The door hung with ribbons of cloth
and meat. The stone walls dripped red for ten feet behind them. Stellan's naked skeleton stood for a moment, still grinning, then collapsed.

Rudi, Menesh and Veidt swore loudly, and frantically scraped at themselves, dislodging the chunks of flesh and scraps of clothing that had
plastered them. Oswald calmly wiped off his face. Genevieve felt her red
thirst rising, but fought it back. This was no banquet for her. She would
rather drink pig's swill than feed like this. Stellan's spirits were gone,
snuffed out with their summoner.

'The walls,' said Veidt. 'They're changing.'

Genevieve looked up at the ceiling. The stones were molten, reshaping themselves. There were faces in the walls and jutting rock claws
reaching out for them. Oswald swung his sword with practiced grace
and a dead hand fell to the floor, shattering as it landed. Rudi drew the
two-handed sword slung on his back and began to hack away at the
emerging creatures.

'Careful, fool outlaw,' shouted Veidt, barely avoiding Rudi's blade.
'That's not a corridor weapon.'

A stone head rolled at Genevieve's feet, its glass eyes milked over,
swollen tongue poked out. One of the creatures, a squat gargoyle, had
detached itself completely from the ceiling and dropped down on her. It
grabbed for her hair. She made a fist and struck it in the chest. It was
like punching a mountain; any human hand would have been pulver-
ized. Pain ran up through her arm to her shoulder and she knew her
wound was reopening.

The gargoyle was shocked to a halt, a hairline crack across its torso,
running from horny shoulder to waist. It lunged for her, stone hands
creaking as it made razor-sharp talons. It was too near for her to draw
sword against it, so she was pushed back. The wall behind her writhed
with life, sprouting claws of its own.

She braced herself against the shifting stones, turning to face the wall,
and kicked out with a booted foot, aiming high, aiming for the crack.
The gargoyle staggered back, split. The top half of its body slid from the
bottom and crashed to the floor. It was a pile of dead stones.

They fought their way through the creatures, smashing them when they could, and found themselves forced through the open door into an abandoned chamber where a great table was set for dinner. The food had long since crumbled to dust. So had the diners, whose dry skeletons were slumped in their chairs in the remains of their finery. Here, there was room to fight properly and Rudi's sword counted. Gargoyles fell.

The bandit chief held the doorway, swinging his blade about him and the creatures flew to fragments. Finally, with a grunt, he kicked the door shut on the last of the enemy. Veidt and Oswald piled in with heavy chairs that could be stacked against the wood. Efficiently, they barricaded themselves into the dining hall of the dead.

Genevieve gripped her aching hand and tried to set the bones in their proper places. She managed to push her fingers back in joint. Her wound was bleeding slightly as she smoothed it over. She hoped no silver traces were caught inside. That could cause gangrene and she would have to have the hand, or the limb, amputated. It might be a hundred years before she grew a new one. It had taken Chandagnac an entire generation to regain an ear lopped off by an overzealous priest of the Old Faith.

She looked down at herself. Her britches, boots and jerkin were filthy and stinking, as if she had crawled through the mud of a plague-pit. The others were in no better condition, although Oswald bore his dirt and rags as if they were perfumed silks. And Veidt had never looked any different; the only clean things about him were his weapons.

'What happened here?' Rudi asked.

'A poison feast,' said Oswald. 'It's one of the worst Drachenfels stories. He appeared alone, on his knees, at the court of the Emperor nearly six centuries ago, and offered to make penance for his sins. He paid generous reparations to all his living victims and abased himself at the graves of many others. He renounced evil and swore allegiance to the gods he had previously cursed. He vowed his loyalty to the Empire. Everyone was convinced he had changed. In ten thousand years, anyone might repent, might wish to cleanse his heart. Any man, that is. He invited the Emperor Carolus and all his court to this place to celebrate his new life, and decreed that Drachenfels would forever be open as a shelter for the destitute. Some of Carolus's advisers spoke against the feast, but the Emperor was a kindly man, and too young to remember Drachenfels's worst deeds. They came here, all of them, the Emperor, and the Empress Irina, their children, and all the nobles of the court. My own ancestor, Schlichter von Konigswald, sat here among them...'

They looked at the abandoned corpses, and saw the jewels lying under cobwebs. One smiling dowager corpse had rubies in her eye-sockets, and a silver-set net of pearls, sapphires and diamonds on her bare ribs. Genevieve picked a tarnished gold circlet from a broken skull.

'The old crown,' Rudi said, eyes alight with avarice. 'It's priceless.'

'We'll return it, my outlaw friend,' Oswald said. 'There'll be plunder for you, but this crown we will return.'

Oswald had promised Rudi Wegener a pardon when they returned to

Altdorf in triumph, but knew, as Genevieve knew, the bandit would not accept it. Once this good deed, this honourable revenge, was done, he would be returning to the forests, to the outlaw life.

Genevieve looked at the corpses and saw flashes of a long-ago day. The chamber was clean and new and brightly-lit. She heard laughter and music. She saw dishes being served. Handsome gentlemen were charming, beautiful ladies fluttered fans. And at the head of the table, a regal man with a crown was attended by a plainly-dressed man in a simple tin mask. She blinked and the dark present was back.

'He poisoned them, then?' Menesh asked Oswald.

'Yes. Only, they didn't die. They were paralyzed, turned to feeling statues. Years later, one of Drachenfels's minions made a confession before he went to the gallows. He told the whole story of the obscenities that took place before the helpless eyes of Carolus and his court. They had brought their children, you see, those foolish and trusting nobles. Heinroth would have understood the horror. After the entertainments were over, Drachenfels left his guests frozen. With a feast laid out before them, they starved to death.'

Oswald struck the table with his sword-hilt. It shook. Brittle crockery broke, a candelabrum fell over, a rat burst from its nest in a ribcage, a skeleton still bedecked in the robes of the high priestess of Verena fell apart. Tears stood out on the prince's face. Genevieve had never seen him betray such emotion.

'Fools!'

Genevieve laid a hand on his shoulder and he calmed instantly.

'After this night, Drachenfels will prey on no more fools.'

He strode across the chamber and pulled open a set of double doors.

'Come on, the minion also drew maps. He bought himself a quick death. Drachenfels's chambers lie beyond these passageways. We're near him.'

IV

The fortress was the man, Genevieve thought. The towers and battlements, the corridors and chambers, the very mountain crag which the bowels of Drachenfels were carved from: they were the Great Enchanter's arteries and organs, his blood and bones. Oswald's band might as well be penetrating Drachenfels's body like knives, striking for his heart. Or they might be fragments of food tumbling down his gullet. And wasn't that a comforting thought?

Erzbet alone was doubtful as they followed Oswald. She was talking to herself, reciting the names of her dead. The corridors were wider here and hung with tapestries. One depicted the Great Enchanter at play and a deal of red thread had had to be employed. Even Veidt paled at what was shown here.

Oswald glanced at the central panels of the hanging and slashed out with his sword. The entire dusty tapestry fell and lay on the floor like a fen-worm's cast-off skin. Menesh touched his torch to it and in an instant the fire spread along its length. The next tapestry, a group portrait of the certain dreaded gods, caught too.

'Very clever, stunted lackwit,' spat Veidt. 'Burning us up now, is it? That makes a change from the traditional dwarfish knife in the small of the back.'

The dwarf pulled his knife and held it up. Veidt had his dart pistol out. There were fires all around them.

'A traitor, eh? Like dead-and-damned Ueli?'

'I'll give you dead-and-damned, scavenger!'

Menesh stabbed up, but Veidt stepped out of the way. Flames reflected in the bounty hunter's dark eyes. He took careful aim.

'Enough!' Oswald cried. 'We've not come this far to fall out now.'

'Veidt cries "traitor" too much,' Rudi said sourly. 'I trust no one who can be bought as easily.'

The outlaw heaved his sword up and Veidt turned again.

'Ethics from a bandit, that's rich–'

'Better a bandit than a trader of corpses!'

'Your corpse is hardly worth the seventy-five gold crowns the Empire has offered for it.'

The pistol came up. The sword wavered in the air.

'Kill him and be done with it,' said Menesh.

This was like Veidt, and like the hot-tempered Rudi. But Menesh had been quiet until now, dodging Veidt's taunts with good humour. Something was working on them. Something unnatural. Genevieve staggered forward as someone landed on her back, pushing her face to the floor.

'Hah! Dead bitch!'

Erzbet's noose was about her neck and drawing in. She had taken her by surprise. Genevieve had to struggle to brace her hands against the flagstones, to give herself the leverage to heave Erzbet off her. The wire constricted. The assassin knew her business: beheading would work, all right. Immortality is so fragile: beheading, the hawthorn, silver, too much sun...

Genevieve got her hand under her, palm flat against the stone and pushed herself up. Erzbet tried to ride her like an unbroken pony, her knees digging into the ribs. Genevieve corded her neck muscles and forced breath down her windpipe.

She heard the wire snap and felt Erzbet tumble from her seat. She stood and struck out. The other woman took the blow heavily and fell. Erzbet rolled on the floor and came up, a knife in her hand. Did it gleam silver like Ueli's?

'The dead can die, leech woman!'

Genevieve felt the urge to kill. Kill the stinking living slut! Kill all these warmblood bastard vermin! Kill, kill, KILL!

'Fight it,' shouted Oswald. 'It's an attack, an enchantment!'

She turned to the prince. Whoreson noble! Sister-raping, wealth-besotted scum! Drenched in perfume to cover the stench of his own ordure!

Oswald held her, shaking her by the shoulders.

Blood! Royal blood! Rich, spiced, hot-on-the-tongue, youthfully-gushing blood!

The vein throbbed in his throat. She took his wrists in her strong hands, feeling their pulses. She heard his heart beating like a steady drum and saw him as a student of anatomy might a dissected corpse. Veins and arteries laid through flesh and over bone. The blood called to her.

How long since she had fed? Properly?

Oswald broke her grip and slapped her.

She found herself and saw only his clear eyes in the dark. He kissed her on the cheek and stood back. The thirst could wait.

Oswald went to each of them in turn, calmed them. Erzbet was the last. She had pressed herself into a corner of the passageway and refused to come out unless coaxed. She waved her knife. Oswald took her hand and pulled the knife out of it. The woman was mad, Genevieve realized, and had been for hours.

Erzbet emerged from her bolt-hole when Oswald talked to her in a low, soothing voice. She clung to the prince like a frightened child to its mother during the daemon king's scenes of a puppet play. Oswald detached the dancer-assassin from his shoulder and passed her to Rudi. The chastened, suddenly serious bandit took her on his arm – had they been lovers, Genevieve wondered? – and Erzbet pressed herself to his side. She sensed Veidt about to make a remark about their new burden, but he kept quiet. Good for him.

The fires were dying. They walked again.

Erzbet was useless now. And Veidt – weather-beaten and hardy Veidt – was ailing. He had sustained a wound during the battle with the gargoyles. It was just a scratch on his face, a newer scar among so many old ones, but it was still bleeding steadily and he had a greyish look. He was moving slowly now, lagging behind them. His sharpness was going and he blundered too often against the walls.

Genevieve heard a clattering and looked back. Veidt had dropped his trifurcate crossbow, his dart pistol and his swordbelt. He was trudging on, trailing them like a prisoner his ball and chain.

This was unthinkable. Veidt would never drag his beloved weapons through the dirt.

Menesh, who had taken so many insults from the bounty hunter, went to him and offered a shoulder to be leaned on. Veidt put out a hand to steady himself, but missed Menesh and fell clumsily against the wall. He crawled on and finally came to rest, gasping for breath, at Oswald's feet. Menesh pulled him upright and propped him against the wall. His face was ashen and he was drooling. He went into convulsions. The dwarf held him down.

'He can't go on, highness.'

Oswald picked up Veidt's dart pistol. It was a fine piece of workmanship, a coil spring-powered gun that could drive a six-inch nail through an oak door. The prince checked it for dirt and blew a cobwebby lump off the barrel. He thrust the weapon into Veidt's hand and he gripped it. The bounty hunter had come through the convulsions.

'We leave him,' said Oswald. 'We'll pass this way again.'

Veidt nodded and weakly raised his hand in salute. He wasn't holding the pistol correctly, Genevieve realized. His finger wasn't on the trigger. If he wasn't helped, he'd be dead by dawn. But they could all be dead by dawn.

Menesh took a stone from his pocket and handed it to Veidt. The bounty hunter tried to pick it up from his lap, but it just lay there. A crude pick was carved on the rounded piece of rock.

'It's the mark of Grungni, dwarf god of the mines. Good luck.'

Veidt nodded. Rudi patted his head as he passed. Erzbet swept her skirts over his legs. Oswald saluted him.

Genevieve looked him in the eyes and saw his future in them.

'Tell me, Mistress... Dieudonné,' Veidt said, each syllable an effort. 'What is it... like?... Being... dead?'

She turned away and followed the others.

Rudi was struck down next, by a simple mechanical device Genevieve would have thought unworthy of the Great Enchanter. A mere matter of a hinged stone set in the floor, of counter-weights and balances, of oiled joints and three iron-hard pieces of wood the length and size of a heavy man. They sprang out of the wall. Two – one at chest height, one at knee height – swung out in front of Rudi, the last – between the others – from behind. They meshed like a three-fingered fist, and the bandit was bent forwards and back between them. They could all hear his bones snapping.

He hung there in the wooden grip, dripping blood and screaming oaths. Then the wooden arms drew back as suddenly as they had leaped out, and he fell in a jellied heap.

Oswald jammed a sword into the wall to hold the arms back and went to him. It was worse than Genevieve had thought. He was still alive. Inside him, whenever he moved, his broken bones would be a hundred knives.

'One by one,' he said. 'The devil is clever, my prince. You must leave old Rudi as you left Veidt. Come back if you can...'

There was blood on the prince's hands. Erzbet was kneeling by the bandit, feeling for his wounds, trying to find the broken places.

'Stay with him,' Oswald told her. 'Be alert.'

So, only three came to the heart of Drachenfels.

V

This was a throne-room for a king of darkness. The rest of the fortress had been ill-lit and dilapidated, but this was spotless and illumined by jewelled chandeliers. The furniture was ostentatiously luxurious. Gold gleamed from every edge. And silver. Genevieve shuddered to be near so much of the stuff. There were fine paintings on the wall. Rudi would have wept to see so much plunder in one place. A clock chimed, counting unnatural hours as its single hand circled an unfamiliar dial. In a cage, a harpy preened herself, wiping the remains of her last meal from her feathered breasts. Genevieve's heart fluttered as it had not done since she was truly alive.

Oswald and Genevieve trod warily on the thick carpets as they circled the room.

'He's here,' said the prince.

'Yes, I feel it too.'

Menesh kept to the walls, stabbing at tapestries.

One wall was a floor-to-ceiling window, set with stained glass. From here, the Great Enchanter could gaze down from his mountain at the Reikswald. He could see as far as Altdorf and trace the glittering thread of the River Reik through the forests. In the stained glass, there was a giant image of Khorne, the Blood god, sitting upon his pile of human bones. With a chill, Genevieve realized that Drachenfels didn't so much worship Khorne as look down upon him as an amateur in the cause of evil. Chaos was so undisciplined... Drachenfels had never been without purpose. There were other gods, other shrines. Khaine, Lord of Murder, was honoured in a modest ossuary. And Nurgle, Master of Pestilence and Decay, was celebrated by an odiferous pile of mangled remains. From this stared the head of Sieur Jehan, its eyes pecked out.

Oswald started to see his tutor so abused and a laugh resounded through the throne-room.

Six hundred years ago, Genevieve had heard that laugh. Amid the crowds of Parravon, when the First Family's assassin was borne aloft by daemons and his insides fell upon the citizenry. A laugh somehow amplified by the metal mask from behind which it came. In that laughter, Genevieve heard the screams of the damned and the dying, the ripples of rivers of blood, the cracking of a million spines, the fall of a dozen cities, the pleas of murdered infants, the bleating of slaughtered animals.

He loomed up, enormous, from his chair. He had been there all the time, but had worked his magics so none could see.

'I am Drachenfels,' he said mildly, the deathly laugh still in his voice, 'I bid you welcome to my house. Come in health, go safely and leave behind some of the happiness you bring...'

Menesh flew at the Great Enchanter, a dwarfish miner's pick raised to strike. With a terrible languor, moving as might a man of molten bronze, Drachenfels stretched out and slapped him aside. Menesh struck a hanging and fell squealing in a heap. Blood was spurting from him. The harpy was excited and flapped her wings against the bars of her cage, smelling the blood.

Drachenfels was holding the dwarf's arm in his hand. It had come off as easily as a cooked chicken's wing. The enchanter inclined his head to look at his souvenir, giggled and cast it away from him. It writhed across the floor as if alive, trailing blood behind it and was still.

Genevieve looked at Oswald and saw doubt in the prince's face. He had his sword out, but it looked feeble set against the strength, the power of the Great Enchanter.

Drachenfels opened a window in the air and the stink of burning flesh filled the throne-room. Genevieve peered through the window and saw a man twisting in eternal torment, daemons rending his flesh, lash-worms eating through his face, rats gnawing at his limbs. He called out her name and reached for her, reached through the window. Blood fell like rain onto the carpet.

It was her father! Her six-centuries-dead father!

'I have them all, you know,' said Drachenfels. 'All my old souls, all kept like that. It prevents me from getting lonely here in my humble palace.'

He shut the window on the damned creature Genevieve had loved. She raised her sword against him.

He looked from one to the other and laughed again. Spirits were gathering about him, evil spirits, servant spirits. They funnelled around him like a tornado.

'So you have come to kill the monster? A prince of nothing, descendant of a family too cowardly to take an Empire for themselves? And a poor dead thing without the sense to lie down in her grave and rot? In whose name do you dare such an endeavour?'

Oswald tried to be strong. 'In the name of Sigmar Heldenhammer!'

Oswald's words sounded weak, echoing slightly, but gave Drachenfels pause. Something was working behind his mask, a rage building up inside him. His spirits swarmed like midges.

He threw out his hand in Genevieve's direction and the tide of daemons engulfed her, hurling her back against the wall, smothering her, weighing her down, sweeping over her face.

Oswald came forward and his sword clashed on the enchanter's mailed arm. Drachenfels turned to look down on him.

She felt herself dragged down, the insubstantial creatures surging up over her. She couldn't breathe. She could barely move her limbs. She was cold, her teeth chattering. And she was tired, tired as she shouldn't be until dawn. She felt bathed in stinging sunlight, wrapped in bands of silver, smothered in a sea of garlic. Somewhere, the hawthorn was being sharpened for her heart. Her mind fogged, she tasted dust in her throat and her senses dulled.

Unconscious, she missed the battle all the ballads would be about. The battle that would be the inspiration for poets, minstrels, sculptors, painters. The battle that would make Prince Oswald von Konigswald a hero famed throughout the Old World. The battle that would cause some to see in the prince the very spirit of Sigmar reborn.

The battle that would put an end to Constant Drachenfels.

Act One

I

It wasn't so much that the food in Mundsen Keep was bad, but that there was so little of it. Detlef Sierck was used to far more substantial daily fare than a measly piece of cheese and a hunk of rough, unbuttered bread served with a half-pitcher of oily water. Indeed, his current accommodations entirely lacked the comforts and services his position entitled him to. And those with whom he was compelled to share his circumstances did not come up to the standards of decorum and intellect he usually expected of his companions.

'I do believe,' he said to Peter Kosinski, the Mad Mercenary, 'that were I to own Mundsen Keep and the Chaos Wastes, I would live in the Wastes and rent out the keep.'

The sullen fellow grunted, belched and kicked him in the head. This was not the sort of treatment usually accorded those of his genius.

The room in which he found himself confined was barely twice the size of the average privy and smelled three times worse. He shared quarters with five others, none of whom he would have, given the choice, selected for his entourage. Each had a blanket, except Kerreth, the smallest, who had, upon the application of some little force, generously given his away to Kosinski, the largest. And they each had a piece of cloth with a number chalked on it.

The cloth was important. Detlef had heard the story of the two comrades who playfully exchanged their cloths, with the result that a clerk who had mischanced to cough loudly during a speech by the high priest of Ulric was sent to the headsman, while a murderer of small children was required to throw three schillings into the poor box at the temple in Middenheim.

'If you can afford it,' he said to nobody in particular, 'never go to debtors' prison in Altdorf.'

Someone laughed and was slapped down by a soul too far gone in misery to see the humour.

When Detlef woke up on his first morning in Mundsen Keep, he found his boots and embroidered jacket taken from him.

'Which of you louts is responsible?' he had asked, only to discover the culprit was not a fellow convict but Szaradat, the turnkey. Guglielmo, a bankrupt Tilean wine importer, explained the system to Detlef. If a

33

man were to stay alive and well-behaved long enough, he stood a good chance of being promoted from ordinary prisoner to trusty.

Szaradat was a trusty. And trusties were entitled to work off the debt that had originally brought them to the Keep by filching whatever could be pawned, sold or bartered from lesser prisoners.

The next night, his shirt and britches disappeared and smelly rags were left in their place. The only thing he had left to call his own, Detlef reflected, was the iron collar welded in place around his neck for the convenience of the warders. But the night after that, he woke up to find himself being held down by uniformed officials while Szaradat hacked away at his hair.

'He sells it to Bendrago, the wig-maker on Luitpoldstrasse,' explained Guglielmo, who was himself sporting an enthusiastic but hardly competent fresh haircut. Detlef knew there were magicians or students desperate for certain other, less dispensible, parts of the human anatomy. He hoped fervently that Szaradat didn't know any of them.

Kosinski, with his wrestler's physique and sore-headed bear's temper, was the only one of the cell-mates not shorn. He was well on his way to being a trusty, Detlef assumed. He had the attitude for it. The others, all of whom sported the identical cropped style, were Manolo, a dusky sailor with an unfortunate fondness for games of chance; Justus, a devotee of Ranald fallen upon hard times; and Kerreth, a cobbler driven to ruin by three or four wives. Kerreth had lost his blanket and much else to Kosinski. Detlef guessed the brawny giant only let the cobbler have a mouthful of his bread and water on the principle that if Kerreth died Kosinski would stop getting the extra ration.

There wasn't much to do in the cell. Justus had a deck of Ranald-blessed cards, but Detlef knew better than to play 'Find the Empress' with him. Manolo had obviously been a blessing for Justus, and had already wagered away a year's worth of food to the trickster-priest. Kerreth had a three-inch sliver of hardwood he had smuggled in, and was working away in vain at the mortar of the walls. He'd barely scraped out half a cupful of dust and the stone blocks were as solid as ever. Detlef had heard the walls were fifteen feet thick.

It was only a question of time before someone turned Kerreth and his sliver in to Szaradat for an extra privilege. Sometimes, he wondered who would betray the sailor. Kosinski, who didn't care about anything, was the obvious choice, but if he hadn't seen this opportunity to grease his way to trusty status by now, he probably never would.

Detlef was honest enough to suspect he would be the one eventually to take Szaradat aside during their monthly exercise period and point out Kerreth's sliver. And decent enough to hope to put off that treachery for as long as possible. But there was only so much an artist could take.

There was a question that always came up. It was about the only conversation the prisoners – the talkative Guglielmo excepted – really took to. There were many ways of approaching the question: What did you do on the outside? Will you ever get out of here? How deep is your hole?

How wide your river? How high your wall? How long your life? What these were all getting at was simple: How much do you owe?

After three weeks, Detlef knew to the penny how much his cell-mates owed. He knew about the sixteen gold crowns Manolo had staked on the unbeatable hand of cards dealt him in the back room of the Gryphon and Star on the Sacred Day of Manann, god of the seas. And the three shillings and fourpence, compounded with interest to eighteen gold crowns, that Kerreth had obtained from a moneylender to purchase a trinket for his latest fiancée. And the ninety-eight crowns Kosinski had spent before learning that he had hired on to an expedition to the Northern Wastes even the most crazed of the other mercenaries thought suicidal. And the two hundred and fifty-eight crowns, twelve shillings and sixpence Guglielmo had borrowed from a certain Tilean businessman to purchase a ship's cargo of fine wines that had gone to the bottom of the Sea of Claws.

He knew about the five hundred and forty crowns Justus had duped out of a spice merchant's wife in return for a course of cream treatments guaranteed to restore her to the full bloom of youth and beauty. He had been lucky to be arrested before the woman's sons returned from overseas to sharpen their swords. Detlef knew about all their debts. And they knew about his.

'One hundred and nineteen thousand, two hundred and fifty-five gold crowns, seventeen shillings and ninepence.'

That was Manolo. But it could have been any of them. They all said it from time to time, sometimes with reverence like a prayer, sometimes with anger like an oath, and sometimes with awe like a declaration of love.

'One hundred and nineteen thousand, two hundred and fifty-five gold crowns, seventeen shillings and ninepence.'

Detlef was getting fed up with the tune. He wished the sum could alter, one way or another. Preferably another. If he had friends outside, patrons or sponsors, he hoped they would feel a generous impulse. But it would take a supernaturally generous impulse to do anything worthwhile to the figure.

'One hundred and nineteen thousand, two hundred and fifty-five gold crowns, seventeen shillings and ninepence.'

'Enough. I'm tired of hearing that.'

'I know,' said Kosinski, with grudging respect, 'but one hundred and nineteen thousand, two hundred and fifty-five gold crowns, seventeen shillings and ninepence. Why, it's an achievement. I've tried to think of it, to see it in my mind, but I can't...'

'Imagine a city built of gold crowns, Kosinski,' said Justus. 'Towers piled high as temples, stacks pushed together like palaces.'

'One hundred and nineteen thousand, two hundred and fifty-five gold crowns, seventeen shillings and ninepence.' There it was again. 'Why, I'll bet the Emperor Karl-Franz himself couldn't lay his hands on one hundred and nineteen thousand, two hundred and fifty-five gold crowns, seventeen shillings and ninepence.'

'I rather think he could. Quite a bit of it was his in the first place.'

Guglielmo shook his head in wonder. 'But how did you do it, Detlef? How could you conceivably spend such a sum? In my entire life, I've barely had five thousand crowns pass through my hands. And I'm a man of business, of trade. How could you possibly spend one hundred and nineteen–'

'…thousand, two hundred and fifty-five gold crowns, seventeen shillings and ninepence? It was easy. Costs kept going up and expenses arose that weren't foreseen in my original budget plan. My accountants were criminally negligent.'

'Then why aren't they in this cell with us?'

'Ahem,' Detlef was shamed, 'well, most of them were… sort of… um… killed. I'm afraid that some of the parties involved were unable to take the long view of the affair. Small minds and money-boxes are the blight of the artistic spirit.'

There was a drip of water at the back of the cell. Kerreth had been trying to catch it in rolled cones made from the pages of a book Szaradat hadn't bothered to steal, but Kosinski kept eating the soggy paper. A mouse had found its way in yesterday and Kosinski had eaten that too. He said he'd tasted worse when campaigning in the Northern Wastes.

'But still,' wondered Guglielmo, 'to spend all that money just on a play…'

'Not just on a play, my dear Guglielmo! On the play. The play that, had it ever been produced, would have lived forever in the minds and hearts of those mortals lucky enough to see it. The play that would have sealed my reputation as the premier genius of my day. The play that would, not to put too sharp a point on it, have earned back tenfold the meagre cost of its staging.'

It was called The True History of Sigmar Heldenhammer, Founder of the Empire, Saviour of the Reik, Defier of the Darkness. Detlef Sierck had written it on a commission for the Elector of Middenland. The epic was to have been staged in the presence of Emperor Karl-Franz himself. Detlef had planned to call upon the full resources of three villages in the Middle Mountains for the production. The entire populations would have been drafted in to serve as extras, a castle of wood was to be erected and burned down during the course of the action and wizards had been engaged to present state-of-the-art illusions during the magical sequences.

The natural amphitheatre in which the play was to have been staged was twelve days' ride from Middenheim, and the Emperor and electors would have to be conveyed there in a magnificent procession. There would have been a two-day feast merely as a prologue for the drama, and the action of the epic would have unfolded over a full week, with breaks in the story for meals and sleep.

Detlef himself, the greatest actor of the age as well as the premier dramatist, had cast himself in the role of Sigmar, one of the few in literature large enough to contain his personality. And Lilli Nissen, the famous beauty and – it was rumoured – sometime mistress of six out of fourteen

electors, had consented to take the role of Shallya, goddess of healing
and mercy. Mercenaries had been engaged to fight nearly to the death
during the battle scenes, an enormous homunculus had been bred especially by skilled wizards to stand in for Constant Drachenfels, an army
of dwarfs had been hired to portray Sigmar's dwarf allies and another
engaged to stand in under masks for the goblin hordes the hero was to
drive out of the Empire – Detlef would have insisted on real goblins, but
his cast baulked at working with them. The crops of three successive
harvests were stored up to fuel the cast and audience, and almost one
thousand professional actors, singers, dancers, animal trainers, jugglers,
musicians, jesters, combatants, prostitutes, conjurers and philosophers
retained to play the major parts in the great drama.

And it had all been ruined by something as petty and uninteresting as
an outbreak of plague among the battlefield extras. Lilli Nissen would
not budge from Marienburg when the news of the epidemic reached her,
and hers was merely the first of the many returned invitations. Finally
the elector himself pulled out and Detlef found himself forced to deal
with a seeming army of angry creditors whose notes against the electoral
coffers were suddenly refused. Under the circumstances, he had found it
necessary to disguise himself as a priestly type and flee to Altdorf, where
the elector's ambassadors unfortunately awaited his appearance. There
had been considerable expenses already, and those who had laid out
the thousand gold crowns he had been asking for a reserved ticket were
clamouring for the refund of their money. Furthermore, the three villages
were rumoured to be clubbing together to petition the assassins' guild.

'It would have been magnificent, Guglielmo. You would have wept to
see it. The scene where I was to best the forces of evil with only my
hammer and my noble heart would have lived eternally in the annals
of great art. Picture it: as Sigmar, all my allies are dead or flown, the
dwarfs have not yet committed to my cause, and I stride – my massive
shadow cast before me by a miracle of ingenious lighting effects – to the
centre of the field of corpses. The goblins creep from their holes. For a
full two hours, I stand immobile as the goblins gather, each more fan-
tastically hideous than the last. Women and children were to have been
barred from this section of the drama, and entertained elsewhere by
acrobats. I had commissioned a choral work of surpassing power from
my regular composer, Felix Hubermann. I had personally designed the
monstrous masks for each of the goblin extras. When the hordes were
finally assembled before me, I would have produced my hammer – my
glowing, holy, singing metal warhammer – and it would have given off
lights the like of which you've never seen. You would have been struck
dumb for weeks by Hubermann's Hammer Theme, and have felt your
youth return as I displayed my heroism and courage in battle against
the goblins and the Great Enchanter. It would have been the triumphant
crowning moment of my altogether glorious career.

'The Tragedy of the Bretonnian Courtesan would have been forgotten, The Loves of Ottokar and Myrmidia would have been completely

eclipsed, and the critics who so sneered at my experimental production of Kleghel's Great Days of Empire would have slit their throats for shame.'

'If words were pennies, you'd have gone free long ago,' said Justus.

'Pennies! That's all I can hope to earn here. Did you note my visitor yesterday? The fellow with the evil eye and the frightful twitch?'

Guglielmo nodded.

'That was Gruenliebe the Greasy. You may remember him. He used to be court jester in Luitpold's day. His speciality was a nauseating little act with trained lambs. When he became too old and fat and slimy to entertain any more, he expanded his business. Now, he owns a string of so-called entertainers who clown and juggle and caper in taverns, and turn over a good three-fourths of their earnings to him for the privilege. If the fumbler drops the balls, the minstrel sounds like a basilisk in pain or the comedian uses lines that might just have been topical in the days of Boris the Incompetent, then you can be certain he belongs to Gruenliebe. Anyway, this piece of offal wrapped up in a human form, this veritable orc in a clown's apparel, had the nerve to propose I work for him...'

The drip dripped, and Detlef burned with the memory of the humiliation, the anger that still boiled...

'What did he want you to do?'

'He wanted me to write jokes for him. To turn out satirical lyrics at a penny a line, to supply his army of witless incompetents with the stuff of laughter, as if one could teach a skaven to play the fiddle or a grave robber to discourse on the cuisine of Cathay. I, whose poems have moved princes to crying fits that will be with them their lives through. I, whose mere offhand remarks have caused hermits under a vow of silence literally to split their sides suppressing laughter...'

'A penny a line,' mused Justus. 'Do you know how many lines it would take to pay off one hundred and nineteen thousand, two hundred and fifty-five gold crowns, seventeen shillings and ninepence at a penny a line?'

'As it happens...'

Justus looked at the ceiling, and his eyes rolled. 'You don't want to know. The great library at the university doesn't have that many lines.'

'Do you think I'd make a good trusty?' Detlef asked.

Kosinski laughed, nastily.

'It was just a thought.'

II

From the terrace of the convent, Genevieve could see the deep, slow, glass-clear waters of the River Talabec, hundreds of feet below. Bordered with thick, sweet-smelling pine forests, the river was like the central artery of the Empire. Not as long as the Reik, which ran a full seven hundred and fifty miles from its rise in the Black Mountains to its mouth at Marienburg, but still cutting across the map like a knife-slash, from the rapid streams of the World's Edge Mountains through the heart of the Great Forest, swelled by its confluence with the Urskoy, to the inland port of Talabheim and then, heavy and thick with the black silt of the Middle Mountains, into the Reik at Altdorf. If she were to cast her kerchief from the terrace, it could conceivably travel the length of the Empire to the sea. Just now, a riverboat – unusual this far up – was pulling in to the jetty that served the convent. More supplies for the Order of Eternal Night and Solace.

Here, secluded from all, she liked the idea of the waters running like the bloodstream. She had come to the convent to be out of the world, but her centuries among men had given her a taste for their affairs. A taste that Elder Honorio discouraged, but which could still not be suppressed. As the comforting dark fell, she saw the tall trees dwindle into shadows and the risen moon waver in the waters. How were things in Altdorf? In Middenheim? Did Luitpold still rule? Was the Crescent Moon still doing business? Was Oswald von Konigswald yet the elector of Ostland? These were not her concerns, and Elder Honorio dismissed her interests as 'a prurient liking for gossip,' but she couldn't be without them. The boat below would be bringing animals, clothes, tools, spices. But no books, no music, no news. In the convent, one was supposed to be content with the changelessness of life, not caught up in its chaotic tumble of events, of fads, of trends. A quarter-century ago, Genevieve had needed that. Now, perhaps she needed to return to the world.

The convent had been founded in the time of Sigmar by Elder Honorio's father-in-darkness, Belada the Melancholy, and had remained unchanged in its isolation down through the centuries. Honorio still wore the buckles and pigtail of a long-gone era, and the others of the order favoured the fashions of their lifetimes. Genevieve felt herself the child again, and sensed censorious eyes criticizing her dresses, her hairstyle, her longings.

Some of the others, the Truly Dead, disturbed her. They were the creatures in the stories who slept by day and would burst into flame at cock-crow if not safely packed in a coffin layered with their native soil. Many bore the marks of Chaos: eyes like red marbles, wolfish fangs, three-inch talons. Their feeding habits offended her polite sensibilities, and caused much hostility between the convent and the few nearby woodland villages.

'What's a child, more or less?' Honorio asked. 'All who live naturally will die before I next need to razor the bristles from my chin.'

Genevieve had been feeding less of late. Like many of the old ones, she was outliving the need. In some ways it was a relief, although she would miss the rush of sensations that came with the blood, the moments when she felt most truly alive. One thing she might regret was that she had never given the Dark Kiss; she had no get, no young vampires to look to her as a mother-in-darkness, no progeny to seed the world.

'You should have had your get while you were still young enough to appreciate them, my dear,' said the graceful, stately Lady Melissa d'Acques. 'Why, I've birthed near a hundred young bloods in my centuries. Fine fellows all, devoted sons-in-darkness. And all handsome as Ranald.'

Chandagnac had been the Lady Melissa's get, and so the vampire noblewoman treated Genevieve as a granddaughter-in-darkness. She reminded Genevieve of her real grandmother in her manner of speech and in her fussiness, although the Lady Melissa would always physically be the golden-haired twelve-year-old she had been eleven hundred years ago. One night then, her coach had been held up by a nameless brigand thirsty for more than money.

According to the grimoires of the order, Genevieve would lose her ability to procreate with the passing of the red thirst. But maybe not: in the libraries of the convent, and through a simple observation of her companions in the order, she had learned that there were as many species of vampire as there were of fish or cat. Some abhorred the relics and symbols of all the gods, others entered Holy Orders and lived the most devout of lives. Some were brutish predators who would drain at a draught a peasant girl, others epicures who would sip only, and treat their human meals as lovers rather than cattle. Some, skilled in sorcery and wizardry, could indeed transform themselves into bats, wolves or a sentient red mist; others could barely tie their own bootlaces. 'What kind am I,' Genevieve would occasionally wonder to herself, 'what kind of vampire am I?'

The thing that marked her bloodline – the line of Chandagnac, reaching ultimately back to Lahmia – from the vampires of dark legend was that they had never died and lain in the earth. The transformation had been wrought lovingly while they still drew breath. She might have no reflection and feel the need for blood, but her heart still beat. The Truly Dead – sometimes known as the Strigoi – were more dead than alive, essentially walking corpses. Few of them were decent, they were the bad ones, the child-stealers, the throat-tearers, haunters of the grave...

Genevieve and the Lady Melissa played cards on the terrace as the sunset faded, the quality of the game improving as their night-senses awoke. Genevieve ran her tongue over her sharp teeth, and tried to think two or three hands ahead.

'Now, now, my girl,' said the Lady Melissa, her child's face grave, 'you shouldn't try to read your granny's mind like that. She's much older and wiser than you, and could easily give you the vision of the wrong cards.'

Genevieve laughed, and lost again, trumped from nowhere.

'You see.'

The Lady Melissa laughed, as she scooped the trick. For the moment, she was genuinely a giggling child; then she was the old lady again. Inside the convent, the Truly Dead were rising. Wolves howled in the forests. A large bat flapped lazily across the sky, blotting the moon for a moment.

Twenty-five years ago, Genevieve had been in at the death of the most evil man alive. The effects had been calamitous, and unforeseen. Throughout the Known World, the agents of evil – some of whom had masqueraded for years as ordinary or even exemplary citizens – were transformed into their true, monstrous selves, or struck down by invisible arrows to the heart, or blasted to pieces by explosions. A castle in Kislev fell silently to the ground, crushing a coven of witches to a paste. Thousands of spirits were freed from their ties to the earth and passed on, beyond the ken of mediums and necromancers. In Gisoreux, the statue of a martyred child came suddenly to life, speaking in an ancient dialect no one could understand, the spell upon him at last lifted. And Prince Oswald and his companions became the heroes of the age.

Emperor Luitpold, shamed by his initial refusal to aid Oswald's expedition, had sent in a troop of the Imperial Guard to clear out the pathetic remnants of Drachenfels's foul servants from his castle. Goblins, orcs, trolls, hideously altered humans, degenerates and hordes of unclassifiable creatures had been put to the sword, or burned at the stake, or hanged from the battlements. The Emperor had wanted to raze the place to the ground, but Oswald interceded, insisting that it should stay standing and desolate as a reminder of the evil that had been. Drachenfels's books, papers and possessions were argued over by the grand theogonist of the cult of Sigmar and the high priest of the cult of Ulric, but eventually found their way into shrines and libraries throughout the Empire, accessible only to the most esteemed and unblemished of scholars.

Genevieve, meanwhile, had refused all offers of reward and returned to the Crescent Moon. Her part in the adventure was over, and she wanted to hear no more of it. There were too many dead and worse for her to make light of the story. But the tavern had changed, and was thronged now with the curious and the disturbed. Balladeers wanted her story, the devout wanted relics of her person, relatives of the monster's victims inexplicably wanted reparations from her, politicians wanted her name to lend to their causes, a clandestine group of young sons-in-darkness wanted to form a vampires' guild around her to lobby the Emperor for the lifting of certain laws against the practices of their kind.

Those loyal to the cause of Drachenfels tried several times to assassinate her. And those narrow-minded worthies who couldn't bear the thing she was decried her part in the fall of the Great Enchanter and tried to make her out as his secret ally.

Most unnerving of all were the flocks of young men who became her admirers, who would bare their throats and wrists to her, begging her to drink deeply, who would sometimes take an edge to their veins in her presence. Some were of that sorry type who plague all the undead, those who crave the Dark Kiss and all it brings. But others claimed they would be content simply to bleed their last for her, to die twitching and ecstatic in her arms.

There was only so much she could stand, and eventually she embarked upon a riverboat for the convent. She had heard such a place existed, and various of her cousins-in-darkness had given her contradictory stories about a remote refuge for vampirekind, but only now did she make the effort to find the truth behind the stories, to petition for admittance into the Order of Eternal Night and Solace. When she had needed to find them, they had got in touch with her. Evidently, they had their agents in the world.

'You're troubled,' the Lady Melissa said. 'Tell me your troubles.'

It was not a helpful suggestion. It was a command.

'I've been dreaming.'

'Nonsense, girl. Our kind don't dream. You know as well as I do that we sleep the sleep of the dead.'

Genevieve saw the masked face in her mind, heard the chilling laughter. 'And yet I've been dreaming.'

They were joined on the terrace by Honorio, the vampire dwarf who was the current elder of the order, and a party of others. One of the party was alive, and nervous. He was a young man, well enough dressed, but obviously not of the first rank. Something about him struck her as being not quite right.

Wietzak, the Truly Dead giant who had once ruled Karak Varn with unparalleled savagery, eyed the young man with obvious bloodlust. Wietzak was Honorio's favoured attendant and would do nothing unsanctioned by the elder, but the visitor wasn't to know that.

'My ladies, I hope you will pardon this interruption,' began Elder Honorio. 'But it seems that though we have left the world behind, the world is not quite ready to abandon all its interest in us. A message – a summons – has been brought here. This gentleman is Henrik Kraly, from Altdorf, and he would have words with you, Genevieve. You may see him or not, as you wish.'

The messenger bowed to her, and presented her with a scroll. She recognized the seal, a crown against trees, and broke it at once. Wietzak ground his teeth as she read. In the forest, there was a commotion as a bat took a wolf.

Within the hour, she was aboard the riverboat, prepared for a long journey. The Lady Melissa gave her a long lecture of farewell, cautioning her against the perils of the world outside and reminding her of the difficulties she would face. Genevieve loved the old lady-child too much to tell her that the hawthorn-wielding Inquisitors she spoke of were three centuries gone and that the cities she remembered as thriving sources of lifesblood were abandoned ruins. Lady Melissa had been with the order for an apparent eternity. They embraced, and the Lady Melissa returned to the jetty where Wietzak, one of those who couldn't bear running water, awaited to accompany her back to the heights of the convent. As her grandmother-in-darkness waved goodbye to her, Genevieve had the disturbing feeling that they were both alive again, and that they were just dearest girlfriends, sixteen and twelve, being separated for a summer.

The next day, prone in her bunk as the oarsmen propelled the craft through the forests, she dreamed again.

The iron-masked man with the hellish laugh would not leave her sleep. Gone he might be, but forgotten was another matter entirely.

She was travelling now to Altdorf. But eventually, she knew, her journey would take her back to the Grey Mountains, back along the course she had followed twenty-five years ago.

Back to the fortress of Drachenfels.

III

When Szaradat came round with the rations, Kosinski let Kerreth keep a little less than usual. Detlef realized the little cobbler was going to die after a few more months of this treatment, and Kosinski would grow stronger. Then, the mad mercenary would need a new source for his extra rations. Guglielmo was nearly an old man, and his legs were spindle-thin. He would be Kosinski's next supplier, his next victim. But, after that...? Manolo was still tough from the seas, and Justus had all the skills one would expect of a follower of the patron god of tricksters and thieves. Detlef knew he was out of condition. His weight only really got down to a comfortable level when he was in the middle of a production, and exercising vigorously every day. He was decidedly flabby now, even on short rations. And Kosinski kept looking stronger and meaner each morning. After Kerreth and Guglielmo died, Kosinski would start taking food from him. And Manolo and Justus would let him, just as he was letting Kosinski steal from Kerreth. As he would let the brute steal from Guglielmo, who was his closest friend in the cell. And if Kosinski took enough, Detlef would himself die.

It hardly seemed a fit fate for the author of The History of Sigmar, the brightest star of the Konigsgarten Theatre in Middenheim. He tried counting the broken hearts he had left among the daughters of Middenheim society, but he was still not cheered. He pondered the roles he had not yet played, the classics he had not yet staged, the masterpieces he had not yet written. Perhaps, if he were ever by some miracle, to get out of the keep, he should consider staging Tarradasch's The Desolate Prisoner of Karak Kadrin as a starring vehicle. Only now, he felt, did he truly understand the plight of the disconsolate Baron Trister.

Someone prodded him out of his reverie. It was Szaradat, rattling his keys in his face.

'What do you want? More hair? Fingers and toes, perhaps, for a cannibal cookpot, or to use as corks for foul wines?'

The trusty spat in the corner.

'You've got a visitor, play-actor.'

'Ach! Gruenliebe again! Tell him I'm unwell, and unable to see him. No, that my social diary is overfull and that I can't squeeze him in. No, that–'

44

Szaradat pulled Detlef upright, and slapped him across the face with the keys. He drew blood.

'You'll see your visitor, or I'll have you transferred to the punishment wing. You won't have the luxuries you have here...'

Detlef did not relish the prospect of learning through their absence precisely with which luxuries his current cell was indeed invisibly equipped. To some, he supposed, it might be deemed a luxury to be in a cell without a ravening wolf in it. Or to have one's bodily wastes taken away once a week. Or not to be neck-deep in the rotten waters of an oubliette.

Szaradat attached a chain to Detlef's iron collar, and dragged him through the door. The genius was led like a dog through the prison, and exposed to the cries and pleas of the other inmates. The keep was centuries out of date, and still equipped with the torture chambers employed during the reign of Hjalmar the Tyrannical, Didrick the Unjust and Bloody Beatrice the Monumentally Cruel. Szaradat looked with longing at a dilapidated rack, and then with disgust at Detlef. It wasn't hard to guess what the trusty was thinking. As emperors go, Karl-Franz was almost reasonable, but who knew what the electors would come up with next. Even Beatrice, to the historian's eye an obvious maniac, had been voted into office by the unanimous decision of the Great and the Good. There was no guessing if or when Szaradat would get to dust off the Tilean boot, oil the spikes of the iron maiden of Kislev, or heat up again the array of tongs and branding implements that now hung forgotten under cobwebs. And when that happened, the trusty would be delighted as a new father... and Detlef would have further cause to regret the day the plausible elector of Middenland came calling at his theatre.

The Great and the Good, pah! Small-minded and Snake-like was more to the point. Vindictive and Verminous! Mean-spirited and Miserly!

At length, Detlef was pushed and jostled into a tiny courtyard. His bare feet froze on the icy stones. It was an overcast day, but the light still hurt his eyes. It was as if he were gazing directly at the sun. He realized how used he had become to the gloom of the cell.

A figure appeared on a balcony overlooking the courtyard. Detlef recognized the black robes, gold chains and superior expression of Governor van Zandt, who had upon his admission given him a lecture on self-denial and peace through suffering. He was one of those officials whose religiosity is such that Detlef suspected them of having taken a vow of stupidity.

'Sierck,' Van Zandt said, 'you may be wondering what that smell is you've been unable to get rid of these last few weeks...'

Detlef grinned and nodded, just to keep in with the governor.

'Well, I'm sorry to have to be the one to tell you this, but I'm afraid the stink is you.'

Gargoyles just below the balcony disgorged streams of water, which fell like a rain of rocks upon Detlef. He was knocked to the ground, and floundered in the jets. He tried to get out of the way, but the streams were redirected and struck him down again. His rags fell apart under the pressure, and great swatches of dirt were scraped painfully from his body. He found fist-sized chunks of ice in the water, and realized he was being washed with melted snow from the roofs. Szaradat threw him a stiff-bristled brush that could well have been one of his prized instruments of torture, and ordered him to scrub himself.

The streams died away. Szaradat tore the remains of Detlef's rags from his body, and prodded him in the bulge of his stomach. He smiled like a rat, showing unpleasantly yellowed teeth. Still dripping, and with the gooseflesh standing out all over, he was marched down a corridor into another room. Szaradat produced a plain robe, hardly stylish but better than nothing, and allowed Detlef to towel himself off before getting into it.

'Gruenliebe must be getting squeamish in his old age,' Detlef said, 'to be offended by a smell far less unhealthy than that given off by his clients' acts.'

Van Zandt came into the room. 'You aren't to see Gruenliebe today, Sierck. Your caller is far more distinguished.'

'Distinguished enough to require the personal attention of the governor of this deathpit?'

'Indeed.'

'You intrigue me. Lead on.'

Detlef waved imperiously, summoning some of the grandeur he had practiced for the roles of the seven emperors in Sutro's great Magnus the Pious cycle. Van Zandt took Detlef's arm impatiently, and steered him through another door. Warmth engulfed him as he stepped, for the first time since his incarceration, into a room properly heated by an open fire. There were unbarred windows to let in the light, and a bowl of fruit – yes, fruit! – stood casually on the table awaiting anyone who might chance to desire a bite or two between meals.

A man of perhaps forty was sitting at the table, polishing a red apple on his generous sleeve. Detlef was struck by his aristocratic bearing and his piercingly clear eyes. This was no ordinary charitable visitor.

'Detlef Sierck,' began Governor van Zandt, an awed quaver in his voice deferring to the man, 'may I present you to Oswald von Konigswald, Defier of the Darkness, Adept of the Cult of Sigmar, Crown Prince and Acting Elector of Ostland.'

The crown prince smiled at Detlef. Detlef had a presentiment that his disasters were only beginning.

'Sit down,' said the man who defeated Drachenfels. 'We have much to talk about, you and I.'

IV

The fate of the Empire was at stake. And the castle was the point that must be held, that must not fail. There were only twenty knights arrayed on the battlements, their plumes stiff on their helms, and barely a hundred common soldiers behind the walls, stoutly prepared to die for the Emperor. Set against them were an orcish horde of some five thousand, reinforced with giants, minotaurs, ogres, undead horsemen, snotlings, greater and lesser daemons and all manner of creatures of darkness. It all fell to the decision of the commander of the castle, His Highness Maximilian von Konigswald, Grand Prince of Ostland.

He pondered the situation, looked about him, and consulted the general. After a brief conference, he knew his plan of action. Maximilian returned the general to his top pocket and gave the order.

'Rain down fire upon the enemy.'

He touched a burning candle to his goblet of Bretonnian brandy, and cast it down at the battlefield. The flames spread, and a thousand or more of the forces of evil were engulfed. They melted, peeling, and the battlefield itself was eaten up by the fire. The smell was quite frightful, and Maximilian himself started back as the orcs hissed and exploded.

The commander-in-chief of the horde looked up and burst into tears.

'Mama, mama,' cried the orcish commander. 'He's burning my soldiers again.'

The commander's mother, the grand prince's nurse, came to the rescue with a pail of water. The soldiers were washed this way and that by the flood, but the fires were put out. The table-top castle became soggy and collapsed, tipping the grand prince's painted lead forces into the melee. Maximilian giggled his high-pitched giggle, and picked out his favourite knights from the mess. Water cascaded onto the marble floors of the palace games room.

'Now, now, highness,' clucked the nurse, 'we mustn't burn down the palace must we? The Emperor would be most upset.'

'The Emperor,' shouted Maximilian, standing to attention despite the pains in his back and limbs, snapping a smart salute. 'To die for the Emperor is the highest honour one can expect.'

The orcish commander, an outsize soldier's helmet strapped to his undersize head, returned the elector's salute.

'Yes, yes, quite,' said the nurse, 'but don't you think it's time for your nap, highness? You've been fighting for the Emperor all morning.'

Maximilian bristled.

'Don't want to nap,' he said, sticking out his lower lip, sucking in his white moustaches and holding his breath. His cheeks went red.

'But an elector needs his rest. You'll be no use to the Emperor if you're falling asleep all over the battlefield.'

'All right. Nap then.' Maximilian began to unbutton his uniform. The nurse stopped him before he dropped his trousers.

'It might be a good idea if you didn't get undressed until you were in your bedchamber, highness. The corridors of the palace are drafty at this time of year and you might catch a nasty chill.'

'Chill? Nasty? Reminds me of the time the Emperor sent me to Norsca. Bloody chilly, Norsca. Lots of snow and ice and white wolves. But cold, mostly. Yes, mostly cold. Norsca is like that. Will there be eggs for supper?'

The nurse manoeuvred the elector away from his battle table as he talked, walking him through the hallways to his daybed room. Behind her, her son wailed. 'Can I be the Emperor's armies next time? I always have to be the orcs. It's not fair.'

Maximilian coughed, deep, racking coughs that came from his lungs and brought stuff up with them. He missed the spittoon, and the nurse had to wipe his moustaches again. He was a very sick elector, they told him, and he needed his rest.

'Eggs, woman,' he thundered. 'Will there be eggs?'

'I think cook had planned on quail, but if you're good and nap until three I think eggs could be arranged.'

They passed a ticking pendulum clock, its face a smiling sun, its workings exposed under glass.

'Nap 'til three! That's hours and hours and hours off.'

'Well, it'll be quail then.'

Two distinguished men, priests of Ulric, saw Maximilian coming and bowed low to him. He poked his tongue out at them, and they passed on without passing comment. He didn't care for priests of Ulric, dried-up old fools who looked down their long noses at heroes of the Empire and tried to get him to read boring papers and things.

'Don't like quail. Like eggs. Good battle food, eggs. Keep you going all day, eggs for breakfast.'

The nurse helped the grand prince into his room. It was decorated with big, bright-coloured pictures of the old emperor, Luitpold, and of glorious battlefields. There was even a portrait of Maximilian von Konigsberg as a young man, with his wife and young son, dressed up for a court affair. Maximilian's hand was on his sword-hilt.

'Sleep 'til three, highness, and perhaps eggs can be found.'

'Half past two.'

'Three.'

The nurse wiped dribble from the elector's moustache.

'A quarter to three.'

'Done.'

The elector bounced on his bed, whooping for joy. 'Eggs, eggs! I'm getting eggs for supper. You can't have eggs, but I can, 'cause I'm a hero of the Empire. The Emperor himself said so.'

The nurse pulled the elector's uniform off, and pulled his bedclothes up over him.

'Don't forget the general.'

'So sorry, highness.' She took the lead soldier out of the elector's jacket pocket and put it on the bedside table where he could see it from beneath his covers. He saluted the figure, who was perpetually saluting him back.

'Say sweet dreams to the general, highness.'

'Sweet dreams, general…'

'And remember, when you've had your nap, you're to see Crown Prince Oswald. You're to put your seal to some papers.'

Oswald. As Maximilian fell asleep to dream of battles and wars, he tried to think of Oswald. There were two Oswalds. His father, the old grand prince, had been an Oswald. And there was another, a younger fellow. It must be his father he was to see, because Old Oswald was important, another hero of the Empire.

But still… eggs!

V

Despite his hard-won distrust of the Great and the Good, Detlef Sierck was impressed with Crown Prince Oswald. Those who carve their names in the annals of history usually turn out to be drooling idiots. The general who kept back the hordes of darkness smells like a cesspool, picks his nose and has pieces of onion in his beard. The courtesan who decided the fate of a city has a missing tooth, a grating laugh and the habit of digging you painfully in the ribs whenever a double entendre creeps into the conversation. And the philosopher whose propositions changed the entire course of Imperial Thought is locked in an infantile battle with his neighbour over a barking dog. But Crown Prince Oswald still looked in every particular the hero who slew the monster, won the lady, saved the kingdom and honoured his father.

He was more handsome than any matinee idol, and his relaxed but alert posture suggested an athleticism superior to most professional swordsmen or tumblers. Detlef, used to being the object of all eyes in company, realized sadly that were a party of ladies to be introduced into the room, they would all, even if unaware of his position in society, flock to Oswald. Detlef would be left to make embarrassed conversation with the inevitable bespectacled, bad-complexioned frump all groups of pretty women haul about with them to throw their attributes into the spotlight.

There was a woman in the story of Oswald and Drachenfels, Detlef was sure. A beautiful woman, of course. What had her name been? He was certain the crown prince was unmarried, so she must have passed out of the story soon after the death of the Great Enchanter. Perhaps she died. That was the fashion in melodrama, for the hero's beloved to die. Heroes had to be free of such attachments if they were to continue their adventuring. During his own dashing hero phase, Detlef had lost count of the number of dying damsels he had vowed eternal love over, and the number of justified revenges he had later claimed.

The crown prince bit into the apple with perfect, even teeth, and chewed. Detlef was conscious that his own teeth were rather bad. He had even taken to wearing his moustaches unfashionably long to cover them up. But he was also conscious now of the hunger that had been with him for months. He knew the crown prince was looking him over, getting the measure of him, but he could only look, with a craving that amounted to lust, at the plain bowl of fruit. He swallowed the saliva that had filled his mouth, and forced himself to meet his visitor's gaze.

What must he look like after these months of Mundsen Keep? He assumed that, even without Oswald to make him seem the male answer to the proverbial frump, he would break no hearts for the while. His stomach groaned as the crown prince threw his apple core into the fire. It hissed as it burned. Detlef would have exchanged a week's bread and cheese for the fruitflesh that had remained on that core.

Evidently, his hunger was all too obvious to his visitor. 'By all means, Mr Sierck, help yourself...'

Crown Prince Oswald waved a gloved hand at the bowl. Pearl buttons at his wrist caught the light. He was, of course, dressed impeccably and in the latest style. Yet there was no showiness about his costume. He wore rich clothes with ease and wasn't overwhelmed by them. There was, indeed, a princely simplicity about his outfit that would look all the better by comparison with the gaudy gorgeousness and over-ornamentation favoured by too many of the nobility.

Detlef touched an apple, relishing the feel of it, like a picky housewife in the marketplace testing for ripeness before making a purchase. He took it out of the bowl, and examined it. His stomach felt as if it had never been full. There were sharp pains. He bit into the fruit, and swallowed a mouthful down without tasting it. The apple was gone in three bites, core and all. He took a pear, and made a hasty meal of that too. Juice dribbled down his face. The crown prince watched with an eyebrow raised in amusement.

Oswald was still a young man, Detlef realized. And yet his famed exploit was some twenty-five years behind him. He must have been little more than a boy when he bested Drachenfels.

'I have read your works, Mr Sierck. I have seen you perform. You are prodigiously talented.'

Detlef grunted his agreement through a mouthful of grapes. He spat the pips into his hand, and felt foolish that there was nowhere else to put them. He made a fist, intending to swallow them later. If Kosinski could eat mice, then Detlef Sierck wouldn't baulk at grapestones.

'I was even granted access to the manuscript of your History of Sigmar. It is held, as you must know, by the elector of Middenland.'

'My greatest work? Did you like it?'

The crown prince smiled, almost slyly. 'It was... ambitious. If impractical...'

'The manuscript would tell you little, highness. You should have seen the production. That would have convinced you. It would have been epoch-making.'

'No doubt.'

The two men looked closely at each other. Detlef stopped eating when there was no more fruit. The crown prince was in no hurry to disclose the purpose of his visit to Mundsen Keep. The fire burned. Detlef was aware of the pleasantness of simple warmth and space. An upholstered chair to sit on, and a table for his elbows. Before he came to the keep, he had insisted on mountains of embroidered pillows, maidservants waiting forever in attendance to gratify his needs, lavish meals served at any hour of the day or night to fuel his genius, and the finest musicians to play for him when he needed inspiration. His theatre in Middenheim had been more imposing, more monumental, than the Collegium Theologica. Never again would he demand such luxuries if he could but have a bed with a mattress, a fireplace and an axe to get wood, and a sufficiency of humble but honest fare for the table.

'The courts have found you responsible for quite a considerable sum of money. You have more creditors than a Tilean kingdom has illegitimate claimants to the throne.'

'Indeed, crown prince. That is why I am here. Through no fault of my own, I assure you. It is not my place to criticize an elector of the Empire, but your honoured colleague from Middenland has hardly acted in the spirit of fairness and decency over my situation. He undertook the responsibility for my production, and then had his lawyers find a way of breaking his contract with me...'

In fact, Detlef had been forced at knife-point to sign a statement absolving the elector of Middenland of any financial liability for The History of Sigmar. Later, the Konigsgarten Theatre had been burned to the ground by a rioting mob of tailors, carpenters, bit-part-players, musicians, ticket-holders, saddlers, bawds, merchants and inn-keepers. When faced with the choice between a pit of lime and a barrel of boiling tar, his trusted stage manager had denounced him. Everything he had had was seized by the elector's bailiffs and thrown to the creditors. And Middenland himself had elected to make an official visit to some southern state with a decent climate and an official edict against stage plays not of a tediously religious nature. No amount of petitioning could recall the former patron of the arts to the aid of the greatest actor-dramatist to put on a false nose since Jacopo Tarradasch himself. And since Detlef had always felt Tarradasch somewhat overrated, the calumny stung even more. He could conceive of no tragedy greater than that his art should be stifled. It was not for himself that he railed against the injustice of his life in prison, but for the world that was deprived of the fruits of his genius.

'Middenland is the beggar among electors,' said the crown prince. 'He has no elephants from the east, no golden idols from Lustria. Set beside the riches of the emperor, his fortune would barely pay for a pot of ale and a side of beef. Your debts are nothing.'

Detlef was astonished.

Seriously, Oswald said, 'Your debts can be taken care of.'

Detlef felt the tripwire coming. Here were the Great and the Good again, smiling and reassuring him that all would be taken care of, that his worries were thrown out with yesterday's slops. He had learned from his dealings with patrons that the rich are a different species. Money was like the fabled warpstone; the more contact you had with the stuff, the less like a human being you became.

His presentiment troubled him again. He was supposed to have a touch of magic in him through some wrong-side-of-the-blanket great-grandfather. Once in a while, he had intuitions.

'You could walk out of Mundsen Keep this afternoon,' the crown prince said, 'with crowns enough to set you up in fine style at any hostelry in Altdorf.'

'Highness, we are straightforward men, are we not? I would indeed relish the prospect of quitting my current accommodations. Furthermore, it would please me greatly to have the burden of my innocently-acquired debts lifted from me. And I have no doubt that your family has the wherewithal to accomplish such miracles. But, as you may know, I am from Nuln, a beneficiary of that city's famed houses of learning. My father began life as a street vendor of vegetables and rose through his own efforts to great wealth. Throughout his life, he remembered the lore of his initial calling, and he taught me a lesson far greater than any the priests and professors were able to impart. "Detlef," he said once to me, "nobody ever gives anything away. There is always a price." And that lesson comes back to me now...'

Actually, Detlef's father had always refused to talk about the days before he assembled the strong-arm gang who enabled him to corner the Nuln vegetable market by smashing the other traders' stalls. He had been too much of a miserable bastard to give his son any advice beyond 'don't go on the stage or I'll cut you off without a penny!' Detlef had heard that his father died of apoplexy during a meeting with the Nuln tax collectors, at precisely the moment when it was suggested that his returns for the last thirty years would bear a close re-examination. His mother had decamped to the coastal city of Magritta in Estalia and taken up with a much younger man, a minstrel more noted for the contour of his tights than the sweetness of his voice. She hadn't exactly encouraged his genius either.

'In short, highness, I would know now, before accepting your generous offer of aid, what is the price for your intervention in my case? What do you want of me?'

'You're a shrewd fellow, Sierck. I want you to write and stage a play for me. Something less unwieldy than your History of Sigmar, but nevertheless a work of some standing. I want you to write and perform my own story, the story of my quest to Castle Drachenfels, and of the fall of the Great Enchanter.'

Act Two

I

It took a full week to negotiate the contract. During that time, Crown Prince Oswald arranged, much to Governor van Zandt's cold fury, that Detlef have his collar struck and be transferred to more comfortable quarters within the keep. Unfortunately for the administration of the prison, the only quarters that even approximated Detlef's idea of comfort were the governor's own official chambers in the central tower. Van Zandt was booted out to seek refuge in a nearby hostelry and Detlef took over his offices for his own business. Although still technically a convicted debtor, he took the opportunity to rearrange his circumstances. Instead of a single dirty blanket, he had an Imperial size bed brought to the governor's rooms; instead of Szaradat's rough treatment, he was attended by a poor unfortunate girl in whose case he took an interest and whose gratitude was memorable and invigorating; and instead of the cheese, bread and water, he was served a selection of the finest meats, wines and puddings.

Even for a week, however, he could not tolerate the drab and tasteless furnishings van Zandt evidently chose to live with. It was hardly the governor's fault that his parents had been a pair of pop-eyed uglies with little judgement when it came to commissioning portraits from cross-eyed mountebanks, but it seemed odd that he should compound the family shame by hanging over his desk an especially revolting daub of the van Zandts, senior, bathed in the golden light of some idiot's palette. After a morning in the room with the thing, imagining the governor's fish-faced mother frowning upon him with disapproval, Detlef personally threw the painting off the balcony and had it replaced with a magnificent oil of himself in the role of Guillaume the Conqueror in Tarradasch's Barbenoire: The Bastard of Bretonnia. He had a generous impulse to leave it behind when he left, to cheer up the cold-hearted official's surroundings with a daily reminder of the keep's most notable past tenant, but then thought better of it. The oil, executed by the Konigsgarten Theatre's art director, was too valued an item to leave for such a poor fellow to gaze dully upon while shuffling parchments and sanctioning the mindless brutality of his staff.

Normally, he would have entrusted the business of the contract to his valued associate, Thomas the Bargainer. But Thomas had been the first to turn on him, and stood at the head of the list of creditors, with his hand out for repayment. Therefore, Detlef took care of the tedious business himself. After all, Thomas had bargained him into his contract with the elector of Middenland. This time, he was certain, there would be no hidden clauses to catch him later.

The agreement was that Oswald pledged to underwrite the production of Detlef's Drachenfels to the depths of his treasury, provided the dramatist himself lived modestly. Detlef hadn't been sure about that particular condition, but then reasonably assumed that the crown prince's idea of a modest living would probably shame a sybarite's decadent dream of total luxury. As Detlef put it, between sips of van Zandt's Estalian sherry, 'all a man like me requires is food and drink, a warm bed with a stout roof over it, and the means to represent my genius to the public.'

Detlef also decided to share his good fortune with his erstwhile cellmates, and insisted that Oswald settle their debts too. In each case, the release could only be obtained if Detlef promised to vouch for their good character and provide them with employment. That was no problem: Kosinski and Manolo were brawny enough to shift heavy scenery, Justus's previous occupation suggested he would make a fine character actor, Kerreth could cobble for the whole company, and Guglielmo would, his bankruptcy notwithstanding, make an admirable substitute for Thomas the Betrayer as business manager. Detlef even arranged, anonymously, for Szaradat's release, confident that the turnkey's base qualities would swiftly return him to prison. It would take years of suffering for him to regain, if he ever did, his unmerited position of privilege within the order of misery that was Mundsen Keep.

Meanwhile, Crown Prince Oswald had a ballroom in his palace reopened as a rehearsal hall. His mother had been fond of lavish parties, but since her death the position of the Empire's premier hostess had fallen to the Countess Emmanuelle von Liebewitz of Nuln. The old grand prince, struck down by ill-health and grief, pottered about with toy soldiers, refighting all his great battles in his private rooms, but the business of the von Konigswalds was done exclusively now by his son. Oswald's men were sent to seek out those remaining members of the Konigsgarten Theatre company who hadn't turned traitor. More than a few actors, stage-hands and creative personnel who had sworn never again to be involved in a Detlef Sierck production were wooed back to the Prodigy of Konigsgarten by the von Konigswald name and the sudden settling of outstanding wages they had long ago written off as another loss in the notoriously hard life of the stage.

Word of Detlef's return spread throughout Altdorf, and was even talked about in Nuln and Middenland. The elector of Middenheim took advantage of the sudden interest to have The History of Sigmar published along with a self-composed memoir blaming the dramatist for the disaster of the production that had never taken place. The book sold well, and thanks to his ownership of the manuscript, the elector was able to avoid paying a penny to Detlef. One of Gruenliebe's balladeers composed a ditty about the foolishness of entrusting another major theatrical event to the architect of the Sigmar debacle. When the song came to the attention of Crown Prince Oswald, the balladeer found his license to jest summarily revoked, his merry face no longer welcome in even the lowest dives and a passage paid for him on a trading expedition to Araby and the South Lands.

Eventually, the contract was drawn up, and Detlef and the crown prince put their seals to it. The greatest dramatist of his generation strolled through the open gates of the debtors' prison, dressed again in flamboyant finery, his grateful comrades a respectful twenty paces behind. It was the first good day of spring, and the streams of melting snow cleaned the streets around the depressing edifice of the keep. He looked back, and saw van Zandt fuming on one of his balconies. Two trusties were carrying a bent and muddy painting up the outside staircase of the tower. Van Zandt shook his fist in the air. Detlef swept the ground with his longfeathered cap and bowed low to the governor. Then, straightening, he gave a cheery wave to all the miserable souls peering out through the bars, and turned his back forever on Mundsen Keep.

II

'No,' screamed Lilli Nissen in her dressing room at the Premiere Theatre in Marienburg, as the fourth of the four priceless jewel-inset cut-glass goblets given her by the Grand Duke of Talabecland shattered into a million pieces against the wall. 'No, no, no, no, no!'

The emissary from Altdorf quaked as the famed beauty's cheeks burned red, and her haughty nostrils flared in unnatural fury. Her large, dark eyes shone like a cat's. The minute lines about her mouth and eyes, totally unnoticeable when her face was in repose, formed deep and dangerous crevices in her carefully-applied paint.

It was entirely possible, Oswald's man supposed, that her face would fall off completely. He wasn't sure he wanted to see what lay beneath the surface that had so enchanted sculptors, painters, poets, statesmen and – it was rumoured – six out of fourteen electors.

'No, no, no, no, no, no.'

She looked at the seal on the letter again, the tragic and comic faces Detlef Sierck had taken for his emblem, and tore it off with lacquered fingernails like the claws of a carrion bird. She had gone into her rant without even scanning the substance of the message, simply at the mention of the name of the man from whom it came.

Lilli's trembling dresser cringed in the corner, the bruises on her face eloquent testimony to the great beauty's hidden ugliness. The dresser had a lopsided face, and one of her legs was shorter than the other, forcing her to hobble on a thick-soled boot. Given the choice, Oswald's man would have at that moment chosen the dresser to warm his bed at the Hotel Marienburg this night, and left the actress who could inspire love in millions to her own devices.

'No, no, no, no.' The screaming was less shrill now, as Lilli digested the meat of Sierck's proposal. Oswald's man knew she would relent. Another starring role more or less meant nothing to the woman, but the name of Oswald von Konigswald must stand out on the page as if written in fire. He would be elector of Ostland soon, and Lilli had a collection to complete.

'No, no...'

The actress fell silent, her blood-red lips moving as she re-read the letter from Detlef Sierck. The dresser sighed, and came out of her corner.

Without a complaint, she got painfully down on her knees and started picking up the pieces of the goblets, separating the worthless glass shards from the redeemable jewels.

Lilli looked up at Oswald's messenger and flashed a smile he would remember every time he saw a pretty woman for the rest of his life. She put her fingers to her temples, and smoothed away the cracks. Again, she was perfect, the loveliest woman who ever lived. Her tongue flicked over one sharp eyetooth – the dramatist had cast her well as a vampire – and her hand went to the jewelled choker at her throat. Her fingers played with the rubies, and then went lower, parting her negligee, revealing a creamy expanse of unrouged skin.

'Yes,' she said, fixing Oswald's man with her glance. 'Yes.' He forgot the dresser.

III

'Have I ever told you about the time when the Crown Prince Oswald and I bested the Great Enchanter?' roared the fat old man.

'Yes, Rudi,' said Bauman, without enthusiasm. 'But this time you'll have to pay for your gin with coin, not the same old story.'

'Surely there's someone...' Rudi Wegener began, sweeping a meaty arm about.

The solitary drinkers of the Black Bat Tavern took no notice of him. His chins shook under his patchy grey beard, and he lurched from his stool at the bar, enormous belly seeming to move independently of the rest of his body. Bauman had reinforced the stool with metal braces, but knew that Rudi would still crush it to splinters one day.

'It's a fine tale, my friends. Full of heroic deeds, beautiful ladies, great perils, terrible injuries, treachery and deceit, rivers of blood and lakes of poison, good men gone bad, and bad men gone worse. And it ends nobly, with the prince destroying the monster, and Good Old Rudi there to guard his back.'

The drinkers looked down into their tankards. The wine was vinegary, and the beer watered down with rat's pee, but it was cheap. Not cheap enough for Rudi, though. Two pence a pint might as well be a thousand gold crowns if you don't have two pence.

'Come on, friends, won't anyone hear the story of good old Rudi? Of the prince and the Great Enchanter?'

Bauman emptied the remains of a bottle into a pot and pushed it across the polished and scarred wood towards the old man. 'I'll buy you a drink, Rudi...'

Rudi turned, alcoholic tears coursing down the fatty pockets of his cheeks, and put a huge hand around the pot.

'... but only on the condition that you don't tell us about your great adventures as a bandit king.'

The old man's face fell and he slumped on the stool. He moaned – he had hurt his back long ago, Bauman knew – and peered into the pot. He looked down at himself in the wine, and shuddered at some unspoken thought. The moment was a long one, an uncomfortable one, but it passed. He raised the pot to his mouth, and drained it in a draught. Gin flowed into his beard and down onto his much-stained, much-patched shirt. Rudi had been telling his lies in the Black Bat ever since Bauman had been old enough to help out his father behind the bar. As a boy, he had swallowed every story the fat old fraud dished out, and he had loved more than anything else to hear about Prince Oswald and the Lady Genevieve and the monster Drachenfels. He had believed every word of the tale.

But, as he grew up, he came to know more about life, and he discovered more about his father's clientele. He understood that Milhail, who would boast for hours of the many women he pursued and won, went home each night to his aged mother and slept alone in a cold and blameless bed. He learned that the Corin the Halfling, who claimed to be the rightful Head of the Moot dispossessed by a jealous cousin, was, in fact, a pick-pocket expelled from his home when his fingers got too arthritic to lift a purse unnoticed.

And Rudi, so far as he knew, had never adventured beyond Altdorf's Street of a Hundred Taverns. Even in his long-gone youth, the old soak couldn't have found a horse willing to go under him, hefted a weapon any more dangerous than a beer bottle – and then only to his lips – or stood up straight to any foeman who came his way. But, Rudi the Bandit King had been Bauman's childhood idea of a hero, and so now he generally had a drink or two to spare for the old fool whenever he hadn't the price in his pouch. He probably wasn't doing the old man that much of a kindness, since Bauman was certain Rudi was floating himself to a coffin on his wines and ales and the burning Estalian gin only he of all the Black Bat's patrons could stand.

It wasn't much of a night. Of the talkative regulars, only Rudi was in. Milhail's mother was sick again and Corin was in Mundsen Keep after a brief and unsuccessful return to his old calling. The others just nursed their miseries and drank themselves into a quiet stupor. The Black Bat was the losers' tavern. Bauman knew there were places with worse reputations – brawlers favoured the Sullen Knight, the unquiet dead flocked mysteriously to the Crescent Moon and the hard core of Altdorf's professional thieves and murderers could be found at the Holy Hammer of Sigmar – but few quite as depressing. After five straight years at the bottom of the street's dicing league, Bauman had withdrawn the tavern from the competition. Somewhere else could lose for a while. The only songs he ever heard were whines. And the only jokes he ever heard were bitter.

The door opened, and someone new came in. Someone who had never been to the Black Bat before. Bauman would have remembered him if he'd seen him. He was a handsome man, dressed with the kind of simplicity that can be very expensive. He was no loser, Bauman knew at once from the set of his jaw and the fire in his eyes. He was at his ease, but he was not the sort to be used to taverns. He would have a coach and horses outside, and a guard to protect them.

'Can I help you, sir?' Bauman asked.

'Yes,' the stranger's voice was deep and rich. 'I'm told that I can generally find someone here. An old friend. Rudolf Wegener.'

Rudi looked up from his pot, and turned on his stool. The wooden legs creaked and Bauman thought that this was finally going to be the tumble he had expected all along. But no, Rudi lurched upright, wiping his dirty hands on his dirtier shirt. The newcomer looked at the old man, and smiled.

'Rudi! Ulric, but it's been a long time...'

He extended a hand. A signet ring caught the light.

Rudi looked at the man, with honest tears in his eyes now. Bauman thought he was about to fall flat on his face in front of his old friend. With a painful thump, Rudi sank to one knee. Buttons burst from his shirt, and hairy rolls of belly fat surged out from behind the cloth. Rudi bowed his head, and took the outstretched hand. He kissed the ring.

'Get up, Rudi. You don't have to be like this. It is I who should bow to you.'

Rudi struggled upright, trying to push his gut back into his shirt and tighten his belt over it.

'Prince...' he said, struggling with the word. 'Highness, I...'

Recovering himself, he turned to the bar, and thumped it with his huge fist. Glasses and tankards jumped.

'Bauman, wine for my friend, Crown Prince Oswald. Gin for Rudi, King of the Bandits. And take yourself a pint of your best ale with my compliments.'

IV

Once established in the palace of the von Konigswalds, Detlef set to work. As usual, the play would grow into its final form as it was rehearsed, but he had to get a structure for it, cast the parts and rough out the characterizations.

He was allowed access to the von Konigswald library, and all the documents relating to the death of Drachenfels. Here was de Selincourt's The House of von Konigswald, with its flattering portrait of Crown Prince Oswald as a youth. And Genevieve Dieudonné's surprisingly slender A Life. My Years as a Bounty Hunter in Reikwald, Bretonnia and the Grey Mountains by Anton Veidt, as told to Joachim Munchberger; Constant Drachenfels: A Study in Evil by Helmholtz; The Poison Feast and Other Legends by Claudia Wieltse. And there were all the pamphlets and transcribed ballads. So many stories. So many versions of the same story. There were even two other plays – The Downfall of Drachenfels by that poltroon Matrac and Prince Oswald by Dorian Diessl – both, Detlef was delighted to find, appalling rubbish. With The History of Sigmar, he had found himself up against too many masterpieces on the same subject. Here, he had new dramatic ground to mark out as his own. It would especially amuse him to trounce his old critic and rival Diessl, and he worked in a lampoon of some of the more shabby mechanisms of the old man's terrible play into his own outline. He wondered if Dorian was still infecting the drama students at the Nuln University with his outmoded ideas, and if he would venture to Aldorf to see himself outstripped by the pupil he had dismissed from his lecture on Tarradasch when Detlef had pointed out that the great man's female characters were all the same.

The title bothered Detlef for some time. It had to have 'Drachenfels' in it. At first, he favoured Oswald and Drachenfels, but the crown prince wanted his name out of it. The History of Drachenfels was impossible: he didn't want to remind audiences of Sigmar, and, also, he was dealing only with the very end of a history that spanned thousands of years. Then he considered The Death of Drachenfels, The Fortress of Drachenfels, The Great Enchanter, Defier of the Dark and Castle of Shadows. For a while, he called it Heart of Darkness. Then, he experimented with The Man in the Iron Mask. Finally, he settled down with the simple, starkly dramatic one-word title, Drachenfels.

Oswald had promised to set aside an hour each day to be interviewed, to be questioned about the truth of his exploits. And he had endeavoured to track down those of his companions in adventure still living, to persuade them to come forward and discuss their own parts in the great drama with the writer who would set the seal on their immortality. Detlef had the facts, and he had a shape for his play. He even had some of the speeches written down. But he still felt he was only beginning to grasp the truths that would lie behind his artifice.

He began to dream of Drachenfels, of his iron face, of his unending evil. And after each dream, he wrote pages of dark poetry. The Great Enchanter was coming to life on paper.

Oswald was not without the aristocrat's traditional vanity, but he was strangely reticent on some subjects. He had commissioned Detlef's play as part of a celebration of the anniversary of his enemy's death, and he knew very well that the event would serve to increase his renown. Detlef gathered that it was important to Oswald to be in the public eye after some years as a background presence. He was already the elector in all but name, and his father wasn't expected to last out the summer. Eventually, he would have to be confirmed in his position and be, after the Emperor, one of the dozen most powerful men in the Empire. Detlef's Drachenfels would silence any voices that might speak out against the crown prince. Yet, for all Oswald's political canniness in backing a production that would remind the world of his great heroism just as he was ready to take part in the running of the Empire, Detlef still found the crown prince occasionally a little too modest for his own good. Incidents that in the accounts of others were hailed as mightily heroic he shrugged off with a simple 'it was the only thing to do' or 'I was there first, any of the others would have done the same.'

It wasn't until Rudi Wegener came forth to speak that Detlef began to understand what had happened in the Reikwald on the road to Castle Drachenfels, and how Oswald had bound together his companions in adventure almost by sheer force of will. And it wasn't until the cult of Sigmar finally allowed him to examine the Proscribed Grimoires of Khaine that Detlef realized quite how monstrously potent Drachenfels's age-spanning evil had been. He began to connect with the research he had done for The History of Sigmar, and – with a nauseating lurch in his stomach – tried to get his mind around the concept of a man, a mortal man born, who could have been alive in the time of Sigmar two-and-a-half thousand years ago and yet who was still walking when Detlef Sierck had been born. He had been four years old when Drachenfels died, exhibiting his prodigious genius in Nuln by composing symphonies for instruments he never got round to inventing.

Detlef wrote speeches, sketched settings, and whistled musical themes to Felix Hubermann. And Drachenfels began to take monstrous shape.

V

The tall, gaunt man who stuttered too badly crept away, his moment in the spotlight over.

'Next!' shouted Vargr Breughel.

Another tall, gaunt man strode onto the make-shift stage in the von Konigswald ballroom. The crowd of tall, gaunt men shuffled and muttered.

'Name?'

'Lowenstein,' said the man in deep, sepulchral tones, 'Laszlo Lowenstein.'

It was a fine, scary voice. Detlef felt good about this one. He nudged Breughel.

'What have you done?' asked Breughel.

'For seven years, I was the actor-manager of the Temple Theatre in Talabheim. Since coming to Altdorf, I have played Baron Trister in the Geheimnisstrasse Theatre production of The Desolate Prisoner. The critic of the Altdorf Spieler has referred to me as "the premier Tarradaschian tragedian of his, or indeed any other, generation".'

Detlef looked the man up and down. He had the height, and he had the voice.

'What do you think, Breughel?' he asked, so low that Lowenstein couldn't hear him. Vargr Breughel was the best assistant director in the city. If there wasn't a prejudice against dwarfs in the theatre, Detlef thought, he'd be the second best director in the city.

'His Trister was good,' said Breughel. 'But his Ottokar was outstanding. I'd recommend him.'

'Have you prepared anything?' Detlef asked, addressing a tall, gaunt man for the first time this morning.

Lowenstein bowed, and launched into Ottokar's dying declaration of love for the goddess Myrmidia. Tarradasch had claimed to be divinely inspired the day he wrote it, and the actor gave the best reading Detlef had ever heard of the speech. He himself had never played in The Loves of Ottokar and Myrmidia, and if he had to be compared with Laszlo Lowenstein, he might consider putting it off a few decades.

Detlef forgot the tall, gaunt actor, and saw only the humbled Ottokar, a haughty tyrant brought to the grave by an obsessive love, dragged into bloody deeds by the most noble of intentions, and only now conscious

that the persecution of the gods will extend beyond his death and torment him for an eternity.

When he finished, the crowd of tall, gaunt men – hard-bitten rivals
who would have been expected to look only with hatred and envy upon
such a gifted performer – applauded spontaneously.

Detlef wasn't sure, but he thought he'd found his Drachenfels.

'Leave your address with the crown prince's steward,' Detlef told the
man. 'We'll be in touch.'

Lowenstein bowed again, and left the stage.

'Do you want to see anyone else?' Breughel asked.

Detlef thought a moment. 'No, send the Drachenfelses home. Then
let's have the Rudis, the Meneshes, the Veidts and the Erzbets...'

VI

The madwoman was quiet. In her early days at the hospice, years ago, she had shouted and smeared the walls with her own filth. She told all who would listen that there were enemies coming for her. A man with a metal face. An old-young dead woman. She was constrained for her own good. She used to attempt suicide by stuffing her clothing into her mouth to stop her breathing, and so the priestesses of Shallya bound her hands by night. Eventually, she settled down and stopped making a fuss. She could be trusted now. She wasn't a problem any more.

Sister Clementine made the madwoman her especial concern. The daughter of rich and undeserving parents, Clementine Clausewitz had pledged herself to Shallya in an effort to pay back the debt she felt her family owed the world. Her father had been a rapacious exploiter of his tenants, forcing them to labour in his fields and factories until they dropped from exhaustion, and her mother an empty-headed flirt whose entire life was devoted to dreaming of the time when her only daughter could be launched in Altdorf society. The day before the first great ball, to which a pimply nine-year-old boy who was distantly related through marriage to the Imperial family was almost certainly going to come, Clementine had run off and sought the solace of a simple, monastic life.

The Sisters of Shallya devoted themselves to healing and mercy. Some went into the world as general practitioners, many toiled in the hospitals of the Old World's cities, and a few chose to serve in the hospices. Here, the incurable, the dying and the unwanted were welcome. And the Great Hospice in Frederheim, twenty miles outside Altdorf, was where the insane were confined. In the past, these cloisters had been home to two emperors, five generals, seven scions of electoral families, sundry poets and numberless undistinguished citizens. Insanity could settle upon anybody, and the sisters were supposed to treat each patient with equal care.

Clementine's madwoman couldn't remember her name – which was listed in the hospice records as Erzbet – but did know she had been a dancer. At times, she would astonish the other patients by performing with a delicacy and expressiveness that belied her wild, tangled hair and deeply-etched face. At other moments, she would recite a long list of names to herself. Clementine didn't know what Erzbet's litany meant, and – as one dedicated to a cult which forswore the taking of any intelligent life – would have been horrified to learn that her patient was recalling all those she had murdered.

Erzbet was supported in the hospice by generous donations. A person named Dieudonné who had never visited had ordered the banking house of Mandragora to set aside a hundred crowns a year for the hospice as long as the dancer was in its custody. And one of the first families of Altdorf also took an interest in her case. Whoever Erzbet had been, she had had some influential friends. Clementine wondered if she was the maddened daughter of some ashamed nobleman. But then again, her only regular caller was a remarkably fat and unsightly old man who smelled of gin and was clearly no one's idea of a leading light in high society. Who she had been was less important to the sister than who she would be.

Now, even Clementine had to admit Erzbet would most likely never again be anybody. Over the years, she had withdrawn into herself. During the hours she spent in the sunny quadrangle at the hospice, she simply stared into emptiness, not seeing the sisters or the other patients. She neither sewed nor sketched. She could not or would not read. She had not danced for over a year. She didn't even have nightmares any more. Most of the priestesses thought of Erzbet's quietness as a sign of merciful healing, but Sister Clementine knew this wasn't so. She was sinking fast. Now, she was a convenient patient – unlike some of the raving creatures the order had to deal with – but she was further into her own darkness than she had been when she was brought to the hospice.

The ravers – the biters, scratchers, kickers, screamers and resisters – got all the attention, while Erzbet sat still and didn't say anything. Sister Clementine tried to reach her, and took care to spend as much as an hour every day talking to her. She asked unanswered questions, told the woman about herself and brought up general topics. She never had the impression Erzbet heard her, but knew she had to try. Occasionally, she admitted to herself that she talked as much for her benefit as for Erzbet's. The other sisters were from a very different background, and were too often impatient with her. She felt a kinship with this troubled, silent woman.

Then, the man came from Crown Prince Oswald. A suave steward with a sealed letter for High Priestess Margaret. Somehow, Sister Clementine was disturbed by the steward's sleekness. His carriage was black, and had discreet bars fitted on it – incongruous next to the generous upholstery – specifically for this mission. The von Konigswald arms – a three-pointed crown against a spreading oak tree – reminded her of her silly mother's silly dreams. She didn't know if her parents had given up searching for her, or simply never cared enough to make the effort in the first place.

Margaret called her to the chapel, and told her to make Erzbet ready to take a trip. Clementine protested, but a simple look from the high priestess of mercy chilled her blood enough to dissuade her. The steward was with her when she went to see the madwoman in the courtyard. She thought the madwoman took notice of the man, and saw the old fears creeping back. Erzbet clung to her, kissing the silver dove on Sister

Clementine's robe. She tried to soothe her patient, but couldn't be convincing. The steward stood aside, seeming not impatient, and didn't say anything. Erzbet had no personal possessions, had no clothes outside the white robe the hospice's residents all wore. All she had was herself, and now, it seemed, she belonged to another, to the whim of a prince.

Clementine took the dove-pin from her robe, and gave it to Erzbet. Perhaps it would be a comfort to her. She stroked some semblance of tidiness into the woman's hair, kissed her forehead and said her goodbyes. The steward helped detach Erzbet's fingers from Clementine's robe. That night, the sister of Shallya cried herself to sleep. The next morning, she was surprised and a little ashamed to find her pillow stiff with dried tears. She made her devotions and returned to her duties.

High Priestess Margaret never told Clementine that in the coach on the road to Altdorf, Erzbet had found uses for the two-inch steel pin on the back of the dove the sister had given the madwoman. She gouged out the steward's eye and, while he was screaming and floundering in his own blood, jammed the pin into her own throat.

As the dancer-assassin died, she named her dead for the last time. The steward had never introduced himself, so she had to miss him out. But, as she finally slipped into the darkness where evil things were waiting for her, she remembered to list her last victim.

'Erzbet Wegener...'

VII

Kerreth had proved skilled with more than simple shoe-making. When he had brought Detlef the samples of his other work, he had been promoted to head of the wardrobe department in what was now being called the Von Konigswald Players' Theatre. He had seamstresses and tanners working under him, and was coming up with impressive designs for the special costumes. His leather suits of armour looked like iron, but weighed a fraction of what they ought to. The battle extras loved wearing them. And, on his own time, he came up with five separate leatherwork masks for Drachenfels. Detlef realized he was lucky to have found the little cobbler in the keep. Otherwise, he would have fainted under the weight of his costume half-way through the first act. At the last estimate, twenty-five per cent of the actresses who had been up for the role of Erzbet had fallen in love with Kerreth, and, after those months in Mundsen Keep, he had been only too happy to oblige them. Detlef felt the barest touch of envy, but ignored it. There was so much to do.

VIII

Lilli Nissen made an entrance while Detlef was busy shouting at Breughel about prop swords.

'Darling!' he screamed, his voice rising a full octave.

'Dearheart,' she answered. They flew into each other's arms and kissed noisily. Everyone stood and watched the greatest actor and actress in the Empire play an impromptu love scene.

'You're twice as lovely as you were the last time I saw you, Lilli. Your radiance knows no bounds!'

'And you, my genius, you have written me the greatest part any actress could hope to fill. I kiss each of your supremely talented fingers!'

Afterwards, Detlef told Breughel, 'It's a good thing that cow is playing a six hundred year-old in this one. It's the first time she's ever done anything near her real age.'

And Lilli shouted at her dresser, 'That fat, smug, oily monster! That foulest of worms! That viper-tongued tyrant! Only a personal summons from the grand prince of Ostland would persuade me to step into a room with that pus-oozing vermin, let alone play opposite him in another of his rot-awful shitguts melodramas!'

IX

Laszlo Lowenstein met his patron at dead of night in the back room of a supposedly empty house. He did not care who the man was, but often wondered what he hid behind his mask. Lowenstein's career had had its ups and downs since he was forced to quit Talabheim a few paces ahead of the witch hunters. A man of his talents and his habits was too easy to find, he reflected. He needed friends. Now he was in the Von Konigswald Players, he was protected by his association with the crown prince, even by his work with Detlef Sierck. But still he returned to his old patron, his original patron. Sometimes, years would go by without the man in the mask. Sometimes, they would meet on a daily basis.

Whenever Lowenstein needed him, the man got in touch. Usually through an intermediary. It had never been the same intermediary twice. Once, it had been a warpstone-altered dwarf, with a cluster of tentacles around his mouth and a jellied-over eye just opening in his forehead. This time, it had been a slender little girl dressed all in green. He would be given an address, and would find the man in the mask waiting for him.

'Laszlo,' the even, expressionless voice began, 'it's good to see you again. I hear you have been having a run of fortune lately.'

The actor was tense now – not all his patron's requests had been pleasant – but sat down. The man in the mask poured him some wine, and he drank. Like all the food and drink his patron had served him, it was excellent, expensive stuff.

'An indifferent house, don't you think?'

He looked at the room. It was undistinguished. Bare plaster, discoloured except where icons had hung. There was a rough table and two chairs, but no other furniture.

'I do believe it's due to be accidentally burned down tonight. The fire may spread to the whole street, the whole quarter...'

His mouth was dry now. He took more wine, and sloshed it around in his mouth. Lowenstein remembered another fire, in Talabheim. And the screams of a family trapped in the upper storeys of a fine house. He remembered the look of blood in the moonlight. It was red, but it seemed quite black.

'Wouldn't that be a tragedy, my dear friend, a tragedy?'

The actor was sweating, imagining expressions on the man's mask, imagining inflections in his voice. But there was nothing. Lowenstein's patron might just as well have been a tailor's dummy brought to life as a real man. He spoke as if he were reading his lines without any effort, just to get the words right.

'You have won yourself a fine role in the crown prince's little exercise in vanity, have you not?'

Lowenstein nodded.

'The title role?'

'Yes, but it's still a supporting part. Detlef Sierck, the playright, is taking the leading role, the young Prince Oswald.'

Lowenstein's patron chuckled, a sound like a machine rasping. 'Young Prince Oswald. Yes, how apt. How, thoroughly apt.'

Lowenstein was conscious of the lateness of the hour. He had to be at the palace early tomorrow, to be fitted by Kerreth the cobbler with his leather-iron outfit. He was tired.

'And you play...?'

'Drachenfels.'

The chuckle came again. 'Ah yes, the man in the iron mask. That must be uncomfortable, don't you think? An iron mask?'

The actor nodded, and the man in the mask laughed outright.

'What do...?'

'Come on now, Laszlo, spit it out.'

'What do you want of me?'

'Why, nothing, my friend. Just to congratulate you, and to remind you of your old attachments. I hope you shan't forget your friends as you achieve the fame you so richly deserve. No, I hope you shan't forget...'

Something small was crying softly in the next room. It bleated like a goat. Lowenstein felt the uncertain stirrings of his old desires. The desires that had led him to his nomadic life, that had made him a wanderer from city to city. Always cities, never towns, villages. He needed a population large enough to hide in. But he needed to hide while putting his face before audiences every night. It was not an easy situation. Without his mysterious patron, he'd have been dead seven times over.

Lowenstein controlled himself. 'I don't forget.'

'Good. You've enjoyed your wine, I trust?'

The crying was quite loud now, not like a goat or a lamb at all. Lowenstein knew what awaited him next. He wasn't as tired as he had thought. He nodded his head to his patron's question.

'Excellent. I like a man who enjoys his pleasures. Who relishes the finer things in life. I enjoy rewarding them. Over the years, I've greatly enjoyed rewarding you.'

He got up and opened a door. The room beyond was lit by a single candle. The thing that cried was tied to a cot. On a table beside it were laid out a trayful of shining silver implements such as Kerreth the cobbler might have, or one of the barber surgeons in Ingoldtstrasse. Lowenstein's palms were slick now, and his nails dug into them. He finished his wine with indecent haste, wiping a trickle from his chin. Trembling, he got up and walked into the other room.

'Laszlo, your pleasure awaits you...'

X

Detlef was discussing sets with Crown Prince Oswald's architects. The crown prince had managed to arrange for the purchase of the actual fortress of Drachenfels, with the intention of staging the play in its great hall. The advantages were obvious, but so were the drawbacks. Some parts of the castle would have to be restored to their original condition, and others remade as dressing rooms, scenery docks and actors' quarters. A stage would be built in the great hall. Initially, Detlef was tempted by the idea of having the play take place in real time, with the audience tagging along after the characters as they made their way to the fortress and then penetrated its interior. But the scheme was too reminiscent of The History of Sigmar for Oswald to authorize.

Besides, while the audience would be few enough in number – only the most important citizens of the Empire would be privileged to attend the performance – they were not likely to be in the first bloom of youth. It would be difficult enough to transport the creaky and antique dignitaries to the fortress by the gently sloping road that had been impassable and daemon-haunted in Oswald's days, let alone the vertiginous path the adventurers had taken. Even if Detlef's cast could brave the perils, it would be likely that some high priest or lord chamberlain would take a nasty tumble from the sheer cliffs on top of which the fortress stood.

This would be the crowning achievement of his career, this single performance. But, all the while, Detlef was planning to prepare a less lavish version of his text more suited to ordinary theatres. He saw no reason why Drachenfels shouldn't enter the repertoire of every company in the Empire, on the condition that substantial royalties were paid him. He already had Guglielmo putting out feelers for a theatre in Altdorf where the play could have a good run after its much-publicized premiere. There was already much interest, with the involvement of the crown prince doing a good deal to offset Detlef's bad reputation. Detlef was waiting for a good bid from a house which would let him stage his play by his own lights, and take the central role himself. Currently, he favoured Anselmo's on Breichtstrasse, but the more experimental Temple of Drama was running a close second. Anselmo's was just a bit too wrapped up in regurgitating two-hundred-year-old productions of

Tarradasch's lesser works for the burghers and merchants who came to Altdorf and felt they had to snore through a play while in the city.

Detlef glanced over the architects' sketches, and put his initials to them. He was satisfied with their suggestions, although he would have to go himself to Castle Drachenfels before making any final decisions. After all, it should be safe now. The Great Enchanter had been dead for twenty-five years.

'Detlef, Detlef, a problem…'

It was Vargr Breughel, waddling into Detlef's chambers with his usual perpetual expression of anxiety. It was always a problem. The whole art of drama was nothing but a succession of problems solved, ignored or avoided.

'What now?' Detlef sighed.

'It's the role of Menesh…'

'I thought I'd told you to settle with Gesualdo. I trust you in matters dwarfish, you know. You ought to be an expert.'

Breughel shifted on his feet. He was not a true dwarf, but the stunted offspring of human parents. Detlef wondered if his trusted lieutenant didn't have a touch of the warpstone in his nature. A lot of people in the theatrical profession had an iota or two of Chaos in their make-up. Detlef himself had had an extra little toe on his left foot which his lamented father had personally amputated.

'There's been some controversy over your selection of the Tilean jester for the part,' said Breughel, waving a long curl of paper covered in blotty signatures. 'Word got out, and some of the dwarfs of Altdorf are presenting this petition. They're protesting against the representation of all dwarfs on the stage as comic relief. Menesh was a great hero to the dwarfs.'

'And what about Ueli the Traitor? Is he a great hero to the dwarfs?'

'Ueli wasn't a real dwarf, as you well know.'

'He's also not likely to be the source of much comic relief, is he? I can't think of many stab-in-the-back gags.'

Breughel looked exasperated. 'We can't afford to upset the dwarfs, Detlef. Too many of them work in the theatre. You don't want a scene-shifters' strike. Personally, I hate the smug bastards. Do you know what it's like being turned out of taverns for being a dwarf when you aren't one, and then being turned out of dwarf taverns for not being a real dwarf?'

'I'm sorry, my friend. I wasn't thinking.'

Breughel calmed down a little. Detlef looked at the illegible petition.

'Just tell them I promise not to make any unwarranted fun of Menesh. Look, here, I'm making some cuts…'

Detlef tore up some already discarded pages. Accidentally, the petition was among them.

'There, no more "short" jokes. Satisfied?'

'Well, there's another objection to Gesualdo.'

Detlef thumped his desk. 'What now? Don't they know that geniuses need peace of mind to create?'

'It's the one-armed dwarf actor we saw. He's insisting he have the role, that he's the only one who can play the part.'

'But Menesh only gets his arm torn off at the very end. I admit we could do some clever trickery with a fake limb full of pig's guts and have a convincing horror scene. But he'd never be able to go through the whole drama without the audience noticing the stiff and inactive hand. Besides, the fool was at least twenty years too old for the part.'

Breughel snorted. 'He would be, Detlef. He's the real Menesh!

XI

The prisoner was going to make an escape attempt. Anton Veidt could see Erno the burglar tensing himself for the break-away. They were only three streets away from the town house of Lord Liedenbrock, the citizen who had posted reward on the man. Once Veidt dropped his charge off and collected his bounty, Liedenbrock would be free to do whatever he wanted to get his property – twenty gold crowns, some jewels belonging to the countess and a gilded icon of Ulric – back. And since the thief had fenced the merchandise in another town and drunk away all the money, Liedenbrock would probably turn his mind towards extracting repayment in fingernails or eyes rather than more common currency. The lord had a reputation for severity. If he hadn't, he would have hardly employed Veidt.

The bounty hunter could tell precisely when Erno would make his run for freedom. He saw the alleyway coming a hundred yards away, and knew his man would try to duck into it, hoping to outdistance Veidt and find some willing blacksmith to get the chains off his arms and legs. He must think the old man wouldn't be able to run after him.

And, of course, he was right. In his youth, Veidt might have raced after Erno and brought him down with a tackle. But, then again, he would more likely have done exactly what he was going to have to do now.

'Veidt,' said the burglar, 'couldn't we come to some arrangement...'

Here was the alley.

'Couldn't we...?'

Erno swung his chains at the bounty hunter. Veidt stepped back, out of range. The burglar pushed aside a fat woman nursing a child. The baby started bawling, and the woman was in Veidt's way.

'Get down,' he shouted, drawing his dart pistol.

The woman was stupid. He had to shove her aside and take aim. The child was squealing like a roasting pig now.

The alleyway was narrow and straight. Erno couldn't weave from side to side. He slipped on some garbage, and fell, chains tangling about him. He rose again, and ran, reaching for a low wall. Sharply conscious of the pain in his twice-broken, twice-set wrist, Veidt brought his pistol up and fired.

The dart took Erno in the back of the neck, lifted him off his feet, and brought him down in a heap of limbs and chains amid the filth of the gutter. Evidently, the alley was used mainly by the inhabitants of the upper storeys of the adjacent houses as a receptacle for their wastes. The stones were thickly-grimed, and a smell of dead fish and rotting vegetables hung like a miasma in the air.

Veidt had been trying for the thighs. That should have brought Erno down, but kept him breathing. The money was the same, dead or alive, but now he would have to haul the deadweight carcass to Liedenbrock's house. And he was breathing hard already. He leaned against a slimy wall, and fought for breath.

A physician had told him that something was eating him up from the inside, a sickness that might be the result of his life-long addiction to the strong cigars of Araby. 'It's like a black crab feeding inside you, Veidt,' the man had said, 'and it'll kill you in the end.'

Veidt didn't mind. Everybody died. If it came to a life without cigars or death with them, he'd not have hesitated about his choice. He took out a cigar now, and his tinderbox. He drew in a double lungful of smoke, and had a coughing fit. He hawked black, ropy phlegm, and made his way down the alley, steadying himself against the walls.

Erno was dead, of course. Veidt pulled out his dart and wiped it clean on the corpse's rags. He reloaded the pistol, setting the spring and the safety catch. Then, he unlocked the chains, and slung them over his shoulder. Chains were an expensive item in his line of work. He'd been using these, forged especially by dwarf blacksmiths, for over ten years. They were good chains, and had kept far more dangerous men than Erno in his custody.

He took the dead man by his bare feet – he'd sold the boots after chaining him up – and dragged him back to the street. As he pulled, there were sharp pains in his chest. The black crab was settling on his ribs, he thought, eating away at the muscles holding bone together, and now his skeleton was grinding itself to dirt inside him. It wouldn't be much longer before he collapsed like a jellyfish, useless to himself.

His aim wasn't so good these days, either. Good enough, he supposed, but he used to be a champion shot. When bounty hunting had been slow, he'd been able to pick up extra income from winning contests. Longbow, crossbow, pistol, throwing knife: he'd been the best with them all. And how he'd taken care of his weapons! Each was honed to the perfect sharpness, oiled if need be, polished, and ready to kiss blood. He still tried to keep up, but sometimes things were more difficult for him than they had been.

Twenty-five years ago, briefly, he had been a hero. But fame passes quickly. And his part in the downfall of Drachenfels had been minor enough to be overlooked by most balladeers. That's why he had allowed Joachim Munchberger to publish Veidt's own account as a book. The mountebank had disappeared with all the profits, and it had taken him some years – working between jobs – to track him down and extract payment. Munchberger must have had to learn to write with his left hand.

Now, the whole thing was about to start up again. Crown Prince Oswald's emissaries had found him, and asked him to come forward and talk to a fat actor for some new version of the tale. Veidt would have refused, but money was offered, and so soon he would have to go through the whole dull story again for this Detlef Sierck – a runaway debtor himself, by all accounts – and again be overlooked while young Oswald luxuriated in the golden glow of glory.

Oswald! He had come a long way down the road since his days as a snot-nosed boy. Soon, he'd be picking his first emperor. While blubber-bellied Rudi Wegener was drowning himself in gin, crazy Erzbet was raving in some cell and Lady Eternity was gorging herself on virgins' blood. And Anton Veidt was where he'd always been, out on the streets, searching for the wanted and unwanted criminals, converting the guilty into crowns. Oswald was welcome to his position.

Erno was getting heavier. Veidt had to sit down in the street and rest. A crowd gathered around him as he watched over his goods, but soon went away again. Flies were buzzing about the dead man's face, crawling into his open mouth and nostrils. Veidt hadn't the strength to shoo them away.

So, haloed by insects, the two proceeded together towards the house of the fine gentleman.

XII

Detlef woke up to find himself face down in a sea of manuscript pages. He had fallen asleep at his desk. By the clock, it was three in the morning. The palace was cold and quiet. His candle had burned low, spilling wax onto the desk, but the flame still burned.

Sitting upright, he felt the dull throbbing in his head that always came with periods of extreme overwork. Sherry would help. He always had some nearby. He pushed his chair back, and took a bottle from the cabinet near the desk. He swigged a mouthful from the bottle, then poured himself a glass. It was fine stuff, like all the luxuries of the von Konigswald palace. He rubbed together his chilled hands to get the warmth back into them.

He ordered the pages on the desk, shuffling them together. His working text was nearly complete. All the alterations prompted by his interviews with Rudi Wegener, Menesh the dwarf and the crown prince were pencilled in, and he doubted whether the testimony of the bounty hunter Veidt or the vampire lady Dieudonné would make much difference. Research was the skeleton of the play, but the flesh on it was all Detlef Sierck's. His audience would expect no less. Oswald had even encouraged him to depart from history at a few points, the better to reach the truth of the matter. Would that all patrons were as enlightened in the matter of artistic license.

His headache began to fade, and he re-read a few pages. He had been working on his curtain speech, the summation of the drama, when he had fallen asleep, and an ink-trail scratched across the bottom of the last sheet of paper.

He'd blotted his soliloquy with his cheek, and guessed the ink would be dried in by now. He must look a fool.

His own words still moved him. He knew only he could do justice to such a speech, only he could convey the triumph of good over evil without falling into bathos or melodrama. Strong men would weep as Detlef-as-Oswald spoke over his fallen foe, finding at last a touch of sorrow for the ending of even a life such as Drachenfels had led. He had planned to have Hubermann underscore the scene with a solo gamba, but now he decided that the music wouldn't be necessary. The lone voice, the stirring words, would be enough.

'Let joyful towers a tintinnabulation sound
That the Enchanter Great is under good ground,
And let th'infernal churches sound their bells
To welcome Constant Drachenfels.'

Outside the window lay the grounds of the palace, and beyond them the sleeping city. There was a full moon, and he could see the immaculately laid-out lawns as if in a monochrome etching. The crown prince's ancestors, the previous electors of Ostland, stood in a row on pedestals, seeming staid and monolithic. Old Maximilian was there, in his younger days, waving a sword for the Empire. Detlef had seen the current elector being assisted about the place by his nurses, blathering to all who would listen about the great old days. Everyone in the household knew the time of Maximilian was drawing to an end, and that the days of Oswald would soon be beginning.

The architects Oswald had engaged to assist in the settings for the play were also planning to remodel some of the palace. More and more, the crown prince was taking over the business of the von Konigswalds. He spent most of his days closeted with high priests, chancellors, Imperial envoys and officials of the court. The succession should be smooth. And Detlef's Drachenfels would mark the start of the Oswaldian era. An artist is not always set aside from the course of history, he supposed. Sometimes, an artist could as much make history as a general, an emperor or an elector.

He scratched his moustache, and drank more sherry, savouring the quiet of the palace by night. It was so long since he had known sustained quiet. The nights of Mundsen Keep had been filled with terrible groans, the screams of those who slept badly and the incessant drip of the wet walls and ceilings. And his days now were a total cacophony of voices and problems. He had to interview actors and the leftovers of Oswald's adventurers. He had to argue with those too hidebound to see how to convert his ideas into actuality. He had to put up with the shrill complaints and the nauseating cooing of Lilli Nissen. And, through it all, there was the clumping of booted feet on wood as actors stamped through rehearsals, the hammerings of the workmen constructing devices for the play and the clatter of the cast members learning to fence for the fight scenes. Most of all, there was Breughel, always roaring 'Detlef, Detlef, a problem, a problem...'

Sometimes, he asked himself why he had chosen the theatre as an outlet for his genius. Then, he remembered...

There was nothing to compare it with.

A cold hand caressed his heart. Out there in the gardens, things were moving. Moving in the shadows of the electors' statues. Detlef wondered if he should raise the alarm. But something suggested to him that these shapes were not assassins or robbers. There was an unearthly languor to their movements, and he thought he detected a faint glow, as of moonlight, to their faces. There were a column of them now, robed like monks, their shining faces deeply shadowed. They moved in complete silence towards the house, and Detlef realized with a chill that they weren't displacing the grass and gravel as they walked. They trod on the air, floating a few inches above the ground, the cords of their robes trailing behind them.

He was frozen to the spot, not with fear exactly, but with fascination, as if under the influence of one of that species of venomous serpent that chooses first to charm, then to bite.

The window was open, but he did not remember unfastening it. the night air was cold on his face.

The monkish figures floated higher now, feet above the ground, drifting upwards towards the palace. Detlef imagined sharp eyes glittering in their indistinct, half-seen faces. He knew with a sudden burst of panic that whatever these beings might be they were here for a purpose, to visit him, to communicate specifically with Detlef Sierck.

He prayed to the gods he'd neglected. Even to the ones he didn't believe in. Still, the figures rose into the air. There were ten or twelve of them, he thought, but perhaps more. Perhaps as many as a hundred, or a thousand. Such a crowd couldn't assemble in the gardens of the palace, but perhaps they were there despite all possibility. After all, men didn't float.

A group of the figures came forward and hovered outside the window, barely out of Detlef's reach. There were three, and the one in the centre must be the spokesman. This figure was more distinct than the others. Its face was more defined, and Detlef could make out a forked, black beard and a hooked nose. It was the face of an aristocrat, but whether a tyrant or a benevolent ruler he could not tell.

Were these the spirits of the dead? Or daemons of darkness? Or some other variety of supernatural creature as yet uncatalogued?

The floating monk looked at Detlef with calm, shining eyes and raised an arm. The robe fell away and a thin hand appeared, its forefinger extended towards the playwright.

'Detlef Sierck,' said the figure in a deep, male voice. 'You must go no further into the darkness.'

The monk spoke directly into Detlef's mind, without moving his lips. there was a breeze blowing, but the apparition's robes weren't moving in it.

'You should beware...'

The name hung in the air, echoing in his skull before it was uttered...

'Drachenfels.'

Detlef could not speak, could not answer back. He was being warned, he knew, but against what? And to what purpose?

'Drachenfels.'

The monk was alone now, his companions gone, and fading away himself. His body suddenly caught the wind and was twisted this way and that, coming apart like a fragile piece of cloth in a gale, and wafted away on the air currents. In a moment, there was nothing left of him.

Covered in a cold sweat, his head hurting more than ever, Detlef fell to the floor, and prayed until he fell into a swoon.

When morning came, he discovered he had watered and fouled himself in fear.

Act Three

1

It was a typical riverboat romance. Sergei Bukharin had travelled down the Urskoy from Kislev, an ambassador to the Empire from Tsar Radii Bokha, Overlord of the North. He joined the Emperor Luitpold just after the confluence of the Urskoy and the Talabec. Genevieve was immediately taken with the tall, proud man. He had won his scars championing the tsar against the altered monstrosities of the Northern Wastes, and wore his hair and moustaches in long braids threaded with ceramic beads. He radiated strength, and his blood was richer than any she had tasted since her retirement to the convent.

Aside from Henrik Kraly, Oswald's steward, Sergei and Genevieve were the only passengers on the Luitpold travelling the length of the Talabec to Altdorf. There was a glum and withdrawn elven poet who had come down from Kislev with Sergei and debarked at Talabheim, but he kept his purposes to himself and was shunned and mistrusted by Captain Iorga and his oarsmen. Of course, Genevieve was shunned and mistrusted too, but they seemed better able to deal with her condition than this alien, unknowable creature. At Talabheim, the cabins were swelled by an influx of merchants, a pair of Imperial tax collectors and a major in the service of Karl-Franz who insisted on debating military matters with Sergei.

Genevieve spent the long, slow days on the long, slow river below-decks, dreaming restlessly in her bunk, and her dizzying nights with Sergei, delicately picking off his scabs and sampling his blood. The Kislevite seemed to enjoy the vampire kiss – as most humans do if only they allow themselves – but was not otherwise all that interested in his deathless lover. When not in her arms, Sergei preferred the company of Major Jarl or Kraly. Genevieve had heard that the tsar's people put little store by women in general, and vampire women in particular. There was the famous example of the Tsarina Kattarin, who had sought the Dark Kiss and extended her reign over Kislev. A conspiracy of her great-great-grandchildren, frustrated at the block she represented to the dynastic succession, had led to her well-merited assassination. The vampires of Kislev and the World's Edge Mountains were all like Wietzak, self-important Truly Dead monsters who at once looked down on human-kind as cattle and feared the day-dwellers for their hawthorn and silver.

She never pressed the matter with Sergei, but she guessed the brave warrior was a little afraid of her. That could well be the attraction for him, the desire to overcome a breath of fear. For her part, she was pleased to pass the dull journey – mile after mile of tree-lined banks, and the eternal grunting and straining of the bonded oarsmen – with a strong taste in her mouth and a roughly handsome face to look at. By the time they were within a few days of Altdorf, she was already growing bored with her Kislevite soldier-diplomat, and although they exchanged accommodation addresses, she knew she would never see him socially again. There were no regrets, but there were no really pleasant memories either.

The Luitpold upped oars as it was hauled to the quayside, between two tall-masted ocean-going merchant ships down from the Sea of Claws with goods from Estalia, Norsca and even the New World. Sergei strode down the gangplank, saluted her from the docks and marched off to court, presumably intending to stop off with Major Jarl at the first bawdy house along the way to remind himself of the feel of a real woman. To her surprise, Genevieve found a tear welling in her eye. She wiped the red smear away and watched her lover walk off with his friend.

'My lady,' said Kraly, impatient now the trip was ended. 'The crown prince's coach is waiting.'

It was an impressive vehicle, and out of place on the malodorous docks of Altdorf, between the stacked-up goods and the dray-carts. Liveried servants waited by the black and red carriage. The arms of von Konigswald were picked out in green and gold. Kraly gave a dock-worker a crown to carry Genevieve's luggage from the Luitpold to the coach. She refrained from mentioning that, for all her girlish appearance, she could best the emissary's bruiser in an arm wrestling contest and pick up a heavy trunk one-handed.

Genevieve bade a respectable farewell to Captain Iorga, who looked relieved to be rid of his half-dead passenger but wasn't afraid enough not to suggest she book a return passage with him if she intended to go back to the convent in a month or so.

After years in the convent, the scents and sounds of Altdorf were again a revelation. The Luitpold had pulled into the docks just after sunset. Torches had been lit to facilitate late workers, and Genevieve could smell, taste and hear as well as any creature of the night. Here was the largest city in the Empire; indeed, in the Known World.

Built upon the islands of the Reik and the Talabec, but extending widely on the banks, Altdorf was a city of bridges and mudflats, surrounded by tall, white walls with distinctive red tiles. Hub of the Empire, home of the Imperial court and the great Temple of Sigmar, and known, so the guidebooks say, for its universities, wizards, libraries, diplomats and eating houses. Also, as the guidebooks omit to mention, its cutpurses, spies, scheming politicians and priests, occasional outbreaks of plague and ridiculous overcrowding.

None of this had changed in twenty-five years. As they pulled into the city, Genevieve noticed that yet another layer of dwellings had been built upon the mudflats, creating a permanently wet, permanently unhealthy beehive structure in which the poor – dock labourers, dwarf wall engineers, street traders – lived in a distinct counterpoint to the fine houses of Altdorf's rich.

There weren't many vampires, because of the bridges. Wietzak and his kind would have found themselves penned in on all sides by running water. Were she ever fully to die and become like them, one of the Truly Dead vampires, a walking corpse with an eternal bloodlust, she would have to avoid this city for ever. For now, she drank in all the sensations, seeking out the pleasant scents of good Altdorf cooking and a ready-to-be-loaded cargo of herbs and ignoring the mud, the rotting fish and the sheer press of unwashed humankind. Left to herself, she would be glutted on blood tonight, but she supposed other arrangements had been made for her. A shame, for here there was life in the night. The Crescent Moon would be opening for business, and other taverns, the theatres, concert halls, circuses, gaming houses. All the rich, gaudy, rotten, beguiling pursuits of the living. The things which, in six-and-a-half centuries, Genevieve had been unable to put behind her.

The door of the carriage swung open, and an elegant man got out. He was so simply dressed that, for a moment, Genevieve took him for another steward. Then, recognition came...

'Oswald!'

The crown prince grinned and stepped forward. They embraced, and she heard again the call of his blood. She touched his bare neck with her wet tongue, connecting electrically between beard and collar with his life force.

He broke the embrace and took a good look at her.

'Genevieve... my dear... it's so hard to get used to it. You're the same. It could have been yesterday.'

Twenty-five years.

'To me, highness, it was yesterday.'

He waved her formality away. 'Please, no titles. It's always Oswald to you, Genevieve. I owe you so much.'

Recalling herself unconscious and at the mercy of the iron-faced fiend of her dreams, she responded, 'Surely, it is I who owe you, Oswald. I still live only by your sufferance.'

He had been a beautiful boy, with his golden hair and his clear eyes. Now, he was a handsome man, with darker colouring, lines of character and a man's beard. He had been slender and wiry, surprisingly strong and agile in battle, but still slightly awkward with a sword in his hand. Now, he was as well-muscled as Sergei. His body felt hard and healthy beneath his jerkin, and his tights revealed well-shaped calves and thighs. Oswald von Konigswald had grown up. He was still barely a prince, but he looked every inch the elector he was soon to become. And his eyes were still clear, still bright with integrity, with emotion, with adventure.

Impulsively, he kissed her. She tasted him again, and this time it was she who drew back, for fear that her red thirst would overwhelm decorum. He helped her into the coach.

'There's so much to tell, Genevieve,' he began, as they trundled through the crowds of the docks towards the city thoroughfares. 'So much has happened...'

A street singer was performing by the Bridge of Three Towers, a comic song about a woodcutter's daughter and a priest of Ranald. When he sighted the arms upon the approaching carriage, he switched to the ballad that told of the death of Drachenfels. Oswald reddened with embarrassment, and Genevieve couldn't help but be a little satisfied to see his flush. This version of the tale was entitled 'The Song of Bold Oswald and Fair Genevieve' and imputed that the prince had taken on the Great Enchanter 'for the love of his long-dead lady.' She wondered, not for the first time, whether there had ever really been anything between them. Looking back on it, Genevieve supposed it would have been strange had they not fallen in love on the road to Castle Drachenfels. But, in his terms if not hers, that was half a life ago. Even Oswald was not about to present a vampire barmaid at court.

When the bridge and the song were behind them, Oswald began to talk of his theatrical venture.

'I have engaged a very clever young man. Some call him a genius and some a damned fool. Both factions are right, but generally the genius outweighs the fool, and perhaps it is the foolery that fuels the genius. You will be impressed with his work, I'm sure.'

Genevieve allowed herself to be lulled by the creak of the wheels, the clap of hooves on cobbles and the pleasant fire of Oswald's voice. The carriage was nearing the Altdorf palace of the von Konigswalds now. They were in the wide streets of the city's most exclusive area, where the mansions of the foremost courtiers stood in grounds spacious enough to accommodate a veritable army of lesser men. Smartly uniformed militiamen patrolled the streets to keep out the bad elements, and torches burned all night to light the way home for the weary aristocrat after a hard evening's toadying and prancing in the corridors of the Imperial palace. Genevieve had not often been in this quarter during her century in Altdorf. The Crescent Moon was back near the docks, in a bustling, lively, dirty avenue known as the Street of a Hundred Taverns.

'I'd like you to talk to Detlef Sierck, to give him the benefit of your recollections. You play a leading part, of course, in his drama.'

Genevieve was amused by Oswald's enthusiasm. She remembered him as a boy declaring that were he not expected by his family to take the role of elector after his father passed on, he would have chosen to be a travelling player. His poetry had won many plaudits, and she sensed that the grown man regretted that the demands of public life had prevented him from continuing to wield his quill. Now, by association, he could return to the arts.

'And who, Oswald, is to play me?'

The crown prince laughed. 'Who else? Lilli Nissen.'

'Lilli Nissen! That's ridiculous. She's supposed to be one of the great beauties of the age, and I'm...'

'...barely pleasing to look upon. I knew that'd be your reaction. In Kislev they say "beware the vampire's modesty". Besides, all is equal. I'm to be played by a dashing young genius who has broken more hearts than the emperor's militia have heads. We are speaking here of the theatre, not of dry-as-dust historical tomes. Thanks to Detlef Sierck, we'll all live for ever.'

'My darling, I'll already live for ever.'

Oswald grinned again. 'Of course. I had forgotten. I might also mention that I have met Lilli Nissen, and, startling through she undoubtedly is, she cannot compare to you.'

'So flattery is still considered an accomplishment at the court of the Emperor?'

The coach paused, and there was a rattling of chains.

'Here, we're there.'

The great gates, inset with a wrought-iron von Konigswald shield, swung open, and Oswald's coach turned into the wide driveway. There was some commotion up ahead, outside the palace itself. Trunks were piled high, and people were arguing loudly. An imposing, slightly over-weight, young man in an elaborate and undeniably theatrical outfit was shouting at a quavering coachman. Beside them, a dwarf was hopping from one foot to another. There were other outlandishly dressed characters present, all serving as an audience for the great-voiced shouter.

'What's this?' Oswald cried. He clambered out of the still-moving coach and strode towards the knot of arguers. 'Detlef, what's happening?'

The shouter, Detlef, turned to the crown prince and fell briefly silent. In an instant, Genevieve felt the young man – the young genius, if Oswald was to be trusted – catch sight of her. She was leaning from the coach. They exchanged a look each was to remember for a long time thereafter, and then the moment was past. Detlef was shouting again.

'I'm leaving, highness! I don't need to be warned twice. The play is off. I'd rather be back in Mundsen Keep than persecuted by ghosts. My company and I are withdrawing from the project, and I strongly suggest that you drop the matter yourself unless you want to be visited by float-ing monks who speak without speaking and carry with them the odour of the grave and a strong suggestion that anyone who defies them will be joining them in the afterlife!'

II

Detlef had taken hours to calm down. But Crown Prince Oswald had spoken reasonably and at length, trying to put some less threatening interpretation upon the monkish manifestations.

'Ghosts can be petty, misleading even, and yet they are not known for their intervention in mortal matters.' He waved an elegant hand in the air, as if conjuring the harmless spirits of which he spoke. 'The palace is old, haunted many times over.'

That was all very well, Detlef thought, but Oswald hadn't stared the deathly things in the face and been given direct orders by the dead.

'It is said that whenever a von Konigswald draws near death, the shades of his ancestors return to bear him away with them. When the grandfather for whom I am named lay comatose with the brain fever, the noseless spectre of Schlichter von Konigswald was seen waiting implacably at his bedside…'

Detlef was unconvinced. He still remembered the ghost monk's piercing eyes and bony forefinger. 'You'll pardon me for mentioning it, highness, but in this case, you seem to be in the pink of good health while it is I, who can boast no relationship to your noble house, who has been placed under the threat of death.'

A grave look came over the prince. 'Yes, Detlef,' he said gently, 'but my father, the elector…'

The crown prince nodded towards the corner of the room, in which the elector of Ostland was coughing gently as he played with his toy soldiers, mounting an assault on the coal scuttle.

'Hurrah for the general,' cried Elector Maximilian. It must have been near his bed-time.

Oswald looked at Detlef, and Detlef felt suitably chastened. The old man was indeed on the point of expiry. His mind had long since crumbled under the sieges of age, and his body was rapidly failing. But there was still the matter of the daemon monks and their levitation tricks.

'A drink, Detlef?'

Detlef nodded, and Oswald poured out a generous measure of Estalian sherry. Detlef took the goblet, and ran his thumb over the embossed von Konigswald shield. Here, in the warmth of a well-lit room, with the calm, unaffected Oswald and a battery of well-armed servants, the phantoms of the night seemed less menacing. If he came to think about it, the monks were far less impressive a manifestation than the tricked-up appearance of Drachenfels's daemon-pig servitors he was planning for the play. If it came to it, the afterlife could not compete with a Detlef Sierck production for supernatural spectacle.

'So, that's settled? Your production will continue?'

Detlef drank, feeling better. There was still something that troubled him, but he instinctively trusted the crown prince. Anyone who could walk alive out of the fortress of Drachenfels must have some experience with the unearthly.

'Fine. But I'll want you to detail some of your guards to watch over the company. There have been too many "accidents," you know...'

Kosinski had broken his ankle thanks to a carelessly anchored – or tampered with – piece of scenery. Gesualdo the Jester had been struck down with a mysterious sweating sickness, and Vargr Breughel was having to read his lines in rehearsal. Someone had broken into Laszlo Lowenstein's rooms and shredded his collection of playbills. And every bit player and scene shifter was telling a spook story of some sort. The only thing that was running as expected about the production was that Lilli Nissen was proving awkward and hiding in her rooms most of the time. She had expended more energy on fluttering her doubtless counterfeit eyelashes at Oswald than on learning her speeches. Detlef had heard of blighted productions before, and none could have been more thrice-cursed than The History of Sigmar, but there were more tripwires and hidden pits along this route than he had a right to expect. And the company had not even made its way to Castle Drachenfels yet.

'That might not be ill-advised, Detlef. We both have more than enough enemies in Altdorf.'

Oswald summoned a servant, and gave him brief instructions.

'There'll be twenty men, under the command of my trusted aide Henrik Kraly, at the disposal of your company tomorrow. Your rooms will be guarded by night.'

The servant hurried off.

'And I'll have your chamber exorcized by the priests of whichever god you favour. I don't hold out much hope, though. This place is too old for exorcisms to take. It's been tried many times, I believe, and there are always new ghosts springing up. There's a story about a bleeding child who trails his grave garments behind him, and there's the skull-faced governess who radiates an eerie blue light, not to mention the phantom dog who recites passages from Tarradasch...'

Oswald seemed to warm to the subject, and was displaying an unhealthy, childish relish in the dark history of his home.

'There's no need to elaborate, highness. I believe I appreciate the situation.'

'And our ghosts are as nothing to the ghosts of the Imperial palace. The first Emperor Luitpold was reputed to have been witness to no fewer than one hundred and eighty-three spectral manifestations in his lifetime.

And Albrecht the Wise's hair was white before he was thirty thanks to the sudden apparition of a daemon of the most frightful appearance dressed in the uniform of the Imperial Guard...'

'The general has triumphed again!' shouted the elector, holding high one particular lead hero. 'Eggs all round! Eggs for the troops!'

The old man's nurse quieted him down, and led him away by the hand to his bedroom. Oswald was embarrassed, but clearly felt for his father's condition.

'You should have seen him as he was when I was a boy.'

Detlef bowed slightly. 'Men are not responsible for their dotage, any more than they are for their infancy.'

There was a brief silence. The troubles passed from Oswald's face, and he turned to his other guest.

'And now, you must meet the heroine of your piece... Genevieve Dieudonné.'

The pale girl came forward, curtsied prettily, and offered her slim, white hand to Detlef. He bowed to her, and kissed her knuckles. She was cool to the touch, but didn't have the dead, slightly rancid appearance of the two other vampires Detlef had met. It was difficult not to think of her as the equal in age and experience of any of the young actresses and dancers Detlef had known in the theatre. She hardly seemed more than a year or two at most out of her schooling, ready to embark upon her first freedoms, fully prepared to be young. And yet she had seen six and a half centuries go by.

'Enchanted,' he said.

'Likewise,' she replied. 'I've been hearing about you. I trust that my reputation is in good hands with your quill.'

Detlef smiled. 'I shall have to rewrite several speeches now that I have seen you. It would be unnatural for anyone to chance across such beauty and not remark upon it.'

Genevieve smiled too. Her eyeteeth were a fraction longer and sharper than a normal girl's would have been. 'Evidently, you and Oswald have studied bottom-kissing flattery under the same tutors.'

The crown prince laughed. Detlef, to his surprise, found the bizarre woman charming.

'We must talk,' Detlef said, suddenly keener on an interview. 'Tomorrow, in the daytime, we could take tea and go through my text. It is still developing, and I would greatly appreciate your thoughts upon the drama.'

'Tomorrow it shall be, Mr Sierck. But let's make it after sunset. I'm not at my best in the daytime.'

III

His patron had done so much for him. It was about time Lowenstein did something for his patron. Even something as distasteful, dangerous and illegal as grave robbery.

Besides, it wasn't really grave robbery; the woman wasn't yet buried. His patron had told him she could be found packed in ice at the shrine of Morr. The corpse was awaiting the Emperor's coroners. And Lowenstein's pleasure. The tall, gaunt actor passed through the door of the shrine, glancing up at the black stone raven that stood on the lintel, its wings spread to welcome the dead, and those whose business was with the dead.

Opposite the shrine was the Raven and Portal, the tavern favoured by the priests of Morr. The black bird on its sign swung in the wind, creaking as if squawking to its cousin across the way. Nearby were the Imperial cemeteries, where the richest, the most lauded, the most famed were interred. In Altdorf, as in every city, Morr's Town was the district of the dead.

The man in the mask had smoothed Lowenstein's way considerably. A guard had been drugged, and lay in the foyer of the low, dark building, his tongue protruding from a foamy mouth. The keys hung precisely where his patron had told him they would be. He had been in mortuaries before, for recreational purposes, and had no undue fear of the dead. Tonight, leather against his face, he had no undue fear of anything.

He pulled the watchman out of the way, so he could not be seen by any late passerby. The shrine smelled strongly of herbs and chemicals. He supposed that if it didn't, it would stink of the dead. This was where those who died questionably were brought. The Emperor's coroners examined the bodies for traces of foul play, or hitherto unlisted disease. It was a shunned place. Just to make sure, he felt for the watchman's heart. It was strong. He pinched the man's nostrils and put a hand to his sticky mouth until the beat was stilled. His patron wouldn't mind. Lowenstein thought of it as an offering to Morr.

There were sounds outside, in the night. Lowenstein pressed himself into the shadows, and held his breath. A party of drunken revellers passed by, singing about the woodcutter's daughter and the priest of Ranald.

'Oh, my pretty laaaad, what you've done to me,

My father will do with his aaaaaxe to thee...'

One of them relieved himself loudly against the marble wall of the shrine, bravely cursing Morr, god of death. Lowenstein grinned in the darkness. The soak would come to know the god eventually, as do all, and his curse would be remembered.

Morr, god of death, and Shallya, goddess of healing and mercy, were the deities who really ruled the lives of men. The one for the old, the other for the young. You could placate the one or beg for the intercession of the other, but, in the end, Shallya would weep, and Morr would take his prize.

Lowenstein felt closer to Morr than all the other gods. In the Nuln production of Tarradasch's Immortal Love, he had played the god of death, and had been comfortable in the black robes. As he was comfortable now in the armour and mask of Drachenfels.

Tonight, he could meet his patron mask to mask, he thought. He had kept his costume with him, and worn the mask for his trip to the shrine. It served to shield his identity, but also he felt a strange ease when hidden behind it. Two days ago, he had noticed horny ridges budding under the skin of his forehead, and felt a roughening of his normally sunken cheeks. He must have caught a touch of warpstone. The mask served to conceal his alterations. With the leather over his face, he felt himself stronger, more alive, more powerful. If his patron had given him this mission in Nuln, he would have been anxious, jittery. Now, he was cool and decisive. He was changing, altering.

The drunks were gone. The night was quiet. Lowenstein proceeded to the back room of the shrine, where the bodies were kept. It was down a short stairway, its walls set into the earth. He touched tinder to a candle, and carefully descended the broad stairs. It was cold, and slow-melting ice dripped to the flagstone floor. Strong-smelling herbal possets hung from the beams, so the nostrils of visitors would not be offended. On raised biers lay the suspiciously dead of Altdorf. Or, at least, the suspiciously dead the Emperor's court cared about.

Here was a well-dressed young blood, his arm ending in a ragged stump, his throat torn out by some beast. Here was a little boy, his face flushed unnaturally red, his belly opened. Lowenstein stopped by the child, seized by a desire to place his hand on the apparently fevered brow, to find it hot or cool. He passed on, glancing at each in turn. Death by violence, death by illness, death by causes unknown. All death was here. The priests of Morr had placed amulets of the raven around the necks of all their charges, to signify the flight of the spirit. To the cult of Morr, remains were just clay. Bodies were revered for the sake of the living; the spirit was in the hands of the gods.

Finally, Lowenstein came to the bier he was looking for. The dead woman was out of place in such a wealthy shrine. In her drab and patched gown, she looked more the type to be left in the streets to rot than to be pored over by the coroners and troubled by the concern of Crown Prince Oswald. All deaths among such people were suspicious, and yet few attracted the attention of the priests of Morr. All the other corpses here were from the monied classes. This woman had clearly been poor.

Her throat had been raggedly cut, and the instrument lay on the ice beside the body. It was the dove of Shallya, blasphemously used in suicide. Lowenstein touched the open wound, and found it cold and wet. He brushed the lank, greying hair from the haggard face. The woman might have been pretty once, but that would have been long before her death.

As a young man, Lowenstein had seen Erzbet dance. It was in Nuln, in a travelling fair in the Grand Square. The woman had performed an exhausting solo, combining the high balletic techniques of the Nuln opera with the wild, primitive displays of the forest-dwelling nomads.

He had been aroused by the performance, by the tanned legs that kicked up her skirts, and by the dark eyes that caught the firelight. She hadn't paid him any notice. That had been the night Bruder Wiesseholle, king of the city's thieves and murderers, was killed. The next day, the fair was gone, and the criminals of Nuln were without a ruler. Erzbet had been good. Twenty-five gold crowns was her price. It had never varied, whether her intended was a mighty lord or a humble beadle. He had heard that – poor fool – she always insisted her clients debate ethics with her, and justify the removal from the world of those they wished to be rid of.

And here she was, Morr's meat at last. Her dead would be waiting for her. Bruder Wiesseholle and the numberless others. He hoped she remembered her ethical discussions now, and could justify each of her assassinations.

He put down his candle by the corpse's head and prepared to take what he had come for. If he were to plunder the other biers, he would doubtless find rings, coins, necklaces, stout boots, silver buttons, golden buckles. But Erzbet had no goods to lose, had nothing Lowenstein's patron could possibly want.

Except her heart.

Lowenstein took the small knives, honed to a razor's edge, from their oilcloth, and tested the one he chose against the ball of his thumb. It stung as it sliced with the merest touch.

And her eyes.

IV

Genevieve took off her tinted glasses and looked up at the fortress of Drachenfels. It seemed different now, smaller. It was a pleasant spring day, and the ride up from the village was almost easy. The last time she had been this way, they had avoided the road – it was littered with the bones of those who had thought they could just walk up to the castle and knock on the door – and scaled the precipitous cliffs. There were other abandoned castles in the Grey Mountains, and they were no more imposing, no more haunted than this one. There were none of the traditional signs of an evil place: birds sang, the local vegetation flourished, milk went unsoured, animals were not mysteriously agitated. Even with her heightened awareness, Genevieve could sense nothing. It was as if the Great Enchanter had never been.

Of course, Oswald's men had prepared the way. Henrik Kraly had sent out a squadron of cleaners, cooks, carpenters and servants to make the place ready for occupation. There had been some initial reluctance among the villagers who had lived all their lives in the shadow of Drachenfels to hire on with the company, but the crown prince's gold had overcome many objections. The lad who saw to her horse after she dismounted must have been born well after the death of Drachenfels. The young of the region were reluctant to believe the stories told by their parents and grandparents. And some of the old were impressed enough by the ballads of Oswald and Genevieve to conquer their aversion to the ruin and take positions with Detlef's troupe.

The genius was in good spirits as he rode at the head of his gypsy caravan of actors, musicians and show people. He was a good conversationalist, and eager to talk with Genevieve. They had been through the minutiae of Oswald's quest, of course, but the dramatist was also interested in the rest of her long life, and was skilled at drawing out incidents she hadn't spoken of for centuries. The breadth of his learning was impressive, and she found him well-informed about the great men and women of earlier eras. She had known Tarradasch, had seen his plays during their original runs, and cheered Detlef greatly with her opinion that the great dramatist was less skilled as an actor and director than as a writer.

'A regional touring company today could better the original Altdorf productions of Tarradasch's masterpieces without breaking a sweat,' she opined.

'Quite! Yes! Exactly!' he agreed.

It was a performance in itself, moving the company from the von Konigswald palace in Altdorf to the remote mountain fastness, and they had been on the road for some weeks. But the journey flew by, with stop-overs at the best inns, and leisurely evenings with the cast discussing their roles and practising their swordfights. By comparison, the original journey had been long, uncomfortable and fraught with danger. Genevieve felt nothing as she passed the sites of battles long-since won. She had made brief pilgrimages to the graves of Conradin – though there had only been bones to bury – and Heinroth, and found the markers Oswald had put up gone. There were no spirits lingering in the forests. Even the bandits had been cleared out years ago by the local militia. Despite it all, Genevieve found it difficult to be in company with Laszlo Lowenstein, the actor cast as Drachenfels. What she had seen of his performance was frighteningly good and, although he seemed offstage to be an ordinary, conscientious craftsman merely happy to be thrown a meaty role, she couldn't forget the impression he made when he pulled on the mask and tried to radiate evil. Even his voice took on the timbre she remembered, and his daemonic laughter, somehow amplified by a device inside his mask, was bone-chilling.

Rudi Wegener was with the caravan, Menesh the dwarf and Anton Veidt too. Veidt was old, lean and ill. He avoided her just as he had avoided her the first time. Rudi was also in poor health, she assumed, with his great girth weighing heavy on his heart and his great thirst similarly straining his liver and lights. Genevieve gathered he had suffered a loss recently, and approached him about it, but he hadn't been eager to talk of Erzbet. That had been a long time ago. It had been a difficult subject to bring up, for Genevieve still recalled the first sign of the dancer-assassin's madness, her unprovoked attack. Otherwise, Rudi was still prone to boasting and garrulousness. He regaled the company with fancifully embroidered accounts of his exploits as a bandit in these very woods, confident that all who might contradict him save Genevieve were dead and in their graves.

Only Menesh, the lack of an arm notwithstanding, was much as he had been. Dwarfs are more long-lived than humans. Genevieve understood that her one-time comrade had become something of a ladies' man since his injury forced him to abandon his life of wandering adventure. He was rumoured to have made several conquests among the girls of the chorus, and to be chasing the amorous record set by Kerreth, the fragile little costume master whose ways with the opposite sex were legendary. There was another dwarf in the company, Vargr Breughel, with whom Menesh was always arguing. Detlef told her that Breughel wasn't a true dwarf, but human born, and that he hated to be taken for one. Menesh was always thinking of cruel jests at Breughel's expense, and Detlef, who held his assistant in high regard, had several times turned uncharacteristically severe and threatened to throw out the one-armed swordsman along the way.

It wasn't the same trip, though. And Oswald wasn't with them. He would have to join the company later, at the head of the second caravan which would bring the audience to the play. Detlef was good company, and there was a spark between them she could not deny. But he was not Oswald, regardless of the role he was to take in the play.

Then again, Genevieve knew she was not Lilli Nissen. The star travelled in her own luxurious caravan, which was driven by a handsome, black-skinned mute from the South Lands who acted as her personal servant and bodyguard. By his scars, Genevieve recognized him as essentially the woman's slave. The vampire had been presented to the actress, and neither party wished to further the acquaintance. Genevieve saw Lilli's face as if it were a-crawl with worms, and the actress pointedly refused to touch the undead woman's outstretched hand. Detlef, too, obviously had little time for Lilli, but excused her on the grounds that, for all her foolishness and temperament, she could indeed be a goddess on stage. 'She had the ability to make audiences love her, even if they would, singly or in twos and threes, find her less appealing than the average monster of the night. She's probably possessed.'

The 'accidents' that had plagued the production in Altdorf abated, perhaps because of the presence of several of Henrik Kraly's pikemen. One inn along the way had been reluctant to accommodate the players, the owner having had bad experience in the past with the theatrical profession, but Kraly's men had quietly convinced him to change his ways. The only peculiar incident had taken place in a village at the foot of the Grey Mountains, where the caravan had been booked to stay overnight at a well-reputed traveller's rest stop.

Detlef had been sampling the excellent food on offer, and quizzing Genevieve about the Bretonnia of her girlhood, asking particularly about the still-remembered great minstrels of the day and the precise qualities of their voices. Breughel had come to their table in some state, accompanied by the owner of the hostelry.

'How many are we?' Breughel asked. 'In the caravan, I mean. Coaches, carts, wagons?'

'Um, twenty-five, I think. No, I was forgetting Lilli's boudoir on wheels. Twenty-six. What's the matter? Have we lost someone?'

'No,' said the hostelier, apologetically, 'quite the reverse. You have one too many.'

Detlef was taken aback. 'You've obviously miscounted.'

'No. The crown prince's messenger specified twenty-six vehicles, and so I set aside space in the yard for that number. The space is filled, and there is one carriage left over.'

'It's Lilli's,' said Breughel.

'It would be,' replied Detlef.

'And she's not happy about leaving it in the road.'

'She wouldn't be.'

The hostelier seemed unduly upset until Genevieve realized he must have recently been shouted at by Lilli Nissen. The famous beauty could be a mad gorgon at times. Detlef continued with his meal, complimenting the hostelier on his lamb chops in wine sauce. The man was from Bretonnia, and justly proud of his fare.

'The thing I can't understand, Detlef,' said Breughel, 'is that we've counted the caravan twice over. No matter where we start we get the same number.'

'Twenty-seven?'

'No, twenty-six. But there are still twenty-seven places filled in the yard.'

Detlef laughed. 'This is silly. You must just have arranged the wagons wrongly, taken up too much room.'

'You know what Kraly's ostlers are like. The wagons are as evenly spaced as old Maximilian's toy soldiers on a board.'

'Well, haul one of the scenery wagons into the road to make room for the human flytrap, and have a drink.'

The next day, at the off, Detlef and Breughel counted the wagons as they trundled up towards the mountain road.

'There, my friend, twenty-six.'

'And our own wagon, Detlef. Twenty-seven.'

It had been a puzzle, but certainly paled when set beside Detlef's experience at the von Konigswald palace. It was hard to take seriously an extra wagon as an omen of evil.

But the next night, Kosinski the scene-shifter, still hobbling on his broken ankle, came up to complain.

'I thought you wanted me to bring up the rear of the caravan.'

'I do, Kosinski. You've the heaviest, slowest wagon. It's the combination of your head and the scenery that keeps it back. You always have to catch up half an hour at the end of the day.'

'Then who's that behind me?'

Detlef and Breughel looked at each other and said in unison, 'The twenty-seventh wagon.'

'And who's that?'

'Who knows?'

They were camped in the open that night, the wagons together in groups. Four groups of six, with three left over. Twenty-seven. Detlef and Breughel independently counted the wagons again, and came up with only twenty-six. But there were still four groups of six, with three left over.

'Detlef,' concluded Breughel, 'there's an extra wagon with us we can't see all the time.'

Detlef spat into the fire. Genevieve had nothing to add.

'So, who is travelling with us?'

Detlef hadn't talked much that evening, and Genevieve hadn't been able to draw him out. He had had a conference with Kraly's men, and had them stand guard until dawn. When everyone else was asleep,

Genevieve had counted the wagons. Twenty-six. She had an assignation with the youth playing Conradin that night, and fed well. He looked white and dazed the next morning, and avoided her for a while, so perhaps she had lost some of her control and taken too much.

But the journey was over now. She looked around for Detlef, but he was busy with Breughel and the architect, arguing over sketches. They could only see the castle as a giant stage set to be exploited for the maximum impact. Guglielmo, the Tilean business manager, was off with the local burgermeister, going over a list of provisions ordered and paid for. Genevieve put her glasses on again, and saw better through the tint.

The rest of the company were going merrily in through the great front gates, looking for their quarters, relieved to be off the road. Lilli Nissen swept past with her little retinue – slave, dresser, astrologer, face-paint adviser – and went into the castle like a queen making a call on the lesser nobility.

Genevieve stood on the road, hesitating. Looking behind her, she saw who else hesitated.

Rudi, Veidt, Menesh.

They each stood alone, looking at the fortress, remembering...

V

The first night in the fortress, Rudi threw a party and invited everyone. There would have been a party anyway, to mark the end of the journey, but Detlef Sierck was kind enough to let Rudi throw it. Of course, Crown Prince Oswald had provided the food and wine, not to mention the fortress itself, but Rudi was there to bring the party to life.

The last weeks, since Oswald found him in the Black Bat, had been good for Rudi. He hadn't been drinking less, but what he was drinking was of a better quality. He'd been telling the old stories again, with his usual 'improvements,' but now there was a marked difference in the interest of his audiences. Detlef had listened attentively to his accounts of the original quest to Drachenfels, and the theatre people encouraged him to recall his other exploits.

Rudi had always liked theatre people. Erzbet had been with her gypsy circus when they first met. He and his band had passed themselves off as strolling players on many occasions. Now, at his party, the company were enjoying his best theatrical story. He was remembering the time when, shortly after holding up a party of noblemen in the Drak Wald Forest, he had been forced to stage a performance for his erstwhile victims in order to convince them that his band were indeed show people rather than bandits. In his retelling, he claimed that the Lord Hjalmar Poelzig had recognized him straight away, but still insisted on the performance to humiliate Rudi. Surrounded by the lord's militiamen, Rudi's bandits had improvised a tragedy about a bandit king and his dancing queen and, at the close of the play, Poelzig had been so moved that he decreed that Rudi should be rewarded and allowed to go free under the lord's own protection.

Detlef roared with laughter as Rudi told his story, impersonating the wily lord, and the brash young man he had been.

Deep inside his drink-besotted brain, Rudi remembered the real lord, and the five good men he had strangled with bowstrings when he caught up with the bandits. He remembered the lord's jailer – hardly more than a boy – and the way he had screamed as Rudi battered him to death against the stones of the prison before making an escape through the castle's stinking drains. Sobbing and befouled, the bandit king had crept away in shame like an animal of the forest. Those had been days of blood and filth and desperation.

The more he spoke of the days of plunder and glory and adventure, the more Rudi came to know that this was the real truth of the matter. What had happened didn't matter any longer. Erzbet was dead, Poelzig was dead, the boy was dead, his brains paste on the floor – the times were dead. But the stories lived. Detlef understood that, with his histories and his dramas. And Oswald too, with his play that would pass all their names down to future generations. Rudi the dirty murderer, Rudi who howled in grief and fear as he smashed in the skull of an innocent child, would be forgotten. Rudi the bandit king, Rudi the stalwart ally of brave Oswald, would be remembered as long as there were stages to dress and actors to walk upon them.

Reinhardt Jessner, the chubby young player cast as Rudi, called for another story. Rudi called for another pot of gin. The fires burned low, and the stories ran out. Eventually, Rudi slumped insensible. He could see the others – Detlef laughing, the vampire Genevieve as pretty as she had ever been, Veidt haggard and silent, Breughel arranging for more wine – but couldn't move himself from his spot by the fire. His belly weighed him down like an anchor. His limbs felt as if he were shackled to four cannonballs. And his back – his never-set-properly, never-right-again back – pained him as it had done for a quarter century, sending messages of agony up his spine.

Detlef proposed a toast 'to Rudolf Wegener, king of banditti' and everyone drank. Rudi belched, the turnip taste filling his mouth, and everyone laughed. Felix Hubermann, the master of the company's music, signed to a few of his players, and instruments were produced. Detlef himself took the shrill rauschpfeife, Hubermann the portative organ, and others the shawms, dulcian, fiddles, lute, curtal, cowhorn, cornett and gamba. The ensemble played, and the singers sang, untrained voices joining with the trained.

The old songs. 'The Miller of Middenheim,' 'Myrmidia's Doleful Lads,' 'Gilead the Elf King,' 'The Lament of Karak Varn,' 'The Goatherd of Appuccini,' 'Come Ye Home to Bilbali, Estalian Mariner,' 'The Reik is Wide,' 'A Bandit Bold' – this over and over, 'To Hunt the Manticore,' 'Sigmar's Silver Hammer,' 'The Pirate Prince of Sartosa.'

Then, the older songs, the near-forgotten songs. Menesh croaked an incomprehensible dwarfish ballad of great length, and six women burst into tears at its conclusion. Hubermann played an elven melody rarely heard by humans, let alone played by one, and made everyone wonder whether his ears weren't just a trifle too pointed and his eyes on the large side.

After some prompting from Detlef, Genevieve sang the songs of her youth, songs long dead except in her memory. Rudi found himself weeping with her as she sang of cities fallen, battles lost and lovers sundered. Bretonnia has always had a reputation for luxuriating in melancholia. Trickles of red ran down the vampire's lovely face, and she was unable to continue. There are precious few Bretonnian tales with happy endings.

Then the fires were piled high again, and the musicians played for dancing. Rudi was unable to stand up, much less dance, but he watched the others at their pleasure. Genevieve capered solemnly with Detlef, a courtly affair with many bowings and curtsies, but the music grew wilder, and dresses flew higher. Jessner took up with Illona Horvathy, the dancer cast as Erzbet, and swung her around in the air, so her skirts brushed perilously close to the fire. Rudi could have been watching his younger self. Illona was a spirited, athletic dancer, and she could perform acrobatic tricks the like of which Rudi had never seen. Jessner, who had taken Rudi into his confidence, assured him that Illona's imagination and physical stamina were not confined to the vertical brand of dancing. But she missed something of the grace, of the abandon, of the seriousness of the original. He had talked to her, and she was a cheerful girl, pleased to give pleasure. But there was none of Erzbet's passion. Illona had never taken a life, had never spared a life. She had not lived at the edge of experience the way Erzbet had.

...and Illona Horvathy wouldn't end her days in self-murder on the road from a madhouse.

A hand fell on his shoulder. It was Veidt's.

'It's over, Rudi. We're over.'

The bounty hunter was drunk, and his unshaven face was like a sagging skull. But he was right.

'Yes, over.'

'But we were here before, eh? Us old men. You and I and the dwarf and the leech girl. We were here when these play-actors were in their cribs. We fought as they'll never have to fight...'

Veidt trailed off, the light in his eyes going out, and keeled over sideways. Like all of them, he'd come out of Castle Drachenfels a different man than he had been outside the gates. Rudi regretted that he had not seen the bounty hunter in twenty-five years. They had shared so much, they should have been lifelong friends. The fortress should have brought them together, especially those hours injured in the dark, waiting for Oswald's return, knowing that the prince would die, and that things with claws and teeth would be coming for them.

The weight of wine shifted inside Rudi, and he desperately felt the need to piss. He shifted upright and staggered away from Veidt, his head spinning like a child's top. Jessner loomed before him, saying something he couldn't make out. The actor clapped him on the back, and sent him stumbling. The musicians were still playing. Illona was dancing alone now.

He made it into the next room, away from the light and the clamour. After he had relieved himself in a cold fireplace, he turned to make his way back to his place by the fire, to his friends.

She was in the doorway, between him and the party. He recognized her slim-hipped figure and long dark hair at once. She wore her dancing dress, slit to the thigh on one side and immodestly tight in the bodice.

'Rudi,' she said to him, and it was twenty-five, thirty years, ago. The days of plunder and glory and adventure.

'Rudi,' she extended an arm to him, her bracelets jingling.

He felt the weights falling away from him, and stood up straight. There was no pain in his back now.

'Rudi,' her voice was soft, yet urgent. Inviting, yet dangerous.

He lurched towards her, but she stepped aside, into the dark. She went to a door, and he blundered after her, pushing through it.

They were in a corridor. Rudi was sure this was where they had fought the living gargoyles, but Oswald's men had cleaned it up, put fresh candles in the sconces, laid down carpeting for the visiting dignitaries.

Erzbet led him on, into the heart of Drachenfels. In the chamber of the poison feast, a man waited for him. At first, because of the mask, he thought it was the actor, Lowenstein. It wasn't.

The man looked up from the table at him. His eyes shone through the slits of his mask. He had cutlery laid out before him, as for a meal. But there were no forks and spoons. Only knives.

The man picked up a knife. It shone like a white flame in his hand.

Rudi, cold inside, tried to push himself away, back through the door. But Erzbet stood before it, blocking his escape. He could see her better now. Her low-cut bodice disclosed the great red gash, like a crushed mouth sideways, in her breast.

She threw her head back, and her hair fell away from her face. He could see that she had no eyes.

VI

Lilli Nissen's favoured method of communicating with her director-writer-co-star was through Nebenzahl, her astrologer. If she was unhappy with a line of dialogue, or the performance of some lesser light of the stage, or the food served in her private rooms, or the noise made by the party she pointedly hadn't attended, or by the way the sun persisted on rising in the east every single solitary morning, she despatched Nebenzahl to whine at Detlef. Detlef was beginning to feel quite sorry for the poor charlatan who was finding his easy berth so unexpectedly rocky. It was the man's own fault, Detlef supposed, for not foreseeing in the cards, stars or entrails what a monster his employer would turn out to be.

The company were in the great hall of Drachenfels, which had been converted into a theatre. Lilli chose to make her entrance over the stage. As usual, she assumed there was no business connected with the play more important than her whim of the moment, and had herself borne in by her chair-carrying giant in the middle of a rehearsal.

It was an early scene, where Oswald, in the palace at Altdorf, is visited by the projected spirit of the Great Enchanter. They debate in verse the conflict to come, and the major themes of the play are foreshadowed. Detlef was having Vargr Breughel read his own lines, so he could concentrate on Lowenstein's performance and the lighting effect that would make him seem insubstantial. With the mask, the thin actor seemed a different creature altogether. Genevieve, who was sitting in on the rehearsal, was shuddering – probably reminded nastily of the real Drachenfels – and Detlef took that to be a tribute to Lowenstein's skills. When he could get perspective on the play, Detlef realized he was in danger of being overshadowed by the villain, and resolved to make his own performance the more masterful. He didn't mind. While he took pride in his acting, he disdained those stars, of whom Lilli was most definitely one, who surround themselves with the most wooden, untalented supporting actors available in order to make themselves seem better.

During the journey to the fortress, Lilli had tried to persuade him through Nebenzahl to cast some of her favourite walking statues in the other female roles in Drachenfels and he had kicked the astrologer off his wagon. Having written, directed and conceived the play,

Detlef felt he could afford to let others shine in it. He planned on taking last billing as an actor in the programme, allowing the weight of his name to be felt as the creator of the piece rather than as one of its interpreters.

Lowenstein-as-Drachenfels was towering over Breughel, vowing that his reign of evil would continue long after the puny prince's whited bones lay in forgotten dust, when Lilli made her unscheduled entrance, trailing her entourage. The black giant carried an oversized armchair without complaint. Lilli sat primly in it, like a child being carried by a fond parent. Her crippled dresser limped a few paces behind, bearing a basket of sweetmeats and fruit – part of the star's 'special diet' – and a few other functionaries whose exact purpose Detlef had never divined were also along to lend weight to their mistress's current gripe.

Nebenzahl strode up to Detlef, visibly embarrassed, but nerving himself to make the complaint. Lilli snarled imperiously, like a mountain cat with delusions of leonine grandeur, and fixed her flaming eyes on him. He knew it was going to be a bad one. If she chose to air the problem in front of the entire company, it was bound to involve a major row. The other actors on stage and in the audience shifted nervously, expecting a firestorm of holocaust proportions.

The foppish astrologer stuck out his fist, and opened his fingers. The teeth were in his hand.

'Lilli Nissen has no need of these, sir.'

He threw them on the ground. Kerreth had carved them especially, working away at scraps of boar's-tusk ivory. The wardrobe man was in the hall now, angry at the treatment of his work, but keeping quiet. He obviously had no wish to go back to being a cobbler, let alone a convict, and had correctly gauged the extent of Lilli Nissen's vindictiveness and influence.

'So, it's a toothless hag, you think I am now, Detlef Sierck!' shrieked Lilli, her face reddening. Her slave put her down, and she flew out of her chair, raging across the stage, knocking Breughel and Lowenstein out of her way. Detlef imagined angry eyes peering out from Lowenstein's mask. Lilli wasn't winning herself any more admirers this morning.

And, of course, it was such a stupid thing to bitch about!

'Lilli, it's no reflection upon your own teeth that I want you to wear these. It's the part you play...'

Lilli rose to the bait. 'The part I play! Ah yes, the part I play! And who cast me in such a role, who created such a disgusting travesty of womankind with me in mind, eh?'

Detlef wondered if Lilli had forgotten that Genevieve was with them. He suspected not. It was plain the women – vampire and vamp – didn't care for each other.

'Never in my career have I been asked to play such a part! Were it not for the involvement of my dear, dear friend Prince Oswald, who personally implored me to step in and fill out your petty little cast, I should have rent the manuscript to bits and flung it back into the gutter where it belongs. I've played empresses, courtesans, goddesses. Now, you want me to play a dead leech!'

Being reasonable wasn't going to help, Detlef knew, but it was the only tactic he could think of.

'Lilli, our play is a history. You play a vampire because Genevieve was... is... a vampire. After all, she lived this story. You only have to recreate it–'

'Pah! And is the drama invariably subject to history? Do you mean to tell me you have changed nothing for the sake of emphasis, to show yourself to the best advantage...'

There were mutterings at the back of the hall now. Nebenzahl was looking distinctly sheepish, patting down his ridiculous wig, self-conscious now he found himself on stage facing an unknown audience beyond the footlights.

'Of course, but–'

Lilli was unstoppable. Her bosom heaved as she drew breath and continued, 'For an instance, are you not somewhat too old and fat to play my good friend the future elector of Ostland as he was when but a boy?'

'Lilli, Oswald himself asked me to play him in this drama. Given the choice, I'd probably want – and no reflection upon you, Laszlo – to play Drachenfels.'

The star flounced towards the lights, and came so far forwards her face was in shadow. The house lights came up.

'Well, if you've rewritten Oswald as an ageing and overweight child prodigy, then you can rewrite Genevieve as something more suited to my personality.'

'And what, pray, might that be?'

'An elf!'

No one laughed. Detlef looked at Genevieve. Her face was unreadable. Lilli's nostrils flared and unflared. Nebenzahl coughed to break the silence.

Elven Lilli might once have been, but she inclined rather to the voluptuous these days. Her last husband had referred to her as having 'the breasts of a pigeon, the lungs of a bansidhe, the morals of an alleycat and a brain like Black Mountain cheese.'

Lowenstein laid a hand on Lilli's shoulder, and spun her round to face him. He was a full foot taller than her, and his built-up Drachenfels boots brought him up on a level with her silent giant.

Unused to such treatment, she raised a hand to slap the impudent actor, but he caught her wrist, and started whispering to her in a low, urgent, scary voice. Her colour faded, and she looked quite afraid.

Nobody else said anything. Detlef realized his mouth was hanging open in astonishment, and shut it.

When Lowenstein had finished his speech, Lilli blustered an apology – an unheard-of thing for her – and backed out, dragging her slave, her minions and astrologer with her. Nebenzahl looked appalled as he was yanked out of the great hall.

After a moment, there was a spontaneous round of applause. Lowenstein took a bow, and the rehearsal continued.

VII

Maximilian stood to attention while the general was speaking. It was late, but the general had awoken him with secret orders. The general told him he must get out of bed, get dressed, and go down to the battlefield, where the fate of the Empire was to be decided. After the Emperor, the general was the most important military leader in the land, and Maximilian always wanted to impress him with his obedience, resourcefulness and courage. The general was the man Maximilian would like to be. Would have liked to have been.

When the orders were finished and understood, Maximilian saluted and put the general into his top pocket. This was a serious business. These were times of grave danger. Only Maximilian stood between civilization and anarchy, and he was determined to do his best or die.

The palace was quiet at this time of night. Quieter in the days too, now that Oswald's theatre friends had gone. Maximilian missed them a little. There had been one dancer who'd been sweet on him, and liked to join in with his battles, making suggestions and asking questions, even though nurse disapproved of her.

Nurse disapproved of a lot of things.

In his slippers, Maximilian was almost silent as he proceeded through the corridors and down the stairs. His breath was short, and he was getting a stitch, but the general would want him to continue. He would not let the general down, no matter what. He thought he saw robed figures in the shadows of one passageway, but ignored them. Nothing could keep him from the fray now he was needed.

The battle room was not locked.

There were several armies on the table. Goblins, dwarfs, elves and men. And in the centre was a castle, the objective. The Imperial standard was flying from the great tower of the castle. The flag was tattered, but waved proud. The armies were clashing already. The room was filled with the tiny sounds of their weapons clanging together, their cannon popping. When they were hit, the soldiers screamed like shrilling insects. The table-top battlefield was swarming with life. Miniature swords scraped paint from lead faces. The dead were melted in grey pools. Puffs of smoke rose. Battle trumpets sounded like echoes in Maximilian's head.

The general had ordered him to hold the castle for the Emperor. He needed a chair to step on before he could reach the table. He put his foot down on the battlefield, crushing a bridge to stickwood, pushing a platoon of wood elf wardancers into the painted stream. He pulled himself up, and stood like a giant on the table. He had to duck to avoid a chandelier as he stepped into the castle. The walls barely came to his ankles, but he was able to stand in the courtyard. The defenders of the castle cheered to have such a champion.

Moonlight came in through the tall, thin windows. The night battle swept across the table, backwards and forwards. The armies had lost all direction, and were turning upon themselves. Sometimes, all four forces appeared to combine to launch a new onslaught on Maximilian's castle. Mostly, every single soldier seemed at war with every other. He detected the claws of Chaos in this business. The felt of the hill was torn as charges fell back from the castle walls, and dark wood showed through the scratches.

The general kept up Maximilian's morale as a wave of goblins clambered up the hill and breached the walls. Dwarf engineers pushed a war-tower forwards. Cannonballs stung his shins. Still he held the fort, at attention, saluting. The castle was in ruins now, and the armies were attacking him, trying to bring him down. The defence forces were sought out and slaughtered. Maximilian stood alone against the enemies.

The wounds inflicted on his feet and ankles were fleabites. Bretonnian soldiers poured fire over his slippers, but he stamped it out, and the fires spread back to their ranks. He laughed. The sons of Bretonnia at war always were noted more for viciousness than valour. Then the battle-wizards came forward, and threw their worst spells at him. Frightful fiends swirled about his legs like fish, and he swatted them away with his hands. A three-headed creature with eyes and a maw in its belly flew for Maximilian's throat, and he caught it. It came apart like cobweb in his hand, and he wiped it away on his jacket.

Spears stuck to his calves, and he felt dizzy to be at such a height above the ground. Goblins were scaling his trousers, hacking through his clothes and sinking hooks into flesh and bone. There were more fires. A ballista and several mortars were deployed. There were explosions all around him. His right knee went, and he was pulled down. Small roars of triumph went up, and his back was riddled with a million tiny shots. Knives small as headlice sawed at him. Spears like needles jabbed. He fell across the battlefield, crushing the remains of the castle, flattening the hill, murdering hundreds beneath him. He rolled onto his back, and the armies reached his face. They set off charges in his eyes, and he was blind. Berserkers set fire to his hair. Warrior wizards opened up channels to his brain. Pikemen attacked his neck. Fresh-conjured daemons burrowed beneath his skin, excreting their poisonous filth.

The general told him he was doing well and that he must keep up the fight. In the dark, the Emperor Luitpold and all his court waited for him. Maximilian knew he would soon be permitted to leave the field of battle, to take his well-earned rest. There were medals and honours and eggs for him. He would receive his just rewards.

The armies moved over him, laying waste to whatever they found. They captured the general, and executed him. To the end, the man was a hero. His lead head rolled across Maximilian's chest and bounced lifeless onto the table.

Tired and relieved, Maximilian sank into the darkness...

The next morning his nurse found him, lying dead among his beloved toy soldiers. Physicians were called for, but it was too late. The old elector's heart had finally given out. It was said that at least his death was sudden and easeful. The sad news was delivered to the new elector with his breakfast.

Oswald von Konigswald wept, but was not surprised.

VIII

Genevieve was on the battlements, watching the sun go down, feeling her strength rising. There was a full moon, and the view was lightly shadowed. With her nightsight, she saw wolves loping in the forests and silent birds ascending to their mountain nests. There were lights burning in the village. She was stretching, tasting the night, wondering how she would drink this evening, when Henrik Kraly found her.

'My lady,' he began, 'if I might beg a favour...'

'Certainly. What do you wish?'

Kraly looked uncertain. This was not like Oswald's smooth and efficient catspaw. His hand rested casually on his sword-hilt in a manner that instantly disturbed Genevieve. During the long trip from the convent, she had gathered that not all his services to the von Konigswalds involved simple message-bearing.

'Could you arrange to meet me in half an hour, and bring Mr Sierck with you? In the chamber of the poison feast.'

Genevieve raised an eyebrow. She had been avoiding that particular place above all. For her, the fortress held too many memories.

'It is a matter of some urgency, but I would appreciate it if you could raise it without alerting anyone. The crown prince has charged me with discretion.'

Puzzled, Genevieve agreed to the steward's terms and left for the great hall. She supposed the dead must have been taken from the table by now and given their proper burial. She would probably barely recognize the poison room. Thus far, she had encountered no ghosts, even in her imagination, at Drachenfels. No ghosts, just memories.

Rehearsals had finished for the day, and the actors were being served in a make-shift canteen. Breughel was haranguing the Bretonnian cook about the lack of a certain spice in the stew, and the cook was defending the recipe handed down to him by his forefathers. 'Dwarfeesh buffeune, yiu 'ave not leeved unteel yiu 'ave taisted Casserole à la Boudreaux!'

Jessner and Illona Horvathy were all over each other in a corner, petting as they joked with other members of the cast. Menesh was talking intently to Gesualdo, the actor playing him, and gesturing extravagantly with his one arm while the other dwarf nodded. On the stage, Detlef and Lowenstein were stripped to the waist, towelling off the sweat they had worked up practising the duelling scenes.

'You've been giving me a fine dash-about, Laszlo. Where did you learn the sword?'

Without his mask and costume, Lowenstein was diminished, seeming rather dull. 'At Nuln. I took classes from Valancourt at the Academy.'

'I thought I recognized that vertical parry. Valancourt taught Oswald too. You'd be a formidable opponent.'

'I hope so.'

Detlef pulled on a jacket, and buttoned it. Although plump, his muscles were well-defined. Genevieve gathered that he too was skilled with the use of the sword. He would have to be, given his fondness for heroic roles.

'Detlef,' she said. 'Could we have a word? In private?'

Detlef looked to Lowenstein, who bowed and walked off.

'An odd fellow, that,' Detlef said. 'He's always surprising me. And yet, I get this feeling that there's something not all there about our friend Laszlo. Do you know what I mean?'

Genevieve did. To her heightened senses, Lowenstein registered as a complete vacuum, as if he were a walking shell waiting to be ensouled. Still, she had met many people like that. In an actor, it was hardly surprising. It did not really matter who Lowenstein was off-stage.

'Well, what's up, elf lady? Do you want me to dismiss Lilli and hire a human being for the role?'

'No, it's something mysterious.'

He smiled. 'You intrigue me.'

She smiled back, on the verge of flirting. 'Kraly wants to see you. Us. In the poison room.'

She caught his scent in the air, and felt the pricking of the old thirst. She wondered how his blood would flow.

'I wish you wouldn't lick your lips like that, Genevieve.'

She covered her mouth, and giggled. 'I'm sorry.'

He grinned. 'The poison room, eh? Sounds lovely.'

'You know the story?'

'Oh yes. Children tortured, parents left to starve. Another one of the Great Enchanter's charming little jokes. He'd have made a good match for Mistress Nissen, don't you think? Imagine the fun they could have had exchanging recipes for the best use of babies. "Yiu 'ave not leeved until yiu 'ave taisted Enfant a la Boudreaux!" Lead on.'

She took his arm and they left the great hall. Detlef winked at Kerreth the wardrobe master as they passed through the door. The little man laughed and rubbed his neck. Genevieve blushed. She could imagine the stories that would be told during rehearsals tomorrow. Oh well, after all these years, her reputation could hardly be more tarnished by an association with an actor.

In the corridor, they continued to talk. Detlef was making a conscious effort to be charming, and she wasn't putting up too much resistance. Perhaps if stories were to be told, she should make the effort to justify them.

'How does it feel to have those teeth anyway? Aren't you forever cutting your lips?'

A witty reply came to mind, but then they entered the poison chamber and saw the looks on the faces of the people grouped around the table. And the mess that lay on it...

When Detlef had finished vomiting, Kraly told him who it was.

IX

Detlef was relieved to learn that he wasn't the first to be sick. The body had been discovered by Nebenzahl the astrologer, and the little parasite had puked his breakfast at once. Even though he spent the greater part of his professional life peering into the entrails of chickens and cats, the exposed insides of a human being caused him much distress. Detlef wondered if there were a way of divining the future through the examination of vomit. Apparently, Nebenzahl had been looking for some trinket misplaced by his mistress and opened the wrong door. He had a talent for awkwardness and, as everyone had noticed but Lilli, absolutely no foresight.

Detlef looked from face to face. Henrik Kraly was expressionless, a hard man faced with a hard situation, intent on not giving anything of himself away. Genevieve seemed beyond caring, but she was not making jokes any more. Besides, it would be difficult to tell if a vampire were shocked pale. Nebenzahl was still sobbing quietly, clinging to one of Kraly's halberdiers, occasionally scraping at the regurgitated matter on his brocaded waistcoat. Vargr Breughel, whom Detlef had insisted on summoning, looked as he always did when faced with yet another problem, as if every disaster in the world were intended personally against him.

And Rudi Wegener did not look like much at all. His face was still there, but it hung loose like a soggy mask thrown over a skull.

Detlef's first thought was that the old bandit had been flayed, but Kraly had already performed the distasteful task of closely examining the corpse and knew exactly what had been done to Rudi.

'The eyes are gone, you notice. Fished out with a dagger or small knife, I'd guess. An unsqueamish man could do the job with his fingers, but he'd best wear gloves.'

Detlef had the unpleasant feeling that Kraly was talking from experience. Electoral houses needed a servant or two with more loyalty than scruples. It was hard to associate open, upright Oswald with this lizard-hearted iceman.

'But that's not what killed him?'

'No.'

'It looks like a wolf got at him, or a ravenous daemon. Something that attacked in a frenzy, devouring, tearing...'

Kraly smiled a one-sided smile. 'Yes, I thought that at first too, but look here.'

He pointed into the body cavity, lifting a flap of skin from the ribcage.

'No bones are broken. The organs are untouched. That, in case you're interested, is what a drinking habit like Wegener's does to your liver.'

The organ was red, swollen and covered with pustules. It was obviously rotted through, even to someone who didn't know what a healthy liver looked like. Detlef thought he was going to be sick again. Kraly poked at the wounds.

'Whoever did this, did it calmly and with great skill.'

Genevieve spoke. 'What exactly was done?'

'My lady, all the fat has been neatly cut out of his body.'

Kraly left the dead thing alone, and the group moved away from it by unspoken mutual consent.

Detlef was outraged. 'Why would anyone want to do that?'

The steward shrugged. Detlef realized that the man was enjoying this brief taste of command. For once, he was at the centre of things, not a simple creature of Oswald's.

'There are many possibilities, Mr Sierck. A religious ritual, dedicating the sacrifice to some dark god. A wizard needing the material for a spell. Many enchantments require peculiar ingredients. Or, it could be the work of a madman, an obsessive who kills in a bizarre manner in an attempt to tell us something...'

'Like "eat less and take more exercise," I suppose! This is insane, Kraly! A man is dead!'

Genevieve took his hand. That helped somehow. He calmed down.

'I'm sorry.'

The steward accepted his apology without sincerity. 'At the risk of being obvious, we must face facts. There is a murderer among us.'

They all looked at each other again, like participants in one of those dim haunted castle melodramas in which the cast drop dead at regular intervals until the high priest of Morr deduces who the killer is and the audience wakes up.

'And we must catch him without word of our troubles reaching the outside.'

'I beg your pardon?'

'Whatever we do must be done in secret. The crown prince would not want this to disrupt the smooth running of his play. I am here to deal with just such occurrences. You need not concern yourself. Know only this, that I will work to bring the murderer to justice as soon as possible.'

Breughel spoke up. 'Detlef, it might indeed be best to leave this to the prince's men.'

'But we can't just go on as if nothing has happened!'

'Can't we? By my interpretation of the crown prince's orders, we have no other course open to us.'

Nebenzahl was still shaking and moaning. Detlef nodded in his direction. 'And how do we keep the popinjay silent?'

Kraly's mouth did something that in another man might qualify as a smile. 'Mr Nebenzahl has just been recalled to Altdorf. He left early this afternoon, and has written to his employer severing their relationship...'

The astrologer started, and stared at the steward.

'I am given to understand that many who quit Miss Lilli Nissen's employ choose to leave in a similar manner.'

Nebenzahl looked like a man just informed of his impending death.

'Don't worry, gut-gazer,' said Kraly. 'You'll be better paid for shutting up and going away than you would have been for staying around and blabbering to everyone. I believe a position could be found for you in Erengrad.'

The halberdier left the room, pulling Nebenzahl along with him. Detlef wondered how the weedy little fraud would get by among the Norsemen and Kislevites of that cold port on the borders of the Northern Wastes. He was furious with Kraly by now, but had learned to be cool in his wrath. Nothing would be achieved if he threw a screaming fit like Lilli Nissen.

'And I'm supposed to continue with the play, and incidentally it is my play not Crown Prince Blessed Oswald's, while people are being slaughtered all the while?'

Kraly was resolute. 'If the crown prince so wishes it.'

'I wonder, my dear steward, if Oswald would entirely approve of your actions.'

This gave Kraly pause, but he soon snapped back. 'I'm sure the crown prince has every confidence in me. He did assign me these duties. I believe I have not been a disappointment to him in the past.'

Genevieve had walked back to the table, and was taking a close look at what was left of Rudi. For the first time, Detlef realized fully that, no matter how she seemed, the woman wasn't human. She had no fear of the dead, and indeed must have some familiarity with them.

'What are you doing?' asked Kraly.

'Feeling for something.'

Genevieve touched the corpse's head, and shut her eyes. She might be praying for his soul, Detlef supposed, or doing arithmetic in her head.

'No,' she said, after a time. 'He's gone. Nothing remains of his spirit.'

'Did you hope to read his murderer's face in his mind?' Kraly asked.

'Not really. I just wanted to say farewell. He was a friend of mine, in case you'd forgotten. He had a hard life, and was not well served by it.'

She left the body alone. 'One thing,' she said.

'Yes?'

'You are aware of the common superstition that a dying man's eyes hold the last sight he beholds? That a murderer may be betrayed by his image in his victim's pupils?'

They all looked at Rudi's face, at his empty eye sockets, and flensed cheeks.

'Of course,' Kraly was impatient now, 'it's rot. Physicians and alchemists no longer think...'

'Quite, quite. The foolishness of another age, like the belief that toad men from the stars ruled the world before the Coming of Chaos.'

'Besides, his eyes are gone.'

'That is precisely the point I wished to make. You and I know the story of the murdered man's eyes is nonsense. But Rudi's murderer might believe it. That would explain why he took the eyes.'

Kraly was taken with the thought. 'A superstitious man, then? A gypsy, or an Ostlander?'

'I make no accusations.'

'Perhaps a dwarf? They are known for their superstitious ways. Brass pennies for luck, black cats drowned at birth...'

Breughel bridled as Kraly turned to him.

'I'm no dwarf,' he spat. 'I hate the little bastards.'

Kraly waved his protest away. 'Still, the vampire lady has a point. My lady, your intuitions are as sharp as they are said to be.'

'There's another possibility,' said Detlef, 'that this was done by no human agency. The supernatural is no stranger to these walls. Drachenfels was famed as a conjurer of daemons and monsters. They were supposed to have been cleared out, but it's a huge building. Who knows what could have lived here all these years, festering in the dark, waiting for its master's murderers to return.'

Genevieve touched a finger to her chin, obviously following Detlef's train of thought. She shook her head slightly, unsure.

'And we have brought back all the survivors of Oswald's adventurers. As easy meat.'

Detlef was concerned for Genevieve – for Menesh and Veidt too – but Kraly had a single thought.

'The crown prince must be warned. He might not wish to come.'

Genevieve laughed. 'You really don't know your master very well, do you, Kraly? This would only make him the more determined to be here.'

'You could be right, my lady. Rest assured, I'll charge the guards with extra vigilance. This will not happen again. You have my word on it.'

X

Alone in his room, Vargr Breughel drank and looked at himself in the mirror. He did not know who had assigned the various quarters for the company, and assumed no cruel slight had been intended. But, his was the only bedroom he had seen here equipped with a floor-to-ceiling mirror. This must have been where some harlot witch painted and primped. The Great Enchanter had had many mistresses down through the millennia. Unlike Vargr Breughel in his meagre forty-seven years.

Moonbeams filtered down through the windows and lit the room, casting a baleful light over everything. Breughel sat in his chair, feet dangling a hand's-span above the carpet, and looked himself in the eye.

He remembered his parents, and the air of disappointment that always hung about them. His sisters, born before him, were above average height. His younger brother had been as tall, straight and handsome as anyone could wish until he fell in battle in the service of the Emperor, giving their parents another reason to be uncomfortable in his presence. His mother and father had blamed each other for his condition, and had spent their lives searching each other for signs of the deformity that had been passed down through their mating to their son. Of course, it had been embarrassing for them to explain to all callers at their home that, no, they didn't have a dwarf servant, they had a dwarf son. And he wasn't a true dwarf.

He was a midget.

He started his second bottle. He was drinking sloppily now. There were stains on his shirt. His skin itched under his clothes, and he wriggled.

He had run away and joined a travelling circus, become a clown. Soon, he was running his own circus – although he had full-sized men to deal with people – and branching out into the theatre. There had been true dwarf clowns working in his circus, but they had not accepted him as one of their own. Behind his back or to his face, they called him a freak, and a warped monstrosity.

Which is what he was.

He had no wife, no mistresses, and bathed in private. His body was a secret, and he kept it well. But he examined himself daily for new changes. Often, there were two or three a month. And with the changes, came new abilities, new senses. The tubers under his arms, held together by bat-like webbing, could tune in to people's emotions. He always knew how others felt, to what degree they were disgusted by him. So far his face had not been affected, but he had had to wear gloves for some years now, to cover the eyes in the palms of his hands. The eyes that could see sounds.

He was a midget. He was also an altered and a freak.

There was a new word for what he was. He had heard scholars use it, first of plants cultivated unnaturally, then of two-headed calves, wall-eyed dogs and the like. And now of humans affected by the warpstone, progressing beyond their flesh, becoming creatures of Chaos.

Vargr Breughel was a mutant.

XI

Karl-Franz I, of the House of the Second Wilhelm, Protector of the Empire, Defier of the Dark, Emperor Himself and the Son of Emperors, had come calling on the palace of von Konigswald. The foyer table was piled high with black-edged condolence cards delivered by messenger, but Karl-Franz laid his down in person. He brushed aside the stewards and guards, and walked briskly through the palace, in search of the new elector.

Others would have visited Oswald. The grand theogonist of the cult of Sigmar and the high priest of the cult of Ulric would have endeavoured to be polite to each other throughout the lying-in-state of the old elector, Maximilian.

Representatives of the city-states and the electoral provinces, emissaries from the major temples of Altdorf and the Halfling Moot would have called with messages of sympathy.

Karl-Franz came alone, without the usual pomp that accompanied his every move, and saw Oswald man to man. There were few others in the land who could warrant such treatment.

The Emperor found Oswald in Maximilian's study – Oswald's study, now – going through old papers. Oswald dismissed the secretaries and ordered wine to be brought.

'Your father was a great friend to me when I was a boy, Oswald. In many ways, he meant more to me than my own father. It's difficult to rule an empire and be the head of a family. As I know too well. Maximilian will be greatly missed.'

'Thank you.' Oswald was still withdrawn, moving as if in a dream.

'And now we must think of the future. Maximilian is buried with honour. You must be confirmed in the crown as soon as possible.'

Oswald shook his head. This must be difficult for him. Karl-Franz remembered the agonizing ceremony that had surrounded his own ascendance to the throne, the days of torture as the electors debated the succession. He had never believed the verdict would be for him. He understood through his own sources that the voting had been eight to four against on the first ballot, and that Maximilian had talked round all but one of the other electors by the end of the session. If he truly ruled, rather than held together a squabbling collection of principalities, then he ruled only on the sufferance of the House of von Konigswald.

'The coronation will be at Castle Drachenfels. After the play. The electors will all be there, and the other dignitaries. We should have no need to reassemble them a few weeks later for another of these stately ordeals.'

'You are right of course, Oswald, but an empire expects due ritual process. Ruling is not enough. One must be seen to rule.'

Oswald looked up at the portrait of his father in his prime. He had a falcon on his hand and stood in the woods, at the forefront of a group. A golden-haired child was by his side. The young Oswald.

'I never noticed before. That youth taking the bird. He's dressed as a falconer, but...'

Karl-Franz smiled. 'Yes, it's me. I remember those days well. Old Luitpold disapproved. "What if the future Emperor should fall from his horse, or lose an eye to an angry bird, or get stuck by a boar?" He thought the future Emperor should be treasured like a painted egg. Your father understood these things better.'

'Yes. I believe he did.'

'And already I see signs that young Luitpold thinks of you as I thought of your father. Maybe I too try to cosset and smother the future Emperor. I hope I'm not the domestic tyrant old Luitpold was, but I see all the signs around me. Circles come around between our houses.'

It was an impressive painting. Karl-Franz wished he could recall the artist. He must have been one of Maximilian's hunting friends. He had certainly had a feel for the forests. You could almost hear the wind in the trees, the cries of the birds.

'Soon, we'll be in the woods again, Oswald. On the road to Drachenfels. There'll be good hunting along the way. I must confess that when you proposed the trip, I wasn't sure about it. But I've always wanted to see the site of your great victory. And I'm weary of the stifling comforts of palaces and courtiers. It's been too long since we stalked a stag, or sang the old songs. And I was sorry that your friend Sierck's History of Sigmar fell apart. Middenland sank a sum of my money in it, you know. I've been looking forward to seeing the fellow act. The ladies of my court tell me he's quite the thing.'

'Yes, Emperor.'

'Emperor and elector, eh? I remember when we were just Karl-Franz and Oswald. There's one thing I've always wondered, though...'

'What, Emperor?'

'When we were young men, when our fathers said you were mad to go up against the Great Enchanter...'

'Yes?'

'Why did you not ask me to come along? I'd have danced for the chance of such an adventure, such a battle.'

Act Four

I

Detlef was not sleeping well. He had retired early, not wishing to be pulled back to the mundane business of the company and the play after having seen what was left of Rudi. Now, he lay awake in bed, wishing, as he had done more than once since this thing began, that he was back in his cell at Mundsen Keep. At least, Szaradat had been someone to hate. And he could see Szaradat, understand his petty nastiness. There weren't any phantom monks pointing their ghostly fingers in Mundsen Keep, and there weren't any fat-taking, eyeball-gouging killers either. Indeed, compared to the fortress of Drachenfels, the keep had been a resort. Perhaps Detlef would turn his prison experiences into the subject of a farce, one day, with the wily debtors outwitting the comically dim trusties and the pompous governor being for ever humiliated by his charges.

It was no use. He could not think of the comic mask tonight.

Not only might there be a madman among them, prowling the darkened corridors of Castle Drachenfels, but also he was worried that Henrik Kraly, Oswald's man, was a potential tyrant who would rather risk the lives of everyone in the company than inconvenience the crown prince in any way. Tarradasch had said "a patron is a man who watches you drowning for twenty minutes and, when you finally manage to drag yourself to the shore by your own efforts, burdens you with help." With the elector of Middenland and The History of Sigmar, and now the crown prince of Ostland and Drachenfels, Detlef appeared to be making a speciality of distinguished backers and doom-haunted productions. He liked Oswald, but he had no illusions about his own importance in the crown prince's ultimate schemes.

The only comfort he could take was that, apart from Lilli Nissen, the play was coming along startlingly well. If they all lived through it, Drachenfels would make their reputations. Laszlo Lowenstein was a revelation. When the play transferred to an Altdorf theatre, Detlef would insist that Lowenstein go with the package. After the performance, he would be a leading light of the stage. Next time, Detlef would consider stepping back to write and direct only, and create a real vehicle for the man's astonishing talents. There weren't any good histories of Boris the Incompetent, and Lowenstein might be right for such a tragic figure. There could even be a good story in the assassination of Tsarina Kattarin by her great-great grandson, the Tsarevich Pavel. If only Genevieve Dieudonné could be persuaded to play the Tsarina…

If only Genevieve Dieudonné could be persuaded to play herself. She'd certainly be less of a pain in the fundament than Lilli Nissen.

Detlef was thinking a great deal of the vampire. He guessed from the murder of Rudi that she was in some danger if she remained at the fortress, and he felt an obligation to her. Yet, how could he hope to protect a 660-year-old girl who could crush granite in her bare hands and had already faced the Great Enchanter and survived? Perhaps he would do better to ask her for protection?

And in addition to the unknown murderer, the ghostly monks and whatever daemons might still cling to the stones of Drachenfels, might they not also need protecting from Henrik Kraly?

Detlef wished Oswald were here already. He had bested the perils of this place once. Furthermore, Detlef hoped the crown prince would be interested to find out what Kraly was doing in his name.

When there came a scratching at his door, Detlef clutched the bedclothes to him like a child who has heard one too many ghostly bedtime stories, and his candle fell over. He knew that it was all going to end here, and the ballads would tell of the genius murdered in his bed before his best work could be done.

'It's me,' hissed a low, female voice.

Guessing he would regret it, he got up and unlocked the door. He had to pull a chair out from under the doorknob.

Genevieve was outside in the corridor. Detlef was at once relieved and excited by her presence.

'Genevieve,' he said, opening wide the door. 'It's late.'

'Not for me.'

'I'm sorry. I was forgetting. Do you ever sleep?'

Genevieve shrugged. 'Occasionally. In the mornings, usually. And not in a coffin filled with my native soil. I was born in Parravon, which was civilized enough even then to pave over their beaten earth roads, so that would be a problem.'

'Come in, come in…'

'No, you must come out. There are strange things happening here by night.'

'I know. That's why I'm staying locked up in my room with a silver throwing knife.'

Genevieve winced, and made a fist of her right hand. He recalled the story of the treachery of Ueli the dwarf.

'Again, I'm sorry. I should have thought.'

She laughed, girlishly. 'No, no, I'm past bothering about all that. I'm a creature of the night, so I have to live with those things. Now, get your clothes on and bring a candle. You probably can't see in the dark as well as I can.'

Her voice was light, flirting, but her eyes were serious. There's a strange quality to vampire eyes.

'Very well, but I'm bringing my knife.'

'Don't you trust me?' Her smile showed teeth.

'Genevieve, just now, you and Vargr Breughel are the only people in this place that I do trust.'

He pulled on his trousers and a jacket, and found a pair of slippers which wouldn't make too much noise on the naked stone floors. He relit his candle, and Genevieve tugged at his sleeve.

'Where are we going?'

'We're following my nose.'

'I don't smell anything.'

'Neither do I. That was a figure of speech. I can feel things, you know. It comes with what I am. There's a great disturbance in this place. When we came here, it was clear, empty, but something came along with us and has taken up residence. Something old, something evil...'

'The twenty-seventh wagon.'

Genevieve stopped and looked at him, puzzled.

'Remember, we could never get straight the number of wagons in the caravan,' he explained. 'There were supposed to be twenty-six, but whenever we weren't looking, there seemed to be twenty-seven. If what you're talking about came with us, perhaps it came in that wagon.'

'That could be so. I should have thought of that at the time. I assumed you were just being artistically inept.'

'Thank you very much. It takes a lot of ineptitude to stage a major play, let me tell you. If it weren't for Breughel, I'd be ploughed under with work. It's not all writing and play-acting. There are finances and accommodation arrangements, and you have to feed all these people. There's probably more organization involved than in a military campaign.'

They had ventured into a part of the fortress Detlef didn't recognize. It was partially in ruins, and the cool night air blew through gaps in the walls. Moonlight flooded in. Oswald's men had not been here, and there had been no attempt to clean the place up or to make it safe. Detlef realized how little of the structure he had seen, had been given access to.

'It's near,' Genevieve said, precisely as a gust of wind snuffed his candle. 'Very near.'

He put the warm stub in his pocket and relied on the moon. He couldn't feel, see or smell anything out of the ordinary.

'What precisely are we looking for?'

'It could be anything. But it's big, it's disturbed and it's not friendly.'

'I'm really glad you told me that.'

She looked good at night, with her long, moonlit hair and floor-length white dress. As dead people go, she was a lot prettier than Rudi Wegener. For a moment, he wondered whether he hadn't been lured to this isolated spot for something more intriguing than a simple exercise in corridor-prowling. His blood ran faster. He had never been bled by a vampire, but he had read the erotic poems of Vladislav Dvorjetski, Tsarina Kattarin's lover, and understood from them that the experience was quite something.

He put his hands on her waist, and drew close to her, smelling her hair. Then, they heard the chanting.

Genevieve turned her head and put a finger to her mouth, shushing him. She stepped from his half-embrace, and pushed her hair back from her face. Detlef couldn't tell whether she was baring her teeth consciously or unconsciously. They looked longer and sharper in the moonlight.

The chanting was only just audible, but it had a horrid quality to it. If this were a religious rite, it would be dedicated to one of the gods whose altars Detlef habitually shunned. If this were some magical incantation, it was the work of an outlaw wizard conjuring up something utterly vile.

Slowly, quietly, they crept down the corridor, passing through alternating patches of light and dark. There were doors in the walls, and one – about twenty feet up ahead – was ajar. The chanting came from beyond that door, Detlef was certain. It grew louder as they approached, and he could make out the low pipe music being played under the vocal. Something about the tune turned his stomach. Something that made him fear he had seen his last sunset.

They pressed close to the wall, and edged nearer.

There were lights beyond the door. And people, moving in a confined space.

Detlef had his silver knife out.

They came to the door, and peered through. The slit only afforded a very limited view of what was taking place inside the chamber beyond, but that was enough to make Detlef feel sick again.

In a circle of black candles lay a small figure. A child or a dwarf. It was impossible to tell, because he had been flayed. His exposed musculature glistened red in the candle-light. Shadows danced around him, cast by unseen participants in this grisly scene.

'Menesh,' whispered Genevieve.

Detlef saw that the red thing in the circle had but one arm. As he gazed at the writhing snakes of the dwarf's intestines, he came to realize that Menesh was still, somehow, alive. He would have vomited then, but there was nothing left in his stomach to come up. Bones stood out white amid the bloody jelly of the remaining flesh.

Genevieve was straining forward, tensing to leap into the room. Detlef held her back by the shoulders. They would have no chance against as many murderers as he thought joined in the chant. She turned, and took his wrists. He felt again the strength of the vampire, and saw red anger flare and die in her eyes. Then, she too realized they couldn't afford to barge in and get killed. She nodded her thanks.

Then they heard the clatter of boots. People were coming down the corridor, and they were caught between the two factions.

Lanterns came out of the dark. Halberds scraped the stone ceiling. Six men-at-arms marched, and Kraly stood at their head. He looked disapproving as he saw Detlef and Genevieve. For once, Detlef couldn't bring himself to be annoyed by the man's presence. Just now, he looked like the Imperial cavalry turning up in the last act to relieve the castle.

The chanting had risen now to a weird ululation that resounded throughout the passageway. Menesh was screaming in time with the music, and the shadows clustered around him.

'What are you doing here?' snapped Kraly.

'Never mind that,' said Detlef, having to shout now to be heard over the chant. 'There's murder being done in this room.'

'So I gather.' He pushed his helmet back, and hooked his thumbs into the pockets of his doublet.

'Kraly, let's end this thing now.'

The steward considered a moment or two. 'Very well.'

Detlef stood back, and let the first pair of Kraly's bully boys crash through the door, knocking it off its hinges. The heavy wood fell with a gust that extinguished the black candles. The chanting and the music shut off suddenly, and there were cries in the dark. Some of the voices were human. Detlef rushed into the room. As he stepped through the portal, the candle he was holding went out and he found himself in total darkness. He had the feeling of being in a vast, exposed plain under a starless, moonless night sky. He stepped in something soft and wet, and heard a groan that told him what it was. Then, he was buffeted this way and that by heavy bodies. There were screams, and the noise of weapons clashing. He was lifted bodily from the ground and thrown across the room. He collided with someone, and went down, his arm twisted under him. There was a wrenching at his shoulder, and he prayed the bone wasn't broken. Kraly was barking orders. Someone stepped briefly on his chest, and he tried to stand up, clutching his agonized shoulder.

Then the lights came in.

Genevieve, a lantern in either hand, stood in the doorway. The chamber was small, and had a dead dwarf in it. Otherwise, Detlef, Kraly and the men-at-arms were alone. In the dark, one of the crown prince's men had been stabbed in the thigh by a comrade, and was bleeding messily as he applied a tourniquet. Genevieve went to his aid, and he cringed away from her as she tied the wound properly. The bleeding stopped and the man seemed somewhat surprised that the vampire let him be.

'Well done, Kraly. Oswald will be proud of you, I'm sure.' Detlef pushed his shoulder back into place, gritting his teeth through the pain.

The steward wasn't rattled by his failure. He was on his knees, examining the dwarf. Detlef was upset to notice the footprint in the new-made corpse's stomach, and thought better of looking at his own slipper.

'The skin's gone, this time. And the kidneys. And the eyes, of course. And… um… the regenerative organs.'

Kraly blushed at having to mention such indecent matters in the presence of a lady.

'He was alive when we came in, Kraly,' said Detlef. 'We probably trampled him to death.'

'He wouldn't have lived.'

'Obviously not, but he might have told us something before he went. We've not done well here.'

Kraly stood up, wiping the dust from his knee-britches. He pulled out a kerchief and tried to get the blood off his hands. He rubbed away at his fingers long after they were clean.

'There must be another way out,' said Genevieve. 'I was at the door. No one came through it after you all pushed your way in.'

They all looked around the room. It was bare stone, with traces of graffiti in a language or languages Detlef didn't recognize as the only adornment. Kraly gave an order, and his men began prodding with their halberds. Finally, when they tried the ceiling, a stone receded above a blade, and a whole section of the wall swung inwards. Beyond lay a hidden passage, its floor thick with the dust of centuries. The cobwebs had recently been parted.

'You first, Kraly,' said Detlef.

The steward, a single-shot pistol in his hand, led the way. Detlef and Genevieve followed, along with four of the halberdiers. They had to leave their halberds behind because the secret passage was too low for the weapons. They all had to stoop.

'This would be a fine escape route for a dwarf,' said Kraly.

'Menesh was the victim, not the murderer,' mentioned Detlef.

'I wasn't thinking of Menesh.'

There was blood in the dust.

'We must have wounded him.'

'Either that or he got covered in the stuff while skinning Menesh.'

'Possibly.'

The passage wound down a spiral staircase, into the heart of Drachenfels. They found a skeleton in centuries-old armour, the skull exploded from within. Detlef shuddered. This place had more horrors than the Northern Wastes. Sigmar himself would think twice at exploring its nether regions.

There were eyeholes in the walls now. Detlef guessed they would peer through the eyes of portraits in the chambers. Either Drachenfels had had a fine sense of irony in his deployment of melodramatic devices, or – more likely – he had invented the clichés later taken up by addlewits out to chill the spines of their audiences. The way things were going, he expected a contested will, devious heirs, corpses concealed in suits of armour and a last-act unmasking of the kindly old steward as a mad killer.

Then they came to a door, and were back in the familiar part of the fortress. This was where the company were billeted.

'Surely that can't be,' Detlef said. 'We descended to the place where Menesh was killed, and now we've come down again, back to where we started.'

'This place is like that,' said Genevieve. 'It's all down, whichever way you go.'

The door swung back, sealing the secret passage. It looked like any other section of the wall.

'Kraly, weren't you supposed to have someone on guard in this corridor?

Someone who might have noticed a murderer covered from head to foot in blood creep out of the wall?'

The steward's face was frozen. 'I had to redeploy my forces to search the castle. That's why you're still alive.'

Detlef had to admit he had a point. 'We're alive, yes, but how do we know everyone in these rooms hasn't been slaughtered in their beds? Only, with our luck, they'd have spared Lilli Nissen.'

'Our quarry was in too much haste to do harm to anyone. Look, he left us a spoor to read.'

There was blood on the carpet. It petered out after a few feet. Outside a door. There was a red smear on the knob.

'I believe we have our killer,' said Kraly, grimly satisfied.

'Don't you think that's just a bit too convenient?' asked Detlef. 'Besides, there was more than one person chanting.'

'That's as may be. We'll round up the confederates later. But first let's take our man. Or whatever he is...'

The door was locked. Kraly discharged his gun at the lock. Others opened up and down the passage, and heads peeked out. Detlef would have to ask later what Kosinski was doing in Lilli Nissen's suite. Kraly kicked the door, and it splintered as it slammed back.

Vargr Breughel had jumped out of bed. Kraly looked at him, and gasped. Detlef pushed through, and felt as if he had been punched in the stomach.

His friend and adviser looked up at him through eyes in his chest and hands.

But it was the look in the eyes in his face that struck through to Detlef.

Breughel, the monster, was crying.

II

There is no pleasure like rising with the sun and finding yourself in the forests of the Empire, thought Karl-Franz I as he made water in the bushes. He listened to the birdsong, naming each individual species in his head as he distinguished it from the rest of the chatter of the morning chorus. It was a fine spring morning, and the sun was already high, streaming through the tall trees. There would be deer along their route today, the Emperor was sure. It was years since he had hunted deer.

In the camp, there were the groans and complaints of those stirred too early from their slumbers. Karl-Franz was amused to find which of his distinguished travelling companions awoke irritable in the wilds, which were nursing heads befuddled by last night's food and drink, and which sprang to their horses enlivened by the call of the birds and the fresh feel of dew underfoot. Herbal tea was being brewed in huge iron pots, and a light breakfast prepared.

Some of the worthies chose to sleep in carriages as well appointed and upholstered as any bed-chamber in any palace, but Karl-Franz wanted only the feel of a blanket between himself and the ground. The empress disagreed, and had opted to stay at home with one of her persistent illnesses, but Luitpold, their twelve-year-old son and heir, was revelling in the freedom of the forests. There were still men-at-arms watching out for the Imperial family at every moment – Karl-Franz couldn't even wander into the woods to empty his bladder without a sword-bearing shadow following him – but there was open air about them. The Emperor felt free of the burdens of state, felt a respite from the stifling procedures of running the country, of resisting the incursions of evil, of defying the dark.

The elector of Middenland, who had been protesting very loudly ever since he learned precisely who Oswald had engaged to stage his play for him, was rubbing his aching back, and moaning softly to the red-haired page who always seemed to be with him. The grand theogonist of the cult of Sigmar, a frail old man for such a robust deity, had not shown a hair of his head outside his coach since they left Altdorf, and his snoring was a source of some amusement. Karl-Franz observed the other electors and their attendants as they shook the sleep from their heads, and took tea. He was learning more of these men and women upon whom the Empire rested on this trip than he had in years of courtly meetings and grand balls.

Aside from Oswald, who rode as if born on a horse and could bring down a pheasant with a single crossbow bolt, the only elector who seemed entirely comfortable on this journey was the elder of the Half-ling Moot, who spent most of his time eating or laughing. The young Baron Johann von Mecklenberg, elector of the Sudenland, was a skilled woodsman, Karl-Franz knew, having spent half his life wandering in search of a lost brother and only recently returned to his estates. Johann gave the impression that he had seen things which made pleasure trips like this petty by comparison. He wore his scars like medals, and didn't talk much. The lady mayoress and chancellor of the University of Nuln, Countess Emmanuelle von Leibewitz, rumoured to be the most eligible spinster in the Empire, was not winning any friends with her whining about the tedious details of the hundreds of masques and parties she had thrown. Karl-Franz was both amused and appalled at the realization that the countess was cooing over Luitpold not in any motherly sense but because she regarded the future Emperor as an ideal marriage prospect despite the obvious disparities of age and temperament between them.

The Emperor took a steaming mug of tea from his attendant, and downed a gulp of the hot, sweet beverage. Middenheim was asking how much longer they would be on the road, and Oswald was making a rough guess. Young Luitpold crashed out of the undergrowth, his jerkin soiled and his hair untidy, pushing Resnais of Marienburg aside, and bore a still-twitching rabbit to the fire. His arrow had taken it in the haunches. Karl-Franz noted that his son took his prize to Oswald for approval. The crown prince deftly snapped the dying animal's neck.

'Excellent, highness,' said the elector of Ostland. 'This was well shot.'

Luitpold looked around, grinning, as Oswald tousled his already wild hair. Resnais fastidiously brushed his clothes. Oswald waved to Karl-Franz.

'Your son will feed the Empire, my friend.'

'I hope so. If it needs feeding.'

Talabecland crawled out of his vast tent, bleary-eyed and unshaven. He looked at the bleeding rabbit in Oswald's hand and moaned.

Oswald and Luitpold laughed. Karl-Franz joined them. This was what the life of the Emperor should always be. Good friends and good hunting.

'Here.' Oswald dipped his hand into the rabbit's wounds, and drew red lines on Luitpold's cheeks. 'Now, future Emperor, you have been blooded.'

Luitpold ran to Karl-Franz, and saluted his father. The Emperor returned the salute.

'Well, my hero son, perhaps you should wash yourself off and have some tea. We may rule the greatest country in the Known World, but we have an empress who rules us, and she would want you well fed and warmed out here. Husbands have been skewered through the eye with tent pegs for less.'

Luitpold took his mug.

'Ah, father, but surely the Emperor Hajalmar was assassinated for being appallingly ill-suited to the throne, rather than for his short-comings as a family man. I seem to recall from my lessons that he died childless, and so could hardly be accused of neglecting the welfare of his heirs, unless you count his failure to produce any as a lack of fatherly spirit.'

'Well learned, my son. Now clean your face and have your tea before I abdicate in favour of your little sister and cut you out of the succession.'

Everybody laughed, and Karl-Franz recognized the deep-throated gen- uine laughter he could sometimes elicit rather than the weak chuckles that came from people who believed an Emperor's joke was automatic- ally funny and that there would be a penalty of death for anyone who thought differently. There was a neighing as the horses were roused in their makeshift pens by the ostlers.

'Father,' asked Luitpold, 'who were the monks who came here last night?'

Karl-Franz was taken aback.

'Monks? I know of no monks. Have you any idea what the lad means, Oswald?'

The elector shook his head, a blank look on his face. Perhaps too blank, as if something were being concealed.

'Last night, when all were asleep save the guards, I was awakened.'

Luitpold told his story. 'I was worried about Fortunato's hoof. His shoe has been working loose, and I thought I heard him whinnying. I got up and went to the pens, and Fortunato was fast asleep. I must have dreamed his cry. But when I returned to my tent, I saw men standing at the edge of the clearing. At first, I supposed them to be the guards, but then I noticed they were dressed in long robes and hoods, like the monks of Ulric...'

The high priest of the cult of Ulric shrugged, and scratched his belly. Talabecland and Middenheim were attentive. Luitpold, enjoying their regard, continued.

'They were standing still, but their faces glowed a little, as if lit by lanterns. I would have called out to them to explain their business, but I didn't want to wake everyone. I was suddenly very sleepy, so I returned to my tent. I assumed you would know what they were about.'

Oswald looked thoughtful.

'Do you suppose my son could have witnessed some apparition? My late father was prone to seeing spirits. The knack could have skipped a generation.'

'I've heard of no such spectral cadre,' said Oswald. 'There are many stories about the hauntings in these woods. My friend Rudi Wegener, whom you will meet at Castle Drachenfels, knows and has told me of dozens of local legends. But these monks do not mean anything to me.'

The Baron von Mecklenberg snorted. 'Then you are less well learned on your own legend than you should be, Ostland. The monks of Drachen- fels are widely remembered by necromancers and spirit-chasers.'

Karl-Franz imagined Oswald was discomforted by his fellow elector's knowledge.

The baron poured the last of his tea hissing into the fire, and continued, 'Drachenfels killed many in his time, and was enchanter enough to make his sway over his victims last beyond their death. Their spirits clung to him, became his slaves. Some even became his followers. They were supposed to be seen in habits like monks. Even after their master's death, they are rumoured to cling together, to form an order in the world of ghosts. We travel to the fortress of Drachenfels, and evidently the Great Enchanter's victims ride with us.'

III

Last night, at precisely the worst point, an assistant stage manager had told Detlef 'things will look better in the morning' and lost two front teeth.

This morning, when, as expected, things looked even worse than they had been, Detlef vaguely regretted his temper. He had fallen into a swoon just before dawn, and woke up now with a pain in his skinned knuckles. His head ached worse than it had ever done the morning after a drunken orgy, and his mouth felt as if it had been filled with quick-drying slime.

The servant who brought him his breakfast on a tray had left it at his bedside and not dared to disturb him. He took a mouthful of cold tea, swished it around to clean the scum off his teeth, and spat back into the cup. The bacon and bread were cold and greasy. He took a bite and forced himself to get it down.

It all came flooding back horribly.

His best friend was a strangely altered monstrosity, and Henrik Kraly claimed he was also the madman who had murdered Rudi Wegener and Menesh the dwarf.

He hadn't bothered to undress last night. Now he did, and found fresh clothes laid out for him. He pulled them on, trying to will the fog out of his head. He rubbed his stubbled chin, and decided to put off shaving until his hands were steady enough to hold the razor.

Detlef found most of the company gathered in the main hall, peering at a notice posted on the door, signed by Henrik Kraly.

It was an announcement that the murderer had been caught and that things would now proceed normally. Vargr Breughel was not mentioned, and no one had yet noticed he wasn't with them.

'I bet it's that bastard Kosinski,' said a small voice.

'No, it's not,' said Kosinski, hitting someone.

'Where's the vampire?' asked Justus the Trickster.

'It wasn't her,' said Detlef. 'Kraly's taken Breughel–'

There were general gasps of disbelief.

'And it wasn't him either. At least, it's not been proved to my satisfaction. Where is Genevieve?'

No one knew.

Detlef found her in her room, dead in her bed. She wasn't breathing, but he felt a slow heartbeat. There was no waking her.

Even in his current state of disturbance, he took the time to look around. There were books on her dressing table, written in an arcane form of Bretonnian Detlef could just recognize but not follow. Genevieve's diaries? They would make interesting reading. A scarf had been hung over the mirror.

It must be strange to lose familiarity with your own face, Detlef supposed.

Otherwise, the room was like any other woman's. Trunks of clothes, a few pamphlets, keys and coins on the nightstand, an icon-sized portrait of a couple dressed in the styles of seven centuries ago. There was a copy of the Drachenfels script on a chair, with annotations in a tiny hand. He would have to ask her about that. Was she studying her own part? Lilli Nissen's part, rather. When she didn't wake up after a minute or two, Detlef left her to the sleep of the undying.

He found Reinhardt Jessner, and told him to take the cast through their lines while he saw to Breughel. The young actor understood immediately, and corralled the company efficiently.

There were Kraly-signed notices up all over the fortress, issuing orders and failing to explain the situation. He must have been up all night putting his signature to them.

Detlef found them in the stables, which had been converted into a makeshift jail-cum-interrogation room. He was drawn to the place by the noise of the thumps.

They'd cleared out one of the stalls, and chained Breughel up naked like an animal in it. Kraly sat on a stool, asking questions, while an inky clerk with a quill taller than his hat scratched down a transcript of the conversation. Detlef wondered how he transliterated the screams.

One of Kraly's halberdiers was naked to the waist, his torso flushed and sweaty. He had armoured gauntlets on, and had been working Breughel over.

The prisoner's human face was bloodied. The rest of him leaked a yellowish fluid.

Even if Breughel had had any answers, he wouldn't have been able to give them, Detlef thought.

'What are you doing here, Kraly? You idiot!'

'Getting a confession. The crown prince will want things sorted out before he gets here.'

'I think if you hit me a couple of times with those gloves on, I'd confess too. Surely, even a cretin like you knows why torture is out of fashion. Unless, of course, you get your amusement this way.'

Kraly stood up. He had Breughel's yellow ichor on his boots. He was freshly barbered and wore an immaculate white cravat. He didn't look as if he had spent the night crawling about secret passageways and leaping to conclusions.

'There are details known only to the murderer. Those are what we are after.'

'And what if he's not the murderer?'

Kraly's lips curled up on one side. 'I think that's unlikely given the evidence, don't you?'

'Evidence! The killer just stuck his bloody hand on a door to point you at a convenient scapegoat, and you've done just what he wanted. A nine-year old wouldn't be taken in by that old trick!'

The torturer took a good shot at Breughel's stomach, disturbing the forest of unclassifiable fronds that grew there. Several of the eyes in his chest had been put out. Another of Kraly's men was heating up a brazier and sticking blacksmithing tools into it. Torture was evidently not a lost art in Ostland. Detlef wondered how Good Prince Oswald would react to all this.

'I was not referring to the bloody door, Mr Sierck. I was referring to... this monstrous abortion, this creature of Chaos...'

Mouths around Breughel's waist snapped open, long tongues darting out. The torturer cried out.

'That stings.' Blue weals rose on his arm.

'You'll be dead in three days,' said Breughel, his voice remarkably unaffected.

The torturer started back, raising his hand to strike. Then panic filled his eyes. He grabbed his arm, as if to squeeze out the infection.

'You can't possibly know that, Breughel,' Detlef said. 'You've never stung anyone before.'

Breughel laughed, liquid rattling in his throat. 'That's true.'

The torturer looked relieved, and cuffed Breughel viciously. Blood flew. The floor of the stall was slippery with various bodily fluids. The place smelled badly. The clerk scribbled down a precis of the incident for posterity.

'Kraly, can I talk to my friend?'

The steward shrugged.

'Alone?'

He nodded his head, got up, and strolled out of the stall. His torturer went with him, rubbing his itching rash. The scribe also withdrew, muttering about judicial procedures.

'Can I get you anything?' Detlef asked.

'Some water would be nice.'

Detlef used a dipper in a bucket that stood nearby, and raised the water to his friend's lips. He found it strange being so close to such a twisted creature, but he swallowed his distaste. Breughel coughed as he slurped, and the water trickled out of his wounded mouth. But his throat worked, and he got some down. He hung there, exhausted, in his chains, and looked expectantly at Detlef.

'Go on,' he said, 'ask me...'

'Ask you what?'

'If I gutted Rudi and took his eyes. And did the same for Menesh.'

Detlef hesitated. 'All right, I'll ask you.'

Breughel's eyes leaked again. He looked betrayed. 'You have to say it out loud. It hurts more that way. The hurting is the most important part of it.'

Detlef gulped. 'Did you kill them? Rudi and Menesh?'

Breughel painfully formed a toothless smile. 'Is that what you think?'

'Oh, come on now, Vargr! This is me, Detlef Sierck, not some total stranger! We've worked together for... how many years now? You stuck by me all through The History of Sigmar, you think I'm going to desert you just because you're a...'

He groped for the word.

Breughel gave it to him. 'A mutant. That's what they're... what we're called, these days. Yes, I'm a creature of Chaos. Look at me...'

Breughel pulsated, strange organs emerging from his torso.

'It's a strange disease. I don't know if I'm dying of it, or being reborn. I wish I were a writer like you, then maybe I could describe what it's like.'

'Does it hurt?'

'Some of the time. At others, it's... quite pleasant, actually. I don't have to feel pain if I don't want to. Otherwise, I'd have given Kraly a nice little confession. Unfortunately, I can't protect myself through ignorance, you see. These tentacles in my belly can see what's uppermost in a man's mind. I know the details of the murders Kraly wants to beat and burn out of me. Just as I know how you really feel about what I've become...'

Detlef cringed inwardly, and blurted an apology.

'Don't be sorry. I'm disgusted at what I've become. I've always been disgusted at what I was. It's nothing new. I don't blame you at all. You're the only one who ever gave me a chance. I'm going to die soon, and I'd like you to know how grateful I've been for your friendship.'

'Vargr, I won't let Kraly kill you.'

'No, you won't. I have the choice whether I live or die. I can stop my heart, tear it apart with the teeth I have inside my chest. And I intend to do it.'

'But Oswald is a fair man. He won't see you hanged for murders you didn't commit.'

Breughel's cilia writhed and changed colour.

'No, but what about seeing me hanged for the murders I will commit? Even seeing me hanged for what I am. I'm changing–'

'That's obvious.'

'Not just in my body. My mind is changing, too. I have impulses. The warpstone warps minds as well as bodies. I've been misremembering things, having strange ideas, strange desires. I'm altering severely. I could go to the Wastes and lose myself in the hordes of Chaos, join with all the other monsters. But I'd not be me any more. I'm losing Vargr Breughel, and I don't think I want to leave behind what I'm about to become.'

Breughel gritted his teeth, and strained against his chains. There was a great grinding inside his chest. His cilia deepened in colour and stuck out like fat sausages.

Kraly and his men came rushing back. 'What's the beast doing?' asked the steward.

Detlef turned and hit him in the gut, hurting his knuckles more. Kraly bent double, swearing and coughing. Detlef wanted to hit the man again, but there was too much else going on for him to bother.

Breughel's torso swelled up, and he snapped his chains out of the wall. Smiling, he advanced on Kraly. The steward screamed as the monster came for him. Breughel rattled his chains and, smiling, slapped his tormentor's face. He continued to expand, rents appearing in his skin. Eyes stood out like boils. He drew a great breath, inflating his lungs. Then, he burst.

Detlef stood back to avoid the splatter. The torturer fell over, putting a hand into the brazier of hot coals to steady himself. He screamed as his hand was roasted through. Breughel fell apart with a great sighing.

As he died, Vargr Breughel said, 'Good luck with the play.'

IV

When, three days later, the Imperial party arrived, things were as nearly back to normal as they ever could be. Detlef had supervised the burial of Vargr Breughel, and informed Henrik Kraly that it would be in his own best interests to keep out of his way. Kraly put up notices announcing that Breughel had been the murderer, and muttered to his men that each day which passed without a fresh atrocity proved him right. If the dwarf had confederates, the steward did not spend too much of his time seeking them out. Privately, he expressed the opinion that the voices they had heard in the room where Menesh was murdered were those of the daemons Breughel was summoning with his unholy ritual.

Murderer or not, Breughel was much missed by the company. Detlef called a halt to rehearsals for an entire morning so that everyone could attend the assistant director's funeral. Detlef had him buried on the mountainside, outside the fortress walls. Justus the Trickster, a cleric after all, read the lesson, and Detlef gave a brief eulogy. The only conspicuously absent face was that of Lilli Nissen, and she hadn't even been much in evidence at rehearsals recently. Breughel had more friends than he knew. When Oswald came, Detlef vowed, there would be a reckoning with Kraly, whom he considered his friend's murderer.

The play was set in its final form now. Detlef went through a complete day of rehearsal without adding, deleting or changing any lines, and an enormous cheer went up from the company. He took out his much-scribbled script and pondered a moment before pronouncing the text whole and finished. Then he delivered a fifty-minute lecture on the finer points of the actual production, browbeating, upbraiding, cajoling and pampering those who deserved it and enthusing his followers with the spirit of the piece. Watching from the audience – with a stand-in taking his role – Detlef thought the only dead spot was Lilli, and there was really nothing to be done about that. At least, she still looked incredible, teeth in or out, and her blankness could just barely be interpreted as undead detachment, even if that interpretation went against the grain of the play and the expectations of anyone who had met the real Genevieve Dieudonné. He could not speak for his own performance. That had been one of Breughel's functions, to keep him alert as an actor while he might be overly concerned with other details of the production. He hoped his friend would not be overly critical from the afterlife, and sought to curb the excesses Breughel had continually pointed out to him.

When runners appeared early in the morning to announce the imminent arrival of the Emperor and the electors, Detlef was confident enough to cancel the day's work and leave the company to their own devices. They would perform all the better for the rest and relaxation. And he knew they would appreciate the opportunity to gawk at rich and famous people. More than one young actress or musician vanished to their chambers to dig out their most fetching, and/or revealing, costumes in the hope of attracting a wealthy patron among the Emperor's entourage.

The Emperor Karl-Franz rode into Castle Drachenfels at the head of his caravan, Oswald – Grand Prince Oswald now – a little behind him, and his son Luitpold doing his best to keep abreast. The Emperor waved, and the assembled cast cheered him. The rest of the caravan creaked and lumbered through the castle gates and the courtyard became a chaos of ostlers and coachmen and servants. The dignified personages spilled out of their carriages and were led to the luxurious apartments that had been prepared for them in the wing of the fortress opposite the actors' quarters. Detlef heard Illona Horvathy commenting enviously on Countess Emmanuelle von Liebewitz's ridiculously bejewelled travelling clothes. He recognized the elector of Middenland, who avoided his gaze and hurried off, grey-faced, to find the privies. Some people don't travel well. Kraly turned out and got to Oswald first. He delivered a concise report, and Detlef saw the elector's face grow serious.

Oswald came over to Detlef, leaving Kraly to liaise with the new influx of guardsmen.

'This has been a bad business.'

'Yes, highness, and made the worse for your servant.'

Oswald was grave. 'So I gather.'

'Vargr Breughel was innocent of any crime.'

'Yet he was an altered.'

'That is, in itself, not illegal.'

'For now, maybe. There are moves in the college. However, I assure you this will not end here. Steps will be taken. You will be heard.'

Young Luitpold ran up to Oswald and tugged at his coat, excitedly. Then, he became aware of Detlef, and turned from a normal boy trussed up in a silly soldier suit to a miniature aristocrat with poise and bearing.

'Detlef Sierck, permit me to introduce Luitpold of the House of the Second Wilhelm.'

The boy bowed, his hand fluttering before his face. Detlef returned the bow.

'I am honoured, highness.'

His duty done, Luitpold returned his attention to Oswald. 'Show me where you slew the monster, Oswald. And where your tutor was killed by Ueli the dwarf, and where the gargoyles came out of the walls...'

Oswald laughed, but without much humour. 'That can wait until Detlef's play. You'll find it all out then.'

The future Emperor dashed off, one silk stocking slipping to bunch at his ankle. Oswald looked more the proud parent than Karl-Franz, Detlef thought. Then, the grand prince turned serious again, as if suddenly aware of the place he had returned to.

'We didn't come in through the courtyard, you know,' he said. 'I only saw this afterwards, in the sunlight. We came in through the cliff gates, which lie beyond that arm of the fortress.'

He pointed. By day, Drachenfels was just an ordinary mountain fastness. Only at night did the dread creep back.

'That's where I saw Sieur Jehan, my oldest friend, with his throat pulled out, bleeding his last.'

'We have all lost friends, highness.'

Oswald stared at Detlef, as if seeing him for the first time. 'Forgive me. So, this place has claimed more victims. Sometimes, I think we should have had it pulled down and scattered the stones, then seeded the site with salt and silver.'

'But then you wouldn't have been able to stage this pageant.'

'Maybe not.'

Detlef could not help but notice that Oswald seemed more disturbed by the death of Sieur Jehan, twenty-five years ago, than by those of Rudi Wegener and Menesh the dwarf within the last week. The aristocrat had grown a tougher skin since his first visit to this place. The boy hero of Detlef's play was buried within the skilled politician, the dignified statesman.

A sprightly man in early middle age approached them. He had doffed his ceremonial coat, and Detlef took a moment to recognize him in a plain black travelling suit.

'Detlef, here is Luitpold's father.'

Emperor Karl-Franz of the House of the Second Wilhelm held out a hand. Detlef didn't know whether to shake it or kiss it, and opted to do both. To his surprise, he found himself immediately liking the man.

'We've heard much of your work, Sierck. I trust you'll not disappoint us tomorrow night.'

'I shall try not to, majesty.'

'That's all we can ask for. Oswald, come, let's eat. I'm starving.'

Karl-Franz and Oswald left, arm in arm.

So these, Detlef thought, are the giants, the true gods whose whims alter the courses of our lives, whose faults slaughter thousands and whose virtues endure for ever. Like the fortress of Drachenfels, they don't seem so much in the daylight.

Genevieve appeared, hidden behind her strange dark glasses, and flew to Oswald.

For a moment, Detlef wondered if what he was feeling was jealousy.

V

While Oswald entertained Karl-Franz and the electors in one wing of the fortress, and Detlef oversaw his dress rehearsal in the other, Anton Veidt was preparing to leave Drachenfels. He took his weapons from their hidden places in his room, and cleaned them. He wrapped a coil of rope around his skinny middle. He packed provisions enough for three days in the mountains. And he allowed himself a cigar, keeping the smoke down, controlling the spasms in his chest.

He was not a stupid man. Erzbet dead. Rudi dead. Menesh dead. He could follow the trend. The vampire lady and the grand prince might be foolish enough to stay and invite their fates, but Veidt was getting out now.

Twenty-five years ago, it had been the same. Conradin dead. Heinroth dead. Sieur Jehan dead. Ueli the dwarf dead. Stellan the Warlock dead. Others whose names he couldn't even remember dead. And Veidt alone in the dark, waiting for death.

Sometimes, he wondered if he really had died in the passageways of this castle, and whether the remainder of his life was just a dream, or a nightmare? As his black crab ate more, he felt himself being tugged back to those hours in the dark with the poison creeping into him.

He would wake up at night, certain that the mattress beneath him was the stone floor of Castle Drachenfels.

Could it be only minutes since Oswald and the others had left him to die here? Could he have imagined the whole course of his life in these few moments of unconsciousness? In the dark, the events of twenty-five years seemed a dream. How could he have ever believed such a hazy, marginal existence was real?

These sick thoughts were a symptom of the dangers of this place. He should never have returned. There weren't enough gold crowns in the Empire to hire a man to commit suicide.

He chose his time well, while Oswald was busy with his feast and Detlef his performance. There would be guards about, but they weren't expecting anyone to attempt an escape. He should have no problem. And if he did come up against some itchy halberdier, he had his dart gun and his short sword.

Actually, he had no reason to believe he couldn't just tell Oswald he was leaving and walk away from Drachenfels in the open. But he did not intend to chance the grand prince's whims. Oswald could as easily have him imprisoned as let him free and there was no telling how important Veidt really was to his pageant.

In his old clothes, his hunting clothes, he left his room and crept down to the courtyard. It was well lit and he could see too many men-at-arms. Kraly himself was supervising the watch, fanatically devoting himself to the security of the Imperial party in an attempt to justify his earlier actions. The great doors were closed, so Veidt would have to scale the walls to escape. The risk was too great.

He would have to leave the castle the way they had come in all those years ago, through the gates at the clifftop. He had rope and his grip was as good as ever. He could descend the mountains, get away into Bretonnia. Oswald would never reach for him there and there were felons enough to keep his belly full. He could grow old with Bretonnian wenches and Bretonnian wine, and maybe burst his heart through excess before the crab killed him.

Weeks ago, when they had arrived at the fortress, he had retraced the steps of their original expedition, searching for the spot where he had lain unconscious while Oswald was killing Drachenfels. He had not been able to find it. One stretch of corridor looked much like another. Now, he paced the route again, reversing their path, pushing for the outside. He passed the great hall, where the play-actors were recreating the death of Drachenfels, then worked his way slowly through the passage where Rudi had been caught in the wooden jaws of the trap. Beyond lay the place of his ordeal, the poison feast chamber, the gargoyle stones, the enchanted door that had killed Stellan, and the outer wall.

His pains had receded in the last few days. Comfortable accommodations and real food will do that to you. He had been lulled by the luxuries, and wilfully ignored the dangers. But now fat old Rudi was gone, and one-armed Menesh, and poor, mad Erzbet. Buried without their eyes. Like him, they should have died here a quarter century ago, but had clung on beyond their time. Veidt intended to cling just a little longer, with just a little more tenacity.

He wandered for hours, longer than he should have, resting for a time in shadowed corners. It was late now. The dress rehearsal would be over, the feast quietening down. This part of the fortress was deserted – shunned, even – and no one stood between Veidt and the safety of the night outside. Rudi had been found here. And the room where Menesh had been skinned was only a few turns of the corridor away.

He was feeling the crab now, feeling it shift inside him. His heart hung like a stone in his chest, and his joints pained him. He was certain he was bleeding inside his clothes. He had to stifle coughing fits lest his noise attract the guards. Or even less welcome presences.

Veidt's feet dragged, as if he were wading through heavy sludge. And he remembered the gargoyle poison seeping through his veins, turning his flesh to the semblance of stone. Perhaps the sickness had just lain dormant in him all these years, awaiting his return to Drachenfels to strike again?

Wet trickled down his face. He touched his hand to the graze, and found it bleeding. The wound made by the gargoyle's horn had opened again.

He stumbled, trying to force himself forwards, and fell headlong. His skull rang as it struck the flagstones. In his convulsive grip, his pistol discharged. He heard rather than felt the dart whizz along the floor under him and bury its tip in his thigh. Then, the pain came. He rolled over, and shuffled back until there was a wall behind him. The shaft was bent, but the head was embedded deep in his muscle. He made a fist around the dart and pulled, but it slipped through his fingers and he was holding nothing. He couldn't get a strong enough hold on the shaft to get it out of his leg.

Tired, he let sleep come...

...then he was awake, alert, the ache in his leg cutting through the fuzziness of his senses.

There were people in the passage with him. His old comrades. There was Erzbet, hanging back, long hair over her face. And Rudi, his loose skin flapping on his skeleton. And Menesh leaking as he held in his guts with a raw hand. There were others. Sieur Jehan with his open neck, Heinroth with his bones on the outside and skin on the inside, a cloud of hanging flesh particles in the rough shape of Stellan the Warlock. And the man in the mask, the man who was not quite Drachenfels, but who would do for the moment, the man who wanted Veidt's eyes.

He realized he had found the spot at last.

VI

At the emperor's feast, Genevieve felt she had been seated with the children. While Oswald and Karl-Franz were at the head table, surrounded by the other electors, Genevieve was considered a suitable adornment to the secondary table, which was lorded over by Luitpold, the Emperor's son. The heir quizzed her excitedly about Drachenfels, but was disappointed to learn she had been unconscious during Oswald's hand-to-hand combat with the Great Enchanter. Genevieve was stuck next to Baroness Marlene's spotty daughter Clothilde, whose entire world was boundaried by her wardrobe and her dance card. Clothilde, who was almost eighteen, insisted on treating her like a very young child in order to assert her own adulthood. With some amusement, Genevieve realized that the girl had no idea who, and particularly how old, she was.

She ate sparingly, and drank nothing. Sometimes, she would glut herself simply for the taste, but she didn't need meat and bread for sustenance and often too much ordinary fare would make her feel constipated and out-of-sorts. She could barely remember eating for the need of it.

Matthias, adviser to the grand theogonist of the cult of Sigmar, nervously asked her if she danced, and she answered rather too emphatically in the negative. He didn't look up from his plate for the rest of the meal.

She kept glancing at the head table, and observing them. Oswald was quiet, sitting back and looking satisfied. The Countess Emmanuelle was endeavouring to outshine everyone in the room, and Clothilde had already rhapsodized about her twenty-foot train with its embroidered tracing of the Imperial family tree and the intertwining line of von Liebewitz, her necklace of three hundred matched sapphires, and her plunging cloth-of-gold bodice. Genevieve assumed the countess's tight clothes were padded. No real woman could fill out that much whalebone and silk.

When the dress rehearsal was over, the feast was joined by a select few invited from the company. Detlef entered, with Lilli Nissen uncomfortably on his arm, and the actress was presented to the court. Some of the electors had the decency to blush, and others the indecency to drool in public. Genevieve was amused to see the look of utter hatred that passed between Lilli and the Countess Emmanuelle. Their gowns were a match for tastelessness and discomfort. Lilli could not compete with the house of von Liebewitz with regards to expense, although she

151

wore enough jewellery to drown a witch, but she could certainly expose more pink skin through cut-away panels and mesh leggings. The countess and the actress kissed each other's cheeks without quite touching lips to skin, and complimented themselves on their youthful appearance, venom dripping from every syllable.

And I'm supposed to be the bloodsucker, Genevieve thought.

'You know,' Genevieve said to Clothilde, who was always forgetting that she was only almost eighteen, 'I must be the only woman in this room who never has to lie about my age.'

The girl giggled, nervously. Genevieve realized she was showing her teeth, and closed her lips demurely.

'I know how old you are,' said Luitpold. 'It's in the ballad of Oswald and Genevieve. You're six hundred and thirty-eight.'

Clothilde choked on her watered wine, quite spoiling her dress.

'That was twenty-five years ago, highness,' Genevieve said.

'Ah, then you must be...'

Luitpold stuck his tongue into his cheek and worked it out in his head. '...six hundred and sixty-three.'

'That's correct, highness.' She raised her glass in salute, but not to her lips.

The meal was over, and the company stood up. Clothilde got as far away as possible, and Genevieve felt a little sorry for the girl. She reminded her of her sister, Cirielle.

Luitpold was attentive now. 'Let's go and see Daddy. He can't stand Middenheim and Talabheim. He'll want to be rescued.'

The future Emperor escorted her to the knot of highly-placed toadies gathered around Karl-Franz. Lilli was doing her best to attract the attention of a tough-looking young man Genevieve believed to be the elector of Sudenland, and not doing terribly well. Countess Emmanuelle was fluttering her eyelashes at Detlef. In the South Lands, Genevieve had seen great black cats being civil to each other over the carcasses of deer and then tearing red flaps from their rivals' glossy hides. Now, she could almost see the claws sliding from their sheaths as the countess and Lilli purred around each other.

Genevieve did feel like a child in this company. Their inter-relationships were so complicated, and the things she could see on the surface of their minds ran so violently counter to the things they said. Still, it was no worse than the court of the First Family of Parravon had been. And she felt better about Karl-Franz than almost any other man of power she had ever met.

Hubermann's musicians were discreetly admitted, and there was dancing. This was not the joyous abandon there had been at the party for poor Rudi, but a courtly ritual that had changed only slightly since it was taught to her as a girl of Luitpold's age. It had nothing to do with enjoyment, and everything to do with ceremony and the reassertion of each dancer's place in the rigid order of the world. In the absence of his wife, Karl-Franz led the dance with the Countess Emmanuelle, looking considerably happier than she as he peered into her cleavage.

Oswald pleaded exhaustion after the journey, and sat at his table. Lilli forced herself on Sudenland, who trampled her feet deliberately and obstinately stayed out of step. Detlef petitioned Genevieve, but she had promised the first pavane to another.

Luitpold was tall for his age, and so they danced well together – the youngest and the oldest in the room. She touched his mind, and sensed his excitement at the occasion. He was looking forward to the play, and to more hunting with his uncle Oswald. In the distance of his life was the Empire and the crown, but he was ignoring them for the moment. She found herself clinging to this ordinary boy in fine clothes, feeling in him a hope for a future she would inevitably have to live to see.

Detlef prised her away from the heir to the Empire, and she realized he was insistent partly because he wished to be with her and partly because he suspected her intentions with regards to Luitpold. Young blood could be so enticing.

They danced together for the rest of the evening. At some point, Oswald slipped away. Genevieve felt his absence less keenly than she felt Detlef's presence, and they continued in each other's arms.

Inevitably, the feast had left her aroused, but unsatisfied. Now, she was thirsty. And here was Detlef, hot blood coursing through his veins.

That night, in Genevieve's chamber, Detlef gave of himself to her. She undid his jerkin and pulled it open, then loosened the drawstrings of his shirt. His hands were in her hair, and his kisses upon her brow. Delicately, with her sharp teeth, she opened a fold in Detlef's neck, just grazing the major artery, and savoured on her tongue the blood of genius. In his blood was everything he was. As she lapped the welling red, she learned of his past, his future, his secrets, his fears, his ambitions. Then, she fastened upon him like a leech as he responded to her caresses, and gulped greedily, smearing her mouth. The blood was warm and salty in the back of her throat as she took it down.

She forgot Oswald von Konigswald, and clung to Detlef Sierck.

VII

Constant Drachenfels stared at his masked face in the mirror, peering into his own malevolent eyes, relishing the powers he felt rising within him. He flexed his hands, feeling the strength soaked into the bones with seas of blood. He passed his pointed tongue over long teeth. Inside his armour, his body was drenched with sweat from his recent exertions. He was so close to the attainment of his purpose. He needed water, to replenish his fluids. A jug and a goblet stood by the mirror. He pushed his mask off his face...

...and Laszlo Lowenstein poured himself a drink.

'Great, Laz. You were terrific!' That fool Jessner thumped him on the back. 'You chilled my blood.'

'Thank you.'

Soon, Lowenstein would have to be polite no more, would bow to no man, neither emperor nor director. He looked at the mask in his hand, and saw his real face.

When Jessner had gone, he worked away at the make-up around his eyes, peeling it off. He renewed the subtle paints he had applied over the discoloration of his face. Tomorrow, he would have no need of deceptions and could show himself as he really was. The changes were mainly under the skin, but soon the new bones would poke through. Soon, he would truly fill the armour of the Great Enchanter. Soon...

Long after everyone had left the dressing rooms, Lowenstein departed. He made his way to the part of the fortress where his patron awaited him. There was more to be carved, and Lowenstein was growing ever more skilled at the task.

The man in the mask stood over a corpse, arms casually folded, unattended by any of his ghosts.

'The bones,' said his patron. 'This time, we need the bones.'

Lowenstein's knives worked quickly. He filleted Anton Veidt expertly, carving away the flesh, and soon had the skeleton unclothed. In the red meat there were stringy lumps of a black stuff he had never seen before, but it parted under the knife like ordinary meat.

'Don't forget the eyes.'

Two scoops, and the job was done. Lowenstein imagined his patron smiling behind his mask.

'A fine job, Lowenstein. We have it all, nearly. The heart, the flesh, the skin, the vitals, the bones. From the vampire lady, we shall need the blood...'

'And from the grand prince? From the murderer of the Enchanter?'

The man in the mask paused. 'From him, Lowenstein... from him, we shall take everything.'

Act Five

I

An hour to curtain-up. There was no feeling in the world like it. Each sensation was amplified a thousandfold. The itches of his love-bites, covered now by the high collar of his Prince Oswald costume, excited him. The air in the dressing rooms was electrically charged. He had sat in his chair, applying his make-up, calming himself, thinking himself into the role. Twenty-five years ago, Prince Oswald had won his greatest victory in the great hall of Castle Drachenfels. Tonight, the battle would be refought, but the triumph would be Detlef Sierck's.

He was the young Oswald, working up his courage before daring to challenge the Great Enchanter.

He felt his freshly-shaved chin, and played with his moustaches. A bottle of wine stood unopened on the table. Good luck notes were sorted in order of importance. There was even a modest message of well-wishing from the elector of Middenland, who must be praying for Detlef to trip over his sword on his first entrance and split his tights in the love scenes. He glanced over his shoulder, at a hunched shape he'd glimpsed in the mirror. A hunched shape where there should be none.

It was a cloak, carelessly flung. He picked it up, folded it, and put it away. Vargr Breughel's small chair was empty.

'For you, my friend,' Detlef vowed. 'Not for the Emperor, not for Oswald. For you.'

Detlef tried to feel that Breughel was present, but it was useless. There was nothing.

He felt nervous, but good. He knew the six-hour performance was going to be an enormous drain on his resources. He had worried that Genevieve had sapped his energies too much. On the contrary, since her kisses he had felt doubly alive, as if her strength were shared with him. He felt able to bear the weight of his role. He had the reserves to perform lengthy soliloquies, to take part in strenuous and spectacular fight scenes, to clash with the powerful stage presence of Laszlo Lowenstein.

He could even overcome his distaste and make love to Lilli Nissen.

He left his room, and went among his cast. Illona Horvathy was being sick in a bucket. 'It's all right,' she choked between heaves. 'I'm always like this. It's a good sign. Honest.'

Reinhardt Jessner was taking a few practice swings with his sword.

'Careful,' said Detlef, 'don't bend it.'

The actor bowed as best he could in his padded jacket with its false stomach. He saluted his director. 'You are right, my prince. Know well that I, Rudi Wegener, king of the bandits, will serve you faithfully. To the death.'

Since Rudi's death, Jessner had been throwing himself into his role almost as much as Lowenstein, as if trying to bring the old man back to life through the power of impersonation.

Gesualdo was pumping pig's blood into the bladder in his armpit, whistling as he did so, in defiance of an old superstition. He gave Detlef the thumbs up.

'Nay problem, chief.'

'Where's Lilli?' Detlef asked Justus.

'No one's seen her all day. She should be in her dressing room.'

'Any idea whether the elector of Sudenland came through...?'

The trickster priest laughed. 'Evidently not, Detlef.'

'Good. Maybe the frustration will build up in her. We might see a performance from the monster yet.'

Justus, a gargoyle below his neck, lashed his tail. 'We've come a long way since Mundsen Keep, eh?'

'That we have. Good luck.'

'Break a leg.'

A piercing scream rang out. Detlef looked at Justus, who looked back in astonishment. There was another scream. It came from Lilli's dressing room.

'Ulric in heaven, what plagues us now?'

Lilli's dresser exploded from the room, blood on her hands, screeching insanely.

'Oh gods, she's killed the bitch!'

Justus held the bowed and bent woman, calming her. Detlef pushed into the dressing room.

Lilli stood in the middle of the room, in her Genevieve dress, a stripe of blood running from her face down her bosom to the floor. She had made fists in the air and was screaming at the top of her considerable voice.

An admirer had sent her a present.

Detlef tried to get through to the hysterical actress. When that failed, he took great delight in slapping her face. She lashed out at him, going for the throat, and he had to get a wrestler's hold on her.

'I knew I should never have come here. If it weren't for Oswald, I'd never have worked with you again, you lowest of the loathsome, you vermin-tongued piece of swine-shit, you leech-spawn!'

She collapsed, sobbing, on a divan, and refused to be comforted. Detlef turned to the mess on the floor, and immediately understood what had happened.

It had been like a jack-in-the-box. Once opened, it had flung its contents up at Lilli Nissen. And its contents were only too recognizable. There was a face in there. The eyeless face of Anton Veidt.

'I won't do it! I shan't do it! You can't make me! I'm leaving this accursed place this hour, this instant!'

Lilli shouted at her dresser, and the poor woman freed herself from Justus. She began packing the actress's things into an open trunk.

'Lilli, the show starts in an hour. You can't leave!'

'Just watch me, worm dung! I'm not staying here to be murdered and abused!'

'But Lilli...'

Word was spreading through the company of this latest calamity. There were crowds at Lilli's dressing-room door, peering in at the star in disarray and the gory garbage strewn across everything. Lowenstein appeared, his costume complete but for the mask, and observed dispassionately. Detlef looked to the other actor, knowing that his career would be ruined too if Lilli betrayed them all.

Lilli sat, arms crossed, watching her dresser pack, barking orders at the crying woman. She scraped at the blood on her face, and wiped away her half-applied make-up. She pulled out her fangs one by one and threw them at the floor.

'All of you,' she snapped. 'Out! I'm changing! I'm leaving!'

Her giant slave prodded Detlef in the chest, and he got the impression he ought to get out of the room.

In the narrow passage between the dressing rooms and the stage, he slumped against the wall. It was all going to be ruined! And Lilli Nissen was deserting him again. He'd never be able to get backing for another production. He would be lucky to get a job carrying spears in a provincial production of some tenth-rate tragedy. His friends would desert him faster than oarsmen escaping from a sinking galleass. It would take all he had to stay out of Mundsen Keep. He saw the Known World falling apart around him, and wondered if he might not do best just to sign up with some forlorn-hope voyage of discovery to the Northern Wastes and have done with it.

'Somebody left it for her,' Justus told him. 'It was wrapped like a gift, a gown or something. And there was a coat of arms on the note.'

'Great. Someone wants this play taken off before curtain-up.'

'Here.' The cleric gave him a bent and bloodied piece of stiff paper. There was an unreadable scrawl of a message, and the smudged impression of a seal. Detlef recognized it, a stylized facemask.

'Drachenfels!'

The Great Enchanter must still have supporters out there, desperate to protect their master's reputation by putting a stop to this recreation of his downfall. Lowenstein stood aside calmly, awaiting orders from his director. Justus, Jessner, Illona Horvathy, Gesualdo and the others were all quiet, intent upon him. He could stop it here, and get out of it with the minimum of dignity. Or he could proceed with the play, simply ignoring the absence of the leading lady. Or...

Detlef tore the paper up, and swore to Sigmar, to Verena, to all the gods, to the Emperor, to the grand prince, to Vargr Breughel and to himself, that Drachenfels would go on, bitch Lilli or no.

The crowds parted, and someone came through, her lovely face shining.

'Genevieve,' he said. 'Just the person I wanted to see...'

II

Emperor Karl-Franz I sat in his box at the rear of the great hall, raised above his subjects, with Luitpold to one side and Oswald at the other. An attendant held out a tray of sweetmeats, which Luitpold had been gluttonously helping himself to.

The red curtain hung in front of the raised stage, sporting tragic and comic masks picked out in gold. He glanced over his programme, gathering from the order of the names listed when each player would make his entrance. Drachenfels boasted a prologue, five acts, and an envoi, with six intervals, including one for a buffet supper. It should run about six hours.

Karl-Franz shifted in his comfortable seat, and wondered whether Luitpold could sit still for the whole thing. It would be a great tribute to Detlef Sierck if the boy could manage it. Of course, Luitpold was eager to learn what his Uncle Oswald had done as a youth.

Oswald himself sat cool and quiet, refusing to be drawn on what he knew of the drama. 'The story is ordinary,' he had said. 'It's the presentation which counts.'

The curtain's rise was a good ten minutes late by Karl-Franz's antique timepiece. He had expected no less. In his Empire, nothing ever started on time.

Countess Emmanuelle was wearing another astonishing creation this evening. It took the off-the-shoulder concept to such an extent that it might almost be classed as off-the-entire-body. The Grand Theogonist was already asleep, but he had his adviser Matthias beside him to prod him if he snored too loudly. As usual, Baron Johann von Mecklenberg looked uncomfortable with a roof over him, but he was wearing his court clothes better as time passed. Talabheim and Middenheim were conferring together. Plotting, probably. The halfling was drunk. Middenland had heard there would be dancing girls wearing very little, and was salivating in his corner, his programme quivering over his padded codpiece. Princes, counts, electors, high priests, barons, burgermeisters, dukes and an emperor. This must be the most distinguished audience in history. Detlef Sierck should be proud of it.

A strange thought came to Karl-Franz. If anything were to happen tonight – if a keg of lighted gunpowder were hurled into the audience, for instance – then a country would fall. The empress could never reign in his stead, and all the other logical successors were here. Like every man to occupy his position since the time of Sigmar, two-and-a-half millennia ago, Karl-Franz was conscious of the precariousness of his seat. Without him, without these men, the Empire would be a writhing collection of warring cities and provinces within three months. It would be like Tilea, but stretching the continent from Bretonnia to Kislev.

'When's it going to start, father?'

'Soon. Even emperors must wait upon art, Luitpold.'

'Well, when I'm emperor, I won't.'

Karl-Franz was amused. 'You have to grow up, prove yourself and be elected first.'

'Oh, that…'

The house lights dimmed, and the chatter died down. A spot struck the curtains, and they split, allowing a man in knee-britches and a wig to emerge. There was a smattering of applause.

'Felix Hubermann,' said Oswald, 'the conductor.'

The musicians in their pit raised their instruments. Hubermann bowed, but didn't produce his baton.

'Your Majesty, my lords, ladies and gentlemen,' he said in a high, mellifluous voice. 'I have an announcement to make.'

There was a ripple of murmuring. Hubermann waited for it to die down before continuing.

'Owing to a sudden indisposition, the role of Genevieve Dieudonné will not be taken at this performance by Miss Lilli Nissen…'

There were audible moans of disappointment from several electors who ought to have known better. Middenland spluttered with indignation. Baron Johann and Countess Emmanuelle, for different reasons, sighed with relief. Karl-Franz looked at Oswald, who shrugged blankly.

'Instead, the role of Genevieve Dieudonné will be taken by, er, by Miss Genevieve Dieudonné.'

There was general amazement. Even Oswald was taken aback.

'Your majesty, my lords, ladies and gentlemen, thank you.' Hubermann raised his baton, and the orchestra struck up the Drachenfels overture.

The first three basso chords, keyed to the syllables of the Great Enchanter's name, chilled Karl-Franz's spine. The strings came in, and the curtains parted on a rocky promontory in the Grey Mountains. The chorus came forward, and began:

'Listen, my masters, and listen well,

For I have a tale of horrors to tell,

Of heroes and daemons and blood and death

And the vilest monster e'er to draw breath…'

III

After the Apparition-in-the-Palace scene, Lowenstein didn't have much to do until the fifth and last act. He had to show his masked face a few times, giving orders to the forces of evil, and he had personally to rip apart Heinroth the Vengeful in Act Three. But it was Detlef's show until the final battle, when he would return to the stage to end it all.

He had the dressing room to himself. Everyone else was watching the play from the wings. Which was a good thing, considering what he had to do.

The material was laid out for him. The bones, the skin, the heart and so on.

A cheer went up from the stage as Detlef-as-Oswald skewered an orc. He heard the dialogue continuing, and the clumping of boots as Detlef strode around the stage, demonstrating his swagger. Lowenstein gathered the vampire wasn't doing badly.

This was the moment his patron had been schooling him for. He read the words from the paper he had been given, not recognizing the syllables, but understanding the meaning.

Lowenstein no longer had the dressing room to himself.

Blue fire burned around the material, as it filled out with the invisible force. Veidt's skeleton, clothed in Rudi's fat and Menesh's skin, sat up. Erzbet's heart began to beat, hungry for Genevieve's blood. The thing had the outline of a man, but was not the man himself.

The eyes were in a box on Lowenstein's dressing table. There were seven of them. One of Rudi's had been squashed beyond use in the struggle. His patron had told him it wouldn't matter. He opened the box, and saw the eyes expressionless and veined in their clear jelly, like a clump of outsized frogspawn.

Lowenstein plucked a blue eye, one of Veidt's, from the sticky mass, and swallowed it whole.

A section of his forehead peeled away.

He took a handful of eyes and, fighting disgust, stuffed them into his mouth. He got them down.

The composite creature watched from its eyesockets.

Pain racked through Lowenstein's body as the changes came upon him fully. Only three more to go. He popped one into his mouth and gulped it back. It stuck halfway, and he had to swallow another to keep it down. Spines sprouted from his knees, and the knobbles of his vertebrae broke the skin.

His bones were expanding. He was in agony. There was one eye left. A brown one. Erzbet's.

As he ate it, the creature embraced him, taking him into its open chest, folding its ribs about him.

The dying and dead sights of Erzbet, Rudi, Menesh and Veidt played back to him.

...himself, masked, bent over a corpse in the Temple of Morr.

...himself, masked, at a table, surrounded by ghosts.

...himself, masked, wielding a red knife in a circle of candle-light.

...himself, masked, crouched in a passageway, pulling bones free from a human ruin.

Fire burned throughout his body, and he completed the ritual, shrieking. It was a wonder no one heard him. But there were wonders enough to go around.

Veidt's bones sank into him like logs thrown into a swamp. Rudi's fat plumped out his gaunt frame. Menesh's skin settled on his own, mottling it. And Erzbet's heart beat next to his own, like a polyp nestling its mother.

He was Laszlo Lowenstein no longer.

Reaching for his mask, he was Constant Drachenfels.

And he was looking forward eagerly to the fifth act.

IV

On the stage, she felt as if she were floating. Unsupported, she tried to find her way through the play without making a fool of herself. Some of the time, she could remember the lines Detlef had written for her. Some of the time, she remembered what she had actually said. Most of the other actors were good enough to work round her. The scenes with Detlef played marvellously, because she still had the flush of his blood in her. She could read the lines of his play from the surface of his mind, and she could see where she was straying from the text.

Her first scene found her behind the bar in the Crescent Moon, surrounded by crowds, waiting for Oswald to walk into her life. The crowds were extras, hubbubbing softly without words, and from her position she could see Detlef waiting in the wings, his Oswald helmet under his arm, and the faces of the audience out in the darkness.

Unlike the living actors, she could see clearly beyond the footlights. She saw the Emperor, attentive, and the real Oswald a little behind him, watching with approval. And yet, she was also seeing the real tavern, smelling again its distinctive smell of people and drink and blood. Individual extras – who would rush off and make themselves over as courtiers, bandits, villagers, monsters, orcs, gargoyles or forest peasants for later scenes – reminded her of the individual patrons she had known then. Through his play, Detlef was bringing it all back.

One of the things about longevity – Genevieve didn't like to think of it as immortality; too many vampires she had known were dead – was that you got to try everything. In nearly seven centuries now, she had been a child of court, a whore, a queen, a soldier, a musician, a physician, a priestess, an agitator, a gambler, a landowner, a penniless derelict, a herbalist, an outlaw, a bodyguard, a pit fighter, a student, a smuggler, a trapper, an alchemist and a slave. She had loved, hated, killed but never had children – the Dark Kiss came too early – saved lives, travelled, studied, upheld the law, broken the law, prospered, been ruined, sinned, been virtuous, tortured, shown mercy, ruled, been subjugated, known true happiness and suffered. But she had never yet acted upon the stage. Still less taken her own part in a recreation of her own adventures.

The story progressed, as Detlef-as-Oswald gathered together his band of adventurers and set out on the road to Castle Drachenfels. Again, as on

167

her recent journey along the same road, Genevieve found herself remembering too much. The faces of her dead companions were superimposed on the faces of the actors representing them. And she could never forget the images of their deaths. As Reinhardt Jessner blustered and slapped his padded thigh, she saw Rudi Wegener's skin draped over his bones. As the youth she had bled conferred with Detlef, she remembered Conradin's chewed bones in the ogre's lair. And as the actor playing Veidt sneered through clouds of cigar smoke, she saw the bounty hunter's face on Lilli Nissen's dressing room floor.

Lilli would be half-way down the mountain now, speeding back to Altdorf and civilization. And the creature who frightened her, who murdered Veidt and the others, would be close by, perhaps coming after her next. Or Oswald.

The play advanced act by act, and the heroes braved peril after peril. Detlef had imagined a jauntiness in their progress Genevieve couldn't remember. There were heroic speeches, and a passionate love scene. All Genevieve could recollect of the first trip were long days – painful for her under the sun – on a horse, and desperate, fearful nights around a fire. When Heinroth was found turned inside-out, the script had her make a vow over his corpse to continue the quest. In fact, she had considered backing out and going home. She played it down the middle, her old fears suddenly reborn, and Detlef improvised a response finer than anything he'd written for the scene. The blanket of pig entrails representing Heinroth looked more real, more shocking, to her than the actual corpse had done.

Illona Horvathy had some difficulty working around the changes in the script, and was nervous in her scenes with Genevieve. But Erzbet had always been afraid of her and the actress's uncertainty worked for the character. Watching Illona's athletic dances – she was more skilled than Erzbet had been – Genevieve worried she would take some knocks in the fight scene in the last act, and that the drama would come to a premature conclusion.

In the love scene, Genevieve, still floating with the wonder of it all, opened the wounds on Detlef's neck. She heard gasps from the audience as blood trickled over his collar. The ballads lied about this. It had never happened, at least not this way. Although – twenty-five years later – she realized how much she had desired it, Oswald had never really responded to her, had kept his blood to himself despite his formal offers. He had once given her his wrist, as a man feeds a dog, and she had needed the blood too much to refuse. That still rankled. She wondered how Oswald would react to the perpetuation of the old story, the old lie. How he was feeling now as he sat next to the Emperor, watching a vampire feed on his surrogate?

The hours flew by. In the play, and without, the forces of darkness gathered.

V

For Detlef, the evening was a triumph. Genevieve was an inspiration. During the comparatively few scenes when the character of Oswald was off-stage, he watched his new leading lady. If she were to apply herself, she could be a greater star than Lilli Nissen. What other actress could really live for ever?

Admittedly, she was drawing on deep personal feeling in the role, and the sheer excitement of the event was getting to her, but she was also a fast study. After a few moments of hesitation in the early scenes, she was growing in confidence and now effortlessly dominated her scenes. There were established, professional actors out there struggling to keep up with her. And the audience was responding. Perhaps the theatre was ready for a vampire star? And he could feel her inside him, whispering in his head, drawing things out of him. Their love scene was the most incredible thing he had ever played on the stage.

Otherwise, the performance was working perfectly, each part falling into place exactly as planned. Detlef keenly missed Vargr Breughel's comments from the wings, but felt by now he could supply them himself. 'Less,' he heard his friend say during one speech; 'more' in another.

The other players gave him what he needed of them, and more. The trick effects functioned on cue, and elicited the proper reactions.

Even Kosinski, drafted in for his bulk in the wordless role of a limping comic ogre, got his laugh and was childishly delighted, begging Detlef to let him come on again whenever a scene could accommodate him. 'Don't you see,' he repeated, 'in the mountain inn, I could be a bouncer... in the forest, a wolf-trapper...'

Detlef had a man stationed near the privies, and after each interval he would report back with what he had heard. The audience – probably the toughest in the Empire, as well as the most influential – was in love with the play. Old men were in love with Genevieve, the character and the actress. Reluctantly, his spy repeated Clothilde of Averheim's gushing enthusiasm for Detlef-as-Oswald, which took in the timbre of his voice, the cut of his moustaches and the curve of his calves. Impulsively, he kissed the man.

Detlef sweated through ten shirts, and consumed three gallons of lemon water. Illona Horvathy shone on stage, and continued to be a total invalid in the wings, clutching her bucket and occasionally throwing up quietly in it. One of the bandit extras was slashed across the arm by Jessner in the duel, and had to be doctored in the dressing room. Felix Hubermann worked like a man possessed, wringing melodies from his musicians that no human ear had ever before apprehended. During the magic scenes, the music became unearthly, almost horrifying.

Detlef Sierck knew this was the night for which he would be remembered.

VI

Then, the last act came.

Genevieve and Detlef were alone on stage, supposed to be at the door of the very chamber in which the play was being performed, the great hall of Castle Drachenfels. Gesualdo, as Menesh, joined them, a miner's pick in his fake right arm. His real arm was strapped beside him, but by squeezing a bulb in his hand, he could control the fake to give it the semblance of life. The musicians were silent, save for a lone flute suggesting the unnatural winds flowing through the haunted castle. Genevieve could have sworn that no one in the audience had exhaled for five minutes. The actors looked at each other, and pushed the door. The scenery descended around them, and the stage seemed to vanish. Genevieve was truly back in...

...a throne-room for a king of darkness. The rest of the fortress had been ill-lit and dilapidated, but this was spotless and illumined by jewelled chandeliers. The furniture was ostentatiously luxurious. Gold gleamed from every edge. And silver. Genevieve shuddered to be near so much of the stuff. There were fine paintings on the wall. Rudi would have wept to see so much plunder in one place. A clock chimed, counting unnatural hours as its single hand circled an unfamiliar dial. In a cage, a harpy preened herself, wiping the remains of her last meal from her feathered breasts.

Detlef and Genevieve trod warily on the thick carpets as they circled the stage.

'He's here,' said Detlef-as-Oswald.

'Yes, I feel it too.'

Gesualdo-as-Menesh kept to the walls, stabbing at tapestries.

One wall was a floor-to-ceiling window, set with stained glass. From here, the Great Enchanter could gaze down from his mountain at the Reikswald. He could see as far as Altdorf, and trace the glittering thread of the River Reik through the forests. In the stained glass, there was a giant image of Khorne, the Blood-God, sitting upon his pile of human bones.

With a chill, Genevieve realized that Drachenfels didn't so much worship Khorne as look down upon him as an amateur in the cause of evil. Chaos was so undisciplined... Drachenfels had never been without purpose. There were other gods, other shrines. Khaine, Lord of Murder, was

honoured in a modest ossuary. And Nurgle, Master of Pestilence and
Decay, was celebrated by an odiferous pile of mangled remains. From
this stared the head of Sieur Jehan, its eyes pecked out.

Detlef-as-Oswald started to see his tutor so abused, and a laugh
resounded through the throne-room, a laugh carried and amplified by
Hubermann's orchestra.

Six hundred years ago, Genevieve had heard that laugh. Amid the
crowds of Parravon, when the First Family's assassin was borne aloft
by daemons and his insides fell upon the citizenry. In that laughter,
Genevieve heard the screams of the damned and the dying, the ripples
of rivers of blood, the cracking of a million spines, the fall of a dozen
cities, the pleas of murdered infants, the bleating of slaughtered animals.

And twenty-five years ago, Genevieve had heard that laugh. Here, in
this great hall.

He loomed up, enormous, from his chair. He had been there all the
time, but Detlef had cunningly placed him so his appearance would be
an unforgettable shock. There were screams from the audience.

'I am Drachenfels,' Lowenstein said mildly, the deathly laugh still in
his voice. 'I bid you welcome to my house. Come in health, go safely,
and leave behind some of the happiness you bring...'

Gesualdo-as-Menesh flew at the Great Enchanter, miner's pick raised.
With a terrible languor, moving as might a man of molten bronze,
Lowenstein-as-Drachenfels stretched out and slapped him aside. Gesualdo-
as-Menesh struck a hanging and fell squealing in a heap. Blood was
spurting from him. The harpy was excited, and flapped her wings against
the bars of her cage, smelling the blood.

Drachenfels was holding the dwarf's arm in his hand. It had come off
as easily as a cooked chicken's wing. The enchanter inclined his head
to look at his souvenir, giggled, and cast it away from him. It writhed
across the floor as if alive, trailing blood behind it, and was still.

Genevieve looked at Detlef, and saw doubt in the actor's face. Gesualdo
was screaming far more than he had in rehearsal, and the blood effect
was working far better. The dwarf rolled in a carpet, trying to press his
stump to the ground.

Lowenstein had torn off his left arm. Gesualdo's real right arm erupted
from his back, displacing the fake, as he tried to stop the flow of blood.
Then, with a death rattle, he fell still.

Lowenstein...

...Drachenfels opened a window in the air, and the stink of burning
flesh filled the throne-room. Genevieve peered through the window, and
saw a man twisting in eternal torment, daemons rending his flesh, lashworms eating through his face, rats gnawing at his limbs. He called out
her name, and reached for her, reached through the window. Blood fell
like rain onto the carpet.

It was her father! Her six-centuries-dead father!

'I have them all, you know,' Drachenfels said. 'All my old souls, all kept
like that. It prevents me from getting lonely here in my humble palace.'

He shut the window on the damned creature Genevieve had loved. She raised her sword against him.

He looked from one to the other, and laughed again. Spirits were gathering about him, evil spirits, servant spirits. They funnelled around him like a tornado.

'So you have come to kill the monster? A prince of nothing, descendant of a family too cowardly to take an empire for themselves? And a poor dead thing without the sense to lie down in her grave and rot? In whose name do you dare such an endeavour?'

Astonishingly, Detlef got his line out. 'In the name of Sigmar Heldenhammer!'

The words sounded weak, echoing slightly, but gave Drachenfels pause. Something was working behind his mask, a rage building up inside him. His spirits swarmed like midges.

He threw out his hand in Genevieve's direction, and the tide of daemons engulfed her, hurling her back against the wall, smothering her, weighing her down, sweeping over her face.

Oswald came forward, and his sword clashed on the enchanter's mailed arm. Drachenfels turned to look down on him.

She felt herself dragged down, the insubstantial creatures surging up over her. She couldn't breathe. She could barely move her limbs. She was cold, her teeth chattering. And she was tired, tired as she shouldn't be until dawn. She felt bathed in stinging sunlight, wrapped in bands of silver, smothered in a sea of garlic. Somewhere, the hawthorn was being sharpened for her heart. Her mind fogged, she tasted dust in her throat...

VII

Like the rest of the audience, the emperor was amazed and appalled. The death of the dwarf had broken the illusion of the play. Something was badly wrong. The actor playing Drachenfels was mad, or worse. His hand went to the hilt of his ceremonial sword. He turned to his friend…

And felt a knifepoint at his throat.

'Watch the play to its finish, Karl-Franz,' Oswald said, his tone conversational. 'The end is soon.'

Luitpold jumped from his seat at the grand prince.

With grace, Oswald stuck out his hand. Karl-Franz's heart leaped as the knife flashed, but the grand prince simply rapped Luitpold's chin with the hilt. Stunned, the boy fell back onto his chair, his eyes turning up into his head.

Karl-Franz drew a breath, but the knife was back next to his Adam's apple before he could let it out.

Oswald smiled.

The audience were torn between the play on the stage, and the drama in the Imperial box. Most of them were on their feet. The Countess Emmanuelle fell into a dead faint. Hubermann, the conductor, had fallen to his knees, and was praying fervently. Baron Johann and several others had their swords out, and Matthias levelled a single-shot hand gun.

'Watch the play to its finish,' Oswald said again, prodding his weapon into Karl-Franz's flesh.

The Emperor felt his own blood soaking into his ruff. No one in the audience made a move.

'Watch the play,' said Oswald.

The audience sat down, settling uneasily. They laid down their weapons. The Emperor felt his own sword being unsheathed, and heard it clatter against the wall as it was thrown away.

Never had the Empire seen such treachery.

Oswald turned Karl-Franz's head. The Emperor looked at the figure of the Great Enchanter, who was swelling on the stage, becoming the giant the original Constant Drachenfels must have been.

The laughter of an evil god filled the great hall.

VIII

His own laughter echoed off the walls.

He could barely remember his life as Laszlo Lowenstein. Since eating the eyes, so many other memories crowded his mind. Thousands of years of experience, of learning, of sensation, throbbed like wounds inside his skull. In the time of the rivers of ice, before the toad men came from the stars, he was battering a smaller creature with a sharp rock, tearing at the still-warm flesh. With each remembered fall of the icy flint, his mind convulsed, drowning in blood. Finally, something small and insignificant was squashed into dirt. His stubby, stiff fingers plucked the eyes from the dead thing, and he ate well through the winter. He felt alive again, and filled his lungs with air flavoured gorgeously by the fear that filled the great hall.

Laszlo Lowenstein was dead.

But Constant Drachenfels lived. Or would live, as soon as his body was warmed by the blood of the vampire slut.

Drachenfels looked from Oswald on the stage, quivering with fear as he had once done, to Oswald in the audience, smiling with resolve as he held his knife to the Emperor's throat.

And Drachenfels remembered…

The harpy squawked in her cage. The vampire lay in a dead faint. The dwarf bled slowly, fingers clamped over his stump. And the boy with the sword looked up at him, tears coursing down his face, maddened by the dread.

Drachenfels raised his hand to strike the prince down, to pulp his head with a single blow and be done with it. The vampire, he would amuse himself with later. She might last for as much as a night in his arms before she was broken, used up and done with. Thus perished all those who defied the dark.

The prince fell to his knees, sobbing, his sword thrown away and forgotten. And the Great Enchanter stayed his hand. An idea formed. He would have to renew himself soon, anyway. This could be used. This boy could be put to good advantage. And an empire could be won.

Drachenfels picked Oswald up, and stroked him as he might a kitten. He began to propose his bargain.

'My prince, I have power over life and death. Your life and death, and my life and death.'

Oswald wiped his face, and tried to bring his sobbing under control. He could have been a five-year-old bawling for his mother.

'You do not have to die here in this fortress, far from your home. If you wish it, you do not have to die at all...'

'How...' he blubbered, swallowing his sobs, '...how can this be?'

'You can deliver what I want to me.'

'And what do you want?'

'The Empire.'

Oswald cried out involuntarily, almost a scream. But he fought himself, forced himself to look at the Great Enchanter. Under his mask, Drachenfels smiled. He had the boy.

'I have lived many lifetimes, my prince. I have outworn many bodies. I have long since traded in the flesh I was born with...'

Unimaginable years earlier, Drachenfels remembered his first breaths, his first loves, his first kills. His first body. On a vast, empty plain of ice, he had been abandoned by squat, brutish tribesmen who would now seem to have more kinship with the apes of Araby than true men. He had survived. He would live for ever.

'I am like that girl in many ways. I need to take from others to continue. But she can merely take a little new blood. Her kind are short-lived. A few thousand years, and they grow brittle. I can renew myself eternally, taking the stuff of life from those I conquer. You are privileged, boy. I'm going to let you look at my face.'

He took off his mask. Oswald forced himself to look. The prince screamed at the top of his lungs, disturbing the dead and the dying of the fortress, and the Great Enchanter laughed.

'Not so pretty, eh? It's just another lump of rotten meat. It is I, Drachenfels, who am eternal. I who am Constant. Do you recognize your own nose, my prince? The hooked, noble nose of the von Konigswalds. I took it from your ancestor, the loathesomely honourable Schlichter. It's worn through. This whole carcass is nearly at its end. You must understand all this, my prince, because you must understand why I intend to let you kill me.'

The harpy twittered. Oswald was nearly himself now, the complete young prince. Drachenfels had read him right, seen the self-interest in the adventuring, the desperate need to outdo his forebears, the hollowness in his heart. He would do.

'Yes, you shall conquer me, lay me dead in my own dust. And you will be a hero for it. You will grow to great power. Some day, years from now, you will have the Empire in your hands. And you will give it to me...'

Oswald was smiling now, imagining the glory of it. His never-admitted hatred of Karl-Franz, Luitpold's brat of a son, rose to the surface. He would never lick the boots of the House of the Second Wilhelm, as his fathers had done.

'For I shall return from dust. You will find me a way back. You will find me a man with too small a soul, a man steeped in blood. You will be his patron, and I shall enter him. Then, you will deliver to me your friends.

I shall take sustenance from them. All who stand with you this day shall die to bring me back.'

An objection fluttered on Oswald's lips, but perished there, unsaid. He looked at Genevieve, prone on the floor, and there was no regret in his heart.

'Then, we shall bend the electors to our purpose. Most will be led by their own interests. The others, we shall kill. The Emperor will die, and his heirs will die. And you will make me emperor in his stead. We shall rule the Empire for an age. Nothing will stand before us. Bretonnia, Estalia, Tilea, Kislev, the New Territories, the whole world. All shall bow, or be devastated as no land ever has been devastated since the time of Sigmar. Humanity will be our slaves, and all the other races will be slaughtered like cattle. We shall make whorehouses of temples, mausoleums of cities, boneyards of continents, deserts of forests...'

The light was burning inside Oswald now, the light of ambition, of bloodlust, of greed. He would have been this without enchantment, Drachenfels knew. This was Oswald von Konigswald as he was always intended to be.

'Kneel to me, Oswald. Swear loyalty to our plan. Loyalty in blood.'

Oswald knelt, and drew his dagger. He hesitated.

'You could not kill the Great Enchanter without earning a scar or two, could you?'

Oswald nodded his head, and slashed at the palm of his left hand, at his cheek and at his chest. His shirt tore, and a line of red ran across his skin. Drachenfels touched his gloved fingers to Oswald's wounds, and raised the blood to his ragged lips. He tasted, and Oswald was his forever.

He roared his triumph, and whirled about the room, smashing articles he had treasured for millennia.

He took the harpy's cage and crushed it between his great hands, squashing the poor thing inside until it was silent, the bent bars of her prison twisted deep in her flesh. He hurled an oak table through his stained glass window, and heard it shatter on the rocks a thousand feet below, a tinkling patter of multi-coloured shards raining around it.

His enchantment reached throughout his fortress, and his servitors were struck down. Flesh turned to stone, and stone turned to ashes. Daemons were freed, or hurled back to their hells. An entire wing crumbled and fell. And, throughout the world, his expiry was felt by the lesser enchanters.

Finally, when enough had been done, Drachenfels turned again to the trembling Oswald. He snapped the lad's sword between his fingers, and hauled a heavy, two-handed blade down from the wall. It had been dipped in the sacred blood of Sigmar, and plated all over with silver, now worn through in patches.

'This is a weapon fit to kill Constant Drachenfels.'

Oswald could barely lift it. Drachenfels fixed him with his stare, and willed strength into the prince's limbs. The sword came up, and every muscle in Oswald's body trembled with the effort, with the fear and with

the excitement. Drachenfels tore open his armour. The stench of his rotting flesh filled the room. The Great Enchanter laughed again.

'Do it, boy! Do it now!'

IX

This wasn't the finale Detlef had written. Something was badly wrong with Lowenstein. Not to mention Genevieve. And Oswald. And the Emperor. And, in all probability, the world...

Lowenstein-as-Drachenfels, who was acting more like Drachenfels-as-Lowenstein, had departed from the script.

Half the house-lights had come on now, and the company were spilling from the wings towards the auditorium. They kept away from Lowenstein, but their eyes were fixed on him. The audience were in their seats, looking between the monster on the stage and their imperilled Emperor. Grand Prince Oswald, the mask off at last, dared them to try for him. And the actor whose mask was the reality surveyed the chaos he had wrought.

Detlef's prop sword felt very puny indeed in his grip.

Lowenstein stood over Genevieve, who was in her stage swoon. Her eyes opened, and she screamed. He bent down to her, hands like claws.

She rolled away from his grasp, and scrambled to her feet. She stood beside Detlef. They faced the monster together. He felt her in his mind again, felt her fear and her uncertainty, but also her resilience and her courage.

'It's Drachenfels,' she hissed in his ear. 'We've brought him back!'

Lowenstein – Drachenfels – laughed again.

Someone in the audience discharged a gun, and a wound opened in the monster's chest. He wiped it shut, still laughing, and threw something small. There was a scream as the gunman went down, writhing in torment. It had been Matthias, the grand theogonist's advisor. Now, he didn't much resemble anything naturally human.

'Does anyone dare defy me?' The great voice said. 'Does anyone dare stand between me and the vampire?'

Detlef was standing between Drachenfels and Genevieve. His immediate impulse was to get out of the way, but the wounds in his neck ached, the wound in his heart kept him where he was. She willed him to go, to leave her to this monster's mercies. But he couldn't.

'Back,' he said, summoning all his acting skills to put the heroic ring into his voice. 'In the name of Sigmar, back!'

'Sigmar!' Spittle flew from the mouthslit of the mask. 'He's dead and gone, little man. But I'm here!'

'Then in my name, back!'

'Your name? Who are you to defy Constant Drachenfels, the Great Enchanter, the Eternal Champion of Evil, the Darkness Who Would Not Be Defied?'

'Detlef Sierck,' he snapped. 'Genius!'

Drachenfels was still amused. 'A genius, is it? I've eaten of many geniuses. One more will be most refreshing.'

Detlef realized he was going to die before the curtain came down on his play.

He would die before his best work was done. To future generations, he would be a footnote. A minor imitator of Tarradasch who showed promise he never lived to fulfil. A nothing. The Great Enchanter was not just going to take away his life, but was going to make it seem as if he had never been, never walked on a stage, never lifted a quill from its pot. Nobody had ever died as thoroughly as he would die now.

Drachenfels's hand fell on Detlef's left shoulder. The fire of agony coursed through his arm as it popped out of joint. The Great Enchanter was exerting enough pressure to crush his bones to fragments. Detlef twisted in agony, unable to break the hold, unable to fall away in ruins. By degrees, Drachenfels applied more force to his grip. His putrid grave-breath was in Detlef's face. The actor's entire left side tried to curl up to escape the merciless pain. Drachenfels's fingers burrowed into his flesh like lashworms. A few more moments of this, and Detlef would be glad of the release of death.

Behind the monster's mask, evil eyes glowed.

Then Genevieve jumped.

X

Three times before had the killing frenzy fallen upon her. She always regretted it, feeling herself no better than Wietzak or Kattarin or all those other Truly Dead tyrants as she wiped the innocent blood from her face. The faces of her dead sometimes bothered her, as the face of Drachenfels had been tormenting her dreams these last few years. This time, however, there would be no regrets. This was the righteous killing for which she had been made, the killing that would pay back all those whose lives she had sapped. Her muscles corded, her blood took fire, and the red haze came over her vision. She saw through blood-filled eyes.

Detlef hung from Drachenfels's fist, screaming like a man on the rack. Oswald – smiling, treacherous, thrice-damned Oswald – had his knife in Karl-Franz's throat. These things she would not tolerate.

Her teeth pained her as they grew, and her fingers bled as the nails sprouted like talons. Her mouth gaped as the sharp ivory spears split her gums. Her face became a flesh-mask, the thick skin pulled tight, a mirthless grin exposing her knife-like fangs. The primitive part of her brain – the vampire part of her, the legacy of Chandagnac – took over, and she leaped at her enemy, the killing fury building in her like a passion. There was love in it, and hate, and despair, and joy. And there would be death at the end.

Drachenfels was knocked off balance but stayed upright. Detlef was thrown away, landing in a heap.

Genevieve fastened her legs about the monster's midriff, and sank her claws into his padded shoulders. Strips of Lowenstein's stage costume fell away, disclosing the festering meat beneath. Worms crawled through his body, twining around her fingers as she dug through his flesh to get a snapping grip on his bones. She had no distaste for this thing now, just a need to kill.

There was pandemonium in the audience. Oswald was shouting. So was everyone else. People were trying to escape, fighting each other. Others stood calm, waiting for their chance. Several elderly dignitaries were in the throes of heart seizures.

Genevieve pulled a hand from the monster's opened shoulder and tore at Drachenfels's mask. The leather straps parted under her knife-sharp nails and the iron plates buckled. It came free and she hurled it away.

There were screams from the audience. She avoided looking him in the face. She retained that much rationality. She wasn't interested in exposing his face anyway. She just needed to get the iron guard away from his neck.

Her mouth opened wide, her jawbone dislocating itself as new rows of teeth slid out of their sheaths, then snapped shut. She bit deep into the monster's neck.

She sucked, but there was no blood. Dirt choked her throat, but she still sucked. The foulest, most rancid, most rotten taste she had ever known filled her mouth and soaked through to her stomach. The taste burned like acid, and her body tried in vain to reject it. She felt herself withering as the bane spread.

Still, she sucked.

The scream began as Lowenstein's last gasp, then grew in sound and fury. Her eardrums coursed with pain. Her skeleton shook inside her body. She felt mighty blows on her ribs. The scream was like a hurricane, blasting all in its path.

A stale trickle flowed into her mouth. It was more disgusting than the dry flesh.

She bit away the mouthful she had been working on, and spat it out, then sunk her teeth in again, higher this time. The Great Enchanter's ear came away, and she swallowed it. She scraped a patch of grey meat away from the side of his skull, exposing the cranial seams. Clear yellow fluid seeped through between the bony plates. She extended her tongue to lick it up.

A hand covered her face, and pushed her back. Her neck strained, near to snapping point. She bit through the thick glove, but couldn't lodge her teeth in his palm. Another hand gripped her waist. Her legs unwound from Drachenfels.

The killing frenzy ebbed, and she felt her vampire teeth receding. Convulsing, she vomited the ear she had eaten, and it stuck to the hand over her mouth.

She felt death touching her again. Chandagnac was waiting for her, and all the others she had outlived in her time.

Drachenfels tore her clothes, baring her veins. Her blood, the blood she had renewed so many times, would make him whole again.

By her death, she would resurrect him.

XI

Detlef was still alive. Half of his body was numb with shock, and the other half crawling with pain. But he was still alive.

Drachenfels's scream filled the hall, pounding like nails into everyone's heads. Stones were shaken loose from the walls by the noise, and fell on members of the audience. Every pane of glass in every window shattered at once. Old people died and young people were driven mad.

Detlef got to his knees, and crawled away.

Genevieve had sacrificed herself for him. He would live, at least for the moment, and she would die in his stead.

He could not allow that.

On his feet, stumbling, he knocked over a section of scenery. The person who had been hiding behind it – Kosinski – fled. Ropes fell around Detlef, and weights from above. Flats collapsed, buckling upon each other. A lantern fell, and a ring of burning oil spread from it.

He had lost his sword. He needed a weapon.

Leaning against the wall was a sledge-hammer. Kosinski had hefted it when the scenery was being put together. It should have been packed away. It was dangerous where it was. Someone could easily trip over it on their way backstage. Detlef had fired people for less.

This time, if he lived, he would treble Kosinski's salary and cast the brute in romantic leads if he wanted it...

Detlef picked up the hammer. His wrists hurt with the weight of it, and his wounded shoulder flared with pain.

It was just an ordinary hammer.

But it was no ordinary strength which flooded from it into Detlef's body.

As he raised the hammer to strike, Detlef imagined a slight glow about it, as if gold were mixed with the lead.

'In the name of Sigmar!' he swore.

His pains vanished, and his blow connected.

XII

Drachenfels took the full force of the swing in the small of his back. He held Genevieve to him, unwilling to give up the blood that would revivify him.

Detlef Sierck swung round with his blow, and faced the Great Enchanter.

Drachenfels saw the shining hammer in his hands, and knew a moment of fear. He didn't dare say the name that came to him.

Long ago, he stood at the head of his defeated goblin horde, humbled by the wild-eyed, blonde-bearded giant who held his hammer high in victory. His magics deserted him, and his body rotted as the hammer blows connected. It had taken a thousand years to claw his way back to full life.

The light that shone in Detlef's eyes was not the light of genius, it was the light of Sigmar.

The human tribes of the north-east and all the hordes of the dwarfs had rallied to that hammer. For the first time, Drachenfels had been bested in battle. Sigmar Heldenhammer had stood over him, his boot on the Great Enchanter's face, and ground him into the mud.

Genevieve struggled free of him, and darted away. Another blow fell, on the exposed plates of his skull.

Deep inside Constant Drachenfels, Laszlo Lowenstein floundered in death. And Erzbet, Rudi, Menesh and Anton Veidt. And the others, the many thousand others.

Detlef jabbed with the hammer, using it like a staff, and Drachenfels felt his nose cave inwards.

Erzbet's heart burst, flooding bile into his chest. Rudi's fat turned liquid and gushed down into the cavity of his stomach. Menesh's skin split and sloughed off him in swathes. Veidt's bones cracked. Drachenfels was betrayed by his kills.

Waiting in the wings, Drachenfels saw the monk-robed figures. That semi-human ape tribesman would be there, and the thousands upon thousands who had followed him into death.

Detlef, paint streaming from his face, berserker foam in his mouth, swung his hammer.

Lowenstein's thin body stood alone in the ruin that would have been the Great Enchanter. Drachenfels cried out again, feebly this time.

'Sigmar,' he bleated, 'have mercy...'

The hammerblows landed. The skull cracked open like an egg. Drachenfels collapsed, and the blows continued to come.

It had been cold on the plains, and he had been left behind to die, too sickly to be supported by the tribe. The other man, the first kill, had chanced by and he had fought to take the life from him. He had won, but now... fifteen thousand years later... he knew he had lost after all. He had only held off death for a few moments in the span of eternity.

For the last time, the life went out of him.

XIII

Karl-Franz was bleeding badly now. Oswald's hand wasn't steady, and the blade was biting deep. It was only luck that had kept him from severing the artery, or poking through to the windpipe.

The spectacle on the stage was not what anyone had expected. The Emperor felt Oswald's body shake as Detlef Sierck demolished the actor playing Drachenfels.

The traitor's plans had gone awry.

'Oswald von Konigswald!' shouted Detlef, bloody hammer held aloft.

The auditorium grew quiet. There was the crackle of flames, but all the crying and shouting stopped.

'Oswald, come here!'

Karl-Franz could hear the elector whimpering. The knife shook in the groove it had carved in his neck.

'Stay where you are or the Emperor dies!' Oswald's voice was weak now, too high, too slurred.

Detlef seemed to shrink a little, as if coming to his senses. He looked at the hammer and at the dead thing on the stage. He laid the weapon down. Genevieve Dieudonné stood beside him, her arm about him when he was ready to sag and drop.

'Kill Karl-Franz and you'll be dead before he hits the floor, von Konigswald,' said Baron Johann von Mecklenberg, his sword raised. The elector of Sudenland was not alone. A forest of swordpoints glittered.

Oswald was looking around desperately for a way out, for an escape route. The back of the box was guarded. The sweetmeat man stood there, in a wrestler's stance. He was one of the Imperial bodyguards.

'Know this, Karl-Franz,' Oswald whispered to him, 'I hate you, and all your works. For years, I've had to swallow my disgust in your presence. If nothing else, I shall end the House of the Second Wilhelm tonight.'

Sssssssssssnick!

Oswald pushed Karl-Franz away, waving his bloodied knife in the air, and vaulted over the side of the box.

XIV

Grand Prince Oswald hit the floor in a crouch and ran down the side of the great hall. A high priest of Ulric stood in his way, but the man was old and was knocked down easily. As he fled, Oswald upturned the chairs the audience had been sitting in, hindering his would-be pursuers.

Baron Johann and his confederates stood before the main entrance, waiting for their quarry.

Oswald backed away from them and made a dash for the stage. Genevieve saw him coming and staggered into his way. She was weakened from her attack on Drachenfels and nauseous from the after-effects of his poison flesh. But she was still stronger than an ordinary man.

She made a fist and struck Oswald in the face, mashing his aristocratic nose. She licked the blood off her knuckles. It was just blood, nothing special.

Detlef stood by, and watched. An audience, for once. Whatever had possessed him – and Genevieve had a fairly good idea about that – during his fight with the Great Enchanter had gone now, leaving him puzzled, drained and vulnerable.

Enraged, Oswald hurled himself at her. She sidestepped, and he fell.

He stood up, his boot slipping in the pool Drachenfels had left of himself. He swore, the knife darted out, and Genevieve's arm stung.

More silver.

He stabbed at her, and missed. He flung the knife, and missed.

Fangs exposed, she lunged for him. He dodged away.

With a clean motion, he drew his sword, and brought the point to rest against her breast.

It was silvered too. A simple thrust and her heart would be pierced.

Oswald smiled sweetly at her. 'We must all die, my pretty Genevieve, must we not?'

XV

A sword arced up from the auditorium, spinning end over end. Detlef stuck out his hand and snatched the hilt from the air, getting a good grip.

'Use it well, play-actor!' shouted Baron Johann.

Detlef lashed out and struck Oswald's blade away from Genevieve's heart. Genevieve stepped away.

The grand prince turned, spat a tooth at him, and assumed the duelling stance.

'Hah!'

His sword swiped, slashed Detlef across the chest, and returned to its place.

Oswald smiled nastily through the blood. Having demonstrated his skill, he would now take Detlef apart piece by piece for his own amusement. He had lost an empire, but he could still kill the fool dressed as his younger self.

Detlef hacked, but Oswald parried. Oswald struck out, but Detlef backed away.

Then they fell at each other with deadly seriousness.

Detlef fought the weariness in his bones, and summoned extra reserves of strength. Oswald wielded his sword with desperation, knowing his life depended upon this victory. But also he had had a courtly education, the private tuition of Valancourt of Nuln, the best blades. All Detlef knew was how to make a mock battle look good for an audience.

Oswald danced around him, slicing his clothes, scratching his face. Tiring of the game, the grand prince came to kill him...

And found Detlef's swordpoint lodged between his ribs.

Detlef thrust forward, and Oswald lurched off his feet, sliding the full length of the sword until the hilt rested against his chest.

The grand prince spat blood, and died.

ENVOI

After the premiere of Drachenfels, everyone needed lots of bed-rest. They all had scars.

The Emperor survived, but spoke in a whisper for a few months. Luitpold suffered nothing worse than a swollen jaw and a severe headache and complained of missing the end of the play. Genevieve fed herself from volunteers and recovered within a day or two. Detlef collapsed moments after the grand prince's death, and had to be nursed back to health with hot broth and herbal infusions. His shoulder was always stiff after that, but he never let it be a handicap.

Baron Johann von Mecklenberg, elector of Sudenland, took over, and saw to the burial of Oswald von Konigswald in an unmarked grave in the mountains. Before leaving it, he spat onto the earth and cursed the grand prince's memory. The remains of the Drachenfels thing he cut apart and threw into the valley for the wolves. What there was wasn't much like anything that had ever lived.

He imagined he saw a group of cowled figures watching him as he disposed of the monster, but when the business was done with they were gone. The wolves died, but few were sorry of that. The grand theogonist of Sigmar, in mourning for his Matthias, and the high priest of Ulric forgot their differences for an afternoon and jointly held a ceremony of thanks for the deliverance of the Empire. It was not well attended, but everyone considered their duty to the gods done.

Detlef's company milled around, loading up their equipment on their wagons. Felix Hubermann and Guglielmo Pentangeli took over the running of the troupe while Detlef was indisposed and was collecting a pile of invitations to stage Drachenfels in Altdorf, with its original ending intact. The conductor held off the many managements, knowing that Detlef would have to rewrite the story in accordance with the known facts. The nature of the conspiracy between the Great Enchanter and the grand prince of Ostland would never be known, but whatever Detlef chose to write would be the accepted version.

The elector of Middenland sent a note of apology to Detlef's bedside, and promised to settle any outstanding debts accrued during the production of Drachenfels, providing he were given a token percentage of the profits of any eventual staging of the work. Hubermann translated

Detlef's reply into a polite 'no', and refinanced the company by asking the actors and musicians to invest their own money. Somehow, he found some old gold and silver artefacts of elven manufacture in a trunk and used them for capital. Guglielmo drafted the business agreements that founded the Altdorf Joint Stock Theatre, and cheerfully signed the running of the company over to Detlef Sierck.

The electorals conferred briefly, one seat around the table conspicuously unfilled, and requested that the Emperor nominate a new elector of Ostland. The princedom was due to pass to a cousin of Oswald's, but the electoral vote, it was decided, should be disposed of elsewhere. The Emperor's first suggestion, that the Imperial family be granted a vote in the college, was turned down. And, in the end, the vote went with the kingdom after all. Maximilian von Konigswald had been a good man, and all the others of his line before him. But the whole family were stripped of power thanks to the treachery of a single son of the house. The Emperor's choice of successor was approved. The new electors of Ostland would in future be the von Tassenincks.

Finally, it was decided that the fortress of Drachenfels should be destroyed, and alchemists were brought in to place explosive charges throughout the structure. Baron Johann watched from the opposite mountain, conscious again of the hooded phantoms in the periphery of his vision, and the whole place exploded most satisfactorily, raining down enough stone into a nearby valley to keep the villagers of three communities supplied with blocks for household repair for generations to come.

Henrik Kraly was arrested and charged with murder. Despite Detlef's deposition, he was acquitted on the grounds that Vargr Breughel had more or less killed himself and was probably a dangerous mutant anyway. However, without a salary from the House of von Konigswald, the former steward ran up a huge legal bill he was unable to settle, and spent the rest of his life as an inmate in Mundsen Keep. His dearest ambition, to become a trusty, was never fulfilled.

Lilli Nissen was briefly married to a successful pit fighter until an accident in the ring cut short his career. Her much-vaunted Marienburg production of The Romance of Fair Matilda was a costly failure, and she retired from the stage soon after being offered her first 'mother' role. After several more marriages, and a well-publicized affair with a cousin of Tsar Radii Bokha, she retired completely from public life and drove to despair a succession of collaborators engaged to help her with her never-to-be-completed memoirs.

Peter Kosinski became a popular jester in a double act with Justus the Trickster.

Kerreth the cobbler became official dress designer to the Countess Emmanuelle von Liebewitz, and was a great favourite with the ladies of Nuln.

Szaradat became a grave robber, and was torn apart by daemons while looting a tomb that happened to be under a particularly severe curse.

Innkeeper Bauman was persuaded by Corin the halfling to re-enter the

Black Bat in the Street of a Hundred Taverns' dicing tourney, and the inn's team swept the event three years in succession.

Reinhardt Jessner and Illona Horvathy were married; they named their twins Rudi and Erzbet.

Clothilde of Averheim discovered a herbalist who successfully treated her skin condition, and she became the most celebrated beauty in this corner of the Empire.

Clementine Clausewitz left the Sisterhood of Shallya and married an apothecary. Wietzak the vampire returned to Karak Varn and was destroyed by a secret society dedicated to the memory of the Tsarevich Pavel.

Lady Melissa d'Acques grew bored with the Convent of Eternal Night and Solace and travelled widely, it was rumoured, in Lustria and the New World in the company of a series of foster parents.

Sergei Bukharin lost an eye in a bawdy house brawl on the Altdorf waterfront and later succumbed to untreated syphilis.

Elder Honorio continued to offer refuge to world-weary vampires, and opened a sister refuge for werewolves and other shape-shifters.

Governor Gerd van Zandt was indicted on charges of corruption, and sent to command a penal colony in the Wasteland.

Seymour Nebenzahl converted to the worship of a new-discovered demi-god of frosts and ice, and became the most influential soothsayer in Norsca.

No one ever asked what happened to Lazslo Lowenstein.

Detlef Sierck recovered and rewrote Drachenfels as The Tragedy of Oswald. He took the title role in the first run at the Temple of Drama in Altdorf, but Genevieve Dieudonné could not be persuaded to repeat her one and only venture as an actress. The play ran for some years, and Detlef followed it up with The Treachery of Oswald, which told the end of the story, and in which he surprised everyone by casting Reinhardt Jessner as 'Detlef Sierck' and himself taking the twin roles of Laszlo Lowenstein and Drachenfels. Then, he produced a succession of mature masterpieces. With the profits of the Oswald plays, he bought a theatre which, by common consent of the company, he renamed the Vargr Breughel Memorial Playhouse. The History of Sigmar was rewritten and staged to some critical acclaim, although it never equalled the popularity of Detlef's later works. Even the critics who hated him personally came to acknowledge him as at least the equal of Jacopo Tarradasch. Although no one ever called him devout, he made substantial donations to the cult of Sigmar and built a shrine to the hammer in his town house. He spent some years with Genevieve, and discovered many new sensations with her. His sonnet cycle To My Unchanging Lady is widely held by scholars to be his best work. They were finally parted by the years, when Detlef was in his fifties, and Genevieve still seemed sixteen, but she remained the love of his life.

Genevieve lived for ever. Detlef did not, but his plays did.

Genevieve
Undead

'When he lost his love, his grief was gall,
In his heart he wanted to leave it all,
And lose his self in the forests tall,
But he answered instead his country's call…'

– Tom Blackburn and George Bruns,
'The Ballad of Davy Crockett'

Part One

Stage Blood

I

He had a name once, but hadn't heard it spoken in years. Sometimes, it was hard to remember what it had been. Even he thought of himself as the Trapdoor Daemon. When they dared speak of him, that was what the company of the Vargr Breughel called their ghost.

He had been haunting this building for years enough to know its secret by-ways. After springing the catch of the hidden trapdoor, he eased himself into Box Seven, first dangling by strong tentacles, then dropping the last inches to the familiar carpet. Tonight was the premiere of *The Strange History of Dr Zhiekhill and Mr Chaida*, originally by the Kislevite dramatist V.I. Tiodorov, now adapted by the Vargr Breughel's genius-in-residence, Detlef Sierck.

The Trapdoor Daemon knew Tiodorov's hoary melodrama from earlier translations, and wondered how Detlef would bring life back to it. He'd taken an interest in rehearsals, particularly in the progress of his protégée, Eva Savinien, but had deliberately refrained from seeing the piece all through until tonight. When the curtain came down on the fifth act, the ghost would decide whether to give the play his blessing or his curse.

He was recognized as the permanent and non-paying licensee of Box Seven, and he was invoked whenever a production went well or ill. The success of *A Farce of the Fog* was laid to his approval of the comedy, and the disastrous series of accidents that plagued the never-premiered revival of Manfred von Diehl's *Strange Flower* were also set at his door. Some had glimpsed him, and a good many more fancied they had. A theatre was not a proper theatre without a ghost. And there were always old stage-hands and character actors eager to pass on stories to frighten the little chorines and apprentices who passed through the Vargr Breughel Memorial Playhouse.

Even Detlef Sierck, actor-manager of the Vargr Breughel company, occasionally spoke with affection of him, and continued the custom of previous managements by having an offering placed in Box Seven on the first night of any production.

Actually, for the ghost things were much improved since Detlef took over the house. When the theatre had been the Beloved of Shallya and specialised in underpatronised but uplifting religious dramas, the offerings had been of incense and a live kid. Now, reflecting an earthier,

197

more popular approach, the offering took the form of a large trencher of meats and vegetables prepared by the skilled company chef, with a couple of bottles of Bretonnian wine thrown in.

The Trapdoor Daemon wondered if Detlef instinctively understood his needs were far more those of a physical being than a disembodied spirit.

Eating was difficult without hands, but the years had forced him to become used to his ruff of muscular appendages, and he was able to work the morsels up from the trencher towards the sucking, beaked hole of his mouth with something approaching dexterity. He had uncorked the first bottle with a quick constriction, and took frequent swigs at a vintage that must have been laid down around the year of his birth. He brushed away that thought – his former life seemed less real now than the fictions which paraded before him every evening – and settled his bulk into the nest of broken chairs and cushions adapted to his shape, awaiting the curtain. He sensed the excitement of the first night crowd and, from the darkness of Box Seven, saw the glitter of jewels and silks down below. A Detlef Sierck premiere was an occasion in Altdorf for the court to come out and parade.

The Trapdoor Daemon understood the Emperor himself was not present – since his experience at the fortress of Drachenfels, Karl-Franz disliked the theatre in general and Detlef Sierck's theatre in particular – but that Prince Luitpold was occupying the Imperial box. Many of the finest and foremost of the Empire would be in the house, as intent on being seen as on seeing the play. The critics were in their corner, quills bristling and inkpots ready. Wealthy merchants packed the stalls, looking up at the assembled courtiers and aristocrats in the circle who, in their turn, looked to the Imperial connections in the private boxes.

A dignified explosion of clapping greeted the orchestra as Felix Hubermann, the conductor, led his musicians in the Imperial national anthem, 'Hail to the House of the Second Wilhelm.' The ghost resisted the impulse to flap his appendages together in a schlumphing approximation of applause. In the Imperial box, the future emperor appeared and graciously accepted the admiration of his future subjects. Prince Luitpold was a handsome boy on the point of becoming a handsome young man. His companion for the evening was handsome too, although the Trapdoor Daemon knew she was not young. Genevieve Dieudonné, dressed far more simply than the brocaded and lace-swathed Luitpold, appeared to be a girl of some sixteen summers, but it was well-known that Detlef Sierck's mistress was actually in her six hundred and sixty-eighth year.

A heroine of the Empire yet something of an embarrassment, she didn't look entirely comfortable in the Imperial presence, and tried to keep in the shadows while the prince waved to the crowd. Across the auditorium, the ghost caught the sharp glint of red in her eyes, and wondered if her nightsight could pierce the darkness that sweated like squid's ink from his pores. If the vampire girl saw him, she didn't betray anything. She was probably too nervous of her position to pay any attention to him.

Heroine or not, a vampire's position in human society is precarious. Too many remembered the centuries Kislev suffered under Tsarina Kattarin.

Also in the Prince's party was Mornan Tybalt, grey-faced and self-made keeper of the Imperial counting house, and Graf Rudiger von Unheimlich, hard-hearted and forceful patron of the League of Karl-Franz, a to-the-death defender of aristocratic privilege. They were known to hate each other with a poisonous fervour, the upstart Tybalt having the temerity to believe that ability and intellect were more important qualifications for high office than breeding, lineage and a title, while the pure-blooded huntsman von Unheimlich maintained that all Tybalt's policies had brought to the Empire was riot and upheaval. The Trapdoor Daemon fancied that neither the Chancellor nor the Graf would have much attention for the play, each fuming at the imperially-ordained need not to attempt physical violence upon the other in the course of the evening.

The house settled, and the prince took his chair. It was time for the drama. The ghost adjusted his position, and fixed his attention on the opening curtains. Beyond the red velvet was darkness. Hubermann held a flute to his lips, and played a strange, high melody. Then the limelights flared, and the audience was transported to another century, another country.

The action of *Dr Zhiekhill and Mr Chaida* was set in pre-Kattarin Kislev, and concerned a humble cleric of Shallya who, under the influence of a magic potion, transforms into another person entirely, a prodigy of evil. In the first scene, Zhiekhill was debating good and evil with his philosopher brother, as the darkness gathered outside the temple, seeping in between the stately columns.

It was easy to see what attracted Detlef Sierck, as adaptor and actor, to the Tiodorov story. The dual role was a challenge beyond anything the performer had done before. And the subject was an obvious development of the macabre vein that had been creeping lately into the playwright's work. Even the comedy of *A Farce of the Fog* had found room for a throat-slitting imp and much talk of the hypocrisy of supposedly good men. Critics traced Detlef's dark obsessions back to the famously interrupted premiere of his work *Drachenfels*, during which the actor had faced and bested not a stage monster but the Great Enchanter himself, Constant Drachenfels. Detlef had tackled that experience face-on in *The Treachery of Oswald*, in which he had taken the role of the possessed Laszlo Lowenstein, and now he was returning to the hurt inside him, nagging again at the themes of duality, treachery and the existence of a monstrous world underneath the ordinary.

His brother gone, Zhiekhill was locked up in his chapel, fussing with the bubbling liquids that combined to make his potion. Detlef, intent on delaying the expected, was playing the scene with a comic touch, as if Zhiekhill weren't quite aware what he was doing. In his recent works, Detlef's view of evil was changing, as if he were coming to believe it was not an external thing, like Drachenfels usurping the body of Lowenstein, but a canker that came from within, like the treachery forming in

the heart of Oswald, or the murderous, lecherous, spiteful Chaida straining to escape from the confines of the pious, devout, kindly Zhiekhill.

On the stage, the potion was ready. Detlef-as-Zhiekhill drained it, and
Hubermann's eerie tune began again as the influence of the magic took
hold. *Dr Zhiekhill and Mr Chaida* forced the Trapdoor Daemon to consider things he would rather forget. As Chaida first appeared, with Detlef
performing marvels of stage magic and facial contortion to suggest the
violent transformation, he remembered his own former shape, and the
Tzeentch-born changes that slowly overcame him. When, at the point
Detlef-as-Chaida was strangling Zhiekhill's brother, the monster was
pulled back inside the cleric and Zhiekhill, chastened and shaking, stood
revealed before the philosopher, the ghost was slapped by the realization that this would never happen to him. Zhiekhill and Chaida might
be in an eternal struggle, neither ever gaining complete control, but he
was forever and for good or ill the Trapdoor Daemon. He would never
revert to his old self.

Then the drama caught him again, and he was tugged from his own
thoughts, gripped by the way Detlef retold the tale. In Tiodorov, the two
sides of the protagonist were reflected by the two women associated with
them, Zhiekhill with his virtuous wife and Chaida with a brazen slut of
the streets. Detlef had taken this tired cliché and replaced the stick figures with human beings.

Sonja Zhiekhill, played by Illona Horvathy, was a restless, passionate woman, bored enough with her husband to take a young cossack
as a lover and attracted, despite herself, to the twisted and dangerous
Mr Chaida. While Nita, the harlot, was played by Eva Savinien as a lost
child, willing to endure the brutal treatment of Chaida because the monster at least pays her some attention.

The murder scene drew gasps from the auditorium, and the ghost
knew Detlef would, in order to increase the clamour for tickets, spread
around a rumour that ladies fainted by the dozen. While Detlef's Chaida
might be a triumph of the stage, the most chilling depiction of pure evil
he had ever seen, there was no doubt that the revelation of the play
was Eva Savinien's tragic Nita. In *A Farce of the Fog*, Eva had taken and
transformed the dullest of parts – the faithful maidservant – and this
was her first chance to graduate to anything like a leading role. Eva's
glowing performance made the ghost's chest swell wet with pride, for
she was currently his special interest.

Noticing her when she first came to the company, he had exerted his
influence to help her along. Eva's triumph was also his. Her Nita quite
outshone Illona Horvathy's higher-billed heroine, and the Trapdoor Daemon wondered whether there was anything of Genevieve Dieudonné in
Detlef's writing of the part.

The scene was the low dive behind the temple of Shallya, where Chaida
makes his lodging, and Chaida was trying to get rid of Nita. Earlier, he
had arranged an assignation here with Sonja, believing his seduction of
the wife he still believes virtuous will signify an utter triumph over the

Zhiekhill half of his soul. The argument that led to murder was over the pettiest of things, a pair of shoes without which Nita refuses to go out into the snow-thick streets of Kislev. Gradually, a little fire came into Nita's complaints and, for the first time, she tried to stand up to her brutish protector. Finally, almost as an afterthought, Chaida struck the girl down with a mailed glove, landing a blow of such force that a splash of blood erupted from her skull like juice from a crushed orange.

Stage blood flew.

Then came the climax, as the young Kislevite cossack, played by the athletic and dynamic Reinhardt Jessner, having tracked Chaida down from his earlier crimes, bursts into the fiend's lodgings, accompanied by Zhiekhill's wife and brother, and puts an end to the monster during a swordfight. The Trapdoor Daemon had seen Detlef and Reinhardt duel before, at the climax of *The Treachery of Oswald*, but this was a far more impressive display. The combat went so far beyond performance he was sure some real enmity must exist between them. Offstage, Reinhardt was married to Illona Horvathy, to whom Detlef had made love in the company's last three productions. Also, Reinhardt was being hailed as the new matinee idol of the playhouse. His attractions for the young women of Altdorf were growing even as those of his genius employer diminished somewhat, although diminishing was certainly not what Detlef's stomach was doing with passing years of good food and better wine.

Detlef and Reinhardt fought in the persons of Chaida and the cossack, hacking away at each other until their faces were criss-crossed with bloody lines, and the stage set was a shambles. Slashing a curtain exposed the hastily-stuffed-away corpse of Nita, and Sonja Zhiekhill fainted in her brother-in-law's arms. Not a breath was let out in the auditorium. In Tiodorov's original, Chaida was defeated when Zhiekhill at last managed to exert himself and the monster dropped his sword. Skewered by the cossack's blade, Chaida turned back into Zhiekhill in death, declaiming in a dying speech that he had learned his lesson, that mortals should not tamper with the affairs of the Gods. Detlef had changed it around completely. At the point when the transformation began, the cossack made his death thrust, and Chaida parried it, striking with his killing glove and crushing the young hero's throat.

There was a shocked reaction in the house to this reversal of expectations. It had been Zhiekhill who had killed his wife's lover, not Chaida. This wasn't the story of the division between good and evil in a man's soul, but of an evil that drives out even the good. Throughout the third act, the ghost realized, Detlef had been blurring the differentiation between Zhiekhill and Chaida. Now, at the end, they were indistinguishable. He didn't need the potion any more. In a cruel final touch, Zhiekhill gave his bloody sword to his wife, of whose corruption he approves, and encouraged her to taste further the delights of evil by killing Zhiekhill's brother. Sonja, needing no potion to unloose the monster inside her, complied. With corpses all around, Zhiekhill then took his wife to Chaida's bed, and the curtain fell.

For a long moment, there was a stunned silence from the audience.

The ghost wondered how they would react. Looking across the dark, he saw again the red points of Genevieve's eyes, and wondered what emotion was hidden in them. *Dr Zhiekhill and Mr Chaida* was hard to like, but it was undoubtedly Detlef Sierck's dark masterpiece. No one who saw it would ever forget it, no matter how much they might wish to.

The applause began, and grew to a deafening storm. The Trapdoor Daemon joined his clamour with the rest.

II

The future emperor had been impressed with the play. Genevieve knew that would please Detlef. Elsewhere at the party, there was heated debate about the merits of *The Strange History of Dr Zhiekhill and Mr Chaida*. Mornan Tybalt, the thin-nosed Chancellor, quietly expressed extreme disapproval, while Graf Rudiger had apparently yawned throughout and glumly didn't see what all the fuss was about.

Two critics were on the point of blows, one proclaiming the piece an immortal masterpiece, the other reaching into the stable for his metaphors.

Guglielmo Pentangeli, Detlef's business manager and former cell-mate, was happy, predicting that whatever a person might think of *Dr Zhiekhill and Mr Chaida*, it would be impossible to venture out in society in the next year without having formed an opinion. And to form an opinion, it would be necessary to procure a ticket.

Genevieve felt watched, as she had all evening, but no one talked to her about the play. That was to be expected. She was in a peculiar position, connected with Detlef and yet not with his work. Some might think it impolite to express an opinion to her or to solicit her own. She felt strange anyway, distanced from the play she'd seen, not quite able to connect it with the man whose bed she shared – if rarely using it at the same time he did – or else able to understand too well the sparks in Detlef that made him at once Dr Zhiekhill and Mr Chaida. Recently, Detlef had been darkening inside.

In the reception room of the Vargr Breughel, invited guests were drinking and picking at the buffet. Felix was conducting a quartet in a suite of pieces from the play, and Guglielmo was doing his best to be courteous to von Unheimlich, who was describing at length an error in Reinhardt's Kislevite swordsmanship. A courtier Genevieve had met – whom she had once bled in a private suite at the Crescent Moon tavern – complemented her on her dress, and she smiled back at him, able to remember his name but not his precise title. Even after nearly seven hundred years in and out of the courts of the Known World, she was confused by etiquette.

The players were still backstage, taking off make-up and costumes. Detlef would also be running through his notes to the other actors.

For him, every performance was a dress rehearsal for an ideal, perfect

rendition of the drama that might, by some miracle, eventually tran-
spire, but which never actually came to pass. He said that as soon as he
stopped being disappointed in his work, he'd give up, not because he
would have attained perfection but because he would have lost his mind.

The eating and drinking reminded Genevieve of her own need. Tonight,
when the party was over, she'd tap Detlef. That would be the best way
jointly to savour his triumph, to lick away the tiny scabs under his beardline and to sample his blood, still peppered with the excitement of the
performance. She hoped he didn't drink to excess. Too much wine in
the blood gave her a headache.

'Genevieve,' said Prince Luitpold, 'your teeth...'

She felt them, sharp against her lower lip, and bowed her head. The
enamel shrank and her fangs slid back into their gumsheaths.

'Sorry,' she said.

'Don't be,' the prince said, almost laughing. 'It's not your fault, it's
your nature.'

Genevieve realized Mornan Tybalt, who had no love for her, was
watching closely, as if he expected her to tear out the throat of the heir
to the Imperial crown and put her face into a gusher of royal blood. She
had tasted royal blood and it was no different from a goatherd's. Since
the fall of Arch-Lector Mikael Hasselstein, Mornan Tybalt had been the
Emperor's closest advisor, and he was jealous of the position, afraid of
anyone – no matter how insignificant or unlikely – who might win favour
with the House of the Second Wilhelm.

Genevieve understood the ambitious Chancellor was not a well-liked
man, especially with those whose hero was the Graf Rudiger, the old
guard of the aristocracy, the electors and the barons. Genevieve took
people as she found them, but had been involved enough with the great
and the good not to want to pick sides in any factional conflicts of the
Imperial court.

'Here's our genius,' the prince said.

Detlef made an entrance, transformed from the ragged monster of the
play into an affable dandy, dressed as magnificently as the company costumier could manage, his embroidered doublet confining his stomach in a
flattering manner. He bowed low to the prince and kissed the boy's ring.

Luitpold had the decency to be embarrassed, and Tybalt looked as if
he expected another assassination attempt. Of course, the reason Detlef
and Genevieve were allowed such intimacy with the Imperial presence
was that, at Castle Drachenfels, they had thwarted such an attempt. If
it were not for the play-actor and the bloodsucker, the Empire would
now be ruled by a puppet of the Great Enchanter, and there would be
a new Dark Age for all the races of the world.

A darker age, rather.

The prince complimented Detlef on the play, and the actor-playwright
brushed aside the praise with extravagant modesty, simultaneously
appearing humble, yet conveying how pleased he was to have his patron
bestow approval.

The other actors were arriving. Reinhardt, a bandage around his head where Detlef had struck too hard in the final fight, was flanked by his wife Illona and the ingenue. Several artistically-inclined gallants crowded around Eva, and Genevieve detected a slight moue of jealousy from Illona. Prince Luitpold himself had asked if an introduction could be contrived to the young actress. Eva Savinien would have to be watched.

'Ulric, but that was a show,' Reinhardt said, as open as usual, rubbing his wound. 'The Trapdoor Daemon should be delighted.'

Genevieve laughed at his joke. The Trapdoor Daemon was a popular superstition in the Vargr Breughel.

Detlef was given wine, and held his own court.

'Gené, my love,' he said, kissing her cheek, 'you look wonderful.'

She shivered a little in his embrace, unconvinced by his warmth. He was always playing a part. It was his nature.

'It was a feast of horrors, Detlef,' the Prince said, 'I was never so frightened in my life. Well, maybe once...'

Detlef, briefly serious, acknowledged the comment.

Genevieve suppressed another shiver, and realized it had passed around the room. She could see momentarily haunted faces in the cheerful company. Detlef, Luitpold, Reinhardt, Illona, Felix.

Those who'd been at the performance in Castle Drachenfels would always be apart from the rest of the world. Everyone had been changed. And Detlef most of all. They all felt unseen eyes gazing down on them.

'We have had too many horrors in Altdorf,' Tybalt commented, a mutilated hand stroking his chin. 'The business five years ago with Drachenfels. Konrad the Hero's little skirmish with our green-skinned friends. The Beast murders. The riots stirred up by the revolutionist Kloszowski. Now, this business with the Warhawk...'

Several citizens had been slaughtered recently by a falconer who set a hunting bird on them. Captain Harald Kleindeinst, reputedly the hardest copper in the city, had vowed to bring the murderer to justice, but the killer was still at liberty, striking down those who took his fancy.

'It seems,' the Chancellor continued, 'we are knee-deep in blood and cruelty. Why did you feel the need to add to our burden of nightmares?'

Detlef was silent for a moment. Tybalt had asked a question many must have pondered during the evening. Genevieve didn't care for the man, but she admitted that, just this once, he might even have a point.

'Well, Sierck,' Tybalt insisted, pressing his argument beyond politeness, 'why dwell on terrors?'

The look came into Detlef's eyes that Genevieve had learned to recognize. The dark look that came whenever he remembered the fortress of Drachenfels. The Chaida look that eclipsed his Zhiekhill face.

'Chancellor,' he said. 'What makes you think I have a choice?'

III

Upon this peak in the Grey Mountains, there had once been a castle. It had stood against the sky, seven turrets like the talons of a deformed hand. This had been the fortress of Constant Drachenfels, the Great Enchanter. Now there was only a scattering of rubble that drifted like snow into the valley, spreading out for miles. Explosives had been placed throughout the structure, and detonated. The fortress of Drachenfels had shaken, and collapsed piece by piece.

Where once there had been a stronghold, there was now a ruin. The intention had been to destroy completely all trace of the master of the castle. Stone and slate could be smashed, but it was impossible to blow away like chaff the horrors that lay in memories.

Buried in the ruins for these five years was the Animus, a thinking creature with no true form. Just now, it resided in a mask. A plain oval like a large half-eggshell, wrought from light metal, so thin as to be almost transparent. It had features, but they were unformed, undefined. To gain character, the mask needed to be worn.

The Animus was not sure what it was. Constant Drachenfels had either created it or conjured it. A homunculus or a spirit, it owed its existence to the Great Enchanter. Drachenfels had worn the mask once, and left something of himself behind. That gave purpose to the Animus.

It had been left in the ruins when Drachenfels departed the world for one reason.

Revenge.

Genevieve Dieudonné. Detlef Sierck. The vampire and the play-actor. The thwarters of the great design. They had destroyed Drachenfels, and now they must themselves be destroyed.

The Animus was patient. Time passed, but it could wait. It would not die. It would not change. It could not be reasoned with. It could not be bought off. It could not be swayed from its purpose.

It sensed the disturbance in the ruins, and knew it was being brought closer to Genevieve and Detlef.

The Animus did not feel excitement, just as it did not feel hate, love, pain, pleasure, satisfaction, discomfort. The world was as it was, and there was nothing it could do to change that.

As the moons set, the disturbance neared the Animus.

* * *

As they made love, Genevieve licked the trickle of blood from old wounds in his throat. Over the years, her teeth had put permanent marks on him, a seal. Detlef had taken to wearing high collars, and all his shirts had tiny red stains where they rested against her bites.

His head sunk deep into the pillow, and he looked at the ceiling, vision going in and out of focus as she suckled his blood. His hand was on her neck, under her blonde curtain of hair. They were joined loin to loin, neck to mouth. They were one flesh, one blood.

He had tried to paint the experience with words, in one of his still-secret sonnets, but had never managed to his satisfaction to catch the butterfly feelings, pain and pleasure. In many ways his chosen tool – language – failed him.

Genevieve made him forget the actresses he sometimes took to his bed, and wondered if she too found this joining more special than her brief liaisons with young bloods. Their partnership wasn't conventional, hardly even convenient. But even as he felt the darkness gathering, this ancient girl was the candleflame to which he must cling. Since Drachenfels, they had been together, sharing secrets.

A thrill shot through him, and he heard her gasp, blood bubbling in the back of her throat, knifepoint teeth scratching the leathered skin of his neck. They rolled over, together, and she clung to him as their bodies joined and parted. There was blood between them, and sweet sweat. He looked at her smiling face under his in the gloom, and saw her lick the red from her lips. He felt himself climaxing, first in the soles of his feet, then...

His heart hammered. Genevieve's eyes opened, and she shuddered, overlapping teeth bared and bloody. He propped himself above her, elbows rigid, and collapsed, trying to keep his weight off her. Their bodies slipped apart, and Genevieve eased herself forwards, almost clambering over his bulk, pressing her face to his cheek, her hair falling over his face, kissing him. He pulled the quilts up around them, and they nestled in a cocoon of warmth as the sun rose behind the curtains.

For once, their sleep came at the same time.

With the play and the party and their private embraces, they'd both been awake the night through. Detlef was exhausted, Genevieve in the grip of the vampire lassitude that came over her every few weeks.

His eyes closed, and he was alone in the dark of his mind.

He slept, but his thoughts still raced. He needed to work on the sword-fight to prevent more accidents. And he would have to give thought to Illona, to balance the blossoming Eva's performance. And the second act could use delicate pruning. The comic business with the Tsar's minister was just a tiresome leftover from Tiodorov.

He dreamed of changing faces.

This high in the Grey Mountains the air was as sharp as a razor; as he inhaled, he felt its cutting pass in his lungs. Trying desperately not to wheeze and thus lose his habitual decorum, Bernabe Scheydt completed his mid-morning devotions to the gods of Law: Solkan, Arianka and Allu-minas. At the dig, the first thing he had ordered was the erection of a sundial. A fixed point on the world, shadow revolving precisely with the inexorable movement of sun and moons, the sundial was the perfect altar for worship of order.

'Master Scheydt,' said Brother Jacinto, touching his own forehead in a mark of respect, 'there was a subsidence in the night. The ground has fallen in where we were digging yesterday.'

'Show me.'

The acolyte led him to the place. Scheydt was used to hopping around the ruin, judging which lumps of rubble were sound enough to be stepped on. It was important not to fall over. Every time someone so much as tripped, two or three of the workforce deserted in the night. The locals remembered Drachenfels too well, and feared his return. Every slightest mishap was laid to the lingering spirit of the Great Enchanter. Many more, and the expedition would be reduced to Scheydt and the acolytes the arch-lector had spared him. And acolytes dug a lot less well than the mountain men.

The superstitious fever of the locals was nonsense. At the beginning of the expedition, Scheydt had invoked the dread name of Solkan and performed a rite of exorcism. If any trace of the monster lingered, it was banished now to the Outer Darkness. Order reigned where there had once been chaos. Still, there had been 'incidents.'

'Here,' said Jacinto.

Scheydt saw. A half-rotten wooden beam was balanced over a square pit. A few slabs angled into the edges, like the teeth of a giant. An earthy, shitty, dead thing smell fumed up from the hole.

'It must have been one of the cellars.'

'Yes,' Scheydt agreed.

The earliest-rising workmen stood around. Jacinto was the only one of the acolytes up from their comparatively comfortable village lodgings this morning. Brother Nachbar and the others were poring over and cataloguing the expedition's earlier finds. Back at the university in Altdorf, the arch-lector must be pleased with the success of this dig. The acquisition of knowledge, even knowledge of the evil and unholy, was one way in which the cult of Solkan imposed order upon chaos.

'We must pray,' Scheydt declared. 'To ensure our safety.'

He heard a suppressed groan. These peasants would rather be digging than praying. And they would rather be drinking than digging. They did not understand the Law, did not understand how important order and decorum were to the world. They were only here because they feared Solkan, master of vengeance, as much or more than they feared the ghosts of the castle.

Jacinto was down on his knees, and the others, grumbling, followed him. Scheydt read out the Blessing of Solkan.

'Free me from the desires of my body, guide me in the path of the Law, instruct me in the ways of seemliness, help me smite the enemies of order.'

Since he had embraced the cult, Scheydt had been rigid in his habits. Celibate, vegetarian, abstinent, ordered. Even his bowel movements were decided by the sundial. He wore the coarse robe of a cleric. He raised his hand to no one but the unrighteous. He prayed at perfectly defined intervals.

He was in balance with himself, and with the world as it should be.

The prayer concluded, Scheydt examined the hole in the ground.

The arch-lector had sent him to Drachenfels with orders to search out items of spiritual interest. The Great Enchanter had been a very evil man, but he'd had an unparalleled library, a vast collection of articles of power, a store of the most arcane secrets.

Only by understanding Chaos, could the cult of Solkan impose order. It was important to carry the battle to the enemy, to meet sorcery with cleansing fire, to root out and destroy the devotees of unclean gods.

Only the strongest in mind could qualify for this expedition, and Scheydt was honoured by his selection as its director.

'There's something down there,' Jacinto said, 'catching the light.'

The sun had risen, and was shining now into the cavity. An object reflected. It was the shape of a face.

'Get it,' Scheydt said.

The acolyte followed the order. Jacinto knew his place on the sundial. Two of the workmen lowered the young man into the cavity on a rope, and then hauled him back out. He handed the article he had taken from the floor of the pit to Scheydt.

It was a delicate metal mask.

'Is it anything?' Jacinto asked.

Scheydt was not sure. The object felt strange, warm to the touch as if it retained the heat of the sun. It was not heavy, and there was no place for a cord to bind it to a head.

His hands tingled as he held the mask up in front of him. He looked through the eyeholes. Beyond the mask, the acolyte's face was distorted. Jacinto seemed impossibly to be sneering at his master, tongue poked out, hands flapping by his ears, eyes crossed.

A flare of wrath went off in Scheydt's heart as he rested the mask against his skin. At once, something leaped into his skull, fastening on his brain. The mask was stuck to his face like a layer of paint. His cheeks convulsed, and he felt the metal move with his twitch.

He saw Jacinto truly now, stumbling back away from him.

He was still Bernabe Scheydt, cleric of Solkan. But he was something else too. He was the Animus.

His hands found the acolyte and lifted him up. With new strength, he held the struggling young man up high and tossed him into the pit. Jacinto crashed through the remaining beam and thumped, broken, against an unseen flagstone floor.

The workmen were running away. Some screamed, some prayed. He enjoyed their fear.

Scheydt, devotee of the Law, tried to claw the mask from his face, horrified at the disorder he'd wrought. But the Animus grew strong in a moment and stayed his hands.

The Animus burrowed into Scheydt, seeking out seeds of excess within his imprisoned heart, encouraging them to sprout. Scheydt wanted a woman, a roast pig, a barrel of wine. The Animus had found desires within its host and was prepared to help him slake them. Then, it would travel.

To Altdorf. To the vampire and the play-actor.

As the workmen tumbled and ran down the mountainside, Scheydt drew a huge breath and laughed like a daemon. The straight trees that poked through the rubble bent in the breeze of laughter.

IV

Detlef got to the theatre in the mid-afternoon, leaving Genevieve sleeping in their rooms on the other side of Temple Street. The rest of the company were there already, poring over the reviews. The *Altdorf Spieler*, which boasted a circulation in the hundreds, was stridently in favour of *The Strange History of Dr Zhiekhill and Mr Chaida*, and most of the lesser broadsheets followed its line. Felix Hubermann picked out phrases to be flagged across the posters, humming superlatives to himself as he underlined them, 'gripping... powerful... thought-provoking... spine-chilling... bowel-churning... will run and run...'

Guglielmo reported that the house was sold out for the next two months and heavily booked thereafter. The Vargr Breughel had another hit. On the set, Poppa Fritz, the stage-door keeper and an institution in the theatre, was on his knees, trying to scrub blood out of the carpet. Detlef had ordered buckets cooked up in anticipation of a long run. When he had burst the bladder in his glove as he seemed to strike Eva Savinien, the whole audience had been shocked. He recalled the spurt of feeling that came at that moment, as if his own Mr Chaida were gaining the ascendant, encouraging him to delight in horrors beyond imagining.

As he entered the rehearsal room, cast and company broke into congratulatory applause. He bowed, accepting the praise that meant the most to him. Then, he broke the cheer up by producing a scroll with 'a few more notes...'

When he was finished, and the girl who played the innkeeper's daughter had stopped crying, he was ready to consider the business matters Guglielmo Pentangeli thrust at him. He signed a few papers and contracts, including a letter of thanks to the Emperor for continuing his patronage of the Vargr Breughel.

'Does that hurt?' Guglielmo asked.

'What?'

'Your neck. You were scratching.'

It had become an unconscious habit. His bites weren't painful, but sometimes they itched. Occasionally, after Genevieve bled him, he felt tired and drained. But today he was refreshed, eager for tonight's performance.

'Did you know the Chancellor had condemned the play? In the strongest of terms.'

'He said as much last night.'

'It's here in the *Spieler*, look.'

Detlef cast his eyes down the column of blocky print. Mornan Tybalt had branded *Dr Zhiekhill and Mr Chaida* an obscenity, and called for a ban on it. Apparently, the horrors of the play were an invitation to the feeble-minded to act in imitation.

Tybalt cited the thumb tax rioters, the Beast and the Warhawk as the logical results of a theatre exclusively concerned with the dark and the depraved, the violent and the vile.

Detlef snorted a laugh. 'I thought those riots were a logical result of the silly tax Tybalt himself devised.'

'He's still a powerful man at court.'

'A ban isn't likely, not with Prince Luitpold on our side.'

'Be cautious, Detlef,' advised Guglielmo. 'Don't trust patrons, remember...'

He did. Detlef and Guglielmo had met in debtors' prison, after the default of a previous patron. After Mundsen Keep, everything seemed like an unconvincing play. Sometimes he was certain the curtain would ring down and he would wake up back in his cell with the other stinking debtors and no hope of release.

Even a terrible death at the hand of Drachenfels would have been preferable to a life slowly dribbled away in the dark.

'Have Tybalt's comments engraved on a board, and hang them outside the theatre with all our good notices. There's nothing that increases queues like a demand something should be banned. Remember the houses they got after the Lector of Sigmar tried to suppress Bruno Malvoisin's *Seduced by Slaaneshi or: The Baneful Lusts of Diogo Briesach*?'

Guglielmo laughed.

'The Trapdoor Daemon is with us, you know,' Detlef said. 'I'm sure of it.'

'Box Seven has been cleaned out.'

'And...'

Guglielmo shrugged. 'The food was gone, of course.'

'It always goes.'

This was a recurring joke between them. Guglielmo claimed the offerings were taken away by the house-cleaners for their families, and that he should be allowed to put on sale tickets for Box Seven. It was only a question of five seats, but they were the most potentially expensive in the house. Guglielmo, like all ex-debtors, knew the value of a crown, and frequently mentioned how much the Vargr Breughel lost by not letting out Box Seven.

'Any other signs of spectral visitation?'

'That peculiar smell, Detlef. And some slimy stuff.'

'Hah,' Detlef exclaimed, delighted. 'You see.'

'Many places smell funny, and slime is easy to come by in this place. A good fumigation, and some new furniture and the box would be good as new.'

'We need our ghostly patron, Guglielmo.'

'Maybe.'

The Trapdoor Daemon heard Detlef and Guglielmo discuss him, and was amused. He knew the actor-manager only pretended belief as a pose. Still, there was an obvious kinship between them. Once, years ago, the ghost had been a playwright too. He was touched that Detlef remembered his work. Few others did.

From his space behind the walls, he observed everything, eyes to the peepholes concealed in the scrollwork of a tall cabinet no one ever opened. There were peepholes all over the house, and passageways behind every wall. The theatre had been built at a time when the reigning emperor alternately persecuted and patronised the players, necessitating the incorporation of multiple means of escape into the building. Actors who failed to please were able to get away without encountering the emperor's halberdiers, who then had a reputation as the harshest dramatic critics in the city.

Several players had got lost in the tunnels, and the ghost had found their skeletons, still in costume, strewn in nooks around the theatre's catacombs.

There was no formal rehearsal this afternoon. Everyone was elated from the night before, and eager to repeat the performance this evening. The test of a hit was its second night, the Trapdoor Daemon knew. Magic can sometimes strike once, and be lost forever. From now on, the company of *The Strange History of Dr Zhiekhill and Mr Chaida* would have to work to live up to their reputation.

Poppa Fritz, who had been with the house almost as long as the ghost, handed out mugs of coffee and flirted with the chorus girls. If anyone was responsible for the endurance of the legend of the Trapdoor Daemon it was Poppa Fritz. The stage-door keeper had encountered him on more than one occasion, usually when in his cups, and always embroidered and elaborated when he told of these incidents.

According to Poppa Fritz, the ghost was twenty feet tall and glowed in the dark, with bright red skulls in the pupils of his huge eyes, and a cloak woven from the hair of slaughtered actresses.

Detlef did what the Trapdoor Daemon would have done, and concentrated on Illona Horvathy and Eva Savinien. They had few scenes together, but the contrast between them was vital to the piece, and last night Eva had outshone Illona to the detriment of the play. The trick was to bring the one up without taking the other down.

Illona was not in a good mood, but tried hard, listening intently to Detlef and following his instructions to the letter. She was intently aware of her position. Having had twins a few years ago, Illona was constantly struggling to keep her figure. Last night she must have realized that in the next Vargr Breughel production, Eva Savinien would be the leading lady and she'd be playing somebody's mother. Reinhardt Jessner, on hand merely to read his lines, gave his wife support, but was careful not to tread in the director's way.

Eva, however, was quietly firm, displaying a backbone of steel in her willowy body. She might step from ingenue to star on the strength of Nita, and was even more careful than Illona. She was not a flirt exactly, but she knew how to flatter without seeming to, to ingratiate without being unctuous, to further herself without displaying a hint of ambition. In the end, Eva would be a great star, an extraordinary presence. The Trapdoor Daemon had seen that from the first, when she had had the merest walk-on as a dancer in *The Treachery of Oswald*. Since then, she'd grown inside. He felt pride in her achievements, but also nagging doubts.

Just now, while Illona and Detlef were playing the scene in which Sonja first meets and is attracted to Chaida, Eva sat on a table, hugging her knees, watching intently, and Reinhardt Jessner was in a huddle with her, massaging an ache in her back.

Before scaling the mountain, you first conquer the foothills, and the gossip was that Eva would doubtless seduce Reinhardt away from Illona before she tackled Detlef. The Trapdoor Daemon discounted this rumour, for he knew the girl better, understood her more finely. She wouldn't have a personal life until her position was assured.

Then, Detlef was working with Eva, restaging their final argument, smiling encouragement when he wasn't spitting hateful lines at her. After their dialogue was over, Detlef lightly tapped Eva on the skull and she fell down as if mightily smitten. The company applauded, and Reinhardt helped her up. The ghost saw Illona watching her husband intently, chewing a corner of her lip. Eva, without cruelty or encouragement, pushed Reinhardt away, and paid attention to what Detlef told her about her performance, nodding agreement at his points, taking them in.

The Trapdoor Daemon realized he'd not misjudged Eva Savinien. The girl didn't need to bestow any favours. She would advance on talent alone. And yet, despite the affection he felt for her, he could not but realize there was something chilling about the girl. Like some great performers, there might not be any real person inside the roles.

'All right,' Detlef concluded. 'I'm happy. Let's go out there tonight and kill 'em.'

V

The mountain whore was snoring, eyes swollen shut, as Scheydt chewed his tough meat, washing the chunks down with bitter wine. He'd returned to his room and made his wishes known to the innkeeper in language blunter than the dolt was used to hearing from a cleric of the Law. The Animus rested inside his head as Scheydt fulfilled the desires that had been revealed to him. The mask was a part of him now, and he could open its mouth to eat, to speak, to gobble...

Scratching himself, he stood over the shrine he had erected in the corner of the room when he first came to the inn. It was perfectly laid out, balanced and symmetrical, the symbol of the strength of order over Chaos, an arrangement of metal rods and wooden panels around a central sundial, engraved with the sayings of the Law, decorated with preserved leaves. He hiked up his robe and relieved himself on the shrine, washing away the leaves with his powerful flow of urine.

The noise woke up the whore, and she rolled away, her head to the wall, sobbing. After years of self-denial, Scheydt hadn't been a gentle lover.

There was a knocking at the door.

'What is it?' Scheydt grunted.

The door opened, and an acolyte ventured in. They must all be chattering about him.

'Brother Nachbar?'

The acolyte goggled at Scheydt, appalled at what he saw. He made the sign of the Law, and Scheydt turned around, the last of his flow making a quarter-circle on the floorboards.

Scheydt let his robes fall.

Nachbar could not speak.

The Animus told Scheydt he did not have to put up with fools like this for much longer.

'Get me a horse,' he ordered. 'I'm leaving this pest-hole.'

Nachbar nodded and retreated. The fool was so brain-blasted by the Law that he would carry out Scheydt's orders even if the cleric told him to consume his own excrement or slide a long sword into his scrawny belly. Perhaps, as a parting gesture, he would so order the brother, and tidy up a loose end. No, there was enough tidiness in the world. Let the end stay loose for someone to trip over.

Scheydt washed his foul-tasting mouth out with the last of the wine, and tossed the bottle out of the window, ignoring the shattering crash below. He hoped someone with bare feet would chance by.

Since the Animus and Scheydt had come to an agreement in their shared body, Drachenfels's creature could afford to slumber a little. It wasn't so much a question of taking over as it was of allowing the host to do what he always had wanted to do. The host was not a slave. Rather, the Animus set him free from himself, from the conventions that restricted his desires. Considering the grey grimness of Scheydt's life, the Animus was doing him a favour.

It would take Nachbar a while to get the horse organised. Scheydt hawked and spat at the steaming ruin of the altar. He slipped back into bed, roughly turning the whore over, thumping her fully awake. He ripped her tattered garment, and forced himself onto her, grunting like a hog.

The moons were up and Genevieve was about. She had wakened to an awareness of her own strength. Having fed well, she wouldn't feel the red thirst for days.

Temple Street was busy, crowds hustling to the Vargr Breughel for the evening performance. She was amused by the excerpted reviews emblazoned upon the boards above the doors.

A broadsheet-seller was exchanging papers for coins, shouting about another Warhawk murder. Obviously, atrocity sold well. Everyone in the city was looking up at the sky half the time, expecting the huge bird to swoop, talons first, out of the dark.

The night tasted fine. The first of a fog lingered around her ankles. In the gutter, an old woman was bent double, scooping up dog turds with her ungloved fingers, dropping them in a sack. She was a pure-gatherer, and would sell her crap-crop to a tannery for use in the curing of hides. The woman shrank away instinctively from Genevieve. A vampire-hater, naturally. Some people didn't object to picking up shit, but couldn't abide the presence of the undead.

Poppa Fritz recognized Genevieve and, with a bow, admitted her to the Vargr Breughel by the stage door.

'The Trapdoor Daemon is about tonight, Mam'selle Dieudonné.'

She had listened to the old man's spook tales for years. Fond of him, she'd become fond of his ghost.

'Does our spectre care for the drama?' she asked.

Poppa Fritz cackled. 'Oh yes. *Dr Zhiekhill and Mr Chaida* is definitely to his taste. Anything with blood in it.'

She showed him her teeth in a friendly way.

'Begging your pardon, mam'selle.'

'That's quite all right.'

Inside, everyone was busy. Tonight, she would watch the play from the wings. Later, Detlef would quiz her in detail, asking her honest advice. In an open space, Reinhardt Jessner was practising his sword moves, bare-chested and sweating, muscles gliding gracefully under his skin. He saluted her with his foil, and continued to fence with his shadow.

She caught the theatre smell in her nostrils. Wood and smoke and incense and paint and people.

A rope dangled beside her, and Detlef came down it from the gods, breathing a little heavily. His belly might be swelling but his arms were still hard muscle. He clumped onto the stage, and hugged her.

'Gené, dear, just in time...'

He had a dozen things to ask her, but he was called away by Guglielmo with some tiresome business matters.

'I'll see you later, before the performance,' he said, dashing off. 'Stay out of trouble.'

Genevieve wandered, trying not to get in the way. Master Stempel was mixing up stage blood in a cauldron, cooking the ingredients over a slow flame like Dr Zhiekhill preparing his potion. He dipped a stick into the pot, and brought it up to the light.

'Too scarlet, don't you think?' he said, turning to her.

She shrugged. It didn't smell like blood, didn't have the shine that excited her thirst. But it would pass for non-vampires.

She went to the ladies' dressing rooms, passing a pile of flowers outside Eva Savinien's cramped quarters and stepping into the largest suite on the corridor. Illona was painting her face meticulously, peering into a mirror. Genevieve cast no reflection, but the actress sensed her presence and looked around, trying to smile without disturbing the drying paint.

Illona was another veteran of Drachenfels. They didn't need to talk to communicate.

'Have you seen the notices?' Illona asked.

Genevieve nodded. She knew what must be bothering her friend.

'"A new star shines"?' Illona quoted.

'Eva was good.'

'Yes, very good.'

'So were you.'

'Hmm, maybe. I'll just have to be better.'

The actress was working on the lines around her mouth and eyes, powdering them over, smoothing them into a mask of flour and cochineal. Illona Horvathy was a beautiful woman. But she was thirty-four. And Eva Savinien was twenty-two.

'She'll be in this room next time, you know?' Illona said. 'She radiates. Even from the stage, even in rehearsal, you can see it.'

'It's a good part.'

'Yes, and it's the making of her. But she has to fill it, she has to be there.'

Illona began to comb her hair. The first strands of grey were there already.

'Do you remember Lilli Nissen?' she asked. 'The great star?'

'How could I forget? She was to play me, and I ended up playing her. My one moment in the limelight.'

'Yes. Five years ago, I looked at Lilli Nissen and thought she was a fool, clinging to a past she should have let go, still insisting she play roles ten or twenty years younger than she was. I even said she should be glad to play mothers. There are good parts for mothers.'

'You were right.'

'Yes, I know. That's why it's so painful.'

'It happens, Illona. Everyone gets older.'

'Not everyone, Gené. Not you.'

'I get older. Inside, where it counts, I am very old.'

'Inside is not where it counts in the theatre. It's all out here,' she gestured in front of her face, 'all outside.'

There was nothing Genevieve could say that would really help Illona.

'Good luck for tonight,' she tried, feebly.

'Thank you, Gené.'

Illona looked back into the mirror, and Genevieve turned away from the empty stretch of glass where her image was not. She had the feeling there were eyes behind the mirror, where hers might have been reflected, looking at her curiously.

The Trapdoor Daemon squeezed through the passage behind the ladies' dressing rooms, looking through the one-way mirrors like a patron in an aquarium examining the fish. The vampire Genevieve was with Illona Horvathy, talking about Eva Savinien. Everyone would be talking about Eva today, tonight, and for a long time...

In the next room, the chorus girls were getting into their costumes. Hilde was shaving her long legs with a straight blade and rough soap, and Wilhelmina was stuffing her bosom with kerchiefs. He retained enough of his maleness to linger, watching the fragile young women, feeling arousal and guilt.

He liked to think himself a guardian spirit, not a peeper.

He pulled himself away, and passed to the next mirror. The passage was narrow, and his back scraped against the wall as he pushed on, feeling pressure on his rough hide.

Beyond the glass, Eva Savinien was already in costume. She sat before her mirror, hands in her lap, looking emptily at herself. Alone, she was like a stored mannequin, waiting for the puppeteer's fingers to come and bring her life.

And what life she would have.

The Trapdoor Daemon gazed at Eva's perfect face, conscious of his own shadow on the glass. He was glad the mirror was not silvered on this side, throwing his hideousness back at him.

'Eva,' he breathed.

The girl looked around, and smiled at the mirror.

The first time, during the run of *A Farce of the Fog*, the actress hadn't been sure what she'd heard.

'Eva,' he had repeated.

She was calm then, certain there was a voice.

'Who's there?'

'Just... just a spirit, child.'

The actress had been instantly suspicious.

'Reinhardt, is that you? Master Sierck?'

'I'm a spirit of the theatre. You'll be a great star, Eva. If you have the nerve, if you have the application...'

Eva had looked down, and pulled her robe around her against a chill.

'Listen,' he'd said. 'I can help you...'

He had been coming to her dressing room mirror for months, giving her advice, passing comment on each nuance of her performance, encouraging her to stretch her instrument.

Now he'd helped her as much as he could. Soon her future would be her own responsibility.

'In the fourth act,' he said, 'when you fall, you are falling away from the audience. You should take them with you as you die.'

Eva nodded, paying close attention.

VI

The horse died under him just before dawn. Thereafter, the Animus kept Scheydt running through the twilight, almost matching the pace of the animal it had driven to a foamy death.

If there was a record time for the trip from the Grey Mountains to Altdorf, Scheydt would beat it. No Imperial mess-enger could best his stamina, his resolve, his purpose.

Scheydt's feet were bleeding in his boots and his joints popped with each step, but the Animus ignored its host's pain. As long as Scheydt's skeleton and musculature were mostly intact, it could keep going. If the cleric of Solkan wore out, the Animus would just find another host.

The road passed under his pounding feet as the sun rose. Scheydt was lagging behind the Animus, ceding control of the body, slumping into occasional dozes during which his consciousness would shrink, giving the creature inside him a clearer hold on the world, a more acute vision of the things around. They were already out of the mountains and into the Reikwald Forest. The road ran straight, bounded by tall evergreens. Scheydt's feet struck holes in the ground-mist. His footbeats and laboured breathing were the only sounds in earshot.

Ahead, the Animus saw a small figure, set side-saddle on a pony, pro-ceeding slowly down the road. It was a plump, middle-aged woman in the robes of a priestess of Shallya. In the countryside, priestesses often passed from village to village, exercising the healing arts, delivering babies, ministering to the sick.

Scheydt caught up with the pony, and pulled the priestess from her perch. She struggled, and he snapped a right-angle into her spine, toss-ing her into a roadside ditch. The pony bent under his unaccustomed weight, and he dug in his heels like spurs. The animal wouldn't last the morning, but would give him speed.

'My shoes,' the girl said.

'Shoes?'

'It's snowing. I can't go into the streets without my fur shoes.' The girl stood up to him, growing in stature, unbending her body, squar-ing her shoulders. There was a dab of red paint on her cheek, a graze from earlier.

He made and unmade fists, then slipped one meaty hand into his studded metal glove. It was an impressive prop.

'Hurry away, Nita, my dove,' he sneered, the false teeth bulging and deforming his mouth. 'Your Mr Chaida has an important appointment. We can't have trash like you lying about while we entertain a lady.'

'My shoes.'

It was the third night. Eva Savinien was even better than in the last two performances. Illona was much improved, but she was still outshone. It was almost eerie. This didn't come from him, Detlef knew. It was something inside the girl, blossoming like a flower.

She moved on the stage, towards the lights. He hadn't directed her in that. In her position, the audience's attention would be focused. He was pushed into the shadows behind if he was to hit his mark and strike his blow.

Clever girl.

'I'll give you shoes,' he said, following her, raising his glove.

He wondered if anyone had been teaching little Eva how to steal a stage. She was becoming an adept thief.

Squeezing the bladder of stage blood, he brought his hand down, thumping her from behind, bursting the sac.

She fell, not to the boards but to her knees. Seeing an opportunity, she was seizing it. Blood dribbling down her beautiful face, she looked out into the audience for a long, silent moment, then fell on her face.

Now that was over, he'd have to take back the scene.

From Box Seven, the Trapdoor Daemon saw his pupil perform, and was pleased. Through Eva, he could reach an audience again, could make them feel joy, despair, love, hate...

He hadn't been so excited by a discovery for many seasons.

Her new death scene was masterly, an unforgettable moment. Now the scene was Nita's, not Chaida's. The audience would remember the play as the story of a street girl's downfall, not of a cleric's double nature.

He was too rapt to join the applause that exploded from the house when Eva Savinien came to take her curtain call. Flowers were conveyed to the stage. The company joined the applause. Even Detlef Sierck tipped a salute to her. She was modest, bowing only slightly.

Exhausted by the performance, she had no more to give. She'd discharged her obligation to the audience, and knew how to take its praise.

She'd have to be cultivated properly. A play would have to be found for her, a suitable vehicle. She might need a patron as well as a tutor.

When they hailed her, they would be doing the Trapdoor Daemon honour.

The girl brushed past Genevieve on the way to her dressing room, an attendant carrying her flowers behind her. Eva Savinien had never spoken with her beyond the demands of conventional pleasantry. Genevieve assumed she was wary of vampires.

'That's a fine creature,' Detlef said, wiping his paint-smeared face. 'A fine creature indeed.'

She nodded agreement.

'She took that scene from me as you'd take a toy from a toddler. It's a long time since anyone's done that.'

'How do you think Illona feels?'

Detlef was pensive, his knit frown dislodging the slabs of make-up that made Chaida's brows beetle. Eva was back in her dressing room now, alone.

'She spends a lot of time in her room, doesn't she? Do you think Eva has a jealous lover?'

He considered the point, and spat out Chaida's false teeth into his hand.

'No. I think she's a devout worshipper at the shrine of self, Gené. She spends her spare time improving herself.'

'Is she improved?'

'In herself, yes. I don't know if the company will be happy to work with her much longer.'

'I understand she has had other offers. There were flowers tonight from Lutze at the Imperial Tarradasch Players.'

Detlef shrugged.

'Of course. The theatre is a nest of vultures. Eva is a tasty morsel.'

'Very,' she said, a twinge of red thirst in her tongue.

'Gené,' Detlef scolded.

'Don't worry,' she said. 'She'd have thin blood, I think.'

'Lutze won't get her. She'd have to apprentice for years to get any-where near a lead. I'll find something for her after *Dr Zhiekhill and Mr Chaida* concludes its run.'

'She'll stay?'

'If she's as clever as I think. A jewel needs a setting, and this is the best company in Altdorf. She won't want to be Lilli Nissen, surrounded by fifth-rate hams to make her look good. She needs the challenge of an excellence that forces her to rise.'

'Detlef, do you like her?'

'She's the best young actress in seasons.'

'But do you like her?'

His shoulders shifted. 'She's an actress, Gené. A good one, possibly a great one. That's all. You don't have to like her to see that.'

A stifled sob caught Genevieve's attention. By the stage door, Rein-hardt was shaking Illona. They were arguing, and Illona was in distress. It was easy to deduce the subject of their dispute. Poppa Fritz shoved past the couple, bowed under the weight of a vast basket of flowers.

Reinhardt pulled Illona to him, and tried to calm her crying with a hug.

'It's this play,' Detlef said. 'It's making us find out things about our-selves we might prefer not to know.'

The darkness was in his eyes.

VII

After three days on the road, Scheydt was approaching Altdorf on foot. The Animus was quiet now, and he recalled the details of his trip as if trying to piece together a vivid but fast-fading nightmare. Animals had died, and people too. Pain was a constant thing with him, now. But it didn't matter. It was as if the pain were someone else's, not connected to his soul, to his heart. His boots would have to be peeled from his feet, blood congealing in them. His left arm was broken, and flapped awkwardly. His robes were ragged and filthy with the dust of travel. His face was frozen, immobile, the replica of the mask fused with it. Unconscious of the hurt, Scheydt walked on, one foot in front of the other, trudging in the deep wheelruts of the back road.

The gates of the city were ahead. People clustered around, queuing with their wares to be passed by the Imperial customs. There were watchmen about, doubtless looking for felons and murderers. And soldiers were taking their tithes from the merchants who came to Altdorf with perishable goods, silks, jewels or weapons.

Two young whores joked with the watchmen. A donkey was defecating spectacularly in the road, causing a commotion of people away from its rear end and a heated argument between the beast's owner and various bystanders. Scheydt joined a group of foot travellers, and waited to be passed. At the gate, an officer of the watch was checking purses. Anyone with less than five crowns was refused entry to the city. Altdorf had enough beggars.

A sweetmeat vendor with a tray of pastries was passed through. Then, it came to be Scheydt's turn. The officer laughed.

'You've no hope, ragamuffin.'

The Animus came awake in Scheydt's head and fixed its gaze on the officer. The laughter died.

'I am a cleric of Solkan. The university of Altdorf will vouch for me,' Scheydt explained.

The officer looked at him in disbelief.

'A tramp from a midden, more like.'

'Let me pass.'

'Let's have your purse then.'

Scheydt had none. It must have fallen away during his journey, gone with his hat and cloak. The officer turned to the next man in the queue, a mariner on his way back to his ship at the Altdorf docks, and started examining his papers.

'Let me pass,' Scheydt said again.

The officer ignored him, and he was rudely shoved out of the way.

Scheydt stumbled away some twenty paces, feet not quite working properly. Then he took a run at the gate, head down. His skull punched between the mariner and the officer, and his shoulders slammed both men back against the iron grille of the gate. A crossbow twanged and a bolt struck his back.

His hands went between the bars, and he swept them aside as if they were curtains. He heard oaths from the soldiers and the rest of the crowd. Iron buckled and broke. On the other side of the gate, the sweetmeat vendor looked on in panic, spilling cakes from his tray.

The mariner was in his way. Scheydt made a fist and put it through the sailor boy's head, punching his nose out through the back of his skull. Pulling his bloody hand loose, he heard a squelch as if he were extracting his fist from a bowl of thick, half-set gruel.

A soldier slashed at him with a short sword, and Scheydt held up his broken arm to parry. The blade bit into his forearm, lodging in the cracked bone. Scheydt pressed forwards with his arm, driving the sword's edge into the face of its owner. The split-headed soldier fell out of the way. There was a hole in the gate. Scheydt walked through it, a sword still stuck in his arm.

'Stop in the name of the Emperor!' shouted the officer.

He felt a blast at his back and was pushed forwards. Without losing his footing, he turned to see the officer through a cloud of smoke. The man was holding a flintlock pistol. Scheydt felt clean air on his exposed shoulderblades. The ball had burst and spread, ripping away his robe and his skin. The officer emptied powder from his horn into the gun, and reached for his sack of lead balls.

Scheydt strode to the officer and, with his good hand, took away his works. He emptied white gunpowder from the horn over the man's face, and held the pistol by its barrel, his finger through the trigger guard. The lock was fixed back.

The officer's eyes widened with panic as he choked.

With his elbow, Scheydt smashed the officer's throat apple, driving him back against the stones. He held the pistol near the officer's clown-powdered face, and worked the trigger with his knuckle. A flint-spark danced from the breech into the officer's eyes. The man's head caught fire in a puff, and Scheydt walked away. As he hurried from the gates, his forearm came off and fell into the gutter.

He needed to practise the transformation. Not the make-up tricks – the palmed teeth, the extensible wig, the greasepaint lines that only appeared under a certain light – but the rest of it. Anyone could make himself into a monster on the outside. To be convincing, Detlef's Chaida had to come from inside.

He sat alone in the theatre's bar, staring at the pitted wooden top of a table, trying to find the darkness in his heart. In the hearts of his audience.

He remembered the eyes of Drachenfels. He remembered his months in Mundsen Keep. Some monsters are born, not made. But hunger and cruelty could drive a man to any lengths. What could turn him – Detlef Sierck – into something as prodigiously evil as Constant Drachenfels? The Great Enchanter had been shaped by centuries, millennia. Sorcery and sin, temptation and terror, ambition and agony. Did men become Chaidas a little at a time, like sands dropping in an hourglass, or was the transformation instant, as it appeared on the stage?

He made fists, and imagined them landing blows. He imagined skulls being crushed.

Eva Savinien's skull.

A black hand clutched at his heart, and slowly squeezed. His fists tightened into knots, and his lips drew back from his teeth.

The darkness throbbed in his mind.

Mr Chaida grew in him, and his shoulders slumped as his body bent into the shape of the monster.

An animal mind expanded inside his own.

There was such pleasure in evil. Such ease and comfort. Such freedom. The space between desire and fulfilment was an instant. There was a fiery simplicity to the savage.

At last, Detlef understood.

'Detlef Sierck,' said a voice, cutting through his thoughts, 'I am Viktor Rasselas, steward and advisor to Mornan Tybalt, Chancellor of the Empire, patron of the Imperial bank of Altdorf.'

Detlef looked up at the man, eyes coming into focus.

He was a reedy character, dressed in smart grey, and he had a scroll in his gloved hands. The seal of the Imperial counting house was his cap-badge.

'I am here to present to you this petition,' droned Rasselas, 'demanding that you cease performance of *The Strange History of Dr Zhiekhill and Mr Chaida*. It has been signed by over one hundred of the foremost citizens of the Empire. We allege that your drama inflames the violent tendencies of the audiences and, in these bloody times, such an inflammation is...'

Rasselas gulped as Detlef's hand closed on his throat.

He looked at the man's fearstruck face and gripped tighter, relishing the squirming feel of the neck muscles trapped under his fingers. Rasselas's face changed colour several times.

Detlef rammed the steward's head against the wall. That felt good. He did it again.

'What are you doing?'

He barely heard the voice. He slipped his thumb under Rasselas's ear, and pressed hard on the pulsing vein there, his nail digging into the skin.

A few seconds more pressure, and the pulse would be stilled.

'Detlef!'

Hands pulled his shoulder. It was Genevieve.

The darkness in his mind fogged, and was whipped apart. He found he was in pain, teeth locked together, an ache in his head, bones grinding in his hand. He dropped the choking steward, and staggered into Genevieve's arms. She supported his weight with ease, and slipped him into a chair.

Rasselas scrambled to his feet and loosened his collar, angry red marks on his skin. He fled, leaving his petition behind.

'What were you thinking of?' Genevieve asked.

He didn't know.

VIII

The pupil was learning faster than the Trapdoor Daemon had expected. She was like a flirtatious vampire, delicately sucking him dry of all his experience, all his skill. She took rapid little sips at him.

Soon, he'd be empty. All gone.

In her room beyond the glass, Eva sobbed uncontrollably, her face a cameo of grief. Then, as one might snuff out a candle, she dropped the emotion completely.

'Good,' he said.

She accepted his approval modestly. The exercises were over.

'You have refused Lutze's offer?' he asked.

'Of course.'

'It was the right thing to do. Later, there will be more offers. You will take one, eventually. The right one.'

Eva was pensive, briefly. He could not read her mood.

'What troubles you, child?'

'When I accept an offer, I shall have to go to another theatre.'

'Naturally.'

'Will you come with me?'

He said nothing.

'Spirit?'

'Child, you will not need me forever.'

'No,' she stamped her feet. 'I shall never leave you. You have done so much for me. These flowers, these notices. They are as much yours as mine.'

Eva wasn't being sincere. It was ironic; off the stage, she was a poor dissembler. Truly, she thought she'd outgrown him already, but she wasn't sure whether she was strong enough to proceed the next few steps without her familiar crutch. And, at the back of her mind, she feared competition, and assumed he would find another pupil.

'I am just a conscientious gardener, child. I have cultivated your bloom, but that does no credit to me.'

Eva didn't know, but she was the first he had instructed. She'd be the last.

Eva Savinien came along only once in a lifetime, even a life as extended as the Trapdoor Daemon's.

The girl sat at her mirror again, looking at her reflection. Was she trying to see beyond, to see him? The thought gave him a spasm of horror. His hide crawled, and he heard the drip of his thick secretion.

'Spirit, why can I never see you?'

She'd asked that before. He had no answer.

'Have you no body to see?'

He almost laughed but his throat couldn't make the sound any more. He wished what she suggested were true.

'Who are you?'

'Just a Trapdoor Daemon. I was a playwright once, a director too. But that was long ago. Before you were born. Before your mother was born.'

'What is your name?'

'I have no name. Not any more.'

'What was your name?'

'It wouldn't mean anything to you.'

'Your voice is so beautiful, I'm sure you are comely. A handsome ghost like the apparition in *A Farce of the Fog.*'

'No, child.'

The Trapdoor Daemon was uncomfortable. Since the play opened, Eva had been pressing him about himself. Before, all her questions had been about herself. About how she could improve herself. Now, uncharacteristically, she was being consumed by curiosity. It was something she'd discovered inside, and was letting grow.

She was wandering about her room now, back to him. A bouquet had arrived from the palace every day since the first night. Eva had made a conquest of Prince Luitpold. She took yesterday's stiff blossoms from their vase and piled them with the others.

'I love you, spirit,' she said, lying.

'No, child. But I shall teach you to show love.'

She whirled around, the heavy vase in her hand, and smashed the mirror. The noise of the shattering glass was like an explosion in the confined space of the passage. Light poured in, smiting his shrinking eyes like a rain of fire. Shards pattered against his chest, sticking to the damp patches.

Eva stepped back, glass tinkling under her feet.

She saw him. Unfeigned, unforced horror burst out of her in a screech, and her lovely face twisted with fear, disgust, loathing, instinctive hate.

It was no less than he had expected.

There was an urgent knocking at Eva's door. Shouts outside the dressing room.

He was gone through his own trapdoor before anyone could intervene, pulling himself through the catacombs on his tentacles, driving himself deeper into the heart of the theatre, determined to flee from the light, to hide himself from wounded eyes, to bury himself in the unexplored depths of the building. He knew his way in the dark, knew each turn and junction of the passageways. At the heart of the labyrinth was the lagoon that had been his home since he first changed.

More than a mirror was broken.

* * *

She broke the lock and pulled the door open. Eva Savinien was having hysterics, tearing up her dressing room. At last, Genevieve thought rather cattily, a genuine emotion. It was the first time Eva had suggested off-stage that she might have feelings. The mirror was smashed, the air full of petals from shredded bouquets.

The actress flinched as Genevieve stepped into the room, others crowding in behind her. Like a trapped animal, Eva backed into a corner, as far away as possible from the broken mirror.

There was an aperture behind the looking glass.

'What is it?' Illona asked the younger woman.

Eva shook her head, and tore at her hair.

'She's having a fit,' someone said.

'No,' said Genevieve. 'She's had a fright. She's just afraid.'

She held out her hands, and tried to make calming gestures. It was no good. Eva was as afraid of Genevieve as she was of whatever had thrown such a scare into her.

'There's a passage here,' said Poppa Fritz from near the mirror. 'It goes back into the wall.'

'What happened?' asked Reinhardt.

Detlef shouldered his way into the room, and Eva threw herself at him, pressing her face to his shirt, her body racked with sobs. Detlef, astonished, looked at Genevieve as he patted Eva's back, trying to quiet her down. Being the director made him stand-in father for everyone in the company, but he was not used to this sort of behaviour. Especially not from Eva.

The actress broke away from Detlef suddenly and, darting between the people crowding the room, ran through the door, down the passageway, out of the theatre. Detlef called after her. There was a performance tonight, and she could not run out.

Genevieve was examining the hole where the mirror had been. A cool breeze was coming from it. And a peculiar smell. She thought she heard something moving far away.

'Look, there's some sort of liquid,' Reinhardt said, dipping his finger into a slimy substance that clung to a jagged edge of glass. It was green and thick.

'What is going on here?' Detlef asked. 'What's got into Eva?'

Poppa Fritz leaned into the cavity and sucked a whiff into his nostrils.

'It's the Box Seven smell,' Reinhardt said.

Poppa Fritz nodded sagely. 'The Trapdoor Daemon,' he said, tapping his nose.

Detlef threw up his hands in exasperation.

Bernabe Scheydt had found the theatre easily. It was on Temple Street, one of the city's main thoroughfares. But, by the time he reached the place, Scheydt was not much more use to the Animus. Although he'd bound his stump as best he could with rags torn from his robes, he had lost a lot of blood. He was leaking badly through the hole in his back, and he still had the head of a crossbow quarrel lodged in his spine. This host was dying under the Animus, just as the horses that had brought him to Altdorf had died under Scheydt.

He managed to haul himself into the alley beside the Vargr Breughel Memorial Playhouse, and slumped across from the stage door. As he lurched into the recess a passing woman pressed a coin into his hand, and gave him the blessing of Shallya.

Gripping the coin in his remaining fist, he let the wall support him. He was aware of the slow trickle of blood from his many wounds, but he felt little. Suddenly, the stage door clattered open, and a girl came running out. She must be from the company. She was young, with a stream of dark hair.

The Animus made Scheydt stand up on weary legs, and totter towards the girl, blocking her path. She dodged, but the alley was narrow. He collapsed against her, bearing her towards the wall, dragging her down. She struggled, but did not scream. Already in the grip of panic, she had no more fear.

As he fell on her, Scheydt's leg bent the wrong way and snapped, a sharp end of broken bone spearing through muscle and flesh below the knee. With his hand, he grabbed the girl's hair, and pulled himself up to her face.

The girl began screaming. The Animus guided its host forwards. Scheydt pressed his face close to the pretty girl's, and it peeled off, sliding down between them.

Suddenly, he was free, and pain poured into his body. He shrieked as the full agony of his wounds fell on him like a cloak of lightning.

Without the Animus, he was lost, abandoned.

The girl, calming, stood up, heaving him off.

He could not stop shaking, and liquid was spewing from his mouth. He curled into a ball of pain, his limbs ending in ragged edges of agony. Looking up, he saw the girl feeling her face. The mask was in place, but not joined to her yet. The white metal caught the moonlight, and glowed like a lantern.

She was not screaming any more. But Scheydt was, letting out a tearing, dying, jagged howl from the depths of his disordered soul.

Detlef examined the hole, and was glad nobody suggested he explore the passage. It would have been hard for him to get through the mirror-sized gap, and there was something about the dark beyond that reminded him of the corridors of Castle Drachenfels.

'They must go back for miles,' he said.

Guglielmo was by his side, with a sheaf of floor-plans and diagrams, shaking his head.

'Nothing is marked, but we've always known these were approximate at best. The building has been remodelled, knocked down, rebuilt, refitted a dozen times.'

Genevieve was nearby, waiting. She was in one of her siege moods, as if she expected a surprise attack at any moment. Stage-hands were out looking for Eva.

Illona was trying to look concerned for the girl.

'And this part of the city is rotten through with secret tunnels and passageways from the wars.'

Detlef was worried about tonight's performance. The audience was already arriving. And they were expecting to see the discovery of the season, Eva Savinien.

There was no time to deal with this.

IX

The new host stood up, the Animus settling on her face. Scheydt was writhing at her feet, scrabbling with his hand at her leg, trying to pull himself up.

'Give it back,' he shouted through his pain.

It was easy to shake him off.

The Animus was intrigued by the cool, purposeful mind of Eva Savinien, and by the recent blot of panic that had been scrawled across the hitherto perfect page of her thoughts. This was the vehicle which would get it close to Genevieve and Detlef. Close to its purpose. It would have to be more circumspect now.

Like Scheydt, this host had her needs and desires. The Animus thought it could help assuage them.

She spread and fisted her fingers, feeling the pull and push of her muscles as far up as her elbows, her shoulders. The Animus was conscious of the perfection of her young body. Her back was as supple as a fine longbow, and her slender limbs as well-proportioned as an idealized statue. She spread her arms, heaving her shoulders, stretching apart her breasts.

The screaming man at her feet was attracting attention. There were crowds in the street, and they passed comment. Soon, someone would intervene.

Scheydt had denied himself everything, and, with the Animus in his mind, had exploded. Eva was more in accord with herself, but there were still things the Animus could do for her. And she welcomed its presence, feeding it the information it needed to proceed towards its purpose.

Detlef and Genevieve were both in the building, but it would stay its killing blow for the moment. The revenge had to be complete. It would be cautious not to wear out this host as fast as it had Scheydt.

'Eva,' said a male voice.

The Animus allowed Eva to turn to the man. It was Reinhardt Jessner, standing in the doorway. He was an actor in Detlef's company, a buffoon but a decent one. He could be of use.

'What's wrong?'

'Nothing,' she said. 'Stage fright.'

Reinhardt looked unsure. 'That's not like you.'

'No, but one shouldn't be like oneself all the time, don't you think?'

She eased past him into the theatre, and darted up a small, hungry kiss at his bewildered mouth. After only a moment, he responded, and the Animus tasted the actor's soul.

The kiss broke, and Reinhardt looked down at Scheydt.

'Who's this?'

'A beggar,' she explained. 'Overdoing his act somewhat.'

'His leg is broken. You can see the bone.'

Eva laughed. 'You should know the tricks that can be done with make-up, Reinhardt.'

She shut the door on the still-kicking cleric of Solkan, and let Reinhardt take her back to the stage.

'I'm perfectly all right,' she kept saying. 'It was just stage fright... just an accident... just a panic...'

'Curtain up in half an hour,' Poppa Fritz announced.

Eva left Reinhardt, and made her way back to her dressing room. The Animus remembered the thing the host had seen beyond the mirror. There was no time to take account of it.

'Poppa,' she told the hireling. 'Get me a new mirror, and whip my costumier into action.'

Below the Vargr Breughel, underneath even the fifth level of the basements, there was a saltwater lagoon. A hundred years ago, it had served as a smugglers' den. It had been abandoned in haste; chests of rotted silks and dusty jewels stood stacked haphazardly on the shores. This was the Trapdoor Daemon's lair. His books swelled up with the damp like leavened bread, but the water was good for him. He could drink brine, and needed to immerse his body every few hours. If his hide dried out, it cracked and became painful.

But not as painful as the heartache he now felt.

He had known how it would end. There could be no other outcome. As a dramatist, he must have understood that.

But...

Collapsed on the sandy slope, his bulbous head in the water, its ruff of tentacles floating around it, he was alone with his despair.

Everything had been a futile attempt to put off the despair.

He heard the constant drip of water down the walls of this dungeon, and saw the rippling reflection of his lanterns on the water's surface.

Sometimes, he wondered if he should just cast himself off, and let his body wash through the tunnels to the Reik, and then to the sea. If he were to throw away the last of his humanity, perhaps he might find contentment in the limitless oceans.

No.

He sat up, head breaking the water, and crawled away, leaving a damp trail behind him.

He was the Trapdoor Daemon. Not a spirit of the sea.

There were age-eaten wooden statues of gods and goddesses around the walls – of Verena and Manann, Myrmidia and Sigmar, Morr and Taal. They had been ship's figureheads. Now, their faces were vertically lined where the grain of the wood had cracked, and greened with masks of moss. Slowly, they became less human. When the Trapdoor Daemon had first found this place – the marks of his own change barely apparent to anyone else – the faces had been plain, recognizable, inspiring. As he had become monstrous, so had they. Yet they retained their human faces underneath.

Underneath his skin, he was still a man.

The Trapdoor Daemon stood up. On two legs, like a man. The water had washed away some of his pain.

Lanterns burned eternally in his lair. It was as richly appointed as a palace, albeit with furniture rescued from the scenery dock.

The boatlike bed where he slept looked like a priceless antique from the Age of the Three Emperors, but was in fact a sturdy replica constructed for a forgotten production of *The Loves of Ottokar and Myrmidia*. Nothing was what it seemed.

Somewhere above, the company would be preparing for the curtain. He had not missed a performance yet. And he wouldn't break his habit tonight. Not for something as inconsequential as a heartless actress.

From a hook, he hauled down a cloak intended to be worn by a mechanical giant in one of the old melodramas.

He wrapped himself up, and slithered towards his trapdoor.

The crowds outside the theatre treated him as a madman, and kicked him into the street. The newly broken bone in his leg sawed through his flesh. On his knees, his hand pressed to his stump, he threw back his head and screamed.

The world spun around him. There was no such thing as a fixed point. A sundial is only useful if the sun is out.

Clouds gathered in the night sky, obscuring the moons.

Bernabe Scheydt yelled, and people hurried away from him. His face had been torn away, and he felt as if he were smothered with a mask of hungry ants, a million tiny mandibles dripping poison into his flayed flesh.

Up in the sky, a speck appeared. A black, flapping speck.

His scream ran out, and he just let the pain run through his whole body. His throat was torn and bleeding inside.

The speck became a bird, and he fixed his eyes on it.

An officer of the watch came near, his club out, and he stood over Scheydt, prodding him with a polished boot.

'Move on,' the watchman said. 'This is a respectable district, and we can't be having the likes of you.'

The bird was coming down like a rocket, beak-first, its wings fixed as if it were a missile.

'I... am... a cleric of the law.'

The copper spat, and kicked him in the knee, sending a jolt of pain through his body.

The bird still came. The watchman heard the whoosh as the hawk sliced like a throwing knife through the air, and turned around. He raised his club, and fell backwards, away from Scheydt, stifling his own yell.

The hawk fastened on Scheydt's head, beak gouging for his eyes, talons fixing about his ears. The bird had razor-edged metal spurs fixed to its ankles, and it had been trained in their use.

There was screaming all around.

'Warhawk, warhawk!'

The beak prised Scheydt's skull open and dug in expertly. It didn't feed, it rent apart. A gush of warmth expelled from the cleric's head, and dribbled down his face.

Then the pain was gone, and the bird was flying away.

Scheydt collapsed in the street, an unrecognizable, torn, broken mess. The clouds passed, and moonlight streamed down on the corpse.

X

'There's been a murder,' Guglielmo announced. 'Outside in the street.'

'What!'

Every new development was like a punch to his head. Detlef couldn't keep up.

Eva was in a corner, trying to reassure everyone that she was all right, that she could go on tonight. She was dressed and made up for Act One, turned into the bedraggled, painted Nita.

Guglielmo had a burly guard placed in Eva's dressing room, but the actress didn't want protection. She'd changed completely, and Detlef wondered if her earlier panic had been an act. If so, she'd fooled him completely. And he couldn't think of any reason for the performance. His own dresser draped Zhiekhill's robes around him, pinning them up. Cindy, the make-up assistant, set the trick wig under his cap. He felt like a baby, fussed over but ignored, an object not a person.

If a play lives through the first week, it can run for an age. Detlef wondered if the players could live through this first week of *The Strange History of Dr Zhiekhill and Mr Chaida*.

Poppa Fritz reported that there were protesters outside. They'd been hired by Mornan Tybalt, and come to picket the lines of theatre-goers. Now, having come to stop a play and stayed to witness a murder, they were on the point of rioting.

'It was another Warhawk killing.'

Detlef couldn't move his face to react as the special greasepaint was laid on.

The watch were on their way.

He had lost track of Genevieve, but could trust her to look after herself. He hoped he could trust her to look after him too.

'It has nothing to do with us,' Guglielmo said. 'A beggar was the victim.'

In her dressing room, Illona Horvathy was loudly filling a bucket with her dinner, as she'd done before every performance of every play she'd ever been in. Cindy stood back and judged her handiwork passable. Outside, he was Zhiekhill. Inside, he didn't know...

He heard the first notes of Felix Hubermann's overture.

'Places, everyone,' Detlef shouted.

Feeling the cold, she made her way down the narrow passage, knowing the floor was likely to give way under her. It was dark, but she was at home in darkness.

Genevieve knew the Vargr Breughel was connected with the labyrinth of tunnels that criss-crossed under the city. Altdorf had suffered too many wars, sieges, revolutions and riots not to be worm-holed through with secret ways. There was a drip of slime from somewhere, and the Box Seven smell was strong in the confined space. It was a surprise, however, to find the body of the building itself so extensively undermined, as if the theatre was a stage set, backed not by solid walls but by painted canvas.

From the passageway behind the ladies' dressing rooms – to which, equipped as they were with one-way mirrors, the management could have charged admission and secured quite a substantial income from the city's wealthier devotees of female flesh – she'd passed into a hub-like space, from which tunnels led off to all the points of the compass. There were also trapdoors in the ceiling and floor, so she supposed this knot was one of the secret junctions, a nodal point in the labyrinth.

There were few cobwebs, which suggested these paths were travelled often. In an alcove in the wall at the junction, a small bowl of matter burned, giving off a glow and a smell. It was longbane, a wood known to burn slowly, sometimes for up to a year.

This was an inhabited lair.

'Anyone home?' she asked, the passages throwing back echoes at her. There was no other answer.

She remembered the dark hallways of Drachenfels, and the unease that had set into her soul when she entered that castle. Even before anything had happened, she'd known that had been an evil place, the haunt of monsters and madness. This was different.

Reflecting upon her emotions, she realized she was depressed, not afraid. Whatever walked here, walked alone, lived alone. It hid away in the dark not from malice but from shame, fear, self-disgust.

She opened a door, and a stench enveloped her.

Her sense of smell was keener than a human's, and she had to hold her nose until the first wave had dissipated. Her stomach convulsed, and she would have vomited if there'd been any food in her. She didn't need to eat, but sometimes did so to be sociable or to sample a taste. But she hadn't taken anything solid for weeks. The nausea spasms were like blows to her abdomen.

Standing up, she looked into the cupboard.

It was something's larder, well-stocked with pale sewerfish, dog-size rats, various small altered creatures. The meat animals of the labyrinth all bore the taint of warpstone: the fish were eyeless or possessed of rudimentary forelimbs, the rats had heads out of proportion with their thin-furred bodies, other beasts were unidentifiable as what they had formerly been. They'd all been killed by something strong that broke necks or took large bites from its prey. Evidently, the epicure would not touch meat that was not yet a few days rotten, and these morsels had been left to putrefy a little, until they were fit to serve the larder-keeper's taste.

'Gods,' Genevieve swore, 'what a way to live!'

Moving on, she came to a drop that fell away into the depths of the city like a cliff. It was covered with what looked like a ship's rigging, a net of thick ropes, sturdy if tattered. It would be comparatively easy to climb down, but she thought that adventure could wait for another night.

Down below, she heard water lapping.

Turning away, she confidently expected to be able to retrace her steps. Within fifty paces, she was in new territory, lost.

She thought she was still on the same level as the theatre, and if she held still she could even hear the distant sounds of Felix's overture. She could not have gone that far into the labyrinth. There were trapdoors all over the place. Some must lead back to the public ways of the house.

Trying another promising door, she found herself surrounded by books and papers, stuffed into floor-to-ceiling shelves. There was a longbane taper burning, giving the room a woody, pleasant smell.

Longbane was known as Scholar's Ruin, because its fumes were mildly euphoric, mildly addictive.

This was a fairly ordinary theatre library. There were much-used and scribbled-on copies of standard works. A full set of the plays of Tarradasch, actors' and directors' copies of other repertory warhorses, some basic texts on stagecraft, a bundled collection of playbills, scrolled posters. A bound folio of Detlef Sierck was upside-down among the other books.

Genevieve looked about, wondering if any unusual book might turn up here, some grimoire of power bound in human skin and holding the key to a vast magical design. There was nothing of the sort.

What she did find was a whole case given over to books by someone of whom she had barely heard, a playwright of the previous century named Bruno Malvoisin. He was the author of *Seduced by Slaaneshi*, which she remembered as a scandalous piece in its day. Apart from that, he'd contributed nothing which still lived in the repertoire. She read the titles of plays from the elegant spines of the books: *The Tragedy of Magritta*, *The Seventh Voyage of Sigmar*, *Bold Benvolio*, *An Estalian's Treachery*, *Vengeance of Vaumont*, *The Rape of Rachael*. A whole life was wrapped up between these covers, a life spent and forgotten. Evidently, Bruno Malvoisin meant something to the inhabitant of the labyrinth. That might help solve the puzzle. She must ask Detlef if he knew anything about the man. Or, more usefully, Poppa Fritz: the stage-door keeper was an inexhaustible fount of theatrical lore.

She stepped back into the passageway, and tried the next trapdoor. It led to a small space that smelled of bread and belched a pocket of warm air at her. Genevieve almost passed it by, but then recognized that the back of the space was a door as well. She pulled herself into the recess, and pushed the door – a heavy, iron flap but unlocked – open.

Slipping out of one of the ovens, she found herself in the kitchens of the Vargr Breughel Memorial Playhouse. A chef turned, gasped, and dropped a tray of intermission pastries.

'Sorry,' she said. 'I thought I was cooked through.'

XI

Throughout the play, the Animus observed Detlef Sierck. In their scenes together, Eva was close to him, and the Animus could see through the filter of her mind. The actor was a huge man, almost swollen, physically strong, a powerful projector. This host wouldn't formerly have been able to best him in a struggle. Even with the Animus guiding her, taking away any restraints of pain or conscience, she might take a long time to overcome him. And Eva knew that, frail as she might seem, the vampire would be even more resilient.

With the rider in her mind, Eva lived the role of Nita as never before, wrestling the piece away from Detlef and the other players. The second act curtain was hers, as she returned on her knees to Chaida, lifting her scarf away from her bruises and throwing herself upon his mercy. The tableau was thunderously applauded.

Once the curtain was rung down, Detlef said, 'Good work, Eva, but, perhaps, from now on, less is more...'

As she stood up, the scene shifters working around them to change the stage set, Detlef looked at her. Sweat was pouring from him, beads glistening through his monster face-paint. His role was exhausting.

Reinhardt swarmed around, and kissed her on the cheek.

'Magnificent,' he said, 'a revelation...'

Detlef frowned, his Chaida brows moving together ferociously.

'She gets better and better, don't you think?'

'Of course,' the actor-manager nodded.

'You're a star,' Reinhardt said, touching her chin with his thumb.

The Animus knew that Reinhardt Jessner wanted sexual congress with its host. From Bernabe Scheydt, it understood lust.

'Just remember,' Detlef said, 'at the end of the play, I kill you.'

Eva smiled and nodded humbly. The Animus sampled the complicated emotions that ticked over inside the host's head. She was more ordered in her thoughts than Scheydt, the supposed devotee of the Law, had been. In her single-mindedness, she was very like the Animus itself. In the near distance she had purposes, and every step she took brought her nearer their achievement. Surprised, the Animus found itself in sympathy with Eva Savinien.

Coolly, professionally, the host stood to one side of the stage, allowing her dresser to change her shawl, and a make-up artist to dab stage blood and blue bruising onto her face.

'More flowers,' said an old man Eva knew as Poppa Fritz. 'Flowers from the palace.'

The Animus allowed Eva a tight smile. She thought the admiration of influential men a distraction. Despite everything, despite her resolve, despite her calculation, her life was for the theatre. She thought of taking lovers, patrons, a place in society. But they were just underpinnings. Her purpose was out in the limelight, out on the stage. Eva understood she was different, and didn't expect to be loved by individuals. Only the audience counted, that collective heart which was hers to win.

'And a special bouquet,' Poppa Fritz continued, 'from a kind spirit...'

A chill struck Eva, surprising the Animus.

Poppa Fritz held out a card, upon which was written, 'From the Occupant of Box Seven.'

'That's the Trapdoor Daemon's perch,' he explained.

A panic grew inside Eva, but the Animus soothed it away. Sampling the girl's memory, it understood her instinctive fears, understood the tangle into which she'd got herself. It could help her overcome these untidy emotions, and so it did.

The Animus was beginning to lose its sense of a distinct identity. It had started to think of itself as herself. Its former existence was a dream. Now, it was Eva Savinien. She was Eva.

Her name was called, and without a thought she took up her place on the dark stage. The curtains parted, and the light came up.

Nita lived.

Eva was different tonight. Of course, the Trapdoor Daemon had expected that. After the shock she'd had, most actresses would not even have gone on this evening.

He couldn't understand, though, how she could be so magnificent. She was a different person onstage. The screaming girl in the dressing room was left behind somewhere, and all the audience could see was Nita. He wondered how much of the luminousness of her playing was down to fear, down to the memory of the thing she had seen.

Having confronted a monster in her real life, was she better able to understand Mr Chaida's mistress? Later, would she come back to her guiding spirit just as the Kislevite drab persistently crawled to her abusive lover?

The ghost was almost frightened. He understood Eva the actress, but he couldn't begin to fathom out Eva the woman. He didn't even really believe there was such a person.

In Box Seven, he was racked with sobs, stifling the noise, feeling the tears leaking from his huge eyes.

On the stage, Nita cringed under a torrent of abuse from Chaida. The monster took a willow-switch to her back, and poured forth a stream of obscenities, insults, taunts.

The Trapdoor Daemon, like the rest of the audience, was held horror-struck.

Detlef Sierck's Chaida capered like an ape, almost dancing with glee as he inflicted hurt upon hurt. As Eva's performance grew in strength, so she pushed her co-star to greater lengths.

Evil was in the Vargr Breughel Theatre. Concentrated under the lights, shining for all to see. Detlef's Zhiekhill and Chaida would be remembered as one of his great roles. It went beyond make-up. It was as if the playwright were truly living out the duality, the heights of nobility, the depths of depravity. Some might fear for the performer's sanity and assume he had gone the way of the notorious Laszlo Lowenstein, the horrors of his stage roles overwhelming his real life until man and monster became indistinguishable.

On stage, Mr Chaida clumped with heavy boots over the prone form of the innkeeper's child, gleefully stomping the life out of her.

Listening from his hiding places, the Trapdoor Daemon had learned that tickets for *Dr Zhiekhill and Mr Chaida* were changing hands at ten times their face value. Every night, masked dignitaries were cramming into the boxes, unable to bear not having seen the piece. More seats were being squeezed into the stalls and circle, and commoners were paying a week's wage to stand by the walls, just to wonder at the spectacle, to be a part of the occasion.

The audience screamed as the innkeeper's daughter's head came off, and Chaida booted it into the wings.

It was magical. And fragile. No one knew how long the spell would last. Eventually, the play might fall into a set pattern, and become a routine entertainment, and those lucky enough to see it early would look with pity upon those who came later in the run.

The scene changed. Nita was alone now, singing her song, trying to beg from unseen passers-by the kopecks she needed to bribe the gate-keeper to let her out of the city. Away from Chaida, she might have a chance. Back in her village, she could find a life.

Half the audience was trying to hide their tears.

Her hands out, she felt the buffeting of the uncaring Kislevites. Her song ended, and she slipped to the stage, fluttering scraps of paper drifting about her to signify the famous Kislev snows. In her ragged clothes, Nita shivered, hugging herself.

Then the shadow of Chaida fell upon her. And her doom was sealed.

XII

It was taking Detlef longer to recover after each performance. There were three major fights, four violent love scenes and six murders in the script, plus the physically gruelling transformation scenes. He was picking up as many bruises as a pit-fighter. He must be sweating off pounds, although that didn't seem to be affecting his gut.

Tonight, he'd barely been able to stand up for the curtain calls. Once the piece was over, the weight of weariness fell on him from a great height. They were all calling for Eva, anyway. He could easily fade into the scenery.

Once the curtain was down for the last time, Reinhardt had to help him off the stage, choosing a path between the ropes and flats.

There was a pile of floral offerings the size of an ox-cart heaped up by the ladies' dressing rooms. All for Eva.

Scraping at his face, pulling off his Chaida deformities, he staggered to his own dressing room, and collapsed on a divan, head pounding like a blacksmith's anvil. He was sure Reinhardt had stabbed him during the fight, but had so many pains that he couldn't isolate any individual wound. His dresser soaked a cloth, and dropped it on his forehead. Detlef garbled out a thanks.

He was still shaking, still in the grips of Mr Chaida.

When he shut his eyes, he saw Eva Savinien mutilated and dismembered. He saw rivulets of blood in the streets of Altdorf. He saw children thrown into open fires. Human bodies rent apart, entrails strewn in the dirt, eyes pecked by ravens, tongues pulled out.

He woke out of his doze, horrors still vivid in his mind.

Guglielmo was there, with the broadsheets. They were full of the latest Warhawk murder.

'The watch don't know who the beggar was,' Guglielmo said. 'The regular beggars in Temple Street claim never to have seen him, although he doesn't exactly have a face you could identify. He wore an amulet of Solkan, but the assumption is that he stole it. There's no connection with the other victims. No connection with the theatre.'

Detlef could imagine the hawk's spiked feet latching onto human flesh, the beak gouging skin, hammering at bone.

'I've ordered an extra patrol of the night guard on the street, and I'm putting a few bruisers in the building tonight. This whole thing stinks of trouble. What with Eva's broken mirror and the Warhawk death, I think we might have the beginnings of a curse here.'

Detlef sat up, his back and arms aching. Poppa Fritz was in the room too, looking solemn.

'This house has had curses before,' the old man said. '*Strange Flower*. It seems the Trapdoor Daemon took against it. The production never got to the first night. Illnesses, accidents, mishaps, assaults, disagreements. The whole thing.'

'There is no curse,' Detlef said. '*Dr Zhiekhill and Mr Chaida* is a success.'

'There've been cursed successes.'

Detlef snorted. But he couldn't summon up the contempt for superstition that would once have burst forth unasked when anyone talked of curses on plays. Actors were quite capable of fouling up a production without supernatural intervention.

'Tybalt's called for us to be shut down again,' said Guglielmo. 'I don't know what's got into him. Some moral crusade or other marched up and down outside all evening. Rotten fruit was thrown at the front of the theatre, and a couple of heavies tried to rough up the ticket takers.'

Genevieve appeared.

'Gené,' he said. 'A voice of sanity.'

'Maybe,' she replied, kissing his cheek. She smelled, peculiarly, of fresh bread.

'Where've you been?'

She did not answer him, but asked a question of her own. 'Who was Bruno Malvoisin?'

'Author of *Seduced by Slaaneshi*? That Bruno Malvoisin?'

'Yes, him.'

'An old playwright. Bretonnian, originally, but he wrote in Reikspiel so he must have been an Imperial citizen.'

'That's all?'

'That's all I know,' Detlef said, not understanding. 'He must have died fifty years ago.'

Poppa Fritz shook his head. 'No, sir. Malvoisin didn't die, exactly.'

Genevieve turned to the old man.

'You know about him?'

'What is all this, Gené,' Detlef asked.

'A mystery,' she said. 'Poppa Fritz?'

'Yes, mam'selle. I know about Bruno Malvoisin. I've been in the theatre a long time. I've seen them come, and I've seen them go. All the greats, all the failures. When I was a young man, Malvoisin was a famous playwright. A director, too.'

'Here in Altdorf?'

'Here in this house. When I was an usher's apprentice, he was resident playwright. He suffered under a curse. Some of his works were banned, suppressed. The emperor of the day branded *Seduced by Slaaneshi* obscene...'

'That, I know about,' Detlef interjected. 'It's pretty filthy, although has a certain style. We might revive it one season, suitably amended and updated.'

'He was a brooding man, obsessed, hard to work with. He fought a duel with the manager of the theatre. Hacked his head half off for cutting a curtain speech.'

'A likable fellow, then?'

'A genius, sir. You have to make allowances for genius.'

'Yes,' Detlef said. 'Of course.'

'What happened to him?' Genevieve asked.

'He began to alter. Warpstone must have got into him. They said *Seduced by Slaaneshi* offended the Chaos gods, and Tzeentch took a terrible revenge on him. His face changed, and he began to turn into... into something not human. He wrote furiously. Dark, delirious, difficult stuff. Mad plays that could never be staged. He wrote an epic verse romance, alleging that the emperor had made a mistress of a she-goat. It was published anonymously, but the watch traced him as the author. He was hardly human, then. Finally, shunned by all, Malvoisin disappeared mysteriously, slipped away into the night.'

Detlef nodded. 'Just the thing Malvoisin would do. His plays never have disappearances that aren't mysterious, and no one in them ever slips away into the afternoon. What has all this nonsense about an old hack got to do with anything?'

Everyone looked at Genevieve.

She thought a while before saying anything. At last, she came out with it.

'I think Bruno Malvoisin is our Trapdoor Daemon.'

XIII

With Bernabe Scheydt and the nameless mountain whore, the act of sexual congress had been a simple thing the Animus had been able to understand. Scheydt had offered money for pleasure, and then promised not to give the girl pain if she acceded to his wishes. Actually, Scheydt had reneged; he had neither passed over coin nor refrained from hurting her. The abuse of the girl, terrorising her even after she proved compliant, had been part of the cleric's desire. It had been as important, or more so, than the simple physical gratification.

With Eva Savinien and Reinhardt Jessner, the act was the same, but the meaning was different. The Animus found itself caught up in Eva's thoughts as she admitted Reinhardt into her body, as she let the actor see in her the fulfilment of his desires. She felt pleasure, genuine pleasure, but exaggerated it for his benefit.

The Animus was an amateur in these matters, and let itself be guided by Eva. The congress was better for the actress than it had been for the cleric, perhaps because she expected less of it.

He had willingly come with her, escorting her home after the performance. She rented a bare garret in the theatre district of Altdorf, one of many identical rooms in the area. Later, she'd have a house, luxuries, many clothes. Now, this was just a place to sleep when she was not at the Vargr Breughel. She'd brought other lovers here – her first acting tutor, one of Hubermann's musicians – but the liaisons had never outlasted her partner's professional usefulness. She had no shrine in her room, no pictures on the walls. Aside from the bed, the main item of furniture was a desk at which she studied her parts, a shelf above it weighed down with reading copies of the plays in the Vargr Breughel's repertoire, with her roles underlined and annotated.

After their companionable, fairly affectionate love-making, Reinhardt was overwhelmed. The Animus was puzzled but Eva understood.

Shaking by her, Reinhardt was thinking of his wife and children. He sat up, the quilt falling away from his chest, and reached for the wine bottle on the stand by the bed. Eva propped herself up on a pillow, and watched her lover gulp down drink. Moonlight shone on his damp skin, making him pale as a ghost. He was bruised from his nightly duel with Detlef Sierck.

She cuddled next to him, and pulled him back down, stroking his hair, quieting his shivers. She couldn't stop his guilts, but she could ignore them. Eva's mind was racing. The carnal warmth had passed from her heart and she was calculating. She'd been able to make Reinhardt want her, but could she make the man love her?

The Animus didn't understand her distinction.

She thought on, pondering the success and implications of her latest move. The Animus wasn't capable of being taken by surprise, but it noted that, for a moment, Eva had gained control of their shared mind. The host dared be impatient with it, dared assume its purpose was subordinate to her own.

Eva had won Reinhardt as an ally. As things stood, she could cajole and blackmail him to her cause with further favours or a threat of exposure. But he'd be a stronger partisan if he loved her outright, if he was bound to her by ties stronger than lust or fear.

She found something inside herself that brought tears to her eyes. She lay still, not overdoing it, letting the tears well and flow. Tensing, she gave the impression that she was fighting against a burst of emotion. She waited for Reinhardt to take notice.

He reared over her, and touched a wet cheek.

'Eva,' he said, 'what is it?'

'I was thinking,' she said, 'thinking of your wife...'

Her words were like a dagger in Reinhardt's throat. The Animus savoured the small hurt.

'What a lucky woman she must be,' Eva said, seeming to be bravely trying to smile. 'People like Illona, she'll always be popular. I know what people think of me. It isn't easy being me and I can't change...'

He was comforting her now, his own doubts forgotten. Deep inside, they were satisfied. The Animus felt the warmth of her achievement.

'Don't cry,' he said, 'my love...'

Eva had him.

'Gené, why do I feel vast schemes are being laid against me?'

She had no answer beyond, 'Because maybe there are,' and had the wit not to say that.

It was late and they were still at the theatre, on the couch in Detlef's dressing room. Captain Kleindienst had wanted to ask them questions about the Warhawk killing but they had honestly not been able to help him. However, the icechip eyes of the watchman – famous as the man who had exposed the Beast – had made Genevieve uncomfortable. He seemed like another vampire-hater.

And his pet scryer, a red-headed young woman named Rosanna Ophuls, had been confused by the tangle of leftover emotions and impressions that clung to the Vargr Breughel. She'd not been able to stand being in the theatre more than a few minutes, and Kleindeinst had allowed her to wait outside in his carriage.

'They'll catch the Warhawk, Detlef.'

'Like they caught Yefimovich? Or the revolutionist Kloszowski?'

Both felons were still at large, on the run. The Empire was overrun with murderers and anarchists.

'Maybe they won't catch him. But it will end. Everything ends.'

'Everything?'

He looked piercingly at her. She remembered Illona Horvathy's similar look when Genevieve had told her everyone grew old.

'I'm thirty-six, Gené, and everyone takes me for ten or fifteen years older. You're, what... ?'

'Six hundred and sixty-eight.'

He smiled, and touched her face with a pawlike trembling hand.

'People think you're my daughter.'

He stood up and wandered to his mirror. Detlef was beginning to frighten her. His shoulders were slumped, and when he walked around the room it was in Chaida's distinctive lope. He always had his dark look now. He examined his face in the glass, pulling actorish expressions, baring his teeth like an animal.

She was at her most awake in the height of the night. She could keenly sense the darkness inside him. It was a cold, sharp dark. She wondered if it were the theatre itself that had disconcerted Rosanna, or Detlef.

Even though there'd been no chance of identification, Detlef had insisted Kleindeinst let him look at the corpse of the Warhawk's latest victim. Genevieve had stood by him while the oilskin sheet was drawn back from the skinless, eyeless face. The repulsive stench of dead blood, spoiled for her, poured off the man in the street. And Detlef had been fascinated, excited, drawn to the horror. Kleindeinst's scryer had certainly noticed this unhealthy interest and been sickened by it. Genevieve felt for her.

'Detlef,' she asked. 'What's wrong?'

He threw up his hands, a typically theatrical gesture. It made people in the back of the stalls feel they knew what he was thinking.

But someone close, someone as close as Genevieve, could see the imposture. The mask was loose, and she was glimpsing something behind. Something that reminded her horribly of Mr Chaida.

'Sometimes,' he said, struggling with something inside him, 'I think of Drachenfels...'

She held his hand, slim strong fingers around his. She too remembered the castle in the Grey Mountains. She'd been there before Detlef.

In truth, she'd suffered more within its walls, had lost more than him.

'It might have been better if we'd been killed,' he said. 'Then, we'd be the ghosts. We wouldn't have to carry on.'

She held him in her arms, and wondered when she had ceased to understand what went on inside him.

Suddenly, he was enthused. 'I think I've found a subject for my next play. It will something Eva can play the heart out of.'

'A comedy,' she suggested, hoping. 'Something light?'

He ignored her. 'There's never been anything good about the Tsarina Kattarin.'

The name scraped Genevieve's spine.

'What do you think,' Detlef said, smiling, 'Eva as the Vampire Empress? You could be a technical advisor.'

Genevieve nodded, non-committal.

'It would be a fine horror to follow *Zhiekhill and Chaida*. Kattarin was a real fiend, I understand.'

'I knew her.'

Detlef was surprised, then brushed it away. 'Of course, you must have. I never made the connection.'

Genevieve remembered the Tsarina. Their association was a part of her life she preferred not to think of too often. There was too much blood in those years, too many hurts, too many betrayals.

'In a sense, we were sisters. We had the same father-in-darkness. We were both Chandagnac's get.'

'Was she...?'

Genevieve knew what he was thinking. 'A monster? Yes, as far as anyone is.'

He nodded, satisfied.

Genevieve thought of the rivers of blood Kattarin had let loose. Her long life had had more than its complement of horrors. And she didn't feel an inclination to conjure them up again. Not to supply an audience hungry for sensation and atrocity.

'There are enough nightmares, Detlef.'

His head rested on her shoulder, and she could see the scabbed-over marks she'd left on his neck. She wanted to taste him, and yet she was afraid of what might be in his blood, what she might catch from him...

How much of his darkness had he caught from her? In his Kattarin play, did he intend to take the role of Vladislav Dvorjetski, the Empress's poet lover? Eva would be perfect casting for the monster queen.

Perhaps she was condemning Detlef too easily. It could be that she was as dark in her soul as he was in his obsessions. His work had only teemed with the macabre and monstrous since he had been with her. Bleeding a man sometimes meant taking things from him other than blood. Maybe Genevieve was a truer sister-in-darkness to Kattarin the Great than she liked to think.

'Never enough nightmares, Gené,' he murmured.

She kissed Detlef's neck, but did not break the skin. He was exhausted, but not asleep. They stayed locked together for a long time, not moving, not talking. Another day crept up on them.

XIV

Last night, the Trapdoor Daemon had heard Detlef and Genevieve talking about him. Poppa Fritz had reminisced about the days before he began to alter.

The days when he'd been Bruno Malvoisin.

The playwright he had been seemed now like another person, a role he had cast off with his human flesh.

In the passage behind the rehearsal rooms, where he was able to look in on the company at work, he stretched his major tentacles to their utmost length. Usually he wrapped himself in a cloak and held the centre of his body high, imagining a belly and two human legs below his chest. Today he let himself flop naturally, six tentacles spreading like the pad of a waterlily, the clump of his other external organs and the hard blades of his beak, protected by the leathery tent of his body.

There was very little of Malvoisin left.

In the rehearsal room, Detlef was reading notes to the company. This morning, he had few comments, distracted by the swirl of events around the play rather than fully involved in the drama itself.

The Trapdoor Daemon was puzzled by Eva.

His protégée sat aside as usual, Reinhardt hovering guiltily while paying overdone attentions to Illona. Eva was calm and in control again, different from last night. It was as if she'd never seen his true form. Or maybe she'd found the strength in herself to accept what she had seen? Whatever the case, she wasn't concerned this morning with the monster she had met last night.

A few of the chorus girls had been prattling about a murder outside the theatre. The Trapdoor Daemon knew nothing of that, except that he'd eventually be blamed.

As Malvoisin, he had written about evil, about how attractive it could be, how seductive a path. When he began to change, he had thought that he had himself succumbed to Salli's temptations, as Diogo Briesach in *Seduced by Slaaneshi* had to his own private daemons. Then, as he became less bound by human thinking, he came to recognize there was no more evil in him when his shape changed than there had been before.

In a sense, he'd been freed by his mutation. Perhaps that was the laugh line of Tzeentch's jest at his expense, that he could only be aware of his humanity once his human form was buried in a morass of squiddy altered flesh. Still, he realized that for others warpstone was a polluter of the soul as well as the body.

Watching Genevieve, who was herself watching Detlef with a new attentitiveness, the Trapdoor Daemon wondered whether a warpstone shard had been shot into his protégée.

Eva Savinien had changed, and she was changing still.

He had allowed the company to break up for lunch, and told them they did not have to come back until the evening's performance. *The Strange History of Dr Zhiekhill and Mr Chaida* was rolling of its own accord now, and Detlef was almost at the point when, even if everything else were not falling apart, he would have been prepared to let it alone. Long run shows develop by themselves, finding ways to stay alive. He was even grateful to Eva Savinien, whose unpredictable luminescence was prodding everyone in the company in unexpected directions.

Illona, for instance, was suggesting that she might have the makings of a tragic heroine as she slipped into the age range for roles like the Empress Magritta or Ottokar's Wife.

In Poppa Fritz's rooms, he found Genevieve surrounded by unscrolled maps, weighted down at the corners with books and small objects. She was with the stage-door keeper and Guglielmo, trying to make sense of the diagrams of the tunnels under the theatre.

'So,' she said, 'we're agreed? This one is a deliberate fraud, to be found by the enemies of someone taking refuge.'

The older-looking men nodded.

'It's too clearly marked,' Guglielmo said. 'Obviously, it's designed to get anyone who relies on it hopelessly lost. Possibly even to lead them into traps.'

'What are you three conspirators up to?' Detlef asked. 'Plotting to join Prince Kloszowski's revolutionist movement?'

'I'm going to try to find him,' Genevieve said.

She was dressed in clothes Detlef had not seen her wear in years. In Altdorf, she was usually found in subdued but elegant finery: white silks and embroidered Cathayan robes. Now she wore a leather hunting jacket and boots, with sturdy cloth trews and a man's shirt. She looked like Violetta, disguised as her twin brother in Tarradasch's *Hexenachtabend*.

'Him?'

'Malvoisin.'

'The Trapdoor Daemon,' Poppa Fritz explained. In the gloom, the old man looked like a crumpled parchment himself.

'Gené, why?'

'I think he's suffering.'

'The whole world is suffering.'

'I can't do anything about the whole world.'

'What can you do for this creature, even if he is Bruno Malvoisin?'

'Talk to him, find out if he needs anything. I think he was as frightened as Eva by what happened.'

Poppa Fritz rolled up the fake map, and slipped it into its tube, coughing in the dust that belched from it.

'He's some kind of altered, Gené. His mind must be gone. He could be dangerous.'

'Like Vargr was dangerous, Detlef?'

Vargr Breughel had been Detlef's stage manager and assistant. A dwarf born of normal parents, he'd been with the actor-playwright-director since the beginning of his career. In the end, he'd turned out to be an altered thing of Chaos and had killed himself rather than be tortured by a stupid man.

'Like you were dangerous?'

Detlef had been born with six toes on one foot. His merchant father had remedied the defect in early childhood with a meatcleaver.

'Like I am dangerous?'

She opened her sharp-toothed mouth wide and made play-claws of her hands. Then, she dropped her monster face.

'You know as well as I do that warpstone sometimes just makes a monster of you on the outside.'

'Very well, but take some of our bruisers with you.'

Genevieve laughed, and crushed a prop candlestick into a squeezed ball of metal.

'I'd only have to look after them, Detlef.'

'It's your life, Gené,' he said, wearied. 'You do what you want with it.'

'I certainly intend to. Poppa Fritz, I'll go in here,' tapping a chart, 'from the stalls. We'll have to break open this old trapdoor.'

'Gené,' he said, laying a hand on her shoulder. A child sometimes, she was also ancient. She kissed him, quickly.

'I'll be careful,' she said.

Reinhardt Jessner knew he was being a fool, but couldn't help himself. He knew he was hurting Illona, and would be hurting their twins, Erzbet and Rudi. In the end, he was hurting himself most of all.

But there was something about Eva.

She was in his blood like snakepoison, and it couldn't be sucked out with a simple bite. Since the first night of *Dr Zhiekhill and Mr Chaida*, the bane was creeping through him. He had known it at the party afterwards. One or other of them was always going to make a move. It had been her, but it could as easily have been him.

He felt physically sick when he was away from her, unable to think of anything, of anyone, else. And when he was with her, there was a different kind of pain, a gnawing guilt, a self-disgust, an awareness of his own foolishness.

The more he loved Eva, the more certain he was the girl would leave him. He could do nothing more for her. He was a stepping stone, half-sunk in the stream. There were larger, sturdier stones ahead. Eva would go on to them.

They had snatched a few hours together away from the theatre in the afternoon, rutting in the hot dark behind the drawn curtains of her upstairs room. She had already outpaced and outworn him, slipping into an easeful sleep while he, exhausted, lay awake next to her in her narrow bed, mind crowded and uncomfortable.

This was not the first time, but it was the worst. Before, Illona had known but been able to bear it. The other girls had not lasted, could not last.

He had half-thought Illona had encouraged him to be unfaithful, and they had been better together afterwards than before. Theatrical marriages were difficult and usually foundered. Little diversions gave them strength to carry on.

Now, Illona was in tears all the time. At home, the twins were forever fighting and demanding. He spent as little time there as possible, preferring either to be with Eva or at the Temple Street gymnasium fencing and lifting weights.

Eva shifted beside him, and the covers fell away from her sleeping face. Daylight dotted in through the rough weave of the curtains, and Reinhardt looked down at the girl.

An ice-kiss touched him.

As she slept, Eva looked strange, as if there were a layer of thin glass stretched over her face. Reinhardt caught strange almost-reflections in the surface.

He touched her cheek, and found it hard, like a statue.

As his fingertips pressed, the quality of her skin changed, becoming yielding, warm. Her eyes opened, and she took his wrist in a surprisingly strong grip.

He was truly afraid of her now.

Eva sat up, pushing him back against the plastered wall, her warm body against his, her face empty of expression.

'Reinhardt,' she said, 'there are things you must do for me...'

XV

The labyrinth was different here. While the passages behind the dressing rooms were cramped, these were almost spacious, the underground equivalents of thoroughfares. Odd items had drifted down from the world above. One corridor was lined with flats from various productions, laid end to end so mountain scenery gave way to Darklands jungle, then to the plasterboard flagstones and painted bloodstains of a dungeon, then to a storm-whipped seascape on springs so it would roll behind a stage ship, then to the corpse-littered Chaos Wastes. Genevieve tried to remember which plays went with each canvas.

She sensed her quarry was close. The Box Seven smell lingered faintly, and she had better nostrils than true humans. Some of the painted scenes had dried-slime smudges on them, indicating that the Trapdoor Daemon used this path. She wondered if she should call out, or if that would drive Malvoisin further into hiding.

Having spent so many of her years penned up in one way or another, she could imagine what kind of life the Trapdoor Daemon had down here. What she couldn't imagine was him finding any other kind of life. Humans barely tolerated her, and were invariably hostile to any of her kind who shapechanged. It wasn't an unfounded prejudice, but it was also not entirely just.

The passageway angled down, and ended in a curtained chamber. She looked around for the trapdoor, and found it, disguised as the top of a large barrel.

Originally the tunnel had had a ladder for human use, but that had mainly been scraped away, replaced by a set of protuberances that gave Genevieve an idea of what Malvoisin must look like. The smell was very strong, a whiff of dead fish and saltwater rising from the depths.

For now, she left the tunnel alone, replacing the barrel-top. Today she was going to search only the uppermost levels. She suspected Malvoisin might choose to loiter near the surface. She'd found many of his peepholes, and been amused by the private rooms into which they afforded a view.

Obviously, the Trapdoor Daemon alleviated his solitude by taking an interest in the company of the Vargr Breughel Memorial Playhouse.

She wondered how many of her own private moments had been over-
seen. From a peephole accessible if she stood on the barrel, she could
see into a stockroom where, among the dusty wigstands and tins of face-
powder, she had once bled Detlef intimately.

The red thirst had come upon her during a reception, and she had
dragged her lover to this forgotten corner of the theatre, taking mouth-
fuls of his flesh and gently puncturing his excited skin, gorging herself
until he was dangerously weak, a half-dozen new wounds opened on
his body. Had once-human eyes witnessed her lustful gluttony?

Retracing her footsteps to the last horizontal junction, she explored
a new fork. Nearby, there was a rapid slithering, and she darted in its
direction, her nightsight enabling her not to slam into a wall. She didn't
call out. Something large was moving fast.

The slithering turned a corner and she followed it. There was no
movement of air, so she guessed this was a closed space. She came to
a wall, and stopped. She couldn't hear anything now. Looking back,
she realized she'd been fooled. They didn't call Malvoisin the Trapdoor
Daemon lightly. Somehow, he'd slipped into the walls, ceiling or floor,
and escaped her.

However, she was canny. And she had time.

The Animus let Eva guide it to the theatre, with Reinhardt as thoroughly
in tow as if he were a pig led by a brass ring through his nose. From
Eva, it had learned that destroying Detlef and Genevieve wasn't enough
for its purpose. Before they died, they must be broken apart, the bond
forged at the fortress of Drachenfels sundered completely. That way,
they'd die knowing nothing lasting had come of their triumph. The
Animus was grateful for the new insight, realizing at last that it hadn't
been prepared to do its master's bidding until it joined with its current host. The Great Enchanter must have foreseen this when he forged
the Animus, realizing his creature wouldn't be whole until it was partially human.

It was gathering about itself the tools it needed. Eva, of course, was
the key, but others – Reinhardt, Illona, the Trapdoor Daemon, even
Detlef and Genevieve themselves – must play their parts. For Eva, the
Animus was very like Detlef, conceiving a drama and then guiding his
company through their parts. The Animus was not above being flattered by the comparison. Created as a cold intellect, it bore the vampire
and the play-actor no malice. It just knew that their destruction was
its purpose. From Eva, it had learned a considerable respect for Detlef
Sierck's prowess as a man of the theatre.

Eva left Reinhardt at the Temple Street gymnasium for his afternoon
exercises, knowing he would come when needed. The host had her own
purpose, distinct from that of the Animus.

For the moment, their ambitions meshed neatly. If a conflict ever arose,
each was confident of victory over the other.

The Animus let Eva go on thinking she was in control.

Outside the theatre, there were three distinct crowds. The largest was an unruly queue at the box office, demanding seats for *The Strange History of Dr Zhiekhill and Mr Chaida*. A few well-known touts were preying on these, charging unbelievable prices for genuine tickets, and slightly more credible coin for badly-forged imitations which would never pass Guglielmo Pentangeli's ushers. Competing with the eager would-be patrons was a line of placard-waving petitioners, mostly well-dressed matrons and thin young men in shabby clothes, protesting against the play.

One placard was a vivid poster of Detlef as Mr Chaida, showing him as a giant trampling over the murdered citizens of Altdorf. Since the last host's death, the protests had increased fourfold.

As Eva neared, the third crowd were aroused to activity. These, she was gradually becoming used to. There were liveried footmen with floral offerings and billets douces and formal invitations, and well-dressed young men keen to pursue their suits in person. Besides romantic overtures, Eva Savinien was daily pestered by professional offers, from all over the Empire and as far off as Bretonnia and Kislev. There could be no doubt that the young actress was the toast of Altdorf.

Graciously accepting flowers, invitations and letters, Eva passed through the crowd, politely fending off the more persistent suitors. Slipping through the front door, she immediately dumped her crop of tributes into the arms of Poppa Fritz, who staggered under the burden. She would go through the letters later.

'You should start sending your flowers to the Retreat of Shallya,' a voice said.

It was Illona. Eva turned, squashing a mouse of irritation in her mind. She didn't want this distraction now.

'That's what I did in the last century, when I was in your position. Flowers move you out of your dressing room and are no real use. The patients at the hospital will at least get something out of them.'

'A good idea,' Eva agreed. 'Thank you, Illona.'

'We should talk, Eva,' the older woman said.

'Not now.'

Illona looked sharply at Eva, eyes penetrating. It was as if she knew something, saw something. The Animus knew this was not possible. Not now.

'Take care, Eva. You've charted a dangerous course. Lots of squalls and shallows, rocks and whirlpools.'

Eva shrugged. This was most tiresome. Illona had fixed her with a look, making a strong-link chain between them.

'I was your age once, you know.'

'Naturally. Most people were.'

'And one day, you'll be my age.'

'The gods willing, yes.'

'That's right. The gods willing.'

The chain between them broke, and Eva bowed slightly.

'This has been most enlightening,' Eva said. 'But if you'll excuse me...'
She left Illona in the foyer, and went in search of Detlef. The Animus
could taste the nearness of its purpose.

XVI

The vampire had invaded his world. The Trapdoor Daemon didn't yet
know how he felt about that. He'd been alone so long. Alone except for
Eva. And she was now lost to him.

From the ceiling, where he could cling to the holds he'd carved, he
angled his eyes down, and watched Genevieve as she carefully made
her way down the main passage.

The Trapdoor Daemon understood Genevieve Dieudonné had been
an actress. Once. He admired her courage, and her caution. The labyrinth had its dangers, but she evaded them with skill. She was used to
prowling corridors in the dark. Eventually, the red glints of her eyes
would find him.

His heart pulsated inside his shroud of darkness.

Once, Bruno Malvoisin had loved an actress, Salli Spaak. No, not an
actress, but a courtesan who used the stage to give her respectability.
She had rejoiced in her celebrity, as the crowds came to gawp at her
rather than see the play. Salli had been the mistress of the then-emperor's
youngest brother, Prince Nikol. The fortunes of the theatre had ebbed
and flowed with her patron's feelings for his lady.

Genevieve reminded the Trapdoor Daemon of the long-dead tempt-
ress. So did Eva, although Salli had never been as gifted on the stage as
Malvoisin's recent protégée.

When Salli and the Imperial Brother quarrelled, laws were passed
against the theatre and halberdiers came to bar the house's doors. And
when she pleased Nikol, gifts and favours were showered upon the
whole company.

Salli had made a conquest of Bruno Malvoisin as she had made conquests of many others. She enjoyed the fear that spread whenever she
bestowed her favours on another. It was not a good idea to sleep with
the mistress of Nikol of the House of the Second Wilhelm. The prince
had publicly duelled and dispatched several of Salli's admirers, and Malvoisin knew a man who won a duel with Prince Nikol wouldn't escape
with his life.

Genevieve looked up, and the Trapdoor Daemon retreated a little in
his cloud of artificial shadow. She didn't seem to see him. He didn't
know if he was disappointed, whether he wanted to be found or not.

Behind Salli's beautiful face, there had been a terrible corruption. And Malvoisin had caught it. Like Genevieve – like Eva, even – she had not been entirely human. Prince Nikol had ultimately committed suicide after being lured into taking part in an unholy rite of the Proscribed Cult of Tzeentch, and Salli had been driven out of Altdorf by a mob. By then, Malvoisin was shambling through backstreets in a heavy cloak, trying in vain to disguise his increasingly obvious deformities. By night, he'd written reams, pouring out words as if he knew he had to discharge the entire rest of his life's worth of work within weeks. The day his swelling head shrugged off his nose, he'd gone underground.

Shaking her head, Genevieve continued down the passage. Eventually, she'd solve all the puzzles of the labyrinth. Then the Trapdoor Daemon would have to consider her as a problem.

Salli had believed in warpstone the way a weirdroot addict believes in dreamjuice. At great expense, she acquired the deadly material and added it to her food, to the food of her lovers. Malvoisin had not been the only one to change. The marks had been on the prince when he was found hanging from Three Toll Bridge.

He was, however, the only one to survive.

Salli had been a secret worshipper of Tzeentch, had enjoyed spreading corruption around her. She'd been the chosen instrument of the Chaos god, and had struck him down. In *Seduced by Slaaneshi*, he had dared to present on the stage things never intended for human audiences. His sins had been registered in the darkness, stirring into action powers from which there was no escape.

When Genevieve had passed, the Trapdoor Daemon let himself down from the roof, and settled on the flagstones. He pushed tentacles against two tiltstones in the wall – spaced far enough apart that no one ordinary man could reach them both – and dropped soundlessly into the slide that appeared in the floor.

He descended several levels, and slid into the comforting cold of the black waters beneath the theatre.

Detlef sat on the stage, in Dr Zhiekhill's chair, alone with himself in the auditorium. There was a lantern on the set, amid the doctor's retorts and cauldrons, but otherwise the huge space was dark. He looked out into the empty black, knowing in his mind the precise dimensions of the hall. Dimly, he could see the velvet of the expensive seats. In his island of light, he might have been alone in the entire building, the entire universe.

Still drained from last night, he wasn't sure whether he'd have the energy for tonight's performance. It always came at the last moment. At least, it always had so far. The bite on his neck was irritating him, and he wondered if it might have become infected. Perhaps, he and Gené should stay away from each other for a while.

Their last time together, after the first night, had been bloodier than usual. The red thirst had been strong in her. Occasionally, through the years, he'd had cause to fear that he might not survive their love-making. In the heat, neither man nor vampire really had any self-control. That, he supposed, was the whole point of the heat. If she wounded him too deeply, he supposed she would feel obliged to let him suckle her blood, to become her son-in-darkness, to cheat death and become a vampire himself.

The prospect, always between them but never discussed, excited and frightened him. Vampire couples had a bad reputation, even among other vampires.

At this time in the afternoon, the theatre was asleep, the actors and the audience hours away. Like Genevieve, the Vargr Breughel was only really alive after nightfall.

Genevieve had been made a vampire almost as a child, before she'd settled on her personality; if it came to it, Detlef would change while a fully-formed human being. 'Vampires can't have children,' his lover had once told him, 'not in the natural way. And we don't write plays.' It was true: Detlef could not think of a single great contribution to the arts – or to much else, besides bloodshed – that had been made by one of the undead. To live possibly forever was an attractive, intriguing prospect, but the coldness that came with it frightened him.

The coldness that could make a Kattarin.

Vampire couples were the worst, becoming more dependent upon each other with the passing centuries, more contemptuous of the rest of the world, more callous, more murderous. Each became the only real thing in the other's world. Eventually, Genevieve told him, they became one creature in two bodies, a berserk feeding beast that had to be stopped with silver and hawthorn.

A hand touched his neck and slipped around his throat with catlike ease. His heart stuttered, thinking the Trapdoor Daemon, angered by Gené's intrusion into his lair, had come to lay a deathsqueezing tentacle on him.

He turned and, in the light of the lantern, saw Eva's face, a mask-like oval in repose, worn and expressionless like the bas-relief on a much-used coin.

Her touch was odd, neither warm nor chill.

She smiled, and her face came alive. After all, she was on stage. Detlef wondered what scene Eva was playing.

Lifting her hand and his head with it, she made him stand up. Eva was tall enough to look him in the eye. Tall enough – like Illona and very few others, and unlike Genevieve – to play love scenes with him that looked good from the most remote box in the house.

He expected the kiss, but it was a long time coming.

Genevieve had been working her way up a peculiar network of stairs and ladders which, she realized, must exist inside the thick walls of the Vargr Breughel. Complicated joists and beams provided support for the thinnest shell of stone. By her reckoning, she was heading for an egress somewhere on the roof of the theatre, between the huge comic and tragic masks carved in stone on the eaves.

Perhaps the laughing or crying mouths and eyes were doorways.

She came to a trapdoor that was thick with dried slime, suggesting repeated use. As she touched the latch, she had one of her rare flashes of precognition. With the dark kiss, Chandagnac had given her a touch of the scrying ability. Now, she knew opening this door would solve mysteries, but that she wouldn't like the solutions. Her hand stayed, fingers on the latch, and she knew that if she left the door closed, her life would continue as it was now. If she pushed, everything would change. Again.

She made a fist of her hand, and held it to her chest. In the close space, her breathing was loud. Unlike the Truly Dead vampires, she still breathed. That made her nearly human. And so did her curiosity, her need to know.

Working the latch and pushing through the trapdoor, she wondered briefly if she'd have been happier in herself if her father-in-darkness had killed her before making a vampire of her. Then, she would have been completely apart from the living. Free from the tangles that wound around her heart.

The Box Seven smell was stronger here than anywhere else she'd been in the labyrinth. And no wonder, for this was Box Seven.

Beyond the curtains of the box, there was a light. It must be down on the stage. She stood up, stretching herself to work the cramps out of her arms and legs. Then, she parted the curtains.

On the stage, Detlef was rehearsing with Eva.

This must be the Act Three curtain, where Nita appeals to Zhiekhill for help, not knowing that the kindly man who has offered her protection is actually her monstrous tormentor. The poor girl tries to persuade Zhiekhill to give her money by making pathetic advances, and, in his arousal, he transforms into Chaida, battering her back onto the divan in Zhiekhill's study for a tableau highly suggestive of the action which must come between acts in the minds of the audience.

Watching them kiss, Genevieve waited for the transformation. One came, but not the one she was expecting.

XVII

The Animus was pressed against Detlef Sierck's face, and picked up his confusion, his desire, his pain. Also the growing cancer of darkness. It was the darkness the Animus needed to touch. It would be a simple matter to have Eva seduce him carnally, as she had Reinhardt Jessner. But what would be the point? Sex was not the thing that would break Detlef away from Genevieve. It was the darkness, the Chaida inside Detlef's Zhiekhill, the suppressed impulse to brute degradation.

Eva gripped Detlef's throat hard, exerting pressure as they kissed, almost choking him.

'Hurt me,' she whispered.

Detlef froze in her embrace.

'No,' she said. 'It's what I need, what I want...'

She was almost, but not quite, quoting from *The Strange History of Dr Zhiekhill and Mr Chaida*. Nita had been hurt so much, the text implied, that she had developed a perverse taste for pain. And Nita came as much from the pen and mind of Detlef Sierck as from the performance of Eva Savinien. He had written about the thrill of hurting and being hurt, and the Animus knew he'd found those feelings, like so much, inside himself, and spread them out on the stage. That experiment would be the destruction of him, just as Zhiekhill's dabbling eventually led to his own obliteration.

Eva's grip grew stronger, her thumb-knuckles digging into the soft pouch of flesh beneath Detlef's beardline.

'Hurt me,' she repeated, darting kisses at his face, 'badly.'

His eyes caught the light, and the Animus saw in them that it had reached inside him to dredge up the wish to inflict pain that had always been a part of the genius. It had been one of the things that gave him the surprising strength he needed to help best the Great Enchanter. It was one of the things that made him attracted to the vampire girl.

A part of Detlef Sierck was obsessed with pain, with blood, with evil. And obsession was so close to love as to be sometimes indistinguishable.

Eva took one of her hands from Detlef's throat, and made a claw of her nails, angling to rake the playwright's face.

He struck her hand aside.

His face was a mask of anger, his features conforming exactly to the actors' textbook image of rage, projecting an emotion he couldn't fully feel.

Detlef gripped the hand at his throat, and broke it away. He hit her, hard knuckles colliding with her cheek, raising an instant bruise.

The Animus was pleased.

Eva taunted Detlef, cajoling and insulting, pleading and prodding. She invited punishment, tempted him to become Chaida.

She slapped his face, and he punched her chest. Thanks to the Animus she felt no pain, but was enough of an actress to present a counterfeit that was better than the real thing.

In the struggle, their clothes were loosened, torn. Between blows, they exchanged hungry caresses.

Eva took a prop retort from the stage table, and smashed it against her face. It was sugar glass, but the sticky shards stuck to her, grinding between them as they kissed, grazing their faces. They scratched each other, drawing lines of blood.

Detlef punched her in the stomach, hard. She doubled over, and he threw her down onto Zhiekhill's divan.

This was the Third Act Curtain.

Eva experienced a surge of doubt, but the Animus washed it away. Everything was fine. Detlef tore at her clothes, rendering her smart dress as ragged as Nita's costume.

Detlef fell on Eva, and the curtains did not close.

Genevieve was horrorstruck, her blood on fire. Her canine teeth slid from their gumsheaths. And her fingernails were talon-shaped diamonds. What she saw on the stage made her want blood.

She didn't understand the unnatural love scene being played out below, but she hated herself for being aroused to the red thirst by it. What was coming out of Detlef had always been inside him, she realized. Perhaps this was no more perverse than their own love-making, a blend of human and vampire embrace that always involved the spilling of blood if not the giving of pain. But here Eva was leading Detlef, tugging at him as Mr Chaida tugged in the finale at Sonja Zhiekhill, trying to awake the monster inside her leading man.

She stood in Box Seven, the sea-stench all around her, and looked down, frozen. She was a typical vampire, she thought. Unable to do anything, but watching all the time, waiting for the scraps to fall from the table.

Then, with a dizzying lurch inside her mind, she had another flash of precognition, a scryer's insight that changed everything.

This was not a private moment she'd happened to oversee. This was a puppet show. Somewhere, somehow, something was working the strings, jerking Eva and Detlef to an obscene dance that was at least partly for her benefit. What her lover and the actress were doing on the stage looked more convincing than it should. They were acting, exaggerating so their violent love-making would register all over the house.

Frightened, Genevieve looked around. There was a playwright, a director. A drama was being played out, and she was a part of it too.

She was in the audience now, but she knew she would be called soon to play a part.

Again, everything was beyond her control.

In the Temple Street gymnasium, Reinhardt Jessner pushed his body up and down, spine a rigid bar, thick arms like pump handles. His nose touched the hardwood floor again and again. His mind was racing so fast he needed to tire his body to catch up.

Arne the Body, his instructor, advised him to slow down, but he could not. Throughout his career, he had taken care of his body, his instrument. If the script were thrown away, Reinhardt could outfight Detlef Sierck in the finale of *Dr Zhiekhill and Mr Chaida* and hardly bring a sweat to his brow.

Now, he swung a heavy weight about, feeling the burn in his forearms and shoulders.

Eva. It was all her fault.

He stood to lose everything. His family, his career, his self-respect. And all for Eva, who was already preparing to throw him away, her eye set on Detlef.

He hoisted the weight repeatedly, muscles thick in his arms and neck, teeth grit together. His back and chest were damp with perspiration, and he felt trickles in his close-cropped hair and beard.

Good luck to Eva and Detlef, he thought.

If it weren't for Detlef, Reinhardt would be a leading man himself. He was certainly drawing more attention as the actor-manager grew flabbier and crankier. Especially if a production afforded him a chance to take his shirt off. Perhaps he should take Illona and found his own company. A touring troupe maybe. Away from the stink of the city, there'd be less glamour, less acclaim, less money. But maybe there'd be a life worth living.

Eva.

He had to end it now. For Illona, for the twins. For himself.

He dropped the weight, and stood back. Arne grinned at him, and made his bicep inflate like a pig's bladder, the veins standing out on it like thick worms.

He would go to the theatre, and end it with Eva.

Then things would come together.

XVIII

'No,' said Detlef, quietly. Having touched something inside himself, he was now letting it go, leaving it well alone, pushing it back into the depths.

Eva stilled, staying her hand from the blow.

'What?'

'No,' he said, firmer now. 'I won't.'

He was ashamed of himself, and uneasy. He stood back, hands by his sides. He didn't want to touch her again.

Eva looked real fury at him, and, leaping from the divan, went for his face. He grabbed her wrists, and held her fast, keeping her away from him, pushing her back.

He felt his bruises, but also a strength inside him. He had resisted temptation. He had not become Mr Chaida.

'Hurt meee,' Eva screeched.

There was something wrong with her face, as if there were a layer of thin steel over it. She had foam on her lips, and was fighting seriously now. Her attacks were not in the least playful.

'What are you?' he asked.

'Hurt me, wound me, bite me...'

He pushed her off, and backed away from her, shaking his head.

From the darkness, a pair of hands clapped, the sound reverberating around the auditorium, turning into a thunder of applause.

The Animus had lost. It knew the fact with a gem-bright certainty. The beast in Detlef Sierck hadn't been strong enough to take over his heart completely. He was as much Zhiekhill as Chaida. He could be tainted and taunted, but not destroyed that way. There was too much else in his spirit, too much light in the darkness.

The host was shaking with the trauma of defeat. She was near the end of her usefulness. If the Animus couldn't destroy Detlef's soul, it would have to make do with ending his life.

Eva pressed her hands to her face, trying to keep the loose mask from coming free. As the Animus faded from her mind, she felt her pain, her shame, her rage.

Her hands were wet with tears. She huddled, sorry for herself, wrapping

266   KIM NEWMAN

what was left of her clothes about her. Detlef was stern, uncomforting. She didn't understand what she'd found inside her.

She had thought the Animus a blessing, but it turned out a curse.

The Animus slowly withdrew its tendrils from Eva, detaching itself at every point from her mind and body, cutting off her feelings, relinquishing its degree of control over her.

Only the purpose remained.

Still applauding, Genevieve latched onto her pride in Detlef. He had defeated something as invisible and beastly as Mr Chaida. She hoped she might have been able to do the same, but doubted herself.

'It's me,' she shouted, 'Gené.'

Detlef shaded his eyes and peered into the darkness. He could never see her like that. He did not have vampire eyes.

He was suddenly self-conscious.

'There's something wrong,' he tried to explain. 'We weren't responsible.'

Eva was sobbing quietly, forgotten, abandoned.

'I know. There's something here, something evil.'

She tried to sense another presence, but her scrying was gone. It was only an occasional thing.

'Gené,' he said. 'Where...'

'I'm in Box Seven. There's a secret passageway.'

She turned to check the open trapdoor, and saw something huge and wet squeezing through it.

The back of her hand covered her still-wide, still-sharp mouth, but she did not scream.

She was beyond screaming.

'It's all right,' the Trapdoor Daemon tried to say.

He knew how he must look.

The vampire dropped her hand, and her eyes shone red in the dark. She swallowed and straightened up. Trying not to be revulsed, she couldn't keep the pity out of her face.

'Bruno Malvoisin?'

'No,' he said, the word long and low from his flesh-concealed mouth. 'Not any more.'

She put out her sharp-nailed hand.

'I'm Genevieve,' she said. 'Genevieve Dieudonné.'

He nodded, his huge lump of a head wobbling. 'I know.'

'What's going on?' Detlef shouted from the stage.

'We have a visitor,' Genevieve said over her shoulder.

It was over with and he was out in the open. The Trapdoor Daemon felt a strange relief. There would be pain, but he didn't have to hide any more.

Poppa Fritz was snoring in his cubby-hole when Reinhardt went in through the stage-door.

His resolve was strong inside him.

'Eva!' he shouted.

He blundered through the backstage dark. In the afternoons, all the lights were down, as Guglielmo tried to save crowns on candlewax and lanternwick. But there was a light somewhere. Out on the stage, perhaps.

'Eva!'

'Up here,' said a voice, not Eva's. It was Detlef.

Reinhardt made an entrance, his heavy boots clumping on the stage. He recognized the tableau. It was Act Four, when the cossack found Chaida in Zhiekhill's study with the beaten and bruised Nita.

Detlef was out of his make-up, but he had blood on his face and his clothes were a mess. Eva was on her knees in her spot, face in her hands. It was hard not to follow the script and take his own place, where the girl would throw herself into his embrace, and plead for him to rescue her from the monster.

But this was not a rehearsal or a performance.

'Reinhardt,' Detlef said, 'send Poppa Fritz for a doctor. Eva needs help.'

'What happened?'

Detlef shook his head.

'Things are complicated just now.'

Reinhardt looked about him.

Eva was really distraught, which was outside his experience of her. Suddenly, her hands still to her face, she stood up, and ran to him. He held out his hands to ward her off, and she slipped between his arms, shoving her head close to his.

'What is it?'

He took her wrists, and prised her hands away from her face.

Genevieve's attention was torn. She was beginning to be able to make out the Trapdoor Daemon properly. He carried his own darkness with him, she realized, like a shroud. His head projected up above a ring of thick tentacles, and had to angle back, huge eyes swivelling forwards, so he could speak through the beak-like mouth in the centre of what must be his chest. The marks of his alteration were unmistakable, giving him some of the aspects of Tzeentch, the Changer of the Ways. His eyes were what she saw most, liquid and human.

But the drama on the stage was not played out. The Trapdoor Daemon had slithered forwards, all his appendages in motion as he pulled himself to the balcony of the box. They both looked down at the tableau.

Eva was with Reinhardt, and Detlef was looking at them, then out into the dark.

Experimentally, she touched the Trapdoor Daemon's wet hide. He shrank away, but relaxed, and let her fingers press his skin.

'Beautiful, huh?' he commented.

'I've seen worse.'

Suddenly, the tableau moved.

XIX

Reinhardt dropped Eva on the stage, and she sprawled at his feet like the stuffed dummies who stood in for corpses in the play. It was as if all the life had seeped out of her.

'She was... sick, I think,' Detlef explained.

Reinhardt was just beyond the island of light, but Detlef could see there was something strange about his face. He was wearing a mask.

'Reinhardt?'

The actor stepped into the light, and Detlef felt a hand of dread fall on his shoulder. Reinhardt seemed taller, broader, his bunched muscles straining his clothes. And his face was a terrible, calm blank, silverwhite and dead. He moved like an automaton, but slowly his motion became easier, more fluid, as if the rust in his joints were being oiled away.

'Play-actor,' Reinhardt said, his voice different.

Reinhardt looked around, head moving like a giant lizard's, and strode briefly into the dark. He returned with a background prop in his hand.

A war-axe from Chaida's collection of weapons.

'In the name of the Great Enchanter, Constant Drachenfels,' Reinhardt said, hefting the axe, 'you must...'

The axe jumped forwards, blade whistling.

'...die!'

The axe-edge slammed against Detlef's forehead, all Reinhardt's strength behind it.

He could hear Gené screaming.

The screech died in her throat as Detlef staggered under the blow. Reinhardt's axe was a ruin, its painted wooden blade crushed against Detlef's hard head. With a snarl of rage, the young actor slammed the heavy handle of the prop against the playwright's neck, knocking him out of the circle of light.

Genevieve was looking for a quick way out of Box Seven. The Trapdoor Daemon was thinking with her, and stretched out a tentacle to pull loose a curtain. There was a chandelier in the auditorium, fixed by a long chain that ran through strong eyehooks across the ceiling and down one wall so the chandelier could be lowered and lit. Malvoisin took hold of the chain, and twined the end of his tentacle around it.

Reinhardt was gone beyond humanity, white face impassive as he stumped towards Detlef on heavy feet.

The Trapdoor Daemon yanked the chandelier chain, and it came loose of its eyehooks. The chandelier was unsteady, dropping the stubs of last night's candles into the stalls as Malvoisin hauled on the chain. It was fixed to the ceiling by only the central hook, and plaster dust was powdering out from its mooring as the chandelier crowded up close, anchoring the chain.

Reinhardt had his hands on Detlef, and had lifted him up, ready for a throw.

'Quick,' the Trapdoor Daemon hissed, giving her the chain.

She was over the side like a sailor, and hurtling through the air, booted feet first. There was a whistle in her ears as her hair streamed out, and she swayed unsteadily as she tried to aim for Reinhardt's expanse of chest.

She heard herself shouting.

The Animus was settled immediately.

The host had been in an excited state when the attachment was made. His confused feelings for Eva were easy to convert into feelings against Detlef.

Detlef had always been in the younger actor's way, keeping him from the leading roles. Years of losing fights and fair maidens and applause to Detlef Sierck had bitten deep into the good humour and big heart of Reinhardt Jessner.

The axe had come apart in his hands, a pretend weapon with no real use, but Detlef was stunned.

Feeling the host's muscles pumping, the Animus lifted Detlef high, preparing to toss him forever from the stage, to break his back on the rows of chairs in the stalls.

A cannonball blow struck Reinhardt in the chest, and he staggered back, dropping Detlef.

The girl who had shot out of the dark on a chain rolled across the stage like an acrobat, and stood up. She had her teeth and claws out.

This was perfect. The Animus could achieve its purpose. Detlef and Genevieve were both here.

Detlef stood up. The Animus slammed Reinhardt's heavy elbow into his face, smashing his nose, knocking him back against the canvas wall of Dr Zhiekhill's laboratory. He shook his head, spreading blood around him like a dog drying itself, and tried to stand up.

The vampire came for him, and met a fist which sent even her reeling. Reinhardt had been strong, but with the Animus in his mind he was a superman.

Doors were opening in the auditorium, as people were alarmed by the noise. The company was arriving, and crowds were building up outside.

Genevieve scratched through his britches, drawing blood but doing no hurt.

The Animus brought up Reinhardt's knee against the vampire's chin, and shoved her across the stage.

Lights were streaming in.

The Animus came down hard on Genevieve, knee pinning her body. Reinhardt's hands went around her head.

Only silver or fire or a stake through the heart could truly kill a vampire. But having her head wrenched off wouldn't do her health any good.

The Animus twisted, feeling the vampire's strong neck muscles stretch, her bones draw apart. She had her overlapping teeth clenched but her lips drawn back. Her eyes were dots of fire.

Detlef was hammering on his shoulders, as pointlessly as a gnat might bother an ox.

The vampire's head would come off in a moment.

Detlef stepped back, giving the Animus the room to do his bloody business. Genevieve hissed through her teeth, and spat hate up at Reinhardt's mask.

'For the Great Enchanter,' the Animus said, 'Constant...'

Something huge and heavy fell on Reinhardt, ropy limbs twisting around his body, hauling him backwards.

XX

The Trapdoor Daemon had made his way across the ceiling, and dropped down onto the stage.

Reinhardt Jessner had gone mad. The way Eva Savinien had gone mad. Malvoisin did not understand, but he realized there was more to the story of *Dr Zhiekhill and Mr Chaida* than an old Kislevite fable. In a sense it was literally true. Something could bring out the Chaida in all men, and that something had afflicted Eva, and now Reinhardt.

He found uses for the limbs of his altered body, constricting Reinhardt's wrists to break his grip on Genevieve's neck. The vampire had shown him a moment of consideration and, for that, he owed her his loyalty.

Reinhardt left Genevieve and stood, turning around in the Trapdoor Daemon's grasp, chopping with his hands at the bases of his tentacles, thumping for the nerves.

The actor was strong, but his body was only human.

Out in the auditorium people were shouting.

A firebrand hurtled through the air, and landed nearby on the stage. Detlef was stamping it out, protesting.

'Look,' someone shouted. 'A monster.'

Yes, the Trapdoor Daemon thought, a monster. Help me fight the monster.

Reinhardt struggled furiously, cold like a machine, methodically trying to throw off Malvoisin.

'Kill the monster,' someone shouted.

A missile bounced off his hide, and Malvoisin realized who the shouters thought was the monster.

'Kill!'

Detlef was confused. Reinhardt had gone mad, and some creature of the depths was wrestling with him all over the stage.

He picked up Genevieve, and tried to get her to run. She was confused, but finally picked up her feet as they descended the steps into the auditorium.

There were actors there, and an officer of the watch, and strangers in from the street. Everyone was shouting. No one knew what was going on. Poppa Fritz was waving a lantern and shouting at the top of his voice.

Genevieve stumbled, but started pulling Detlef away from the stage, towards the exit. She wanted them to run.

Detlef looked back. Reinhardt wore the monster like a cloak now, but was free of its grip. With a flex of his shoulders, the actor shrugged the thing off, and threw it away. It landed with a wet thump, spreading out, and some people cheered.

Reinhardt walked forwards, and stepped off the stage, falling six feet but landing perfectly. He stood up straight, and kept walking, wading through bolted-to-the-floor seats as if the stalls were a wheatfield.

The people started quieting down as Reinhardt's legs crushed through solid wood and upholstery.

The watchman was in the way. Reinhardt smashed his chest with a sideswipe, and bloody foam came from his mouth and nose as he went down, coughing.

Gené was tugging him.

'It's after us,' she said, 'and it won't give up.'

Reinhardt had said something about Drachenfels.

'Is it him? Come back?'

Genevieve spat. 'No, he's in Hell. But he sent something back to fetch us there.'

'Ulric's teeth!'

Reinhardt tore the arm off a man, and tossed it aside, walking calmly through the fountain of blood. He was turned into a golem of force, unstoppable, single-minded, unreasoning, unmerciful.

Detlef and Genevieve ran into the foyer, and found a crowd pressing in. Ticket-holders mostly. The seeds of panic were sprouting. They had to fight forwards.

Reinhardt exploded through the double doors, and everyone started screaming at once. Windows were smashed out in the rush as the crowds tried to back away, and furniture was trampled underfoot.

Detlef and Genevieve were caught by the crowd, and pulled away. Reinhardt just fixed his cold eyes on them, and began killing his way towards them, breaking the backs and necks of the people in his way as if he were a poulterer processing chickens. The foul smells of death – blood, shit and fear – hung in the air.

They were out in the street now, and night was gathering. The crowd was running this way and that. Detlef collided with a matronly woman wearing a Moral Crusade sash and carrying a 'DOWN WITH DETLEF SIERCK' placard. She screamed at his bloody face and fainted. He picked up the placard, and held it like a weapon.

He heard a rattle of hooves and wheels. Some kind of help was coming. Gené still had his hand.

'This won't do any good,' she said. 'We've got to keep running.'

The Animus stood on the pavement, dead bodies all around.

The vampire and the play-actor were scurrying, but they wouldn't escape it.

A carriage got between it and its prey, and men in armour piled out, weapons ready. The Animus recognized the Imperial militia.

'By the order of the Emperor Karl-Franz,' began an officer. 'I demand–'

The Animus took off the officer's head, and squeezed it between flat hands until it burst like a pumpkin.

A subordinate gulped, and ordered an attack.

Crossbow bolts struck the Animus's head but it ignored them. Swords slashed its chest, cutting to the bone. It didn't care.

The vampire and the play-actor were still in its sight. They were scrabbling back into the theatre.

The Animus turned around.

'Fire!'

Pistol balls slammed into its body, making it stagger. It picked up the headless officer's heavy sabre.

Reinhardt Jessner had been a great swordsman.

Whirling the blade about it, lopping off everything that got in the way, it strode towards the Vargr Breughel Memorial Playhouse, intent on the attainment of its purpose.

A pistolier threw his weapon at the Animus, and it spanged off the flying blade. With a lunge, the Animus split the pistolier's neck, opening a gap under his chin. Drawing the sword out of the already-dead man, it passed the blade across the face of a Moral Crusade protester, making a blood-edged crease of his eyes and the bridge of his nose.

Detlef Sierck was closing the doors of the theatre, drawing the nightbolts. The Animus punched two holes in the doors, where the bolts were, and then kicked its way back into the foyer.

It stepped over the earlier dead.

The prey were not in sight. It fixed its eyes on one side of the room, and then raked its vision across to the other. It was looking for the slightest trace of the fleeing couple.

A trapdoor on the floor was slightly askew, the corner of a carpet flapped around it. Disguised as a flagstone, it would normally not have been noticeable.

It bent down, and pulled up the trapdoor, wrenching it off its hinges.

A gallon bottle, wrapped in rush matting, was lobbed from one side of the foyer, and smashed against its chest, stabbing the skin with tiny shards of glass. A thick, sweet liquid sloshed all over it, soaking the tatters of its clothes, clogging in its hair and beard.

A thin, elderly man was the culprit.

From Reinhardt's memory, the Animus recognized Guglielmo Pentangeli.

The Tilean business manager had a lamp in his hands, a naked flame with the glass off it.

'Brandy?' he asked.

Guglielmo tossed the lamp at the Animus.

There was an explosion, and the Animus was in the middle of a man-shaped statue of flame.

XXI

As people kicked him with heavy boots, shouting, 'Death to the monster,' Malvoisin remembered why he'd spent all these years in his catacombs. Reaching across the stage, the Trapdoor Daemon hauled itself away from his persecutors, shrinking from the light, shrieking through his beak.

He knew where the nearest trapdoor was, and slid through it, feeling a burst of relief as the wood slammed behind him, cutting him off from the chaos out in the upperworld.

The slide took him down towards the waters.

He needed to get his hide wet and he needed to sleep. Here in the dark – in his dark – there was peace.

But he could hear footsteps. And shouts. And fire.

Even here, they came for him. There'd be no peace now, ever.

Genevieve kept running, Detlef at her heels. There were miles of tunnels down here. The thing in Reinhardt might not be able to follow them. They were in one of the main passageways, heading down towards the Trapdoor Daemon's domain. When they found a bolt-hole, they would rest, and think out what to do.

She should have died thirty years ago, on her first wander in the fortress of Drachenfels. That would have saved a lot of trouble, a lot of bloodshed.

Detlef was babbling, but she didn't have time to listen. She could feel a great deal of heat. There was a fire down here. A fire that was growing closer.

A curtain fell in front of them, and she knocked it aside. It was a dusty cobweb, and came apart, leaving filthy scraggles of sticky stuff on her face and clothes. Small animals and large insects scuttled around their feet.

The fire was behind them, back near the trapdoor they'd come through.

She was back to being an animal again, pure instinct and bloodlust, running from a bigger cat, crushing smaller things underfoot. That was her Mr Chaida, the cruel heart beating inside, ever ready to take over.

They slammed into a wall. Looking round, she realized they were in a magazine. A rack on one wall was loaded with swords and daggers, all angled dangerously outward. They were lucky not to have run straight into them.

She shouldn't have forgotten there were likely to be traps throughout the labyrinth.

'In the floor,' Detlef said, indicating a manhole cover. She was on her knees, tugging at a ring. They heard footsteps, and she pulled harder. The ring came off, with a screech of protest.

'It's bolted from the underside.'

'There must be a trick.'

The footsteps were huge, thumping the ground like giant fists. The tunnels shook. She could smell smoke, and her eyes were watering. In the dark, distant flame flickered.

'It's iron,' she said. 'It leads into the sewers.'

'So? We're in the shit already.'

She shrugged and made awls of her fingers, piercing the metal with agonising slowness. She made fists, and pulled. Pain came alive in her shoulders and elbows.

A walking furnace squeezed into the chamber. A walking furnace with Reinhardt Jessner's face.

Genevieve pulled and heard the bolts breaking. The manhole burst free, and she choked on a gasp of truly foul air. Then, they were all in the middle of an explosion.

Detlef realized that pulling the manhole had let out a cloud of sewer gas. He felt a liquid heat on his face – beard and eyebrows singeing – and was thrown against a hard wall. Even with his eyes screwed shut, the light was brighter than the sun.

He knew something was broken inside him.

Trying to stand up, he realized his left leg wasn't working. He opened his eyes, and saw the explosion had blown itself out. Scraps of cobwebs and detritus were burning, but most of the fire was gone.

Reinhardt had been smashed against a rack of old weapons. His body was blackened with soot and burns, but bright blades shone where they pierced him. Three swordblades stood out of his chest, points glinting. He'd been cooked alive, and now he was spitted. The stench of burned human meat was bitter in Detlef's mouth and nostrils.

Apart from anything else, Reinhardt's head hung wrongly, his neck broken.

Genevieve was on her feet. Her face was sooty, and her clothes were ruined. But she was all right. She was in a better shape than him.

'It's gone,' she said.

She took him in her arms, and checked his wounds. When she touched his knee, pain shot through him.

'How... bad?'

She shook her head.

'I don't know. I think it's just a clean break.'

'Sigmar's holy hammer.'

'You can say that again.'

He touched her face, wiping the black grease away from her girl's skin. Her teeth were receding, and the red spark in her irises was dying.

'It's all right,' she said.

Behind her, Reinhardt Jessner's eyes opened wide in his black face, and he lurched forwards, pulling the rack of swords that pierced him away from the wall.

He roared, and Genevieve hugged Detlef hopelessly.

If Reinhardt fell on them, they'd be transfixed many times. All three would die down here.

XXII

Malvoisin launched himself at Reinhardt for the second time, bearing him away from Detlef and Genevieve, crashing him against a smoke-smeared wall. Reinhardt broke in several places, and swords tore through his flesh, revealing angry red gashes in his burned-black body.

He had his tentacles around the madman, and was squeezing. The body was already a corpse, but it clung to life. Malvoisin squeezed desperately, using his altered body as he'd never done before. He had grown strong in his lair, he realized. He'd wasted himself loitering in the depths of his own dark.

In the sea, he might have had a chance.

Reinhardt's face came off, and stuck to his own.

The Animus left its ruined host, and latched onto Bruno Malvoisin, burrowing into his altered body, seeking his still-human brain. He must have a core which could be soured, turned against the Animus's prey. A core of bitterness, self-hate, misery.

This would be the final, and most powerful host.

It rose from Reinhardt's body, and stretched out its tentacles, reaching for Genevieve.

The vampire girl stood, wide-eyed. 'Malvoisin?'

The Animus was about to tell her 'no.' But the Trapdoor Daemon said, 'Yes, I'm still here.'

Angry, the Animus prepared for its final, fatal blows.

The monster came for them, and Detlef offered up his final prayers. He thought of all the parts he'd never take, the plays he'd never right, the actresses he'd never kiss...

Tentacles slipped around his broken leg, and latched onto his burned clothes, creeping up his body. Genevieve was entwined too. The Trapdoor Daemon was all around them.

In the centre of its head was a blank white face.

Then the monster froze like an ice statue.

Genevieve gasped, unwanted red tears on her cheeks.

She reached for the mask, but it seemed to elude her fingers, sinking into Malvoisin's hide as if it were disappearing under the surface of a still pond.

The mask was swallowed.

Inside his mind, Malvoisin wrestled the Animus, swallowing the creature of Drachenfels at a gulp.

It was hot inside, and he knew he would not last.

'Salli,' he said, remembering...

He had been altered by warpstone, but he had never truly been the Trapdoor Daemon. That was just a theatre superst-ition. Where it counted, he'd always been Bruno Malvoisin.

He had changed as much as he was going to in his lifetime.

And the Animus wasn't going to change him more.

The Animus didn't even regret its failure as it died. It was a tool that had been broken. That was all.

Malvoisin slumped, the fire burning inside him.

A white tunnel opened in the dark, and a figure appeared. It was Salli Spaak, not old and bent as she'd been when she died, but young again, ripe and beckoning.

'Bruno,' she purred, 'it was always you I loved, always you...'

The white tunnel grew and grew until it was all he saw.

Genevieve left Detlef and crawled over to Malvoisin. He was shaking, but he was dead. The thing had gone, forever.

Something about him was changed. The bulk of his body was still the sea creature he had become, but his head was shrunken, whiter. Where the mask-thing had touched was a face. It must have been his original face. It was in repose.

The mask was like Dr Zhiekhill's potion. It brought out what was inside people, buried in their deeps. In Eva and Reinhardt, it had brought out cruelty, viciousness, evil. In Bruno Malvoisin, none of those things had mattered, and it had only brought out the goodness and beauty he'd left behind.

'Is it dead?' Detlef asked.

'Yes,' she said. 'He is.'

'Blessings of Sigmar,' he breathed, not understanding.

She knew now what she must do. It was the only thing that could save the both of them. Crawling over to him, she made sure he was comfortable and in no immediate danger.

'What was it?'

'A man. Malvoisin.'

'I thought so.'

She stroked the burned stubble of his scalp.

'I suppose we'll have to take the play off... for a while.'

She tried to find the strength.

'Detlef,' she said. 'I'm leaving...'

He knew at once what she meant, but still had to prod her. 'Leaving? Leaving me?'

She nodded. 'And this city.'

He was quiet, eyes alive in his blackened face.

'We're no good to each other. When we're together, this is what happens...'

'Gené, I love you.'

'And I love you,' she said, a thick tear brushing the corner of her mouth. 'But I can't be with you.'

She licked away her tear, relishing the salt tang of her own blood.

'We're like Drachenfels's thing, or Dr Zhiekhill's potion, bringing out the worst in each other. Without me, you won't be obsessed with morbid things. Maybe you'll be a better writer, without me to anchor you in darkness.'

She was nearly sobbing. Usually, she only felt this way when a lover died, old and decrepit while she remained unaged, their youth flown in a mayfly moment, leaving her behind.

'We always knew it couldn't last.'

'Gené...'

'I'm sorry if it hurts, Detlef.'

She kissed him, and left the chamber. There must be a way out of this sewer.

XXIII

In the dark with his hurts and a dead thing that had been a man, Detlef overcame his urge to cry.

He was a genius, not a poltroon. His love would not die. Nothing he could do would stifle that. He would end up expending millions of words on it, and still never be able to snuff it out. His sonnet cycle, *To My Unchanging Lady*, was not complete, and this parting would inspire the third group of poems. It would spur him perhaps to his greatest work.

The smell was terrible. It was the smell of death. The familiar smell of death. Detlef felt a kinship with the dead playwright.

'Bruno,' he said, 'I'll revive all your plays. You've earned that much of me. Your name will live again. I swear it.'

The dead thing didn't answer, but he'd not expected him to.

'Of course, I might make some revisions, bring your work up to date just a little...'

Genevieve was gone, and she would never come back. The loss was worse than any wound he'd sustained.

He tried to think of something – anything – that would make the hurt go away, would make it better.

Finally, he spoke again, 'Bruno, I'm reminded of something Poppa Fritz told me. It's a story about a young actor visiting Tarradasch himself, when he was producing his own plays in Altdorf, running the old Beloved of Ulric theatre across the road, although I've also heard it about a young minstrel visiting the great Orfeo...'

His breathing was stronger now, and the pain in his leg was going away. Soon, they'd come for him. Gené would send people back for him. Guglielmo wouldn't let him lie broken for long.

'Anyway, Bruno, here's the story. A young actor from the country comes to the big city in search of fame and fortune on the stage. He can sing, he can dance, he can juggle, and he was a star in his university players' company. The young blood gains an audition with Tarradasch, and the great man is quite impressed. But not impressed enough to offer a place in his company. "You're good," Tarradasch says, "you've got a lot of talent, you've got the looks of a leading man, you've got the strength of an acrobat, and you've the grace of a dancer. You've learned your audition pieces very prettily. But there's one thing you haven't got. You haven't got experience. You're not yet eighteen, and you know nothing of life. You've not loved, you've not lived. Before you can be a great player, and not just a talented mannequin, you must go out and live life to the full. Come back to me in six months, and tell me how you've fared."'

Detlef's face was wet with tears, but his trained voice didn't break.

'So, Bruno, the lad leaves the theatre, Tarradasch's advice going round and round in his head. Six months later, he comes back, and he has a new story. "You were so right, master," he tells the great man, "I've been out there in the city, living for myself, experiencing everything. I've met this girl and she's shown me things about myself I could never have imagined. This has never happened before. We're in love, and everything in my life dances like blossom on a spring breeze."'

Detlef looked at the slumped bulk of the man who'd been the Trap-door Daemon.

'"That's perfect," Tarradasch says, "now if only she would leave you..."'

Part Two

The Cold Stark House

I

Lying in his bed, he heard music from far away. To him, the music seemed to fill the endless rooms and passageways of Udolpho like a sweet-scented but poisonous gas, drifting with invisible malevolence through the towers and turrets, suites and stables, garrets and gables of the immense, rambling, mostly derelict estate. Down in the great hall, the harpsichord was being played, not well but with a sorcerer's enthusiasm. Christabel, dark daughter of Ravaglioli and Flaminea, with her supple hands and sinister smile, was practising. It was a dramatic piece, expressing violent emotions.

Melmoth Udolpho understood violent emotions. Thanks to Dr Valdemar's potions and infusions, he was a prisoner in his own shrunken body, his brain a spark of life in an already rotting corpse. But he still had violent emotions.

He thought again of his will. Poor Genevieve must come out, or she would hold up the succession forever. She was fresh now, but – like him – she would live long, too long. Pintaldi must be recognized as Melmoth's grandchild, in order to pass the fortune on to his current favourites, the twins. Young Melmoth was the purest Udolpho of the lot of them, and Flora would make a grand consort for him when he grew up and took his position in the world. Only the long-gone Montoni, whose bastard Pintaldi claimed to be, could possibly have matched him.

A few nights ago, Young Melmoth and Flora had surprised Mira, one of the maids, and tied her up. They had placed a mouse on her stomach, and then clapped a cup over the animal, fixing it in place with a scarf. After an hour, the mouse had got hungry, and tried to eat the soft floor of its cell. Young Melmoth thought that a fine experiment, and had kissed Flora on the lips to celebrate its success. They were of Montoni's line, undoubtedly; although Ulric alone knew what their mother had been.

The will must reflect the purity of Udolpho blood. Several times in past centuries, brothers had married sisters, cousins married cousins, simply to keep the blood pure.

Old Melmoth was nearly blind, but he hadn't left his bed in perhaps thirty years and didn't need his sight. He knew where the curtains hung around him, and where his tray was placed each day.

He could no longer taste food, and his sense of smell was also completely gone. He couldn't lift his limbs more than an inch or two and only then with great effort, or even raise his head from its deeply-grooved pillow. But he could still hear. If anything, his hearing was sharper than it had been when he was younger.

He heard everything that went on within the walls of Udolpho.

In the ruined west wing, where the roofs were gone and the exquisite mosaic floors designed by his mad great-uncle Gesualdo were open to the elements, wolves sometimes came to root around. In the stables, flies still buzzed around the neglected and dying horses. In the cellars, rats scratched against old oak doors, wriggling between the bones of forgotten prisoners. And, in her rooms, poor Mathilda, her swollen head almost insupportable, sometimes raged against her fate, smashing the furniture and attacking the servants with an energy Old Melmoth could only envy. There must be provision in the will for Mathilda. So long as she remained human, she would be a beneficiary.

In the darkness that was forever before his face, a light appeared. It was small at first, but it grew. The light was blue and sickly, and there was a face in it. A familiar face. A long nose, and sunken hollows where eyes had been.

Old Melmoth recognized the features of his eldest son. 'Montoni,' he gasped, his papery throat spitting out the name like a hairball. The rightful heir to the House of Udolpho, vanished into stormy night sixty years earlier, looked down at the ruin of his father, and his empty eye-sockets filled with pity.

Old Melmoth's face cracked as he smiled. His gums hurt. Not yet. He wasn't ready yet. He clung to his bedclothes as he clung to life. There was more to be done, more to be changed. He was not ready to die.

II

Prince Kloszowski prayed to gods in which he no longer professed to believe that none of his travelling companions had died of the Yellow Ague. He guessed most of them had succumbed to simple malnutrition or the ministrations of an overenthusiastic torturer, but one of Marino Zeluco's permanent guests might have carried disease enough to provide a swift escape of the duce's dungeons. As the cart trundled along the rough road towards the marshes, he felt several of the bodies leaking onto him, and clamped his hand tighter over his mouth and nostrils. This close, he could taste the stench of the corpses. Breathing was becoming a problem. Naturally, Kloszowski was at the bottom of the pile, and the press of bodies was becoming insupportable. He could no longer feel his legs and feet, and his elbows burned every time he tried to move his arms. The darkness was hot, and getting hotter with every uncomfortable mile.

The duce had told him the only way out of the dungeons of Zeluco was in a corpse-cart, and here he was proving the parasite right. Unless the ordeal were to end soon, Kloszowski would sadly not be alive to benefit from the irony. His mother, the Dowager Princess, wouldn't have approved of his current situation. But his mother hadn't approved of any of his situations since early infancy, so that was hardly a novelty. He needed to cough but the weight on his back was too much. He could only choke feebly, grinding thinly-fleshed ribs against the rough wooden planks of the cart.

Of all his daring escapes, this was the least enjoyable. Through the cracks between the planks, he sucked cold, clean air, and occasionally caught glimpses of reflected light from puddles in the road. The novice of Morr, comfortable on his padded driver's seat, was humming a gloomy melody to himself as he transported human waste to the marsh that served the dungeons as a markerless graveyard. There were things in the marsh the Zelucos liked to keep well-fed, in the hope of dissuading them from forsaking watery homes in search of live meat. Tileans were like that, keener to come to an accommodation with the creatures of Chaos than on crusading against the filthy monstrosities.

Zeluco had too cosy a life extorting from the peasants to bother much with good works. He was a typical parasite, the fruit of ten generations of inbreeding, oppression and perfumed privilege. Come the revolution, Kloszowski swore, things would be different...

The weather was unpredictable in this benighted land where marsh met forest, and Kloszowski had several times heard the patter of rain on the canvas cart-cover. He was sure the occasional rumble of thunder stirred in with the steady creaking of cartwheels. This was flash-flood country. Most of the roads were little better than ill-maintained causeways.

Kloszowski rebuked himself again. His predicament was, as usual, his own fault. Along the road to revolution, there were always distractions, and too often he let himself be tempted. He had first preached the cause to Donna Isabella Zeluco, impressing upon her, between more conventional attentions, the justice of his struggle. She had seemed convinced the rule of the aristocracy was an obscenity that should be wiped, through violent revolution, from the face of the world. However, it proved unwise to proceed from his philosophical and amorous conquest of the duce's wife to pursue, in rapid succession, both of his daughters, Olympia and Julietta. The girls had been eager to learn of the revolution and of the casting-off of chains, especially when Kloszowski had demonstrated that the outmoded and hypocritical chastity fostered by their parents' class would be swept away along with any notions of rank and title. But as the sisters' enthusiasm rose, with enormously satisfying results, so that of their mother abated.

The cart bumped over a stone in the road and someone's protruding bone stabbed into his side. He definitely heard thunder. The superstitious said thunderclaps were tokens of the anger of Ulric, god of battle, wolves and winter. Kloszowski, who knew gods were fictions invented by the parasite clergy to excuse their position over the toiling masses, prayed to Ulric for delivery from the bottom of this corpse-pile. A flash of lightning lit up the crack beneath his eye, and he saw the mud of the road, a tuft of grass white in the instant's lightburst. Very close, thunder drum-rolled again. There must be a storm coming.

One night, emerging in disarray from a tryst with one or other of the girls, he'd found himself seized by men-at-arms and hauled up before the duce for a lengthy lecture on the rights and duties of inherited wealth. Donna Isabella, her conversion forgotten, stood dutifully beside her gross and wealthy husband, nodding at every point as if his speech were not the self-interested prattle of an ape-brained idiot. After Zeluco had concluded his address, failing to give Kloszowski adequate opportunity to refute his infantile arguments through reasoned debate, he had ordered that the revolutionist be confined to the depths of the dungeons of Zeluco for the remainder of his life. The duce had introduced the prisoner to Tancredi, a hooded minion reputed to be the most exquisitely skilled torturer in all Tilea, and assured him, Kloszowski, that their acquaintance would deepen into a full and mutually entertaining relationship that would provide him, Zeluco, with many enjoyable hours. The duce was looking forwards to screams of agony, retractions of deeply-held political convictions and heart-rending, though futile, apologies, offers of restitution and pleas for mercy.

The bone broke his skin and cut deeper. The pain was good. It made Kloszowski aware he could still feel. His blood trickled and clogged under him. The fog that had been creeping into his brain dissipated. The cart was speeding up, as the novice tried to get his unpleasant task over with before the storm broke.

Were it not for the warmth, generosity and sympathy of Phoebe, the jailer's comely and impressionable daughter, Kloszowski would be in the dungeon still, stapled to the wall, waiting for Tancredi to heat up his branding irons, dust off his knuckle-cracking screws, and start leafing through anatomies for inspiration.

He might yet fail in this escape, if the breath were crushed out of him by the other corpses. He fought to draw in a double lungful of air, and held it inside as long as he could, exhaling in a steady, agonising, stream. Then, he fought for the next breath. Fires of pain were burning up and down his back. He could feel his feet now, as if they were being pierced by a thousand tiny knives. He tried to move, to shift the weight of the dead from his spine.

He vowed, if he survived, to write *The Epic of Phoebe*, which would celebrate the jailer's daughter as a heroine of the revolution, worthy of comparison with the martyred Ulrike Blumenschein. But he recalled that he had frequently vowed to write epics, and invariably lost impetus after fewer than a score of pages had been filled. As a poet, he was more successful with more concise pieces, like the six stanzas of his well-remembered *The Ashes of Shame*. He tried to frame the first canto of *The Ballad of Phoebe*, planning a mere dozen or so verses. Nothing much came of it, and he wondered whether *Phoebe: A Sonnet* would suffice to repay his debt of gratitude.

The cart was slowing. Kloszowski wondered what was bothering the novice.

These were bad days for the revolution. In the dungeons, he realized he had not written a word of poetry since his flight from Altdorf, shortly after the Great Fog Riots. Once, verse had spewed from his mind like liquor from a stabbed wineskin, carrying his passion to those who heard him recite or read his pamphlets, stirring up suppressed dissent wherever it reached. Now, there was rarely anything. The revolutionist leaders were scattered, imprisoned or dead, but the cause lived on. The fire might be dwindled to a flame, but so long as there was breath in him, he would fan that flame, confident that it would eventually burn away the loathed worldwide conspiracy of titled thieves and murderers.

The cart halted, and Prince Kloszowski heard voices.

He could speak the elegant Tilean of the parasitical classes, the dowager having ensured his complete education, but he found it hard to follow the coarser argot of the oppressed masses. That had proved an embarrassment during his stay in Miragliano, where he had hoped to seed a revolt but found himself mainly ignored by potential revolutionists unable to understand his courtly speech. In the end, he had left the city when the Yellow Ague began to spread, and people started frothing yolky dribble in the streets. Tilea had more diseases going round than there were ticks on a waterfront dog.

Three different voices were engaged in a spirited conversation. One was the novice of Morr, the others men he had encountered on the road. The men were on foot and the cart was being drawn by two adequate horses from the duce's stables. The men obviously saw the inequity as an injustice, and were arguing that it should be rectified at once. Any other time, Kloszowski would have supported their just cause, but if this trip were extended any further, there was quite a chance that his absence from the dungeons of Zeluco would be noted, and a cadre of men-at-arms sent in pursuit.

The duce was not one to forgive a man who had, he alleged, wronged his wife and daughters, let alone spread sedition throughout his estates, suggesting his tenant farmers be allowed to retain the greater part of their produce for themselves rather than turning over nine-tenths to the castle granaries. And Donna Isabella was unlikely to look favourably upon a lover who had, she claimed, deserted him in favour of greener olives, no matter how much he had told her that fidelity was merely another of the chains society used to confine the true revolutionist into a dungeon of conformity.

The novice of Morr was insistent. He would not give up the horses, and be stranded on an open road with a cartload of fast-spoiling bodies.

Suddenly, the novice changed his mind. There were other voices. Other men, not on foot, had come out of a copse at the side of the road, and were insisting the novice turn over the duce's horses to their comrades, whose own mounts had been killed. There were voices all around and Kloszowski heard horses snorting as they drew near. The cart was surrounded. One of the horsemen spoke surprisingly well, addressing the novice in cultivated Old Worlder. He claimed his men had been unhorsed during a bloody battle with a band of foul skaven, the ratmen who were such a problem in the Blighted Marshes, and that the novice should be proud to help out such heroes.

The novice at least pretended to believe the man, and the horses were unharnessed. The foot-weary travellers strapped their saddles to new mounts, and the whole band rode off, hooves thumping against the soggy road.

'Banditti,' spat the novice when the party was out of earshot.

Kloszowski wondered if his back had snapped under the strain. If he tried to stand up, would he find his bones turned to knives, carving inside his flesh like Tancredi's white-hot skewers. Certainly, the pain was spreading.

The cart wasn't going any further. Thunder sounded again.

He moved his arms, testing their strength, hoping his spell in the dungeons had not sapped him too much. Then, he pressed against the bottom of the cart, pushing his back upwards. It was an agony, but he felt bodies parting as he fought his way up through the pile. His head pushed against the canvas sheet that had been tethered over the corpses. It was leashed tight, but the fabric was old and rotten. Making a fist, he punched upwards, and felt the material give. He stood up, the canvas

tearing as he forced his way through the hole he had made. There was
a sigh of escaping corpse-gas, which fast dispersed, leaving only a vile
taste in the back of his throat.

It was evening, night not quite fallen. In early spring, the swamp
insects were already active, although not the murderous nuisance they
would be at the height of summer.

He breathed clean air, and stretched out his arms in triumph. He was
not broken inside.

The novice, a very young man with his hood down around his shoulders, screamed and fainted dead away, slumping in the road.

Kloszowski laughed. He could imagine what he looked like, exploding from among the dead.

The sky was thick with irritated clouds, and neither moon was visible. The last of the sunset spilled blood on the horizon, and scattered
orange across the marshlands to the south. A light rainfall began, speck-
ling Kloszowski's shirt. After the heat and the grime, it was pleasant,
and he looked up at the sky, taking the rain on his face, feeling the
water run down into his beard. It began seriously raining, and he looked
down, shaking his head. The rain was purer water than he had tasted
in weeks, but it felt like just-melted chips of ice, freezing him to the
bone in a minute.

The poet-revolutionist clambered down from the cart, wondering where
he was and what he should do next.

To the south were the Blighted Marshes, currently agitated by the down-
pour of pebble-sized drops. To the north was a thin, scrubby forest and
a thick mountain range that ran along the Bretonnian border. Neither
direction was particularly inviting, but he'd heard especially vile stories
about the marshes. It was sound sense to stay away from anything that
announced itself on the map as being blighted.

In the distance, he heard horsemen. Coming this way. They would be
in pursuit of the banditti, but they wouldn't be averse to recapturing an
escaped prisoner. His decision was made for him.

III

The library of Udolpho was one of the largest privately-owned collections in the Old World. And the most neglected. Genevieve stepped into the huge central gallery, and held up her lantern. She stood on an island of light in an ocean of shadows.

Where were Ravaglioli and Pintaldi?

There was dust thick on the floor, recently disturbed. Ravaglioli and Pintaldi were in the book-walled labyrinth somewhere. Genevieve paused, and tried to listen. Her ears were abnormally sensitive. Ravaglioli often said there was something strange about her.

She could hear the rainwater blowing against the five thirty foot high windows at the end of the gallery. She knew there was going to be a daemon of a storm. Often, storms raged around Udolpho, besieging the mountain fastness as surely as a hostile army. When the rains fell thick, the passes became gushing culverts, and there was no leaving the estate.

Somewhere in the library, a wind blew through a hole in the walls, producing a strange, flutelike keening. It was tuneless, but fascinating. Vathek claimed the cries were those of the Spectre Bride, murdered four centuries previously by her jealous brother-lover on the eve of her wedding to Melmoth Udolpho's great-great-grandfather Smarra. Genevieve believed few of Vathek's ghost stories. According to the family lawyer, every stone of Udolpho, every square foot of the estate, was triply haunted by the ghost of some ancient murdered innocent. If he were to be taken on trust, the estates would still be knee-deep in blood.

Blood. The thought of blood made Genevieve's heart race. Her mouth was dry. She'd been off her food lately. She imagined nearly-raw beef, bleeding in a tureen.

She was walled in by ceiling-high cases, weighted down with more books than were imaginable. Most of the volumes had been undisturbed for centuries. Vathek was always rooting around in the library, searching for some long-lost deed or long-forgotten ghost story. The cases were the walls of a maze no one could completely map. There was no order, no filing system. Trying to find a particular book would be as futile as trying to find a particular leaf in the Forest of Loren.

'Uncle Guido!' she shouted, tiny voice bouncing between bookcases. 'Signor Pintaldi?'

Her ears picked up the clatter of sword on sword. She had found the eternal duellists. A cloud of dust descended around her. She held her breath. Between the tinkling clashes, she heard the grunts of men locked in combat.

'Uncle Guido?'

She held up her lantern and looked towards the ceiling. The cases were equipped with ladders to provide access to the upper shelves, and there were walkways strung between them, twenty feet above the flagstone floor.

There were lights above, and shadows struggled around her. She could see the duellists now, clinging to the bookcases, lashing out with their blades.

Guido Ravaglioli, her mother's brother-in-law, was hanging by one arm from a ladder, leaning into the aisle. Genevieve saw his bristle beard above his tight white ruff, and the white splits in his doublet where Pintaldi's swordpoint had parted the material. Pintaldi, who claimed to be the illegitimate offspring of Old Melmoth's vanished son Montoni, was younger and stronger, leaping from case to case with spiderlike dexterity, but her uncle was the more skilled blademan. They were evenly matched, and their duels usually resulted in a tie.

Very rarely, one would kill the other. No one could remember what their initial argument had been.

Genevieve called to the duellists, begging them to stop. Sometimes, she felt her only position in Udolpho was as family peacemaker.

Ravaglioli hurled an armload of heavy books at his unacknowledged cousin-by-marriage. Pintaldi swatted them out of the way, and they fell, spines breaking, to the floor. Genevieve had to step back. Ravaglioli thrust, and his swordpoint jabbed into Pintaldi's shoulder, drawing blood. Pintaldi slashed back, scribing a line across Ravaglioli's forehead, but he was badly thrown by the wound and his hand couldn't grip the sword properly.

'Uncle, stop it!'

There were too many duels in Udolpho. The family was too close to get along. And with Old Melmoth still on his deathbed, nobody could bear to leave for fear they'd be cut out of the will.

The fortune, she understood, had been founded by Smarra Udolpho's father, a plunder-happy pirate who had ravaged the coast with his galleass, the *Black Cygnet*. Down through the centuries, the money had been compounded by a wide variety of brigandry, honest endeavour and arranged marriages. There was enough for everyone but everyone wanted more than enough. And, despite the visible fortune, there were forever rumours that the Black Cygnet had concealed the greater part of his treasure in a secret location about the estate, prompting many persistent but fruitless searches for buried gold.

At least, this was what she understood. Details were often hazy. Sometimes, she was unsure even of who she was. She remembered only Udolpho, one day much like the last. But she did not remember ever being younger than her sixteen summers. Life in this house was unchanging, and sometimes she wondered if she had lived here all her life or merely for a moment. Could this be a dream? Dreamed by some other Genevieve, intruding into an entirely different life, forgotten entirely when the dreamer was awake?

Pintaldi staggered across a walkway. Its ropes strained, and Ravaglioli hacked through the support ties, laughing madly.

Her possible second cousin fell to his knees. He was bleeding badly, the red standing out against the white of his open-necked shirt. Pintaldi had finely-trimmed moustaches and, understandably, a face lined with old sword scars.

Shouting with triumph, Ravaglioli used his sword like an axe, parting another thick rope.

The walkway fell apart, wooden planks tumbling to the floor, one single rope remaining. Pintaldi fell, his unwounded arm bent around the rope, and dangled in mid-air. He cried out. His sword plunged down, and stabbed into a fallen book.

Ravaglioli was sagging against one of the shelves, squeezed against a row of huge, thick books. He didn't look triumphant now. There was blood in his eyes.

Pintaldi tried to get a firmer hold on the rope, reaching up with his hurt arm. But his fingers wouldn't make a gripping fist. Her uncle wiped his face off, and made the last cut, parting the rope. Genevieve gasped. Pintaldi swung heavily into the bookcase, bones breaking, and fell badly before her. His head was at an unhealthy angle to his body.

There was nothing she could do but wait.

Wearily, Ravaglioli descended from his perch. He'd been hurt himself during the duel, and was bleeding into his clothes. He couldn't get up the energy to hawk enough phlegm to spit on his slain opponent.

Genevieve looked at him, not needing to restate her complaint. He already knew this family feuding was pointless, but couldn't stop fighting any more than she could stop peacemaking. That was the way of Udolpho.

Why did the blood seeping from his shallow headwound excite her so? She could smell it, taste it. It glistened as it trickled. She felt a thirst she didn't understand.

A forked spear of lightning struck the ground beyond the windows, filling the library with a painful flash. The thunder sounded instantly, shaking the whole edifice of Udolpho.

She supported Ravaglioli, helping him to a couch, and sitting him down. He would need sleep.

Later, she would have to give a full report to Vathek, and he would take it up with Old Melmoth. The will, a much-discussed secret between the patriarch and his lawyer, might have to be altered. The will, the main topic of conversation in the halls of Udolpho, was always being altered, unknown clauses being added, taken out, restored, substituted, reworded or rethought. Nobody but Melmoth and Vathek knew what was in the will, but everyone thought they could guess...

She walked to the window, and looked out into the night. The library was the heart of the southern wing of Udolpho, a mansion built like a vast cross on its plateau, and from its windows there was a view of the slopes which descended towards the plains. When the weather was clear, admittedly a rare occasion, you could see as far as Miragliano and the sea. Now there was only a spectacular cloudscape, and a fascinating pattern of rain splatters. One of the sickly trees by the ruined Chapel of Manaan had been struck by the lightning blast, and was burning like a lamp, a tattered flame amid the dark, fighting lashing sheets of rainwater. Its flickering light made the stones of the chapel seem to dance, animated, Vathek would have claimed, by the souls of the victims Smarra's pirate father had sent to the bottom of the Tilean sea.

A hand fell on her shoulder, and she was spun around.

'Fire,' Pintaldi said through his twisted throat. 'Pretty fire...'

Pintaldi had a fascination with fire. It often got him into trouble. His head still hung at the wrong angle, and his shoulder was caked with dried blood.

'Fire...'

Gently, with strong hands, she took his head and shifted it, setting it properly on his neck. He stood up straight, and experimented with nods. He was put back together again. Pintaldi did not thank her. His eyes were fixed on the burning tree. There were flecks of foam on the ends of his moustache. She turned away from his gaze, and watched with him as the fire was crushed by the storm.

'It's like a struggling soul,' Pintaldi said, 'at the mercy of the gods.'

The flames were wiped off the tree, and it stood, steaming, its branches twisted black and dead.

'Its defeat is inevitable, but while it burns, it burns bright. That should be a lesson for us.'

Pintaldi kissed her, the taste of his blood biting into her tongue, and then staggered back, breaking the contact. Sometimes, he was her lover. Sometimes, her sworn enemy. It was hard to keep track. The variations had something to do with the will, she was sure.

He was gone. Beyond the window, the storm attacked ferociously, tearing at the stones of Udolpho. The house was colder than ice tonight.

IV

The novice's robe was heavy with chilled water, and Kloszowski missed the warmth and security of his heap of dead people. He was lost in the forests. By the ache in his legs and knees, he could tell he'd been climbing upwards. The ground beneath was sloping more sharply, water running in hasty rivulets around his feet. If there were men-at-arms out searching for him, he couldn't hear them over the din of the weather. He would have pitied anyone trying to get through this storm on horseback in armour, and guessed Zeluco's men would have given up by now. Not that that was much consolation.

Lightning struck, imprinting the black and white image of the forests on his eyes. The trees around here were all twisted and tangled, as if lumps of warpstone in the earth, seeds of Chaos sprouting amid the other roots, were turning the forestry into a nightmare distortion. With each javelin of lightning, certain trees seemed to leap forwards, sharp-twigged branches reaching out like multi-elbowed arms. He told himself not to be superstitious, and tugged at his borrowed hood. Freezing water trickled down the back of his neck.

Underfoot, soft ground was a sea of mud. Soon, there'd be little difference between the forest and the marshes to the south. He was wading, and the novice's boots were too loose, already filled with a soft, cold mush of mud that settled a chill into his toebones. If he stopped, he would be drowned where he stood.

He fought onwards, the rain as tough an obstacle as the ever-changing wind. His robes flapped like the ragged wings of a dying raven. The symbol of Morr picked out on his chest was very apt. He must look like death.

Finding shelter was his only priority. None of the trees offered any cover against rain and wind. His knees were on the point of giving out and his exposed hands were wrinkled like those of a drowned sailor who'd been in the water long enough for the fish to eat his eyes. It could be that, with another irony, he'd escaped from the dungeons of Zeluco only to perish of his freedom, not murdered by the malice of the duce but impersonally snuffed by uncaring elements.

The ground was sloping upwards, and there were slow waterfalls of mud streaming around. Surely there must be a hunting lodge somewhere, or a woodsman's hut. Even a cave would be welcome.

Up ahead, Kloszowski imagined he saw a light.

He felt a surge of strength in his legs and shouldered his way through the rain, pushing towards the glow. He hadn't been wrong, there was a light. Somehow, it wasn't reassuring. A pale blue luminescence, it was constant, distorted only by the curtains of rain hanging between Kloszowski and it.

He pulled himself up over a bank that had been reinforced with stone and logs, and found himself on the remains of a road. He could see the light clearly now. It was a blue ball, hovering a few feet above the ground like a small, weak sun. And beneath it was an overturned carriage.

A horse, its neck broken, was mangled between the traces, legs sticking out in the wrong direction. There was a liveried coachman sprawled face-down in the mud, not moving, a fallen tree across his back.

Kloszowski ran, boots slapping the pebble-and-hard-earth surface of the road. At least the coach would offer some shelter.

He didn't like to look at the blue light, and tried to keep his eyes away from it. In its centre, the blue became a tinted white, and there were thick smudges, changes in the consistency of the glow, that reminded him of a face.

There was a screeching in with the wind. Someone was crying out. The carriage was on its side, rain streaming in through one of the open windows. There were people inside, arguing. Blue flames fell like little raindrops, and evaporated against side of the vehicle. He reached the carriage, and saw himself bathed in the blue light. It didn't radiate any heat.

'Hello there,' he shouted. 'Friend, friend.'

He climbed up, and looked through the open window.

There was a puff and a fizz from inside, and a woman shouted.

'You idiot, I told you it wouldn't work if the powder got wet.'

Kloszowski tried to pull himself in, but the carriage was overbalanced. He heard a wheel snapping as the vehicle righted itself, and jumped back so it wouldn't break his legs. The people inside were dumped on the floor, and sounded shaken up.

'Back, monster,' a man said.

Kloszowski could see a shaking pistol pointed at him. Its flashpan and barrel were black with soot and still smoking. It wouldn't fire again. He pulled open the door, and forced himself in, slapping the firearm away.

Inside, it was wet but at least the rain wasn't whipping his face. It sounded like a thousand drum beats on the wooden roof of the coach.

There were two passengers, the man with the pistol and a young woman. He was past middle age and had once been sleek and corpulent, and she was in her twenties and probably attractive.

Her face was lovely, and she had a mass of coppery gold ringlets.

They must have been expensively dressed when they set out on their journey. Now, they were as wet, muddy and bedraggled as the meanest peasant. Nature was as great a leveller as the revolution. The passengers were obviously afraid of him, and shrank together, clutching each other.

'What manner of fiend are you?' the man asked.

'I'm not a fiend,' Kloszowski said. 'I'm just lost in the rain.'

'He's a cleric, Ysidro,' said the woman.

'Thank the gods,' the man said. 'We're saved. Exorcise these daemons and I'll see you're richly rewarded.'

Kloszowski decided not to tell them his robes were borrowed. He'd seen the light outside, but no daemons.

'This is Ysidro d'Amato,' said the woman, 'from Miragliano. And I'm Antonia.'

'Aleksandr,' Kloszowski said.

Antonia was less scared that d'Amato and better able to deal with the situation. He knew straight away that she wasn't a parasite.

'We were travelling when this storm blew up,' she said. 'Suddenly, there was this burst of lightning, and the coach turned over...'

'Daemons,' gasped d'Amato. 'There were daemons and monsters, all after my... after...'

He shut up. He didn't want to say what he thought the daemons were after. When the man was dried off and tidied up, Kloszowski imagined he wouldn't much like Ysidro d'Amato. The name was familiar, and he believed he'd heard it during his stay in Miragliano.

'There's a house ahead,' Antonia told him. 'We saw it through the trees before it got dark. We were trying to get there, to get out of the storm.'

Lightning struck, near. Kloszowski's teeth were rattled by the thunder-clap. The blue ball had grown, and was all around the coach. Its light was almost soothing and made him want to sleep. He fought the impulse. Who knew what might happen if he were to close his eyes.

'We'd better make a dash for it,' he said. 'We can't stay out the storm here. It's dangerous.'

D'Amato hugged a valise to his chest like a pillow and wouldn't budge.

'He's right, Ysidro,' said Antonia. 'This light is doing things to us. We must go on. It's only a few hundred yards. There'll be people, a fire, food, wine...'

She was coaxing him as if he were a child. He didn't want to leave his carriage. The wind pulled the door open, slamming it against the side of the coach, and rain came in as if thrown from buckets. The face in the light was very definite now, with a long nose and chasms for eyes.

'Let's go.'

Kloszowski tugged Antonia, and they broke out of the carriage.

'But Ysidro–'

'He can stay if he wants.'

He pulled the woman away from the broken coach, and she didn't struggle much. Before they'd gone ten steps, d'Amato stuck his head out of the door and emerged at a run, valise still in a tight embrace.

He was a fat man, not light on his feet, but he splashed enthusiastically as he staggered, and both Kloszowski and Antonia were able to catch him before he fell. He shook free of them, trying to keep them away from his valise. It was obviously a favourite toy.

'It's this way,' said Antonia, pointing. The road was rising slightly, and curving. Kloszowski couldn't see anything in the wet darkness.

'It's a huge place,' she said. 'We saw it from miles away.'

D'Amato was standing transfixed, looking into the empty eyes of the blue face. Antonia pulled at his elbow, turning him round. He shook his head, and she slapped him. Hard. He woke up, and began to walk with them.

Together, they struggled into the darkness. Kloszowski wanted to look back, but didn't. He felt he would never be warm again.

It was impossible to see clearly, but the firm road beneath their feet was as good a path as any.

'They can't have it,' d'Amato was muttering. 'It's mine, mine...'

There was cold water between Kloszowski's eyes and eyelids, and ice forming inside his skull.

'Look,' Antonia said.

There was a wall along the side of the road, partly carved from the mountainside, partly built from great stone blocks. Now, they were standing by a set of huge ironwork gates, rusted and sagging. They could easily get through between the railings. Beyond was the outline of a huge house, and there were faint lights.

Kloszowski stood back, and looked up at the gates. This must be a substantial estate. A family of the parasite classes would live here, sucking the lifeblood from the peasantry, grinding their bootheels into the faces of the masses.

In the scrollwork at the top of the gates, a word was picked out. It was the name of the estate, and probably the name of the family.

UDOLPHO.

Kloszowski had never heard of it.

V

Word of the duel had reached Schedoni, Ravaglioli's father-in-law and Old Melmoth's son, and his disapproval hung over the dinner table like marsh gas. The old man, reputedly a notorious libertine in his nearly-a-century ago youth, sat at the head of the table, still waiting to inherit a position as head of the household from his bedridden father.

At his side was the empty chair and place always maintained for his wife Mathilda, an invalid whom Genevieve had never seen, and beside them were the two outsiders upon whom the family most depended, Vathek the lawyer and Dr Valdemar, the physician.

Both had lived at Udolpho forever, and both had gained the family look, long faces and deep-set eyes. Valdemar was bald but for three cultivated strands pasted across his shining scalp, while Vathek was so thickly-haired that his eyes seemed to peer from a black ball of fur. At separate times, it had been rumoured that Vathek or Valdemar were either Schedoni's long-lost brother Montoni – Pintaldi's alleged grandfather – or the result of an adulterous or incestuous union contracted by Schedoni in his wild days. None of the rumours had ever been proved or disproved.

Vathek and Valdemar hated each other with a fervour that went beyond any emotion Genevieve could conceive of nurturing, and each was convinced the other constantly plotted his death. The currently favoured means of murder was poison, and neither had touched food of whose provenance they were even remotely uncertain for some weeks. The lawyer and the doctor stared at each other over full plates of meat and potatoes, each silently daring the other to take a perhaps contaminated mouthful. Vathek was charged with the custodianship of the will, but it was Dr Valdemar's duty to keep Old Melmoth alive long enough for it to be finished and signed.

Old Melmoth, who still held court in his master bedroom, was well over a hundred and twenty, and preserved long past his expected death by Dr Valdemar, who had travelled many years ago in Cathay, Lustria and the Dark Lands, in search of the magical ingredients necessary for the prolongation of life. He was a blasphemer and a sorcerer, her aunt said. But Old Melmoth was still alive, chuckling over each new intrigue in the unfolding saga of his family.

At the other end of the table, Ravaglioli sat opposite Pintaldi, pouring himself a generous goblet of wine while his wife Flaminea glared disapproval at him. She was the last remaining adherent of Claes Glinka's long-discredited Moral Crusade, and disapproved of most earthly pleasures. The family had to have someone to criticise its morals, and Flaminea had elected herself, taking every opportunity to preach damnation. A few months ago, she'd taken a hammer to the indecent sculptures of the Hanging Gardens, and destroyed, in the name of modesty, many priceless and irreplaceable works of ancient art. After that, the will, apparently, had been severely rewritten against her interests and her crusade had relaxed minutely. Ravaglioli, who had long since ceased to share his wife's rooms, made an exaggerated display of drinking, sloshing the wine around in his mouth and sighing with satisfaction as a mouthful slipped down his throat. Aunt Flaminea snorted her disdain, and carved her meat into tiny pieces with deft, cruel cuts of her serrated eating knife.

Genevieve was seated next to the empty chair that had been Flamineo's. He had been her father, and Flaminea's brother, before his still-unexplained death. On her other hand was a throne-like piece of furniture, decorated with intricate carvings of which Flaminea definitely did not approve, occupied by her father's fleshly uncle, Ambrosio, a monk of Ranald who'd been expelled from the Order of the Trickster God for an excess of vices. She edged her chair towards her late father's place, specifically to keep her unprotected knee and thigh out of range of Ambrosio's creeping fingers.

Ten feet away, across the table, were the beautiful twins, Young Melmoth and Flora. Pintaldi's ten-year-old offspring by a woman of dubious humanity, their ears were slightly pointed. Their curls fell on thin, delicate shoulders. The twins rarely spoke, save to each other. They had finished eating, and were sitting quietly, unnervingly blinking in a synchronized pattern.

The dinner party was completed by Christabel, Ravaglioli and Flaminea's daughter, as dark as Genevieve was fair, who was at Ambrosio's other side, her fork ready to deal with any exploratory graspings. She'd been educated in the Empire, at the academy in Nuln, and was recently returned to Udolpho, scandalising her mother with the habits she appeared to have acquired during her time away from the family estates. Once, after a dispute about the ownership of a bonnet, Christabel had ominously told Genevieve that she had taken a course under Valancourt, the master swordsman, and would be only too pleased to give a demonstration of her carving skills. Genevieve knew also that her cousin was a devotee of weirdroot, and often sought escape from the cold, stark walls of Udolpho in juicedreams. Just now, she was eating languidly, her hands not quite co-ordinated, and Genevieve suspected she'd been chewing the root earlier.

Genevieve looked up and down the table. It was hard to keep track of her family, to remember their relationships to her and to each other. Sometimes, they changed, and a relation she believed to be her uncle would turn out to be her cousin, or a cousin would become a niece. It was all to do with codicils to the will, which changed everything.

Beyond the tall windows, lightning forked.

Odo Zschokke, the chief steward, served as head-butler, supervising the three maids – Lily, Mira and Tanja – as they brought course after course to the table. Zschokke was seven feet tall, with broad shoulders only now bowed by years. He had been the captain of the Udolpho guard during the last major family war, when Old Melmoth's now-dead necromancer brother Otranto had raised daemons and the dead in an onslaught upon the estates.

Zschokke had sustained wounds from a Slaaneshi daemon's claw that carved three deep grooves diagonally across his face, twisting his nose, tearing his lips and making his eyes seem to stare through the dead skin bars of a cage-mask. His voice had been torn from him, but he was still a capable man, and Old Melmoth trusted him more even than Vathek and Valdemar. No one doubted that Zschokke stood to benefit from the will.

Genevieve didn't want to eat. Her meat was overcooked, grey through to the heart, and she didn't care for vegetables, particularly the black-eyed grey-white potatoes produced by the estate's garden. She took a little red wine, ignoring Flaminea's dagger looks, but it only served to sting her palate. She thirsted, but not for wine, and she hungered, but not for cooked-through beef...

The meal was mainly eaten without conversation. The clatter of knives and forks on plates was backgrounded by driving rain, and the constant crescendo of thunder.

The storm excited Genevieve, aroused in her a hunting instinct. She wanted to be outside, slaking her thirst.

The maids took away her uneaten main course, and there was a pause. Zschokke signalled, and new bottles of wine were presented to Schedoni for his approval. He blew dust off a label, coughed, and nodded.

'I hardly think innocent children should be exposed to such vice and debauchery, father,' snapped Flaminea, thin lips pinching as she enthusiastically chewed her morsels of meat. 'We do not want to raise another generation of sybarites and libertines.'

Flora and Young Melmoth looked at each other and smiled. Their teeth were tiny and sharp, their eyes nearly almond-shaped. Genevieve had seen them playing games with the castle cats, and could not think of them as innocents.

She sipped her wine.

'You see,' Flaminea said, 'my niece is on the slope to degradation already, swilling wine at her tender years, wearing silks and satins to inflame the lusts of vile men, combing out her long, golden hair. The rot has started. You can't see it yet, but it will show on her face before long. Another sixteen years, and her face will be as corrupted and monstrous as...'

There was a loud thunderclap, and Flaminea refrained from naming the name. Schedoni stared her down, and she collapsed in her seat, shut up by her father's glance.

Genevieve had heard her grandmother was hideously disfigured by disease, and that she was always veiled as she grovelled in her rooms, awaiting Morr's last kiss.

Genevieve raised her goblet in a toast to her aunt, and drained it. The wine was as tasteless and unsustaining as rainwater.

Ambrosio had shown some interest when the subject of inflamed lusts was raised, and his swollen, purple-veined face wobbled as he licked his lips, his hand under the table fastening upon the upper thigh of Lily, the maid pouring his wine. A smile spread over his features as he reached higher, and Lily betrayed no sign of the attentions he was paying to her. A thin string of drool dangled from the cleric's mouth. He wiped it away with a finger.

Schedoni drank, and surveyed the family and its retainers. His face was the template from which everyone else around the table – even the beautiful Christabel – seemed to have been struck. But before Schedoni, the long nose and deep eyes had belonged to Old Melmoth. And before Old Melmoth, there were generations of the House of Udolpho, all the way back to Smarra's father, the Black Cygnet. There was a portrait of the pirate, standing aboard the deck of his vessel supervising the execution of an Araby captain, and he too bore the Udolpho features. He must have been the originator of the line, Genevieve realized. Before the pirate, there had been no family. It was his stolen fortune that had created the house.

Ravaglioli and Pintaldi were arguing quietly, their old quarrel revived again, and making threatening gestures with their dinner knives. Once Pintaldi had ended an argument by thrusting a skewer into Ravaglioli's throat between the meat course and the game, and then, with a flourish, taken his soup spoon to the other man's eyes. Ravaglioli had not forgotten or forgiven that.

'After dinner, I shall play the harpsichord,' Christabel announced. She was not contradicted.

Genevieve's cousin had learned music in Nuln, and possessed a pleasant although not outstanding voice. At the academy, she had also begun to get the measure of her own charms, and was clearly more than a little frustrated to be removed from the society of the Empire back to Udolpho, where her opportunities for breaking hearts were severely limited. Since she had driven Praz the gamekeeper to suicide, there had been no one to torment with her sable-black hair, liquid eyes and silky skin. She spent much of her time wandering the broken battlements of Udolpho, fretting and plotting, shroudlike dresses flapping in the breeze, petting the ravens.

'In Nuln, my playing was often praised by the Countess Emmanuelle von Lie...'

Christabel's boast was interrupted by thunder and lightning. And another crash of noise. At once, it was colder and wetter. Everyone in the great hall turned to the floor-to-ceiling windows which had just been blown in. Rain was pouring into the hall like shot, and stung on Genevieve's face. The wind screamed as the candles placed down the spine of the table guttered and went out. Chairs were pushed noisily back, Flaminea gave a polite little squeak of fright, and hands went to swordhilts.

It was dark, but Genevieve could make everyone out. Her eyes were fine at night. She saw Zschokke moving slowly, as if in a dream, across the hall, reaching for a lantern. One of the maids was wrestling with the opened windows, forcing them shut. The wind and the rain were shut off, and the light came up again as Zschokke turned up the wick of the lantern. There were strangers, dripping wet, standing behind Schedoni's huge chair. While the windows were open, someone had come into the hall.

VI

The company was gloomy, with funereal clothes and long faces, and their great hall was ill-lit and dusty, the upper walls covered with filth and cobweb.

Some of the diners looked barely alive, and they all had an unhealthy pallor, as if they'd lived all their lives in these shadows, never emerging into the sunlight. There were two pretty girls among them, though, a pale, lithe blonde and a lush, dark-haired beauty. They immediately excited Kloszowski's revolutionary interest. Trapped like Olympia and Julietta by the conventions of their class, they might make enthusiastic converts to the cause.

'We were lost,' he explained. 'We made for your light.'

Nobody said anything. They all looked, hungrily, at the newcomers.

'There's a storm outside,' said Antonia, unnecessarily. 'The road is washing away.'

'They can't stay,' said a thin old woman, voice cracking with meanness. 'Outsiders can't stay.'

Kloszowski didn't like the sound of that.

'We've nowhere else to go. There's no passable road.'

'It would be against his will,' the woman said, looking up at the shadowed ceiling. 'Old Melmoth can't abide outsiders.'

They all thought about that, looking at each other. There was an ancient man, a halo of cotton-spun white hair fringing his skull, at the head of the table. Kloszowski took him to be in charge, although he didn't seem to be this Old Melmoth. By his side stood a tall, scar-faced servant, the muscle of the family, typical of the type that leaves their own class and helps the aristocracy keep his brothers and sisters in chains.

A dangerous brute, to judge by the height and breadth of him and the size of his hairy-backed hands. Still, his face showed he had, at least once in his life, taken second prize in a fight.

'Shush, Flaminea,' the old man told the woman. 'We've no choice...'

Several men of the company had swords out, as if expecting banditti or beastmen.

Kloszowski noticed a pronounced family resemblance. Long noses, hollow eyes, distinct cheekbones. He was reminded of the phantom face in the blue light, and wondered whether perhaps they wouldn't be better off taking their chances with the storm.

'See here,' said d'Amato, who seemed to inflate as he dried. 'You'll have to shelter us. I'm an important man in Miragliano. Ysidro d'Amato. Ask anyone, and they'll tell you. You'll be well rewarded.'

The old man looked at d'Amato with contempt. 'I doubt if you could reward us, signor.'

'Hah,' d'Amato said. 'I'm not without wealth.'

'I am Schedoni Udolpho,' the old man said, 'the son of Melmoth Udolpho. This is a rich estate, weighed down with wealth beyond your imagination. You can have nothing we could want.'

D'Amato stepped back, towards a fireplace the size of a stable where whole trees burned, and looked away. He seemed smaller with the fire behind him, and he was still clinging to his bag as if it contained his beating heart. With typical bourgeois sliminess, he'd been impressed by talk of 'wealth beyond your imagination.'

Kloszowski remembered where he'd heard of d'Amato. Miragliano, a seaport built on a network of islands in a salt marsh, was a rich trading city, but it suffered from a lack of drinkable water. Fortunes had been made via water-caravans and canals, and d'Amato had been the leading water merchant in the city, carving out his own empire, forcing his competitors out of business. A year or so ago, he had achieved an almost total control over the city's fresh water, and been able to treble the price. The city fathers had protested, but had to give in and pay him.

He had been a powerful man indeed. But then the Yellow Ague had come, and investigating scryers laid the blame on contaminated water. That explained why d'Amato was leaving home...

Schedoni signalled to the scarred hulk.

'Zschokke,' he said. 'Bring more chairs, and mulled wine. Our guests are in danger of catching their deaths.'

Kloszowski had stepped as close to the fire as he could and felt his clothes drying on him.

Antonia had stripped her soaked shawl, and was raising thin skirts to toast her legs. Kloszowski noticed that at least one of the Udolpho clan was especially intrigued by the spectacle, the flabby old fellow with a cleric's skullcap and a lecher's look in his eye.

Antonia laughed gaily, and did a few dance steps.

'I'm a dancer sometimes,' she said. 'Not a very good one.'

Her legs were shapely, with a dancer's muscles.

'I used to be an actress too. Murdered by the end of Act One...'

She stuck her tongue out and hung her neck as if it were broken. Her blouse was soaked to her skin, leaving Kloszowski in no doubt as to her qualifications for the entertainment business.

D'Amato swarmed around Antonia, making her drop her wet skirts to cover herself.

'Sorry,' she said. 'Bought and paid for, that's me. The Water Wizard has exclusive rights to all performances.'

She was remarkably cheerful, and d'Amato was obviously embarrassed by his plaything's boldness.

'Harlotry is the path to Chaos and damnation,' said the shrivelled kill-joy. 'This house was always plagued with harlots and loose women, with their painted cheeks and their sinful laughter. But they're all dead now, and I, righteous and ridiculous Flaminea, am still here. They used to laugh at me when I was a girl, and ask me if I was saving my body for the worms. But I'm alive, and they're not.'

Kloszowski had Flaminea marked as a cheerless maniac straight away. She seemed to derive considerable enjoyment from contemplating the deaths of others, so she wasn't denying herself every earthly pleasure.

The hulk found him a place at the table, next to a moustached gallant who couldn't hold his head properly.

'I'm Pintaldi,' the young man said.

'Aleksandr,' Kloszowski returned.

Pintaldi reached for a candle, and brought it close. Kloszowski felt the heat on his face.

'Fascinating stuff, flame,' he said. 'I've made a study of it. They're all wrong, you know. It's not hot, it's cold. And flames are pure, like sharp knives. They consume the evil, and leave the good. Flames are the fingers of the gods.'

'Very interesting,' said Kloszowski, taking a swallow of the wine Zschokke had decanted for him. It stung his throat, and warmed his belly.

Flaminea glared at him as if he were molesting a child in her presence.

'You are a cleric of Morr,' said a hairy-faced beast sat near Old Melmoth. 'What are you doing out in the storm?'

Kloszowski was befuddled for a moment, then remembered his borrowed robe.

'Um, death is everywhere,' he said, holding up his stolen amulet.

'The dead are everywhere,' said the hairy man. 'Especially here. Why, in this very hall the ghostly disembodied hands of the Strangling Steward frequently take shape, and fix about the throats of unwary guests.'

D'Amato coughed, and spat out his wine.

'Only those guilty of some grave crime need fear the Strangling Steward,' said the folklorist. 'He only visits the guilty.'

'My apologies,' said Schedoni. 'We are an old family, and our blood has grown thin. Isolation has made us eccentric. You must think us strange company?'

Everyone looked at Kloszowski, hollow eyes seeming to glow blue in the gloom. 'Oh no,' he said, 'you've been most hospitable. This certainly compares favourably with the last noble house in which I was a guest.'

That much was true, although Kloszowski suspected Zschokke might share certain talents with Tancredi. All these aristocratic menages kept a pet killer.

'You must stay the night,' Schedoni said. 'The house is large, and rooms can be found for you.'

Kloszowski wondered how long he could maintain the deception. Since the great fog riots, his name had been a byword for insurrection. If he were to be revealed to the Udolpho clan as Prince Kloszowski, the revolutionist poet, he'd probably find himself defenestrated. And the far windows of the great hall overlooked the gorge below. It would be a fall of seven or eight hundred feet onto jagged rocks.

Pintaldi had picked up the candelabrum now, and was holding his palm close to a flame.

'See,' he said. 'It burns cold.'

His skin was blackening, and there was a nasty, meaty smell.

'Harlots will rot,' said Flaminea.

Kloszowski looked across the table at the fair young girl. She had sat quietly, saying nothing, her eyes demurely cast down. She didn't have the Udolpho look, yet she was obviously part of this bizarre collection. Her lips were unrouged but deep red, and she had white, sharp teeth. She looked up, and caught his gaze. She seemed about sixteen, but her clear eyes were ancient.

'Without harlots, where'd be the fun in the world?' said Antonia.

Flaminea shook a bony fist at the dancer, and spat a chunk of gristle onto her plate. The woman had a fuzz of beard on her chin and her hair was scraggy grey. Dried out, Antonia was as healthy as a ripe apple, and made a distinct contrast with this withered crew.

'I shall play the harpsichord,' said the dark girl sitting by the fat cleric. Schedoni nodded, and the girl got up, daintily walking across the hall to the instrument. She wore something long, black and clinging, like a stylish shroud. Kloszowski was feeling warm again, but somehow the cold was still settled in his bones.

VII

As Christabel played, Genevieve considered the outsiders. Something about them disturbed her. She saw Ambrosio's lips tighten as Antonia showed her legs. She felt the strange hostility between the cleric of Morr and the merchant of Miragliano. These men hadn't chosen to travel together. And both had things to hide.

She imagined travelling, coaches crossing the Old World, from Estalia to Bretonnia, from the Empire to Kislev. There were great cities – Parravon, Altdorf, Marienburg, Erengrad, Zhufbar – and unknown, far-distant countries – Cathay, Lustria, Nippon, the Dark Lands. She believed she had spent all her life at Udolpho, never leaving its walls, as much a prisoner as invalid Mathilda or the altered son Ravaglioli and Flaminea were rumoured to have penned in a cellar, fed only on human flesh.

All she could remember was Udolpho, and she couldn't even remember much of that. There were huge gaps in her recollection. And yet, impressions of things she could never have known sometimes came to her.

Christabel played strangely, letting her juicedreams seep through as she embroidered around the edges of a familiar piece. Her tangle of black hair flew back as she nodded her head in time to the savage music.

The music disturbed Genevieve more. In her mind, she was a predator, tearing out the throats of her prey, her teeth sinking into flesh, delicious blood gushing into her mouth, trickling over her chin, flowing over her bosom.

Her nails had become sharp, and her teeth shifted in her mouth, the enamel reshaping...

There were other dream memories, crowding in. Faces, names, places, events. Things she could never have known, she experienced. She remembered a crowd attacked by invisible forces, and the kiss of a dark, handsome man who had changed her. She remembered a queenly woman, her face and arms red with blood, dressed in the costume of an earlier age. She remembered an iron bracelet and a chain, tying her to a rough-faced man, and a night in an inn. She remembered twice venturing into a castle to face a Great Enchanter. She remembered a theatre and a striking actor, and her flight from him, from his city. She remembered a thing with the body of a sea-creature and the eyes of a man. All these things were more than dreams, and yet they did not fit with the life Genevieve knew she had lived, a quiet, secluded, forgotten life in this castle.

Christabel's shoulders heaved, and sweat fell from her face.

Flaminea grunted from time to time. Music was sinful in her mind, and she rejected her daughter's talent. Sometimes, Christabel killed her mother, choking the life out of her with a silken scarf, or battering her with a stone torn out of the walls of the house.

Sometimes, when Flaminea worked up a righteous frenzy, it was the other way around, and she would denounce her daughter as a witch, standing by smugly while the villagers dragged her to the stake and Pintaldi lovingly nurtured the bonfire.

The cleric of Morr was looking at her. He was a foreigner, and didn't strike her as being a real cleric. Even Ambrosio had something about him that suggested holy orders, no matter how many times his hands reached into skirts or bodices. Aleksandr was not the type to bow to any god, or to any man.

Was it just that he was too good-looking to be a celibate of Morr?

His hood was down, and his throat was exposed. She saw the delicate blue vein threading up into his unkempt, still-wet beard, and imagined she could detect its pulse by sight.

Genevieve licked her lips with a rough tongue.

VIII

This was a strange brood, Antonia Marsillach thought to herself, and no mistake. For the millionth time, she wondered whether it wouldn't have been cleverer to stay in Miragliano and throw herself on the mercy of the city fathers. She'd had nothing to do with Ysidro's damned poison water, and suspected he was only taking her away with him to his luxury bolt-hole in Bretonnia because she knew a lot about the careless way he'd pursued personal profit at the expense of public safety. She should have turned the hog in and petitioned for a reward instead of sticking by him. He was no use anyway, never had been. Even when things were going well, he'd been more interested in the counting house than the bedroom. She should go back to the stage, and try to get out of the chorus and into a featured spot. She could act better than some, dance better than most, and the customers always liked to look at her legs. She was still young. She wanted some fun.

And here she was surrounded by refugees from the kind of melodrama the city fathers had banned from the Miragliano playhouse as overly morbid and liable to incite public disorder. Before the ban, she'd been in them all, shaking herself during the prologues and getting murdered during the first acts of Brithan Cragg's *Ystareth; or: The Plague Daemon and Orfeo's Tall Tale; or: The Doom of Zaragoz*, Detlef Sierck's *The Treachery of Oswald* and *The Strange History of Dr Zhiekill and Mr Chaida*, Ferring the Balladeer's incredibly violent *Brave Konrad and the Skull-Face Slaughterer*, Bruno Malvoisin's obscene *Seduced by Slaaneshi; or: The Baneful Lusts of Diogo Briesach*. Those plays had dark and stormy nights, and weary travellers forced to stay the night, and puritanical harridans, and family curses, and secret passages, and much-altered wills, and ghouls, goblins and ghostliness.

And here she was in one again, promoted from the chorus to a featured role. She'd have to watch herself before the first act curtain.

The witch pounding the harpsichord was competing with the thunder and lightning, while the aunt who hated harlots was foaming at the mouth with righteous hysteria, and the cleric of Ranald was sneaking looks at her cleavage whenever he thought he was unobserved. Schedoni seemed courteous enough, but Antonia wasn't convinced he was still alive. She suspected he might be a wired-together corpse used as a ventriloquist's dummy by the scarred butler. She looked around the great hall, wondering where the entrances to the secret passages were.

Ravaglioli, the harridan's husband, was still eating, while everyone else was paying attention to his dark daughter. He was a noisy, messy eater, and food fragments were scattered about his place at the table.

Antonia was tired, and looking forwards to a big, warm, fresh-laundered bed without Ysidro d'Amato in it.

They had brought out Estalian sherry, and it was doing her good inside. Her clothes had dried on her body, and she relished the thought of peeling them off, and towelling herself down. Maybe she could find skilled hands to help her with that. Aleksandr seemed likely enough, and Father Ambrosio would doubtless be keen to volunteer his services.

She wasn't that wonderful as a dancer. But she had other skills. She could always find a comfortable place somewhere. She always had. Zschokke poured her some more sherry. She was feeling quite tipsy.

Ravaglioli scooped a spoonful of some flavoured gruel into his mouth. Antonia wasn't sure whether it was savory or sweet. He gulped it down with a slurp, and reached out for more.

Then, he paused, and his cheeks ballooned, as if he had bitten into a whole pepper. His face reddened, and the veins in his temples throbbed purple. Tears leaked from his eyes, and slipped into the cracks of his swelling cheeks.

He slapped the table with both hands, his full spoon splattering gruel around him. Christabel continued to play, but everyone else looked at the suffering man.

Ravaglioli held his throat, and seemed to be struggling, trying to swallow something.

'What is it?' asked Schedoni.

Ravaglioli shook his head, and stood up. His throat apple was bobbing, and he was breathing uneasily. His eyes were wide open, bloodshot, and panicked.

'It's justice,' snarled Flaminea. 'That's what it is.'

Zschokke tried to help the man, holding him upright, giving him a goblet of water.

Ravaglioli looked worse than the poisoned plenipotentiary, in Sendak Mittell's *Lustrian Vengeance; or: 'I Will Eat Their Offal!,'* when he was told that the deathbane-laced tripes he had just eaten were pulled from his beloved grandmother while she was still alive.

He pushed the servant away, but poured the water into his mouth, sucking vigorously. He gulped, and the blockage in his throat went down towards his stomach. He drained the rest of the water, and reached for the sherry, laughing.

'What was it?' Schedoni asked.

Ravaglioli shrugged and smiled, wiping the spittle off his chin. 'It felt like a little metal ball. I've no idea what it was doing in the gruel, or what it could have been. It was coated with something sticky.'

Then he grabbed his stomach as a spasm hit him.

'It... hurts...'

Ravaglioli began shaking, as if lapsing into a fit. He held the edge of the table, and grit his teeth.

'Burning inside... it's growing... hot...'

Suddenly, he bent backwards, his spine audibly snapping against the chair rest. His swelling stomach burst through the hooks of his doublet, and was exposed.

Christabel stopped playing, and turned on her stool to look at the commotion her father was causing.

Zschokke backed away from the flailing man, and several people moved their chairs to give Ravaglioli room. His eyes were showing only white. His stomach was distended like a pregnant woman's, about to deliver triplets. Red stretchlines were appearing in the skin. The man was groaning, and there were noises inside him, breaking and tearing noises.

Antonia couldn't look away.

With a sulphurous bang, Ravaglioli's stomach exploded. Gobbets rained around him, and his chair collapsed.

A whisp of blue smoke curled out of the gaping hole in his midriff.

Somebody screamed, and screamed, and screamed...

...and Antonia realized it was her.

IX

That had been disgusting!

Kloszowski wiped his sleeve with a napkin, and watched everyone panic. D'Amato quieted Antonia down with a slightly overenthusiastic slap, and the dancer sat back, appalled.

A bald fellow with bow-legs, who'd been sitting near Schedoni, scuttled over, dusty coat-tails trailing the floor, and examined the corpse of Signor Ravaglioli, prodding around the edges of his yawning stomach wound with a bony finger.

'Hmmmn,' he said. 'This man is dead.'

Obviously this was a physician of some insight.

'Some explosive device, I suspect,' the doctor added. 'Designed to react to the inside of a human stomach...'

He took a fork, and poked around inside the mess.

'Ah yes,' he said, holding up a small shiny scrap of something. 'Here's a fragment.'

'Thank you, Dr Valdemar,' said Schedoni. 'Zschokke, have this mess cleared away and then bring us coffee.'

Kloszowski got up and thumped the table. Cutlery rattled. Ambrosio stopped his still-full wine goblet from falling over.

'I don't think you understand,' he said. 'This man is dead. Murdered.'

'Yes?' Schedoni seemed puzzled by his outburst.

'Someone must have killed him.'

'Indubitably.'

'Aren't you going to find the murderer? See that he, or she, is punished?'

Zschokke and two servants brought an old curtain to carry off Ravaglioli in, and a maid with a bucket and mop appeared to tidy up the quarter of the room that had been splattered.

Schedoni shrugged. 'Of course, murderers are always exposed, always punished. But first we should finish our meal. The habits of Udolpho will never be disturbed by something as crude as a mere killing.'

Everyone at the table appeared to agree with the old man and so, feeling foolish, Kloszowski sat down. Not only was this family the epitome of the parasite classes, they were all mad.

Christabel, piqued because her father's death had interrupted her recital, returned to the table, and took her seat. Ambrosio made a grasp at her bottom but she brushed his hand away.

Ravaglioli's chair was tipped back and he was lifted onto the sheet, and quickly wrapped. The maid wiped up.

'Put him in the cold storage room,' Dr Valdemar instructed the steward. 'I shall examine further later. There may be much we can learn.'

'Perhaps our guest might say a blessing for the dead,' suggested Vathek the lawyer. Everyone looked at Kloszowski, and he resisted the urge to look behind him.

He kept forgetting he was a cleric of Morr.

Kloszowski mumbled something and made gestures in the air, vaguely trying to imitate clerics he'd seen at funerals. No one questioned his impersonation, and the coffee arrived in several steaming pots.

'I must tell Old Melmoth,' Vathek said, addressing himself to Schedoni. 'This will affect the will. Ravaglioli was in the direct line of succession.'

'No he wasn't,' snapped Flaminea, between thirsty little sips at the boiling black coffee. 'I was.'

Vathek scratched his bristle-covered cheek.

'My late husband married into Udolpho. I am the direct heir, am I not, father?'

Schedoni shook his head, as if unable to remember.

'I thought father was grandfather's son,' said Christabel, 'and that you, mother, married into the family.'

'That was my impression,' said the lawyer.

'Well, your impression was wrong,' snarled Flaminea. 'I have always been the heir. Father Ambrosio will confirm the truth, won't you, uncle?'

Ambrosio, who was dividing his attention between Antonia's thighs and Christabel's breasts, applied himself to the question.

'I'm not your uncle,' said the father, 'I'm your father. Before I entered the cult of Ranald, I was married to my cousin Clarimonde. She was abducted by the banditti and never heard from again, but she left me with a daughter.'

Ambrosio's hand had dipped below the table, in Christabel's direction. He winced, and brought it up again. Christabel still had her meatfork.

'Uncle, you are confused,' said Flaminea. 'You are a father, not *my* father. Surely, you concede that Christabel is your grand-niece, not your grand-daughter.'

Ambrosio drank his coffee, the prong-marks red against the white skin of his hand, and said, reasonably, 'I believe Christabel is Pintaldi's sister, is she not?'

'Christabel?' said Flaminea, eyes glowing blue.

The dark girl shook her head, and said, 'It's nothing to me.'

Outside, the thunder had receded to a dull rumble every few minutes, and the main noise was the steady tattoo of the rain against the walls, and the rattling of the windows. Inside, Kloszowski's head was beginning to ache.

'More coffee?' asked Schedoni, courteously.

X

She had lost track of time, and could not tell how many years she'd been imprisoned. Her life before she came to Udolpho was a distant, vague memory. She had been married, she thought, and had children. She had lived in a city near the sea, and her husband had been a mariner, eventually the owner of his own boat, his own shipping line. Then, she'd travelled, and come, during one of these damnable thunderstorms, to Udolpho.

Her captors called her Mathilda, but that wasn't her name. Her real name was...

Mathilda.

No. It was...

She couldn't remember.

Zschokke, the tall man with the twisted face who brought her her meals, could not speak. But he was often accompanied by a bent, mad old man named Schedoni, and he always called her Mathilda. He spoke to her as if she was pitiably altered, but there was nothing wrong with her.

She was not a victim of warpstone. She was a normal woman.

She tried to lift her head, but the weights Zschokke fastened around her skull while she was asleep were too heavy.

There had been a slit window once, but it had been bricked up.

She could never tell whether it was day or night but she knew when there was a storm. She could hear the thunder, and the stones of the ceiling would become wet, occasionally dripping on her.

She didn't know why she was held prisoner. At first, she'd begged for her release, then for an explanation. Now, she didn't bother. They called her Mathilda and were sorry for her, but they'd never let her free. She would die in this room and be buried under a slab carved with the name of Mathilda Udolpho. That was to be her fate.

Once she had secreted a chicken bone from one of her meals, and snapped it, making a sharp tool. For months, she'd scraped away at the mortar between the stones, loosening large blocks. She'd rested her head against the cold wall while she worked away with her bone-trowel, and had flattened a part of her face.

In the end, Zschokke had caught her. She had tried to sever the vein in his throat with the sharp bone, but it had just broken on his skin.

He didn't abuse her for her attack. But she'd eaten filleted meat and fowl ever since.

She tried to remember her real husband, her real family. But she could only picture the face of Schedoni Udolpho, and recall the names of the children he repeatedly told her they'd had together: Montoni, Ambrosio, Flaminea...

She tried to stand, but couldn't. Her head was heavy as a cannonball, and her neck had long since withered away. She could draw her knees up and crouch but her head stayed anchored to the floor.

She dragged herself, pulling with her hands and pushing with her feet, across the floor of the room, the carpet bunching up under her. One day, Mathilda would get out. And then they'd all be sorry.

XI

Zschokke stopped and grunted, tapping d'Amato on the chest. The water merchant staggered back as if he'd been dealt a weighty blow.

The huge steward pushed open a door. It creaked, of course. Zschokke shoved d'Amato through it. Then, he lifted up his candle, and proceeded down the corridor.

Kloszowski didn't know where they were within the house. They had been led a long way away from the great hall, through passages and up staircases. They could be either deep in the depths of Udolpho, or high up in one of the towers.

They had passed through a derelict part of the building, and he had imagined that Zschokke was a little afraid, casting too many careful looks about him, flinching away from the holes in the walls and the screened-off rooms. Kloszowski hated to think what might put a fright into the giant brute.

These were the guest apartments.

Antonia was trying to smile, and talking to the steward, asking him questions about the family, and about the house. Zschokke interjected a few groans into his grunts.

'This reminds me very much,' the dancer was saying, 'of the daemon-blighted inn of von Diehl's *The Fate of Fair Florence; or: Tortured and Abandoned*.'

They came to another door, and Zschokke pushed it open. There was a fire burning in a grate in the room beyond, which was decorated in the Cathayan style, with silks and low tables and pieces of porcelain. The steward pointed a finger at Antonia.

'For me?' she said. 'Thank you. It looks lovely. Very homey.'

Kloszowski was in the room next door, a tiny cell with a bare cot, a single candle, and a thin blanket. This was what they thought fitting for a cleric, obviously. Next time he was forced to take a disguise, he'd pick something likely to win him better accommodation. Zschokke slammed the door behind him, and he was alone.

There was a thin window, and the rain steadily spattered against it. Kloszowski peered through, but couldn't see anything beyond the trick-les of water.

He stripped off his habit, and got out of the novice's boots. His feet were still filthy from the forest mud. The rest of his clothes were ragged and grimy from his spell in the dungeons of Zeluco. He undressed, tearing his britches to pieces, and unpicking the rags of his shirt from his chest and arms.

There was a basin of water by his bedside. He remembered d'Amato's Yellow Ague, but assumed that up here in the mountains they wouldn't be buying from a bloodsucker like him. Obviously, they had enough rain to fill their own butts. He washed himself thoroughly, and felt better than he'd done in months.

Oddly, there was a full-length mirror in the room, the one non-ascetic touch of the furnishing.

He stood naked before it, and held up the candle.

The dungeon hadn't been good for him. There were bruises on his wrists, ankles, back and chest, and he had scabbed-over wounds on his knees and hips. He could see his bones too clearly through his skin, and his face was more haggard than romantically gaunt.

Still, that particular ordeal was over.

Then, his image in the mirror shook, and distorted, as if a ripple were travelling across a still pond. The frame lurched forwards, and the mirror swung open like a door.

Kloszowski tried to cover himself with a towel. His heart beat too fast. Something came out of the dark space behind the mirror, and seized him by the neck, pulling his head down.

XII

There was nothing for it but to do the deed herself. Vathek was too spine-less for the business. And, in any case, she would never have trusted him to carry it through.

In the months since she had first seduced the lawyer, Christabel Udolpho had learned many things. She knew now that there was not one will, but many different, mutually irreconcilable wills. Old Melmoth Udolpho changed his mind daily, and insisted on newly-drafted testaments. Some he would sign, some he would abandon.

She dressed carefully, in tight riding britches and a loose blouse, then pulled on her soft leather boots and spent some time braiding her hair. Vathek watched her, chattering about nothing, going over and over the plan. He was confused about the details, but she had them down cold.

The lawyer touched her neck, and let his thin fingers creep into her hair. She felt a thrill of disgust, but suppressed it and gave him a win-some smile in the mirror.

Vathek was a vile creature, hirsute all over his body, and given to sweating. There was some animal in his soul, she was sure. A pig, or a bear. But he wasn't strong, not in his limbs or in his mind. He was easy to lead.

Christabel touched the furred back of Vathek's hand, and rubbed her cheek against his arm.

Soon, it would all be over. Soon, all the fortune of Udolpho would be hers. Then, she could take lovers for herself, gratify her own wants. Aleksandr, the cleric of Morr, had seemed interesting in a reedy, sly sort of way. And she'd heard the maids talking about the giant, Odo Zschokke, and how his manly parts were in proportion to the rest of him. A tiny flare of desire raised her hackles.

Her hair crackled with electricity, and expanded a little, giving Vathek a slight shock. He withdrew his hand, and tried to laugh.

'Be sure to finish him,' he said. 'You must be sure.'

Christabel smiled as she pulled the falconer's gloves on. They were fine leather, and felt good on her hands. She had strong hands, from hours of practice with harpsichord and duelling sword.

After the fortune was disposed of, and the Black Cygnet's treasure found, she would have to turn her attention to Lawyer Vathek. Perhaps an accident might be arranged. A fall from the south wall. An encounter with wolves.

She stood up. She was taller than the lawyer, and he had to look up to meet her eyes. His smile was shaking. He was afraid, of what they were about to do, afraid of her...

She patted his shoulders.

She had dictated the final will, naming herself sole heir to the house and fortunes of the family. Old Melmoth, the blind fool, had signed it, imagining himself to be dealing with a minor business matter. All the other wills were bundled up in scrolls in Vathek's office, waiting to be burned.

Melmoth could not live much longer. Not without Dr Valdemar's infusions to keep him going.

Christabel opened a drawer, and pulled out a ball of copper wire. It was supposed to be for the harpsichord. She unravelled a length and held it up before Vathek's face. His eyes wavered.

She bit through the wire, and held up a loop of about four feet, the ends tied around her thick-gloved hands.

She pulled the loop tight, and it straightened with a musical twang. It would do the job.

'I'll be back,' she told Vathek, and stepped out into the dark hallway, moving silently through the gloom towards the doctor's rooms.

Very soon, she would be very rich.

And then they'd all tremble.

XIII

At least, the last surprise had been relatively pleasant.

'I knew there'd be a secret door, somewhere...'

They were cramped on his cot, but after weeks in a dungeon, Kloszowski was not about to complain. Antonia was soft, and expert. Being a dancer gave her a lot of control. She wore bells on her anklets, and they had tinkled amusingly as her legs wrapped around him, ankles crossed tight against the small of his back. His neck was cricked as his head was propped against the headboard, but the enjoyable warmth of Antonia's body, pressed close to his own, made up for that.

'I searched my room, and found some levers by the fire. I didn't want to be alone in this place.'

Kloszowski wondered if Antonia would be a convert to the cause. She evidently had an attachment to that bloated bourgeois exploiter d'Amato, but it could hardly be very strong. After all, she'd sought out his company.

'You're not really a cleric, are you?'

He admitted it. She snuggled closer, settling her head on his chest.

'I knew it. No one is what they say they are.'

'Are you really a dancer?'

'And an actress. Not now, I admit. But I was. The city fathers closed down the Miragliano playhouse, and I had to find something to do. And there was Ysidro, lolling about in the street with his purse clinking...'

'What about d'Amato? Is he what he says he is?'

She pouted. 'He's running away from the city fathers. The Yellow Ague is his fault. He poisoned everyone.'

He had been right about the water merchant.

'Coins are all he cares about, Aleksandr. Coins, and the things they can buy. Things like houses and horses and clothes and statues. Things like me.'

She rubbed a warm knee up his leg, exciting him again.

'Don't worry,' she said. 'This is compliments of the management. Selling it never got me anywhere but into trouble. Even dancing is better than that. Ysidro took me to a municipal ball once, before everyone started foaming yellow and dying, and all the city fathers' wives ignored me. There was this one woman, Donna Elena, who was a real cow, and

322

made jokes behind her fan that set all her henfriends off on that horrible pretend laughing. I wanted to kill them all, scratch their eyes out.
Donna Elena's husband, Don Lucio, was a commissioner of public works.
Ysidro wanted him to grant him a city contract, to provide water for the
watch stations. After the ball, Ysidro told me to go to a waterfront inn
with Don Lucio and let him do what he wanted.'

'Did you enjoy it?'

'Not it, itself. There wasn't much to Don Lucio, if you get my meaning.
But I kept thinking of Donna Elena, and her fan and her laugh. She'd
sold it too, but for life. I was only stuck with Don Lucio for the night.
She had him forever, and good luck to her too, the slag...'

'There's injustice in the world, my love.'

'Too bloody true,' she said, rolling on top of him, flicking his neck
with her tongue. 'But forget that for now...'

He did.

XIV

Genevieve couldn't sleep. She only really felt alive at night.

In her nightgown, she paced her room, listening to the noises of the night. There were creatures in the storm, calling to her.

Her room was modest. She had no mirrors.

Above her mantel was a portrait of Flamineo, her father. He had looked much like Flaminea, his twin, but had been wild where she was puritanical.

A flash of lightning lit up her father's face, making his eyes glow blue. He was painted standing on the mountainside, with the silhouette of Udolpho in the background, and tall trees all around. Sometimes, people imagined they saw things moving in the trees in the picture, bright-eyed and sharp-clawed things.

Her father had been a huntsman, an associate of that famous devotee of the chase, Graf Rudiger von Unheimlich. He had died of a fall during a hog course. He had been obsessed with dangerous game, and had even been known to set out after creatures with near-human intelligence – werewolves, goblins, elementals. No wonder he was dead.

Genevieve couldn't remember him. He had the Udolpho face, but so did everyone else she knew.

There was more lightning. She looked at the portrait, and it was a landscape. The trees were there, and the hillside and the silhouette. But her father was missing.

It had happened before.

XV

Her strangling wire before her, she crept down the passage.

Vathek had told her these were the corridors haunted by the Bleeding Baron, a houseguest of Smarra Udolpho who had been stabbed by his sons but refused to die.

She kept to the shadows, trying to stay silent.

Christabel thought of what she'd do with the fortune when it came to her. First, she would expel her relatives from Udolpho and cut them loose in the world. They wouldn't last a month apiece. Then, she'd dismantle the house, stone by stone, until she had the Black Cygnet's treasure. Then, the wealthiest woman in the Known World, she would return to the great cities – of the Empire, of Bretonnia, of Kislev – and make all men her slaves. Countries were hers for the taking.

She heard something, and pressed herself into an alcove, blending with the dark. Something heavy was coming down the passage.

She held her breath, and waited. Heavy footsteps sounded out, and there was a metallic creaking. Blue light filtered through from somewhere.

Christabel tried to shrink into a ball, her killing loop ready just in case. A man-shaped thing rounded the corner. It was taller than Zschokke by a full three feet, and had to bend its head to fit into the high-ceilinged passage. The apparition was clad in a full set of antique armour. It was burnished iron, with fiery designs inlaid, and moved like an animated statue. It had a species of clanky grace that was almost bewitching.

Christabel stood up, and was ignored as the thing walked past. Vathek had not told her about any mailed monster. This was a new addition to the Histories of Udolpho.

The armoured giant moved slowly, but with purpose. Its visor was down, but there was a blue glow behind the slits.

Not knowing why, she stepped out into the thing's path, and looked up at it. There was an unfamiliar crest on its helmet.

The giant halted, and stood over her, its arms outstretched.

She was impressed with its sheer presence, its size, its power. If she stretched her arms out to their limits, she could barely touch both the thing's shoulders. She touched her fingertips the iron chest. It was smooth, and slightly warm, metallic but living. She let her palm linger on the sculpted muscles.

The giant made Lawyer Vathek seem truly pathetic.

It embraced her. She felt a flush of pleasurable fear, as she was lifted by the giant. It could crush her with no effort. She slipped her arms around its neck, and hung in its grip. Sensing a male presence beyond the visor, she felt drawn into the blue light.

After a moment, he set her down gently, and pushed past her, continuing on his way. She watched his armoured back as he turned the next corner. Her heart, she realized, had nearly stopped. She felt faint, but overcame her weakness. Her body was still vibrating with the pleasure of the giant's touch.

She could not yield to womanish feelings. Less carefully than before, she strode through the passages towards the doctor's apartments. She wanted this over with.

Dr Valdemar sometimes worked late in his laboratory, distilling the infusions which had been keeping Old Melmoth alive all these years. He would always be found surrounded by bubbling retorts and smoking crucibles. When she had done her business with him, she would set a fire and no one would suspect anything. The elements and chemicals he was fooling with were dangerous. There had been more than one unfortunate explosion in his rooms.

The doctor's door was open. She held her loop ready, and slipped in. There was a fireplace, its blaze shrunken to embers, its orange glow cast through the room. A chair was outlined before the fireplace, and Dr Valdemar's bald head shone above its back. He was staring into the hot coals.

On the points of her toes, she crossed the floor, and, with a swift movement, fixed the loop around Dr Valdemar's head. She pulled tight, and felt the wire through her gloves as the struggled to choke the life out of the doctor.

He didn't resist.

Immediately, she realized why. Dr Valdemar was tied to his chair, and shoved close to the fire. His legs had been pushed into the grate when the coals were burning high. Now, his boots and britches were partly burned away, and his feet were stubby cinders at the end of blackened legs.

The doctor's head rolled in her strangling grip, and she saw that his mouth had been stuffed with pages of parchment. In his forehead three metal pimples were shining. They were nailheads.

Damn, she thought, the twins have been here first!

XVI

'Did you hear that?'

'What?'

Someone was singing. A mournful lament, wordless and haunting. Kloszowski would never forget it.

'That.'

'Ignore it,' he told her. 'It'll be more trouble.'

The melody was far away, but getting louder.

'But...'

He kissed her, and pressed her head against the pillow.

'Listen, Antonia. Here's my plan. We stay here, and pass the night pleasantly. Tomorrow when the storm is over, we get up early, steal some clothes and get away without looking back.'

She nodded her agreement as he slipped his hand down to her cleft, and teased. She bit her underlip and shut her eyes, responding to his touch.

The singing was almost that of a choir.

Kloszowski kissed her shoulder, and tried to forget the song. It was no use.

Antonia sat up.

'We can't do it.'

This wasn't going to work.

'We have to find out.'

'I think that'll be a very bad idea.'

She was out of the bed, and pulling on the nightgown she had been wearing. Kloszowski was cooling off.

He got up, and wrapped the novice's robe around him. He looked around for a weapon. He could probably smash someone's skull with the basin, but it was hardly convenient.

He tried to open the door. It was bolted, from the outside.

'We're locked in,' he said, fairly relieved.

Antonia pulled the mirror open. 'No we're not. There are tunnels and stairways. I saw them on the way here.'

She picked up the candle and stepped into the passage. Suddenly, it was dark in the cell. He heard her ankle bells tinkling tinily.

'Come on.'

He blundered his way into the boots, and followed.

XVII

Genevieve heard a rap at her door, and the scurry of small feet. It was the twins playing knock-and-run-away again, she knew. She didn't open the door. It would only encourage them.

She sat in the dark and listened. The Wailing Abbess was going again, guiltily confessing over and over again to the stifling of her baby boy, the result of her indiscretion with a dwarfish wizard. The whole family was supposed to be buried behind one of the walls in the east wing somewhere.

Her father wasn't back in his portrait yet.

There was a creak. Her door was bending a little, as if something heavy were propped against it. Knowing she'd regret it, she walked over, unlocked the door, and pulled it open. Her visitor fell to his knees, then pitched chest forward onto the carpet at his feet. She recognized Lawyer Vathek from his clothes.

But where was his head?

XVIII

Aleksandr was keeping up with her but wasn't happy about it.

There must be an entire system of these tunnels, like the dwarf labyrinths under many of the cities of the Empire. They kept having to push through dust-heavy curtains of cobweb, and crunching old bones underfoot. She could hear rats scuttling in the dark.

They still couldn't tell where the song was coming from.

'It's odd,' she said, scything away a cobweb with her arm. 'Lots of webs, but no spiders.'

Aleksandr huffed. 'I don't like spiders.'

'Who does?'

'Christabel Udolpho?'

Antonia laughed. 'Maybe.'

She rubbed the cobweb between her fingers and thumb. It came apart.

'This isn't like webs, you know. It's like the cotton stuff they use in the theatre. I remember in the company of *Cobweb Castle; or: The Disembowelment of Didrick* that it got everywhere. People were choking on it.'

'So this is a melodrama, then?'

'Well, have you ever seen a dinner guest explode before? Or a hulking butler with more scars than pimples? Or found a place like this on a dark and stormy night?'

'You have a point. A small one, perhaps, but a point.'

They came to a dead end. They turned and retraced their steps, and came to another.

'That wall wasn't here. Look, our footsteps come out of it...'

She lowered the candle. It was true.

The singing had stopped. There was a steady grinding sound now, much nearer.

'Antonia,' Aleksandr said, 'hold up your candle.'

She did. The ceiling was slowly descending.

'Merciful Shallya,' Aleksandr said.

XIX

Ysidro d'Amato knew he wouldn't be able to sleep until he'd counted it all out again, just one more time.

He had his valise open, and was fingering the bags of coins. He opened each in turn, loosening the drawstring, and sorted through the different denominations. He always had as much as he could in coinage, and kept it in his own hiding places rather than the banking houses of Miragliano. That had proved to be a wise course.

He cursed the marsh-trader who had offered him such an irresistibly low price for two barge-tankers of supposed rainwater. When the watchmen, and anyone whose business took them to a watch station, started dropping dead, sickly foam leaking from every orifice, d'Amato had instinctively known it was time to leave the city, and move into his Bretonnian household.

His coins clinked as he passed them from hand to hand. He would leave Antonia Marsillach along the way somewhere, he'd decided. Given the choice between hard, cold coin and soft, warm skin, he would always choose the former.

This was a strange house. He'd be happy to leave.

He began to replace his coinbags in his valise, carefully slipping them in. Something in the bag moved, and he pulled his hand out quickly, tucking it into his armpit. He had felt a small, warm body. It was the size of a rat, but it hadn't been furred. Rather, its back had been covered with tiny quills that made his skin sting.

Blue eyes peered up from the dark of the bag.

He was unable to make a sound. He watched in horror as the valise tipped over, unbalanced by the shifting weight of the thing inside.

Then, in a black blur, the thing shot out, and, squeaking, disappeared. A moneybag chunked against the floor, and a scrap of parchment drifted out. It was an old bill from his counting house that he'd used to line the bottom of the valise.

He picked up the paper and looked at it. It wasn't covered in the jotted figures he remembered. It was a plan of some sort, but it wasn't complete. The lines were broken up, as if he only had half of the design, the scribe having been interrupted before he could ink in all the faded pencil lines. There were the remains of a seal on the paper, a baby swan's head in black wax.

Behind him, a door opened. He turned. D'Amato clutched his dagger. No one would steal his coins and live.

'Montoni,' the newcomer said. 'Grandfather, it's me.'

It was Pintaldi. He slumped forwards into the room. He held up his arm. Three of his fingers were missing, and the stumps were still pumping blood.

'It was Flaminea and Schedoni,' he gasped. 'They're trying to cut our branch out of the will.'

'The will?'

'Yes. The fortune should be ours, grandfather. I know you have returned to put our case.'

'I'm not...'

Pintaldi threw himself into a chair, and started binding his hand with a scarf.

'I recognized you from the portrait in the gallery, grandfather. You haven't changed that much in sixty years. Still the same Montoni.'

The merchant was confused. He knew he was not this Montoni, and yet, there was something...

'The fortune, you say?'

Pintaldi nodded. 'It's vast, by now, the interest compounded since the time of Smarra's father. Unimaginably vast.'

D'Amato tried to imagine an unimaginably vast fortune. He tried to see it in coins. A pile of moneybags the size and shape of a city, or a mountain.

'And, grandfather, I still have my half of the map. It's tattooed on the backs of my children. With your half, the pirate's treasure shall be ours! And damn these silly stories about the Black Cygnet's curse!'

Treasure! D'Amato's prick hardened. Treasure! He looked at the paper from his valise, casually cast aside, and back at Pintaldi. Alert now, he listened. But he didn't mention the half-map he'd found.

'They're plotting all the time. Flaminea, Ravaglioli, Schedoni, all of them. Plotting to cut us out. Vathek is with us, but Valdemar isn't. I can win Christabel round. She likes a handsome face. But Genevieve is a witch. We'll have to kill her.'

He was beginning to follow. 'A witch, yes. A witch.'

'Ambrosio is the real problem. Your brother. Zschokke knows you were exchanged in infancy, and that he is really Montoni and you Ambrosio. But that can be dealt with. You were Montoni when you ran off, when you fathered my father with that bandit queen, when you slew the wood elf who could have given testimony against us.'

Montoni remembered. He had only been using the name of d'Amato as a disguise. He had forgotten, but returning home had brought it all back. The fortune was rightfully his. The treasure was rightfully his. Schedoni and Flaminea were usurpers. Not a coin would go to them.

'Pintaldi, my beloved grandson,' he said, embracing the youth. 'Our cause will prevail.'

Pintaldi cringed, binding his hand tighter.

'We must kill Genevieve. And Ambrosio.'
'Yes,' he said. 'Indeed we must.'
'Tonight.'
'Yes, tonight.'

XX

The space was barely two feet high. They were pressed against the floor, and tangled together, their limbs sticking out the wrong way. The ceiling was still coming down.

Kloszowski couldn't take this seriously. It was such a stupid way to die.

'Antonia,' he said, 'I should tell you that I'm a notorious revolutionist, condemned to death throughout the Old World. I'm Prince Kloszowski.'

Her face, near his, smiled feebly.

'I don't care,' she said.

They tried to kiss, but his knee got in the way. Eighteen inches. This was worse than the corpse-cart. The floor was wet. Water was leaking in from somewhere.

He thought of all the things he could have had if he hadn't devoted his life to the cause of the revolution. The approval of the dowager princess, a fine house, quality clothes, a large estate, a pretty wife and wonderful children, accommodating mistresses, an easy life...

'If we ever get out of this,' he said, 'I'd like to ask you to...'

There was an inrush of air, and the ceiling was withdrawn, hurtling upwards. The wall slid into a slot onto the floor, and there was a clear passage ahead.

'Yes...?'

Kloszowski couldn't finish his sentence.

'Yes?' said Antonia, her eyes heavy with happy tears.

'I'd like to ask you to... to...'

The pretty girl's lower lip trembled.

'...to get me a couple of complimentary tickets next time you dance. I'm sure you're a wonderful performer.'

Antonia swallowed her evident disappointment, and smiled with her mouth, shrugging her shoulders. She hugged him.

'Yes,' she said, 'sure. Come on, let's get out of these tunnels before anything more happens.'

XXI

Ravaglioli's stomach felt empty, as if he hadn't eaten for months.

He struggled out of the thick material in which he had been wrapped, and straightened up. Ulric, but his stomach hurt!

He was laid out on a stone table in one of the vaults. He tried to remember what had happened. There had been something in his gruel. He had swallowed something. It was Flaminea, he was sure. She was the poisoner. Pintaldi would have used fire, Christabel her hands.

He staggered across the flagstones, and collapsed against the doorslab. He would have to use all his strength to push it out of the way. Then, he'd find Flaminea and have his revenge.

His wife hated insects, and Ravaglioli knew where he could find a nest of young lashworms. He would take their eggs and force them down her throat, letting them hatch inside her, and eat their way out. That would pay her back.

He pushed against the stone, straining hard. He thought of revenge.

XXII

In the great hall, lying on a hog-length platter, she found Schedoni. He had a skewer in his chest, but he was still alive and bleeding.

The blood excited Genevieve. Something in her stirred.

Lightning struck, and shadows darted across the hall. She saw Zschokke standing by the window, blood on his hands. He had been drinking, and was a stupefied statue. One of the maids was with him. It was Tanja, naked and oiled, on all fours like an animal. She wasn't fully human, staring eyes where her nipples should be, and a tiny, scaled tail poking from her buttocks.

Schedoni was breathing irregularly, his blood spreading in a puddle around him.

Genevieve ran across the room, to the table. Tanja hissed, but Zschokke held her back.

Was Schedoni her grandfather, or her great-grandfather? She couldn't remember.

The old man's shirt was torn open, and the skewer rose and fell with each gasp of his ribcage. Genevieve's mouth was full of blood. Her eye-teeth slid out of sheaths. An ancient instinct took over. She pulled the skewer and threw it away, then fixed her mouth to Schedoni's wound. She sucked, and the old man's blood was pumped into her.

Her mind cleared, and she swallowed.

These people were nothing to her. She was a visitor, like Aleksandr and d'Amato and the girl. They had made her play her part, but it wasn't her. She wasn't Genevieve Udolpho. She was Genevieve Dieudonné. She wasn't sixteen, she was six hundred and sixty-nine. She wasn't even human. She was a vampire.

Genevieve drank, and became stronger.

Rough hands took her by the back of the neck, and pulled her off Schedoni. Her teeth came out of the wound, and blood bubbled free from her mouth.

Zschokke threw her across the room. She landed like a cat, and rolled upright.

The steward roared through his ravaged throat, and Tanja leaped at her.

She made a fist, and punched the animal girl's face. Tanja bounced away, nose pushed in.

It had been a subtle trap, she remembered. She'd been running, and that was part of it. She had wanted to change her life, and that had been her weakness. She could no longer live with Detlef, no longer be domesticated in Altdorf. Travelling to Tilea, she had been caught in a storm, and been forced to take refuge in the House of Udolpho. Then, she had been sucked into their game...

Zschokke had a pike, taken down from the wall. Twenty feet long, it looked manageable in his hands. He prodded at her. Its tip was silver. She stepped back. He was trying for her heart.

Schedoni was sitting up now, wound scabbing over. That was part of the spell. Now she was out of its influence, and she suspected it wouldn't work for her. A thrust of silver and wood through her heart, and she'd be as dead as anyone.

Zschokke came for her.

XXIII

In his bed, Old Melmoth smiled, weak muscles pulling at his much-lined skin. As a boy, he had loved to read melodramas, to see them on the stage. As a young man, he had been the foremost collector of sensational literature in the Old World. Now, on his deathbed, thanks to the magic spells his pirate forefather had brought back from the Spice Islands, he was at the centre of the greatest melodrama the world had ever seen. He pulled the strings, and his puppets schemed, murdered, loved and prowled...

Vathek sat by his bedside with his head in his lap, another draft of the will laid out on the clothes. Dr Valdemar, pulling himself around by his hands, was in the corner, preparing the next infusion.

Outside, it was a dark and stormy night...

XXIV

They came out through a door in the fireplace of the grand hall. There was a fight going on. Genevieve, her eyes red and her teeth sharp, was backing around the long table, and Zschokke, the steward, was after her with a pike.

'Do something,' Antonia suggested.

Kloszowski didn't know. He wasn't sure whether Genevieve stood between him and the fortune of Udolpho or not. Maybe her death would take him one step nearer to the mastery of this pile, to the fulfilment of his destiny.

He stepped into the room.

'I am Montoni,' he announced. 'Come back from the sea to claim my birthright!'

Everyone paused, and looked at him.

He stood tall, determined to show through his bearing that he was indeed the rightful heir. His years of wandering were forgotten. Now, he was home, and prepared to fight for what was his...

'No,' said another voice, '*I* am Montoni, come to claim my birthright.'

It was d'Amato, dressed up as a ridiculous comic bandit, with sashes and a cummerbund, and a sword he could hardly lift.

'Are you crazed?' asked Antonia. 'First you're a revolutionist, now you're the missing heir.'

'It just came to me. I must have had amnesia. But now I remember. I am the true Montoni.'

D'Amato was affronted, and waved his sword. 'You'll never cheat me out of my inheritance, swine. Out of my treasure! It's mine, you understand, mine. All the coins, the mountains of coins. Mine, mine, mine!'

The merchant was a pathetic madman.

D'Amato's sword wobbled in the air. Kloszowski had no weapon.

'Mine, you hear, all mine!'

Antonia handed him a three foot long poker with a forked end. He remembered how d'Amato had abused his beloved. Antonia was a gypsy princess, sold in infancy to the vile Water Wizard, and mistreated daily. Kloszowski held up the poker, and d'Amato's sword clanged against it.

'Fight it, you fools,' Genevieve shouted. 'It's not real. It's Old Melmoth's spell.'

The merchant slashed wildly, and Kloszowski barely avoided taking a cut. He got a double-handed grip on the poker, and brought it down heavily on d'Amato's head, knocking him against a heavy chair.

So much for the usurper!

D'Amato fell in a heap, mumbling.

'It's mine, all mine. I am Montoni, the true Montoni Udolpho...'

Kloszowski drew Antonia to him, a strong arm around her heaving shoulders, and kissed the girl he would make mistress of Udolpho.

'I am Montoni,' he said.

He looked at everyone, waiting to be accepted.

'NO,' roared a familiar voice.

The word hung in the air, echoing like a thunderclap.

'NO.'

Zschokke had spoken. He was no mute after all.

'I can stay silent no longer.'

The steward had the voice of a bull. Kloszowski had heard his voice earlier, before nightfall, before the storm. Zschokke had been the bandit chieftain who had robbed the cleric of Morr. He must have known all along that Kloszowski was in disguise.

'*I* am the true Montoni Udolpho,' he said.

The suits of armour ranged against the far wall came to life, their visors raised.

'And these are my loyal servants.'

They were swarthy banditti, many missing eyes and noses.

'This house and all in it rightfully belongs to me.'

Zschokke thumped his chest for emphasis. The point of the pike appeared between his neck and collarbone, and speared upwards. Zschokke looked at the thing sticking out of him, and opened his throat in a deafening sound of rage.

He was lifted off his feet like a toy, and slid down the pike. Gouts of blood spurted around his face. There was a giant in armour behind Zschokke, hoisting him on his own pike. With the giant had come Christabel, dressed as a bride in a moth-eaten white train and veil. Kloszowski was astonished.

XXV

She finally reached the door, her head pushed first against it, and found it unlocked. For the first time in many years, Mathilda was out of her room. With an effort, cradling her head in her hands, she stood up. There was a window at the end of the corridor, and beyond that she saw the valley.

For an instant, she was her old self – Sophia Gallardi of Luccini – and then she was at the window. Her head broke the glass and the casement, and she fell with the rain towards the slope hundreds of feet below. She felt as if the fall would never end. But it did.

XXVI

Antonia was lost. She no longer knew, nor cared, who everyone was.

Zschokke was twisting like a worm on a fishhook, and the giant was standing like a statue. The armoured banditti clustered around the giant, striking useless blows with maces and swords.

One of the windows blew in, a cloud of glass shards spreading through the hall with the wind and rain. It was more spectacular than the finale of Jacques Ville de Travailleur's *Accursed of Khorne; or: Death of a Daemon Lord*.

The table was knocked over, disclosing Father Ambrosio, his habits askew, entangled with two of the serving maids and a squealing piglet.

He appeared to be having some form of seizure, doubtless brought about by overexertion. He was trying to dislodge something unseen from around his neck. Antonia believed she saw the red imprint of invisible fingers in the white flab of his neck.

She took Kloszowski's arm, and held him close.

Genevieve, her chin bloody, took Kloszowski's other arm. She seemed to be the only other person in Udolpho who was awake.

'We've got to get out of here,' the vampire said.

'Yes,' Antonia said.

'Now.'

'Yes.'

Kloszowski didn't struggle.

The giant slowly threw his pike like a javelin. With Zschokke still spitted on it, it travelled the length of the gallery and its point sank into the wall about fifteen feet from the floor. The pike sagged, but the servant bandit was pinned fast, blood dribbling from his back.

Antonia wondered about d'Amato. She left Kloszowski to Genevieve, and bent over her former protector.

The double doors flew open, and Pintaldi burst into the great hall, bearing a blazing torch in either hand, shouting, 'Fire, fire!'

'Ysidro,' she said. 'Ysidro, wake up.'

'It's all mine, do you hear? I am Montoni! Montoni!'

'Ysidro?'

He pushed her away, and she stumbled against Flaminea.

'Harlot,' she said, scratching.

The giant was moving fast now, wringing the necks of the bandits one by one, and tossing them in a pile. Christabel was playing the harpsichord in ecstasy, her train flowing in the wind.

'Come on, girl,' said Genevieve, who was tugging at a blank-eyed Kloszowski.

Antonia allowed herself to be led out of the hall.

'Mine, mine...'

'Fire, fire!'

XXVII

Christabel couldn't remember who she really was. It didn't matter. Since she had come to Udolpho, she had been home.

Her new lover had killed Zschokke. Now, he would ravage the rest of her enemies. The last of the steward's bandit crew was down, dead inside his crushed armour.

She slammed the harpsichord lid shut, and held out her arms, feeling the cold caress of the wind on her body.

Ravaglioli was crawling out of the vaults into the hall. She nodded, and the giant stepped on her father's back.

Tanja, the lizard-maid, flicked out a long, forked tongue and caught a fly.

'Merciful Shallya,' said Flaminea as the strangling cord went around her neck. Christabel pulled tight.

'Fire, fire...'

Pintaldi tossed a torch into the air, and it came down in burning pieces.

Christabel's train caught light, and the flames licked up around her in an instant, spreading to Flaminea.

'Harlot,' her mother croaked, spitting.

Christabel kept the noose tight, even as the fire grew around them. Pintaldi was right. The flames were cold, and cutting. Pintaldi was on fire himself, spreading his flames everywhere, embracing everyone.

They were all there. Schedoni, Ravaglioli, Vathek, Ambrosio, Dr Valdemar, Flaminea, Zschokke, Pintaldi, Montoni, the maids. The fires spread throughout the great hall. Another wing would be ravaged before the storm extinguished it all. The giant stood unmoved by the blaze. There were others with him. Flamineo, the Phantom Huntsman. The Blue Face of Udolpho. The Strangling Steward. The Wailing Abbess. The Spectre Bride. The Bleeding Baronet. And many, many more.

Christabel felt her face melting...

...and knew it would not be forever.

XXVIII

The rain was dying out, and it was nearly dawn.

Kloszowski lay on the ground while Genevieve and Antonia watched the House of Udolpho burn.

'Will it be forever?'

'No,' Genevieve said. 'It'll remake itself. It's a strange spell. Something Old Melmoth whipped up.'

'Was anyone part of the original family?'

'I don't know. I think maybe Schedoni. And Dr Valdemar is a real doctor.'

Kloszowski sat up, and the women turned to him.

'M-Montoni?' Antonia asked.

He shook his head.

'He thought he was a revolutionist,' Antonia explained to the vampire.

'I am a revolutionist,' he protested.

'It'll pass.'

'But I am.'

Another tower toppled into the ruin, gold gleaming for an instant in the first light before a belch of black smoke obscured it. As one section of the house crumbled, another grew like an accelerated plant, walls piling up, windows glassing over, roofbeams stretching creakily across the spine. The House of Udolpho was unbeatable.

'We can't stay here,' Genevieve said. 'We've got to skirt round the estate, keeping well clear of it. The spell is far reaching, and persistent. Then maybe we can make our way to Bretonnia.'

'Will they go on?'

Genevieve looked at him. 'I think so, Aleksandr. Until Old Melmoth finally dies. Then maybe they'll all wake up.'

'Fools.'

'We all believe in fairy tales,' the vampire said.

XXIX

Alone in his room, Old Melmoth enjoyed the climax of tonight's plot. Fire was always satisfying, always purgative.

The armoured giant was good. He had been an excellent addition. One had escaped. But one was new. A fair exchange. The cast was the same size it had been at nightfall.

Broken Mathilda was back in her room, more altered than ever.

There was just drizzle outside now, and the first blotches of dawn in the sky.

Christabel was screaming as she burned, her wedding dress crumpling and crinkling, melting against her skin. And Tanja was hissing venom in Ambrosio's face, repaying him for his attentions.

Schedoni was cooked where he lay on his platter. Perhaps he could be eaten cold for breakfast. It would not be the first time human meat was served at the table of Udolpho.

He relaxed, and waited for sleep.

It would be interesting to see what happened with Montoni's map fragment. The Black Cygnet's curse had claimed many treasure hunters down through the years. Perhaps Flamineo should creep from his portrait more often, with his hunting dogs, and seek out a new dangerous game.

He had first made his spell in the library, pledging a portion of his soul to the dark powers on the condition that he never be bored again. His early life had been neither tragic nor comic, but merely boring. Now, he was a part of his beloved melodramas, constantly entertained by the dances of his scheming puppets. He drifted, but was brought back by a tiny sound. His door opening.

'Vathek?' he croaked. 'Valdemar?'

Two sets of footsteps, light and surreptitious. His visitors didn't answer him.

He felt the tug of his bedclothes, as they climbed up onto his bed, forcing through his curtains. They were light, but he knew their finger-nails and teeth would be sharp, and they would use them skilfully. He heard them giggling together, and felt their first touches. The curtain of his bed collapsed, falling to the floor.

'Melmoth,' he said, with love. 'Flora?'

It had been the final curtain.

Part Three

Unicorn Ivory

I

Tall, straight trees stood all around like the black bars of a cage. If Doremus looked up, he could barely see the blue-white tints of the sky through the foliage canopy of the Drak Wald forest.

Even at midday, it was advisable to travel these paths with a lantern. Advisable, that is, for the traveller. The huntsman had to forgo safety for fear his light would alarm his quarry.

Calmly, Graf Rudiger, his father, laid a hand on his shoulder to get his attention. He squeezed, pinching too hard, betraying his excitement. He jabbed his head towards the north-west.

Not turning too fast, Doremus looked in that direction, and caught the last of what his father had seen.

Points of reflected light. Like short silver daggers scraping bark.

His father tapped two fingers against Doremus's shoulder. Two animals.

The sparks of light were gone, but the beasts were still there. The breeze was from the north, and they would not get the hunters' scents in their nostrils.

His father silently pulled a long shaft from his quiver, and nocked it in his warbow. The weapon was longer than the reach of a tall man. Doremus watched Rudiger draw back the bowstring, the cords in his neck and arm standing out as the tension grew. The graf made a fist around the fletches of his arrow, and its sharp triangle rested against his knuckles.

Once, on a wager, Graf Rudiger von Unheimlich had stood for a full day with his bow drawn, and, at sunset, struck the bullseye. The friends against whom he had bet had barely managed an hour or so apiece with their bows drawn, and they had forfeited their weapons upon their loss. The trophies hung in the hunting lodge, elegant and expensive pieces of workmanship, finely inlaid and perfectly turned. Rudiger wouldn't have used such trinkets: he put his faith in a length of plain wood he'd hacked himself from a sapling, and in a craftsman who knew a bow was a tool for a killer, not an ornament for gentlemen.

The graf stalked towards the quarry, bent over, arrow pointed at the hard ground. The beasts' spoor was visible now, delicate hoofprints in the mossy, rocky soil of the forest floor. Even this late in the day, there was still frost. Beyond the length of a finger into the pebbly leaf-mulch, the earth was iron hard, frozen solid. Soon the snows would come and put an end to Graf Rudiger's sport.

Making an effort to keep his breathing quiet, Doremus took an arrow of his own and lined it up in his supple bow, pulling the string back two-thirds of the way, feeling a knot of shoulder-pain as he fought the catgut and wood. As everyone kept pointing out, Doremus von Unheim-lich was not his father.

The others fell in behind the pair. Otho Waernicke, under special orders not to blunder around like a boar and give the hunters away, was mov-ing carefully, meaty arms tucked around his belly, checking under every footstep for treacherous twigs or slippery patches.

Old Count Magnus Schellerup, the last of the soldiers the former Emperor Luitpold had called his Invincibles, was flashing his thin-lipped skull's grin, the scars that made a tangle of one cheek reddening as the hot blood of the chase flushed his face. The only concessions he made to the passing years were the many-layered furs which made a hunch-back of him. Magnus might complain about his old bones, but he could keep up with men forty years his junior on a forced march. Balthus, the thick-bearded guide, and his slender night companion, were the rear guard, along to pick up the pieces. The girl clung to her man like a leech. If Doremus thought about her, he had to suppress a shudder of distaste.

He watched his father. These brief moments were what he lived for, as he neared his prey, when the danger was at its height, when there could be no foreknowledge of the equality of the contest. Count Magnus was the same, hanging back only out of deference for the graf, but con-sumed with a lust for the honourable kill. Doremus had had it explained to him from the cradle, listened to the stories of trophies won and lost, and still it meant nothing to him really.

A muscle in his arm was twitching, and he felt the bowstring biting into his fingers as if it were razor-edged.

'It's no good if you don't bleed,' his father had told him. 'You have to carve a groove in your flesh just as you carve a notch in your bow. Your weapon is a part of you, just as, when the time comes, you are a part of it.'

To fight the pain, Doremus made it worse. He pulled further, draw-ing the arrowhead to the circle of his thumb and forefinger, its points scratching the flesh-webbing of his hand. The tendons of his shoulder and elbow flared, and he bit his teeth together, hard.

He hoped his father was proud of him. The Graf Rudiger did not look behind him, knowing his son wouldn't dare fail.

Rudiger stepped around a tree, and stood still, straightening up. Doremus advanced to stand at his shoulder.

They saw the quarry.

There had been a subsidence in the last fifty years, bringing down several of the trees. They lay, broken but still alive, branches shot out in odd directions, and the hollow had filled with still rainwater. This part of the forest was full of subsidences, where the old dwarf tunnels had fallen through. The ground was as dangerous as any creature of the wilds. The pool was still, covered with ice as thin as parchment, dappled with red-brown leaves.

At the other side of the pool, where the ice was broken, the quarry stood, heads dipped to drink, horns trailing in the water.

Behind them, someone drew audible breath at the sight. Balthus's bedmate. The girl would be cursed.

As one, the unicorns looked up, eyes alert, horns pointed at the hunting party.

It was a frozen moment. Doremus would remember every detail of that fragment of a second. The unicorn horns, sparkling from the water, shining like new-polished metal. The steam from the beasts' flanks. Clouded amber eyes, bright with intelligence. The shadows of the twisted branches of the fallen trees. The croak of the greentoads at the pool's edge.

The unicorns were stallions, slender and small as young thoroughbreds, white with the characteristic black flecks of their tribe in the matted hair of their beards and underbellies.

Graf Rudiger's arrow was in flight before the girl had finished her noisy inhalation. And it was speared into his kill's eye before Doremus had his aim. Rudiger's unicorn neighed and thrashed as the arrowhead emerged from the back of his head, and reared up.

The shock of death came fast, blood pouring out of its eyes and nostrils.

Doremus's unicorn was turned and away before his arrow was released and, as he let go the fletches, he had to bring up his left hand to adjust the aim.

The arrow flew wonkily from his hand, and he felt a burning up and down his arm.

'Good shot, Dorrie,' blurted Otho, clapping his agonised shoulder. Doremus winced, and tried not to let his pain show.

The unicorn was almost out of sight before the arrow found him. It slid past his flanks, carving a red runnel in his white hide, and bit deep beneath his ribs.

It should be a heart-shot.

Doremus's unicorn stumbled and fell, but got up again. Blood gouted from his wound.

The animal screamed, emptying his lungs.

'A kill,' Count Magnus said, nodding approval.

Doremus could not believe it. From the moment he had chosen his arrow, he had been sure he would miss. He usually did. In wonder, he looked to his father. The Graf Rudiger's heavy brows were knit, and his face was dark.

'But not a clean kill,' he said.

Doremus's unicorn staggered on, vanishing between trees.

'He won't get far,' Balthus said. 'We can track him.'

Everyone was looking to Rudiger, waiting for his verdict.

Grimly, he stepped over the crest of the subsidence, choosing his footmarks well among the leaf-encrusted floor-vines. His bow was slung on his back again, and he had his dwarf-forged hunting knife out now. The von Unheimlich fortune was one of the greatest in the Empire, but, beside his bow, this knife was the graf's most prized possession.

They all followed the master huntsman, edging around the still pool to the fallen beast.

'A shame it was only a stallion,' Count Magnus said. 'Otherwise, it would have been a fine trophy.'

His father grunted, and Doremus remembered the hunters' lore that he had been made to learn by rote as a child. The unicorn horn his great-grandfather had brought to the von Unheimlich lodge was from a mare. Only unicorn mares made trophies.

Rudiger's unicorn was already beginning to putrify, suppurating brown patches spreading on his hide like the rot on a bruised apple. Unicorn males did not last long after the kill.

'You'll soon have your arrow back, Rudiger,' Count Magnus said. 'That's something.'

Rudiger was on his knees by his kill, prodding with his knife. The animal was truly dead. As they watched, the rot spread, and the stinking hide collapsed in on the crumbling skeleton. The remaining eye shrivelled, and plopped through its socket. Maggots writhed in the remains, as if the carcass were days dead.

'That's amazing,' Otho said, making a face at the smell.

'It's the nature of the beast,' Balthus explained. 'There's some magic in their make-up. Unicorns live well beyond their time, and when death catches up with them, so does decay.'

The pale girl tutted to herself, face blank. It could not be pleasant for her to see such a thing, to know this must eventually be her lot.

Rudiger put his knife away, and scooped up a handful of the unicorn's cooling blood. He held it up to Doremus's face.

'Drink,' he said.

Doremus wanted to back away, but knew he could not.

'You must take something from the kill. Every kill makes you stronger.'

Doremus looked to Count Magnus, who smiled. Despite the bright red mess a wildcat had made of his face, he was a kindly-looking man, who often seemed more willing than his own father to overlook Doremus's supposed weaknesses and failures.

'Go on, my boy,' Magnus said. 'It'll put iron in your bones, fire in your heart. Libertines in Middenheim swear by the potency of unicorn blood. You'll partake of the virility of the stallion. You will sire many fine sons.'

His courage stiffened, Doremus shoved his face into his father's hands and swallowed some of the thick red liquid. It tasted of nothing in particular. A little disappointed, he did not feel a change.

'Make a man of you,' Rudiger said, rubbing his hands clean.

Doremus looked around, wondering if he were seeing more clearly. The guide had said there was some magic in the make-up of the beast. Perhaps the blood did have its properties.

'We must follow the wounded stallion,' Balthus said. 'He mustn't be allowed to reach the mare of the tribe.'

Rudiger said nothing.

Suddenly, Doremus wanted to be sick. His stomach heaved, but he kept it down.

For an instant, he saw his companions as if they wore masks, masks reflecting their true natures. Otho had the jowly face of a pig, Balthus the wet snout of a dog, the girl a polished and pretty skull, Magnus the smooth and handsome face of the young man he had been.

He turned to look at his father, but the vision passed, and he saw the graf as he always did, iron features giving away nothing. Perhaps there had been magic in the blood.

The unicorn was just a sack of bone fragments now, flat against the forest floor, leaking away essence. Otho prodded the corpse with his foot, and opened a gash in the hide, through which belched a bubble of foul air and yellow liquid.

'Euurgh,' Otho said, with an exaggerated grimace. 'Smells like a dwarf wrestler's loinstrap.'

Rudiger took his arrow from the unicorn's head, breaking it through the papery skull. He considered the shaft for a moment, then snapped it in two and dropped the pieces onto the messy carcass.

'What about the horn?' Otho said, making a grab for it. 'Isn't there silver in a unicorn's horn?'

The horn powdered in his grip, the traces of silver glittering amid the white pulpy ash.

'A little, Master Waernicke,' Magnus explained. 'It goes with the magic. Not enough to be worth anything.'

Doremus noticed that the girl was staying well away from the kill. Her kind didn't care for blessed silver. She had a fair face and shape, but he couldn't forget the skull he had seen.

Balthus was on edge, eager to continue.

'If the wounded beast gets to his tribe, the mare will know what we've done. The whole tribe will be warned. That could be dangerous for us.'

Rudiger shrugged. 'Fair enough. We're dangerous for them.'

The graf was not concerned. After a kill, he was always distracted, triumph followed by irritability. Doremus recognized that he was the same way after he had been with a woman. No matter how wonderful it was, it was never up to the anticipation. Rudiger kept his trophies dutifully, but Doremus wondered if they were only reminders of his disappointment. The lodge was full of magnificent horns and heads and pelts and wings, but they might just as well be handfuls of dust for all his father cared for them.

It was the moment of the kill that was all to the graf, the moment when he was the power of life and death. That was his fulfilment.

'You bagged a beast, Dorrie,' Otho blustered. 'Bloody well done. That merits a good few hoists of the ale jar, my friend. You'll have a special place at the table in the League of Karl-Franz from now on. We'll down you a good few toasts before the term's end.'

'Balthus,' said Rudiger, in a dangerously even tone.

The forest guide turned to pay attention to his master. His mistress stood a little behind him, quivering a little.

'In future, have your vampire whore keep quiet or leave her behind. You understand?'

'Yes, excellency,' Balthus said.

'Now,' the graf said, 'day is done. The hunting has been good. We shall return to the lodge.'

'Yes, excellency.'

II

Vampire whore.

Genevieve had been called worse.

But if she were to be serious about not killing Graf Rudiger von Unheimlich, it would have helped if he wasn't such a bastard.

After three days at the von Unheimlich hunting lodge, Genevieve had to admit the graf appeared to incarnate all the vices which Prince Kloszowski claimed were endemic among the aristocracy.

He treated his son like a broken-spirited dog, his mistress like a slow-witted servant and his servants like the frosty leaf-mould they had to spend so much time scraping from the soles of his highly-polished hunting boots. With the fuzzy close-to-the-skull haircut typical of the noblemen of this northern region of the Empire and an assortment of supposedly glamorous scars all over his face and arms – and, presumably, the rest of him – he looked like a weathered granite statue that had once been of a handsome young man and was now due for replacement.

And he murdered for sport.

In her time, she had met many people who richly deserved killing. Since her time encompassed six hundred and sixty-nine years, most of them were dead, of violence, disease or old age. Some were dead by her own hand.

But she was not a murderer for hire. No matter what Mornan Tybalt thought as he sat in the Imperial palace in Altdorf, moving people around like chesspieces, tugging the strings of his many puppets.

Puppet, that was a new entry for her collection of professions. And assassin?

Perhaps she would have been better off staying with poor Detlef? It would have been some years before time overcame him and left her stranded with her eternal youth, carrying another grandfather-aged lover through his final years.

She was still quite fond of him, even.

But she had left Detlef and Altdorf. Journeying to Tilea, she had become caught up in the intrigues of Udolpho, and been extricated only through the intervention of Aleksandr Kloszowski. Then, she had accompanied the revolutionist and his current mistress, Antonia, back to the Empire, travelling with them for the lack of other companions.

She had debated politics with the revolutionist, pitting her cool, cautious experience against his fiery, self-delighted idealism.

That association had been her mistake, the first hook that Tybalt had needed to catch her. She hoped Kloszowski was in Altdorf now, plotting the downfall of the Empire, and, especially, the ruination of the scheming and one-thumbed keeper of the Imperial counting house.

In the cramped quarters she was sharing with Balthus, she stripped out of her hunting clothes – tight leathers over linen – and chose one of the three dresses she was allowed. It was simple, white and coarse. Unlike everyone else in the lodge, she didn't need furs or fire after nightfall. Cold meant nothing to her.

Recently, as the full moons shrank for the last time this year, she was becoming more sensitive. She hadn't had blood for over two months. Kloszowski had let him bleed her one night, when Antonia was distracted, and there had been a young wall guard in Middenheim. Since then, nothing, no one.

Her teeth hurt, and she kept biting her tongue. The taste of her own blood was just a reminder of what she was missing. She must feed, soon.

She looked at Balthus, who was at his devotions before the shrine of Taal by his bed. Her partner-in-crime, Tybalt's puppet had broad shoulders and a thick pelt over his muscled chest and arms. He might be weak in spirit, but he had strength of body. There would be something in his blood, if not the tang of the truly strong then at least enough flavoured substance to quench her red thirst for a while.

No. She was forced to share enough intimacy with the forest guide. She did not want to extend their acquaintance. She had too many blood ties, tugging at her memory.

Blood ties. Detlef, Sing Toy, Kloszowski, Marianne, Sergei Bukharin. And the dead ones, so many dead: Chandagnac, Pepin, Francois Feyder, Triesault, Columbina, Master Po, Bloody Kattarin, Chinghiz, Rosalba, Faragut, Vukotich, Oswald. All wounds, still bleeding.

From the slit window, she could see the slopes descending towards the Marienburg-Middenheim road, the major path through these trackless woods. A rapid little stream, ice-flecked, ran past the lodge, providing it with pure water, carrying the sewage away.

Kloszowski would have made a poem of that stream, coming pristine to the house of the aristocrat, flowing away thick with shit.

With his blood, she had taken some of his opinions. He was right, things must change. But she, of all people, knew they never did.

Balthus didn't speak to her when they were alone, or even much when they were with the others. She was supposed to be his mistress, but he wasn't much for play-acting. By some peculiar turn, that made the imposture a lot more convincing that in would have been if he had always fawned over her and pestered her with public advances.

She was sensitive enough to pick up any suspicions, had there been any. The puppet-assassin had passed the first test.

Graf Rudiger was too arrogant to think himself vulnerable. He travelled with no men-at-arms. If he remembered Genevieve as the mistress of Detlef Sierck, he gave no sign of his recognition. He had been at the first night of Detlef's *Strange History of Dr Zhiekhill and Mr Chaida*, but gave no indication that he had then noticed the vampire.

It had been a week after she had parted from Kloszowski and Antonia. She had been drawn to Middenheim, the City of the White Wolf, needing the distraction of people around her, needing to satisfy her red thirst.

She had found the wall guard and shared herself with him, taking as her due a measure of his blood. He had gone cross-eyed with pleasure as she lapped at the pool of his throat.

Then the watchmen had come for her and taken her, naked under a blanket, to an inn in the better part of the city where she had been sat in a darkened room, tied to a chair.

She broke the ropes after a minute or so of straining, but it was too late. The puppet master arrived, and commenced their interview.

She had seen the olive-skinned Tybalt at the Imperial court, trotting around behind Karl-Franz in his grey robes. She had followed his attempts to impose a levy of two gold crowns annually on all able-bodied citizens of the Empire. Known popularly as the thumb tax, this had led, two years earlier, to a series of riots and uprisings during which Tybalt himself had suffered the loss of a thumb. Despite the injury, he had emerged from the riots with an increased measure of power and influence.

His principle rival for the Emperor's ear had been Mikael Hasselstein, lector of the cult of Sigmar, but Hasselstein had been grievously hurt by some scandal and retired to a contemplative order. He had also been at the first night of *Dr Zhiekhill and Mr Chaida*, grimly protesting. Lipless, humourless, pock-marked and balding, the righteous Tybalt frightened Genevieve more than most servants of the Chaos gods. Coldly devoted to the House of the Second Wilhelm, Tybalt had the makings of a tyrant. And underneath his patriotic fervour and the network of new legislation, Tybalt was at the centre of a web of intrigue and duplicity, his puppets tied to his own standard rather than that of the Emperor, his activities beyond the reach of any legal authority.

Of course, the minister had enemies. Enemies like the Graf Rudiger von Unheimlich.

In that darkened room, Mornan Tybalt, one hand a bandaged paw, had given her a choice. If she refused to do his bidding, then he would bring her to trial, charged with being a confederate of the notorious revolutionist Kloszowski. She would be implicated in a tangle of plots against Karl-Franz and the Empire. Her past association with the well-remembered and ill-regarded von Konigswald family would tell against her, and, as Tybalt reminded her, no one really liked or trusted her deathless kind. She would be lucky to be beheaded with a silver blade and be remembered as the inspiration for Detlef Sierck's *To My Unchanging Lady* sonnets. Tybalt would press for a harsher punishment, silver-shackled life imprisonment in the depths of Mundsen Keep, each endless day identical to the next for as long as the persistent spark remained in her unaging, undead body. But if she became his puppet and carried through his plan, she could go free...

Had she followed her instincts, she would have torn out the Minister's scrawny throat. At least that way she would have earned her punishments. But he had another hook: Detlef. Tybalt promised that if she did not enter his service, he'd use his considerable influence to have the Vargr Breughel Memorial Playhouse closed down, and to prosecute various suits against the playwright. Tybalt insinuated it would be easy to break Detlef who, lately, was not the man he had been. Genevieve carried enough guilt over Detlef, and knew she couldn't be the cause of further hurt to him.

Tybalt did not need to explain the situation between him and the graf. It was well-known. Tybalt was the son of a palace clerk, who had risen through the ranks through his wits and determination, and blackmail, extortion and duplicity. He had about him similar men, colourless toilers without breeding or lineage, quill-scratching achievers who insinuated themselves into the workings of the Empire and became indispensable. Tybalt and his like had never wielded a sword in battle or taken the trouble to acquire the manners expected of the court. They dressed in a uniform drab grey as a protest against the highly-coloured fopperies of those thin-blooded aristocrats they saw as parasitical hangers-on.

Graf Rudiger von Unheimlich was the patron of the League of Karl-Franz, the famous student society of the University of Altdorf, and he was the unelected, unofficial leader of the old guard, the families who had served the Emperor since the times of Sigmar, the battered and hulking truebloods who commanded the Empire's armies, and who brought glory to the name of Karl-Franz with their victories.

The graf rarely deigned to visit any of the great cities of the Empire, but Karl-Franz and his heir Luitpold had many times been his guest at the hunting lodge the von Unheimlich family maintained in the great forest of Talabecland. Karl-Franz trusted Rudiger, and the graf was not the man to keep silent when he saw a plague of grey men with ledgers sapping the strength of the Empire. After the thumb tax riots it had been the alumni of the League of Karl-Franz who had helped restore order, not the ink-stained bureaucrats of the treasury.

While Mornan Tybalt had been in hospital screaming over his lost thumb, and the Empire had been shaking a little as the news of the Altdorf uprisings spread out, it had been the Graf Rudiger who had convened the electoral college and the nineteen barons of the first families at his lodge, and formulated the plans which had forestalled a revolution.

'We shall be the Invincibles again,' he had said, and the Empire had remembered the old days, the days of warrior-statesmen like Count Magnus Schellerup. After bloody months, all had bowed again to the House of the Second Wilhelm.

Later this year, Graf Rudiger and the Emperor would meet again at the ceremony by which Prince Luitpold would attain his manhood. The electors would be there, and the nineteen barons. And Mornan Tybalt was afraid that a quiet conversation between these descendants of the Empire's great families would lead to the downfall of one grey clerk's son.

'The graf must die,' Tybalt had told her, 'and in such a way that there are no questions. An accident, if you can. Simple violence, if you must. Whatever, the finger of guilt must point away, to the winds. Von Unheimlich is a hunter, the foremost in the Empire. And you, Mademoiselle Dieudonné, are a predator. The match should be intriguing, I think.'

Tybalt already had one puppet in place, Balthus. But the guide was just a spy. The minister needed a murderer.

Genevieve suited the requirements.

Balthus finished his oblations and stood up. Genevieve wondered what Tybalt's hook was in his case. There must be something about him that could cause his ruin.

He hadn't mentioned her trespass of this afternoon. If anything, the slip made her seem more like an empty-headed plaything. The graf might have utter contempt for Genevieve now, but he wasn't afraid, or suspicious, of her.

She remembered his conduct in the woods. His treatment of his son, Doremus. His intolerance, impatience.

He had called her a vampire whore.

Her eyeteeth touched her lower lip, and she felt their keenness. There would be red in her eyes.

She remembered Doremus, gulping down the unicorn's blood to make a man of himself. She'd heard of the custom, but never seen it practised. It struck her as barbaric. And, born into an age of barbarism she'd outlived, she had a horror of such things.

'As an afterthought,' Tybalt had said, 'the graf has a son and heir, Doremus. A sensitive youth, I'm told. The hope of the von Unheimlich line. There are no brothers or male cousins to carry the name. It seems unlikely that Doremus could replace his father among the nineteen, but I detest loose ends left to dangle. They have a habit of snagging on something, and the whole design unravels. Once the graf has been eliminated, take care of the son as well. Take good care of the son.'

III

'The Grafin Serafina was a beautiful woman,' Count Magnus said. 'To die so young is a tragedy.'

Doremus had been looking again at the portrait in the dining hall, wondering what lay behind the face of the mother he had never known.

She had been painted in the woods, kneeling by a brook, surrounded by flowers of spring. There was an impossible touch of the elfin in her sharp, delicate features. And the trees above cast shadows upon her face, as if the painter had foreseen the accident that would befall her. Twenty years ago, in these woods, she had been thrown from her horse, and her slim neck had been snapped.

'If you are ever inclined to judge your father harshly, my boy, remember his great loss.'

Magnus laid a hand on his neck, and fondly squeezed, ruffling his hair.

'What was she like, uncle?'

Magnus had been 'uncle' to him ever since he was a child, although he was not a blood kinsman.

The count smiled with the half of his mouth that worked, and his scar blushed.

'Lovelier than the painting. She had gifts. She took away the cruelty of men.'

'Was she... '

Magnus shook his head, cutting off his question. 'Enough, boy. Your father and I have too many old wounds. Past Mondstille, when the year grows old, they ache.'

The servants were setting the fire in the alcove, and a supper had been laid out. A hunt supper. Meats from the day's chase, fruits from the woods.

His father was at the head of the table, emptying his third horn of ale, recounting the day's exploits to his mistress of the moment, Sylvana de Castries, and to Otho, who had been on the hunt but seemed no less interested for that.

The graf had crawled out of the momentary gloom that had come upon him after his kill, and was enthused, explaining every step of the chase, every creak of the bow, every twitch of the quarry.

There was something about Sylvana that put Doremus in mind of his mother's picture although, nearing her twenty-sixth birthday, she was already five years older than Serafina had been at her death. He supposed the resemblance was what attracted his father to the otherwise undistinguished woman, an unmarriageable younger daughter – servants whispered she was barren – of a wealthy merchant of Middenheim. At twenty-six, Sylvana was getting too old for her station. The graf always bedded child-women. Doremus, astonished and appalled, had seen his father look at Balthus's vampire. Rudiger saw only the face of sixteen, not the soul of six hundred.

The graf held an invisible bow out, smile tight as he demonstrated his sure aim.

Otho Waernicke was matching Rudiger drink for drink, and showing it badly. He was the serving lodge master of the League of Karl-Franz at the University of Altdorf, and hence merited the patronage of the graf, who had once held the position himself.

Otho was a grand-duke of somewhere obscure, elevated from the commonplace not through any martial distinction of his family but because a toadying money-lender of a grandparent had extended unlimited credit to a profligate elector. After this term, Otho would leave the university to pursue his interests – gambling, whoring, drinking, brawling, spending – elsewhere, and it was his duty to choose his successor. It was important to his father that Doremus become the next lodge master, and continue the family tradition. In Altdorf, Doremus was a member of the League of Karl-Franz, but rarely chose to participate in its legendary, orgiastic celebrations, aligning himself with the more studious faction, the 'inkies,' within the university.

Otho laughed too loud at some remark of Rudiger's.

Otho had presided over Doremus's initiation ceremony, when the pledges had been made to pick up a crab-apple with clenched buttocks and run trouserless around the courtyard of the college three times without dropping the fruit, then required to consume five deep horns of heavy beer while reciting backwards the lineage of the House of the Second Wilhelm.

Doremus had not exchanged more than a few sentences with Otho since that memorable occasion and had been surprised to find Waernicke invited to this hunting party. Of course, Otho, the first lodge master of the league not to have come from among the families of the electors or the nineteen barons, had been impressed to be summoned by such an important personage as the Graf Rudiger. He had been annoyingly solicitous and matey towards Doremus ever since they set out from Altdorf for Middenheim, and then to the hunting lodge.

The graf released his invisible arrow, and laughed as he recalled his true aim and clean kill.

Sylvana clapped, arranging her face so as to express amusement without cracking the mask of powder around her eyes and mouth.

Otho was staring directly into Sylvana's valley-like cleavage, and dribbling beery spittle.

Rudiger, of course, must notice his guest's interest in his mistress. Doremus wondered just how hospitable his father was prepared to be to upstart Otho.

Doremus looked away from Sylvana, back to his mother's portrait. The Grafin Serafina had died on another of Rudiger's unicorn hunts. If there was any gossip, it had never been repeated within Doremus's earshot.

Magnus stood in front of the rising fire, toasting his behind, drinking wine from a goblet. Balthus sat at the table, on hand to give expert testimony should the graf need a detail of his stories confirmed or expanded. His vampire was about somewhere, lurking.

Doremus sat down at the table, and carved himself a slice from a haunch of venison.

'Fine meat, my son,' Rudiger shouted. 'The finer for its freshness.'

Actually, Doremus would have preferred it hung for a day or two, but his father was insistent that what he killed this morning should be consumed this evening.

'To fully appreciate the taste of a meat, you have to kill it for yourself,' Rudiger explained, loudly. 'It is the way of the forest, the path of tooth and nail. We are all hunters, all animals. I simply remember better than most.'

Doremus chewed the tender meat, and cut himself some bread. Anulka, the dark servant girl with the distracted eyes, brought him a jug of spiced wine. His legs and back ached from his day in the woods, but he was hungrier than he'd thought.

From somewhere, Otho found a lute, and began to sing bawdy songs. Tired of the noise, Doremus poured himself a goblet of wine, and hoped the liquor would make the racket go away.

'Oh, the bold Bretonnian barber has a great big pole,' Otho sang, 'And the doughnut-maker's daughter a fine-sugared hole...'

IV

'A pity we couldn't have unicorn on our table, graf,' Otho ventured, voice tired from the fine entertainment he had granted the others. Some blasted servant had taken his lute away. He assumed Rudiger would have the fellow roundly flogged and booted for his impertinence, although the graf had unaccountably failed to intervene. He probably didn't want to make a fuss during dinner.

'Unicorn is not a game animal,' the old sportsman said. 'Unicorn is barely an animal at all.'

'Is that a unicorn horn on the wall?' Otho asked, knowing damned well it was, but wanting to keep Graf Rudiger occupied with stories. While he was boring everyone with tales of the hunt, he wasn't looking at Sylvana. And when he wasn't looking at her, the woman was nuzzling his leg under the table with nimble fingers, pinching his thigh, exciting his interest.

Sylvana de Castries had been eyeing up Otho for days, and tonight, if old Rudiger got sozzled enough, things would pass between them that would brighten up this dull holiday jaunt. It was a week since his last harlot, and his balls were bursting.

Otho choked back a laugh as Sylvana's hand strayed into his lap. From here, he could see down the front of her dress, almost to her belly-button. She had a ripe body, lightly freckled the way Otho liked his whores.

After a day of hunting, there was nothing better than an evening of food and drink, and a night of well-upholstered harlot. Among his league brothers, Otho was famous for his appetites in all directions. It was a point of honour in the fraternity that the lodge master be insatiable. Although, looking at weedy Dorrie, that tradition was due to take a nosedive in the new year.

Otho wondered if there were any way he could keep Doremus out of the office, and pass the cap on to one of the real bloods, Baldur von Diehl, Big Bruno Pfeiffer or Dogturd Domremy.

The unicorn trophy was mounted on a shield bearing the von Unheimlich coat of arms. Three feet long, and regularly polished, it was a perfectly tapered spear, threaded through with veins of silver. In the lodge, it was traditional for a little blood from any notable kill to be rubbed into the horn as a tribute, and the trophy's background was overlaid with crusted stains.

Rudiger emptied his horn, and called for it to be refilled. Anulka, the juicy maid-slut with the blue lips of a weirdhead, complied. If Sylvana didn't come through, Anulka was Otho's number two choice. She looked just the sort for a midnight game of hide-the-sausage.

'Yes, Lodge Master Waernicke,' Rudiger replied, 'that is the horn of a unicorn mare. A magnificent beast, hunted down and killed by my grandfather, the Graf Friedrich. As you know, only the female unicorn yields ivory. The stallions we saw today were poor things beside a unicorn mare. They are taller, swifter, beardless, possessed of an almost human intelligence. Among unicorns, things are different than among men. Each tribe consists of a mare and six or eight stallions. Lusty bitches, unicorn mares. Mothers gore their female foals at birth. Only the strongest survive to adulthood, to gather their own tribes. Unicorn mares are the longest-lived of natural animals, surviving several generations of stallions to tup with their grandsons and great-grandsons.'

Otho laughed loud, and elbowed Sylvana. Under the table out of Rudiger's eyeline, he slipped a spit-slicked forefinger into his fist and wiggled it in and out. Sylvana laughed like music, and her breasts shook like jellies.

Otho's mouth went dry with lust, and he had to gulp down a swallow of wine to keep himself from choking.

He had been drinking ale, wine, Estalian sherry and coarse Drak Wald gin. He believed in mixing his drinks, and his stomach had never let him down yet.

'You have hunted a unicorn mare?'

Otho looked around. Genevieve, the vampire girl, had dared to ask the graf a question.

There was a pause. Otho expected the graf to lash out at the intemperate bloodsucker. Instead, he sipped his ale, and shook his head.

'No, but I shall. Tomorrow. And you shall all accompany me.'

In the quiet that fell, Otho could hear the fire crackling.

'A two-edged privilege that,' Magnus said, 'considering the saying.'

Everyone looked at the old northerner.

'And what saying is that?' Otho asked, jollying the party along.

'"Of those who hunt the unicorn mare, one comes home and he alone."
It's commonplace in the Drak Wald, and in the north.'

'A superstition,' Rudiger snorted.

'Nevertheless, it is often true. As a child, I was a guest in this lodge when Graf Friedrich set out to bring home his ivory. And I was here when he came up the hill, horn in his hand. Five had set out. Including your father, Rudiger. And only one returned.'

The graf fell quiet. Although Friedrich was often remembered in story and song, little was said about Dorrie's grandfather, Lukaacs.

'Are you afraid, old friend?'

Magnus shook his head. 'No, Rudiger, not afraid. I'm too old for that.'

'"One comes home and he alone," eh?'

Rudiger had explained earlier that he had waited years for the chance to go after a unicorn mare. Traditionally, they could only be stalked between the winter solstice of Mondstille and the new year celebrations of Hexenstag. And, despite the proliferation of stories, they were rare creatures.

'Today, we robbed our mare of two consorts. That will have angered her. Tomorrow, we must hunt her down, or she will come for us. That is all there is to it.'

Otho felt he better show some enthusiasm. 'Fine sport,' he said. 'I'm in.'

He slapped the table, rattling the cutlery, and shoved a hunk of meat into his mouth, washing it down with more ale.

Sylvana sat primly back, her hand withdrawing. 'Tonight,' she had whispered. 'Outside...'

That would be cold, but a league man fears no discomfort.

'It will be an adventure,' Otho said, through a mouthful of food. Then, he belched.

Rudiger looked askance at his guest, but he too was drunk, although with a quieter, more dangerous inebriation.

'Sorry,' Otho said. Rudiger shrugged, and smiled.

'And I,' Magnus said.

Dorrie kept his mouth shut. But there was no way out of it for the little inky, Otho knew. When Graf Rudiger called his unicorn hunt, he had spoken for his son too. The milksop would have to rush about in the open air, keeping up with the graf. If it weren't for his lineage, Doremus would come in for a lot more barracking at the university. He was just the type the league men liked to tar and feather, or tie naked to the statue of the Emperor in the courtyard. Didn't drink, didn't brawl, didn't wench. Nose in a bloody book all the time. The dead woman in the portrait must have put it about as much as Sylvana, because little Dorrie certainly didn't seem to be the type to have an old man like Graf Rudiger. Come to think of it, he had heard stories...

The threads of silver in the mare horn caught the last of the fire, and shone like lines of molten metal.

'The unicorn mare is the most dangerous quarry in the world,' Rudiger said.

'And what's the second?' the vampire asked, boldly.

'Man's mare,' the graf said, smiling. 'Woman.'

V

After midnight. Here she was, again, creeping through dark corridors, night senses alive.

Rudiger would have understood, Genevieve thought. He was a hunter. In him, it was a need as keen as her red thirst.

This afternoon, she had thought Otho Waernicke might be a possibility. He was a fat-head, but certainly strong in his way, impulsive, hot-passioned. But now his blood would be thick with ale and wine, and she had tapped too many drunks in her barmaid days. She didn't need his hangover. Sylvana had been drinking heavily too, and she wasn't sure she should try her anyway. The graf might find out, and take extreme measures. That silver-and-ivory unicorn horn would be a very effective way of ending her vampire life. Doremus was off-limits for the same reason, although the youth appealed to her. He had depths that weren't immediately apparent, and that made him attractive.

The last moons of the year, just past full, shone in through the glassed window at the end of the corridor. The pale light was cool and soothing to her skin, but the thirst burned in her throat and stomach.

Soon, she would be forced to Balthus. The puppet could hardly resist, and everyone already assumed she was bleeding him in his bed. But, for the moment, she could afford to be more fastidious.

The forest guide had taken to laying garlic flowers on his shrine to Taal, to protect him from her. And he had a silver knife under his mattress. She had picked it up with a cloth around her hand, and dropped it into the commode. She didn't want Balthus panicking and hurting her.

She made her way back down to the dining hall. The embers were still glowing in the ashes of the fire, and the servants were clearing up by candlelight, bearing away the crockery to the kitchens, arguing over the leftovers of the venison and fruit.

They all froze as she stepped into the hall, but, recognizing her, shrugged and got back to work. They knew what she was, but also that she was only barely their superior in the von Unheimlich household. Compared to the caprices of Graf Rudiger, she was no threat.

There was a servant girl in her early twenties, dark where the others were corn-blonde, sultry where they were lumpy. At dinner, Genevieve had sensed this girl's interest. Her name was Anulka, and she was from the other end of the Empire, the World's Edge Mountains. In that region, there were Truly Dead vampire lords and ladies, and the peasants competed to please their masters. Anulka had lingered by Genevieve, bringing her wine and food which went untouched, and bestowing smiles and glances.

The girl would do.

Anulka was by the fire, waiting. Genevieve beckoned her, and she curtseyed, crossing the room with a certain smugness of expression, calculated to irk the other maidservants. They turned their backs, and shook their blonde plaits, muttering prayers to Myrmidia under their breaths.

The dark girl took Genevieve by the hand, and led her out of the dining hall into a dressing room. It was sparsely furnished, but there was a cot, with pillows rather than straw.

Anulka sat on the cot, and, smiling, loosened the drawstring of her shirt, lowering her collar away from her swan-white neck. Genevieve's eyeteeth grew longer, sharper, and her mouth gaped open. There was red desire behind her eyes. She felt her fingernails extend like claws, and brushed her hair away from her face.

She must have blood. Now.

'No, child,' someone said, a hand upon her shoulder. 'Don't cheapen yourself.'

She wheeled around, razor-tipped fingers up to strike, and saw the interloper was Count Magnus. Just in time, she held herself back. It would not do to harm this nobleman, the friend and mentor of Graf Rudiger.

'The slut's looking for a protector, for gold, for a way out of this place.'

Anulka's blouse was in her lap now, and her flesh was pale and cold in the moonlight. There was a trickle of blue juice seeping from her mouth, spotting her breasts.

'She's a weirdroot chewer, Genevieve,' Magnus said. 'You'd be poisoning yourself.'

Anulka smiled as if Magnus weren't there, teeth stained, and caressed herself, inviting Genevieve's sharp mouth to fasten upon her body.

If she hadn't been so consumed with the red thirst, she might have noticed Anulka's addiction. She was far gone into it, weirddreams floating in her eyeballs. The servant lay back on the cot, and convulsed as if Genevieve had bitten her. She moaned, welcoming a long-gone, or half-imagined lover.

Magnus found a blanket and, not unkindly, put it over Anulka's slow-writhing body.

'She'll sleep it through,' he said. 'I know the addiction.'

Genevieve looked at him, asking without words...

'No,' he said, 'not me, my father. His brother was one of the five who didn't come back when Friedrich won his ivory. He thought it should have been him, and tried to bury the guilt with dreams.'

She was weak now, and enervated. She was shaking, her gums split and her stomach empty. She had been close to drinking, but not close enough...

368

KIM NEWMAN

'Dreams,' Magnus said, wistfully.

There was nothing for it. She must find Balthus and take him. He would fight, but she could find a burst of strength to overcome his struggle. Her teeth would meet in his neck.

She turned, and her knees gave way. Magnus, surprisingly fast for someone his age, caught her.

'It's been too long, hasn't it?' he asked. She didn't have to answer.

Magnus laid her down on the flagstones, which were ice-cold through her dress, and propped her up against the wall.

The red thirst was an agony.

The Count was undoing the seven tiny buttons at the end of his jacket sleeve. He rolled the cloth back, and loosened the cuff of his shirt.

'It'll be thin,' he said, 'but we're a fine-blooded family. We can trace our line back to Sigmar himself. Illegitimately, of course. But the blood of the hero is in me.'

He presented his wrist to her, and she saw the blue vein pulsing slightly. His heart was still strong.

'Are you sure?' Genevieve asked.

Magnus was impatient. 'Child, you need it. Now, drink.'

She licked her lips.

'Child...'

'I'm six hundred years older than you, count,' she said.

Gently, she took his wrist in her hands, and bent her head to the vein. She licked a patch of skin with her tongue, tasting the copper-and-salt of his sweat, then delicately scratched the skin, sucking up the blood that welled into her mouth.

Anulka moaned in her weirddream, and Genevieve suckled, feeling the warmth and calm seeping throughout her body.

When it was over, her red thirst receded and she was herself again.

'Thank you,' she said, standing up. 'I am in your debt.'

The count still sat, his bare arm extended, blood filling his tiny wounds. He was looking distractedly at the window, at the larger moon. A cloud drifted across the moons.

'Count Magnus?'

Slowly, he turned his head to look up at her. She realized how weak he must be after her meal. Invincible or not, he was an old man.

'I'm sorry,' she said, gratitude gushing. She helped him upright, hugging his great barrel chest as she got him standing. He was heavy-set, big-boned, but she handled him as if he were a frail child. She had taken some – too much? – of his strength.

'Child, take me to the balcony. I want to show you the forests by night. I know you can see better in the dark. It will be my gift to you.'

'You've done enough.'

'No. Rudiger wronged you today. What Rudiger does, I must make amends for. It's part of our bond.'

Genevieve didn't understand, but she knew she must go along with the count.

They passed through the dining hall, which was cleared of servants, and towards the balcony doors. The cloud passed the moons, and light poured in, striking the portrait given pride of place among the von Unheimlich trophies.

Magnus paused, and looked up at the picture of the young woman in the woods. Genevieve felt a shiver of motion run through his body, and he said a name under his breath.

Serafina.

The doors were open, and a night breeze was blowing in, scented by the trees. Genevieve could taste the forests.

The doors should have been fastened.

Genevieve's night senses tingled, and she intuited something. Not a danger, but an excitement. An opportunity.

Count Magnus didn't even know she was there. He was years ago in his memories.

Silently, she manoeuvred him onto the balcony, keeping in the heavy shadow of a pillar.

The balcony ran the length of the lodge, and afforded a view of the slopes beneath. The lodge was built against a sharp incline, and could only be approached from the side paths. The pillars held the lodge up, and the balcony between them was level with the tops of the nearest trees. Beneath, the stream ran.

There was a man at the other end of the balcony, bent over the balustrade, looking downwards, a bottle clasped in one hand.

It was the Graf Rudiger.

For Genevieve, it would be a simple matter. She had to put Count Magnus down, trusting him to fall asleep. Then, she simply had to pick up Rudiger and throw him, head-first, off the balcony. His skull would be crushed, and it would seem like a drunken, regrettable accident.

And Mornan Tybalt would be unopposed in the councils of the Emperor.

But she hesitated.

Replete, she felt benevolent, grateful. Count Magnus was the graf's friend, and her goodwill towards him spilled over onto the von Unheimlich family. She could not, with honour, carry out Tybalt's mission while Magnus's blood was still in her.

Magnus lurched away from her, standing shakily on his own. She was afraid for a moment he would tumble over the balustrade. It was fifty or sixty feet to the jagged rocks of the streambed.

But Magnus was firm on his feet.

Rudiger didn't notice them. He was deep in his own brooding. He took a pull from his bottle, and Genevieve saw he was shaking. She wondered if the graf were human enough to be terrified by the goal he had set himself. He was more likely to come home on a bier with a hole in his chest than in triumph with his ivory in his fist.

And that, too, would let Genevieve off Tybalt's hooks.

Rudiger was looking at something below, out in the woods.

Genevieve heard a woman's laughter. And a man's, deeper and out of breath.

Magnus was almost level with the graf now. Genevieve followed him, worry rising.

Out in the woods, white bodies shone in the moonlight.

Magnus embraced the graf, and Rudiger struggled in his friend's grip, teeth gritted.

Graf Rudiger von Unheimlich was shaking with rage, angry tears on his face, his eyes red-rimmed and furious. With a roar, he crushed his empty bottle in his hand, and the glass shards rained down from the balcony.

Genevieve looked over the balcony.

Down by the stream, Otho Waernicke, a fat naked pig-shape, was covering a woman, snorting and grunting, his belly-rolls and flab-bag buttocks shaking.

Rudiger shouted wordlessly.

The woman, eyes widening in horror, noticed the audience, but Otho was too carried away to be aware of, or care about, anything but his lusts. He rutted with vigour.

Genevieve saw fear in the face of Otho's partner, and she pushed at the bulky youth, trying to get free of him. He was too heavy, too firmly attached.

'Rudiger,' Magnus said. 'Don't...'

The graf pushed his friend aside, and made a fist of his bleeding hand, cold sober fury radiating from him.

The woman was Sylvana de Castries.

VI

Doremus was in the woods, hunting with his father.

'The second most dangerous quarry,' Graf Rudiger had said. 'Man's mare...'

They were running fast, faster than horses, faster than wolves, darting and weaving between the tall trees.

Their quarry was forever just out of sight.

Magnus was by Doremus's side, his scar fresh, face bloody.

Balthus was with them, doglike, snapping at their heels, licking his nose and forehead with a long tongue. And his vampire glided above them on butterfly-bat wings stretched between wrists and ankles, lips pulled back from teeth that took up half her face. Rudiger kept on, dragging them all with him.

They moved so fast they seemed to be standing still, the trees rushing at them with ferocity, the ground ripping out from under their feet.

Doremus had a stitch as sharp as a daggerthrust.

They were closing on the quarry.

They burst from the trees into a clearing, and caught sight of the prey.

Rudiger cast a stone from his slingshot. He caught the quarry low on her legs, and she fell, a jumble of limbs, crashing down against a fallen tree, bones snapping loud inside it.

Moonlight flooded down onto the fallen prey.

Rudiger howled his triumph, steam rising from his open mouth, and Doremus saw the face of the fallen.

He recognized his mother...

...and was awake, shaking and covered in sweat.

'Boy,' Rudiger said. 'Tonight we hunt.'

His father was standing in the doorway of his bedchamber, bending his bow to meet the loop of its string, neck straining taut under his beard.

There was a servant ready with Doremus's hunting clothes. He stepped out of bed, bare feet stung by the cold stone floor.

The shock of the chill wasn't enough to convince him he wasn't still dreaming.

Count Magnus was with his father, and Balthus and Genevieve.

Doremus didn't understand.

'The second most dangerous quarry.'

He pulled on his clothes, and struggled into his boots. Gradually, he came awake. Outside, it was still darkest night.

Unicorns were hunted by day. This was something different.

'We hunt for our honour, Doremus. The name of von Unheimlich. Our legacy.'

Dressed, Doremus was pulled down the corridor towards the entrance of the lodge.

The night air was another shock, cold and tree-scented. Magnus had lanterns lit and was tending them. Balthus had the two dogs, Karl and Franz, and was whipping them to a frenzy.

There was a dusting of snow on the ground now, and flakes were still drifting down lazily. Cold, wet spots melted on his face.

'This harlot has dishonoured our house,' Rudiger said. 'Our honour must be restored.'

Sylvana was shivering, standing between two servants who were careful not to touch her, as if she carried the plague. She was dressed in a strange combination of man's and woman's clothes, some expensive, some cheap. A silk blouse was tucked into leather trousers, and a pair of Rudiger's old hunting boots were on her feet. She wore a cowhide waistcoat. Her hair was a tangle over her face.

'And this fool has insulted our hospitality, and shown himself unworthy for his position.'

The fool was Otho Waernicke, dressed similarly to Sylvana, and laughing with an attempted insouciance.

'This is a joke, isn't it? Dorrie, explain to your father...'

Coldly, Sylvana slapped the lodge master of the League of Karl-Franz.

'Idiot,' she said. 'Don't sink further, don't give him the satisfaction...'

Otho laughed again, chins quaking, and Doremus saw he was crying.

'No, I mean, well, it's just...'

Rudiger stared at Otho, impassive and hard.

'But I'm the lodge master,' he said. 'Hail to Karl-Franz, hail to the House of the Second Wilhelm.'

He saluted, his hand shaking.

Rudiger lashed him across the face with a pair of leather gloves.

'Poltroon,' he said. 'If you dare to mention the Emperor again, I shall have you killed here and let the dogs eat your liver. Do you understand?'

Otho nodded vigorously, but kept quiet. Then, he clutched his stomach and his face went greasily grey-green.

He burped, and a dribble of vomit came out of his mouth.

Everyone, including Sylvana, stood back.

Otho fell onto his hands and knees, and his whole body shook like a stuck pig's. He opened his mouth wide and, in a cascade, regurgitated every scrap of the food he had consumed earlier. It was a prodigious puke, worthy of legend. He choked and gagged and spewed until there was nothing but clean liquid to bring up.

'Seven times,' Count Magnus said. 'A record, I suspect.'

Otho heaved painfully, and made it eight.

'Get up, pig,' Rudiger said.

Otho snapped to it, and stood up.

'The wolf has its fangs, the bear its claws, the unicorn its horn,' Rudiger said. 'You too have your weapons. You have your wits.'

Otho looked at Sylvana. The woman was calm, defiant. Without her face paint, she looked older, stronger.

'And you have these.'

Rudiger produced two sharp knives, and handed them to Sylvana and Otho. Sylvana got the balance of hers, and kissed its blade, eyes cold.

Otho didn't know quite how to hold his.

'You must know,' Rudiger told Sylvana, 'that when I hunt you, I love you. It is pure, with no vindictiveness. The wrong you have done me is set aside, washed away. You are the quarry, I the hunter. This is the closest we could ever be, closer by far than we were as man and mistress. It is important you understand this.'

Sylvana nodded, and Doremus knew that she was as mad as his father. This game would be played out to the death.

'Father,' he said, 'we can't...'

Rudiger looked at him, anger and disappointment in his eyes. 'You have your mother's heart, boy,' he said. 'Be a man, be a hunter.'

Doremus remembered his dream, and shuddered. He was still seeing things differently. The unicorn blood was in him.

'If you see dawn,' his father told Sylvana and Tybalt, 'you go free.'

Rudiger took a waxed straw from a servant, and touched it to the flame of one of Magnus's lanterns. It caught, and began to burn slowly.

'You have until the taper is gone. Then we follow.'

Sylvana nodded again, and stepped into the darkness, silently vanishing.

'Graf Rudiger...' Otho choked, wiping his mouth.

'Not much time, hog.'

Otho stared at the burning end of the straw.

'Get you gone, Waernicke,' Count Magnus said.

Making his mind up, the lodge master pulled himself together and jogged away, fat jouncing under his clothes.

'The snow is slowing down,' Magnus said, 'and melting on the ground. A pity. That would have helped you.'

'I don't need snow to follow tracks.'

The taper was nearly half-burned. Rudiger took the dogs from Balthus, gathering their leads in one hand.

'You and your bloodsucking bitch stay here,' he ordered his guide. 'I'll only take Magnus and my son. We should be enough.'

Balthus looked relieved, although Genevieve – who was more alive somehow tonight – was irked to be left behind. For some reason, the vampire had wanted to be in on the hunt. Of course, she must be used to the second most dangerous quarry.

The straw was a spark between Rudiger's thumb and finger. He flicked it away.

'Come on,' he said, 'there's hunting to be had.'

VII

Otho Waernicke felt as if someone had just run him through the gut with a red-hot poker, and dug around a bit in his vitals.

He didn't know where he was in the forest. And he was more frightened than he'd ever been.

Brawling was more his line. Going out into the Altdorf fog with his League mates and tangling with the Hooks or the Fish on the docks, or with the thumb tax rioters along the Street of a Hundred Taverns, or with the blasted revolutionists. That was real fighting, real bravery, real honour. A good brawl, with a good booze up and a good bedding afterwards.

Rudiger was just a maniac out to slaughter him. The Graf von Unheimlich was no better than the Beast, that altered revolutionist who had ripped apart half a dozen whores in Altdorf two years ago. Otho had brawled well the night they had exposed the fiend.

Yefimovich was the sort of creature who should be hunted through the night. He would probably take to it.

His feet hurt in the unfamiliar boots, and he was cold to the bone.

Where was Sylvana? She had got him into this; now it was her duty to save his fat from the furnace.

His fat was weighing him down now. It had never been such a nuisance before. Meat and drink gave a fellow a figure.

Running was all very well, but he kept banging into trees and cutting his face open or ripping his clothes. He had fallen on his ankle a few minutes ago. It was already throbbing, and he was afraid he had broken something.

This was a nightmare.

He couldn't remember how it had happened. He had only been on that harlot Sylvana a moment or two when he was being hauled off, and slapped silly.

Graf Rudiger had hit him.

That was why he had been so sick.

A treebranch, ridiculously low, came out of the dark and smashed his face. He felt blood pouring out of his nose, and just knew his teeth were loose.

He wished he were back in Altdorf, snoring in his bed at the League's lodge house, dreaming of hot women and cold ale.

If he got out of this, he would enter the Order of Sigmar. He would take vows of temperance, celibacy and poverty. He would offer to all the gods. He would donate his money to the poor. He would volunteer for missionary work in the Dark Lands.

If only he were allowed to live...

He ducked under the branch, and stepped forwards.

All the blood he had been spilling and the trees he had been bashing would be a trail the graf could follow. Huntsmen were good at all that rot, tracking their quarry through scratches on bark and bent twigs on the ground.

Merciful Shallya, he wanted to live!

He kept seeing the graf's arrow going through the unicorn's head, the amber eye bursting, arrowpoint prodding out of the mane.

At once, there wasn't any ground under his feet, and Otho fell. His knee struck stone, and then his back, his head, his arse. He rolled down a slope, stabbed by stones and branches. Finally, he came to a halt, face up.

He would just lie and wait for the graf's arrow.

It couldn't be any worse than running in the dark.

Above him he saw the moons, Mannslieb and Morrslieb.

He prayed to Morr, god of death, pleading with him to hold off. He had exams to pass, a life to live.

He remembered the pain in his stomach, and rolled over. There couldn't be anything more inside him to come out, but his belly clenched and he coughed, choking on bile.

This was how he would die.

He ground his face into the icy dirt, and waited for the arrow in his back.

Behind him he would leave three unacknowledged bastards that he knew of, and unpaid bills in a dozen taverns. He didn't know if he had killed any men, but he had thrown stones and knives in brawls and any number of his opponents might have died of the pummellings he had given them. He had served his Emperor, and he had looked forward to a lifetime of defending the House of the Second Wilhelm from his enemies.

A point jabbed him between the shoulderblades, and he knew it was over.

'Kill me,' he said, rolling over to present his belly to the sword. 'Kill me to my face.'

The graf was not standing over him.

Instead, he found himself staring into a pair of huge amber eyes, set either side of a long face. A sparkling horn stuck out from between the animal's eyes and prodded him.

The unicorn mare breathed out, and plumes of frost shot from its nostrils.

Unicorns are horses with horns, but horses have no range of expression.

This unicorn was smiling at him, mocking him. The stallions' eyes had been cloudy, but the mare's were bright, glowing, alarming.

He froze, and felt his bladder giving out, flooding his trousers with warm wetness.

The unicorn whinnied a laugh at him, and took its horn away.

It was taller than the tallest cavalry horse Otho had ever seen, and long-maned, powerfully muscled. Immensely strong, it was also sleekly feminine.

Horrified at himself, Otho couldn't help but respond to it as he would to a woman.

For the first time in his life, Otho Waernicke saw something he considered beautiful.

Then, with a ripple of white in the darkness, it was gone.

Otho could not believe his luck. He sobbed relief, and laughed out loud, choking on the emotions unloosed from him.

Then he heard the other animals coming.

They were growling, barking, tearing across the distance between him and them.

The two dogs exploded out of the night, and sank their teeth into his fat.

Otho screamed.

VIII

Doremus skidded down the slope, arms out to keep his balance, towards the yapping, screeching tangle.

'Karl! Franz!'

He called the dogs, but they didn't hear or didn't care.

Behind him, Rudiger stood on the crest of the ridge, watching the dogs go for Otho.

This had gone far enough. He wasn't going to let the fat idiot get killed. It wasn't as if his father really cared about his mistress. As far as Doremus could judge, he would have thrown Sylvana away soon. It was only natural the woman should cast around for another protector. Admittedly, she had shown poor taste, but Otho was a duke, albeit a thin-blooded parvenu of a duke.

'Karl,' he shouted, and the dog looked up, red on its teeth.

He took Karl's collar and pulled him away. Franz was chewing Otho's knee, tearing through cloth to get to the flesh.

The lodge master was still alive. He didn't even seem to be hurt that much. He had scratches on his face and neck, but the dogs hadn't a taste for human meat.

Doremus pulled Franz away.

Calmed, the dogs sat and slavered. Doremus patted their heads.

Otho moaned and cried.

For some reason, Doremus remembered Schlichter von Durrenmatt, the undersized lad who hadn't passed the initiation into the League of Karl-Franz. Otho and his fellows had mercilessly kicked and pummelled the boy, throwing him naked into the Reik, advising him to swim home to mother. Doremus wished Schlichter, now a novice of Manaan, were here to see Otho Waernicke fouled and humiliated.

Doremus threw Otho a kerchief.

'Clean yourself up,' he said.

His father and Magnus were with them now. Rudiger made no attempt to intervene, and watched coldly as the sobbing Otho, his boy's eyes streaming in his fat libertine's face, wiped his wounds, wincing as he touched the cuts.

'This quarry was poor,' Rudiger said. 'Not worth taking a trophy from.'

'You should clip his ears, at least,' Magnus said, half-smiling to show he was joking.

Otho, who didn't see the smile, whimpered.

'I should have his balls for what he's done,' Rudiger said, not smiling. 'But a man's a man, and bears little responsibility for the actions of his loins.'

'The mare,' Otho said. 'She was here...'

Rudiger smiled, 'Was she, indeed? A finer quarry than you, jostling for position. But it's no use. The unicorn is tomorrow's animal. Tonight we're after man's mare.'

Magnus was concerned. 'It could be dangerous. Unicorns don't believe in hunters' etiquette.'

Otho was hugging himself, shivering with fear and the cold.

'Master Waernicke,' Rudiger said, 'listen well...'

Otho shut up, and half-sat, looking to the graf.

'Go back to the hunting lodge, and a carriage will take you to Middenheim. Tell the coachman to leave before I return from this hunt.'

Otho nodded, relief dawning on his face. He bent forward, to kiss Rudiger's boot. The graf prodded him in the chest, and snarled disgust.

'My son will be the next lodge master?'

Otho said 'yes' several times, tears flowing freely.

'And he will restore the honour of the League of Karl-Franz.'

Magnus helped Otho stand up. It was clear the quarry had wet his trousers. Even Doremus had no more disgust for the fool.

'Get out of my sight,' Rudiger said.

Otho bowed nervously, and scrambled up the slope, grunting and huffing, foam falling from his mouth.

The last Doremus saw of Otho was his ample behind vanishing over the crest of the ridge.

'He'll find his way back by dawn,' Magnus said. Rudiger shrugged, and plodded on.

'The woman took the left fork back there,' he said. 'She'd have headed for the stream, to break her scent.'

'Father?' Doremus said.

Rudiger and Magnus both turned to him.

'What?' Rudiger asked, glaring dangerously.

'Nothing.'

'Come on then. It'll be dawn in an hour, and the quarry will have flown.'

Doremus felt shamed, but fell in step with the two huntsmen.

Rudiger had been right. The dogs followed Sylvana's trail to the stream, then hesitated. The graf set them loose, knowing they would find their own way back to the lodge.

'It's just us now. A man hunts a woman. That's the way of the world, my son. A man hunts a woman.'

'Until she catches him,' Magnus said, completing the saying.

They followed the stream into the woods. The pre-dawn light was already in the skies, filtering down through the trees as an eerie glowing.

'Plenty of time,' Rudiger said.

'We're near Khorne's Cleft,' Magnus said, making the sign of Sigmar at the mention of the dread power's name.

Khorne's Cleft was a deep subsidence, some three or four hundred feet, cutting through the forest as if a giant axe had struck the hillside. There was a waterfall gushing into the Cleft, and local legend had it that the water ran red whenever a mortal crime was committed by the fall. That, of course, was nonsense, although Doremus had heard the waters did have unusual properties. Natural healing, the woodsmen's wives called it. As a child, he had cut himself badly on the forehead and Magnus had washed his face with waters from Khorne's Cleft, wiping away and closing up the wound as if it had never been.

'Good,' the graf commented. 'She can't get over that.'

They emerged from the trees, and stood on the edge of the Cleft. Doremus heard the water crashing to the thin, deep lake at the bottom, and saw the rush of the fall from the opposite side of the gorge.

'Where is that harlot?' Rudiger swore, nocking an arrow and drawing back his bow.

It was impossible that Sylvana could have climbed down. The Cleft had no bottom, just the lake. Too many woodsmen had left their bones down there.

Doremus looked down, around and, finally, up.

The Cleft was the beyond the length of even an athlete's jump, but the spreading trees above met and mingled, creating one canopy. He couldn't see the woman, but he could see where the branches were moving, weighed down by something heavy.

Doremus said nothing, but his father looked up anyway.

'Cunning minx,' he said, aiming at the moving branches.

Magnus laid a hand on his friend's shoulder.

'Rudiger,' he said. 'No. This ends here. Your honour is restored.'

The graf shook off Magnus, and cold fury burned in his face.

'My honour, Magnus? That has not always been your first concern.'

Magnus stood back as if slapped, and his eyes fell. Rudiger took aim again. Doremus could see Sylvana now. She was almost across, her legs hanging down over the waterfall.

'Rudiger,' Magnus shouted...

Then, things happened, quickly and together. Doremus was whirling around, trying to follow it. Inside his mind, there were explosions of clarity.

His father let loose his arrow, and it flew straight. Nearby, in the woods, there was a crashing as something large loomed. Sylvana didn't scream as the arrow pierced her side, but Doremus heard the tearing of her clothes and flesh as the barb slid into her. Magnus's protest died in his mouth. Hooves struck hard ground, and young trees bent aside. A huge head burst from the trees behind them, amber eyes aflame, hornpoint flashing like lightning. Rudiger had another arrow ready and away. Sylvana shook the branches she was clinging to, and leaves fluttered down like dead birds, swept away by the torrent of the fall. The mare's horn sliced through the distance, and Doremus knew the unicorn would stab his father, spearing him, shoving him from the edge of Khorne's Cleft. Rudiger's second arrow took Sylvana higher up, in the shoulder, and she lost one handgrip. Boughs creaked and cracked. Magnus made a wrestler's grasp for the unicorn's neck, and she turned her horn to slice at him.

The unicorn mare was a vast, awesome creature, silver-white and ancient. Sylvana fell, impossibly slow, towards the waters. The mare's horn caught Magnus below the ribs, and gored him. With a splash, Sylvana hit the lip of the waterfall, and scrabbled at a rock which divided the rushing waters. The unicorn tossed its head, and Magnus was lifted off the horn, a rope of blood bursting from his wound. Rudiger had still another arrow ready.

Magnus hit the ground, spilling over the edge of the Cleft and Doremus, unfrozen at last, reached for him. Sylvana's hands were torn from the rock, and she was swept over the fall. The unicorn bellowed, its sound joining with the woman's scream. Rudiger turned from his kill, and met eyes with the mare. Doremus had hold of Magnus, and was hauling him back from the precipice. Sunlight broke through, and shone off Rudiger's arrowpoint and the tip of the mare's horn. Magnus was babbling. Rudiger and the unicorn looked at each other, his arrow pointed to the ground, her horn to the sky.

'My boy,' Magnus said, through agony. The unicorn withdrew, without turning, and was gone into the woods.

It was over, for the moment.

'My boy, I must tell you...'

Doremus listened, but Magnus had fainted. His chest still rose and fell, but his furs were soaked with blood.

'Father,' Doremus said. 'Help me with uncle, help me.'

He looked at the graf, who had relaxed his bow. Doremus's father was staring across the Cleft.

In the first light of day, the waters of the fall seemed red with blood.

IX

First, Otho had limped out of the night, dogs at his heels, screaming for a coachman. One was ready, and without a word to Genevieve, the lodge master of the League of Karl-Franz left, his hastily packed bags rattling around the carriage with him.

Then, shortly after dawn, the others came back, Rudiger and Doremus supporting Magnus.

'Keep away from him, leech,' Doremus warned her as she went to help.

Magnus, barely awake, shook his head at him.

The count broke away from his companions, and Genevieve took his weight in her arms. It was nothing to her.

She laid him down on cushions in the dining hall, and tore his clothes away from his wound.

'It's deep,' she said, 'but clean. And nothing has been broken or punctured. He's been lucky.'

She had picked up a deal of doctoring in her years, among many other skills. Balthus tore up a tablecloth for bandages. Magnus, drifting in and out of consciousness, winced as she wrapped him up tight. A little blood seeped through his bandage.

'The wound should knit,' she told the others.

Doremus was concerned for the Invincible, but Rudiger hung back, not interested in the count's survival.

'We should go out soon,' the graf said. 'The mare is still around.'

Genevieve couldn't understand the man she was supposed to kill. His best friend was sorely hurt, and he thought only of chasing a unicorn.

'He'll be avenged,' he explained, answering her unasked question.

'He's not dead; he doesn't need vengeance.'

Magnus was quiet, compliant.

'Balthus,' Rudiger ordered. 'Be ready to leave within half an hour. Today, we'll bring back the ivory.'

Balthus saluted, and went off to get his hunting gear.

A door opened, and Anulka wandered in, eyes vacant, bodice badly laced, hair in rat-tails.

'You,' Rudiger said. 'Look after Count Magnus.'

The servant obviously didn't understand. Her lips and chin were blue with weirdjuice.

'Vampire,' Rudiger said. 'You come with us.'

At that moment, Genevieve decided – Tybalt or no – that she would kill the Graf von Unheimlich. She knew there was blood on his hands. He must have killed his mistress. And Sylvana de Castries had not been the first 'hunting accident' in the vicinity of Rudiger's lodge.

Magnus, exhausted, was looking at the portrait of the graf's dead wife.

'Serafina,' he said to himself. He was exhausted, hurt, delirious.

'Anulka,' she said to the maid, using her vampire eyes to penetrate the dreamfog. 'Get some weirdroot. I know you have it. Grind a little into a herbal tea. Give it to the count. You understand?'

The servant nodded, fearful. Weirdjuice, much diluted, could help take away Magnus's pain.

She let Anulka take Magnus, and stood up.

'Get ready,' Rudiger told her. 'Perhaps you'll learn something about hunting by daylight.'

Genevieve bowed and withdrew, trotting down the corridor to her quarters.

Balthus was already dressed in jerkin and furs, and taking his knives and snares down from the shrine of Taal.

'We'll do it today,' she told him. He nodded, his back to her.

'You keep Doremus occupied, and I'll finish the graf. Then we'll be free of Tybalt.'

Genevieve pulled on trousers and a waistcoat. She took one of Balthus's feathered caps, and tucked her hair under it.

'What's his hook, Balthus?' she asked. 'What makes you Tybalt's puppet?'

The guide turned to her. His beard had grown recently, and was creeping up his cheeks towards his eyes. A thatch of ruddy fur swarmed up from his chest and around his neck.

'I might change,' he said. 'Some day.'

'A touch of warpstone, eh? Poor faithful dog-altered. Well, you can find a new master and fetch all the sticks you like after this.'

Balthus didn't look happy about it.

Back in the hall, Rudiger was impatient to leave.

Magnus, already drifting into the dream from Anulka's tea, was trying to say something, trying to talk to Doremus. The graf's son knelt by his 'uncle,' trying to listen, but Rudiger was pulling him away.

'Time for that later,' the graf said. 'We must be on the trail before it cools.'

Genevieve squeezed Magnus's hand, and followed the three men out of the lodge. The dogs were tired, so the hunters would have to do without.

Around the lodge, where the trees were cleared, it was a pretty morning. The sun was heavy on Genevieve's eyes, but in the dark of the woods things would be better.

The graf was striding off. He had told Balthus they were heading for Khorne's Cleft, to pick up the mare's trail there.

Genevieve hesitated, looked back at the lodge, and followed the others. It would be no trouble for her, keeping up.

They travelled a recently beaten path, the way Rudiger and Doremus had brought Magnus. Genevieve smelled blood on the ground. Under some circumstances, she was more sensitive than a good dog. But she did not volunteer to stand in for Karl and Franz.

Rudiger was grimly exultant. He sang under his breath, hunting songs of the Forest of Shadows.

Unaccountably, Genevieve did not just want to kill him. She wanted to break him, humble him and drink his blood. What he had told Doremus yesterday was true: you could take strength from your kills. Genevieve wanted his strength.

Rudiger had changed since he had killed his woman. He wanted Genevieve by his side, and kept tugging at her, keeping her up with him.

She guessed his interest in her, and planned to use it against him. When Balthus led Doremus away, she would take her teeth and claws to him. Once it was over, she could pitch him into Khorne's Cleft, and his body would be gone forever.

They came to the Cleft. This, she understood, was the site of the kill. Genevieve noticed Doremus looking into its depths, hoping for a glimpse of Sylvana.

Rudiger was unaffected, down on his knees, looking for hoofprints.

'Here,' he said, tapping the frosted ground.

Genevieve examined the spoor, noting the distance between prints.

'She must be huge,' she said.

'Yes,' grinned Rudiger. 'An old bitch unicorn, seventeen or eighteen hands, ivory longer than my arm.'

She smelled his arousal.

Rudiger took her slender wrist, and encompassed it with his mighty fist. She could break his back with her slim hand.

'I want her horn,' he said.

He stood up, and followed the mare's hoofmarks into the trees. Doremus followed, reluctantly it seemed. Genevieve thought the way they were taking was familiar.

'She took her time,' Rudiger said, pointing to a chewed branch well out of human reach, 'had some breakfast. She's a cool one, trying to gull us all the time. She'll take a lot of killing.'

The graf strode ahead, following the path the mare had made.

Genevieve looked to Balthus, and the guide turned away. She knew she couldn't count on him, but she hoped she wouldn't have to.

'Look,' Rudiger said, pointing to a flattened area, 'you can see the outline.'

There was a blanket of thin scum on the leafy ground, and the last traces of a skeleton.

'This was your kill of yesterday, son,' Rudiger said. 'Your wounded stallion must have found her, set her off against us. That's war, of course. We must kill the mare, Doremus, before she kills us. This is what it is to be a man.'

She had heard raving lunatics make more sense.

Rudiger went on ahead, came back, and called them on, urging them to run.

She got the feeling Doremus was at the end of his patience with his father. He shouldn't be difficult to distract.

'Come on, come on,' Rudiger said.

Genevieve realized what it was that had been plucking at her mind. 'I know this path,' she said.

'Yes, yes,' Rudiger agreed. 'The track to the lodge. The mare has doubled back, gone on the attack. Very clever, but we aren't fooled.'

She was appalled.

'But the count...'

'An old huntsman's trick, my dear. Leave the wounded as bait. Magnus taught it me when I was a child.'

Rudiger laughed, and Genevieve could have struck him down. Her nails were lengthening, sharpening, and her anger was keen.

But the graf was gone, running ahead, all caution flown, enthused by the chase.

Balthus caught her eyes, and nodded towards a fork in the trail. He could mislead Doremus, and she could end it.

She shook her head.

'We've got to get back to the lodge,' she said. 'Count Magnus is in danger.'

'Uncle...' Doremus said. 'How?'

'The mare has his scent, his blood,' Balthus explained. 'She'll want to finish him.'

'And my father...?'

'Knew?' Genevieve asked. 'Of course he knew. Come on.'

Stirring Doremus out of his doziness, she ran on, following Rudiger, following the mare.

The trees thinned, and they neared the lodge.

From ahead, she heard a howl. A man's howl of grief and fury.

Outpacing Doremus and Balthus, she ran, dodging trees, pushing against the ground. She was fast as a leopard when she had to be.

But she was not fast enough.

The doors of the lodge hung open, and Rudiger stood before them, still shouting his anger.

Genevieve pushed past him, and saw she was too late.

Anulka was crumpled in the entrance, a bloody hole gouting under her chin, twitching in her last dream. Count Magnus Schellerup lay beyond, beside the overturned and smashed table. He was twisted like an old blanket, and the deep gores in his chest exposed ribs and vitals. The mare must have tossed him on and off her horn like a child playing with a cup and ball toy.

She skidded on the blood, and fell to her knees.

The smell of the blood was in the air around her, and she salivated. The blood of the dead was repulsive to her, tainted food. She had been reduced to drinking it too many times, but it still made her stomach turn. Magnus's blood, in her, cried out.

Doremus was with her now, the wind gone out of him.

'Uncle...'

It was too late.

Behind her, Rudiger was striding back into the woods, determined to have his revenge.

Genevieve took a cushion, and laid it against Magnus's bloody head, covering his scar. She looked at the unblemished half of his face, and at Doremus. Then, she shivered, the world turning around and coming down, with a nauseating lurch, in a new configuration.

She understood. And she understood what she had to do.

Leaving Magnus, pushing past Doremus and Balthus, she followed Rudiger into the forests.

Her foreteeth slid out of their gumsheaths.

X

Doremus wept in his heart, but no tears came.

Uncle Magnus was dead, and there was nothing more to do for him. He looked at the old man's face, his scar covered by the vampire girl's curiously tender gesture. For all his life, Magnus had been there, the old Invincible, warm where his father was cold, understanding where his father was indifferent, encouraging where his father was demanding. The count had not been invincible, in the end. But he had died quickly, of a mortal and honourable wound, not lingered with some disease, leaking uncontrollably from all orifices, mind befuddled, body diminished.

It was not such a bad death, Doremus told himself. Then he looked at the blood, at the ripped wounds, and knew there was no such thing as a good death.

Balthus was waiting, in attendance. There were servants all around now, chattering, tutting. Where had they been when the mare was killing the count? Hiding for the sake of their skins?

Doremus followed his father and the vampire, Balthus jogging along with him.

No matter what he felt about his father, about hunting, about the kill, Doremus swore he would track down this thing that had slaughtered his uncle and end her life.

He would find the mare before Rudiger, and this time he would have a clean kill. Then, he would burn his bow.

The forests swallowed them up.

XI

Following his trail, Genevieve hunted the huntsman.

This had nothing to do with Tybalt.

This hunt was hers.

She imagined the mare's horn gouging against Magnus's ribs, sinking deep into his belly, pulling out his intestines.

And she remembered the cold madness of the Graf Rudiger von Unheimlich.

At this moment, there was no more dangerous beast in the forests than a she-vampire.

Always, she had kept herself apart from the Truly Dead, those vampires who preyed on the living for pleasure. She had listened to them enthuse about their sport and felt superior to the grave-grown things with their foul breath and red eyes, faces set in beast's snarls, clinging to their coffins and catacombs by day, gliding on the winds by night in search of juicy necks, relishing the fear they cast about them like a shroud.

She remembered those she had known: the Tsarina Kattarin, bloody tyrant who reigned for centuries, exultant with the blood of her subjects flowing over her body; Wietzak of the World's Edge, a mouthful of teeth like razor-edged pebbles, chewing the flesh of a peasant child; even her father-in-darkness, Chandagnac, dandyish as he dabbed the gore from his lips with a lace handkerchief, old and alone behind his handsome face and manners.

For the first time in nearly seven hundred years, Genevieve Dieudonné understood the righteousness of the red thirst.

She regretted those she had spared: Tybalt, Balthus, Anulka, Otho. She should have gutted them, and drunk the blood fresh from their bellies. She should have drunk an ocean from them.

Rudiger was travelling fast, keeping ahead of her.

She knocked young trees out of her way, enjoying the crack of breaking wood. Birds flew from their falling nests, and small animals scurried out of her way.

'Halt,' a voice said, piercing her red rage, and striking her at the heart.

She stood still, and found herself in a small clearing.

Barely half a dozen yards away, the Graf Rudiger stood, warbow raised, arrow ready.

'Silver head, wooden shaft,' he explained. 'In an instant, it would be through your heart.'

Genevieve relaxed, stretching out her arms, opening her empty hands.

'Normally, I'd tell you to throw down your weapons, but I can hardly expect you to pluck out your teeth and nails.'

Her red rage flared, and she saw Rudiger's face coloured by a bloody film. She fought to control herself, to let the killing thirst die.

'That's right,' Rudiger said. 'Get a leash on your temper.'

He gestured with his arrowhead, and Genevieve sank to a crouch. She crossed her legs under her, hands tucked under her bottom.

'That's better.'

Her teeth slipped back, shrinking.

'Tell me, vampire, how much has that grey book-keeper put on my head? How many of his precious crowns will he part with to get his way?'

Genevieve kept quiet.

'Oh yes, I know all about your mission here. Balthus has the soul of a dog, and the loyalties too. I've known from the beginning. Tybalt doesn't understand that there's more to a man than a price.'

Calm in triumph, Rudiger reminded Genevieve of Mornan Tybalt, eyes glittering as a scheme was fulfilled.

'I'd kill him if it would do any good. But once Balthus gives testimony, there wouldn't be any point. The jumped-up clerk's son will be back where he belongs, toiling in some tiny office, struggling for every scrap of food, for every tarnished pfennig.'

Could she get to him before his shot her?

'You're better than that, vampire. Tybalt must hold you to some crime to make you his tool.'

Behind Rudiger, in the woods, something large was moving. Genevieve could sense her, could feel her excitement.

'Let's make a truce?'

Rudiger relaxed, and let his arrow slide loose.

Genevieve nodded, needing the time.

'See,' Rudiger said, holding the bow in one hand and the arrow separately. 'No harm.'

He came to her, but not within her arm's reach.

'You're pretty, Genevieve,' he said. 'You remind me...'

He extended his arm, and his fingertips touched her cheek. She could grab his arm, maybe tear it off...

'No, you're an original,' he said, taking his hand away. 'You're a huntress, like the mare. You'd be good with me. After the hunt, there are other pleasures, rewards...'

She felt his lust curling out at her. Good. It might blind him.

'Strange to think you're so old. You look so green, so fresh...'

He took her and kissed her, rough tongue pressing against her lips. She tasted the blood in his spit, and it was like pepper in her mouth. She did not fight him, but she did not join him.

He let her go.

'Later, we'll raise your enthusiasm. I'm skilled with more than the bow.'
Rudiger stood up.

'First, there's ivory to be had. Come on...'

He stepped into the woods, and she got up, ready to follow. She did not know what would happen next.

She had the mare's scent. And so, obviously, did the graf.

XII

They were back at Khorne's Cleft. On the other side, from which Sylvana had fallen.

For Doremus, this would be a haunted spot now.

By day, it was stranger than it had been at night. The waterfall sparkled, and it was possible to see all manner of colours and lights in the water.

Balthus was down on all fours, smelling the ground. His backbone had lengthened, straining his jerkin, and his ears were pointed, shifting back on his skull.

It seemed only natural. Even Doremus could sense the call of the woods.

He was still seeing things. And hearing them.

The trees whispered, and the rush of the waterfall was a hissing chatter, talking to him, singing him strange music.

It was bewitching.

He felt like sitting down, and listening hard. If he paid attention for long enough, he was sure he could make out what was being said to him.

It was the unicorn blood in him.

Balthus sat up, snorting, slavering. Then, he bounded off into the woods. Doremus should follow him, but he felt a lassitude creeping over him. The whisperings held him back.

Balthus was scurrying away.

Doremus followed the guide, trailing after his noise. Balthus was yapping like a hound.

Tonight, he would want to be kennelled with Karl and Franz, leaving the leech alone in his bed.

He found Balthus at the edge of a clearing, pointing. He pressed his back to a tree, and caught his breath.

Something was moving between the trees, something with a silver-white hide that flashed.

Doremus had an arrow ready.

He kicked Balthus, sending him off to the right, hoping to attract the mare's attention. If she charged the guide, Doremus would get a perfect shot. He could take her in the neck, or the eye, or the withers. Then, he could use his knife to finish the job if it needed finishing.

He would prefer a clean kill. It would make his father proud.

The mare came to a halt and raised her head, listening. Doremus knew the true kinship of hunter for prey, and understood her thinking.

She suspected a trap, but was measuring her chances. Was she confident enough to charge anyway?

Balthus barked, and the mare went for him.

The unicorn galloped out of the woods, and exploded, bigger by daylight than Doremus had imagined last night, into the clearing. Doremus stepped out from behind the tree and advanced a few paces, arrow coming up...

There was a shaking in the ground as the unicorn's hooves struck. Then, the rumbling increased and became a sharp, earthy scream.

The ground was giving way.

Doremus fired, but his arrow shot upwards, skittering above the unicorn's eyes and clanging against her horn as she batted it aside, its force spent.

The earth tipped like an unbalanced stone, and Doremus slid down it. The unicorn lost her footing too, and whinnied a long stream of forest oaths.

Doremus lost his bow and started tearing at the rippling ground, pulling himself out of the subsidence.

The mare, heavier than he and stuck with hooves rather than fingers, just floundered, and sank further.

Turning his head, Doremus saw the unicorn's head shaking, horn waving, as she fell through into the abandoned dwarf tunnel beneath.

He had lost her.

XIII

They ran to the sound, and found where the earth had given way. Doremus was squatting by the hole.

'The mare's down there,' he said.

Rudiger needed no more. He scrambled into the hole, calling for them to follow.

'I can see down there,' Genevieve said. 'You can't.'

Balthus, part-way through some change, fumbled a tinderbox and a candle out of his pouch and struggled with them. His pawlike hands couldn't work the flint. Doremus took the candle, and struck a light to it.

Carefully, they let themselves into the hole. It was about twice as deep as a man is tall, and led into a tunnel.

'This must be an arterial route,' Genevieve said. 'It's tall enough for us, and for the mare.'

There were much smaller side tunnels, cobwebbed over, which neither man nor unicorn could have got through.

'An easy track,' Rudiger said. 'We just follow the broken webs.'

Balthus whimpered as a spider the size of a housecat scuttled out of its lair.

Rudiger took the point of his boot to it, and it squealed as he crushed it against the wall.

Rudiger was ahead again, and they were behind. This was going round and round, hunting the hunter hunting the hunter and being in turn hunted. Genevieve wanted it finished.

The tunnel sloped downwards, deeper into the earth. She hoped the engineers had built to last. Nearer the surface, things were falling apart.

These workings had been abandoned since the time of Sigmar. None of the higher races had set foot here for centuries.

'There's light ahead,' she said, feeling it in her eyes.

'That's impossible,' Rudiger snorted.

Doremus covered the candleflame, and they all saw it.

'Evidently not,' the graf admitted. 'My apologies.'

The mare had headed for the light.

It was cold down here, and wet. Water trickled down the walls and around their boots.

Their way was barred by a sparkling curtain, and the drumming of water was loud in their ears.

'We're behind the waterfall,' Doremus said.

It was true. Genevieve stepped forwards, and put her hand in the icy curtain, feeling the water splash onto her arm and face.

'The mare must have plunged through,' Rudiger said.

It was a pretty sight.

'Come on,' the graf grunted, holding his nose and throwing himself into the water.

For an instant, he was visible in the water like a bug frozen in ice, then he was swept away.

Doremus was startled.

'There must be a way through to the Cleft,' Genevieve said. 'He should come out with the mare.'

Balthus leaped after his master.

'Are you the kind that doesn't like running water?' Doremus asked.

'I didn't think I was yesterday.'

Still, neither of them made a move to the curtain.

'Can you hear the voice in the water?'

Genevieve listened, and thought she could hear something frail and pleading in the rush of the fall.

'I've been hearing that all day.'

'It must come from around here somewhere.'

Genevieve looked about. To a human, this would be almost as dark as night. To her, it was almost as bright as day.

'Douse the candle, I'll see better,' she said.

Doremus complied.

The rock chamber behind the waterfall became plainer. There were murals carved into the walls, depicting Sigmar wielding his hammer against the goblins. It was indifferent as art, but showed some dwarf-ish enthusiasm.

The noise was a mewling, singing, crying...

They found her in an alcove, mossy blankets pulled around her, face pale and thin, almost elfin.

'Sylvana?'

The woman didn't answer her name.

'She must be dead,' Doremus said, 'I saw father shoot two arrows.'

Genevieve knelt by the woman, and saw how changed she was. The arrows were still in her flesh, but they had sprouted, grown. Green shoots emerged from the wood, and the fletches were heavy with blossom. Her face was changed too, supple as young bark with a green undertone, her hair was the consistency and colour of moss, her thin arms were wrapped around her soft, pulpy body. She had taken root where she lay, been absorbed into the nook. Where she was, she had water and light.

Genevieve had heard that these waters had properties. As she looked at Sylvana, flowers blossomed around her face.

KIM NEWMAN

'Doremus,' Sylvana whispered, her voice coming not from her filmed over mouth but from her breathing nostrils, 'Doremus...'

The young man didn't want to get near the changing woman. But she had something to tell him.

Her head raised, neck growing like a branch beneath it.

'Rudiger killed your mother,' she said.

Doremus nodded, accepting what Sylvana told him. Obviously, that had occurred to him.

'And he killed your father too,' Genevieve added.

Doremus's eyes went wide with incomprehension.

XIV

'Clever, clever,' a voice said behind them.

Rudiger stood, dripping, before the waterfall, his knife out, its blade glistening.

'Doremus,' he said, 'to my side. I have kills to claim.'

Doremus froze, not knowing what to do.

'Serafina?' he said. 'Mother?'

'A whore, like all women,' Rudiger shrugged. 'You did well to grow up without her warping you with her fussing and fiddling.'

The vampire stood up, slowly. In the dark, her eyes seemed to shine red.

'I waited for you outside, but only the faithful dog came.'

The thing that had been Sylvana shrank, her head sinking into its bed of greenery.

'So I returned.' He beckoned with his knife.

'That's a poor thing, graf,' Genevieve said. 'Where's your other weapon?'

Rudiger laughed, as he did at the height of the chase. He tapped his quiver.

'In with the arrows.'

'Father,' Doremus said. 'What does this mean?'

'You don't have to call me that any more.'

'It was Magnus,' Genevieve told him. 'I saw it in his face. You have his face.'

Suddenly, Doremus understood his 'uncle,' understood the care he had always bestowed on him, understood the glances he had always given Serafina's portrait.

'He was a good friend, and no more to blame for the betrayal than that fat fool last night,' Rudiger said. 'It was the harlot I married, that was all.'

Genevieve had been creeping nearer to Rudiger, by inches, whenever the graf was paying attention to Doremus. He didn't know which one to help.

'Vampire,' Rudiger said. 'Keep your distance.'

Genevieve stood still.

'How did you know I did for Magnus?' he asked.

'The count was killed with a horn. The mare would have used her hooves as well.'

Rudiger smiled. 'Ah, that's a hunter's observation.'

From his quiver, he pulled out his grandfather's trophy.

'So pretty, so sharp, so dangerous,' he said, looking at Genevieve.

The horn was still red with Magnus's blood.

'I couldn't let him take my heir away,' Rudiger explained. 'The name of von Unheimlich must continue, even if the bloodline is interrupted. Honour is more important even than blood.'

Doremus knew the count had been trying to declare himself as his father. When Magnus was wounded, he had wanted him to know, had wanted him to carry the memory.

'It was eating him inside,' Rudiger continued. 'He would have spoken out in public, taken you away, taken you for his heir. Now, the threat is gone. The family is whole.'

Doremus turned away from the graf, and cried for his father.

XV

Genevieve went for Rudiger, and collided with him, arms going around him, pushing aside the deadly horn.

Together, they hit the curtain of water.

She clung tight as they plunged down, deep into the lake at the bottom of Khorne's Cleft. Under the surface, it was quiet, all sound muffled.

She could stay under longer than the graf.

She could drown him. But he was struggling, fighting her.

Underwater, he was strong, pushing her away. She felt the point of the horn scrape across her thigh, the silver stinging like a lashworm eating in the wound.

They broke the surface, and the noise was unbearable. Rudiger was shouting, and the water was hammering down around her.

Her blood was all around her.

Rudiger ducked under, and she saw his boots kick the air as he went down. She trod water, paddling with her arms.

Rudiger rose from the waters, horn held in both hands like a heavy sword, angling down at her.

She knifed her legs, and twisted out of the way, and the horn stabbed the unresisting water.

Making a fist, she punched Rudiger in the side, feeling but not hearing his ribs give way. He turned like a wounded fish, and stabbed out, forcing her back. A wave hit her, and she had to keep her balance. The horn came for her again, and she swam back.

She found rock behind her, and the waterfall pressed her down.

Slowly, thinking her pinned down, Rudiger came for her, horn ready for her heart.

'Die, vampire bitch,' he snarled.

The horn jumped, and she let herself be sucked down.

Rudiger stabbed the stone, and she shot out her hand, latching onto his throat, feeling his stiff wet beard in her grip.

The horn broke and she hurled her whole bodyweight at the graf.

She slammed against him and he lost his fragment of horn, his hands grabbing for her hair.

She had lost her cap, and her hair was loose.

Genevieve ignored the pain in her scalp, as Rudiger wrenched. He was

397

under her, and as she swam for the mouth of the culvert, she kept pushing the graf under the surface. He gulped down icy water, and choked out bubbles of air.

There was hard rock under her feet now, and she scraped the graf across it.

At the edge of Khorne's Cleft, the water flowed into a stream, and there was firm ground she could strike for.

Her eyeteeth were points of pain in her mouth, and she felt the red rage again.

She could hear the graf's heartbeat, feel the blood pounding in his throat. Her nails had dug in, and the beaten man was bleeding.

The waterfall had worn a bowl-like indentation in the rock, and at the edge of the culvert there was a ridge that almost breached the surface.

Genevieve slammed Rudiger against the ridge, cracking his spine.

She stood up, the water pouring out of her clothes, and looked down at her quarry.

He was still kicking, but he couldn't hurt her any more.

The graf's warbow and quiver were washed away, floating down the stream. His knife was at the bottom of the lake. His grandfather's ivory trophy was broken and gone. The fight was out of him.

Behind her, Doremus emerged from the waterfall.

The need was in her throat, her heart, her stomach, and her loins.

She fell upon the graf like a beast, nuzzling his neckwounds with her mouth, and tearing through the skin, chewing into the veins with her sharp teeth.

The blood, iced cold by the water flowing around, gushed into her mouth, and she swallowed greedily.

This was not loving, this was preying.

She drank long, sucking the wounds dry, opening fresh ones, and sucking them too. She tore the graf's clothes, and ripped his flesh. She felt him shrinking inside her, sniffed his passions as they were extinguished, swallowed him whole and digested him completely.

She heard his heartbeat slow to a halt, felt his waterlogged lungs collapse, sensed his blood slowing...

At once, she had dead blood in her mouth, and it tasted of ashes. She spat it out and stood up.

Graf Rudiger von Unheimlich was beyond the healing of the waters of Khorne's Cleft.

At the bank of the stream, the unicorn mare stood, amber eyes fixed upon the predator.

Genevieve felt the last of Rudiger's blood rush through her heart, and she strode through the water, kicking waves around her. The mare waited for her.

Wading ashore, she walked up to the unicorn.

They both knew the hunt was over.

She placed her arms around the mare's neck, and rested her head next to the unicorn's, feeling the fur rise against her cheek.

She sensed that the mare was as old as she, that she had known the last of her stallions, that this was the last hunt...

Looking into the mare's eye, Genevieve knew it must all be over. With a sudden wrench, she turned the beast's head around, hearing its neck break like the crack of a gun.

The old mare went down to her knees, and died in peace.

There was a final reward.

She grasped the horn, feeling the nasty tingle of its silver threads, and plucked it from the mare's forehead. It came loose as easily as a ripe fruit is freed from the bough.

The red rage passed from her like a cloud.

XVI

'Here, Master Doremus,' Genevieve said, handing him the ivory. 'A present. A replacement for the trophy that was lost.'

He was shivering, his clothes heavy with water.

Balthus, almost completely a dog, was crouched by the dead mare. He bared his teeth, and worried the unicorn's belly.

Genevieve kicked him away, and he slipped, yapping, into the woods. He was part of the wild now, like Sylvana. The Drak Wald was well known for claiming its own.

The vampire stood between her kills, between the unicorn mare and the Graf von Unheimlich.

'This is what hunters are for,' she said, 'for killing the things that need killing, the things that have outlived their time, have gone beyond their glory.'

The ivory felt smooth and beautiful in his hands.

'Go home, Doremus,' Genevieve said, 'and bury your father. Bury him with honour. Take his name, if you want. Or Count Magnus's. Use your position to harry Mornan Tybalt, whatever...'

He was still confused about all this.

'And as for him,' she said, nodding at the graf, who lay face up in the water, mouth open. 'Forget that he killed Count Magnus. Remember that he knew what he knew but let him live as long as he did. That must mean something.'

The vampire girl was different, now. Commanding, strong, confident. She didn't disgust him any more. She was old, but she looked younger now than ever before.

'And you?' he said.

She looked thoughtful a moment. 'I'll stay here a while, and lose myself in the forests. I'm a wild thing, too.'

Genevieve reached up and kissed him, her cold lips against his. Doremus felt a thrill course through him.

'Be the man your father would have had you be,' she said.

He left her there, and made his way down, past the stream.

When he was out of her sight, he took one last look at the ivory and tossed it into the water. It sparkled on the streambed, the current flowing over it. That was a better background for the trophy than any dusty wall.

Nearing the lodge, Doremus realized the saying was true: *One comes home and he alone.*

Beasts in Velvet

'All men and women are beastly,
and when skinned,
a beast in velvet
is a beast for all to see.'

– Jacopo Tarradasch,
'The Desolate Prisoner of Karak Kadrin'

PROLOGUE

Margarethe

Her last pfennigs had gone on gin and now all she had to warm her was the sting in her throat. It was late and her legs felt like lead weights threaded through with pain. There were thin, dark clouds overhead, obscuring first one moon, then the other.

The summer was long dead and the autumn month of Brauzeit twenty-six days old. Soon, the winter would set in and there would be lumps of ice in the river. It was cold now, but it would be colder then. The weather scryers were predicting a traditional Altdorf fog.

She trudged down Luitpoldstrasse towards the Street of a Hundred Taverns, noting which hostelries still had 'VACANCY' chalked up on their boards. She could not read, but there were words she could recognize. By the watch station, there was a notice the height of a tall man, covered in scroll-like writing. She could pick out a few words: 'wanted,' 'murderer,' 'fifty gold crowns' and, larger than the rest, 'THE BEAST.' A sergeant stood outside the station, wrapped in a warm wolf's-fur coat, his hand resting on a swordhilt. She kept her head down and walked past.

'Watch out, old woman,' the watchman shouted, 'the Beast is about!'

Not looking up, she swore at him and turned a corner. The officer had called her an old woman. That hurt worse than the cold. She could not stop shivering and wrapped her old shawl tighter about her shoulders. It did little against the fishhook-sharp blast of the wind.

She had no idea where she could sleep. Ten or fifteen years earlier, she could have earned a bed for the night by servicing the night man at one of the waterfront hostelries. Not that she would have bent so low when she was in her prime. She had given herself only for gold crowns. But not now. There were younger girls to collect the crowns. There were always younger girls. She admitted to twenty-eight, but felt twice that and knew that at this hour, by the light of both moons, she must look older still. Next year, she would be forty. Her youth had been used up too quickly. Rikki Fleisch's knife had taken out one of her eyes and left a deep groove in one cheek, a repayment for some imagined wrong, but time had wrought an almost equal damage to the rest of her face.

Her shawl had been good once, embroidered with gold thread. The gift of Friedrich Pabst, a gentleman who had been her admirer, it was now patched and ragged. She was going through her shoes, and they had never been the right size. Her feet hurt more than anything else, ruined by years of tottering on ridiculously high heels through the cobbled streets and across the rickety bridges of Altdorf. The gold crowns were all spent now, mostly by Rikki. He had been sweet to her in the beginning and had bought her clothes and jewels. But the clothes were rotted and the jewels pawned, sold or stolen. They hadn't been worth much anyway. And the few good pieces had had to have the original owners' crests filed off.

Across the rivers, there was music. The Emperor's palace rose above all the other buildings and could be seen from almost everywhere within the city's walls. That was too far away to be the source of the music, but there were other great houses. She had been at balls in her youth, taken along by Rikki as a gift for important men, or even invited on her own by her gentleman – Fritzi, she had called him – during their brief summer together, before his wife had returned from her cousin's place in Talabheim. The ladies had known what she was and shunned her, but their men had come sniffing around her skirts, begging her to dance with them and later soliciting other favours. She remembered their perfumes and their velvets. The music of those days had gone out of fashion, but the gentlemen must still be the same, unchanging, smooth, calculating. Undress them and they were just like Rikki Fleisch.

Once, she had been the prize in a dicing game and was taken upstairs by a courtier. He had been some remote cousin of one of the electors. He was fumbling and clumsy and had popped a dried weirdroot flake into his mouth before joining her in the bed, needing the dreams to inflate his courage. Now, she could not remember his face, just his magnificent suit of clothes. That night, she had woken up to find him twitching beside her in his dream. On an odd whim, she had got out of the bed and pulled his distinctive courtier's green velvet cloak over her naked body, relishing the soft kiss of the fabric on her skin. The courtiers all wore these cloaks when they were in the presence of the Emperor. It was an old tradition. Then, that night, Margi Ruttmann had been fit for an emperor. She hawked and spat in the gutter, tasting the gin again as spittle filled her mouth.

There was no music on this side of the river. At least, not music like that. She shivered, the memory of velvet on skin like a phantom's embrace. It was a long time since she had lain with a man who used perfume. Or even soap.

On nights like this, the wind blew off the rivers, filling the air with the stink of dead fish and dead men. No wonder this was where the Beast chose to do his bloody business. More people died every year around the wharfs than on all the glorious battlefields of the Empire. Margi had been in the Black Bat earlier, making the few pfennigs she had taken from Gridli Meuser's child last on a tall glass of gin, combing her stringy red hair over the damaged side of her face, pouting at the few sailors and dockhands who came in. They all knew her and no one was interested. Twenty years ago, they would all have been around her, as they were around that pigeon-chested tart Marlene, or the dark girl from the north, Kathe Kortner. But that had been twenty years ago, when she had been ripe. Now, she only got the drunkest of the drunk and then only on nights when it was too dark to see her face. It was a question of on your back under one of the bridges or standing up in an alley and holding your breath so you don't catch the stench of sweat and beer in your throat, hoping it would be over with soon enough to get back before closing time for a glass or a chew. Five children, born in backrooms and sold by Rikki before they could be named, and Ulric knows how many herb-induced miscarriages had ruined her inside anyway. She could never feel anything, which was probably just as well.

Her standards had been slipping recently, she knew that. Where once she would have insisted on the finest wines, now she was guzzling the roughest gin. Anything to dull the pains. She couldn't remember the last time she had made the effort to get any real food. All the coins she could scrape together went on gin. She would take weirdroot when she could afford it and escape into dreams. But these days her dreams were as dull as waking life and she was always pulled back in the end and dumped in her own self, waking up to the pain. It wasn't just in her legs. Her back hurt more and more, and her neck. And the gin was settling into her brain, making her head throb most of the time.

Business was bad all through the docklands, she knew. In the Black Bat, Bauman had been talking about the Beast and how trade had fallen off since the murders started. There were still the waterfront rats and the sailors fresh off the boats, but most of the citizens of Altdorf were staying away from the Street of a Hundred Taverns. If you didn't get cut up and spread around, you were likely to get hauled in by the watch and questioned. Most people said that the Beast was a nobleman from the Imperial court. Or else he was a cultist of the Dark Powers, disgustingly altered by the warpstone, his fingers turned to sharp knives. Kathe said she had seen the Beast once, stalking a child through the Old Docks, his huge eyes glowing green. She said he had three mouths, one in the usual place and two high up on his cheeks, that his teeth had been inches long and that his breath had been poisoned steam. But Kathe had already discovered the dream-delights of weirdroot and was out of her skull most of the time, not caring who took her. She wouldn't last long. Bauman said he heard that the Beast was a dwarf, killing because he had vowed to cut the big people down to his size. The watch didn't know anything. There were posters up in all the taverns and she had heard drinkers laboriously reading them aloud. The watch were offering good crowns for any information leading to the capture of the murderer. That meant they were desperate.

To Margi, it didn't make any difference. All men were beasts, more or less, with fangs and claws, and women were fools for thinking anything else of them. Besides, she had a claw of her own, a nice sharp blade.

She needed a bed now, more than she needed a weirdroot dream. She had spent too many nights curled up under sacks down by the docks. That was dangerous. Even if the rats didn't bother you, the company watchmen always came round and used their sticks on you. She would always offer herself to them, asking to be left alone in return. It had been months since one of the brutes – that hog Ruprecht at the Reik and Talabec Trading Company – had taken her up on it, and he had been too bloated to do much. Afterwards, he had kicked her a few times and still put her out on the streets. She thought Ruprecht had cracked one of her ribs. With all her other pains, it was hard to tell. One night, she would go back to the Reik and Talabec and take out her blade, just to see how many layers of fat the company man had around his belly. It would be worth doing soon, before they caught the Beast. He could take the blame for it.

She leaned against a wall and felt her whole body sag. Things were bad for Margi Ruttmann.

Whoring wasn't much of a trade at the best of times and it wore you out in a few short years. She knew that now, but she had been a stupid girl once, painted and simpering with the rest of them, dreaming that she would latch on to the younger son of some courtier and become his adored mistress. Marlene and Kathe were like that, but they would learn better soon. She smiled at the thought, imagining the giggling girls gone to rot, shunned by their current crop of admirers. Red-cheeked, plump-titted Marlene would run to fat and drop bastard children yearly in piglet-like litters, and Kathe, who danced like a serpent, would shrivel away to a scarecrow, living more and more in dreams until she walked off a bridge or under a carriage and four. She knew how people aged, had seen it over the years. Margi had just got tough, her soft skin turned leathery, her heart a dead lump like the stone of a peach.

For the hundred millionth time, she cursed Rikki. Without his mark on her face, she would still have been able to get by in her old business. Months after he had carved her, she had slipped into his bed, his own blade in her hand, and cut him a little. She had made holes and let pieces leak out. The memory, too, made her smile. An old woman needed her comforts. The watch had questioned her, but Rikki had too many enemies for them to spend time choosing a likely candidate. That had been during the Waterfront War, when the Hooks and the Fish had been killing each other off up and down the riverbanks. Rikki had been with the Hooks for a while, so he just got listed as another reprisal. The War had not really ended, it just got boring and the gangs lost interest. Earlier, Margi had seen Willy Pick, the current head man of the Hooks, wearing a Citizens' Vigilance armband and walking with an officer of the watch. Until the Beast was caught, there would be some unusual alliances. Most of the Fish were with that agitator Yefimovich, making speeches outside the palace and throwing rocks through shop windows.

Under her shawl, she gripped the handle of Rikki's knife. It was the one he had taken to her eye. It was the only possession she had never pawned. After all, it was her living these days. Her face and body might be ageing like fruit left too long in the bowl, but the blade stayed keen. Tonight, her blade would reap a harvest. Enough for a bed, she hoped, with maybe enough for a few chews of weirdroot to help her sleep, to help her dream.

She tottered down the Street of a Hundred Taverns, looking for a likely prospect. Outside the Sullen Knight, two young, drunken sailors were pummelling each other bloody while a crowd of drinkers looked on and cheered. Kathe was at the centre of the knot of onlookers, her hair loose, her eyes wild and moist, waiting to relieve the winner of his last voyage's wage. Bets were being placed, but neither lad looked to be up to much. That was no good, anyway. Too many people around.

Margi crossed the road rather than walk by the Crescent Moon. She knew what kind of clientele that hostel attracted and she wanted nothing to do with *them*. She didn't mind spending dead men's money, but she was nervous about doing it if the dead man was still walking around.

The Black Bat was closed by now and so was the Beard of Ulric. There was a middle-aged man lying unconscious in the gutter outside the Dancing Dwarf, dressed only in his underwear. He had already been worked over thoroughly: his purse was inside-out and empty beside him, and his knuckles were bloody where the rings had been pulled off.

Two officers of the watch marched past, ignoring the robbed drunk, their clubs out ready to break up the brawl at the Sullen Knight. She stepped into a narrow alley between Bruno's Brewhouse and the Mattheus II, and shrank into the shadows. There was a flickering torch still lit above the door of the Mattheus II and she had to edge close to the wall to avoid its light. There were still a few warrants outstanding on her and the watchmen often pulled her in for questioning. Once, years ago, she had had to service all the men in the Luitpoldstrasse Station just to win Rikki a favour. The watchmen were just like the Hooks or the Fish, with the crest of the House of the Second Wilhelm on their tabards rather than tatty gang emblems. What with the Beast, there were a lot more of them on the streets, hauling in whoever they could find just to prove they were doing something.

She heard the watchmen shouting at the brawlers and the yelps of those who were getting their lumps from the clubs. She hoped they knocked Kathe's silly teeth out for her. Or took her back to the station for a backroom party. That would teach her, the wiry bitch.

Why the watch couldn't catch the Beast and leave the rest of the waterfront alone, Margi didn't know. Perhaps it was because only the drunks and losers who fouled up everywhere else got assigned to the docks. All the shipping lines hired their own men to guard the warehouses and any skipper worth his pay would post his own watches when moored in Altdorf.

It was a long-standing joke in the city that thieves didn't get sent to Mundsen Keep, just assigned to the Dock Watch. The back room at the Luitpoldstrasse Station, where she had conducted her business, was a treasure trove of pilfered goods, stored until the weekly divvy-up. Every once in a while, some officer got too greedy and was hung in chains from the Fork Wharf, but for the most part it was crime as usual. The shipping companies found it cheaper to let their goods be tithed than to make a fuss and suffer from those mysterious fires which often raged around the boats and warehouses of merchants who complained about law and order.

The watchmen passed again, their leather jacks creaking, and she heard the crowd from the Sullen Knight moaning about the spoiled fight. Each of the officers had a chastened sailor on the end of a chain, his thumbs locked together. One of them started singing 'Come Ye Back to Bilbali, Estalian Mariner,' his voice cracked by drink and loose teeth.

'Shut up you,' said one of the officers, administering a thump with his club. The sailor fell down. The officer kicked him. Margi slid down the wall, hugging her bony knees, trying to stay out of sight. A small animal crept by her, brushing her hand with a velvet-furred side. It was gone. Both the officers were kicking the would-be minstrel.

'That's seen for Orfeo here,' said the downed man's keeper, unlocking his thumb-cuffs and wrapping the chain around his hand. 'Let's give his bunkmate some of the same.'

The other officer laughed and also started to free his prisoner. The sailor, a lot less drunk now, protested and demanded to be taken to the station and put in a cell. He was sorry for disturbing the peace.

'Why aren't you out catching the Beast?' said the sailor, his voice wavering, 'instead of–'

The first officer smashed his link-gloved fist into the sailor's stomach, knocking the breath out of him. He took a few more well-aimed shots at the prisoner, then stepped aside to let his friend have a go. The other officer used his chain like a whip and lashed the sailor across the face. The sailor tried to run towards the alley. Margi scuttled back, scraping herself against the wall. The officer flicked the chain out and it wrapped around the sailor's ankles, bringing him down face-first onto the cobbles. His head banged stone and he was probably knocked out. The watchmen kicked him a few times, spat on him and left, laughing. They were typical of the Luitpoldstrasse Station crew.

It was cold in the alley and there was water running somewhere. A chill crept through her. She turned and saw the glitter of water pouring from an aperture in a wall. It didn't smell clean.

There was someone else in the alley. She couldn't make out who or what, but she had the impression of a long cloak. A tall figure, most likely a man. Leaning against the back wall, washing something in the stream. At last, a prospect. She hoped the watchmen were out of earshot.

Margi smiled and pouted. She had practised the expression, to cover up her bad teeth. Under her shawl, she slipped the blade from its sheath.

'Hello, my love,' she said, her voice silly and fluttering like Marlene's, 'lonely this evening, are we?' The figure turned. She could not see a face.

'Come now, come to little Margi, and we'll take care of you...'

She unlaced her blouse and stepped into the light, hoping her skin would look all right. No one would want her if they got close enough to see her. But by then, it would be too late. The prospect would be just where she wanted.

'Come on, my love,' she cooed, her blade behind her. She beckoned with her left hand. 'This'll be a night you'll never forget.'

The figure moved. She heard the rustle of thick material. Fine clothes. She had hooked herself a rich man. Was it her imagination, or did she hear gold crowns rattling in a full purse? This could set her up for a month. She could almost taste the weirdroot in her mouth, feel the dreams blossoming in her skull.

She hung her head to one side and licked her lips. She pulled her blouse away from her shoulder and let her fingers caress her breast, play with her hair. She was like a fisherman, hooking a record-breaking catch.

The figure was close now. She could see a pale face.

She brought out her blade. You could get too old for whoring, but you were never too old to rob a drunk.

She could hear heavy breathing. Obviously, the prospect was interested.

'Come to Margi...'

The shadow-shape was close enough. She imagined a tall man and fit him into the outline she could see, considering where the best spot would be for a first strike. She stabbed out with her blade, aiming for the throat apple.

A hand closed on her wrist, incredibly strong, and she felt her bones grinding, then breaking. Her blade fell and clattered on the cobbles. She opened her throat to scream, sucking in a lungful of cold night air. Another hand, rough-palmed, clamped her mouth, shutting off her cry. She saw bright eyes, aflame, and knew her life was over.

The Beast pulled her into the dark alley and opened her up...

Part One

Murder

I

Baron Johann von Mecklenberg, the Elector of Sudenland, was a good servant to his Emperor, Karl-Franz of the House of the Second Wilhelm. He could not refuse his master a thing, not even an archery lesson for Karl-Franz's son, Luitpold.

'Higher, Luitpold,' Johann told the youth. 'Keep the quarrel and the sight in line.'

The straw targets were set up in the courtyard by the palace stables, and all horses and men had been cleared out of the sometimes erratic path of the future Emperor's bolts. The heir would have preferred to practise in the great ballroom – the only place inside the palace which had the distance to make target practice a real challenge – but an inventory of the priceless paintings, hangings and antiques in the possible line of fire had convinced the Emperor that it would not be a good idea to grant his son that particular wish.

'There,' said Luitpold as he released the crossbow string. There was a satisfying twang. The quarrel brushed the outermost edge of the target and embedded itself with a thud in the wood of a stable door. A horse in the next stall whinnied.

Johann did not laugh, remembering his own shortcomings as a boy. His ineptitude in archery had caused a lot more trouble than merely frightening a horse.

Luitpold shrugged and slipped another bolt into the groove.

'My hands shake, Uncle Johann.'

It was true. It had been true for three years, since the heir had been knocked down by the traitor Oswald von Konigswald during the one and only performance of the original text of Detlef Sierck's *Drachenfels*. No one who had been in that audience came out of the theatre in the Fortress of Drachenfels the person they had been before. Some of them, for instance, had been carried out under a sheet.

Johann was perhaps an exception. For him, life had had its horrors as long as he could remember. Even before Drachenfels, he had become used to struggling with the creatures in the darkness. Most people chose to ignore those things at the edge of their vision. Johann knew that such wilful blindness simply allowed the dark to close in. His years of wandering might be over, but that did not mean the threat was ended.

The warpstone was still working its wretched magic on the hearts, minds and bodies of all the races of the world.

Luitpold fired again. He hit the target this time, but his bolt was stuck askew in the outermost ring.

There was applause from above and Johann looked up. On the balcony, Karl-Franz stood, his voluminous sleeves flapping as he clapped for his son. Luitpold reddened and shook his head.

'It was useless, father,' he shouted. 'Useless.'

The Emperor smiled. A thin man with a mass of curly gold-grey hair stood by Karl-Franz, his monk's hood down around his shoulders, his hands in his sleeves. It was Mikael Hasselstein, the Emperor's confessor. A lector of the Cult of Sigmar, Hasselstein was rumoured to be a likely candidate to fill the post of Grand Theogonist once old Yorri finally got through with the business of dying. Johann worshipped at the Cathedral of Sigmar whenever he could, but he could never bring himself to like men like Hasselstein. Clerics should perhaps not be courtiers. Now, Hasselstein stood by his Emperor, his face unreadable, waiting to be called upon. No one could be all the time as cool-headed and even tempered as Mikael Hasselstein seemed to be. No one human. And Johann was hardly more impressed with his Emperor's other companion, the pock-marked and olive-skinned Mornan Tybalt, the Keeper of the Imperial Counting House, who was intent on replenishing the palace's coffers by levying an annual tax of two gold crowns on all able-bodied citizens of the Empire. The agitators were calling Tybalt's scheme 'the thumb tax,' and gamblers were already wagering on the percentage of citizens who would rather have their thumbs clipped than part with the crowns.

'Johann, show me again,' Luitpold asked.

Reluctantly, aware that he was being put on show, Johann took the crossbow. It was the best design Imperial coin could buy, inlaid with gold filigree along the stock. The sights of the weapon were so precise that it would take a fumblefingers of Luitpold's stature to miss.

Without appearing to look at the sight or the target, Johann released the quarrel. The target was marked with a series of concentric red and blue circles. Instead of a bullseye, it had a tiny red heart in its centre. Johann's bolt split the heart. A tear of red paint dripped from the wound in the straw.

In his mind, Johann heard the echoing cries of all those he had had to kill during his ten years of wandering. His ten years on the trail of Cicatrice the Chaos champion and his followers, the altered monstrosities that called themselves Chaos Knights and his own brother, Wolf. When he had set out, with his family retainer Vukotich at his side, he had been as bad a bowman as Luitpold. But he had learned. When you shoot at straw targets, it is easy to be lazy, to settle for less and wait for the next turn. When you face bestial creatures in battle, you shoot true or you do not live to draw a bowstring again. Johann would never be as elegant in battle as a court-educated warrior, but he was still alive. Too many of the people he had known along his route were not. Vukotich, for one.

Luitpold whistled. 'Good shot,' he said.

The Emperor said nothing, but nodded at Johann and, with Hasselstein and Tybalt at his side, walked on, vanishing from the balcony into one of the palace's many conference rooms. Karl-Franz had a lot to worry about these days, Johann knew. But then again, everyone had a lot to worry about.

Johann held up the crossbow to his eyeline, checking the sight. He felt the wooden stock against his cheek. Back in the forests of Sudenland, he had learned archery with a longbow. He remembered the tight string against his face, the shaking arrowhead resting on his thumb. When he had fired at a target, they called him Deadeye. But whenever an animal had been in front of him, he had ended up nicking his knuckle and firing wild. Strange to think that, all those years ago, he had had an unjumpable fence in his mind. He had been unable to kill. Now, sometimes, he wished he had never been cured of that particular failing.

One skewed shot and he had lost ten years. At sixteen, he had been too compassionate to kill a deer, and had fired wild, piercing his brother's shoulder. That one mistake had meant Wolf had to be sent home while Johann and Vukotich remained in the forests to finish the hunt, and when Cicatrice and his Chaos Knights rode by intent on ravaging the von Mecklenberg estates, Wolf had been stolen away. Vukotich and Johann had followed Cicatrice across the face of the Known World, learning more and more of the mysteries, the horrors, that were hidden from most. In the frozen wastes of the north, on a battlefield where the monsters of the night fought forever, it had come to an end and Johann had found himself confronting young Wolf, grown into a beastman himself, twisted by a hatred that still writhed in his old wound. Vukotich had sacrificed himself and, by a miracle that Johann still gave daily thanks for, Wolf had been restored to him, a boy again, given another chance. The power of innocent blood had saved his brother and that had been the end of the wandering for Johann.

He gave the crossbow back to Luitpold.

'Again,' he said. 'Try to keep your shoulders loose and your hands still.'

The youth grinned and wrestled another bolt into the groove, cocking the string with a grunt.

'Careful,' Johann said, 'or you'll put a bolt through your foot.'

The heir brought the crossbow up and fired. The shot went wild, the quarrel breaking against the flagstones. Luitpold shrugged. A door behind them opened and Johann turned his head.

'Enough,' Johann said. 'It's nearly time for your fencing lesson.'

Luitpold gently leaned the crossbow against the back of a chair and turned round to greet the newcomer.

'Viscount Leos,' he said, 'welcome.'

Leos von Liebewitz saluted and clicked the heels of his polished boots. Most famous duellists were distinguished by their scars. Johann, with more experience of ungentlemanly scraps than polite contests, was covered with them. But Leos, who had fought countless times, had a face as unlined and soft as a girl's. That, Johann knew, was the mark of a master swordsman. Leos switched his green cloak over one shoulder, disclosing his sheathed sword. The young nobleman had watery blue eyes and cropped gold hair that made all the ladies of the court go weak, but he never seemed to return their interest. Clothilde, grand daughter of the Elector of Averheim, had very ostentatiously made romantic overtures to him very soon after her startling transformation from spotty, spoiled brat to ravishing, spoiled young woman and was now suffering from a severely broken heart. Johann supposed that the young viscount's sister, the notorious beauty Countess Emmanuelle von Liebewitz, had enough devotion to the amorous arts for any one family.

Leos smiled sweetly. 'Highness,' he said, nodding. 'Baron von Mecklenberg. How is our pupil coming along?'

Johann didn't say anything.

'Fearfully bad,' Luitpold admitted. 'I seem to have more thumbs than are strictly required by law. I shall have to pay extra tax.'

'A sharp mind will serve you better than a sharp sword, highness,' said Leos.

'That's easy to say when you're the best swordsman in the Empire,' snapped Luitpold.

Leos frowned. 'My teacher, Valancourt, at the Academy in Nuln, is better. And that fellow they sing songs about, Konrad. And a dozen others. Maybe even the baron here.'

Johann shrugged. He certainly did not intend to get dragged into an exhibition match with deadly Leos.

'I'm rusty, viscount. And old.'

'Nonsense.' Leos drew his sword with one clean, fluid movement. The thin blade danced in the air.

'Would you care to make a few passes?'

The swordpoint darted by Johann's ears, whipping through the air. Luitpold was delighted and clapped encouragement.

'I'm sorry,' Johann said. 'Not today. The future Emperor is impatient to receive the benefit of your learning.'

The viscount's arm moved, too fast for Johann's eye, and his sword was sheathed again.

'A pity.'

An attendant was already clearing away the straw targets and archery impedimenta. A trolley had been wheeled into the courtyard. A fine array of swords lay on the upper tier, while masks and padded jackets were bundled below.

Luitpold was eager to get into his gear. He tried to strap himself into his protective jacket and got the wrong buckles attached. The attendant had to undo the Prince and start all over again. Johann was reminded of Wolf, the old Wolf of their childhood, not the strange young-old boy he had brought back from the Chaos Wastes. His brother was three years younger than him, twenty-nine, and yet he had lost ten years to Cicatrice and seemed no older than his late teens. His body had been restored and his soul purged of all the horrors of his years with the Chaos Knights, but the ghost of the memory was still with him. Johann could still not stop worrying about Wolf.

Luitpold made a mock ferocious face as he pulled his mask down and cut up the air with his foil.

'Take that, hellspawn algebra teacher,' he shouted, thrusting forwards and twisting his blade in the air. 'This, for your calculus and this for your dusty abacus!'

Leos laughed dutifully, fastidiously strapped on his chest-protector and pointedly did not bother with the mask. Luitpold capered, administering a death thrust to his imagined opponent. 'Lie there and bleed!' Johann could not help comparing the lively, unspoiled heir with the withdrawn, brooding Wolf.

He had come to Altdorf not just to do his duty at the court, but to be close to Wolf. His brother was supposed to be studying at the University, catching up on his long-lost lessons. And Johann was worried by the reports he kept receiving from Wolf's tutors. Sometimes, the student would disappear for weeks on end. Frequently, his temper would snap and he would get into some ridiculous fight or other and, holding back at the last moment, would be roundly pummelled by an opponent he should have been able to beat without effort. Whenever Johann saw his brother's face bruised and drained of expression, he could not help but remember that other face he had seen on the battlefield. His brother had been a fang-snouted, red-eyed, luxuriously-maned giant. How deeply had that creature been embedded in Wolf's soul? And how clean had his slate been washed by the power of innocent blood? Which, after all the House of von Mecklenberg had been through, was the real Wolf?

Leos was giving Luitpold a work-out now. Johann saw that the viscount was slowing himself, fencing as if wearing weighted boots and gloves. But he was still an elegant murder machine, prodding the prince's quilted torso with every strike, perfectly parrying the youth's counterthrusts. In a genuine duel, he would have cut the future Emperor into thin slices like a Bretonnian chef preparing a cold meat buffet.

There were a lot of stories about the Countess Emmanuelle's many love affairs and her strange preferences in the boudoir, but they were never told where Viscount Leos might hear them. The exclusive graveyards of the Empire were full of well-born swordslingers who thought they were better with a blade than Leos von Liebewitz. The countess had a lot to answer for.

The viscount was making Luitpold break into a sweat now and the heir wasn't disgracing himself. He was less clumsy with a foil than with a crossbow, and he had the strength. It was the strength of a runner, not a wrestler, but that was what he would need to be a swordsman. Once he learned the moves, Luitpold would be a fine duellist. Not that Karl-Franz would let him get anywhere near a serious fight while still alive and Emperor. Luitpold was enjoying the lesson, even clowning a little for Johann's benefit, but Leos was taking it all seriously. The future

Emperor's thick jacket was marked with a hundred tiny tears and the stuffing was leaking.

Watching Leos, Johann wondered about the viscount. During his lost years, Johann had fought many duels to the death, had survived many battles. He had bested men so grievously altered by the warpstone that they resembled daemons. He had killed many. The blood of all the races of the Known World was on his hands. That had not been a courtly game, with seconds and stewards and rules of etiquette.

He was sure that, if it came to it, if it ever got serious, he could take Leos von Liebewitz. But he was not looking forward to it. Not one bit.

Behind the clash of steel on steel, Johann heard something else, a clamour outside the palace walls. Luitpold and the viscount did not notice and continued with their fake combat, Leos ticking off the heir's errors and praising his good moves.

People were shouting. Johann's ears were good. They had had to be, in the forests and the wastes.

Six halberdiers, stumbling as they buckled on their chestplates and helmets, rushed across the courtyard. Luitpold stood aside and Leos, hands on hips, frowned.

'What's going on?' Johann asked.

'The main gate,' huffed a young soldier, 'there's a mob there. Yefimovich is making a speech.'

'Sigmar's Hammer,' spat Leos, 'that damned agitator!'

The halberdiers ran off through the archway, heading for the palace gate. Luitpold turned to follow them.

'Highness,' Johann said, sharply, 'stay here.'

It was Luitpold's turn to frown. Anger sparked in his eyes, but died immediately.

'Uncle Johann,' he complained, 'I–'

'No, Luitpold. Your father would hang me in irons for the crows.'

Leos was pulling off his padded jacket. Johann could see trouble coming to the boil.

'Viscount,' he said, 'if you would remain here to protect the future Emperor. Just in case...'

Leos bridled, but a glance from Johann convinced him. He touched his sword to his nose and bowed his head for an instant. Thankfully, he was not one of those aristocrats – like Luitpold – who had been taught to question every order. The von Liebewitz household must have had a good, strict nanny in charge of the nursery.

Johann followed the halberdiers and found himself in step with a growing number of men as he followed a path through the interlocking courtyards. The noises beyond the gate were getting louder and there were more voices being raised. He heard a rattle and recognized it as the sound of the main portcullis coming down. It was as if the hordes of Chaos were inside the walls of the city, and the Imperial Guard were falling back to the last position of defence. But that could not be the case.

There was such a crowd of soldiers by the gate that Johann could not see through. He judged by the din that there were a lot of people beyond the portcullis gate, and that they weren't happy. It was always something. If it wasn't the incursions of Chaos it was the thumb tax, and if it wasn't some new religious zealotry it was a mob demanding that some unpopular felon be turned over to them for swift justice. The mob of Altdorf was a byword throughout the Empire for unruliness.

He heard one of the halberdiers saying something about the Beast and knew this was worse than any of the other causes. A ball of dried mud and dung sailed through the railings and burst against an arch, showering dirt down on a troop of the Imperial Guard. Halberds were being rattled.

Johann found himself standing next to a tall cleric of the Cult of Sigmar. His hood was up, but he recognized the man as Hasselstein.

'What's happening?'

Hasselstein turned his face and paused a moment – Johann imagined him weighing in his mind whether the Elector of Sudenland was important enough to be told anything – before giving a curt report. 'It's Yevgeny Yefimovich, the rabble-rouser. He's been whipping the mob up into a frenzy about the Beast murders.'

Johann had heard about the Beast murders. The news of each pathetic drab butchered down by the docks had filled him with a secret dread. The slayings were so savage that many could not believe a human being was responsible. The Beast must be a daemon, or a beastman. Or a wolf.

'But Yefimovich is an insurrectionist, isn't he?' Johann protested. 'I understood he was always rabbiting on about the privileges of the aristocracy and the suffering of the peasants. Just a typical fire-breather.'

'That's what's so silly,' Hasselstein said. 'He alleges that the Beast is an aristocrat.'

A phantom blade slipped between Johann's ribs and he felt his heart stop. After a long pause, it beat again, and again. But he would remember that thrust for quite a time.

Very deliberately, he asked, 'What evidence does he have?'

Hasselstein sneered. 'Evidence, baron? Yefimovich is an agitator, not a jurist. He doesn't need evidence.'

'But there must be something.'

Hasselstein looked into Johann's eyes and for the first time the elector noticed how ice-sharp the cleric's gaze was. Something about the man reminded him of Oswald von Konigswald. There was the same ferocious deadness in his eyes, the same compulsion for total control. Johann would not have liked to face Leos von Liebewitz over duelling swords, but he fancied that Mikael Hasselstein would be an even more dangerous enemy.

The cleric reached into his robe and took out the emblem of his cult. It was a heavy-headed hand-hammer. Obviously, it had some religious significance, but it looked as if it would be mainly useful if the Emperor's confessor ever felt the need to smash in someone's skull. Johann got the impression that the calm and suave Hasselstein often felt like smashing in someone's skull. It was always these icewater-for-blood, no-emotion-on-the-surface types that ended up in the town square taking an axe to the market-day shoppers in the name of some unheard-of lesser godling.

'Let me through,' the cleric said. The halberdiers parted and a path was cleared to the gate. Another dirt bomb exploded and Hasselstein shrugged it off. Johann stood back.

Yefimovich was held at shoulder height by his followers and was ranting.

'For too long have the titled scum of the noble houses of the Empire trampled us under their perfumed boots!' he was shouting. 'For too long has our blood been spilled in the services of their pointless squabbles. And now one of them walks the night, dagger in hand, carving up our women...'

Hasselstein looked up calmly at the fire-breather, gently slapping his hammerhead into his palm.

'If it were duchesses and the like being butchered, you can be sure that the Beast would be in Mundsen Keep by now, properly chained and tortured. But no, just because these women don't have lineages dating back to the time of Sigmar, the Imperial court doesn't give two pfennigs for them...'

Hasselstein spoke calmly to a captain of the guard. Johann couldn't hear their conversation. Yefimovich was shouting too loud. However, musketeers were joining the halberdiers. Surely, the cleric wasn't planning to fire on the crowd. The Emperor would never allow that.

'We know who the beasts are!' Yefimovich shouted, his hands gripping the bars of the portcullis gate. 'You can see them in their cage, just like in a zoo...'

He shook the bars, his long hair flying behind him. One of the musketeers propped his rifle on its stand and took aim at the agitator, flicking back the flint catch with his thumb.

Johann knew he couldn't stand by and watch Hasselstein start a riot that would lead to a massacre.

He looked up at Yefimovich. He had heard a lot about the man, had even read some of his pamphlets, but this was the first time he had seen the agitator. He really was a fire-breather. His face seemed to glow as if there were flames under the skin and his red eyes shone like a vampire's. He was from Kislev originally and had got out a few horselengths ahead of the Tsar's cossacks. Some said his family had been killed at the whim of a nobleman, others that he was himself of the aristocracy, tainted by the blood of the vampire Tsarina Kattarin, and had turned against his own kind.

'Here I am!' he shouted. 'Are you afraid of me, you lackeys and minions? I drink the blood of princes, break the backs of barons and crush the bones of counts!'

Johann could see why Yefimovich had such a following. He was as magnetic as a great actor. If they ever wrote a play about him, only Detlef Sierck could take the part. Although, considering the fervour with which he advocated bloody revolution, perhaps the late and unmourned Laszlo Lowenstein would have been better casting.

Beside Johann, someone gasped. 'So that's Yefimovich.'

Johann turned. It was Luitpold. Johann felt a knot of anger, but pulled it straight.

'Highness,' he said, 'I thought–'

'It's always "highness" when you're being dutiful, Uncle Johann.'

Leos was with him, his hand on his swordhilt, his face blank. A man like the viscount could be useful just now. Like Johann, he was sworn to protect the House of the Second Wilhelm, and if Luitpold got into trouble, he would need the protection.

Hasselstein had finished talking with the captain, who rushed off to execute some order or other. Calmly, the cleric looked up at Yefimovich. If they had strained, they could have touched one another.

Johann felt as if he were witnessing an invisible battle of wills. It was almost intriguing, the man of fire outside, the man of ice inside. In their hearts, they must have a lot in common.

'Where is he?' Yefimovich was shouting. 'Where is the arch-coward himself? Where is Karl-Franz?'

Luitpold started forward, about to shout back. Johann laid a hand on the heir's shoulder.

'My father is a good man,' Luitpold said, quietly.

Johann nodded.

'Does he care about the murdered women of the dockland? Does he?'

Yefimovich drew breath, preparing for another speech, but said nothing.

'Citizens,' Hasselstein said in the pause, his voice surprisingly loud and strong, 'you are requested to disperse and return to your homes. Everything possible is being done to catch the Beast. I can assure you of that.'

Nobody made a move. Yefimovich was smiling, the sweat pouring from his burning red face, his hair streaming behind him like flames. He wore many badges on his tunic: the hammer of Sigmar, the sickle of the outlawed Artisans' Guild, the fish of the waterfront gang and the red star of the Kislevite underground. So many symbols, but just one cause.

'The palace, as you may remember, is equipped with many defences,' Hasselstein said. 'During the War of Succession, the troops of the false Emperor Dieter IV besieged this place and Wilhelm II repelled them by disgorging molten lead from the row of exquisitely carved gargoyles you see perched above the main gate. Note the fineness of the detailwork. Dwarfish, of course. The faces are caricatures of the five daemon princes the young Wilhelm encountered and overcame during his years in the wilderness.'

The crowd, as a man, started to edge back. Yefimovich was sweating hatred and glaring death. Hasselstein continued with his lecture, as if pointing out features of architectural interest to a visiting dignitary.

'Of course,' the cleric continued, 'those were barbarous times and the current Emperor would never consider using such methods on his loyal subjects.'

Held breaths were released and the crowd pressed forward. Yefimovich grabbed the bars again and showed his teeth. He snarled like an animal and seemed fully capable of chewing his way through the portcullis.

'However, it is a simple matter to connect the palace's ingenious sewage and waste disposal system to the old defence pipes...'

He nodded and the gargoyles vomited filth.

A stream of liquid waste hit Yefimovich full in the face and he cried out in rage. His bearers deserted him and he was left hanging from the gatebars. Behind him, the crowd was running from the rain of ordure. People were knocked down and trampled in the panic. The smell wafted through the gates and Johann covered his mouth and nose.

Luitpold laughed out loud, but Johann wasn't sure if it was funny or not.

Yefimovich fell away from the gate. Someone had jabbed him with the blunt end of a halberd. Johann wondered whether it wouldn't have been more sensible to use the business point. The fire-breather slipped on a lump of fecal matter and fell badly. This experience certainly wasn't going to make the agitator change his views and become a lover of the nobility. Children were crying and people, covered in filth, were limping away. The halberdiers were laughing and jeering and making comments.

'You talk it,' one shouted, 'you might as well be covered in it!'

Yefimovich stood up, holding his side, blood leaking from his nose. Bright eyes opened in his brown-coated face. He had a scary kind of dignity, even in his current condition. He spat through the bars of the gate and walked away. The last of the crowd went with him, wiping themselves off.

'There,' said Hasselstein, a thin smile on his face, 'that is that dealt with. The Emperor has authorized me to say that there will be an extra ale ration this evening as a reward for your valorous service in his defence.'

The halberdiers cheered.

'What started this?' Luitpold asked an officer of the guard.

'Some whore down by the docks,' the man replied. 'The Beast got her, ripped her apart.'

Luitpold nodded, thinking.

'The fifth, she was,' the officer continued. 'They say it's a bad business. The Beast just tears them up. It's like he was an animal or something. A wolf.'

A wolf! Johann's heart stopped again as he remembered the face of a boy who was also a beast.

'Uncle Johann,' Luitpold said, 'if the people are unhappy because of this murderer, then it is our duty to catch him and make things right again.'

Knowing better, Johann lied to the boy. 'Yes, highness.'

II

The Beast's first memories are painful, but exciting.

'Don't touch yourself there! That's disgusting!'

Then, blows. The Beast tastes blood in its mouth. It sees a face in the mirror, with bruises. A face that could be anything, anyone. It doesn't have to recognize the face as itself. It is lumpy and bleeding, pathetic. It is just the face of the boy-shell. For the first time, the Beast roars. It does not have claws yet, but knows they will grow.

Later: 'Here, kitty-kitty... here, let's play together. There now, there's a nice cat. Whose mama loves you, then? That's right. That's nice. Purr, purr for your mama...'

A sharp claw appears in the Beast's hand. It slides through fur and skin, and punctures muscle.

The cat shrieks like a daemon.

'Here, kitty-kitty... come to mama. Kitty? Kitty!'

Still later, a different voice.

'There now, slip into your trousers. What a fine, handsome boy you are. You'll make your father proud. What's this in your pocket? Careful, you'll tear the cloth. It's expensive. It's velvet. Like they wear at the Emperor's court in Altdorf. There now, you've torn it. I told you to be careful, boy!'

More blows. By now, the Beast is used to blows. It doesn't feel them, no matter how hurt the boy-shell is. The boy-shell stops crying eventually and with each hurt the boy recedes and the Beast becomes stronger.

When they are ten years old, the Beast kills again, for the first time since the kitten. The Beast is clever. It knows it is not yet as strong as it will become. So it picks Old Nikolas, the family's retired game-keeper. Old Nikolas had to retire on a pension when gored by a hog during a hunt. His legs are bent and he spends most of the day in his hammock in the old lodge. He is slow and will not be able to escape the Beast. The boy-shell thins and the Beast pokes out its claws, taking down father's two-edged sword from his last campaign. It is heavy in the Beast's hands, but not too heavy. The weight is important. If the Beast can heft the weapon up high enough, the weight will increase the force of the blow, compensate for the weakness of the boy-shell's arms. It has all been thought out perfectly. The sword slices down and parts

Old Nikolas's neck as if it were soft cheese, chopping also through the canvas hammock.

The gamekeeper's head rolls free and the Beast kicks it like a ball.

'It's horrible, horrible, horrible. My little boy mustn't see. He mustn't. Don't you understand?'

The Beast waits for a long time, pretending to be the boy-shell. They grow up, are educated in the arts of a gentleman.

On their twelfth birthday, the Beast comes out again and takes an axe to a drunken guest in the garden. It's Uncle Sergius, who had bounced the boy-shell up and down on his knee. He looks strange with the split in his face. The wound reminds the Beast of the forbidden places of the female body. Then the Beast makes its first and only mistake. Kneeling by Uncle Sergius to get a better look at the split, the Beast dips the boy-shell's fingers into the blood, probing the wound.

'Sigmar's hammer!'

It is Natasha, the girl who travels with Uncle Sergius. The boy-shell's father calls her his brother's mistress. The Beast knows what that means. They think that sort of thing is disgusting.

Natasha just stands there, not saying anything, her mouth getting rounder, her arms stuck out like a scarecrow. She looks funny. The boy-shell smiles at her and the Beast takes out the claw from its waistsheath.

'It's all right, 'Tasha. Don't be sad.'

The boy-shell gets up and slips an arm round Natasha's waist. She is shaking, but can't move. The Beast licks her face with a rough tongue. She doesn't flinch.

She enjoys it really, the Beast knows that. Women are disgusting like that. Absolutely disgusting.

The Beast takes its hard, straight claw – eight inches of sharpened steel – and puts it into Natasha's stomach.

She gasps in delight and blood comes out of her mouth.

The Beast takes its claw out of Natasha's stomach and puts it into her chest. Then, it puts the claw somewhere else. And somewhere else.

Split-face Uncle Sergius looks up at the moons. And Natasha doesn't say anything.

This is the best thing the Beast has ever known. From now on, it will hunt only women. It will kill only women. The boy-shell agrees.

Women, it has finally realized, are its natural prey.

Women. Disgusting women.

III

As usual, the tally was coming up three barrels short. Benning, the clerk, was scratching his chin with his quill, squirting a little ink into his beard as he looked in bored bewilderment at the cargo barge moored up by the Reik and Talabec Trading Company Warehouse. Ruprecht, the night man, was yawning enormously, making the point that he wanted to go home and sleep. Judging by his breath, the fat hog could have accounted for all three casks of l'Anguille wine by himself. If the ship-yard dog licked Ruprecht's sweaty crotch one more time, it would be as drunk as a priest of Ranald on Trickster's Day.

'Count it again,' snarled Harald Kleindeinst.

Benning, who was sensibly afraid of him, complied, and began checking the cargo against his manifest.

The *River Rat*, pride of the Reik and Talabec line, had the Marienburg to Altdorf run, carrying wines from Bretonnia, cloth from Albion and scrimshaw baubles from Norsca. And, during its twenty-five year life, it had never arrived in Altdorf with exactly the same cargo that had left Marienburg. Rather, while the cargo might have entered Altdorf intact, it always seemed peculiarly diminished by the time the unloaded goods were inventoried.

Harald was going to do something today that would change that record.

'I wish you'd hurry up,' said Warble, the supercargo, 'I have business in the city that won't wait.'

Warble was a halfling, but he wasn't the fey, childlike creature half-lings were supposed to be. He was chewing a cheroot and sitting on a deckstool, calmly waiting for Harald to let him disembark.

'Take your ease, Warble,' Harald told him. 'Nobody leaves the wharf until the cargo is accounted for.'

'I'm here on business, thief-taker,' the halfling said.

'So am I.'

Sam Warble shrugged and looked at the pointed toes of his boots.

The dock crew were also sitting around, impatient. Krimi, the young foreman, was fraying the end of a rope with a marlinspike and casting the occasional threatening glance at Harald when he thought the day watch wasn't looking at him. Krimi was a Fish, and in addition to the colours sewn onto his jerkin, had fish tattooed on his cheeks.

That marked him as a war chief and made him think he was a tough character.

Harald knew better. Harald had met a lot of people who thought they were tough characters. They usually turned out to be pussies.

The Fish were losing ground to the Hooks and trying to get back by throwing in their lot with Yefimovich the fire-breather. The clerk continued his count, mumbling under his breath.

It had been a cold night, but it was a warmish day, the last of the autumn. The heat meant that the docks smelled worse than usual. The next barge was unloading a cargo of seafish that might possibly have been caught within the last ten years, although Harald wouldn't have put a bet on it. Chunks of ice were fast melting in the sunshine and the dockers were hurrying the job, trying to get the barge unloaded before the smell got too bad to bear.

Harald's hand rested on his right hip and happened to brush against the hilt of his throwing-knife.

After all these years, the weapon still hung comfortably in its sheath.

'Come down in the world, haven't you, thief-taker?' said Warble.

Harald raised his upper lip a little.

'The last time I was in Altdorf, you were a captain of the watch. Now, you're just doing sums for merchants.'

Harald looked at Warble, trying to place the face.

'Have I heard of you, halfling?'

Warble shrugged again. 'I doubt it. I keep to myself, mostly. I have a lot of respect for the law.'

'Still three barrels short,' said Benning.

The clerk looked at Krimi before he looked at Harald, which was their second mistake. Deciding to steal from the Reik and Talabec Trading Company, of course, had been their first.

Ruprecht could have stayed out of it, but he was too stupid. He was leaning against a stack of cotton bales on the dock, flapping a meaty hand at a fly that was buzzing around his eyes.

'I told you, Kleindeinst, there's no mystery. The barrels slipped their moorings and rolled overboard. They're with the fish.'

Harald just looked at the night watch. He felt sick to his stomach, as he always did around stupid, contemptible people.

'It's funny how many things just roll overboard on this run, isn't it?'

Ruprecht was sweating more than usual. He must be nursing a hangover from that l'Anguille wine. It had quite a kick and fat people could rarely hold their liquor.

'With the fish, huh? That's a believable story.'

Krimi looked up from his rope and raised an eyebrow. The Fish had originally got their name because they were always the people who seemed to come into possession of goods that 'rolled overboard.'

'Apart from that,' the clerk said, 'the tallies match.'

'Benning,' he said, 'if your tallies match, then you're either a terrible book-keeper or a clever thief. And I don't think you're a terrible book-keeper.'

The clerk jumped, almost falling off the quay. He turned round and his eyes stuck out.

In the quiet, he could hear the creaking of the barge as it drifted into the quay, grinding against the pilings and floated away again. The shipyard dog was panting, waiting for something to happen. Like everyone else.

'Do you have any idea how stupid you've been? These others don't know any better than to steal. But you're an educated man. You should never have doctored the tallies.'

The clerk looked around. Neither Krimi nor Ruprecht met his panicky eyes.

Warble pretended not to be interested and spat the wet end of his cheroot into the water.

'Three barrels, Benning. It's always three barrels. Whenever you count, Mr Fish here unloads and Ruprecht stands around watching, the cargo always comes up three barrels short. You should have varied it. You thought the company wouldn't believe it if there was no pilferage, so you decided on three barrels.'

Ruprecht was shaking, ready to explode. Krimi was gently lashing the dock with his rope. His gang lolled around, half on the barge, half off, leaning on things, waiting.

The halfling exhaled smoke. 'I've been over all the tallies and it comes to a lot more than three barrels a trip. You're a conscientious man, you must know exactly how much you've cheated the company out of.'

Benning was about to crack. Harald could see the water in his eyes.

'I-I-I was... I was fuh-fuh-forced...'

'Shut up, quill-pusher,' shouted Ruprecht, leaning forwards. He slapped his own face, setting his chins wobbling, but still missed the fly.

Harald turned on the night watch and his knife was in his hand, the blade against his palm, hilt pointed at Ruprecht. It was a fine piece of workmanship, with an eighteen-inch blade honed to razor edges. Some men had daggers with designs carved into their hilts and the names of gods etched on the blades. But this was unadorned, a thing of smooth curves and sharp lines. It was not for show.

'It's a tradition of the docks, Kleindeinst... nobody begrudges old Ruprecht his cut...'

Harald didn't say anything. He always felt sick to his stomach when thieves broke down. And thieves always broke down.

Krimi said, 'Yevgeny Yefimovich says that property is theft.'

'Yes, well theft is theft too.'

Harald held up his knife.

'This was made by Magnin the steelsmith,' he said. 'It is the heaviest throwing knife in the known world. To be effective, such a weapon has to be balanced to within a thousandth of an ounce. To be thrown properly, the knife-wielder has to have an accurate sense of time, an unusual strength of wrist and the eye of a hawk.'

Ruprecht backed against the bales. The fly settled on his ear. The night man was blubbering, sweat darkening his shirt.

'You'd better hope, scum, that those five bottles of wine I drank last night have not affected my aim this morning...'

Ruprecht sucked in a breath and closed his eyes, and the knife left Harald's hand, flipping end over end as if travelling through thick liquid...

There was a thud as the knife embedded itself up to the hilt and Ruprecht yelped.

The insect had stopped buzzing.

Ruprecht opened his eyes and found that the knife was stuck into the cotton bale, between his right ear and his skull. He was not even cut.

'Now, do I get a confession, or do things get unpleasant?'

Ruprecht was too busy praying to answer the question, but the Fish weren't impressed. They saw a man without a knife and made the familiar error of thinking he would be easy to take.

Krimi made a move with his eyes and came for Harald. He whipped out with his rope and raised his marlinspike to smash Harald's skull.

It was just like the old watch days. The scum seemed to move slower than a thick syrup, while he darted like a dancer.

Harald caught the rope as it snaked through the air and, with a deft turn, wrapped it around his wrists. He pulled and Krimi was off his feet.

When the Fish was within Harald's reach, he brought his knee up sharply into the other man's groin.

Krimi gasped in agony and his marlinspike fell onto the quay.

Harald let him go and pushed him away.

'Hurts, doesn't it?' he said.

The Fish would be too busy thinking about pain to be any more trouble. Harald picked up the rope and, pulling Krimi's hands away from his bruised balls, tied his wrists.

'Ruprecht,' he said, 'bring me my knife.'

Without thinking, the night man pulled the Magnin out of the bale and handed it to him. Harald sheathed it.

He looked at the remaining dockers. None of them wanted any more trouble.

'What are you waiting for?' he said. 'Get the cargo on the dock and don't forget the secret compartments in the fore hold.'

The Fish snapped to and started moving barrels and boxes like the marionettes of an especially dextrous puppeteer.

Warble stepped off the barge and looked at Krimi, who was still rolling on the dock, his knees locked together.

Harald yanked on the rope, hauling Krimi upright, and slipped an iron collarbrace around the Fish's neck, clicking the catch tight. Spikes dimpled the criminal's throat, drawing a little blood. If he struggled, he would gore himself badly. Harald playfully tugged the collar, drawing a howl from the Fish.

'Tell me,' Warble said, 'is that why they call you "Filthy Harald"?'

IV

'Let me through, I'm on the Emperor's business.'

It was not strictly true but, along with his distinctive green courtier's cloak, it impressed enough people to get Johann through the crowd on the Street of a Hundred Taverns. Even discounting the curiosity-seekers and ghoulish layabouts, there were more people in the narrow alley between the Mattheus II and Bruno's Brewhouse than he would have thought possible.

'Captain Dickon,' an officer of the watch was saying to his superior, 'one blanket isn't enough to cover the corpse.'

'Sigmar's hammer,' swore the captain.

More than one person had been sick in the gutter.

'It's incredible,' said a slender elf in minstrel's clothes. 'She's all over the place.'

'Oh, shut up, pointy-ears!'

A scuffle was in the offing. Several, in fact. Johann got the impression that this crowd could be even more dangerous than Yefimovich's mob.

They had already been given their first whiff of blood and now they were thirsty for more.

The officers were standing with two battered sailors, one sergeant asking questions. A watchman produced a pair of handcuffs and rattled them threateningly in a sailor's face.

'It's that sailor boy,' shouted an old man. 'He's the Beast!'

'String him up!' someone shouted.

'It's too good for him,' put in someone else. 'Cut him up like he cut up poor old Margi!'

The crowd was pressing forwards, pushing Johann towards the alley. He felt fingers reaching for his purse and slapped them away. Someone small apologised in a high, shrill voice and scuttled off to rob someone else.

The captain turned, and raised his voice. 'Back, all of you. This man is not a suspect. He found the body.'

There was a palpable air of disappointment. The crowd had wanted to do someone violence. Now, it was cheated. The sailor looked relieved, but his shipmate was too sick to notice his narrow escape.

'Captain,' said Johann. 'I am Baron von Mecklenberg.'

'The Elector of Sudenland?'

KIM NEWMAN

'Yes.'

The captain stuck out his hand. 'Dickon of the Dock Watch.'

Johann shook the watchman's hand. Lying, he explained, 'The Emperor has asked me to observe your investigation. He is very concerned with these Beast killings.'

Dickon tried to look as if he was pleased to have an aristocratic overseer. He wore a long coat and a peaked cap with a tiny feather. His nose had been broken and badly set some time in the past. He wasn't in uniform, but he had his watchman's copper badge pinned to his breast.

'Really? Could you do something about my requests to the palace? I've been trying to get the troops down here. The Dock Watch can't cope by itself. We're undermanned.'

Johann wondered if he had got himself in too deep without thinking. 'I'll try my best, captain.'

The crowd were pushing in towards the alley again.

'Look, it's her arm!'

'That's disgusting.'

'I can't see, mama. Hold me up.'

'Ought to be strung up.'

'Where's my purse? I've been robbed!'

'She was a mean old cow, though, that Margi. Vicious.'

'*Disgusting!*'

'Ought to be burned at the stake in the Konigsplatz.'

'Bloody coppers. Never around when someone's ripping your bowels out.'

'They say he eats their hearts.'

'I bet it's a Bretonnian. Filthy people, Bretonnians.'

'Nahhh, it's a dwarf. All the wounds are below the chest. Never touches their faces.'

'It's a curse.'

'We're all doomed. Repent, repent. The wrath of the gods has descended upon the unrighteous.'

'Bloody coppers.'

'Shut up.'

Johann was pushed against Dickon. The crowd was turning in on itself, a few blows had already been exchanged. The dwarf-hater and the woman who had no love for Bretonnians were squaring off against each other. The ragged cleric of no particular god was starting a sermon.

'This is ridiculous,' said the captain. 'You men there, get these people out of here.'

Four officers, one looking distinctly queasy, pulled out their clubs and advanced at the crowd. Luckily, they didn't have to hit anyone. Grumbling, the people dispersed. The taverns were open. Murder was evidently good for business. At least, it was in the daytime when the Beast wasn't about. The cleric loitered a while, telling the officers that the gods were angry. But when a sergeant remarked that the man resembled a pickpocket due to have his fingers trimmed if he were ever caught, the cleric disappeared in the direction of the Black Bat.

'Where's that scryer, Economou?' Dickon asked the sergeant.

'On her way from the temple, sir.'

'I wish she would damned well hurry up.'

Johann and Dickon were near the entrance to the alley now.

'Would you care to take a look, baron?' the watch captain asked, a little insolence oozing into his habitual deference to the green velvet.

'Uh, yes,' Johann said. He realized that the captain thought he was a morbid sensation-seeker, using his position to get an eyeful of the latest atrocity. The watchman evidently had a very low opinion of people. Just now, Johann couldn't bring himself to mind. If Dickon thought he were just another degenerate, then he would never think of checking with the palace to expose his story of being the Emperor's representative. That would make things a lot easier.

Dickon nodded to an officer in the alley and the watchman bent down to lift the blanket.

In his years of wandering, Johann had come across a great many dead bodies in a great many states of abuse and decay. But this was the worst thing he had ever seen.

'Was it a woman?'

He couldn't relate the remains to anything human, much less distinguish their sex.

'Oh yes,' said Dickon. 'Her name was Margarethe Ruttmann. She was a whore and a thief, and probably killed her pimp a few years back.'

Dickon spat. The officer let the blanket fall. The stains were spreading on the cloth.

'A proper little minx with a blade, too. Let's hope she put up a fight and marked our man.'

An officer who had been on his hands and knees at the rear of the alley, where water was dribbling from a hole in the wall, cried out. Dickon and Johann walked to him, carefully stepping around Margarethe Ruttmann.

'It's her knife, sir.'

He held up a pathetic little pig-sticker.

'...and here's her other hand.'

'Merciful Shallya!'

The hand lay under the stream, washed white and clean. It looked like a fat, plucked bird.

'Put it with the rest. The scryer will want to see it.'

The copper took out a kerchief and wrapped his fingers, then plucked the hand out of the stream and, holding it with his thumb and fingertips, walked very fast over to the blanket and popped it under the cover. Standing up, he rubbed at his hand with the kerchief. He was shaking.

'Not like thumping drunks and roughing up weirdroot suppliers, is it, Elsaesser?'

The young officer shook his head.

'It's what I have to work with, baron,' Dickon told Johann. 'This is the

Dock Watch, not the Palace Guard. These people don't just have copper badges, baron, they have copper heads.'

The sun was shafting down into the alley. It was almost overhead. The morning was gone. Shadows were thin and things not meant to be seen were in full view.

'And put that knife in a bag, Elsaesser. Maybe the scryer can get something from it.'

They came out of the alley. Dickon pulled out a pipe and a tobacco pouch. He lit up and inhaled a suck of thick, foul smoke. He did not offer Johann a chew.

Carts were trundling by, mainly carrying barrels to the street's famous hostelries. Life was going on. Across the way, three young women were soliciting passersby. The watchmen took no notice, so Johann assumed they had met their payments to the Luitpoldstrasse Station this month. He wondered how much it would cost to get the watch to be unwatchful while a murder was being committed. Not too much, he supposed.

'Skipper,' asked one of the sailors, 'can we go now? We were supposed to rejoin our ship just after dawn. Things will go bad for us if we're any later. Captain Cendenai is a hard woman.'

Dickon looked at the man and he shrank visibly.

'No you cannot go, sailor boy. I stopped that crowd ripping you apart because I don't want you dead until I'm completely sure you didn't cut old Margi up, you understand?'

The other sailor was heavily bruised about the face and holding his stomach. He was standing in a pool of his own vomit and still heaving occasionally, even though there was nothing left inside to come up.

'Bloody amazing isn't it, baron? This fellow is so used to the rolling waves that he gets seasick on dry land.'

Nobody bothered to laugh.

'What do these men have to do with the killing, captain?'

'Who bloody knows? They were on leave last night and were responsible for a bit of a disturbance down at the Sullen Knight. Incidentally, if you ever want a good punch-up that's the inn to drink in. A couple of our officers broke them up and administered a street sentence–'

'What's that?'

Dickon grinned. 'That's when the cells are too full to bother with idiots like this, and you give them a couple of headaches with the clubs, then leave them somewhere where people won't trip over them. They invariably wake up with a few lumps and a newfound respect for the Emperor's laws.'

'Damn the Dock Watch,' said the less-sick sailor. 'Bastards all!'

The officer holding the sailor stuck an elbow in the man's ribs, chuckling. The seaman bent double, feeling an old wound flare up.

'Find them a cell,' said Dickon, 'and give them some breakfast...'

The sick sailor finally brought something else up, a thin gruel laced with blood.

'...then keep them for some more questioning. Oh and find a herbalist for the puking champion.'

The sailors were dragged off, protesting feebly.

'They're all scum round here, baron. You see what I have to deal with.'

Johann thought he had seen enough to judge Dickon's methods. He was a watchman of the old school. Faced with a crime and no obvious culprit, his inclination was to haul in someone obscure and helpless and hit them until a confession came out. That looked tidy on the court books, but didn't do much about the actual problem. And it wouldn't work on the Beast. Looking at Margarethe Ruttmann, Johann knew that the Beast was a man who enjoyed his nightwork and he wasn't going to stop unless someone stopped him.

'Ulric,' said Dickon, 'but I could do with a cup of tea.'

Dickon walked over to the bench and grabbed by the ears the two officers who had beaten up the sailors. They must have been around at the same time as the Beast, but evidently they couldn't remember seeing anything or anyone more suspicious than usual. They yelped like dogs as Dickon wrung a report out of them.

'Useless scum,' Dickon spat.

'Sorry, captain,' said one of the coppers. Dickon slapped him with his open hand.

'You're mucking out the cells for a month, Joost.'

Johann looked around, wondering if any of these officers were capable of doing a job which required more than brute force and stupidity.

Most of the Dock Watch had a familiar look, with heavily-ridged brows, bruised knuckles and three days' beard. Big, hard arm muscles from hefting the club and big, soft stomachs from hefting the tankard. Two of the older men were laughing and joking in an attempt to impress the others with their hard-heartedness, trying to remember whether they had ever purchased temporary use of the deceased's body.

'Tell you what, Thommy,' said one, 'I don't fancy her much now.'

'Shut up, you ghoul bastards,' said Elsaesser. 'This was a person, not a lump of meat.'

'Not been on this watch long have you, son?' said Thommy. 'You'll learn.'

The young officer turned away in disgust and got back on his knees, looking closely at the ground.

There was a puff and the torch above the door of the Mattheus II was alight. The hostelry must have some sort of gas lighting, or a tame wizard in the tap-room. The landlord came out with a tray of free ale for the officers. Dickon got his first. 'It's not tea,' the captain said, 'but it'll do.' Only Elsaesser wasn't interested.

Johann stood by the young officer and watched him work. Elsaesser was sorting through the scraps of rubbish that had been strewn around during the Beast's work. There was a lot of it. He picked up each item, examined it, and put it back in its place.

'Is this your first?' Johann asked.

'No,' said Elsaesser. 'Third. I've been on the watch for a month. I missed the first four.'

'You're not from Altdorf?'

Elsaesser turned a piece of broken beermug over, looked at a maker's mark, and put the shard back.

'No, baron. I'm from the Reikwald Forest originally.'

'You're here from the Forest Rangers?'

'No, just out of the University.'

Elsaesser cast a cursory look at some waxed paper, an old food-wrapper.

'You have a degree?'

'Law. With a little military history and alchemy thrown in.'

The officer picked up a long strip of green material and held it up to the light. There was mud and blood on it.

'Then what are you doing on the Dock Watch? The service doesn't seem exactly suited to scholarship?'

'I *asked* for it, baron. They always need men.'

'You asked for the Dock Watch? But–'

'It's the crookedest watch in the city? I know. But the docks are where the Beast works. And I want to see the Beast caught.'

Elsaesser was a good man, obviously.

The officer stood up, brushing off his knees. He draped the piece of cloth over his hand and looked at Johann.

'What is it, Elsaesser?'

The officer's open face showed puzzlement.

'Look,' he said, holding the scrap against Johann's shoulder.

It was green, exactly the shade of his own cloak.

Johann took the cloth and felt the nap of the velvet. It was familiar.

Johann looked at Elsaesser and they both felt the world changing. Johann gripped the velvet strip and tried to feel something from it. He was no scryer, but he could not help trying. It didn't take a seer to draw a conclusion from green velvet.

'Yefimovich is right,' Johann said. 'The Beast is a courtier.'

Elsaesser shook his head. 'We don't know that. This could have been in the alley for days.'

'No, it's fresh. Look at this edge. It's been torn recently. And it's bloody.'

Johann held the strip up. It was a thin triangle, with two ragged edges and a hem. It came from the trailing edge of a garment. He looked at the hem. It was stitched with gold thread, and the velvet was a little worn where it would have scraped the ground.

Dickon was with them. 'What's this?'

'Green velvet, captain,' Elsaesser said. 'Like the baron's cloak.'

Dickon raised an eyebrow and laughed. 'So we have our man, eh?'

Johann explained, 'Green velvet cloaks are worn by tradition at the palace. By electors, courtiers, ambassadors, ministers. Even members of the Imperial family.'

For the first time, Dickon looked upset. He clamped his pipe between his teeth.

'You're saying the Beast is from the court? Merciful Shallya, that'd be worth a boatload of trouble.'

'It could as easily be a tailor or a servant,' said Elsaesser. 'Or a thief who's stolen the cloak, or someone who wants us to think that the Beast is a courtier.'

'It's not just the velvet, captain,' Johann said. 'It's the gold thread. That's expensive.'

Dickon was thinking it through, balancing justice against his career. Johann could imagine his rat's mind struggling through the maze of conclusions. The captain of the Dock Watch knew that there would be little thanks for anyone who proved that the Beast was an aristocrat. An altered of the warpstone, yes, or, better still, someone usefully unimportant and disgusting. Someone everyone could hate without complication. But a courtier, an ambassador, a minister... That would be too much trouble. A watchman who arrested and convicted a nobleman might win a medal, but he would never again be advanced in the service, he would never again have the trust of his betters.

'Good work, Elsaesser,' the captain snapped, snatching the scrap from Johann and scrunching it into a ball. 'You've seen through this trick. The Beast is trying to stir up trouble. With Yefimovich spreading sedition throughout the city, the murderer is sending us on a false path. But we're not fooled. The Dock Watch isn't that stupid.'

Dickon tossed the velvet in the air and it landed on the Mattheus II torch.

'Captain,' protested Johann. 'That's important evidence.'

The velvet burned and fell as ash.

'Nonsense, baron. It was just a false trail. The Beast is a clever creature. We know that. He wants us chasing all over the place, harassing important people, while he stays about his bloody business. I mean, can you imagine a minister of the Emperor chopping up harlots in a back alley?'

For some reason, Johann thought of Mikael Hasselstein. And of the late Oswald von Konigswald.

'Or even, perhaps, an *elector*?'

Elsaesser looked at the black scraps on the cobblestones. Dickon stamped on them, grinding them into nothing. Johann watched him do it. He could not have stopped the man, but he was also not sure he wanted to.

After all, he had several of these cloaks. And so did most of the people he knew at the court. Leos von Liebewitz had been wearing one this morning. The last time he had seen Wolf, he had lent the boy one of his courtier's cloaks for an Imperial function. He had made his brother a gift of it.

'There, that's that trouble dispensed with. Now, let us hope that our scryer accomplishes something. Unless I miss my guess, this is her right now.'

A watch coach drew up outside Bruno's and the door was pulled open. A young woman dressed in red, her red hair done up in a scarf, stepped out. She wore a simple hammer symbol amulet. Dickon extended his hand to her.

'Captain Dickon of the Dock Watch,' he said.

The woman looked at him, looked into the alley, looked up at the sky, and collapsed in a faint.

'Sigmar's bloody hammer,' said Dickon.

V

In his dream, Wolf was running through the forests. He was not quite an animal and resisted the urge to fall on all fours and propel himself with his hands as well as his feet. He was clothed and armoured, like a man, but he was also a wolf, with a wolf's teeth, a wolf's fur and a wolf's claws. He ran at the head of his pack, many of whom were also caught halfway between beast and human. Snow crunched under his feet as he dodged around the trees that stood tall and dark in his path. And ahead of him somewhere was his prey of the night. The pine trees smelled strong but his prey's scent was stronger. His snout was wet with his own saliva and he could already taste the copper and salt tang of the blood with which he would soon be filling his mouth and belly.

He sighted his prey and leaped, his strong hind-legs kicking against the hard-packed snow, his claws extended.

Something smaller than he cried and went down under him. His claws sliced into flesh.

The two moons were full in the night sky. As he rended his meat, he looked up and howled...

With the last of his howl still in his ears, Wolf awoke. He was damp with his own sweat and the thin sheet was sticky over his body. His thick coat of hair itched and his head swam with the fast fading remains of his elation.

He had had the dream again and felt nothing but shame.

Above him was the familiar lath and plaster ceiling of Trudi's room at the Wayfarer's Rest. He must have ended up here last night rather than returned to his apartment at the University. He wondered when he had last been at his college. Last night, he remembered someone saying that Professor Scheydt had been asking after him. And his brother, Johann.

Exhausted rather than refreshed by his sleep, he lay still in the narrow bed, feeling the warmth of Trudi, who was still sleeping soundly, her body pressed against his.

He tried to banish the dreams, but they would not go away. By day, he had no memory of the time he had spent with Cicatrice's Chaos Knights, although he had been able to draw out of Johann as much of the story as his brother knew.

For ten years, he had been under the influence of the scar-faced bandit king, and for ten years the warpstone had steadily worked its magic upon him, giving him a body and a mind to match his name. Only the sacrifice of Vukotich, the family's loyal servant, had restored Wolf von Mecklenberg to his original form. And while his form might have been changed back, there was still the question of what had happened to his mind.

He was twenty-nine years old and yet now, six years after his rescue, he seemed to be nineteen. At nights, his lost years crowded back in. But how much of his dreaming was memory and how much delirium?

At first, he had hidden away in the family estate, trying to cling to childhood, refusing to talk of any current matters, resisting Johann's attempts to tell him what had happened during his ten-year 'absence.' Then, he had tried to run away, to live wild in the woods, in the hope that he would find peace of spirit. Two chance meetings had given him examples to follow and he had returned to the von Mecklenberg estates and then travelled to Altdorf to enrol in the University.

The first had been with a nobleman whose face was tattooed with the mask of a beast. His name was Wolf too, Wolf von Neuwald, and he had lost a brother to Chaos. He had lived through many hardships and become an adventurer, a one-time associate of the hero, Konrad. Wolf met this other Wolf in a country inn and gradually each had drawn the other's story out. Wolf was confused by the other Wolf's cynicism and thought him cruel and hard, but he also admired the man's persistence in playing out the hand of cards fate had dealt him. Born a rich man, he was reduced to poverty; raised for the church, he was a wandering mercenary, callously certain that his next job might mean his death. From him, Wolf had learned acceptance.

The second encounter had been in Marienburg, where Wolf wanted to spend one summer learning his way around boats and the sea. Johann had arranged a position for him as midshipman with a trading boat on a regular route between the port and Norsca. Erik was a Norseman and, like the other Wolf, a mercenary. They had met on the docks and been drawn to one another at once, by a kinship they could hardly speak of. Both of them were, to some extent, shunned by their fellows and they both had a touch of Chaos in them.

For Erik, things were worse. Whereas Wolf had to live with having been a monster, the Norseman lived with the fear of constantly becoming one. The call of the moons was strong in him, but he had fought it successfully so far. Wolf dreaded hearing the news that Erik had succumbed to his wolfishness, for if the giant warrior didn't have the strength to resist, then how could he hope to deal with his inner daemon? The last he had heard, though, Erik had been still human.

It had been easier for Johann, who had caught up on his ten years' absence in a few short months and taken on the rights and responsibilities of an elector of the Empire. For Wolf, progress would always be much slower. And he would always need crutches.

Lately, he had taken to chewing weirdroot. It was easily available around the colleges of the University, or on the Street of a Hundred Taverns, and the dreams it brought were not of bestiality and violence.

Last night, Wolf thought, he must have gone through several roots. He tried to remember...

He and Trudi had gone underground, into the old dwarf tunnels, to a raucous party. There had been music and dancing and coloured lanterns. Wolf had been invited by Otho Waernicke, the Chancellor of the League of Karl-Franz, to a celebration of some mainly forgotten hero. The League was the oldest, most distinguished student fraternity at the University and – as an elector's brother – he was due to be admitted as soon as he had passed his first exams. If he passed his first exams, rather. However, if someone as party-obsessed as Otho had scraped through the academic requirements, there was no reason Wolf should fail. Wolf remembered dancing with Trudi, their bodies moving together to the noise of a band of elven minstrels. Then, things got vague...

He reached out to his bedside table and found his root pouch. It was full, whereas it had been nearly empty yesterday. He must have visited one of his usual suppliers, Philippe at Bruno's Brewhouse or Mack Ruger at the Breasts of Myrmidia.

Sitting up, he took a root from the bag and examined it. It had been cut in half with a blade and the wound had already dried over.

Trudi stirred and flopped an arm over his body.

He had met her during his first week in the city and they had been together ever since. He had known women before – and who knows what he had done during his wandering years – but Trudi was his first proper girlfriend. She was a serving maid at the Wayfarer's Rest and although no virgin priestess, she was not as loose as most you could pick up along the street.

She was young, of course, and illiterate. Sometimes, she asked him to teach her her letters, but mostly she was disdainful of any learning. Books had nothing to do with life, she usually said. Wolf, who had not spread a book open in months, had to agree with her.

He lay back and let Trudi edge herself over him, pressing him down with her body.

'I didn't feel you get into bed,' she said. 'You must have been very late...'

He did not want to tell her that he could not remember himself.

She chortled, 'But I knew when you woke me up...'

She pressed her hips against him, gently rocking, and ran her fingers through his chest hair, making little curls.

Wolf's body was responding to the girl. He tipped her chin up and kissed her, tasting the nightfilm on her teeth.

'You, you're insatiable,' she said.

She brushed her hair back out of her eyes and blinked.

'Just let me wake up. Ulric, but it must be past lunchtime.'

His mouth was dry. He snapped the half-root in two and offered her a piece. She waved it away and he popped them both into his mouth, chewing hard.

She stroked his sides, then bent down and pressed her face to his chest. As she nibbled around his neck, he stroked her long, fair hair.

He felt the dreams seep into his mind and chewed harder. The room expanded and his mind shrank.

He held up his hand and, for a moment, saw a clawed paw, tearing at Trudi's head, taking off her ear and half her face.

He froze and looked again.

'What is it, Wolf?'

His hand was normal. Her head was unhurt.

She kissed his mouth and he pushed a lump of rootpulp against her tongue. Accepting it, she swallowed and their dreams melted together.

They lost their perception of time but continued, slowly, to explore each other.

Finally, Trudi straightened up and took hold of her shift. She pulled it up over her head and shook out her hair, so it rested on her shoulders.

She put her hands on his chest and moved, gently.

He closed his eyes and touched her, moving from her shoulders, down across her breasts...

Something felt strange. He opened his eyes and looked. Trudi was lost in the moment, her eyes open but unseeing.

His hand had found four lines on her body, starting in one armpit, crossing her ribs and tapering off on her stomach. They were shallow cuts, already scabbed.

He tried to match his fingers to the marks, but they were too widely-spread. He managed to touch all four, but only by straining his knuckles.

He traced the lines, feeling Trudi shudder with something between pleasure and pain. Her stomach was ticklish, so when he touched her there, she laughed.

'Wolf,' she said, 'last night, you were a beast.'

VI

'There,' said a voice, 'she's awake.'

Rosanna awoke to the stench of tobacco in her nostrils. It stung and she shook her head. Her scarf was gone and her hair was loose.

She had been back in the village in her dream, choking on the thick smoke of a spring clearance fire, hearing the sap hissing as green branches were eaten by the flames. Her father had been there, and her mother and sisters. She had been standing on her own, the rest of her family joined with the rest of the villagers as they sampled mulled wine to keep away the chill. Amid the sibilances of the fire, she heard voices hissing 'witch' and remembered the punishments formerly inflicted upon gifted little girls. Her grandfather's aunt, the last in the family to have her scrying talent, had been burned by one of the inquisitions. Rosanna only survived because the Cult of Sigmar had put her under the seal of protection as soon as their village cleric had reported her gift. From the earliest, she had been raised to be sent to the Temple in Altdorf to serve the cult. Her cold hands were bleeding from her long hours with rough needles, pretending that she might have a future as a seamstress. She knew from their thoughts that her family would be as relieved to see her go as the rest of the village. She knew all their secrets. The thick smoke was wafted around her by the strong wind and her eyes watered. The smoke thinned and her dream was over. She was back in Altdorf.

Someone was holding a smoking pipe under her nose.

'Take that thing away,' another voice said. 'You'll poison her.'

She sat up on the cobblestones and hugged herself. There were three men around her, two officers of the watch and a distinguished-looking gentleman in the green cloak of a courtier. One of the watchmen, the captain in ordinary clothes, was waving the pipe.

Dickon, she remembered, of the Dock Watch. He had introduced himself before it overwhelmed her.

It. The fear.

'You must have had a shock,' said the courtier. 'Did you scry anything?'

She tried to remember. There was just a blackness, with flashes of red. It made her head ache. She thought there were eyes in the dark, but she couldn't tell if they were human or animal.

'Useless,' muttered the captain. 'They've sent me an imbecile.'

'No,' said the courtier, 'I don't think so. Sister, may I help you up?'

He offered his arm and she accepted.

On a plain of bleached bones and cast-off armour, men and monsters were fighting. She felt the cold wind and parried a blow. She was facing a hulking creature with a shaggy mane and finger-length teeth.

The courtier got her onto her feet and she walked a few experimental steps. She shook the vision out of her head. She was too used to them to take too much notice. Her ankles were weak, but otherwise she was all right.

'I'm not a sister, sir,' she said, 'I'm a miss. Rosanna Ophuls.'

'Baron Johann von Mecklenberg, at your service. But I understood you were sent from the Cathedral of Ulric.'

'Yes, but I am not a cleric, just a scryer. I was born with a gift, but that doesn't make me any more spiritual than the next woman. Sorry.'

The baron bowed his head slightly. Rosanna had seen him, she realized, at a state affair in the cathedral. He had flanked the Emperor himself. He was an elector. She would have to mind her manners. She remembered a story she had heard about him and thought she understood the scene she had picked up.

'Miss Ophuls,' said the watchman who had not spoken, 'did you see anything?'

'This is Elsaesser,' said the baron. 'He's one of the smarter people on the Dock Watch.'

Captain Dickon snorted and put his pipe in his mouth. Rosanna did not have to be a scryer to imagine his attitudes. The watchman thought that Baron von Mecklenberg was an interfering dilettante, and young Elsaesser a naive hothead who would soon learn better.

Elsaesser shook her hand and she got the impression of tall trees and heady air.

'The Reikwald,' she said.

Elsaesser was impressed.

'Don't be. It's just a party trick.'

'When you arrived,' said the baron, 'did you scry anything?'

She thought back beyond the blackness of her fainting spell. She remembered opening the coach door and setting her foot on the cobbles. Then there were flashes of red in the dark. She heard the ghost of a scream and received the image of someone in a long, voluminous garment, bent over a shrieking animal, working away inside it. No, it was not an animal. It was – had been – a woman.

'It was horrible.'

'Did you see the Beast?'

She nodded: yes.

'What did he look like?' asked the baron.

'Long... green... coat,' she said.

'A coat?' He held her elbow. She saw his cloak rippling and was fascinated by the gold stitching amid the velvet.

'Long... green...'

'This is pointless,' said Dickon. 'She's on the same false trail.'

'No,' she said, 'not a coat...'

'A cloak?' Elsaesser asked.

'Like this one?' said the baron.

'Yes... no... maybe.'

'Wonderful,' snapped Dickon. 'Yes, no or maybe. That narrows our options enormously.'

'Give the girl a chance.'

The watchman looked sullen and coughed out a brown cloud. 'Yes, baron. Although it's my guess that she couldn't scry a rainshower if the sky were full of clouds.'

Rosanna was annoyed by the captain. She pretended to be unsteady and put her hand out to balance herself. She placed her palm on Dickon's chest and let her mind reach out to him.

'Ahh, captain, you are impatient, I see. You would like to be back at home with your wife and children.'

'You are mistaken, Miss Ophuls,' Elsaesser said. 'The captain has a wife but, I believe, no children.'

Dickon looked dark and shifty.

'Oh, I'm sorry. I had such a clear impression. It happens sometimes. I see now that your wife is childless.'

'That's right,' Dickon said, 'not that it's any of your business.'

'But you do have children. Two of them. A boy and a girl. August and Anneliese. Four and two. And there's a woman, too. What is her name?'

'The captain's wife is called Helga, Miss Ophuls,' said Elsaesser. Rosanna wondered whether the young watchman were really as naive as he seemed, or whether he was enjoying his superior's embarrassment.

'Helga, eh? I must be badly mistaken. The name I'm picking up is...'

'I think we've wasted enough time,' said Dickon.

'...Fifi.'

Elsaesser tried not to smirk and Dickon took a keen interest in the cobblestones, pulling his cap down low.

'If you'd come this way, Miss Ophuls,' said the baron. She consented and took his arm again. Dickon stayed away, making sure not to touch her.

Rosanna was afraid of what she would have to do now. She had volunteered for this job out of a sense of duty. The Cult of Sigmar had spent a lot of money educating her, a poor barefoot seamstress from the Grey Mountains, even though she had no intention of becoming an initiate. She owed the Cathedral the use of her gifts. And the Cathedral owed a debt to the city of Altdorf, which it had succoured for three thousand years. So, with debt piled upon debt, she would have to step into the alley between the two inns and die again...

The baron helped her, as if he were assisting a very old duchess out of a carriage and escorting her to a ball. He led her to the alley, the watchmen keeping pace like train-holding servants.

'Everybody back,' said Dickon. 'She has to go in alone.'

Officers emerged from the alley and stood in the street.

Rosanna could see a form lying under a blanket and could see red patches on the blanket itself.

The first time, when she was a little girl, she had been asked to kiss her dead grandmother's forehead before the funeral. She had felt her lungs fill up with thick liquid and had coughed until her throat bled. By then, her parents were used to little Rosie's 'feelings' and understood only too well. She stayed away from graveyards after that but death was impossible to avoid. Lying in a bed at an inn, with her first boyfriend, she had experienced in succession the last moments of three people who had died in the bed: an old man with a fading heart, a young hunter with most of his chest shot away in an accident and an unwanted child stifled with a pillow by a mother barely in her teens. It was not a sensation she would ever get used to.

'This is your first time with the Beast?' asked the baron.

'Yes.'

'We've never called in a scryer before,' said the captain. 'It's a new approach.'

'What do you know about the murders?'

'That the Beast kills women, tears them apart.'

She was picking up the baron's own beast again. He was called Wolf. She smelled his breath, saw the steam rising from his pelt.

'You think you can go through with this?'

She took a deep breath. 'Yes, baron, I think I can. I believe it's important.'

'Good girl.'

'The first thing,' said Elsaesser, 'is to make sure that this is like the others. You understand?'

Rosanna wasn't sure.

'Many people die, many are murdered. Especially in the alleys off the Street of a Hundred Taverns. This woman might have killed a man herself, a few years ago. He could have friends or relations who see the Beast as a way of evening the score without attracting attention. Or it could be a monkey-see-monkey-do madman.'

'I don't understand.'

Elsaesser was patient. 'Violence is like a plague, it spreads without reason. The Beast could have inspired an imitator. It happens with most killings like these.'

'I see. What should I look for?'

Elsaesser blushed, obviously embarrassed. 'Well... ah... first, you should see whether she was... ah... molested, um, before or after...'

'He means was she raped, Miss Ophuls,' put in Dickon.

Rosanna remembered being led to a stone suspected to have been used as an altar in the Geheiminisnacht rites of a Chaos cult. Literally dozens of sacrifices had been raped in that place and she had felt for every one of them. Afterwards, their throats had been cut and the cultists had drunk their blood.

'Were the others?' she asked.

'We don't think so. The thing with sex crimes as vicious as these is that they are usually instead of rather than as well as, if you get my meaning.'

'Clearly.'

'These madmen usually turn out to be impotent, or inadequate. Mama's boys, most of them.'

The woman in the alley was getting no deader, but Rosanna could feel the residues fading fast.

'And be sure that we are dealing with a human,' said the baron. 'I'm still not convinced that the Beast is not an actual beast, or an altered.'

'So far,' said Elsaesser, 'the wounds have been consistent with some sort of hooked weapon. But it could also have been a set of claws.'

'Does the killer eat his victims?'

Elsaesser looked shocked. 'No, miss. We don't think so. It's hard to tell, but we think she's all there.'

'Well, that's something to be going on with.'

The baron and Elsaesser stood back. Rosanna tottered a little, but didn't feel faint any more. The Beast was gone, leaving only a memory behind. A memory couldn't hurt her.

She stepped across the entrance stone of the alley and the direct sunlight was blocked. The noises of the street were faint in her ears. She could have been distant from everyone, rather than a few steps away.

She walked in a little way and came to the blanket.

Bright blood seemed to run under her shoes in a river, washing into the street. Cries echoed between the walls and there was a dreadful rending sound, as a body was torn apart.

Her heart grew cold.

She felt an ache in her joints and the sting of gin in her throat. One of her eyes wasn't seeing properly. There was someone in the alley with her. Someone tall, in a long coat or cloak. She saw a flash of green and the glare of mad eyes. Then, something sharp went into her stomach.

She staggered back, breaking the contact.

Now, she was standing over the bloody work, watching shoulders heave. She saw a woman's white face. She was old, one-eyed. Her hair was stringy. Blood splashed across her face.

She was the Beast, but she knew nothing. She felt a tangle of impulses driving her, felt the desire to kill. Her cloak flapped around her as she tore away the skin and the flesh. Her mind contained just one idea. She must kill.

She broke the contact again. She had learned nothing. Her knees and ankles were going. The baron was there to catch her and to pull her out of the alley.

'There she goes again,' complained Dickon. 'Useless, useless.'

The baron unlaced her collar and let some air in.

'Well?' asked Elsaesser.

'I felt both of them,' she said. 'The woman had one eye.'

'And the Beast?' asked the baron.

She concentrated. 'The Beast is...'

She tried to find the words.

'The Beast is two people.'

Dickon thumped a fist into his palm. 'The sailors,' he exclaimed. 'I knew it! The sailors.'

'No,' said Rosanna, 'you don't understand. The Beast is two people, but with only one body.'

'This is insane.'

'No, captain,' said the baron. 'I think I see what Miss Ophuls means. The Beast is an ordinary person most of the time, as sane and rational as you or I...'

Rosanna nodded.

'...but sometimes, when the mood or whatever takes him, he is something else, a Beast.'

'Is the Beast a werewolf?' asked Elsaesser.

Rosanna wondered. In the dark, she had seen nothing but the eyes.

'Yes... no... maybe...'

'The same old tune, eh?'

The baron turned on the watchman. 'Captain, I'll thank you to leave this woman alone. She is obviously trying her best and I hardly think you are helping her.'

Dickon was chastened.

Elsaesser had darted into the alley and come out with something.

'Here,' he said, 'try this...'

He handed her a small bag.

'What is it?'

'It's Margi Ruttmann's knife.'

'Who?'

'Margi Ruttmann... her... in the alley.'

'Oh, yes... of course...'

She had not picked up the woman's name. That happened quite often.

'She may have tried to defend herself. She may have cut the Beast.'

She pulled the drawstring loose and let the bag fall. She turned the knife around in her hand, feeling the hilt.

'If he were wounded in a specific way, we could look for a man with that wound. It would be something to go on.'

She gripped the knifehandle and held the blade up.

Her cheek stung as the blade slipped in, piercing her eye. Half her vision went red and then black.

She was shaking.

She pinned him down and slid the blade into him, ignoring his screeches.

'Rikki,' Rosanna said. 'She killed someone called Rikki.'

Dickon snorted again. 'Well, that's that old case closed. At least we've accomplished something here.'

'Try holding it by the blade,' Elsaesser suggested.

Rosanna considered and then flipped the knife over, catching it in her fingers. It was sharp but she didn't cut herself.

'Excuse me,' she said, holding the knife up. She positioned the point against the bridge of her nose and then tilted the blade up, resting its flat against her forehead. It was cold as an icicle.

'This helps sometimes.'

Elsaesser and the baron looked on, radiating encouragement. They were both, she realized, interested in her.

The blade leaped in the dark and the point sank into heavy cloth. The blade was pulled away. The cloth tore. The ripping sound was extended for longer than was possible. Amplified, she heard it tearing forever.

'Well?' someone asked.

'Green velvet,' she said.

Elsaesser and the baron looked at each other, their hearts sinking.

'Green velvet,' she said again, 'like the baron's cloak.'

VII

Dien Ch'ing bowed low, in the Celestial fashion, prostrating himself and touching his forehead to the flagstones. They were cold.

'My humble and unworthy self is honoured to be graciously admitted into your estimable presence, noble sir.'

The ambassador knew that Hasselstein had no patience with Cathayan courtesy, but conducted himself impeccably anyway. That was important. His mask must not slip.

'Get up, ambassador,' he said, 'you make yourself ridiculous.'

Dien Ch'ing stood, wiping non-existent dust from his robes. The palace floors were as clean as a virgin's conscience.

The Emperor's confessor was not wearing his lector's hood. He was dressed like any other courtier, in fine white linen and a green velvet cloak. Out of his habit, he did not look especially ascetic.

'Nevertheless, noble sir, I am pleased to be granted this audience.'

Hasselstein was obviously distracted. Dien Ch'ing assumed that the man had actually forgotten their appointment. He was unprepared for their discussions and that made him irritable. He was too much the smooth courtier to give offence to the representative of the Monkey King, but he had other, more pressing business, and he would prefer to be seeing to it. That was interesting. The cause of the Lord Tsien-Tsin could be assisted by such distractions.

Besides, it was just as well. Dien Ch'ing wondered how generous the welcome would be if Hasselstein and his Emperor knew that he did not, in fact, serve the Monkey King and that the real ambassador, despatched two years ago from far Cathay, was resting with his throat cut in an unmarked grave somewhere in the Dark Lands. He assumed that things would be very different indeed.

'Has the Emperor found the time to consider the Monkey King's petition, noble sir?'

Some memory of the matter surfaced in Hasselstein's mind and he dredged the facts together. Behind him, rolled up in tubes, were all the petitions. Dien Ch'ing could see his perfect forgery stuffed in with the others.

'Your proposed expedition to the Dark Lands, eh?'

Dien Ch'ing touched his thumb to his forehead and bowed again.

'Even so, noble sir.'

Hasselstein was playing with the papers on his desk, pretending to be busy. It was not like the man. Dien Ch'ing understood the Emperor's confessor to be a skilled politician, not a distracted curmudgeon. There was something seriously amiss at the court of Karl-Franz.

'It is being considered. The undertaking would be costly and difficult to put together. I'm sure you understand.'

'Indeed, noble sir. That is why the Monkey King proposes a joint venture. The Lord of the East should shake hands with the Emperor of the West. And the encroachments of evil grow greater every day. The time is right for a full-scale campaign.'

'Um,' said Hasselstein, 'possibly.'

Dien Ch'ing smiled inside, but let nothing show. He must be humble, he must be patient. One does not ascend the Pagoda of Tsien-Tsin at a single leap. One must take the steps individually and pause for rest and reflection at each level. The plan for this trap had been laid years earlier, in the Dark Lands, and there would be no haste in springing it. Dien Ch'ing remembered how haste could spoil a recipe, and did not intend to fail his master a second time.

'You will pardon me, noble sir, for daring to express an intuition, but is there perhaps some pressing matter which occupies your thoughts?'

'What?' said Hasselstein.

'In Western parlance, what is wrong?'

'Oh, that...' Hasselstein almost smiled. 'You're sharp, Dien Ch'ing, aren't you? You "noble sir" and "unworthy humble self" a lot, but you don't miss much.'

Hasselstein shifted his papers again. They were conferring in the antechamber to one of the waiting halls of the palace. From their alcove, they could see de la Rougierre, the Bretonnian ambassador, waving his plumed hat and trying to attract the attention of a pretty maidservant. And that idler Leos von Liebewitz was swishing his cloak and fingering his sword, waiting for someone.

'A few hundred years ago,' Hasselstein began, 'no one was allowed in to the palace without a mask. The Empress Magritta forbade anyone to enter her presence without what she called "their true face" on.'

The maidservant was walking away, leaving de la Rougierre to stump off in a snit. The Bretonnian was a dwarf and fancied himself as a ladies' man. He was the subject of many amusing stories, mostly obscene. The stunted popinjay's assignment to the court was obviously a subtle Bretonnian insult to the Emperor and yet no one was willing to make any complaint. The situation was amusingly absurd.

'And you feel that nothing has changed?'

Hasselstein fingered his chin. 'So many masks, Dien Ch'ing. And who is to say whether the mask or the face tells the truth.'

Leos was joined by his sister, the Countess Emmanuelle, and de la Rougierre came back, his hat off and scraping the floor again, trying for another conquest. Leos's gloved hand went to his swordhilt.

'There was a disturbance outside the palace today.'

'Yes, Dien Ch'ing. It was Yefimovich, the fire-breather...'

Dien Ch'ing knew Yefimovich. He knew what lay underneath the Kislevite's mask. Hasselstein would be surprised if he ever saw that particular true face in all its fiery splendour.

'I have heard he is agitating the citizenry against the privileges of the aristocracy. In Cathay, such impudence would be rewarded in a civilized manner. The miscreant would be stretched out between four willow trees, with fine nooses of catgut around his ankles, wrists, neck and testicles, and left to hang until he changed his opinions. We are a reasonable people.'

Hasselstein laughed, bitterly. 'Indeed, Dien Ch'ing. I wish we could serve Yefimovich in the Celestial fashion. But, under the House of the Second Wilhelm, the people have their rights. It's the law.'

Dien Ch'ing knew that was a joke. Like the Monkey King, Karl-Franz might talk endlessly about the rights of his people, but he would rescind them in a moment if it meant bringing a cream horn to his table a few seconds faster or adding three gold pieces to his treasury.

'Of course, noble sir, what the fire-breather alleges is absurd. Some are born to rule and others to be ruled. That is the eternal truth.'

Leos and Emmanuelle were laughing at some joke of de la Rougierre's. Powdered buffoons, all of them. Parading their fine silks and their exquisite manners, weighed down by their lineage, made stupid by generations of in-breeding. The von Liebewitzes were like porcelain dolls, wrapped from birth to death in a cocoon of spun cotton. It would be so easy, so amusing, to snap their arms and legs off and then to crush their tiny, painted heads to powder. As they argued over the correct way to fold a napkin, children sold themselves in the streets outside. No wonder Yefimovich's speech-making found such an eager audience.

'That's it, exactly,' said Hasselstein. 'The Emperor rules by the sufferance of the gods and of the electoral college.'

Countess Emmanuelle was laughing like a girl. It was a trained laugh, polite and pretty, and nothing to do with an honest emotion.

'I have heard of an experiment tried some years ago in a few of the Tilean city states. Democracy, or some such nonsense. The rule of the people. A failure, I believe.'

'The people!' Hasselstein thumped the table, making his inkwells jump. 'Sigmar knows our Emperors have not always been fit to rule – this Empire has withstood Boris the Incompetent and Bloody Beatrice the Monumentally Cruel, after all – but the people! That mob outside our gates, howling for blood! They can hardly even feed themselves, or wipe themselves off after a visit to the privy. Could they ever rule anything?'

De la Rougierre was fussing around the Countess Emmanuelle's skirts, trying to touch her legs while pretending to demonstrate some dance step. If he did not show some caution, the dwarf would find himself spitted by Leos's deadly blade. And serve him well.

'And yet, heroes have come from among the people, have they not?

The man Konrad, of whom all the minstrels sing; is he not a peasant? And Sierck, who saved the Emperor's life a few years ago, was a mere actor, I believe. Sigmar himself was hardly born to the green velvet, as it were. Many men of genius have risen through their own merits. Minister Tybalt is the son of a grocer, is he not? And the Cults of Sigmar and Ulric are well-remembered for the humble-born servants who performed such great feats. You yourself, I assume, have no especially notable antecedents...'

Dien Ch'ing was taunting Hasselstein, so subtly the man would never realize it. 'Well,' the cleric said, 'actually, my eldest brother is a margrave. Our family is very old. I dropped the "von" from my name when I entered the temple.'

'Ahh, so Yefimovich's taunts are personal?'

'He does not single me out for especial contempt. He hates all aristocrats.'

'A foolish man, not to know how the world is ordered.'

'A foolish man, yes, but also a dangerous one.'

'Surely not. You have the palace guard, the militia, the watch.'

'You are right, Dien Ch'ing. The Empire has nothing to fear from Yevgeny Yefimovich.'

The Celestial smiled and bowed. Hasselstein had spoken half a truth. By himself, Yefimovich was no real threat; but, in partnership with Dien Ch'ing, and with the blessings of the Lord Tsien-Tsin, Yefimovich could do more than spread fire.

An Empire always rests unsteady on its foundations. Plans were well-laid and already coming into operation. It was up to Dien Ch'ing to take advantage of any circumstances that arose. He had cast the yarrow sticks this morning and believed he saw a useful catspaw in the near future, a creature who could seed a panic which might spread throughout the city and perhaps topple a throne or two.

'Tell me, noble sir,' Dien Ch'ing asked Hasselstein, 'what do you know about this fellow they call the Beast?'

A cloud passed over the cleric's face. For a long while, he didn't say anything.

Then he began to tell Dien Ch'ing the whole story.

Part Two

Fog

I

He was entitled to the use of one of the luxurious coaches the palace put at the disposal of the electors, or of the most important ambassadors. When he was down at the stables picking his horses, he saw footmen in the von Liebewitz livery harnessing a couple of magnificent animals to one of the electoral coaches and he took a moment to examine the gold filigree-encrusted monstrosity. It looked like a giant decorated egg, with jewelled lanterns, painted panels depicting the life of Sigmar and enough glitter to light a street. Obviously the Countess Emmanuelle was off to another of her balls this evening. Back in Nuln, she was the foremost hostess in the Empire; during her sojourn in Altdorf, she was trying to even things up by being the most expensive guest in the capital. The whisper was that the countess always went to these functions escorted by Leos, but that he came back alone, leaving his sister in the arms of her amour-of-the-moment.

Johann wondered which lucky noble house would have to lay down the red carpet and slow-bake the quail tonight. There was a ball at the house of the von Tassenincks, he knew. His invitation had been delivered a few days ago, but, even if he did not have other urgent business, he would not have been happy to attend. The parvenu elector, called in on a compromise to replace the dead and disgraced Oswald von Konigswald, had been trying to impress the city with his style and grace, but Grand Prince Hals and his sullen heir Hergard were simply clowns, straining too hard to apply their tongues to the bottom of the Emperor, and Johann always thought the college had made a bad decision granting a seat to the von Tassenincks. There had been a dreadful scandal involving the Grand Prince's mad nephew a few years earlier. In fact, that incident had given Johann the inspiration for tonight's adventure.

He could have taken out the twin to the von Liebewitz carriage, but opted instead for a plain black coach. Rather than bother with five footmen to ride on top and carry the torches, he chose only Louis, his usual driver. A few extra crowns would be useful to the man, whose wife was expecting their thirteenth or fourteenth. All sons. Louis joked that he would soon be able to field a football team, with substitutes and line-keepers. The coachman was dependable and could keep his mouth shut. His loyalty was to who bribed him first, not who bribed him most.

With a good, strong, ugly horse between the shafts, the coach slipped anonymously through the palace gates, rumbled past the Temple of Sigmar and took a turn towards the river, crossing at one of the trade bridges. Then they were in the Street of a Hundred Taverns. It was well-placed, with the University and its environs to the left and the docks to the right. Even with the Beast at work, there were students and workmen enough to keep the beer and wine flowing. Of course, the streetwalkers and tavern girls were wandering about in gangs of five or six – all, presumably, with daggers tied to their thighs and blackjacks hanging from their girdles – but perhaps they did more business that way. Last night, Margarethe Ruttmann would have been one of them. Now, she was in several separate piles at the Temple of Morr, beyond even the reach of the watch's pet necromancers.

He wondered if Wolf were back at his rooms within the University buildings yet. He had asked a few days ago, but the bursar at Wolf's college said the student hadn't been seen for over a week. Then Johann wondered what the University life was like. He had had a place open for him at the University – all the von Mecklenbergs had been educated there, for centuries – but Cicatrice's raid had changed the course of his life. It was literally a miracle of Sigmar that Wolf was getting a second chance. While Johann's contemporaries had been learning dead languages and studying the outcome of battles on maps, he had been in the forests somewhere, learning how to stay alive.

The last time he had been driven up this street, the street girls had pressed close to the coach whenever it slowed down, explaining the services they offered, citing unrealistically low prices and championing their own abilities. Now they hung back, talking only to faces they knew. The black coach must look faintly sinister, Johann supposed. The word out on the street was that the Beast was an aristocrat from across the river. Green velvet would not be a popular fashion here for a while, even if bright gold was never quite out of favour. Dickon might have burned that scrap of evidence from the alley, but the story was already out.

The most fantastic rumour was that the Beast was Prince Luitpold's insane twin brother, reared in secrecy since birth and let out at night to prevent him preying on the palace's important and wealthy guests. This afternoon, an old woman in the crowd had described the Phantom Prince as having hair down to his waist and talon-like fingernails. Apparently, he ate only raw meat and howled at the moon.

The coach had to stop because of a disturbance. It was outside the Sullen Knight, where men were shouting and scuffling. Johann noticed that there was a thin carpet of mist covering the cobbles. An Altdorf fog was coming down.

His first impression was that a bunch of students and a gang of dockers were working up for a major fight.

Two of Dickon's Dock Watch were strolling by on the other side of the street, unconcerned. That, apparently, was typical. There were women at the upper windows of the taverns, egging their men on.

A broad-shouldered youth wearing the cap of one of the University's fraternal societies was haranguing a group of roughly-dressed loafers. The student's friends were trying to calm him down, but the loafers were already throwing punches, and more students were appearing from somewhere.

'Nobody mixes it with the League of Karl-Franz!' shouted the trouble-maker, waving a clay stein with an embossed coat of arms.

One of the loafers spat.

'Spit on the League, will you?' roared the student. 'You'll earn yourself a bloody nose like that.'

Johann noticed that the loafers all had a cloth emblem patched to their breasts. It was a docker's hook. Most of them had real hooks dangling from their broad leather belts.

He had heard of the Hooks. They were one of the gangs that tried to run the waterfront, ensuring that their friends were suitably employed on the docks, tithing a percentage from everyone's pay. They were usually feuding with a similar faction, the Fish. During the Beast crisis, some of them were even pretending to be a Citizens' Vigilance Committee, although Johann understood that was just another excuse for beating people up. Now, they seemed ready to take on the League of Karl-Franz.

The students were singing now, a song which involved a great deal of beer drinking and stein clashing. It sounded defiant.

'Louis,' said Johann, 'isn't there a way around this?'

The coachman shook his head.

'A pity.'

Caps were flying into the air and someone was throwing vegetables. A rotten cabbage exploded against the coach door.

This was a nuisance.

Johann saw a figure hurrying through the crowds, coat collar turned up, and recognized him.

He opened the door and shouted out, 'Elsaesser. Over here.'

The young watchman heard and darted through the students towards the coach. More trays of beer had been brought out onto the street and the League of Karl-Franz were getting rowdier.

Elsaesser climbed into the coach, wiping a pulped tomato from his jacket. Tendrils of mist trailed in with him, dissipating swiftly. The watchman was out of uniform and off-duty. Johann had arranged to meet the officer at the Black Bat, but luckily their routes had crossed before that particular inn. The coach wouldn't be able to get through until the fight was over. There were other vehicles stalled in the road, including a cart piled high with beer barrels and a flashy gig in which a well-dressed young man was escorting two fluttery young ladies.

'Baron Mecklenberg,' the young officer said, 'good evening.'

'Von Mecklenberg, actually.'

'I'm sorry. I have a problem with titles.'

'You sound like a follower of Yevgeny Yefimovich.'

Elsaesser looked sheepish but stuck his neck out. 'The man has some sound ideas, baron. I don't trust or like him, but he is a genuine reaction to problems that are not going to go away.'

Johann was impressed with Elsaesser's bravery. Not every young watchman would dare to come so close to sedition in conversation with an elector of the Empire.

'At the University, I signed the petition against the dismissal of Professor Brustellin.'

'Funnily enough, so did I.'

Elsaesser looked at the baron with a new respect. 'I shouldn't have quibbled about my name,' Johann admitted. 'I've spent too much of my life away from palaces and estates to have many noble illusions about the aristocracy, in the Empire or elsewhere. In fifty years, Brustellin's book will be recognized as the masterwork of philosophy it is.'

The Professor had published a volume entitled *An Anatomy of Society* that had been banned upon the orders of the Emperor. He had likened the Empire to a human body and drawn a parallel between the aristocracy and a bone-sapping cancer.

'But now he's an outlaw.'

'All the best people are. Sigmar was an outlaw.'

Elsaesser made the sign of the hammer.

'Well,' said Johann, 'did you find out where our man is?'

Elsaesser grinned. 'Oh yes. Nobody wanted to tell me, but I found an old sergeant who wanted drinks money for this evening. I have to say we're not talking about a popular individual here.'

'You're telling me. I mentioned his name to Mikael Hasselstein and got an icy blast of disapproval.'

'Still, I think you're right. He's the man for the job.'

The student leader was drunk enough to be bold. Or stupid. He strolled through the melee and found the biggest, meanest-looking member of the Hooks and poured the dregs of his stein over the man's head. Then he gave a swift punch with a blocky fist and broke the appalled Hook's nose.

A cheer went up from his comrades and from the women on the upper storeys on the left side of the road. The student turned round and raised his hands in triumph, accepting the applause, and a club came down on his head, denting his cap and probably concaving his skull. He was lucky not to find a hook spearing into his kidney.

Elsaesser was nervous.

'That's Otho Waernicke, Grand Duke of Somewhere-or-Other,' he said of the downed student. 'He's an absolute cretin. The League of Karl-Franz are always burning down some dormitory or other, or bothering the novices at the nunnery of Shallya. If their degrees weren't bought and paid for by their daddies before they enrolled, they would never graduate from the University.'

'You weren't a member then?'

'No, you have to have a lineage for that. I was an "inky".'

'What?'

'That's what the Leaguers call students who actually study. Inkies. It was supposed to be an insult, but we became rather proud of it. We formed a League of our own in the end and always swept the debating contest.'

'I bet they hammered you at boxing, duelling and drinking, though–'

'Oh yes, and pox-catching, dying young and long-distance vomiting. It must be a hard life, being born to the green velvet.'

A chill passed over Johann's heart. 'Yes, a hard life...'

He was thinking of Wolf.

'I'm sorry, baron, I meant no slur.'

The Hooks were laying into the Leaguers, mainly using their fists and steins. There was blood on the cobbles, but the hooks weren't out. Yet. The women on the upper storeys were betting with each other and a little man was running around making odds and taking credit notes.

Otho Waernicke was sleeping it out, but his friends were putting up enough resistance to do him credit.

Johann took out a document and handed it to Elsaesser. The watchman noted the seal and was impressed.

'You spoke with the Emperor then?'

'Ah, no,' Johann admitted, 'but I spoke with young Luitpold and I did borrow the Imperial seal.'

'So, what does this say?'

'Nothing. It's just a blank sheet of paper inside. No one will dare break the seal. So, we have approval to bring our man out of retirement...'

'Isn't this dangerous?' Elsaesser asked.

'I don't think so. I do have influence with Karl-Franz. I should think that the Emperor outranks Dickon of the Dock Watch.'

Elsaesser's eyes were round and his face pale. 'But, ah, I...'

Johann saw what the officer was worried about. 'I shall make sure that you do not suffer, Elsaesser. This is all my responsibility. Your future is assured.'

'I'm glad to hear it. Dickon transferred me from the Beast case to the vagrancy squad. As of tomorrow, I'm supposed to walk up and down this street harassing tarts and pimps. If they're on the streets, they must be destitute, and that's a crime so I'm supposed to fine them three pfennigs on the spot. Dickon gets half the take at the end of the month and the rest is parcelled out to the other watchmen.'

'What if they really are destitute and don't have three pfennigs?'

'Then I'm supposed to thump them with my club. That's how justice works on the docks.'

Johann made a fist inside his suede glove and pressed his signet ring to his chin. 'When the Beast is caught, I shall make sure that things change at the Dock Watch. You have my word on it.'

'Thank you, baron.' Elsaesser did not sound convinced.

The fight was dying down, inconclusively. Most of the battlers had gone back to their inns, or been carried off to apothecaries, and only the hardiest, toughest and stupidest were still exchanging punches and kicks.

An old woman was checking patches of blood in the cracks between cobbles, looking for gold teeth.

Louis was able to drive on and the coach continued. The last of the brawlers got out of its way.

Johann saw that Otho Waernicke was sitting up and singing now.

Elsaesser gave Louis the directions to the warehouse of the Reik and Talabec Trading Company. Their man should still be at work, to judge by what Elsaesser had learned about his current situation.

'It was the only thing he could get when he was kicked out of the watch,' the officer explained. 'He's a glorified stock-keeper, really.'

The coach turned off the Street of a Hundred Taverns and started threading down through the odd byways of the docks.

'Just one thing puzzles me,' Johann said. 'Have you found out why they call him "Filthy Harald"?'

II

It was a slow night at the Wayfarer's Rest, so Wolf and Trudi headed, arm in arm, up the street for some livelier entertainment. They had stayed in bed, mainly dozing, until nearly nightfall. Like most students, Wolf was used to keeping vampire's hours. He felt better with the rising of the moons, more alive. He was hungry and not just for food.

There was a thin mist rising around their ankles, bubbling slightly. Wolf recognized the makings of a proper Altdorf fog and was glad all the taverns in this area of the city were on the same, well-lit thoroughfare. An Altdorf fog crept off the two rivers once every few months or so and descended upon the city for a couple of days. The citizens were used to it and had long contrived good reasons for staying in their hearth-warmed homes for the duration, but to Wolf it was still almost exciting, almost glamorous...

Anything could happen in an Altdorf fog, as if the city instantly became engulfed in a giant weirdroot dream. Lovers could meet for a few hours and then be separated forever. Certain creatures which usually kept to the sewers and backrooms would come out for a few nights on the streets, masked by the thick, grey clouds. There were many stories of adventures in an Altdorf fog, or jokes about romantic entanglements. At the Vargr Breughel Memorial Playhouse, Detlef Sierck was appearing in *A Farce of the Fog*, based on one of the oldest of the jokes, and Wolf had taken Trudi a few nights ago. They had laughed continually at the fools' parade of lecherous husbands, ravenous mistresses, ardent lovers, innocent wives, vulgar midwives, comic watchmen and absurd clerics, and marvelled at the fog effects contrived on the stage.

Tonight, the fog did not seem quite as jolly as it had in the play. It rose fast and hung thick in the air. It was impossible to see from one side of the street to the other. Even the inn lanterns were shrouded, Trudi was shivering under her shawl and not saying much. Wolf knew what she was thinking about. The girl couldn't read the posters, but she had heard the rumours. And there was a new poster up, unmistakable even to the illiterate, with a caricature of a bestial face – indistinct and yet unmistakable – over a pledge of a substantial reward.

The fog was all around them now and the innkeepers were all out lighting extra torches and laying in for a siege. Those hardy drinkers prepared to venture out in any weather would keep all the taverns in business for the next few days and the landlords wanted to be sure their patrons could find their way to their establishments.

'Halt,' said a voice. 'You there...'

Wolf turned to look and realized that he was the one who was being asked to halt. A tall, wide figure was coming through the fog at him. He did not wear the helmet and badge of a copper – not that that would necessarily have made Wolf feel safer, what with all the stories he had heard about the Dock Watch – and so Wolf surreptitiously slipped his arm from around Trudi's and rested his hand on the pommel of his dagger.

He had some gold in his purse and a pouch of weirdroot slung under his jacket in the small of his back. He did not want to lose either.

'Let's have a look at you.'

A lantern was held up and shone in his eyes. Trudi flinched and pressed close to him. Wolf could still not see the man's face, but in the light he saw the docker's hook hanging from his belt and the embroidered symbol on his overcoat.

'Student, are you?'

Wolf nodded. It was best not to provoke trouble.

'Pleased to meet you, sonny-boy...'

The Hook's tone was mocking, unpleasant. Wolf guessed from his voice that he was a youngish man himself, still in his twenties. Sometimes, Wolf did feel his age, did feel too old for all this...

'This your girlfriend?'

Trudi tried to hide behind him, like a night-animal getting behind a rock.

'Pretty one, isn't she? Students get all the pretty ones. Not like us honest working men.'

Wolf could see the Hook wore a Citizens' Vigilance armband. He was one of the unofficial patrolmen the waterfront faction had put out on the street while the Beast was loose.

'Still, that'll change come the Revolution...'

Obviously, this vigilante was a disciple of Yevgeny Yefimovich.

The Hook reached out and stroked Trudi's hair. Wolf made fists and felt his sharp nails digging into the meat of his hands.

'How about a little sample?'

Wolf could smell gin on the Hook's breath. None of these vigilantes were taking seriously their mission to protect the locals. The CV was just an excuse for more bullying.

'Excuse me,' Wolf said, in protest.

The Hook chuckled. Wolf realized now there were others in the fog. The vigilantes never went around on their own. He could make out the shapes. Even more, he could distinguish the smells. He still had some of the senses he had developed during his time with the Chaos Knights, especially after dark, especially when the moons were full, especially in the fog.

The Hook leered, greenish teeth shining in his shadowed face, and leant forwards. His features appeared, horridly distorted, in the lantern's beam and he poked out his tongue.

'Raaaahh!'

Trudi swallowed a scream and her fingers dug into Wolf's shoulder.

'You should be careful who you go with, love,' the Hook said, 'or the Beast'll get you!'

Trudi spoke, slowly and quietly, to Wolf. 'Make... them... go... away...'

The girl didn't like the Hooks. She hadn't told him much about her life before they met, but he had picked up bits and pieces. She had been with the Fish for a time, passed from man to man, and had had friends killed in the Waterfront War. Some of her clothes still had the stitches in the fish shape where the insignia had been ripped off. She was out of the gang life, but still remembered some of the bad times. She had a few scars, where they didn't show.

Wolf did not want a fight. He was as afraid of what he might do to the Hooks as what harm they might do him.

'They say the Beast is from over the river,' the Hook began, conversationally. 'Yefimovich says the killer is a palace lackey or a rich merchant. Obviously, the monster comes from the overprivileged classes.'

Wolf realized he was wearing his best clothes. He might look like a beggar by the standards of the court, but he was still a pampered prince to these men.

'Me, I reckon different. The Beast is rich scum, sure as Sigmar's mighty hammer. But I think he's from this side of the river. I think he's from the University. I think he's a bloody student.'

The Hook's lantern made a little bubble of visibility in the fog. Wolf and Trudi and the Hook were in it, and his comrades were on the edges, lurking like deep sea predators. Wolf did not know where on the street they were and how close he might be to a friendly inn.

'Let them go, Brandauer,' said one of the other vigilantes. 'They're just kids.'

Under other circumstances, Wolf would have taken objection to that.

'Need to be taught a lesson,' Brandauer said.

'This isn't catching us the Beast,' said the more conscientious vigilante. Brandauer grumbled, but let his lantern fall from their faces.

'Watch yourselves,' he said, turning away. Wolf could have put a dagger between his shoulderblades with a single, easy move. He knew precisely where to strike if he wanted to pierce the heart. Or the liver. Or the kidneys. He had learned his anatomy in a forest university, cutting and hacking with a short sword.

But that had been another life, another person. That had been a beast, not a man.

The Hooks were gone. Even their lanternlight was obscured in the fog.

Wolf realized he had been sweating. Trudi relaxed her grip.

He wondered about the Beast. He did not like to think of the murderer, stalking through the night as he had through the forests. The thing that made him afraid was that he could understand the madman, know the pleasures he experienced in his alleyway hunting expeditions. Perhaps the Beast was a Chaos Knight, as he had been. Some alterations were easy to conceal with a mask or a cloak. And some were impossible to detect at a glance. In Cicatrice's company there had been knights who appeared to be children or old men, but who were frenzied berserkers in battle, stronger than the armour-skinned, axe-handed giants. It was unnervingly easy to imagine the Beast as someone like that. An old beggar, a lost child, a street woman. Any face could be a mask.

Wolf and Trudi walked towards the faint luminescence of the tavern lights. Reading a few signs, he knew exactly where he was. There was the Drunken Bastard, the hostelry that catered exclusively to the miserable, solitary drinker. And the Crooked Spear, well-known as the pick-up place for young men who preferred the company of their own sex. And the Crescent Moon, which attracted the unquiet dead, they said. None of them were exactly promising. Alone among so many illuminated signs, the Crescent Moon's ironwork symbol hung in darkness. Its patrons did not need torches and lanterns to find their way.

Suddenly a pulse of desire throbbed in his brain. He needed to chew the root. Sometimes, the urge hit him at the oddest times: during lectures, in polite conversation, on long coach trips, in bed with Trudi. If it ever became a problem, he would deal with it…

His mouth went dry and the fog swirled inside his head. He saw sparks like fireflies, dancing before his eyes…

…but it was not a problem.

'Wolf?'

Trudi held him tight, again.

'It'll be all right,' he mumbled, reaching round under his coat for the pouch. Trudi let him go and stood apart a little, her outline blurring in the fog.

Wolf shook a fresh root into his hand and took his knife to it. He slivered off a slice and took it onto his tongue, relishing the sting as the juice seeped out.

'That's better,' he said, putting the root back and concealing his pouch again. 'That's a lot better.'

Someone came out of the Crescent Moon: a slender girl in a long cloak. She turned up her collar and walked with confidence, dodging out of the way of a drunk stumbling blind through the fog. Even through the fog, Wolf could see the red tint in her eyes and knew why she could see in the murk. She was whistling an old Bretonnian tune. Wolf envied this creature for whom the night and fog held no terrors. The man she had avoided made the sign of Sigmar as she passed and continued, stumbling faster towards the Drunken Bastard, hand in his purse dredging for coins.

The girl came close and stopped. She smiled, her teeth sharp pearls, and looked with curiosity at Wolf.

'Do I know you?' the vampire asked. She spoke Reikspiel with a faint, attractive Bretonnian accent.

Wolf would have remembered. She was lovely, fascinating. She looked perhaps sixteen, but there was no way to judge her age.

'I don't think so.'

'Genevieve,' she said, extending a slim, cold hand to be kissed. 'Genevieve Dieudonné.'

Trudi did not like the girl. She had problems with dead people. It was one of the prejudices of her class.

'I've heard of you,' Wolf said.

The vampire's smiling face closed a little. Her hand became a little colder.

'You have met my brother, Johann. We look quite like each other.'

'Johann is a common name.'

'Johann von Mecklenberg, the Elector of Sudenland.'

Genevieve smiled again. 'Ah yes, not such a common person.'

'Wolf,' he said, 'and this is Trudi.'

'Hello, Trudi,' the vampire said.

Wolf could not be sure whether Genevieve was trying to put Trudi at her ease, or slyly enjoying the girl's discomfiture.

The juice was beginning to affect him. He stared at Genevieve's face, seeing strange things in it. Sometimes portraits grow faint with age and flake to reveal other pictures that have been painted over. Genevieve's girl's face was like that, with another face underlying it: an old, predatory face, with needle teeth, hollow cheeks and eyes burning like red lamps.

'I don't care much for the court, I'm afraid,' the vampire said. 'Too many bad memories. Perhaps I'll see you again at the theatre.'

Terror gripped Wolf as he felt his brain seizing up. He was losing touch with the functions of his body. His face was frozen and he was retaining the mask of courtesy, exchanging politenesses with the ancient girl. But he felt as if Wolf were shrinking inside his body and someone else gaining the ascendant.

The fog was pressing in, driving his consciousness down into the depths of his person.

'Watch yourself in the fog,' Genevieve said, slipping into it. 'There are hunters about.'

He heard her walk away, her shoes slapping tinily on the cobbles. Her smell – sweet with an undertaste of blood – lingered a few moments and was dispersed in the fog.

Genevieve, he had heard, had come to live with what she was. Like the other Wolf and Eric, she did not fear the beast inside. Wolf felt an urge to run after her, to talk with her further. There was something he should learn from the vampire.

The fog grew thicker, clinging to his clothes. Even Trudi was hard to see. He breathed in the cold, tasting weirdroot as the air rushed over his tongue. The dreams were in his blood by now.

There were shapes in the fog. He could see them now. They called to him.

'Wolf?'

Trudi seemed a long way in the distance, shouting to him as if he were at the top of the highest mountain in the Empire.

There were colours in the grey fog. And music.

His feet were uncomfortable, confined in their heavy boots, the toe-nails pressed into flesh, the toes constricted. Pain and strength mingled in his limbs.

'Wolf?'

He was Wolf and he was not Wolf. The taste of the blood was still in the air.

The girl tugged at his sleeve. A burst of anger exploded inside him.

Hissing, he turned on the girl, his sharp-fingered hand lashing out...

III

'I think that's why they call him Filthy Harald,' someone said.

He turned around, throwing-knife in his hand. Two men had come into the warehouse, one in his early thirties, the other ten years younger. They didn't make him feel sick on sight, so they were probably all right.

'You have shit on your boots, sir,' said the older man. He wore his green velvet cloak as if born to it. A courtier.

He shrugged and sheathed his knife. He saw no threat from the two newcomers.

'I was just beating it out of someone,' he snarled.

The gentleman in velvet and the off-duty watchman looked at each other and shrugged.

He let them hang for a moment, then explained, 'Someone has to clear out the sewer inlets when they get blocked. It's part of my contract with the Reik and Talabec.'

He wiped his boots on a rough mat. He would have to sluice them off properly later.

The gentleman looked a little upset. But he didn't wrinkle his nose in distaste. He was rich and probably titled, but he was not queasy about messy realities. Harald knew that this was not a typical court popinjay. If it came to a fight, the courtier would take quite a bit of killing.

'Well,' said Harald, 'what can I do for you?'

'We have a commission,' said the aristocrat.

Harald didn't say anything. He took a wet rag from a hook on the wall and wiped the last of the dirt from his boots.

'This is Baron Johann von Mecklenberg, the Elector of Sudenland,' said the officer.

Harald didn't bow and scrape. It wasn't his style.

'How is Dickon?' he asked.

'What?'

'Dickon. Is he still captain of the Dock Watch?'

The youth was astounded.

'You've got the copper smell, boy. It can't be mistaken.'

'I'm Helmut Elsaesser. And I am from the Dock Watch.'

Harald didn't like the feeling that he was being called upon to demonstrate his skills, like a conjurer at a children's party.

'You have sharp eyes, thief-taker,' said the baron.

Harald nodded, agreeing with him.

'Dickon is still captain.'

'I'm sure he's the best money can buy.'

The boy laughed. He was all right.

The baron looked around the warehouse. Goods were piled up, with chalk marks on the boxes to indicate their eventual destination. Room and board came with the job. A cot in a cupboard and three company meals a day. You could call it a life.

'You used to be with the watch?'

'Yes, baron. Used to be.'

Harald's boots would pass. He looked up at his visitors. They had brought a little of the fog with them. Outside, it would be cold, difficult. Ideal weather for cutpurses, pimps, pickpockets and ruffians. Bad weather for coppers.

'I understand you resigned.'

Harald spat out a short laugh.

'That's what you heard.'

Elsaesser was passing a document from hand to hand.

'They say you were the best copper in Altdorf.'

'I'd heard that too.'

'But not recently.'

Harald sat down. A pot of tea was stewing on the small table.

'I'm in the mercantile business now. I've retired to make my fortune.'

'By unblocking sewers?'

'And catching pilferers, and stock-taking and sweeping the place out if I have to.'

Without being asked, the baron sat down at the table. Elsaesser stayed upright, like a dutiful footman. He was clutching his document as if it were a charm blessed of Verena. Harald saw the Imperial seal. He wasn't impressed. He'd seen it before.

'Quite a descent in the world.'

'You could look at it that way, baron. A man should make the best of his circumstances. Whatever they are.'

He had been with the Reik and Talabec Trading Company for three years now and he couldn't think of the first names of the merchants who employed him.

'I've heard stories about your resignation.'

'You can take your pick of them.'

'What's your story?'

Harald didn't see why he should go through all this again. But it was expected of him.

'I killed a man. Several, in fact. But one in particular.'

'Ulli von Tasseninck.'

Harald remembered. The weight of the knife in his hand. The arc of the throw. The satisfying thud of impact.

'You knew him, elector. I'm not surprised.'

'The nephew of Grand Prince Hals von Tasseninck, Elector of Ostland.'

'Yes, a distinguished family.'

The young man, a corpse already, taking five more steps then crumpling onto the flagstones. It had been a neat job. No blood spilled.

'And a powerful one.'

'Show me an elector who is not powerful. You should know.'

Harald poured himself a mug of tea. He did not offer any to his visitors.

'Couldn't you have used a little more tact? Ulli was headstrong, yes, but he was born to the green velvet.'

Harald felt his bile rising and gulped down tea to calm his stomach.

'Baron, I saw a naked man chasing a girl, with his cock in one hand and a meatcleaver in the other... Well, I guess I forgot to enquire as to his lineage–'

Ulli had left his green velvet courtier's cloak draped over a statue of Verena, presumably hoping to blind the goddess of justice. Harald had wiped his knife on the cloak and thrown the garment over the dead man.

'The girl was Ulli's property, was she not? A bonded slave?'

Harald shrugged. 'It was dark in that temple. I didn't see the brand of ownership burned into her back.'

The baron had no answer. Harald knew that the man approved of his actions. Most people approved of him. That didn't help much. What people – especially those in green velvet – thought, and what they did were two separate courses.

'She was thirteen years old,' Harald said, 'and your friend had been using her since she was eight.'

Dark points appeared in the baron's eyes. 'Ulli von Tasseninck was not my friend.'

'Did you know that the Grand Prince endowed a college in his name at the University? There's a statue of him outside it, looking like a saint, brandishing the spear of learning. The Ulli von Tasseninck School of Religious Studies.'

A slash of a smile split the baron's neatly trimmed beard.

'Actually, the statue was damaged recently. Someone smashed its head and replaced it with a pumpkin lantern.'

'That's a crime.'

'You wouldn't know anything about it.'

'I hate crime.'

'I thought so.'

Steam rose from Harald's tea. He understood the baron a little better now. He was a good man, too.

They were all good men. A dying breed.

'What happened to the girl? You bought her, didn't you?'

Harald remembered. She could hardly speak and would hide under a table whenever anyone new came into the room. When he had asked her what her name was, she had not known what he had meant. When he had explained that her name was what everybody called her, she smiled and said, 'Bitch.'

'No, I freed her.'

'I understood that cost you a lot.'

'Everything I had. My house, my savings, my horse, everything. Even my job. That was Grand Prince Hals's price.'

The baron nodded.

'I kept something back, though,' Harald said. 'Most of the weapons came with the commission. They belong to the watch. But this,' he patted his knife, 'is mine, bought with my own crowns.'

'Fine workmanship. Magnin the steelsmith?'

Harald nodded.

'I have one of his swords.'

Harald took out the knife and looked at his face in the polished steel. His reflection curved with the blade.

'She's married,' Harald said. 'Ulli's plaything. She married a chandler and got fat. She has hundreds of babies.'

'All named after you?'

'No, none of them. We don't see each other. She has too many memories.'

He kissed his blade, feeling the stone cold hardness against his lips.

'So, you have a steel mistress?'

'You could call it that,' he said, slipping his knife away. 'But it's just a good tool.'

'You were married, weren't you?' It was the first thing Elsaesser had said in a while.

Harald's stomach boiled again.

'I was. My wife died.'

'I'm sorry to hear that,' said the baron. 'Plague?'

His gut felt as if lashworms were eating through it.

'Hooks,' he said. 'Or Fish. They never found out.'

'That was back during the Waterfront War,' Elsaesser explained to the baron. 'Just before it petered out. It was strange. One day, both gangs were at each other's throats. Then, the fighting stopped. The war chiefs of the Hooks and the Fish just disappeared.'

Harald remembered the faces looking up at him from under the water, disappearing as the weights on their boots pulled them down.

'Another unsolved case,' he said. 'Dickon has a barrelful of them.'

'I've met Dickon.'

'Then you know what kind of a copper he is. Money at the end of the week and anything for a quiet life.'

The baron held out his hand and Elsaesser put the document in it.

'This is an Imperial warrant, Mister Kleindeinst.'

The baron laid it carefully on the table, squaring the corners.

'For what?'

'For anything you say. Immediately, it's an order reconfirming you in your old position.'

'Dickon will love that.'

'You won't be under Dickon. You'll report to me and I'm answerable only to the Emperor.'

Harald's stomach was calming down but there was a tightness in his belly replacing the ache. He could almost taste the desire. This warehouse was a grave and he could feel the earth shifting as he struggled out of it.

'Then, these are sealed orders giving you the authority to go anywhere, question anyone, do anything...'

There was a great deal of darkness in the baron's eyes. Harald felt as if he were looking into a knife-mirror again.

'And, finally, this is a warrant of arrest for a certain criminal,' said Elsaesser.

'A warrant of arrest,' explained the baron, 'or, if necessary, a warrant of execution.'

Harald picked up the document and sniffed it.

'This isn't real, is it?'

'No,' said the baron, 'but that will be our secret.'

'Boy,' Harald said to Elsaesser. 'Get a chair and sit down. Do you want tea?'

Elsaesser brought two cups from a shelf. Harald poured drinks for his visitors.

'I suppose I had better enjoy this,' he said, drinking again. 'This was the only perk of the job, imported tea from Kislev. And I don't work here any more.'

The document was in his shirt pocket, above his heart.

'I brought this,' Elsaesser said, pulling out a small, cloth-wrapped packet. 'It was in a desk at the Luitpoldstrasse Station.'

He unwrapped the object and let it fall on the table. The copper badge hadn't changed. It bore the watch code number for the Luitpoldstrasse District, 317, and his own service serial number, 89. Harald picked it up and felt it in his hand. His stomach wasn't bothering him now. It was as if he had regained the use of a crippled limb. He slipped the badge into his pocket.

'What do you know about the Beast?' asked the baron.

'Seven,' Harald said, imagining them laid out in a row. 'Seven so far.'

'And there will be more.'

'Yes. He can't stop. A womanslayer is the worst kind of criminal there is.'

'Can you catch him?'

The baron was serious now. Harald felt the weight of the badge in his pocket. For a small scrap of metal, it felt awfully heavy.

'You know,' he said, putting his boot up on the table, 'this is why they call me "Filthy Harald".'

The baron looked at Elsaesser, puzzled.

'I don't understand.'

'Every filthy job, baron. That's when people come to me. That's what I get. Every filthy job.'

IV

She had missed the main service at the temple, but attended a late evening ceremony. There were no pews. Worshippers at the Temple of Sigmar were expected to stand up, or to kneel on the hard stones. After her day, she decided on kneeling, although that meant a chill seeped into her knees and crept up through her body. Contact with the ground brought her closer to the god anyway, as she picked up the residue of the many devout prayers that had been offered in this small chapel. There were ignoble, ungodly thoughts too – even ignoble, ungodly prayers – but Rosanna was used to weeding them out and allowing herself to sink into the centuries of pious converse with the patron deity of the Empire.

They had kept her down at the Luitpoldstrasse Station well into the evening, sorting through odd items of clothing left over from the victims. And bits of irrelevant rubbish found lying around at the scenes of the killings. She was not a necromancer; she could not communicate with the dead and quiz them about their last moments. She was a psychometrist, picking up images and impressions from inanimate objects, usually strong emotions that had been associated with people who had been in contact with the things she scried from.

It had been a ghastly task, living through seven deaths, and all she had picked up was a tangle of confusion and spilled blood. She thought the Beast was a madman with a knife, but could not rule out the persistent suggestion that he was an altered creature. Through the pain, she only had the vaguest impressions of staring eyes. And she kept seeing green velvet.

But almost as bad as the shocking detritus left by violent death were the aching impressions she picked up of the lives the women had lived before their murders. Hunger, cold, poverty, lifelong abuse, joyless love. One woman had had maybe seventeen children, none surviving. Another had been introduced to weirdroot in infancy by her father, and had not spent a day outside her dreams for the rest of her life. The Beast would eventually go from the docks, but the misery would remain, unchanged.

She prayed to Sigmar, trying to cleanse herself of the deaths of seven women. In the centre of the octagonal chapel, looking up at the stylised image of the warhammer above the altar, she tried to reach out to the god who had been a man. Sometimes, her gift brought her epiphanies.

But she was never sure of them, never sure that she had not merely tapped into the shared delusions of three thousand years of devout souls rather than reached the gods themselves.

Most people did not see enough, but Rosanna Ophuls frequently saw too much. It was worse, ultimately, than seeing nothing.

The graveyard shift cleric concluded the service and she stood up. Her only fellow communicants were an old woman who attended every service available at the Temple, from the earliest in the morning to the latest at night, and Tilo, a distracted-looking novice with ink on his fingers and a terrible stutter. She rubbed her knees and tried to get some warmth into them.

'R-R-R-Ro…'

'Yes,' she said, not waiting for him to finish.

He was going to ask her out to a coffee house. She could pick it up from his mind. His forehead was bright red and his hair, even in his early twenties, was thinning. His scalp glowed scarlet.

She felt kindly towards him.

'I'm sorry, Tilo. I've been summoned by the Lector.'

'Muh-muh-muh…'

Maybe some other time?

'Maybe, Tilo.'

His lips twitched in a smile.

'Excuse me.'

She stepped past him, through the doorway of the chapel. Tilo seemed to stumble slightly and pressed against her.

Inside her brain, a bubble of Tilo's mind exploded.

…she was looking down at herself, naked and tied to a bed, flames licking upwards from her flesh. Her face was painted and she was grinning like an empty-eyed weirdroot imbecile. Her breasts and hips were as exaggerated as those of dwarf goddess carvings. She was covered in a thin film of some perfumed oil and it was burning without pain. Her body rippled as she writhed against her bonds, lifting her back off the bed in an arch, invisible clouds of warmth and musk radiating from her hot centre. She was begging for something, words dribbling out of her mouth…

She pushed away from the novice, breaking the contact.

In his eyes, she read his horror.

'You saw,' he said, not stuttering, 'you *saw!*'

He ran away, his robe flapping about his legs.

There was a fountain outside the chapel. She pushed her face into the jet of water and tried to wash Tilo out of her.

'I am not a pretty girl,' she told herself, lying. 'What other people see is not me.'

She rubbed cold water into her face. She never wore rouge, tried to cover her long, red hair with a scarf. She did not lead men like Tilo on. And yet, wherever she went, she could feel men's eyes following her. All women experienced much the same thing, she supposed, but not all women could feel what she felt, could feel the dirty tendrils of men's desires slinking into her mind.

'Rosanna,' a voice said.

She stood up, her face dripping. The front of her dress was wet and clung.

Siemen Ruhaak, an initiate of the Order of the Torch, stood in the corridor, his hood up. The Order of the Torch was the cult's administrative arm. Ruhaak was always fetching people for audiences. The novices were afraid of him, because he always appeared when they were due for a scolding. Rosanna always felt slightly sorry for him, seeing the doubts that writhed beneath his sternness. If the Lector, Mikael Hasselstein, was a Knight of the Cult of Sigmar, then Siemen Ruhaak was his squire.

'Am I late?' she asked.

Ruhaak shook his head. 'I was just coming for you.'

'Is the Lector ready to see me?'

'Yes. He has just returned from a palace function. I would appreciate it if you did not disturb him overmuch. He seems distracted. He has so many things to consider.'

Rosanna couldn't quite understand. She couldn't even scry what Ruhaak was getting at. Something vague was troubling the man and he didn't even know what it was.

Ruhaak knew more about her than Tilo. As they walked through the passages towards the Lector's office, she noticed that he was careful not to touch her. He even held the sleeves of his robe tightly against his side to avoid a casual, accidental brushing.

There were two kinds of men: those who wanted her and those who were afraid of her.

Outside the Lector's office, two Knights of the Fiery Heart stood to attention, in full armour. Hasselstein did not usually bother with such precautions, but in a crisis he almost always called for the cult's military wing. For a powerful man – in Altdorf, Hasselstein was second only to the Grand Theogonist Yorri XV in the hierarchy of the cult – the Lector was remarkably easy to spook.

The knights stood aside and Ruhaak opened the door for her. She bowed her head as she entered the office. The door was closed behind her and she was with Mikael Hasselstein, the Emperor's confessor. Ruhaak had not come in with her.

She had talked with Hasselstein before, but never alone. Mostly, she saw him in the distance as he was about the business of the cult and of the Empire. Usually, he was getting into or out of a carriage, holding up his expensive robes. She knew he was convinced that Mornan Tybalt, the Master of the Imperial Counting House, was his deadly rival and was always embroiled in scheme and counter-scheme to gain the most favour with Karl-Franz. Hasselstein spent more time at the palace than the Temple and spoke eloquently about the need for the cult to remain at the centre of the court's political life. Sigmar had a hammer but the Lector fought with a quill and a ledger.

She looked up.

The Lector was lying on a couch with his boots off. He wore his cleric's robes, but open like a coat. Underneath, he was in a courtier's finery. He looked a little ill. The office was large but cluttered. There was an indifferent portrait of the Emperor up on one wall, given pride of place. An antique screen in the Nipponese style, decorated with images of Sigmar wielding his hammer, was set up before the slit windows. The room was lit with a single candelabrum. Rosanna got the impression that the Lector had just extinguished most of the lamps to save his eyes from hurt. The desk was piled high with books and papers, and an array of seals was set out on the blotter, neatly ordered by size and function of etiquette.

Hasselstein fixed her with his eyes and sat up.

'Ophuls,' he snapped, 'stay where you are.'

She stood as stiff as the knights sentry outside.

'There's a stool behind you,' Hasselstein said. 'Sit down.'

She did so, demurely tucking her dress around her legs. It was a low, wooden footstool and made her feel like a child.

'That's better,' he said, breathing again. If Ruhaak was cautious about touching a scryer, then Mikael Hasselstein was terrified. As the Emperor's confessor, she supposed, he carried a lot of things in his head that he could, even if threatened with torture, share with no one but his god.

'Ophuls,' he said. 'Rosanna, isn't it?'

'Yes, lector.'

Hasselstein stood up and began pacing the room in his stockinged feet, describing a half-circle around her. Even without contact, she could feel the storm of concerns surrounding his head. They crackled in the air like lightning. Ruhaak was right the Lector had a lot on his mind.

'Child, you've been with the Temple for some years?'

She nodded.

'You are a good and faithful servant of Sigmar. I have only excellent reports of you.'

He poured himself a glass of Estalian sherry. The Lector was not known for his asceticism. A cold bird sat in a dish on the floor by the couch, its ribs exposed and its legs twisted off. Rosanna remembered that she had not had time to eat today.

The chicken had led a happy life, pecking at corn, scratching around in the straw. It had been the special pet of the farmer's daughter. But the farmer's daughter had not been fond enough of it to neglect a profit. One day, she had gathered the bird up in her arms and neatly strangled it. Rosanna had sampled plenty of animal lives like that. She was a vegetarian.

Hasselstein stood still, sipping his sherry.

Uppermost in his thoughts was a woman. Rosanna scried a flurry of skirts, a lingering trace of perfume and the warm press of a body. So far as she knew, Hasselstein had no official mistresses. She pulled her invisible feelers back in and let them lie like her hands, folded in her lap.

Hasselstein drank more of the liquor. He was tired.

'You have been down at the docks today?'

'Yes, Father Wallraff sent me to help the watch.'

'Wallraff, eh? A man with initiative. Good for him.'

Rosanna had the impression that the Lector did not want to reward the father for his initiative. She would not have been surprised to learn that the sharp young cleric had suddenly been assigned to missionary duty beyond the Sea of Claws.

'I've been trying to help in this case of the Beast.'

Hasselstein drained his glass. 'The murderer, yes. I have heard of him.'

Rosanna could not help herself. The impressions pouring from Hasselstein were too strong to ignore. There was the laughter of a woman and the sticky taste of sweat. The Lector did not think like Tilo, constructing fantasies for the night. He was not imagining, he was remembering. She scried bodies pressed together in a hurry, lovemaking with a hard edge, blood and bruises in with the kisses and caresses. There was also a great darkness, as if the cleric were trying to blot out part of his memory.

'A bad business. What have you learned?'

Rosanna forced herself to ignore the pictures in Hasselstein's mind.

'Little, I'm afraid. The murderer is a man, I think. A human being, that is. Or of some closely related race.'

Hasselstein's face knit. Anger burned like a halo around him.

'I had imagined from the savagery associated with the slayings that we were dealing with a monster of Chaos.'

'I don't think so. The Beast is twisted in mind, not in body. At least, that is my impression. It's not very clear. There is something strange about the murderer, physically. I've scried that much from the scraps the watch have kept. I keep feeling that something important is just within my grasp, but that I cannot pick it out from the confusion.'

'You are young,' Hasselstein said, 'your gifts are not fully trained yet.'

'Perhaps the cult would care to assign someone with more control. There is always Hannelore Zischler or Beate Hettich.'

The Lector thought for a moment and then made a decision. 'No, Rosanna. You must have your chance. Bringing in another scryer would confuse matters. Besides, the others are not in Altdorf. These murders show no sign of pausing to allow us to send for Zischler or Hettich. The Beast must be caught soon.'

'Yes.'

'Can you tell me *anything* more about the murderer?'

Rosanna wasn't sure whether to mention it, but, 'It's not something I scried, but before I arrived the watch found some important evidence that was destroyed.'

Hasselstein was keenly interested.

'Yes,' he said, impatiently, 'what was it?'

'A scrap of green velvet, lector. Like the courtiers wear.'

Hasselstein made a fist and his glass shattered in it. Rosanna flinched as his rage filled the room.

His face was set and inexpressive, but his mind was in a turmoil.

He took out a handkerchief and bound his cuts.

'Rosanna, have you taken any vows? I know you're not a novice, but you are attached to the cult?'

'I have pledged allegiance and obedience.'

'Obedience? Good. The cult must come before anything, you understand? This is a precarious time for the Empire and only we have the best interests of the Empire as our first concern.'

Hasselstein had said as much during his private sermons to the Temple staff. Father Wallraff had been amusing about the speech, asking her if she could think of a time in history which had not been a precarious one for the Empire.

'Whatever you learn about the Beast, you must bring first to me. If I am not available, confer with Ruhaak. This is vitally important.'

'I... I understand.'

'Be sure you do. We have the Order of the Fiery Heart, remember. Anything the watch can do, our own Templars can do better. I do not trust the watchmen. Too many criminals have escaped from them.'

Rosanna did understand. The Dock Watch, as she had seen, were greedy bullies. If the Beast was a rich man, he would find it easy to purchase his freedom. She could not be responsible for that.

'And we must have secrecy. This may not be a story it would be useful for many people to know about.'

Hasselstein was thinking of his woman again. She was crying out in passion as they coupled.

Didn't anyone in this Temple think of anything else?

'I understand.'

'We are a wealthy order, Rosanna. I see no reason why you should not profit from your labours in this case.'

Rosanna could not have been more shocked if the Lector had slapped her.

'Should you acquit yourself to my satisfaction, I believe I can authorize a healthy pension. Enough to set you up in any corner of the Empire, in any business you might choose. You would have a substantial dowry should you prefer hunting a husband to hunting a murderer. Should you be tired of your own name and family history, a new background could be contrived for you.'

This was an astonishing suggestion.

'What I mean is that this is such an important matter to me – to the Cult of Sigmar – that your performance is of the most immediate interest to me. Serve us well and there is little you might desire that is not within my gift.'

Rosanna bowed her head. Her scarf was slipping from her hair.

Forgetting himself, Hasselstein advanced and extended his hand in a familiar gesture, as if to lay the cleric's healing touch upon a suppliant. It was the traditional way of ending a confession, symbolising the priest's assumption of the sins of the communicant.

A fraction of an inch away from her hair, which was rising slightly to meet the charge of his body, Hasselstein's hand froze.

In his mind, he was pleasuring a woman in a dark, cramped space, a cupboard or a small room. Her knees were braced and she was gripping a chairback to stay unsteadily upright. They both grunted as he ground inside her and the odour of sex hung in the air like an Altdorf fog. Her skirts and his robe were disarrayed, bunched between them, and his hands were in her clothes, fastened like leeches to her body. His face was in the woman's hair. It was red, like Rosanna's. But then it was blonde and silk-fine. As the couple peaked, she turned her head to look into his face, to lick hungrily at his chin. Looking through his eyes, she saw her own face again, but rippling like the surface of a disturbed pond. Has-selstein's desires were superimposed upon his memories. Rosanna saw her eyes changing colour, from green to blue, and her features shifting. The face distorted and became several other faces. One of them, she was sure, belonged to Margarethe Ruttmann, the Beast's last victim. And oth-ers, just beyond her recognition, seemed similarly familiar.

The Lector snatched his hand away and rubbed it against his robe.

'You have my blessing,' he said. 'Now, go...'

V

The girl runs through the fog, but the Beast is faster than anything in the city. It doesn't know whether it runs on two legs or four, but its claws strike sparks from the cobbles. The girl is limping, her ankle turned on some loose stone. She is sobbing, knowing what comes next.

She is already marked, the scratches across her face are still bleeding.

There aren't cobbles under their feet any more. Wooden planks shift and rumble as they run down the jetty.

They are on the docks. The old, disused docks. There is nobody else around. They are alone together. The Beast is pleased.

The boy-shell holds back, allowing the girl a few moments to make a move. She finds a ladder and climbs down from the wharf, towards the shingles of the riverbank.

The Beast dispels the boy-shell and grabs the wooden posts that stick up beyond the ladder.

Below, the girl is climbing. She has sunk into the fog, but it can hear her mewling and the beating of her heart. It can smell her fear.

The Beast knows her. It knows her name: Trudi.

The fog is wonderful. It feels like part of the Beast, as if its breath were solidifying in the air around it. The Beast was born for the fog and feels comfortable in it. The fog is its friend, like the crooked alleyways are its friend, and the tangle of piles under the docks, and the night that falls as thick as velvet upon the city.

The ladder is old and rotted through. A rung snaps and the girl falls. The Beast hears her sob as she lands badly, the wind knocked out of her.

Somewhere out on the river, a foghorn sounds. Two barges pass dangerously close to one another. The Beast hears the night watches swearing at each other. They are very far away.

Not bothering with the ladder, the Beast leaps. The river is low at this time of night, so it falls in shallow water, its knees and ankles bending as its bulk is forced into a crouch.

It feels pebbles under its feet and hands, and fragments of clay pipes thrown away by sailors and dockers for centuries. Sometimes seashells are shifted this far inland, scraped from the hulls of the ocean-going ships that sail down the Reik from Marienburg.

The Beast stands on two legs, slicing its claws through the air. The boy-shell is lost in the fog, lost forever...

The girl is near, huddled up against a thick, wooden post, trying to still her breathing.

The Beast lopes towards her, shingles crunching under it.

It tries to say her name, as it has tried to say the others. The word will not come from its mouth. Its jaw doesn't work as it should.

The Beast finds the girl...

...and the girl screams.

VI

Dien Ch'ing reflected that he was not as young as he had formerly been. His face was still as smooth as new vellum and his hair had been white since childhood. Few could guess his age, but he knew. Sixty-five. He had been serving the Lord Tsien-Tsin – Tzeentch, as the Master was called in this barbarous land – all his life. There had been rewards. Continued strength, health and vitality were among them. Tsien-Tsin, Lord of the Fifteen Devils, repaid faithful service with longevity. Ch'ing could reasonably expect to live to a very great age, far greater than that enjoyed by even the most venerable of his ancestors.

His life had taken him across the face of the Known World many times. He had visited each of the continents, had amassed and squandered fortunes, had seen his enemies suffer and perish, had tasted the delights afforded only to the initiates of his proscribed cult. And still, he felt, he was only a few tiers up the pagoda. He had served the Invisible Empire for the length of his days. It was time, he believed, that a little more of the greater purpose of Tsien-Tsin were revealed to him.

Tonight, he would meet with his immediate superior and perhaps a little more would be explained.

He had slipped out of the quarters allotted to him in the palace and taken advantage of the fog to travel unseen across the city. It was a skill he had cultivated for many years. In a sense, the helpful fog spoiled the trick. Any fool could skulk and hide in fog, but only an adept of Ch'ing's stature could pass unnoticed through a crowded city at the height of midday on a clear, cloudless day.

Using the key that had been delivered to him, he let himself into one of the rooms at the back of the Holy Hammer of Sigmar on the Street of a Hundred Taverns. It was not the rowdiest, most decadent of the many hostelries in the vicinity. Indeed, it was one of the quietest, best-ordered and neatest, as befitted a private club open only to the most desperate thieves and professional murderers in the city. Only those with a key were admitted and securing a key was more difficult than gaining an audience with the Emperor.

In the darkness of the passage, Ch'ing could hear a conversation being conducted in the tap-room.

'I say it gives the business a bad name,' claimed a man with a Tilean lilt to his voice.

'I agree with you, Ettore,' said a more cultivated, suave-sounding man, 'but what can we do? The matter is in the hands of Sigmar and, of course, the Dock Watch.'

There was some laughter. Ch'ing smiled. So this was what murderers sounded like when they were relaxing.

'The Beast is just a butcher,' said Ettore. 'He gives murderers a bad name.'

'You strangled your last wife with her nightcap, I believe.'

'That was a personal matter.'

'And then you took a red-hot poker to your children.'

'They were disobedient. Besides, your hands are hardly clean, my friend Quex.'

'I don't deny that,' purred the suave murderer, 'but I have never killed without being paid for it.'

'I say we should trap the Beast ourselves,' a third, gruff-voiced, assassin said.

'What?' spluttered Ettore. 'Us, help the Dock Watch?'

'They've been poking around too much since the Beast started killing tarts. They're not catching him, but they are harassing us. When was the last time old Dickon actually caught anyone?'

Nobody knew.

'Well, he pulled in Fagnar Brisz today and a couple of coppers roughed up Schatten.'

'That's terrible. They'll be refusing bribes next.'

'Brisz is an animal,' said Quex, 'little better than the Beast. His use of the bandsaw on the Widow von Praunheim was simply unnecessary and distasteful.'

'Well, Quex, if the Beast keeps it up, you can debate etiquette with Brisz in Mundsen Keep.'

'The Beast is an amateur, gentlemen, and amateurs always get caught. Or disappear without trace.'

'I say good luck to him and let's have another drink.'

'A fine idea, my man.'

A hand clamped down over Ch'ing's shoulder and he twisted, his hands up, ready to defend himself.

He favoured the crane-style, arms out for balance, feet kicking like the lightning-fast pecks of the bird's deadly beak.

'Careful,' said a familiar voice. 'The corridor is narrow, you'll break your wrists.'

Ch'ing relaxed and bowed. In the darkness, Yefimovich's eyes glowed like hot coals.

'It is good to see you, my friend,' the High Priest of Tzeentch said. 'How long has it been since we first met?'

'More than thirty years. Not since Zhufbar.'

'Ah yes, a failure. I still regret it. We were out of favour after that.'

'Quite so.' The marks on Ch'ing's arms, where the daemon sting had appeared, still pained him.

'The man died, you know. In the north, on the Great Battlefield at the Top of the World.'

Ch'ing bowed in gratitude for the news. 'I'm pleased to learn of that.'

'And the vampire woman… well, you must know of her subsequent history. She lives in this city.'

'Genevieve Dieudonné. Our personal business is not over. But she must wait for the while. After all, neither of us is getting any older.'

Yefimovich laughed. 'I have a room upstairs. Come on.'

They climbed to the first floor, in the pitch dark. Yefimovich glowed slightly, a red undertone to his skin.

'Where is your familiar?' Ch'ing asked.

'Respighi? Don't let him hear you call him a familiar. He thinks he's an acolyte. He is out in the fog somewhere, doing my work.'

'Give him my most pleasant wishes.'

'I'll be sure to.'

Inside the room, the agitator lit a lamp. He had a cot and a table, and more books than the palace library. There were many copies of his own seditious pamphlets, tied up in bundles: *Sons of the Soil, Arise!, Casting Asunder the Chains, You and Your Betters* and *Come the Revolution.*

Ch'ing picked up a book. It was new and neatly-bound, but had no title embossed on the spine.

'This is my most popular work,' Yefimovich said. 'It's called *Beasts in Green Velvet.* It is an analysis of the misdeeds of the ruling classes. It will inflame the peasantry of the Empire, with its stories of men, women and children trampled under the iron heel of privilege.'

The High Priest sounded pleased with himself. Ch'ing cast his eye over a few lines. The book was like a gazeteer of the first families of the Empire, with a list of their crimes down through the centuries. This page was about the Kreishmier family of Ferlangen. He had never heard of them, but they seemed to be a long line of petty tyrants, hanging, branding, torturing, raping, robbing and enslaving the local peasantry as the whim took them.

'All cunning lies, I trust?'

'Oh no, that's the clever part. This is all true. These people allege that, as disciples of the proscribed cults, we serve evil. And yet, look at all their works and accomplishments…'

Baron Otto Kreishmier, since deceased, had once hanged twenty-seven of his tenant farmers between sun-up and sun-down on the Feast of Mitterfruhl to collect on a wager with his sister.

Ch'ing set down the papers. 'Things are not ordered very differently in Cathay. The Monkey King sits in his Eternal Gardens boasting of his youthful exploits, while his ministers rob him blind and use the people as chattels. And, as you know, Kislev suffers under an absolute monarch.'

The High Priest's eyes grew. 'Yes, but only in the Empire are the people told they are free even as they are being wrapped in chains. Our kings and tsars do not claim to be anything other than tyrants. Karl-Franz is an elective ruler, and a precarious one at that. This will shake him a little...'

Yefimovich tapped a pile of papers. The ink was still wet.

'Tomorrow, this pamphlet will be on the streets. The Empire is a tinderbox...'

Yefimovich took his lower eyelids between his thumbs and forefingers.

'...a tinderbox waiting for a flame.'

He pulled his skin and his face came off in one piece. It dangled, a dead mask.

Knowing what to expect, Ch'ing averted his gaze.

'That's better,' said the High Priest. 'Now my skin can breathe again.'

Ch'ing turned around and looked into the true face of his comrade in Chaos.

Yefimovich was thoroughly human in his features, but they were as transparent as moulded glass. Under his face-shaped bubble of skin raged an eternal fire. Ch'ing could see the lines of his skull, but rather than being covered with flesh and muscle they were clothed in forever-burning fire. No heat came from him, but the flames still writhed.

'You know, there are people in this city who think I am a fire-breather.'

VII

She woke up and instantly forgot her dream...

...but her heart still beat at ramming speed and the terror was still upon her. She shivered in her own sweat. The echo of her cry was still dying in the small, stone-walled cell.

Rosanna sat up, the last blanket falling away from her. She had been writhing in her sleep and almost all the bedclothes had been thrown off her cot.

Outside the slit window of her cell, where the moons should have been, was a wedge of grey. A night-candle burned on her writing desk, casting a small pool of light upon the piles of books jumbled there. She always needed a flame in the dark. It was her last connection with childhood.

She hugged herself, until the trembling subsided.

Sometimes, she was gripped with raptures in the night. But mostly, her dreams were terrible. It was a part of the gift to which she could never become used.

As always when the horror was squirted directly into her mind, she wished she had been born fat, stupid and normal like her sisters. She would have married a hunter or a woodcutter, and dropped five children by now. The only thing to disturb her nights would have been her husband's snoring.

She disentangled herself from the last of the blankets and walked across the tiny cell – the flagstones were shockingly cold under her bare feet – to the stand where there was a basin of fresh water.

Although not a cleric or a novice, she was still under the strict regime of the Temple. There was no mirror for her vanity. Just now, she was grateful for the absence. She did not think she could look into her own face without remembering too much...

She slipped her hands into the cold water and was fully awake. Her heartrate had slowed to normal. She splashed water on her face and rubbed away the sweat and sleep.

...parts of her dream came back to her...

She pressed her fists against her eyes, trying to keep the dream away.

...she was running through the fog and there was someone – something – coming after her. She could hear its rasping breath and fancied the clatter of its claws on cobbles. The smell of dead fish was all around her.

She was running on wooden boards now, desperate to get to the end of a quay. A ladder stood out in the fog. If she reached it, she might be safe...

She knelt, letting the dream that was not a dream come back.

...she climbed down quickly, her long skirts caught and tore on some neglected nail. Looking up, she could see the silhouette on the lip of the jetty, its eyes shining. Green velvet. Sharp teeth. Claws. It was unmistakably the Beast. Her face still stung from the rakemarks. She was afraid, but not just for herself...

Rosanna was confused. As so often in her intuitive visions, identities were scrambled. She could not make out any names. The girl she was dreaming she was worked in a hostel called the Wayfarer's Rest and had brothers called Jochim and Gustav, but her own name did not swim in her head with these other scraps. The thing that followed her had the faces of many men she had known, but Rosanna could not sort out which was the real aspect of the Beast and which the confused overlay of memories. There was a name uppermost in the girl's mind as she ran. Wolf. Wolf was the girl's lover. But the face that went with the name was mixed up with the dark blur of the Beast. The scryer tried to separate the two, and could not. There was an idealized Wolf, but she guessed he existed only in the girl's imagination: this noble, handsome, kindly face resembled that of the Baron Johann von Mecklenberg. That was another layer, prompting her to wonder just what the elector's interest in these crimes was. In the girl's mind, Wolf's face was constantly changing.

...the Beast caught her, and her body was opened...

Rosanna fought the dream. Despite her duty to learn, she kicked against the vision. She did not want to know any more, but the momentum was too great. She was forced to dream through until the end, until the complete darkness descended.

...after an eternity of pain, she died.

The dream shut off and Rosanna was herself again, the other girl gone from her mind as if she had never been there.

Rosanna did not believe in any of the gods. Not even Sigmar. No gods could allow such things.

The dead girl had known her attacker and yet not been sure of his identity. Like the others, she had died in a state of panic and confusion. The rustle of velvet was as strong with this girl as it had been with Margarethe Ruttmann. Green velvet.

Reliving the dream had made her void her bladder. She took off her wet nightdress and washed herself thoroughly, as if trying to wipe away any trace of her contact with the dead girl.

It was quiet outside. Beyond the fog, the sun would be rising soon. The work of the day would begin.

Rosanna returned to her cot and pulled the blankets over herself. She curled up small and wrapped the bedclothes tight around her, like a prickly cocoon.

What she had dreamed had happened. And it had happened tonight, probably at exactly the moment she first dreamed it. This murder was distinct from the seven others.

Somewhere out there, undiscovered, was an eighth corpse.

Part Three

Duel

I

As the bells of the Temple of Sigmar sounded the hour of seven, the sun rose over Altdorf. The city, however, remained in the dark under its blanket of fog.

The lamplighters stayed in their beds late, knowing that they would not be needed to extinguish the city's street-torches until the fog lifted. Later, the Imperial Militia would kindle the traditional fogfire in Konigsplatz and, across the river, the Temple would open its refectory for those stranded away from their homes by the weather.

Along the city's miles of riverfront, lanterns would be strung to guide the ferrymen and the bargees. The business of trade must continue, even if the fog slowed the riverboats and barges to a crawl.

Meanwhile, with the tax collectors blundering about in the murk, the influx of contraband into the city would increase tenfold. With harvest produce just due to flow into the docks, some rapid and illegal profits would be made and the Fish would make thankful offerings to Manann, God of the Seas, for sending the fog and enabling them to circumvent the revenue men.

At the palace, a victory procession arranged in honour of the heroes of the Empire who had recently defended Averland from the goblin hordes was quietly cancelled. Karl-Franz did not care much for the fog and had a superstitious dread of venturing out into it. His great-grandfather, Matthias IV, had gone out among his people in the fog, using the gloom as a disguise so he might learn their true feelings about their Emperor, and had disappeared without a trace. Even a century later, white-bearded vagrants were turning up regularly, claiming to be the rightful Emperor.

The fog having descended the evening before, a notice had gone up in the barracks across the square from the palace and a platoon of the Imperial Militia had been routinely seconded to the city watch to help out with the extra duties required. Later, this traditional measure – practiced in every fog – would be the cause of controversy and confusion, and not a little spilled blood.

The fog spilled over the high walls of the city, but tended to dissipate into thin streamers of mist in the surrounding forests. The city was a bowl, cupping the thick grey and brown broth to itself. The fog came off the Reik and the Talabec, shrouding at first the docks and the water-front. But by this morning it had spread to every quarter.

The fog affected everyone, from the Emperor in his palace and the Grand Theogonist in the Temple to the boatmen and workmen of the docks, the students and professors of the University, the gamblers and harlots of the Street of a Hundred Taverns, the Hooks and the Fish and a dozen other lesser factions, the toll-keepers of the bridges, the merchants of the north-eastern business quarter, the beggars and paupers of the East End, the staunch servants of the Law and the furtive worshippers of the Dark Powers, and the actors and artists of Temple Street. Some hated the damp, clinging curtain that permeated everything; but some loved the fog, and ventured out in search of the possibilities it offered.

It was a good time for crime and a better one for intrigue.

Schygulla, the dock manager, was an old Hook and Per Buttgereit's cousin was with the Fish. So, without ever having been involved in either faction, the apprentice was caught up in their pointless, continuing struggle.

He had wanted to be a student, but he couldn't master his letters. His father had told him that 'apprenticeship is a wonderful opportunity,' and signed him up for five years of shit work on the docks at a minimum rate of pay. His father, at forty-eight, was still apprenticed to Lilienthal the stonemason. He still talked about the opportunities that would open up to him when he finished his training, just in time to drop dead from a heart attack after thirty-five years of hefting huge blocks of granite and making pots of tea.

Buttgereit was supposed to turn up at the Beloved of Manann dock before everyone else and get the kettle boiling. Then, he was to wait for Schygulla to think of something crappy for him to do. Usually, it was scraping something off something, or sorting out the good fish due to go on sale across the river in the Marketplatz from the bad fish due for a fast turnover into soup in the East End. Today, of course, it was string-ing lanterns underneath the docks. If a task involved going where the smell was worst, Schygulla always assigned Buttgereit.

The lanterns – slow-burning candles surrounded by polished reflec-tors in tin cages – were easy to break and any damage would have to come out of his apprentice's wage. He had carried them carefully down to the end of the dock and was having to take them down two at a time.

'This ladder is rotted through,' he complained to himself. 'Someone will probably take a nasty fall and be swept away.'

There were fifteen lanterns and fifteen spots along the dock, above the high watermark, where they were supposed to go.

Probing his way through the fog, Buttgereit could hear Schygulla laugh-ing with some of his old cronies. They were relating stories about the lascivious Elector of Nuln and her elite cadre of strapping guardsmen. To the Countess Emmanuelle von Liebewitz, they said, remaining faith-ful to a true love meant not going to bed with more than ten men at the same time. The old men, thrown out of the Hooks long ago, all laughed

meanly at that one. The countess was rumoured to be so vain of her
beauty that she had a summerhouse constructed only of mirrors and
insisted that her female servants always wear masks so that she might
shine all the more by comparison.

Buttgereit took the rungs one at a time, barely able to see his feet,
and afraid that a slat would break. When he put a foot into the water,
he knew that he was at about the right place. The river would cover the
shingles at this hour in the morning. He pulled his wet shoe out and
shook it. There was a rope strung from the ladder to the pilings that supported the dock. It was supposed to mark high-water but it had sagged
a little and looped under the surface. The first lanternhook was on the
ladder, just above the rope.

He had seen the Countess Emmanuelle at a river procession once and
she hadn't looked especially decadent. She was undoubtedly the most
beautiful woman in the Empire, though. She reminded him a bit of his
mother, only with more facepaint and expensive clothes. Admittedly,
she had had several young men – some no older than Buttgereit – in
the ceremonial barge with her and they had all been gussied up in tight
uniforms with lots of braid and polished leather. Some of them wore as
much paint as she did. Buttgereit had hated them all personally. Their
job seemed far more rewarding than making tea and scraping barnacles.

'Hurry up, fishface!' Schygulla shouted down at him. 'The Reik and
Talabec have all their lamps strung and are unloading already. We'll lose
trade if you don't stop dreaming and get to work.'

Buttgereit grumbled under his breath and, holding onto the ladder with
his left hand, hung the first lantern from the hook, which was just by
his knees. With the second lantern dangling from his teeth, he let himself down two rungs and crouched, still trying to keep out of the water.
This would be just the time for the ladder to fall apart and drop him
into the scummy waters of the Reik.

Schygulla was a fiend for palace gossip. Now he was repeating unthinkable stories about the Countess Emmanuelle's brother, Leos. According to
the dock manager, the viscount had been spoiled for all women by the
ravages of his sister and sought solace with the Countess's cast-off male
lovers. Buttgereit would have liked to see the old fool tell that story to
the Viscount Leos's face. The man was reputedly the most deadly duellist in the Empire and he would make a fine carving job of Schygulla's
face. Of course, those born to the green velvet didn't deign to match
swords with over-the-hill dock ruffians, but it made a pretty picture.

'I said hurry up, not play with yourself!' shouted Schygulla. He said
something about Buttgereit that the apprentice couldn't hear and the
cronies barked with laughter.

Bastards, all.

Buttgereit applied his tinderbox flame to the wick of the first lantern.
Light grew and he could see a little better.

Beyond the rungs of the ladder was a dark space. There were criss-cross
wooden pilings, reinforced with rusted iron stays and cables, rooting the

Beloved of Manann quay in the shingles of the riverbank and anchoring it in the stone walls of the docks.

Water lapped at the pilings and fog swirled in the enclosed space. There was something floating in the water, wrapped up in cloth, caught by one of the cables.

Buttgereit couldn't make out what the lump was. Then, he saw the threads of blood in the water.

'Buttgereit,' shouted Schygulla, 'what in Sigmar's name are you doing?'

The apprentice's stomach was roiling.

He wanted to call up to the manager, but he was afraid that if he opened his mouth to speak his breakfast would burst out.

The floating lump was shifting in the water, being dragged towards him.

'Buttgereit, I'll take my hook to you!'

There was a face just under the surface of the river. The empty eye-sockets stared up at him, bloody tears pulled away by the current.

Finally he found his voice and yelled.

II

It was easy to lose track of the time in the fog. Shortly after dawn, Genevieve Dieudonné entered the quarters she shared with Detlef Sierck on Temple Street, just across from the Vargr Breughel Memorial Playhouse, where the actor-playwright was still appearing in *A Farce of the Fog*. The six hundred and sixty-seven year old girl pulled off her cloak and hung it on the back of the door. She admired it. A gift from the future Emperor Luitpold, who had something of a crush on her, it was a splendid garment of green velvet. If she were to visit the palace more often, she would fit in easily.

She thought of Oswald, the corrupt calculating machine in green velvet. She turned her back on the cloak.

Tendrils of fog had come in with her. Satiated from her night's feeding, she felt the somnolence that came upon her every few weeks. She would sleep for several days and awake replenished.

But she did not want to retire just yet. Her blood was still flowing and she could still taste what she had taken...

In the next room, Detlef was sleeping. He kept late hours himself, dining after his performance, but they had not been together last night. Genevieve could not remember the last time they had actually slept together, rather than find a mutually convenient time for love making. The human and the vampire cycles were too different.

There were pictures of Detlef up on the walls, posters showing him in his greatest role: as Lowenstein in *The Treachery of Oswald*, as Baron Trister in *The Desolate Prisoner of Karak-Kadrin*, as Guillaume in *Barbenoire: The Bastard of Bretonnia*, as Ottokar in *The Loves of Ottokar and Myrmidia* and as the Daemon Prince in *Strange Flower*.

They had been together for four years now, since their experiences at the fortress of Drachenfels. The years had been good, but they had been kinder to her than to him. Detlef's weight had increased and he had put on so many old-man make-ups to play the great roles that he seemed much older than his actual age. She, however, was unchanging. Her mind was old, but her blood was still young.

An unthought tear, a bubble of red, appeared in her eye and trickled down her cheek. She wiped it away with the back of her hand and licked it clean, relishing the tang.

After so many years, she ought to be used to transience. Everybody changed. Even her.

There was a great deal of clumping about inside and Detlef stumbled in, his nightshirt ballooning over his stomach, his hair and moustaches in a mess. He did not bid her good morning.

'The house was half-empty last night,' he said. 'There was too much fog outside the theatre for our farce to have much appeal.'

'Attendance has been falling off for weeks, my dear.'

'You're right, Gené. We are nearing the end of our run.'

Genevieve caught his meaning, and sadly agreed.

'Where were you last night?' he asked, wearily.

'Feeding,' she said, remembering...

Mrs Bierbichler, Helmut Elsaesser's landlady, had practically adopted him, claiming that a young man so far away from his birthplace would tend to neglect himself and that a woman should step in and sort things out for him. His landlady was childless herself, but several of her friends had young female relatives and chance meetings were forever being contrived. To be fair, Elsaesser quite liked the Widow Flickenschildt's niece, Ingrid, whose blonde braids reached nearly to her knees when uncoiled, and had arranged to see the girl again one night next week. However, it was hard not to resent such smothering care and attention.

'Eat, eat,' his landlady told him, piling yet another plate of oatcakes onto the table, 'or you'll grow thin and die.'

Elsaesser's protests were hopeless. Mrs Bierbichler ladled syrup onto the cakes and slipped the plate in front of him.

He took his knife and fork to the food. When, full-mouthed, he nodded his approval, she let slip that this was a Flickenschildt family recipe she was trying out.

Elsaesser was surrounded by women who wanted him to hurry up and get married. He felt as if he were the victim of a huge conspiracy. The cakes were good though.

'Hot coffee,' Mrs Bierbichler said, pouring some into a bucket-size container. 'It will settle your stomach and keep you warm. If you eat too fast, you could get indigestion and die.'

Elsaesser took a swig. The coffee was strong, black and bitter. Mrs Bierbichler did not believe in sugar or cream in coffee. She said that made you fat, and if you were too fat you could die.

'You shouldn't go out in a fog. You could catch a chill and die.'

Swallowing coffee-soaked cakes, Elsaesser replied, 'It's my job, Mrs B. It's a duty.'

'Well, it should be some other man's duty. Someone less vulnerable to nasty colds.'

'It's important.' Elsaesser was serious. 'The Beast must be caught.'

Mrs Bierbichler raised her hands to the gods. 'The Beast! Ach, he only cuts down girls who are no good. Why should you run after such women, when there are lovely girls I could name so much closer to home, so much nicer for you. Such good cooks! Such hips for child-bearing! You could catch a disease and die, you know, from girls who are no good.'

'Nobody deserves the Beast,' he said, slowly, feeling his resolve build.

Since the first murder, Elsaesser had been following the crimes. His last few weeks at the University had rushed past, as he passed his exams with the expected ease, but he had spent more time thinking about the Beast than of his future. He could have had a position with any watch in the city, but he had insisted on the docks. His professors had been appalled but he had insisted. In his head, he knew all the victims intimately, their names, their lives, the circumstances of their death: Rosa, Miriam, Helga, Monika, Gislind, Tanja, Margarethe. To get Professor Scheydt to approve his posting to the Dock Watch, he had told the man that Rosa May, the first victim, had been his mistress. He had never met the girl, but he needed to give the pragmatic professor a reason for his need to catch the Beast. Scheydt, a cleric of the law, could understand revenge better than he could justice.

Elsaesser told himself he wanted the Beast brought in to serve the cause of justice, but sometimes he was not sure. Sometimes he wondered why he burned with the need to stop these particular murders. People died by violence throughout the city, throughout the Empire, every day, but Elsaesser only took the Beast personally. The facts of the case would creep into his dreams and he would find himself surrounded by the images and impressions he had of the women's last hours. He knew all the women, all the victims. But also, after these months of intensive study, he knew the Beast.

The murderer was becoming more active: the first three killings had taken place over four months, the last four had been within the last five weeks. In the madman's mind, something was coming to the boil. Four out of the seven victims had died during fogs or on nights when the fog seemed to threaten to appear. Some maniacs killed by the moon, but the Beast was stimulated by the fog.

'No,' said Elsaesser, 'nobody deserves the Beast.'

He shoved his plate away and got up. His uniform coat was hanging from its stand, the copper badge new-polished. He slipped it on and felt better. Merely by becoming a watchman, he was doing something.

Mrs Bierbichler came for him with a long scarf and wrapped it around his neck, muffling his chest and face.

'You must wrap up warm. If the cold gets into your lungs, you could die.'

Mrs Bierbichler knew a lot of ways that you could die.

The long table in the dining hall rattled as Otho Waernicke thumped it, sending plates and cups jumping into the air.

'Bow, you heathens,' he shouted.

There was a massed moaning from the soreheads and hangovers who had crawled down to this late breakfast, unshaven, bleary-eyed and mainly bruised. Last night, the League had been in three serious fights and an assortment of minor scraps.

The chaplain, startled, continued to offer up thanks to Ulric for the new day, albeit with a more attentive audience.

Otho thumped the table again and roared for the steward.

His head hurt. A lot. Some time last night, he had offered to drink a dwarf under the table and asked his opponent to name the poison. This morning, he had woken up under the table with a dwarf snoring in his ear. They had gone on from Alte Geheerentode brandy to gin laced with gunpowder. If he belched, Otho could kill a man at fifty paces.

There was some squealing and shouting from the vestibule as last night's whores were kicked out into the street with a few extra pfennigs for their trouble. The League's hall was sacred to Ulric and the Emperor, and it was traditional to eject all women between the chaplain's morning thanksgiving and nightfall.

Otho's chest and legs hurt too. He couldn't remember where the bruises had come from. There was a long scrape up his side that made him think of a docker's hook.

The thanks given, and the women out of the building, the chaplain turned around the bust of Ulric that stood on the great mantelpiece. Ever since the League had been founded, the eyes of its patron deity had been turned to the wall between nightfall and thanksgiving, so the god would not have to look upon the trespasses of his youthful, high-spirited worshippers.

With the eyes of Ulric on them, the students of the League became models of gentlemanliness, moderation and propriety.

At least until nightfall…

Inside the man-shell, the Beast rested. Last night's work had been satisfying and momentarily succoured the creature. But it was becoming hungrier sooner. It had ventured out two nights in a row. Tonight, it might make it three…

III

When Johann awoke, his chambers in the palace were eerily quiet. Suites were kept open in the west wing for any of the electors whose business might bring them to the city. He occupied his with only a few servants, while down the passageway was quartered the huge retinue required by the Countess Emmanuelle von Liebewitz and her brother. Usually, he was awakened by the flurry of activities required by the countess-elector's levée. Today he slept well past that.

He dressed himself but called in Martin, his valet secretary, to trim his beard. Afterwards, as he ate a breakfast of fruit and cheese, he went through the day's communiqués. There was a long letter from Eidsvik, his steward back in Sudenland, reporting on the harvests and request- ing his approval for certain charitable gestures. The von Mecklenberg estates had done well enough this year not to need to draw on the tithe of farm goods it was entitled to collect from the outlying farms and Eids- vik suggested contributing the offerings to the poor. Johann decided to go along with it and dictated a brief assent to be sent off along with a document granting the steward power of attorney for a further two months while he concluded his 'business' in Altdorf.

Then there was a note in precise script from Professor Scheydt at the University, setting out simply Wolf's attendance record for the past few terms and hinting in more complex terms that Johann's brother could only remain enrolled on his course if he were to attend more lectures or pay larger bribes. Johann had no immediate answer. He could not bring himself to think of Wolf in connection with the murders in the docks, but he could also not forget the wolf-faced giant he had faced at the top of the world. Could innocent blood really wash away such a mon- ster forever? Before Harald Kleindeinst found the Beast, Johann would have to find Wolf.

There was a notice of the cancellation of the victory parade and a cir- cular of the Emperor's orders for the day. The Imperial Militia were to take up their 'fog positions' to perform 'fog duties.' Johann, still rela- tively new to the capital city, didn't know what that meant, but Martin explained that it was a traditional measure. Even the palace guard would find employment in the fog. Under the circumstances, Johann thought that putting more armed men on the streets was a compromised blessing.

Finally there was an invitation to a private party at the Matthias II, to be hosted by the Bretonnian ambassador, de la Rougierre. Johann was about to crumple that card and throw it away, when he remembered that Margarethe Ruttmann had died next to the Matthias II. What was de la Rougierre's connection with the place? And who else was included in the invitation? Martin did not know. He decided to put off a decision. It might perhaps be a sound idea to attend this party. There were people who said that the Beast was a dwarf.

Today, Johann wanted to seek an audience with the Emperor, to discuss the Beast. He had been doing too much in Karl-Franz's name without having strictly gained the right to use it. Before this went any further, he wanted official approval.

There was a commotion and Luitpold exploded into the room in a flurry of velvet.

'Uncle Johann,' he said, 'come quickly–'

'What is it?'

'Von Liebewitz is fighting a duel in the gymnasium. To the death.'

Siemen Ruhaak made Rosanna wait until Hasselstein had finished his breakfast. She stood outside the Lector's chambers, fidgeting. If she was wrong, she would look foolish. But she was not wrong.

On her way to Hasselstein's office, she had seen Tilo, emerging guiltily from the confessional. She wondered how much he had told his cleric about her and his feelings. Impure thoughts were as much sin as impure deeds. But that didn't make people any more comfortable around someone who could genuinely judge them by their thoughts.

She still felt the dead girl's wounds.

Rosanna was not even the first to have an audience with the Lector. Hasselstein's door opened and Adrian Hoven, the cleric-captain of the Templars, stepped out. He was wearing his breastplate and helmet, as if prepared to dash off on some military venture for the greater glory of Sigmar. Hoven took no notice of her and barged past. She recognized a packet of sealed orders in his mind, concealed even from her prying thoughts and understood that he had been charged with some secret, urgent task.

'Enter,' decreed Hasselstein.

She stepped into his chambers and found him dressed exactly as he had been last night. He had either slept in his clothes, or not at all. A breakfast tray was abandoned on the floor and he was drinking tea from a monogrammed mug.

'Lector,' she said, without formalities. 'The Beast has killed again. I saw it in a dream.'

Hasselstein choked and spilt tea down his shirt.

As he dressed, she prepared for her sleep. In the fog, the heavy curtains weren't necessary, but she drew them all the same.

Watching Genevieve, Detlef Sierck was conscious of the difference, apparent and real, between their ages. Another sonnet was forming in his mind. When she was asleep, he would set it down. He had been writing sonnets almost since the beginning, since the play in the fortress, but he had not shared them with her, had not sought to publish them. The plays were for everybody, but the poetry was private. When the time was right, he would have the whole cycle printed and bound up for her. He had a title: *To My Unchanging Lady.*

Pulling on his trousers, he was aware that he would need a new wardrobe soon, unless he lost some weight. He was prepared to do anything to become healthy and slim, except take exercise, eat less, go to bed early or give up wine.

Detlef sat with her as she lay on the bed, waiting for the deep sleep to come, to give her a little of the death she had staved off for so long. They talked, not the high-flown talk of new lovers, but the intimate, ordinary talk of an old married couple. However, lately, people who did not know Genevieve was a vampire had begun to mistake her for his daughter.

There were always actresses to tempt him and Genevieve did not tap him overmuch for fear of bleeding him dry. So they both had to pursue outside interests, but they were very special to each other. Without Genevieve, he might never have built his genius into a real career. He could easily have spent his life boasting of the theatre he would one day create without actually doing anything.

'The farce is played out,' he was saying, 'our audiences don't want to laugh any more. It's the Beast. He has brought horror to the city and the people can't shake it off even for the length of a play.'

Genevieve nodded, comfortable in her near-doze, and murmured agreement. She was at her most child-like when she slept.

'I shall close *A Farce of the Fog* at the end of the month and present something else.'

'Horror,' Genevieve said, almost under her breath.

'Yes, that's a good idea. If they can't laugh, perhaps they can still scream. We have done Drachenfels to death, but there is still the story of the Wittgenstein family and its monster. Or of the horrid fate of the von Diehl brothers. Either of those would make a play that would curdle the spine and shiver the blood...'

Genevieve mumbled.

'You know what I mean, Gené.'

Detlef thought some more. 'Of course, those are stories of monsters and daemons. Perhaps the Beast requires something a little closer to home, a little more intimate in its horror.'

Genevieve's eyes were closed, but she could still hear him.

'The Beast suggests the story of a man who is outwardly a mild, devout, conscientious individual, but inwardly a fiend thirsting for blood... no offence, Gené. Some citizens say our murderer is a beast-man or a daemon, but my informants in the watch tell me they are definitely looking for a human culprit. There's that old Kislevite play by V. I. Tiodorov, *The Strange Case of Dr Zhiekhill and Mr Chaida.* It is the story of a humble, respectable cleric of Shallya who samples the forbidden potion and becomes a raging, animalistic libertine. It's dross, of course, but I can prepare a loose translation, with some improvements. Some major improvements.'

The vampire was asleep but Detlef was seized by his idea.

'Of course, the transformation scenes will require all my stagecraft. I want a scene to make people forget the Beast, to make them confront their real horrors, the horrors that come from inside. It will be a masterpiece of the macabre. The critics will quake and foul their britches, women will faint all over the house and strong men will be reduced to abject terror. It will be wonderful. Gené, my darling, this will frighten even you...'

IV

Graf Volker von Tuchtenhagen looked less arrogant this morning.

'Surely, there is some other way we can settle this?'

He had obviously been dragged from his drunken bed by his second and could barely remember the grave offence he had given the family of von Liebewitz.

Leos slashed the air with his rapier. It felt like an extension of his body. Bassanio Bassarde had once jested that it was the only sexual organ the viscount possessed. The noted Marienburg wit was dead now, his windpipe laid open by an elegant manoeuvre.

'We are all gentlemen here,' von Tuchtenhagen blathered as his seconds stripped his jacket. 'No offence was meant.'

Leos said nothing. He had risen early, untired after his late night in the fog, and taken his usual run around the palace grounds. Men who neglected their bodies were fools.

'Whatever it was that I said, I retract.'

Leos stood, arms loose, ready. That calm that always came upon him before combat was like a cloak. He never felt more alive.

'Ambassador,' he said to Dien Ch'ing, the Celestial who had consented to serve as referee, 'convey to my honoured opponent my apologies...'

Von Tuchtenhagen sighed with relief, stepping forwards.

'...this is no longer a personal matter. It gives me great regret to kill him...'

Von Tuchtenhagen froze, his flabby face a mask of fear. Tears were trickling from the corners of his eyes. He was unprepared. The sleep was still in his eyes, the stubble on his face. Leos rubbed his own smooth, beardless chin with the back of his hand.

'...but this is a matter of the honour of a lady.'

Last night, at the von Tasseninck ball, Leos had overheard von Tuchtenhagen discussing the Countess Emmanuelle with a cleric of Ranald. The graf had suggested that Leos's sister resembled a rabbit, not in appearance but in conduct.

'And of my family.'

The Celestial nodded gravely. He did not need to relay the message.

'Leos, I have money,' said his opponent. 'This need not happen...'

A cold fury burned in the viscount's breast. The suggestion was unworthy even of von Tuchtenhagen. The family were new to the register, elevated by Matthias IV a short century ago and still striving to obscure the memory of the merchants and tradespeople they had been. Von Liebewitzes had fought alongside Sigmar at the birth of the Empire.

Leos brought up his foil, bent at the knees and hung his left hand in the air.

'You have accepted the terms of this combat,' Dien Ch'ing said in his high, musical voice. 'This is a matter between gentleman and no other may intervene.'

Von Tuchtenhagen brought up his shaking sword and Dien Ch'ing held its point against Leos's weapon.

'The duellists shall fight until the matter is settled.'

'First blood?' Von Tuchtenhagen suggested, a flare of hope in his tone. Leos shook his head, impatient to get on with it.

'The victor shall be the gentleman left alive at the end of the duel.'

Dien Ch'ing took a handkerchief from his sleeve. It was silk, embroidered with dragons.

When the silk touched the polished wooden floor, the duel would commence.

The Celestial's hand went up.

Countess Emmanuelle von Liebewitz, elector, lady mayoress and Chancellor of the University of Nuln, examined her face minutely in the ornate mirror and plucked a stray hair from her arched eyebrows.

'There,' she said, 'perfect.'

Yevgeny Yefimovich was getting tired of wearing his hood. He had sent Respighi out late last night to get him a new face, but his servant had not yet returned.

In his upstairs rooms at the Holy Hammer of Sigmar, he addressed his most fervent followers in the Revolutionary Movement. Prince Kloszowski, the radical poet, lolled as usual, a cigarette dangling from his lips, his beard a studied mess. Stieglitz, a former mercenary who had served with Vastarien's Vanquishers, was fingering the stump where his left arm had been and groaning softly, as was his habit. The man's face was a mass of scars, the result of a few too many brushes with the aristocratic oppressor. Professor Brustellin, recently forced to resign in disgrace from the University, was polishing his round eyeglasses and drinking steadily from his ever-present, never-emptied silver bottle. And Ulrike Blumenschein, the angel of the masses, was combing out her long, tangled hair before a mirror. Between them, these people would bring down an Emperor. They believed this would usher in an age of justice for the common people, but Yefimovich knew it would lead only to a power vacuum which would allow for the triumph of Tzeentch.

'We must seize the opportunity,' he told them, 'and exploit it for all we can–'

'But what proof is there,' put in Brustellin, 'that the Beast is of the hated classes?'

Yefimovich explained patiently, 'None, of course. It was destroyed by the lackeys of the Emperor.'

'Proof that has been destroyed is the best kind,' said Kloszowski, with a sardonic smile, 'one never has to produce it.'

'Remember, Dickon of the Dock Watch was seen to burn something at the site of the last killing,' Yefimovich said. 'That was our proof.'

'The Ashes of Shame,' declared Kloszowski. 'That shall be the title of my next work. I'll have it written, copied and distributed by nightfall. It'll be sung in every tavern, to a dozen different tunes, by this time tomorrow.'

Brustellin, disenchanted with words, sneered, 'More poems, just what the revolution needs!'

The poet was angered. 'Clothhead academic! My poems do more for the cause than your dusty tracts. Poetry is for the people, not for ink-blotched scholars and dried-up prunes of clerics.'

'I was flogged, you know,' said Brustellin, loosening his cravat, preparing to bare his back to exhibit yet again the marks left by the punishment that had preceded his expulsion. 'Twenty years of teaching and that young dolt Scheydt had me flogged and thrown into the streets.'

He was down to his shirt and everyone was telling him not to go further. They had all seen a sight too much of Brustellin's ravaged back.

'You were flogged and Stieglitz here was mutilated and crippled,' spat Kloszowski. 'But only I have been hanged by the hated classes...'

Dramatically, with a practiced movement, the poet pulled his scarf away to reveal the burn. The rope had been rotten and snapped itself instead of Kloszowski's neck. He had written several poems about the experience. 'I was face to face with the gods,' he claimed, 'and they were working men like ourselves. Not a plutocrat or popinjay in the lot of them.'

Brustellin muttered something about the arrogance of princes. Kloszowski stamped his feet like a child in a temper tantrum. He hated to be reminded of his noble origins, although he was reluctant to drop the title from his name.

'You cannot argue that I have not suffered with my working brothers, professor. My soul has been dragged through the dirt with the best of them.'

Yefimovich spread his hands and the revolutionaries stopped arguing.

'The Beast is the best thing to happen to this city since the thumb tax, my friends,' he said. 'For once, the people are angry with their masters. That anger is our strength.'

'It's a shame that the Beast has killed only worthless drabs,' said Ulrike. 'The people would be more inflamed if he were to prey on decent, humble womenfolk. A good mother, or a precious daughter. Maybe a priestess of Verena.'

'That can be arranged, my dear,' Yefimovich said. 'People are putting every crime in the city off on the Beast. If a few deaths would prove politically useful, we have people who can take care of them.'

Ulrike nodded, pleased that her idea had been taken up.

These people all had their reasons. Stieglitz had seen too much injustice, Brustellin had thought it through and reasoned that the rule of the Emperor was wrong, and Kloszowski thought the revolution sounded romantic, but Ulrike Blumenschein roused the rabble because she was mad. That made her the only one in the group who could pose a threat to Yefimovich. The mad often have insights that a sane person would not. If he were swept away, she would become the figurehead of the movement and, her hair trailing and eyes shining, would lead them all to be happily slaughtered by the Imperial Guard outside the gates of the palace.

'Be ready to move at a moment's notice,' he said. 'The day is coming soon.'

Kloszowski clapped, tobacco ash falling onto his loose shirt. He pulled on his workingman's coat and hat – Yefimovich was sure he had spent an afternoon rubbing his clothes between two stones to get that authentically proletarian tattered look – and left the room. Yefimovich nodded and the bent professor and the one-armed mercenary went after him. They all had their orders for the day. By nightfall, the city would be rumbling with dissent. The fog helped. It made everyone angry. Yefimovich fancied that he could deliver a speech blaming the Emperor for the fog and everyone would believe him.

Ulrike was the last to go. She had taken to lingering around him lately. Being an Angel of the Revolution was a lonely job. Eventually she followed the others, on her way to the underground chambers where her trained scribes copied out the movement's pamphlets and poems, and she posed for inspirational pictures to be distributed on cards and posters.

Yefimovich only had to wait a few minutes before a rat-like scratching at the window told him that Respighi was back.

He unlatched the window and his assistant crawled in. Respighi was an extraordinary mix of races. His father, it was said, had been a dwarf trollslayer and his mother a human woman under the influence of warpstone. He could usually pass for a dwarf if he wore loose pantaloons to cover his tail, although his face was pushing out recently, becoming more rodentlike. With his boots off he could climb walls and with his tail out he could hang from the ceiling. The creature loved Tzeentch as much as he hated his long-lost father.

For the moment, he was the high priest's servant and it was his job to find Yefimovich the skins which concealed his true nature from the world.

Respighi laid a pouch on the table.

'How fresh is it?'

The altered shrugged and whistled. 'Some time late last night. I've been on the dodge. Lots of watchmen out.'

Yefimovich knew Respighi had just got lost in the fog. It didn't matter. It would be fresh enough.

Yefimovich doffed his hood and enjoyed the slight flinch Respighi gave as he saw the high priest's face of fire. Then he pulled the new face out of the pouch and pressed it over his own.

His flesh tingled as the magic worked, binding the stolen skin to his own. When it was fixed, he wiped the traces of blood away from around his still-burning eyes and licked his new lips. He tasted rouge.

'What did you get me, Respighi? A man's face or a woman's?'

The altered shrugged. 'Who knows? It was foggy.'

Yefimovich felt his face. The mask was shifting, settling on to his old features. His skin was smooth, unstubbled.

'I can tell you one thing,' Respighi muttered. 'It's human.'

Dickon had known Schygulla for years. The dock manager had been a war chief in the Hooks long before Willy Pick's day, when the watchman had been walking the waterfront with his eyes closed and his hand out. They had stroked and threatened each other many times, and the Beloved of Manann still sent him cases of wine and sweetmeats every festival day. The company brought in more goods and paid less excise than any other crew on the docks.

When the body was discovered, Schygulla had sent a runner not to Dickon's family house but to the rooms of his mistress. The Hooks knew him too well, he reflected as Francoise 'Fifi' Messaen berated him for having her early morning despoiled by the interloper. The great Detlef Sierck had kicked Fifi out of his repertory company for being 'a talentless slut,' but the actor-manager had been wrong: Fifi was a girl of many talents, most of them horizontal. After a night with her, Dickon needed to go home to his wife and get some rest and a cup of tea. But today that wasn't going to happen.

The runner had guided him through the fog to the wharf, where the Beast's leavings had been dragged up and gathered together on a sheet of soaked canvas. This one was worse than the others.

'Merciful Shallya,' Dickon swore.

A young man was sobbing at one corner of the dock. Schygulla looked at him with contempt and spat. 'That's Buttgereit,' he said. 'He found the thing.'

Dickon understood why Schygulla called the corpse a thing. It was hard to imagine that it had ever been alive, much less a woman.

'Do you know her?' he asked the dock manager.

Schygulla looked disgusted. 'Are you kidding me, captain? Her own true love wouldn't recognize her after a night with our Beast.'

It was true.

The fog was getting into his bones. It would be time soon for Dickon to go into the back room at the Luitpoldstrasse Station and take his savings out from the hollowed statue of Verena. He had been supplementing his salary very well and should have enough to take Fifi and the children and retire to the country, somewhere far away from Hooks and Fish and smugglers and slashers.

'Let's get some coppers down here and clear this up, captain,' Schygulla said. 'I'm losing business.'

Dickon agreed.

V

The gymnasium doors opened and a huge man strode in, his heavy boot-steps like bass drumbeats.

Dien Ch'ing paused, his arm still upraised. His kerchief fluttered but remained in his grip, hanging.

This was all absurd, but amusing. Only trousered barbarians could bind themselves with so many rules in such a simple matter as murder.

Graf Volker pulled his sword away and barked with panicky laughter. Viscount Leos stayed cool, his weapon still at the ready.

'Hold,' said von Tuchtenhagen. 'I invoke the rules of chivalry.'

Leos straightened up and let his sword rest by his side. He was a chilly character and strange for a Westerner. Ch'ing wondered if the beardless young aristocrat had any Cathay in his blood. There was certainly something subtle in his eyes.

'I am unable to fight and so I request that my champion, Toten Ungenhauer, stand in for me.'

Leos did not seem concerned. Von Tuchtenhagen's champion was a full foot and a half taller than the youth and had a chest as big as a barrel. He wore a tunic emblazoned with the von Tuchtenhagen arms. It left his massive arms bare.

At the Second Siege of Praag, Ch'ing had seen Gotrek Gurnisson, the dwarf Trollslayer, in action, wielding a two-edged axe against a horde of beastmen. Toten Ungenhauer was proportioned like Gotrek, but nearly twice his size. Leos von Liebewitz was rumoured to be the greatest duellist in the Empire, but surely he could not stand against such a monster.

Ungenhauer stepped into his master's place and took a sword. It looked like a knitting needle in his ham-sized fist. Ch'ing assumed he would throw it away and simply wrench the viscount's head off, ignoring any feeble cuts he might sustain in getting past Leos's foil. That would not be against the rules of chivalry.

Although it was not strictly according to the code, spectators were filing in to the chamber and taking seats. A knot of von Tuchtenhagen creditors who had hoped to see the Graf Volker shredded were leaving in disappointment, but other courtiers were settling in. Ch'ing saw Johann von Mecklenberg and the future Emperor sitting high up, near the back of the hall. Hergard von Tasseninck, who had been present when the original insult was delivered, was there with his mistress. And, veiled, Marquess Sidonie of Marienburg, whose husband Bassanio had been efficiently despatched by Viscount Leos late last year in a similar duel. The most notable absence was that of the Countess Emmanuelle, who supposedly didn't care for the sight of blood.

Von Tuchtenhagen had overcome his fear and was excitedly walking back and forth, chortling to himself and to the audience, working himself up.

'Von Liebewitz,' he said, 'I should like to elaborate upon my comments of the last night. Your sister, I understand, spreads her legs for servants and sailors...'

The audience gasped. Leos seemed unmoved.

'If it were dark enough, she would take a dwarf or a halfling into her bed. Or an altered... if he were freakish in the right direction...'

Leos brought up his sword slowly and placed its point against Ungenhauer's outstretched blade. The giant grinned, displaying gaps in his teeth.

'I believe it would take a beast to pleasure her to her full satisfaction,' von Tuchtenhagen spat, 'an absolute beast!'

Ch'ing raised the kerchief and let it flutter to the floor.

The swords clashed and parted with a resounding *chink!*

Karl-Franz I of the House of the Second Wilhelm, Protector of the Empire, Defier of the Dark, Emperor Himself and the Son of Emperors, poured sugar into his coffee. He was mildly surprised that his son had not turned up yet for their hour together. It was part of the palace ritual. Karl-Franz would quiz Luitpold on his lessons and try to impart some of the wisdom he had acquired in his years of office. Still, it was not the first time the future Emperor had found some distraction elsewhere. He yawned. These days, nothing ever seemed to happen...

There was a '317' worked into the headstone above the door. On the docks, there was a joke that the sign signified the average number of bribes the Dock Watch accepted in any given week. The watchmen at the Luitpoldstrasse Station admitted him without question. The older ones recognized him and the youngsters had heard of him.

Elsaesser said good morning and he nodded to the young officer.

He found Economou, a sergeant he remembered, and enjoyed the burst of rage and fear in the man's face.

'What...?!'

Harald curled his lip and held up his fist.

A couple of bullies came up behind Economou.

'Joost,' Harald said, 'Thommy. Have you missed me?'

A slow grin spread over the sergeant's face. 'You're trespassing, Kleindeinst. You two, strip your tabards and eject this intruder from the station.'

The bullies enthusiastically pulled off their apron-like garments, embroidered with the emblems of the city and of the Dock Watch and rolled up their sleeves.

'I've looked forward to this for a long time, Kleindeinst,' said Joost. 'It took me years to work off the black mark you put on my record.'

'Yes,' agreed Thommy, unconsciously massaging his once-broken collar bone. 'It's a delight to see you again, especially now you're a civilian...'

Harald held up his fist and uncurled his fingers, letting the officers see his badge.

Economou's jaw hit his chainmail choker.

'You came back?'

Harald let a slow smile spread. 'Yes, sergeant. I came back.'

Joost and Thommy hustled back into their tabards and backed off.

'Find me a desk, sergeant. And get me what you've got so far on the Beast.'

Economou hurried away. Joost and Thommy crammed into the door, trying to follow him.

Harald miaowed at the retreating watchmen.

'I beg your pardon,' said Elsaesser.

'Pussies,' Harald explained. 'Just a pair of pussies.'

The young officer nodded. 'Oh.'

The double doors pushed inwards and a pocket of fog belched into the station. A man stepped out of it, gasping. It was a messenger and he had run a long way carrying a fog lantern.

He put the dripping lamp down and got his breath back.

'There's been another one,' he gasped, 'down at the docks. Another killing.'

'The Beast,' said Elsaesser.

The messenger said, 'Yes.'

'Come on, boy,' Harald told the younger man, 'let's go goose Dickon and get this investigation underway.'

Etienne Edouard Villechaize, Comte de la Rougierre, the ambassador from Charles de la Tete d'Or III of Bretonnia, inflated his chest like a peacock as he prepared to explain, for the millionth time, that yes, he was a dwarf and yes, did also hold high office in one of the kingdoms of men.

'My parents were hostages for life, Gropius,' he told the dancing master. 'I was raised in the household of one of the king's ministers. My brothers were content to become jugglers and jesters. I have always felt a higher calling...'

He twirled his waxed moustaches and waved his puffed sleeve at the man, allowing a shower of lace to flutter around his arm. The auditorium of the Flamingo Club, a private theatre located on the wrong side of Temple Street, was small, but still encouraged de la Rougierre's flair for the dramatic gesture.

'I have repudiated my dwarfish name and taken that of my noble benefactor. My body may be that of a dwarf, but my soul is Bretonnian to the core. I am the best of both races, strength and style.'

KIM NEWMAN

'Pardon my ignorance,' beseeched Gropius, 'but I was not aware that
there was any great population of dwarfs in Bretonnia–'

'If there were, do you think they would have allowed my parents to
be hostages for life. You are a very stupid man and I decline to explain
further. I am not a freak to be gaped at and petted. I am a powerful
individual in my own right and my abilities are of the highest. I must
uphold the honour of King Charles wherever I go.'

The dancing master was properly cowed. He applied a taper to the
lights that fronted the stage.

'Your prowess is indeed legendary,' he admitted, his astonishment overcome and his natural inclination to fawning and toadying returning. 'We
have heard of your many... um... conquests.'

De la Rougierre strutted, hand on hip, dismissing the subject with a
wave. He took his seat.

'And those stories about the Countess Emmanuelle,' he licked his lips,
'are they–'

'Please, I insist! There is a reputation at stake here...'

...namely, his own, should it come out that the countess had persistently refused his advances.

'...there are matters a de la Rougierre does not discuss with a
tradesman.'

The dancing master bowed and let the subject drop.

'Now,' the ambassador said, 'bring on your finest.'

'Uh, certainly, your excellency.'

Gropius snapped his fingers and said, 'Miele.' A pert, petite girl stepped
out from behind the curtains and stood on the tiny stage. She simpered
and danced a few steps.

'Enough,' said de la Rougierre. 'Show me another.'

Her face fallen, Miele slouched off, trailing her fur boa.

'This is Tessa Ahlquist,' Gropius explained.

A slender dancer with long, ladylike legs – adequately displayed by
an immodest costume – replaced the first girl. The ambassador was
more interested, but quickly tired and had her dismissed. Tessa Ahlquist
stormed off in a flurry of feathers.

Angry, de la Rougierre turned on the dancing master. 'I thought I made
my instructions quite clear. This is a very special function and I have
very special requirements.'

Gropius paid attention, nodding like an imbecile.

'I want a big woman, you understand. Big!'

Gropius chewed his moustache. 'Ah, of course, your excellency. I understand perfectly. You want a dancer of stature.'

'Why yes, that's it exactly. Stature! The girl should be heroically proportioned, you understand. Heroically.'

A ratty smile spread across the dancing master's face.

'Milizia,' he shouted, 'would you come out and dance for the gentleman!'

The next girl appeared...

...and de la Rougierre fancied that he was again in love.

VI

It was the most incredible thing Luitpold had ever witnessed. And it was over in seconds.

He was just about to intervene, invoking the ancient rights of the Imperial family to save his fencing teacher, when Johann laid a hand on his arm and shook his head. The elector was right. Leos von Liebewitz would never forgive him if he were robbed of his honour that way. The viscount would rather die.

Luitpold had imagined that the duellists would step back, take the measure of each other and then join in combat. That was what he had been taught to expect.

Instead, they stepped forwards. Ungenhauer, the von Tuchtenhagen servitor who was rumoured at court to be affected by the warpstone, lunged for Leos, his arms out...

Leos seemed to move casually, as he half-bent out of the champion's way. He just touched Ungenhauer's neck with his foil, then danced out of his reach, coming around behind the man.

A gigantic gusher of blood came from Ungenhauer's throat, spraying the floor in a circle as he turned. Dien Ch'ing raised the skirts of his robe and scuttled away from the mess, but Graf Volker had his boots ruined and one of the seconds got a faceful, forcing him to retire, choking, against the wall.

A roar began in Ungenhauer's chest but it came out of the new mouth in his neck, not the old one in his face.

He raised his hands, as if in triumph, and collapsed to his knees. The whole gymnasium shook.

Leos picked up Dien Ch'ing's silk and wiped off the point of his sword.

Ungenhauer toppled forwards and tiles broke under his face.

There was a moment of incredulous silence and then the applause started.

Leos was indifferent. He was busy wrapping his weapon and handing it to his second. Graf Volker was on his knees praying to Sigmar.

The Celestial raised his hand for quiet and was rewarded.

'By the rules of chivalry, honour is restored. The life of Graf Volker von Tuchtenhagen is the property of Viscount Leos von Liebewitz, to be disposed of as he sees fit...'

Von Tuchtenhagen was crawling towards the viscount, incoherently begging for forgiveness. Doglike, he licked Leos's boots.

'Call for a cleric,' Leos told Dien Ch'ing, 'and a barber. I will not kill a man who is unshriven, much less unshaven.'

'It is confirmed, Lector,' said Ruhaak. 'A messenger has brought the news from the docks.'

Mikael Hasselstein was preoccupied. His junior repeated what he had just said. It sank in. He rolled the facts around his mind and worried at them.

'I did not doubt it, Siemen. Miss Ophuls has an extraordinary gift.'

He could not keep his thoughts on the murders. Last night had been a bad one. At the von Tasseninck ball, Yelle had been threatening to break it off, had been insistent. It had taken all his persuasion and all his skills to bring her round. That, and a quick coupling in an ante-chamber, made all the more exciting by the possibility of imminent discovery. But his attachment was becoming a nuisance. It was affecting his work.

Ophuls sat in the corner, knowing everything and keeping it inside. Hasselstein resented the girl. How simple his life would be if he were able to read thoughts.

Yelle had changed him, he realized. Loving her was draining him, leeching time from his days that he could not afford to spare.

Ruhaak waited for orders. He was a fine instrument, but had no initiative. The Grand Theogonist had not been the same since his bastard Matthias was killed and the whole burden of the Cult of Sigmar had descended upon the shoulders of Mikael Hasselstein. Until now, they had been broad enough to stand it, but the strain was pressing him close to the ground.

Being the Emperor's confessor was a unique privilege, but the sins Karl-Franz worried and fretted over were so paltry, so insignificant. Hasselstein envied the Emperor his uncomplicated nature. He was a truly good man and truly unselfconscious about it. Not so the cleric who gave him absolution. If the Emperor could unload his sins on Mikael, who was there for Mikael?

Yelle was such a harlot, too. There had been other men even when things were good between them. Too many other men. He had even seen her making up to that grey-faced toad, Tybalt.

Hasselstein tried to look as if he were pondering the problem of the Beast, not wrestling with his own heartaches. Ruhaak was respectfully silent, but Ophuls was near to fidgeting. How much did the witch know?

Perhaps he should take the girl as his confessor. She could see his sins anyway, he was sure. They might as well formalise the relationship. No, she was a woman. She reminded him of Yelle. All women were harlots. Even the novices of the Sisterhood of Sigmar were always clustering around the Knights Templar, showing their ankles and bending over on any flimsy pretext. Vixens, harlots and temptresses, the lot of them. Sometimes, Hasselstein thought women were all creatures of Chaos, their bodies shaped by the warpstone to taunt men, their hearts those of daemons, their instincts essentially cruel.

If only Ophuls were a man, like Ruhaak or Adrian Hoven or Dien Ch'ing. Then they could use her gift together. But these witches were always women. In past centuries, the cult had branded them as creatures of Chaos and sought to burn them. That had been a waste. Even if uncontrollable, Rosanna Ophuls was of great use to the cult.

'Miss Ophuls,' he said, 'do you have any more bright thoughts?'

She was surprised to be consulted before Ruhaak and took a moment to put the words together.

'Nothing immediately, lector…'

But there was something. 'Yes?'

'Yesterday, at the site of the last killing, I met with Johann von Mecklenberg.'

'The Elector of Sudenland?'

'Yes. He was taking an interest in the Beast. I don't know why. He is a rare type. He was unconsciously screening his thoughts.'

Hasselstein thought about von Mecklenberg. He was a handsome young man, with just the right amount of roughness to take the boyishness out of his face. He was Yelle's type. Had they been lovers? He didn't know if they even really knew each other, but there was something furtive about the elector, something not quite right.

'Screening his thoughts? That suggests he has something to hide.'

'Not necessarily. I do not think he was deliberately trying to keep me out. Nor was I setting out to read him. I just noticed his mental shields and was curious.'

'You've done well, Miss Ophuls. This is interesting news.'

Rosanna Ophuls was a dangerous dog, Hasselstein thought. She could turn and snap at her master as easily as she could tear out the throat of an enemy. But she was a strong dog all the same.

'I shall send you to help the Dock Watch again,' he said. 'If von Mecklenberg shows up again, get close to him, find out what you can. This business keeps leading back to the palace.'

And Yelle, he added silently. But silence was still too loud. Ophuls wrinkled her brow, as if trying to catch a misheard name.

Hasselstein tried to shut up his mind tight.

Deliberately, he addressed Ruhaak. 'Simeon, get Adrian Hoven back. I want an escort ready to accompany Miss Ophuls and I want more men ready to put on the streets. The watch have had their chance and it is time that the Cult of Sigmar intervened. The Beast will be brought in under our banner.'

Milizia danced for the funny little creature, the dwarf who acted like a Bretonnian, until her breasts and belly were tired of jiggling.

De la Rougierre was clearly delighted with her performance and she knew how to take advantage of that. She leaned close and let him stare at her, his stubby fingers curling his moustaches. She knew what she looked like from beyond the footlights. Melons in a sack. But some men made such a fuss.

Gropius was standing back, marking time with his long forefinger. There was no music, but she knew the pieces she danced to so well that she could do without it. She was accompanied only by the slapping of her bare feet on the stage, the discontented mumbles of the other girls and the strange little noises de la Rougierre kept making.

The ambassador was enchanted and his eyes followed her every movement. There was spittle in his beard.

Finally he could bear it no more and asked her to stop.

'My dear,' he said, 'you are truly a magnificent creature. Seldom have my eyes beheld such... such *ample* beauties...'

Backstage, Tessa, Miele and the others were complaining. Big, ridiculous Milizia, with her big ridiculous tits, was showing them up again. Usually, when she stepped on a stage, the customers thought that not all of her was real. However, after a few of the scarfs had come off, they changed their opinion and were astounded.

'...you will be richly rewarded,' the dwarf babbled, 'in gold crowns. I shall have a carriage call for you.'

She bowed gracefully and thanked him. Gropius pursed his lips, but nodded his approval. He would take a cut, of course. If this worked out, Milizia might look for new management, or even handle her career herself. Perhaps de la Rougierre might offer her a permanent position, as a dancer or as something else.

The ambassador walked out of the theatre, striding as if his legs were as long as Tessa's. Turning as he got to the door, he doffed his hat to her, scraping the floor with its feathers. Winking and kissing his fingers, he left.

Gropius looked up at her and told her to put her clothes on.

VII

Sam Warble was impressed.

He had taken the uncomfortable barge journey to Altdorf – a thing he was loth to do – only on the condition that he be paid in advance. He had asked for a higher fee even than usual, firstly because his employer could well afford it, and secondly because the commission had sounded deeply boring.

He had not expected to see Toten Ungenhauer killed. And to get a front row seat. Even if it meant dressing up as a footman and wearing a false beard, the entertainment was worth the price of admission.

He remembered when Ungenhauer was the chief enforcer for the Marienburg Fish. Warble visited his friends' graves whenever he could and that kept putting him in mind of the big thug-for-hire. The Marienburg Fish had tactfully expelled Ungenhauer when it became too much trouble to saw off his horns every month and keep pretending he was a real human being.

He looked around the gymnasium for his employer. Sure enough, the marquess was there, recognizable by the big nose that stuck out under her veil. He nodded subtly to her and she did everything but get up, bare her buttocks and blow him a kiss. Rich widows were all fools.

Von Tuchtenhagen was in one corner with a cleric of Verena, either delivering a lengthy and detailed confession or begging to be spirited out under the divine's robes. He had ignored the viscount's suggestion that he take advantage of some skilled barbering and meet the deity of his choice in a presentable manner. Warble sympathised with the man. When you were dead, nobody gave a plugged pfennig for hair-oil and perfume. You could ask Ungenhauer, even if you weren't going to get much of an answer.

It was well within the viscount's rights to kill the graf. Nobody was going to argue with that. There was also no question in Warble's mind that von Tuchtenhagen deserved to die. He had read Yefimovich's *Beasts in Green Velvet* and knew that enough of it was true to make him believe the anecdote told about Graf Volker, the three shepherdesses, the missing cufflink and the pit of quicklime.

Leos wasn't even being especially impatient. He had put away his gentleman's sword and selected a common garotte for the task.

Most of the audience had gone. This wasn't the show, this was a distasteful but inevitable aftermath.

Finally, even the cleric had had enough and left the grovelling von Tuchtenhagen to Leos.

The Celestial, whom Warble didn't like the look of, held the graf by the shoulders while Leos looped the garotte around his neck, making sure there was silk between the wire and the flesh. That was the privilege of a gentleman. Not to be touched by the thing that killed him.

Von Tuchtenhagen gave everyone a chance to see what he had eaten for breakfast.

Then, with a swift move, Leos yanked the noose tight and let the graf fall next to his champion.

Smiling, he stood back. The Celestial checked von Tuchtenhagen's pulse and breath. The green velvet scum was dead.

Everyone packed up and got ready to leave.

'You,' a full-size human servant said to him, 'shorty.'

Warble reached for his dagger but realized it was in his other pair of boots. He was dressed as a servant and servants in the palace weren't armed unless they wanted to be tortured as suspected assassins.

'Help me clear this mess up.'

Warble shrugged. Harald Kleindeinst wasn't the only one who got stuck with all the filthy jobs.

Unseen and yet aware, the Beast smelled blood and knew that it would prowl again tonight...

'This is Rosanna Ophuls,' said Elsaesser. 'She's from the Temple.'

Harald acknowledged the girl's presence and hoped she wouldn't get in the way.

'Don't worry, I won't,' she said.

'Rosanna is a scryer.'

'So I see.'

The body had been dragged out of the water by a couple of Schygulla's dockhands, and laid out on a table in the warehouse of the Beloved of Manann. Dickon, still sulking about the return of Harald Kleindeinst, was busy shepherding official investigators through his ring of guards while keeping out trouble-makers. It was the most useful thing Harald could think of for him to do. It wasn't really demeaning enough, he reflected. Now he had some Imperial authority over his old captain, he wanted to settle a few old scores.

Revenge was an ignoble and fruitless pursuit, but he was just a weak-willed human being and couldn't be held responsible for his base impulses.

If he wanted suspects, this place was full of them. Schygulla, the manager, used to run with the Hooks. Most of his employees were familiar faces from Harald's pilferer-rousting days. But, come to that, few of them had as many unsolved crimes to their credit as the watchmen on this case. Walking through the crowd of bystanders, Harald had felt his stomach going again.

He looked at the eyeless, faceless corpse and knew he wasn't after an ordinary criminal. The Hooks and the Fish often mutilated their kills if they wanted to make a point to the dead men's comrades, but even the gangs' berserkers didn't do this sort of thing to women.

'Scryer,' he said, 'what can you tell me?'

The girl didn't want to touch the dead thing, but she laid her hand on the flayed flesh of the victim's forehead.

'Wolf,' she said.

'A wolf did this?'

She shook her head. Her eyes closed and her whole body shook. She turned her head on the axis of her neck, as if straining for a sound or a scent.

'Wolf,' she said again. 'That's the word that was on her mind.'

'Wolves don't usually hunt in the city,' he said, 'and they usually eat at least part of their kill. An animal wouldn't have rolled her off the jetty, but left her in case he wanted to come back for another meal.'

'Not a wolf. *Wolf*. I think it's a name.'

She took her hand away and wiped it off on her dress. She was not nervy about this business. She didn't want to stick her fingers into human meat, but if it had to be done she wasn't going to complain. Rosanna Ophuls was all right.

'There's a famous Wolf,' said Elsaesser. 'Wolfgang Neuwald.'

'Neuwald? That's a familiar name. Ah, you mean Wolfgang von Neuwald.'

'That's right, captain. He's in Ferring the Balladeer's songs about the hero, Konrad. They say he wears a wolf's face tattooed over his own.'

'Hero? That's an interesting word, Elsaesser. I've met people who think Constant Drachenfels was a hero.'

'Neuwald... ah, *von* Neuwald's supposed to have killed before. And he was from Altdorf originally.'

Harald shook his head. 'I know about Wolf von Neuwald, watchman. I didn't like him, but slaughtering bawds wasn't his style.'

'It's not an uncommon name,' said Elsaesser.

'I'll have every Wolf, Wolfgang, Wolfie, Wulfrum, Wolfgard and Wulfric pulled in and put to the torture,' snapped Dickon.

Harald, Rosanna and Elsaesser looked at the captain of the Dock Watch as if he were an idiot.

'You're an idiot, Dickon,' said Harald.

The captain looked as if he had an answer ready, but made himself forget all about it.

'Just because this woman died thinking of Wolf doesn't mean he was her killer. Most men I've seen die call for their mother, or their girl–'

'Brilliant, Kleindeinst,' sneered Dickon. 'So Wolf is the whore's mother?'

Rosanna was annoyed. 'She wasn't a whore, captain. She worked in the Wayfarer's Rest. She was a maid.'

Dickon huffed and walked away, taking out his pipe.

Harald looked at the corpse, examining every detail of every wound. He wanted to build up a picture of the kind of animal he was after. He wanted to know what made the Beast get hot, what gave the killer his pleasure. His stomach was filling with acid, but he could imagine the thing he was up against.

'I think you're right,' Rosanna said. 'Wolf was the girl's lover. I can make out a face. I think I'd recognize him.'

Harald broke out of his concentration on the corpse. He pulled the blanket over, tucking it gently around the dead girl.

'Can you draw?'

Rosanna started to ask him what he was talking about, then caught up with him.

'Yes. I could draw him.'

Harald took Schygulla by the ear and told him to get some paper and a pencil. The manager rummaged through a desk piled with ledgers and found some loose leaves.

Rosanna sat down and began to sketch.

'The runner should bring back the landlord of the Wayfarer's Rest soon,' said Elsaesser. 'Then we'll be able to get her name.'

'Really? If this were your girl, could you recognize her?'

The boy was shocked. Just now, Elsaesser was in the dangerous stage. He got too involved with the job, but it was all still much like a game. If he survived the waterfront watch, he would learn. He might make a good copper.

Rosanna handed him the sketch. He looked at it.

'You've drawn Johann von Mecklenberg without a beard, scryer.'

She bit her lip. 'Yes, I know. I tried not to. The face I'm seeing isn't quite the baron, but it's very close.'

'This could be Baron von Mecklenberg as he was ten years ago, as a student,' said Elsaesser.

'Ten years ago, this girl would have been about seven,' said Rosanna.

Harald looked at her, not needing to ask a question. 'I can scry her age,' she said, 'but not her name. It's like fishing in the dark, you don't always get what would be most convenient.'

'Hmmmn.' Harald examined the girl's sketch. She was a good draughts-woman. He wondered about the Baron Johann. He still hadn't worked out what von Mecklenberg's interest in all this was. He instinctively trusted the man – which wasn't exactly his usual attitude to electors and aristocrats – and intended to stick by his first feeling. But there were questions he would have to find answers for.

'You've met the elector?' he asked Rosanna.

'Yesterday. When they found the last girl.'

'What did you make of him?'

She was surprised to be asked the question, but did not try to get out of answering. 'He's concerned. I don't think he's the Beast.'

'Neither do I,' chipped in Elsaesser. 'If he were, he would be stupid to set you to catch him.'

Harald thought about that. 'Unless he wanted to be caught...'

The warehouse door was opened and Dickon let a watchman in. He was dragging a bald, middle-aged man who had put a cloak and boots on over his nightshirt.

'This is Runze, of the Wayfarer's Rest.'

The landlord looked at the thing on the table. Harald lifted the blanket.

'Sigmar's mighty hammer,' Runze swore, 'it's Trudi!'

The man turned, clutching his belly and was sick over Dickon.

'Pathetic,' Harald said to himself. 'Another weak stomach.'

'Trudi?'

There was no answer.

Wolf turned over in the bed and found no one there. He was not at the University, or in the room at the Wayfarer's Rest.

'Trudi?'

He tried to remember the night before, but could not.

Water was dripping somewhere and the floor was shifting. He wondered if he were on a boat.

There were questions he would have to answer. Where was Trudi? Where was he? What had he done last night?

And why was he covered in blood?

Part Four

Riot

I

When it was all over, there would be an Imperial inquiry, presided over airily by the Grand Theogonist Yorri. Whether the titular head of the Cult of Sigmar could possibly be impartial in the matter of the Great Fog Riots was a question that many asked but few answered to anyone's satisfaction.

However, when all the allegations and rumours were discounted and the more fabulous lies disproved, these facts were definitely ascertained.

Firstly, this particular fog was the thickest, heaviest, foulest, longest-lasting and most debilitating to descend upon the city within living memory. Since the term 'living memory' included that of Genevieve Dieudonné, 667, it was a simple matter to amend the statement to the effect that this was the worst the fog had ever been.

For the rest of their lives, weather bores who had happened to be in the city during the Great Fog would annoy their friends and relatives and any total strangers who could be trapped into paying attention with fantastic, but dull, tales of the fog's duration, quality, quantity and climatic peculiarity.

Secondly, at some time in the early afternoon, members of the revolutionary movement began to distribute a fresh pamphlet authored by Yevgeny Yefimovich, featuring the first publication of Prince Kloszowski's poem 'The Ashes of Shame,' in which it was alleged that the Beast was finding shelter within the palace of the Emperor. Among other things, this handbill claimed that Dickon of the Dock Watch, never an especially popular public figure, had found a green velvet cloak in the alley next to the murdered body of Margarethe Ruttmann, and that he had personally burned this piece of evidence. Yefimovich concluded his pamphlet with a call for all honest men to rise up against the hated oppressors and bring down the corrupt rule of Karl-Franz.

Thirdly, in a jurisdictional dispute typical of a city with more Imperial, religious, local and political factions than many nations, a surprising number of mutually hostile armed bands of men ventured out into the foggy streets, ostensibly to protect the citizens from the twinned dangers of the fog and the Beast. The watches were first reinforced by detachments of the Imperial Militia, augmented by the palace guard in the richer sections of the city. Meanwhile, under the command of Adrian Hoven,

patrols of the Knights of the Order of the Fiery Heart combed the area
of the palace and the Temple of Sigmar, tactlessly putting to the question many citizens lost in the fog.

In addition to these official forces, a group of Hooks under the command of Willy Pick, flying the spurious standard of a Citizens' Vigilance
Committee, took up tactical stations on the city's bridges and casually
terrorised passersby. And the League of Karl-Franz, vowing that a little
weather was not going to halt their traditional Imminence of Winter
wine-drinking contest, flowed in numbers from the colleges of the University towards the Street of a Hundred Taverns. Of course, the list of
armed factions was swelled by many of Yefimovich's agitators, by a number of harlots who had decided it best that they carry weapons with the
Beast at large, and by sundry fools and adventurers who thought this
seemed like an interesting time to wander around in search of excitement.

Between them, these three factors set off the most serious outbreak
of urban violence Altdorf had ever known.

The first clashes occurred in the early afternoon, when an inex-
perienced Imperial Militia lieutenant ignored the advice of the Dock
watchmen he was detailed to assist and attempted to persuade a group
from the Citizens' Vigilance Committee to abandon their positions at
the north end of Three Toll Bridge connecting Temple Street in the west
with Luitpoldstrasse in the east. No one was seriously injured, but the
lieutenant was pitched into the slow-flowing Reik and had to struggle
out of his armour to escape drowning. He learned a valuable lesson and
peace was briefly restored.

Just as the temple bell was sounding the hour of three – in the afternoon, although the fog made it hard to distinguish from three in the
night – Don Rodrigo Piquer de Ossorio Serrador Teixiheira, the seventeen
year-old second son of an Estalian duke, was returning with a severe
headache from the House of von Tasseninck, where he had succumbed
to an excess of wine during the ball of the night before, to his quarters
at the University, where he was endeavouring to master alchemy and
siege engineering. Angry at having missed the duel everyone was discussing and feeling in need of the proverbial 'feather of the chicken that
pecked you,' he rapped on the door of the One-Eyed Wolf, insisting that
the landlord open up and serve him some sherry. The landlord wasn't
at home, but the front bar of the hostelry was currently occupied by a
chapter of the Fish, who were listening attentively while the one who
could read was explaining the contents of 'The Ashes of Shame.'

Barging in, Teixiheira swished his green velvet cloak in a manner he
considered quite stylish and requested, in somewhat belligerent tones,
that he be served, insisting that his breeding demanded that these commoners do all within their power to oblige him. He was discovered
hanging under the Old Emperor Bridge, his cloak having been cut into
strips and used to fashion a crude but functional noose. Yorri's Commission decided that Teixiheira was the first official casualty of the riots.

By the hour of five, seventeen others had come to violent ends and the riots had not even really got underway yet. These souls lost their lives in simple skirmishes between individuals or groups of not more than three or four. Typical was the case of Ailbow Muggins, a halfling fruit and vegetable merchant, who mistook an approaching pair of Knights Templars for revenue men intent on discovering the load of contraband harvest goods he had just taken delivery of from a Fish. Muggins was surprised trying to pour powder and shot into the horn of his state-of-the-art flintlock pistol and died, not from the swordblow to his head, but because a spark struck from his hat buckle by the blade ignited the powder in his horn. Cleric-Sergeant Rainer Wim Herzog, who inflicted the stroke and lost an eye in the explosion, was later decorated by Cleric-Captain Hoven and commended for valour, if not in the field, then at least in the fog.

Yorri's Commission could not later account for the activities of Dien Ch'ing, the ambassador of the Monkey King, who apparently spent the day visiting several peculiar establishments scattered throughout the city, purchasing disparate elements that might well be connected with sorcery. Some criticism was also passed on Etienne Edouard Villechaize, Comte de la Rougierre, the ambassador of Charles de la Tete d'Or III, who was believed to have spent the afternoon and early evening at the Matthias II tavern in the company of Milizia Kubic, an exotic dancer of heroic proportions, and to have conducted himself in a manner unbecoming a diplomat of Bretonnia. The sworn testimony of Norbert Schlupmann, a keghand at the Matthias II, who spent the afternoon peering through a small hole bored in the ceiling of de la Rougierre's rented apartments, was examined closely by the Grand Theogonist and then placed in the great library of the Temple with many other proscribed works, its contents sealed forever from the public eye and ruled not germane to the investigation.

At some time in the afternoon, Harald Kleindeinst, while questioning the staff of the Wayfarer's Rest in an effort to piece together the last hours of Trudi Ursin's life, survived an assassination attempt and managed, after a very brief chase, to subdue Watchman Joost Rademakers, his would-be murderer. Unfortunately, Rademakers did not survive long enough to explain his motives for attempting the crime. At the time, however, Kleindeinst expressed the opinion that his fellow officer was acting upon the orders of an unnamed third member of the Dock Watch. An autopsy conducted in the Temple of Morr revealed that Rademakers expired due to complications following a crushed windpipe and that the thirty-six bone fractures sustained during his encounter with Kleindeinst were not necessarily contributory factors in his demise.

The corpse of Graf Volker von Tuchtenhagen, suitably cleaned up, was delivered from the palace to the house of the von Tassenincks, following the tradition that the responsibility for the body of a losing duellist devolves, if his family are unavailable, on the owners of the property where the original insult was delivered. Grand Prince Hals, never particularly close to the deceased, had the graf packed in precious ice and sealed up for shipping back to his estates in Averland, where, upon the delivery of the news, his mother would die of grief and his tenants would hold an unofficial and unauthorized three-day festival of merry-making and licentiousness. Toten Ungenhauer was turned over to the local Temple of Morr, where a cursory examination revealed that he had indeed been drastically altered by warpstone. After scientific dissection, von Tuchtenhagen's champion would be disposed of in the same lime pit that would, after a respectful period, receive the unwanted, much-abused bodies of Margarethe Ruttmann and Trudi Ursin.

The first of the fires was set just after nightfall, at the house of Amadeus Wiesle, an unpopular moneylender active in the East End of the city. The Commission was never able to determine whether this fire was the responsibility of a citizen with a specific grievance against Wiesle or by an agitator in the thrall of Yevgeny Yefimovich, and the watch – given a list of the creditors evicted, abused, physically disabled, sold into servitude or executed thanks to their involvement with the usurer – decided not to pursue the matter further. By then, the watch had far more pressing affairs to consider.

If it had not been for the fog, word of the fire in the East End might have spread faster and caused a panic. As it was, there was a panic anyway, for a surfeit of other excellent reasons.

Although no one was yet aware of it, the Beast was awake and was beginning to stalk its prey of the evening...

II

Harald Kleindeinst had arranged to meet them at the Wayfarer's Rest in the middle of the afternoon, but was late. Rosanna had the impression that the officer was the sort of man who kept to his word unless an immovable object got in his way. He had given her Helmut Elsaesser as an escort and told her to poke around Trudi Ursin's room, to see if she could pick up anything useful about the girl. So far, the investigation had been proceeding on the assumption that the Beast was a random murderer, striking merely as the opportunity presented itself. But it would be a lot easier to build up a case if the victims were selected according to a system, no matter how insane. Kleindeinst had had Elsaesser reassigned to the case and put him in charge of finding connections between the dead women. Obviously, the young officer had already been thinking along that course, since he had memorised a great deal of information about the Beast's previous victims: Rosa, Miriam, Helga, Monika, Gislind, Tanja, Margarethe. And now Trudi.

Elsaesser seemed to know them all intimately. Rosa, Monika and Gislind had worked for the same pimp, a Hook named Maxie Schock, and Miriam and Margarethe, older than the others, had at different times been involved with Rikki Fleisch, the small-timer Margarethe had murdered. Three blondes, two indeterminate brown, one black, one redhead and one shaven with dragon tattoos. Six prostitutes, one fortune-teller and, now, one hostel maid. Miriam, 57, was the oldest and Gislind, 14, the youngest. They had all worked in the same area, the rough sprawl around the Street of a Hundred Taverns, and those with homes had lodged within walking distance. The watch had already been through over two hundred husbands, ex-husbands, children, boyfriends, 'protectors,' 'admirers,' customers, associates, friends, enemies, acquaintances and neighbours. A few people had cropped up in connection with more than one of the women – there were jokes being told at the Luitpoldstrasse Station about the appetite of that dwarfish Bretonnian ambassador, de la Rougierre – but no one could be tied in with all of them. The only thing the eight had in common was their deaths, unmistakably the work of the same hand.

Rosanna sat at the dressing table and looked into the cracked but clean mirror, trying to see a dead girl's face as it had been. She was trying to forget the red ruin she had seen at the Beloved of Manann warehouse, the blood sucked away by the water, greyish patches of skull showing through. Elsaesser searched the room, apparently at random, looking for things he had seen before. 'Helga had shoes like this,' he said, going through a box in the wardrobe. He made a discovery. 'And most of them used this stuff.'

She looked over. He had found a cache of weirdroot. He scraped one of the dried roots with his fingernail and dabbed his tongue. 'This is snakeshit,' he said. 'Last year's crop. Maybe older.'

Rosanna looked back at the mirror. Her face was cut in half by the crack.

She touched the hairbrush and got the impression of long, thick hair, crackling as it was combed out. From the corpse, she hadn't been able to tell what the girl had looked like when she was alive.

'Two people lived here,' said Elsaesser, holding up a maidservant's apron and a man's jacket. 'See, I can scry too. It's called deduction.'

He seemed pleased with himself. That worried Rosanna a little. She wasn't sure why Elsaesser was so hot on the Beast. Partly, she saw, it was because he liked puzzles. The only thing she had caught from his mind was the feeling of his fingers working away at difficult knots, trying to get them loose. His hands were always restless. The whole process of tracking the killer excited him. He was like a first-time huntsman, exhilarated by the chase but not yet blooded, not yet forced to see a kill. And there was some other motive, something harder to define.

It was really much simpler when you did something you were told to. There were no motives to untangle and ponder. She was here because the Lector wanted her here. And, after yesterday's session with the left-overs of the victims, she was here because she wanted the Beast stopped.

Elsaesser dropped the apron on the bed and examined the jacket. It was obviously of a good cut. Trudi had had a rich boyfriend, or a light-fingered one with access to a tailor's shop.

'The League of Karl-Franz,' the officer said. 'Look.'

He tossed the jacket at her and she caught it. On the lapels was the Imperial seal, picked out in gold.

'The Leaguers all wear these things. I should have recognized it straight away.'

It was like holding an angry animal. The jacket struggled in her grip and she heard growling, spitting and snarling. Claws slashed, teeth were bared. There was snow underfoot and a trail of blood to follow. Yellow and red eyes shone and she realized they were her own, thrown back at her by the mirror.

'Trudi's boyfriend is a first-year, not fully inducted,' said Elsaesser. 'He'll be able to put on some extra braids if he passes his first exams.'

She dropped the garment.

'What's wrong?'

Rosanna could not stop shaking.

'Wolf,' she said.

Elsaesser was attentive, contrite. 'I'm sorry, I should never have just thrown the thing at you. I keep forgetting about your gift.'

'That's all right, it would have happened anyway. I can feel it in this whole room. It's strong, like a musk.'

'You should act more like a witch...'

She hated that word, but was willing to put up with it from the well-meaning young officer.

'...cover your clothes with symbols and emblems. Wave your hands and mutter hocus pocus.'

The gooseflesh under her sleeves subsided. Elsaesser stroked her hair, as if he were fifty years older rather than six years younger than her. He had none of the caution Mikael Hasselstein exhibited around her and that made her realize how few of the people she knew were willing casually to touch her in the way ordinary people did each other. She didn't even scry anything more from the officer, beyond a general attempt to soothe her after her nasty contact.

'I'm not a witch, or a sorceress. This isn't something I learned, it's something I was born with. It's like being double-jointed, or having a good singing voice.'

He was serious again. 'Is it Wolf?' he asked.

'I think so. Names are difficult, sometimes. There are odd things about him. He must be a student, but he feels older. He has been through a period of his life he barely remembers, but is constantly plagued by. He's not an altered, but he has undergone some... some transformation...'

Elsaesser was paying close attention.

Kunze, the landlord, had said that Trudi had a boyfriend who stayed with her sometimes. Aside from being a student and not short of the odd crown, he didn't know anything about the man. However, Kunze had described him as 'a hairy devil' even though, when pressed, he had admitted that the boy didn't wear a beard.

There was a knock at the door.

'Come in.'

A girl in an apron entered the room and curtsied. Rosanna felt the wave of fear coming off her. She had been crying.

'I'm Marte,' the girl said. 'Mr Kunze said you wanted to see me.'

'You were Trudi's friend?' Elsaesser asked.

Marte said, 'We worked alternate shifts, officer. She was a good girl and filled in when I was sick. I'm sick a lot.'

Rosanna noticed that the girl was a little lame and her skin colour was not good.

'Did you know her boyfriend?' she asked.

Marte's face twisted and Rosanna tried hard not to flinch. The maid had just switched from passive fear to active fear.

'Him,' she said, loathing in her voice, 'he was a bad one. An animal. He was sweet as sugar one minute, then a vicious beast. I don't know why she stuck with him. I'd never let a man use me as he used her. We bathed together, every week, and she always had some new bruise or scratch that he'd given her.'

The yellow and red eyes burned in her mind.

'Do you know his name?'

Marte was more angry than scared now. 'Did he do it? I always said he was a bad one.'

'His name?'

'Merciful Shallya, was he… was he *the Beast?*' Marte was on the point of fainting.

Elsaesser took her by the shoulders and held her up. 'What was his name?'

'Oh yes. His name. It was Wolf…'

Elsaesser and Rosanna looked at each other.

'Aristocracy, he was. He kept it quiet, but Trudi told me his brother was an elector…'

Inside her mind, something vague was coming into clear, hard focus. Rosanna remembered the sketch she had made for Captain Kleindeinst and the face that had kept trying to impose itself over the one in Trudi's mind.

'His name was Wolf von Mecklenberg.'

III

The barge was empty. Wolf tried to remember coming aboard, but couldn't. The cabin door was splintered and he guessed that he had broken in.

He had slept in his clothes and woken up feeling grimy next to the skin.

He had gone out last night, with Trudi. There had been a thick fog. He remembered an argument.

But nothing else.

He wished Johann were here. Johann would know how to save him from the animal inside him. Johann had spent ten years tracking him, trying to rescue him from the Chaos knights.

Those had been bad years, but they were gone now. Gone forever.

He could remember some things. He could remember that day in the woods when he had got in the way of Johann's arrow.

His shoulder still hurt when it was damp, and sometimes bled. Now there was an ache between the bones, precisely where Johann's shaft had pierced.

That day, he had been snotty. He had been taunting his brother for his faint heart. As a boy, Johann had not been a natural killer. Wolf had been the huntsman in the family. He had lived for his time in the woods, loping along in the tracks of some stag or hog, his bow always ready. If it swam, flew, ran or burrowed, Wolf could kill it.

Now, he wished he had been more like Johann, instinctively turning away from murder.

His trophies were dusty and forgotten in some storeroom on the estate. And he wished he could get rid of his urge to kill.

It must have been easy for Cicatrice to work on him. The seed of Chaos had always been there, nestling in his heart, waiting to sprout. He had been a monster inside long before the warpstone had given him a body to match.

These last weeks had been foggy, if not in the city then in his mind. He remembered the feel of Trudi, the feel of her flesh...

And he did not want to remember any more.

He must have been weird-juicing last night. Purple squiggles still came and went in the periphery of his vision. And then he must have been brawling. One of his teeth was loose and he had bled from cuts on his face. But not all the blood on his clothes was his own.

On the floor of the cabin he found a docker's hook, like the ones carried by the waterfront gang. It was blooded.

For some reason, he took it with him when he left.

Emerging onto the deck, he found that the barge was moored near the Three Toll Bridge, at one of the public quays.

He took three crowns from his pouch, to cover the damage, and left them by the wheelhouse, under a coil of rope so they wouldn't shine and attract attention.

The barge was on a loose mooring, to rise and fall with the river, and it was played out. The rope was stretched tight and the quay was ten feet away. There was nothing for it but to get wet.

He lowered himself into the icy waters, almost relishing the shock of the cold, and got a strong grip on the rope. The current pulled at his legs. There was a surface mist trailing off the water, joining the thick fog in the air.

He could barely see the dock.

He worked his way, hand over hand, feeling the rush of water washing him clean.

He hauled himself up and stood on the planks of the jetty. He tried to shake himself dry, like a dog, but his shirt and britches hung on him like ice slabs.

He wanted to go back to Trudi, but wasn't sure that was a good idea. He could not remember what their argument had been about, but it had been a bad one. He thought he had used his hands on her. Again. And that made him burn with shame.

Dripping, he walked off the docks, fumbling his way in the fog...

There were ruffians fighting on the Street of a Hundred Taverns, but it was more serious than the usual Hooks-and-Fish or Students-and-Dockers clashes. Those did not usually leave many dead, but Dien Ch'ing could tell that at least five people had been killed in the fighting so far. It would be a good night for his lord.

Disdaining the ostentatious carriage that was his right as ambassador, he had chosen to go for a walk in the fog. At the palace, there were those who thought he must be mad, but the ways of foreign diplomats were not often questioned.

The duel this morning had given him quite an appetite.

He honoured the purpose of Lord Tsien-Tsin and heard in his head the orchestra of the Fifteen Devils. He longed for the Pagoda, and to be far away from this barbarous and cold country. He remembered the sweet teas and fragrant blossoms of his homeland, and wondered humbly how soon it would be before his master chose to summon him back to Cathay to work towards the downfall of the presumptuous Monkey King. That monarch had reigned for too long over the greatness of the east, and it had always been the intention of Tsien-Tsin that he be brought low. Ch'ing had promised himself the position of executioner and imagined the scimitar describing a graceful arc towards the throat of the Monkey

King and the look in his enemy's eyes as his befuddled head was expertly detached from his unworthy neck.

His pleasant thoughts were interrupted.

'You,' said a rough voice, 'Green velvet!'

There were three of them, each taller than he. They blocked his path. They were indistinct in the fog, illuminated by the fires behind them. He looked from outline to outline. Two men and a woman. They each held docker's hooks in their fists.

'Off your patch, aren't you?' said the one who had already spoken.

Ch'ing bowed. 'Might I humbly request that you let my meagre and contemptible self past. I have urgent business.'

They laughed at him and he sighed.

'We don't want your sort here,' said the woman.

'Palace scum!'

'Parasite!'

A hook sliced out of the fog at him. He clapped his hands over it, halting it an inch from his nose.

'Moves like a rabbit,' someone said.

He let the hook go and it was withdrawn.

He saw the dagger coming and tapped it away with his palm. It struck a wall.

The fog swirled around them as the three Hooks spread to surround him. The fire nearby was rising and Ch'ing realized that there was a carriage overturned in the street, burning steadily. He could see their stupid faces. They all had grotesquely large noses, skins the colour of a pig's belly and peculiar moon-round eyes, and the men were disgustingly bearded, with thick hair like growths of moss about their chins and necks. Typical unwashed barbarians.

He drew up his knee and spread his arms in the crane position.

'He's a loony,' said the woman.

He hopped into the air and kicked where her voice had come from. She was out of the ring instantly, consciousness knocked out of her.

Ch'ing landed a little unsteadily on the cobbles, but quickly regained his balance.

'Did you see that?'

'What did you do to Hanni?'

'Swine!'

The two Hooks circled him and he turned, preventing either from getting behind him.

Finally, he became tired of the game.

For the one who had spoken first, he employed the Drunken Master technique, weaving unsteadily from side to side, then head-butting the Hook to the ground and stamping on his face, as if trying to put out a burning patch of lamp-oil. It was most comical.

For the other, he switched to the Sleeping Fist. Yawning loudly, he stifled himself with the back of one hand and leaned backwards, as if falling into a hammock. His outstretched elbow smashed into the Hook's ribcage, breaking a few bones. The man coughed and fell, and Ch'ing sliced his neck between his scything legs.

He left two dead and one sleeping. Sparing the woman was his concession to the mores of the Empire where, for some extraordinary reason, it was not considered polite to kill a female. Not, of course, that that stopped anyone. This Beast fellow, for instance...

Standing over his fallen enemies, he heard someone clapping.

A creature scurried monkey-like out of the fog, its hands slapping together.

Ch'ing bowed. He recognized Respighi.

'My master sends his greetings, Celestial.'

'They are accepted with thanks.'

'He is busy elsewhere...'

There was a sound from across the river. It was a large building gently bursting into flames. There were a lot of fires in the fog. In the distance, people were shouting.

'...but has asked me to accompany you to the Matthias II. I am to represent his interests.'

Ch'ing spread his hands. 'We all have the same interest, Respighi. The greater glory of Lord Tsien-Tsin.'

'Tzeentch.'

'As you will. Names do not matter. We all eventually serve the same purpose.'

Respighi giggled.

IV

Having decided to accept de la Rougierre's invitation for the evening, Johann was now faced with the problem of making his attendance at the soirée not seem extraordinary. He had cultivated, he now realized, an unusual unsociability, regularly avoiding the balls and receptions that proliferated around the Imperial court. It was not that he hated these things so much, but that he had been away from the world of titles and etiquette for so long that he no longer had the desire to enter it. The latest dances, current fashions in hemlines and the petty schemings of rival court factions simply did not seem important, or even interesting, to him.

And yet, it was now clear that he must be at the Bretonnian ambassador's soirée. He knew, with a certainty that was unusual, that this was not just an innocent social occasion. The scent of the Beast was in the air.

In the afternoon, he had encountered Leos von Liebewitz, who was in ominously good spirits, and discovered that the viscount and his sister were also on de la Rougierre's guest list. Leos had offered him a place in their carriage and he had accepted with practiced off-handedness.

Johann found it creepy that the undemonstrative, unemotional, humourless viscount was only able to be anything approaching friendly if he had spilled blood that day. Before leaving him, the youth had clapped Johann on the shoulder and shaken his hand. He fancied that Leos had kept up physical contact a moment or two longer than was necessary. There were stories told about the viscount, not to his face... Stories about why he had rejected the undeniably appealing Clothilde of Averheim as a marriage prospect, or even as a sweetheart-of-the-month...

De la Rougierre was away from the palace, making preparations, so Johann had to ask around to discover who else would be at the table. That meant paying his respects to the Countess Emmanuelle and listening to her for longer than he would have chosen to.

The countess was genuinely the most beautiful woman he had ever seen, but she was so self-absorbed as to qualify also as one of the most boring. He found her surrounded by a flurry of notably unattractive maidservants, endeavouring to make a choice between seven equally magnificent, overly decorated and borderline immodest gowns. She had been relying on the judgement of Mnoujkine, the guests' steward, to assist her and the man was notably relieved to have a superior to take over the duty from him. She asked Johann to give advice and he had to sit in her rooms while she darted behind a screen to struggle out of and into each in turn. Mnoujkine, with the tact of a born underling, withdrew to leave his betters unchaperoned.

All the while, she talked. Johann learned that the party was to be graced by the presence of future Emperor Luitpold. Mikael Hasselstein was due to make an appearance and Dien Ch'ing, the Cathayan ambassador, and Grand Prince Hergard von Tasseninck. Also, the Marquess Sidonie of Marienburg, which prompted Emmanuelle to remark that 'the Bretonnian would have to be careful with the seating arrangements since Leos killed her husband last year on a matter of honour.' Johann wished the countess would take the trouble to watch her brother butcher his opponents and then try to talk about matters of honour.

Three electors, the future Emperor and a Lector of the Cult of Sigmar. If one was to assume that Luitpold could influence his father, and that Hasselstein was more or less charged with the powers the Grand Theogonist was neglecting to wield these days, then one would see that this small, exclusive gathering concentrated more political power in one room than had gathered since the last meeting of the Electoral College. The thing that puzzled Johann most was where the Celestial fitted in. What could be the common interest of Bretonnia and Cathay? Also, it was well-known that de la Rougierre had little actual power at the court of King Charles de la Tete d'Or, the ridiculous perfumed dwarf having been appointed to the ambassadorship as a cruel joke against Karl-Franz that no one had yet had the nerve to explain to the Emperor.

'Which do you prefer, baron?'

He paid attention. The countess was in her robe again, playing artfully with her lapels to show off her well-shaped bust.

'The green velvet,' he said, distractedly.

She seemed surprised and chewed a strand of her hair like a teenager. It was well known that the countess had been twenty-nine for some years now.

'Very well, the green velvet. A good choice. Traditional. You have an admirable eye, Johann.'

He shrugged, uncomfortable. He did not know where to put his hands and opted to leave them in his lap.

She gave her maids directions in a low, serious voice. The dress was to be cleaned, pressed, aired, perfumed and laid out. She listed the underwear and accessories that went with it, and handed one girl the key to her jewel-box, with instructions to fetch several bracelets, brooches and rings, and a specified tiara-and-necklace combination. Obviously, the life of the Countess-Elector of Nuln was one tough decision after another.

Johann made an excuse and left.

He thought about Wolf. And he thought about Harald Kleindeinst, wondering if he had done the right thing by setting the watchman on the trail.

It was too late to step back.

In an hour, he would join the von Liebewitzes and venture out into the fog.

Perhaps there would be answers out there.

They were waiting for him at the Wayfarer's Rest. He had been delayed by the business with Joost Rademakers. Dickon was being stupid and would suffer for it later. He should have known that Rademakers on his own wouldn't have a chance against Filthy Harald. The captain always had underestimated him.

The whole city was going mad in this fog. The Luitpoldstrasse Station had been snowed under with bleeding citizens, complaining of assaults, robberies and arson. Harald had seen three Knights Templars roughing up a couple of Fish and left them to it. There were Imperial Militiamen hanging around with the watch, getting in the way.

Dickon had sent a runner to the fire-fighters, to help with the burning carriages in the Street of a Hundred Taverns, but he had either got lost, got killed or found the fire service busy elsewhere.

He could tell straight away that Rosanna and Elsaesser had news for him.

'Out with it,' he said. 'Elsaesser, speak slowly, no repetitions, no gabble.'

'Trudi Ursin's missing boyfriend is Wolf Mecklenberg...'

'Von Mecklenberg,' put in Rosanna.

'The elector's brother.'

Harald bit down hard on the nugget, to see how it tasted. It wasn't good.

'But the baron was interested in the Beast *before* Trudi turned up dead,' he reasoned. 'Which suggests that he knows something we don't.'

'There's more,' said the scryer. 'It's common knowledge that the baron's brother was abducted as a child, by Chaos knights...'

'It was a bandit called Cicatrice,' said Elsaesser. 'I'd heard the story, but never made the connection...'

'Wolf was rescued,' explained Rosanna, 'and purged of the warpstone. But maybe there's still something inside.'

Harald imagined a young man in a frenzy, tearing at a girl with claws and teeth.

'Scryer, is Wolf the Beast?' he asked.

She thought hard, not wanting to say anything until she was certain.

'I'll put it this way: do you *think* he's the Beast?'

'It's... it's not impossible. I've been through some of his clothes, trying to find traces. He has an aura of violence, of confusion. Also, he suffers from terrible guilt.'

'But that doesn't make him our killer?'

'No,' she admitted. 'There are a lot of violent people in this city.'

She was looking at him. There was still a splash of Rademakers's blood on his coat.

'That's true,' he said.

'What should we do?' asked Elsaesser.

'You take Baron Johann,' he ordered. 'Get over to the palace and stick to him like a lashworm in case his brother shows up. Tell him I've sent you for his own protection. Make up some story. Convince him that there's a rumour going around that he's the killer and the vigilantes are after him. That's probably true. There are rumours going around that everyone's the killer. Dickon is trying to convince the Hooks that it's me, and hopes they'll put me out of the way.'

Elsaesser saluted.

'Rosanna,' Harald continued, 'you stick with me. We'll try and find this Wolf of yours. He may not be the killer, but he's certainly got some questions to answer.'

'He's a Leaguer,' Elsaesser said. 'You could start at their hall. It's not far.'

'Also,' said Rosanna, 'he's on weirdroot. He might be trying to buy some of the stuff.'

'That's something to start with.'

Elsaesser pulled on his peaked cap and left.

'Lad,' Harald said after him, 'be careful.'

The officer said, 'I will be,' and left.

Harald felt the aches of his fight with Rademakers disappearing. The old copper feeling was coming back. It wasn't just nausea, it was a tightness in the pit of his stomach that he recognized as excitement.

'You want him, don't you?' said the scryer.

'Yes, I do.'

'Dead or alive?'

'Either way, Rosanna. Just so long as we stop him, I don't care.'

'Dead, then.'

'That's safest, I admit.'

'Dead, yes. I agree. Dead.'

'Selecting your sword, viscount?'

There was a perfume in the air that he recognized. Knowing he was in for a tedious scene, Leos ran a chamois leather along the edge of his blade and turned to pay attention.

'Dany,' he said, pointing at a comely throat with the foil, 'do not overestimate your importance in the order of things.'

The favourite pouted, ringlets shaking.

'Testy this evening, aren't we?'

'I have to go out.'

'With the countess? You are much in her company.'

The sword point did not shake. It was fixed in the air. He was still in perfect condition, the muscles of his shoulders, arms and legs gave him pleasure as he stretched, extending his steel. Von Tuchtenhagen's champion hadn't strained him at all.

'I could kill you, you know. Quite easily.'

'But would that be honourable?'

'Honour is a matter for gentlemen. Between us, it's different.'

Dany laughed, a girlish giggle, and brushed Leos's sword away.

'It certainly is, dearest.'

Leos scabbarded his blade and felt its weight on his hip. With his weapon in place, he felt whole again.

'You killed this morning?'

'Twice.'

'Did it give you an appetite?'

Dany tried to kiss him, but he pushed the favourite away.

'Not now.'

'Temper, temper. You know, Leos, when you are angry I can quite see the quality in you that made poor Clothilde of Averheim swoon so dramatically. I hear the little fool is ruined for all other men after your callous treatment of her. Such a shame. Hot little bitch too, I'd heard. The young men of her city must curse you in their prayers.'

'Dany, you can be extraordinarily tiresome at times.'

'I thought I had a certain degree of license. After all, I am an *intimate* of the family...'

Leos felt the killing chill in his heart.

'You're sailing into choppy waters, Dany. You might well encounter the odd wreck.'

'Wrecks by the name of the Graf von Tuchtenhagen, or the Bassanio Bassarde, or... what were the other names?'

'You know them as well as I do.'

'Not quite as well. No one ever forgets their kills.'

Dany was playing with silk handkerchiefs, running fingers under them, examining the shifting patterns.

'My sister has tired of you, you know,' Leos said, spitefully. 'She has a more important admirer.'

'Bitch,' spat Dany.

Leos gave one of his rare laughs. 'Hurts, doesn't it? Have you met the current paramour? Very distinguished, they say, and highly influential. Between them, the countess and he could decide the fate of the Empire.'

Dany made a fist, crumpling silk.

'Before von Tuchtenhagen and Bassarde, I had to kill others. You are right. I remember the names: Cleric-Captain Voegler of the Order of the Fiery Heart, young von Rohrbach, even a commoner or two, Peder Novak, Karoli Vares...'

Dany tried to counterfeit a lack of fear.

'It's a long list. Perhaps my sister provokes too many insults for her own good. But many of them were quite close to her at one time or another. The ways of her heart are unpredictable.'

The favourite looked away.

'And so, Dany my dear, are the ways of mine.'

Leos took the favourite's shoulders and turned a pretty face around to look into his eyes. Dany's pupils were contracting, a sign of overfondness for weirdroot.

'Aren't my hands strong, Dany dear?'

Leos forced his mouth against Dany's and kissed him. The viscount tasted the favourite's fear.

'Maybe you won't be the favourite much longer?'

Dany broke away and wiped his mouth with his silk, spitting into it. He had been shaking, but now his confidence was coming back.

'I'll never duel with you, Leos,' he said.

Leos smiled. 'And I'll never ask you.'

'After all,' Dany said bitterly, 'now the countess has done with me, it is not as if I lacked for female company?'

The favourite smiled.

'And my girlfriend's name is still von Liebewitz.'

Leos backhanded Dany across the mouth, rouging his lips with blood.

'You should be more careful, family favourite. If it ever entered your head to tell what you know, or what you think you know, you would be dead before the first story crept out of your mouth. Remember that.'

Dany slunk away and flung himself face-down upon the bed. He was not crying out loud.

Leos finished dressing. Johann would be waiting at the coach. Emmanuelle would be late, as usual.

Leos was interested in spending some time alone with the Elector of Sudenland. The man had a mysterious, attractive air.

And he was after something.

V

'Etienne,' said the dancer, Milizia, 'is this appropriate?'

The Bretonnian ambassador cast an eye on the girl's costume. It was tight in the right places and cut away to display her body. It was a gravity-defying miracle.

'Wondrous to behold, my sweet,' he said, 'now leave us alone. We men have business that must be discussed. The landlord will feed you in your dressing room and I shall send for you later.'

Milizia curtseyed, setting herself wobbling like a jelly on a plate and withdrew. De la Rougierre felt his amorous spirits rising again and fingered the waxed ends of his moustaches.

'The lady,' began Dien Ch'ing, 'is most substantial.'

De la Rougierre laughed out loud. The Celestial was a sly one.

'You have no women the like of our Milizia in Far Cathay, I'll bet.'

'No, indeed we do not.'

'More's the pity, eh? Tell me, those sailors' stories about the girls of the East...'

Ch'ing waved his serious anthropological inquiry aside and tapped the papers on the desk.

'This treaty, de la Rougierre. Tonight, I would like to see our guests put their seals to it. It is most important.'

'Of course, of course, but nothing is more important than love, my friend, nothing...'

The Celestial gave a thin smile. 'As you say.'

'But after love, there must be war, eh?'

De la Rougierre thumped his barrel chest. 'The Bretonnians are as renowned for their prowess on the battlefield as in the boudoir, my friend. The foeman trembles when the armies of Charles de la Tete d'Or III are on the march.'

'So I am given to understand. I am a poor stranger in these lands, but even I have heard of the high reputation of the Bretonnians.'

The dwarf clapped his hands like an excited child and lifted his goblet. The Celestial was a fine man, a fine diplomat.

'This treaty will be the start of a great campaign against the Dark Lands, a campaign that will strike at the goblins in their homes. It will be magnificent.'

'Of course,' the Bretonnian agreed, 'with a de la Rougierre in it, it could hardly be anything but magnificent!'

'That is indeed so.'

'I'm glad to hear you agree with me. I'll call for another bottle of this establishment's best Quenelles rosé and we'll drink a toast to our victory over the dark.'

Ch'ing laughed softly, almost under his breath.

For an instant, de la Rougierre felt as if someone were tickling his skeleton with a rocfeather. There were shadows in this room and he could swear that there was something small lurking up in one of the corners, hanging from the ceiling, spying on them with glittering eyes. When he looked again, there was nothing there.

The wine arrived.

'Our guests will be here soon,' de la Rougierre told the landlord. 'Make sure they are conducted up here with no trouble. These are important people.'

The landlord, who was taking more money for this private party than he usually did in any given three month period, was nervously obsequious and assured the Bretonnian that all that could be done would be done or he would know the reason for it and be using a stick on his staff.

The Celestial sipped his wine.

'Wonderful vintage, is it not? The best wines in the world are Bretonnian. And the best wine-drinkers.'

De la Rougierre drained his goblet, then refilled it.

He thought of Big Women.

Getting across the city to the palace had not been easy. Two of the main bridges had been blocked, Emperor Karl-Franz Bridge by the wreckage of a couple of carts and an armed band of Hooks, and Three Toll Bridge by the Knights Templar and the Imperial Militia, who had sealed off each end and were keeping some unfortunate travellers penned between their positions.

In the end, Elsaesser found a lone ferryman and paid him over the odds.

Out in the fog, everything seemed peaceful. But he could see the flickering of distant fires in the East End and hear shouts of anger and pain.

'Bad fog,' said the boatman, 'worse than the coronation year and that was as bad as it's ever been.'

A rowing boat floated by, keel-up.

'Nothing as bad as fog, unless it's torrential rain with thunder and lightning.'

There was a series of splashes. Some people were being thrown off one of the docks.

'Maybe an earthquake would be worse, if we ever got them. Or the Southlands hail where the stones are the size of coaches.'

Everyone was busy tonight: the watch, the Templars, the Hooks, the Fish, the militia, the fire-fighters.

That would make things easy for the Beast if he wanted to venture out.

'Of course, an invasion of hideously altered beastmen would put a bit of a dent in trade and spoil everyone's day.'

To Elsaesser, it was personal now. He felt as if it were just him and the Beast. That wasn't true, of course. There was Captain Kleindeinst and Rosanna.

'And a rain of fire from the skies, called down by a black wizard, would be just *awful.*'

And Baron Johann? He was with them, wasn't he?

'You have to look on the bright side in the ferry business.'

Elsaesser was sure the baron wasn't trying to protect the Beast. That would not make sense. Even if his brother were the killer, the baron would want him stopped, if not necessarily executed.

'Here you are, sir. Have a nice evening.'

He paid the man and ran all the way to the palace. He passed more Knights of the Fiery Heart, marching from the Temple, armour clanking.

Reinforcements. They were talking about taking on the enemy and putting them to the rout, but none of them seemed to know which enemy. After some discussion, they decided they were probably supposed to put down a rebellion in the notoriously slack and untrustworthy palace guard.

The portcullis was down, but Elsaesser had wound up with Baron Johann's imperially-sealed document and that was enough to get him into the palace. None of the men on the gate knew where the baron was, and neither did the steward he bumped into in the courtyard.

Elsaesser had never been inside the palace before and was surprised at how big it was. You could fit his entire town into its walls. Even without the fog drifting through the courtyards, it would be easy to get lost in the place.

He saw a slim young man striding across towards some outbuildings, looking as if he knew where he was going.

'Excuse me, sir,' Elsaesser asked.

The man turned. He wore one of those damned green velvet cloaks that were causing such trouble.

'I beg your pardon,' he said, 'do I know you, officer?'

'No,' he admitted and the courtier sneered, as if Elsaesser were committing a grave offence by talking to someone to whom he had not been introduced.

The officer remembered Professor Brustellin's lectures. This man was typical of the aristocratic cancers the great man had diagnosed, handsome in an unmanly sort of way, with a bred-in-the-bone contempt for anyone without a lineage.

'I'm with the watch,' Elsaesser explained. 'I need to see Baron Johann Mecklenberg.'

'Von Mecklenberg, I think you mean.'

'Yes, of course, von Mecklenberg,' said Elsaesser, impatient. 'Do you know where he is?'

The youth looked amused. 'I'm going to meet him now, at our carriage. Is it really necessary that you disturb him?'

'Oh yes, he'll thank you for conveying me to him. It's to do with the Beast.'

The aristocrat dropped his effete pose and looked serious, a single line appearing between his fine brows.

'Viscount Leos von Liebewitz,' he said, not extending his gloved hand. 'Come on, hurry up.'

They walked through the fog and soon the outlines of a coach were discernible. The baron stood beside it.

'Elsaesser,' he said, 'what are you doing here?'

The viscount stood back, faint in the fog, and Elsaesser wondered why the man was so brittle. There was more than just aristocratic distance in it. He was acting like a jealous girl.

'Captain Kleindeinst sent me. I'm your bodyguard.'

The baron laughed, not unkindly.

'You don't seem the type.'

'Sorry, sir.'

'No, fine, it's a good idea. You can fill me in on your progress...'

Elsaesser knew that would come up and wondered whether he should tell the baron what they had learned about his brother's relationship with the last victim.

'You've met Leos, I see.'

The viscount emerged from the fog, his face a mask.

'Elsaesser and I have been hunting the Beast.'

'The murderer of commoners? I'm surprised at your interest, Johann.'

Elsaesser felt something pass between the baron and the viscount. All these titles confused him and the subtle tensions that went along with them were worse. He was glad he only had to deal with Hooks and Fish, and murderers.

The baron ignored the viscount's implied criticism and turned to talk with Elsaesser. 'Leos is a champion swordsman. He'll be useful in the fog, I think.'

The viscount smiled sheepishly and tried to shake off the compliment.

'Leos, will you throw in with us? Will you join the hunt?'

The man was uncomfortable, torn between two impulses. He wanted not to have anything to do with a nasty common series of killings, but he desperately needed the baron's approval. In the end, he did not have to make a decision, for someone arrived to interrupt the impromptu conference.

'Elsaesser,' said Baron Johann, 'may I present the viscount's sister, the Countess Emmanuelle.'

A lady, wrapped up in transparent gauzes to protect her dress and face against the fog, appeared out of the gloom.

Elsaesser's knees went unaccountably weak.

He was travelling in distinguished company. He wondered what Mrs Bierbichler would say.

Undoubtedly, he would be told that he could die.

* * *

The Beast smelled the fog and crept out of the man-shell, claws extending.
    It tasted the blood in the air and howled for joy. With each night, this
city became more hospitable.
    Tonight would be magnificent...

VI

Their cart rattled through the streets of the East End, drawn by two stolen horses. He stood up, no longer even needing to speak. The crowd was with him, surging behind the cart. In the back, Stieglitz was making torches with efficient skill, using his teeth to compensate for his missing arm. Dipped in pitch, they were then handed to Brustellin and Kloszowski to be lit and, flames growing, to Yefimovich and Ulrike to be thrown.

A torch spun into the air, spinning wooden end over flaming head, and disappeared into the fog. He heard it land and then the soft whump! of the flames spreading.

'Down with the green velvet!' shouted Ulrike, her long hair streaming behind her, her face aglow in the torchlight.

A hundred voices in the crowd echoed her.

This was her moment. She was like Myrmidia, Goddess of War, leading her armies against the Chaos Powers.

Of course, Ulrike, unknowing, was serving those same powers.

Yefimovich could capture a crowd with his words. As he had discovered, there was even a sexual charisma to his fire-breathing. He could pull people in and make them his, convert them to any cause. Tomorrow, he could enlist in the service of the Emperor and turn these people around, making them into ardent supporters of the aristocracy. His slogans came from dozens of mouths and seemed to have been born there.

But he would never have what Ulrike had.

She was truly the Angel of the Revolution. In her, the madness glowed like the fire of the gods. She believed with a passion in the cause and her belief was contagious.

Of course, she was beautiful. Of course, she was young. And, of course, she had suffered mightily during her rise from house-slave to angel. But there was something else, something inside. Some actors had it, too few leaders of men, and all gods.

There was not a man in the street who would not follow Ulrike to the death. Men as disparate as Kloszowski, Brustellin and Stieglitz were desperately, hopelessly in love with her. It was rumoured – incorrectly, as it happened – that she had enslaved electors, courtiers and even the Emperor with her looks.

She sang songs of the revolution and her high, clear voice could be heard above the chorus of the crowd.

She gently tossed a torch through a second-storey window and cheers went up as the flames grew.

The crowd were hailing her even as she set fire to their homes. There was nothing a woman like this could not do.

Yefimovich's inner fires burned. The face Respighi had found for him was not settling well. He would need another before morning. That was an annoying distraction. There were too many important matters to take care of tonight.

'They'll be trembling in their palaces,' said Kloszowski. 'I'll write poems about this night. They'll live when the House of the Second Wilhelm is forgotten.'

The cart stopped. There was a press of bodies in the street.

'What is it?' Yefimovich asked.

'Templars,' said one of the ringleaders, a Fish called Ged. 'Blocking the bridges, trying to keep us on this side.'

Yefimovich grinned. There could not be enough of them.

The fires had been started in the East End, the smallest of the three triangular wedges within the city walls that made up Altdorf. To one side was the wedge with the palace and the Temple and to the other the one with the docks and the University. His plan was to take the docks and swarm through the Street of a Hundred Taverns to link up with the radical students of the Ulli von Tasseninck School. He had anticipated, even counted on, the blockade of the bridge.

'Stieglitz,' he said. 'You're the tactician. We have the weight of numbers. Can we break through?'

The ex-mercenary fingered his stump. He grunted. 'Boats. We'll need boats. And archers.'

'Done,' Yefimovich said. 'Ged, get him what he needs.'

'And you,' asked Kloszowski, 'what will you do?'

'I shall get across and make sure that we can surprise the Templars from the rear. I'll take Ulrike. She can stir up some support on the docks.'

'It's a good plan,' said Brustellin. 'Similar to the tactics of Bloody Beatrice the Monumentally Cruel in her campaign against the Thirteen Rebel Electors.'

Ulrike wasn't hearing them. She was still singing, still exulting in her communion with the crowd. Yefimovich pulled her down and helped her off the wagon. People got out of her way, treating her respectfully. A young man threw himself at her feet and kissed the hem of her dress. She smiled and made of him a radical for life.

Yefimovich's gloves were itching. His inner fires were troublesome tonight.

'I have a boat ready,' he told Ulrike. 'It's disguised. We're meeting friends on the other side.'

Ulrike allowed herself to be led like a child through the cheering multitude. It was slow going, but she did not stop too often to dispense blessings or accept embraces.

Five or six city blocks were burning now and the fires were spreading through the close-packed tenements. There would be plenty of burned meat for Tzeentch.

Finally, Yefimovich got Ulrike to the boat. Respighi had killed its own-ers earlier and had it covered with canvas, moored unobtrusively at a near-derelict jetty. People flowed by, swarming towards the bridges, as he pulled away the covering and helped Ulrike step into the boat. She shouted encouragement at them, but they mainly couldn't hear. Amid the crowds, they were strangely alone.

'Get down low, we don't want you to be seen.'

She crouched, looking up at him with adoration. He took a satisfaction in that.

'Here,' he said, 'roll this up and use it as a cushion.'

She took the cloak. 'It's green velvet,' she said.

'Come the revolution, we'll all wear green velvet.'

She laughed. 'Come the revolution...'

He began to row. His gloves chafed as he worked the oars. He would have preferred to have someone else do this, but Respighi was busy at the Matthias II.

The oars slapped water and the fog was all around them. Beyond Ulrike, Yefimovich could still see the glow of the fires in the East End.

'Are we there yet?' Ulrike asked.

'Past the half-way mark.'

They were well away from any of the bridges. He could not see the fog lanterns on either bank.

This was about right.

He upped oars.

'What is it?'

Yefimovich took the hook from under his seat.

'The Beast, Ulrike...'

'What? Where?'

He stood up. 'The Beast is about to kill you.'

He struck. Blood spurted and his shoulder felt wrenched.

The look of surprise stayed in her eyes, even with the hook sunk into her forehead.

He pulled the weapon free and began his Beast-work.

VII

The Luitpoldstrasse Station was a bedlam. When Harald had been there in the afternoon, just after his fight with Joost Rademakers, there had been a loose crowd of annoyed people outside, hurling curses and pebbles at the front of the building. Now there was a tight crowd of furious people and they were hurling more than words and small stones. The front windows had been smashed out and flaming torches were being lobbed into the station, lying on the floor to be stamped out by one of the officers of the watch. Harald wished he had not taken the trouble to push through the crowd to get into the place, since the crowd seemed to have closed behind him like a trap. And, to cap his carelessness, he had brought the scryer with him and needlessly subjected her to danger. This was what the Second Siege of Praag must have been like.

'Damn it,' said Thommy Haldestaake, an old skull thumping copper, 'I'm going to break out the crossbows. That'll dispel the bastards.'

Thommy looked at Dickon, who was sitting glumly in the corner, having evidently given up on the whole thing. He had a steaming pot of tea on his table and was occasionally gulping down cups of the stuff.

The captain didn't stamp on Thommy's suggestion and so the officer picked the station keyring off Dickon's desk and walked towards the armoury, sorting out the keys to the double lock.

'No,' said Harald.

Thommy stopped and turned round to outstare him.

Harald stood up and rubbed his forehead, where he still wore one of the bruises Rademakers had given him, and let his hand fall to rest on the hilt of his Magnin knife.

When he was first appointed to the watch, he had been partnered with Thommy. The old officer had shown him all the ways that a cunning copper could augment his salary, by accepting the occasional crown or two and turning his back on the odd crime, or by insisting on a modest cut of the profits of any pimps, dicers, weirdroot vendors or pickpockets who wanted to stay in business on his beat. Harald had gone straight to Captain Gebhardt, Dickon's predecessor, and set out his evidence against the bent watchman, and been surprised when Gebhardt simply turned him out of the office.

Thommy explained that he had forgotten to mention that, in addition to making a profit, it was traditional for a watchman to tithe a portion of his personal earnings and turn them over to the captain. Then Thommy had tried to beat Harald to a bloody pulp.

That had been a long time ago and Thommy had been younger. But it had been an even match and neither had emerged the clear victor. Thommy's cheekbones were still asymmetrical and Harald still had the trace of a knife-slash across his hip.

Thommy put the first key in the lock and turned it. The works creaked. 'Thommy, I said no.'

The old copper turned, growling, and came at him like a wrestler.

This time it would be decisive. But Harald didn't have time for a head-to-head. So it would also have to be quick.

Harald pulled out his Magnin, tossed it in the air, caught it by the blade and hurled it.

He was merciful and the hilt slammed into Thommy's skull, stopping him in his charge. He blundered forwards, but was already senseless. Harald picked up his knife. Thommy was in an instant deep sleep, stretched out on the rough wooden floor.

Dickon didn't complain. His tidy world of regular bribes and comfortable corruption was falling down around his helmet. He swallowed some tea.

A torch came through the window and Harald caught it in the air, returning it to the foggy night with a powerful throw.

He and Rosanna had come back to have Dickon put the word out that Wolf von Mecklenberg was wanted for questioning. But the captain was no longer able to take care of that simple job, or even interested in Harald's case. The Beast was taking a very low priority this evening.

'Dickon,' Harald said, 'this place will catch fire eventually. Get your men out.'

Dickon looked up, but didn't seem to know where he was.

Harald stood over him and slapped his face with his open hand. The captain mumbled.

Rosanna stood by him. She picked up Dickon's half-full mug and sniffed the tea sloshing in it.

'Weirdjuice,' she said.

Harald tipped Dickon's head back and looked into his eyes. The captain wasn't seeing anything real.

'You dolt,' he said, with feeling. Dickon smiled, drooling a little.

There was a crash and a wagonwheel smashed through the window, sweeping in most of the casement. There were burning rags tied to it. The whole thing had been soaked in lamp-oil.

Thommy moaned and tried to get up.

The keyring was dangling from the armoury door. Harald got it and tossed it to Rosanna.

'Find someone half-decent and have him open up the cells. There'll only be whores, drunks and vagrants down there. Get the prisoners out and tell any watchmen you find to leave as well.'

The scryer went without question.

Harald looked at Thommy and Dickon. It was up to him to make sure that neither of these deadweights got burned to death in a fire.

He was tempted to leave them, but resisted.

The fire was spreading from the burning wheel. Dickon's potted plants were aflame and the blaze was spreading to a cabinet stuffed with arrest scrolls. The Luitpoldstrasse Station was a lost ship and it was up to Harald to get everyone evacuated.

Outside, people were shouting, 'Death to the watch!'

Great.

Harald picked up Thommy in a fireman's hold. The old officer accepted too many bribes in pies and cream, and Harald's knees buckled. But he stayed upright.

'Death to the Emperor!'

In the narrow passage outside, there were drunks and watchmen scrapping with each other and trying to get out of the front doors. They were emerging into a hail of cobblestones and bits of wood.

A lieutenant of the Imperial Militia was trying to keep order, rattling off tactical instructions which everyone was ignoring.

'Down with green velvet!'

Two coppers were deliberately stripping their tabards and insignia, arguing over a civilian's cloak. That was one way to resign from the watch.

'Death to Sigmar!'

Harald butted his way through and dumped Thommy on the steps of the station, rolling him towards the crowd. A pebble stung against his hand and he heard the crowd call for his blood.

'Death... Death... Death!'

The militiaman came out of the station and his shiny breastplate made a fine target. Stones put dents in it and the lieutenant staggered. Harald pulled him out of the way and tossed him into the crowd.

It was like a game. Once you were part of the crowd, you weren't the enemy any more. Harald heard the lieutenant shouting, 'Death to the watch!' with the worst of them.

He fought against the thinning stream of watchmen and petty criminals, and got back into the station. Almost everyone else was out. There were fires everywhere now, steadily growing. A wall collapsed and a ground-cloud of dust swept around his shins.

'Death to everyone!'

Rosanna came up from the jail area. 'All the cells are empty now,' she said.

'Get out,' he said. 'I'll find Dickon and follow you. We're closing down this station. It was a shithole anyway...'

Dickon staggered into the passage. One sleeve was on fire, but he couldn't make his hand work to smother it. He rubbed against a wall but the flames persisted.

Harald ripped the captain's jacket off and threw it away. Dickon looked offended.

'Good coat, that,' he said. 'Briechs Brothers of Schwarzwasser-strasse.'
Like a child, Dickon allowed himself to be led out of the station.

As the three of them came out of the station, the roof fell in and a
cloud of hot air, smoke, dust and cinders exploded through the doors
behind them, pushing them down the stairs.

The crowd was retreating now. A few watchmen were down in the
street, being thoroughly kicked. Harald saw one of the officers who had
been struggling into civilian gear standing shoulder to shoulder with the
mob, putting the boot in to his former sergeant.

'Death to the tyrants!'

The whole quarter was in flames.

He looked around for Rosanna and saw her struggling. Two militiamen and a Fish wearing the insignia of the Revolutionist Movement were
fighting over her like dogs arguing over a scrap of meat.

They all wanted death for someone-or-other, he had gathered that much.

Harald thumped one militiaman and pulled Rosanna out of the melée.
The revolutionary raised a club, but caught the look in Harald's eyes
and backed off.

'Filthy Harald,' he muttered, panic growing, 'Filthy Harald is back!'

The revolutionist – whom Harald could not remember ever having
met – turned and ran, spreading the news.

Harald felt a kind of exhilaration in the man's instinctive fear. The
urge to shout was contagious.

The mob was breaking and retreating. 'I'm back,' he shouted at them.
'Filthy Harald is back!'

The fog was still thick, but the fires made it easier to see things. The
crowd was swarming away from the burning station, flowing like a tide
of molten lead, streaming into side-streets.

There were cloaks and coats underfoot. People had ventured out wrapped
up for the fog and found themselves next to the bonfires. There would be
chills and fevers when the blazes died.

Rosanna was saying something. 'There isn't one Beast... they're all
Beasts...'

The rioting had passed on to some new battlefield. It would hit the
Street of a Hundred Taverns in force next. Later, it would run and either
sweep across the river to the palace or head north towards the University. Maybe it would split in two. Maybe it was not that localized. It
could be happening like this all over the city.

Luitpoldstrasse was empty now and a terrible quiet fell. Harald heard
the crackle of burning buildings and the low groaning of people in pain.
There was blood in his mouth. He spat it out.

Thommy was lying face down and bloodied. He might have been alive.
Dickon was sitting cross-legged in the street, trying on a succession of
cast-off garments to replace his Briechs Brothers coat. He was a broken
man, which at least saved Harald the bother of breaking him.

The fog was agitated, still swirling to fill in the spaces so recently
occupied by the mob.

He turned to Rosanna.

She was standing stiff, arms by her sides, as if fighting a sudden paralysis. The vein in her forehead was pulsing and her eyes were wide.

He reached out to shake her, but stopped himself before he touched her. He didn't want to break her contact, whatever it was.

'What can you see?' he asked.

Her lips moved and she croaked a word. He couldn't understand. 'What is it?'

Despite the fires, it was a cold night. Harald felt a chill.

Rosanna croaked again, clearer this time.

'Near,' she said, 'near.'

VIII

There had been some rowdiness out on the street, but nothing the Templars couldn't handle. He had charged Cleric-Captain Hoven with keeping order and knew he could depend on the man to be a true servant of Sigmar.

As his coach trundled through the checkpoints, Mikael Hasselstein was deeply troubled.

He had not heard from Yelle all day. His nerves were drawn as tight as bowstrings.

At the Matthias II, the green velvet carpet was laid down in the street. There were footmen with torches to light the way through the fog to the inn.

Hasselstein hurried across the pavement and through the doors. The Matthias II was empty of its usual patrons, being staffed only by footmen and waiters in the livery of the Bretonnian ambassador. It had been redecorated in the colours of Bretonnia for the occasion and a buffet was laid out against one wall.

'Lector,' said de la Rougierre, bowing low, 'welcome...'

Hasselstein was polite to the silly little dwarf and presented his ring of office to be kissed.

'You are the first of my guests. The company tonight will be most distinguished. Can I interest you in a Bretonnian vintage?'

'No, I think not... well, maybe, yes.'

The ambassador grinned broadly and snapped his stubby fingers. A servant girl in a tight bodice decanted a full goblet of sparkling Vin de Couronne.

The drink might relax him a little.

The girl flounced off and Hasselstein noticed just how close the cut of her uniform was. He suspected that the buffoon dwarf had had a hand in the design of the outfits worn by his female servants.

Leos von Liebewitz might be the best duellist in the Empire, but Etienne de la Rougierre could lay claim, in another sense, to being the most prominent swordsman.

He thought of his mistress and her moods. She was as unpredictable as an Altdorf fog and as dangerously deep. Tonight, he must confirm his position with Yelle, or risk madness.

Of course, de la Rougierre must have some diplomatic scheme or other to propose, and he should pay attention to that as well.

The next to arrive was the future Emperor Luitpold, attended by two huge guardsmen in full armour.

'Rough night,' he said. 'Half the city is on fire.'

The young man was still a child in many ways and prone to exaggeration.

'Really, highness?' Hasselstein said, politely. 'You surprise me.'

'It's the fog,' the young man said. 'It always makes people funny in the head.'

'The fog, yes.'

He was thinking of Yelle, of her lips, her eyes, the delicate softness of her...

'Fog.'

The serving girl gave the Prince a drink and he thanked her. She nearly swooned, obviously smitten with the young man, for his stature as future Emperor if not for his ordinary good looks. For his part, Luitpold was equally obviously staggered by her, especially when she leaned forward to fill his goblet. The palace maids certainly didn't look like that.

'You know,' the heir to the Empire said, 'I could have sworn I saw something in the corner of the room... something small, with bright eyes...'

De la Rougierre was offended. 'Highness, that is impossible. I had all the rats caught and killed this afternoon...'

...and they would be gracing the table this evening, if Hasselstein's prejudices about Bretonnian cuisine were to be confirmed.

'...I have ensured that this establishment is fit for the most high-born and courtly of guests...'

The dwarf winked, his grin taking on a lascivious tone.

'...if, however, graced with a manner of entertainment one would not find at the stuffier court sort of affair.'

De la Rougierre was practically dancing a jig. He would be more fitted to the position of jester than ambassador. It really was time the Emperor protested to King Charles about the little idiot.

'I've secured the services of a variety of entertainers the like of whom one rarely sees. They appeal, I hope, to the more *sophisticated* tastes, to the more *liberated* palate...'

Hasselstein thought he knew what the dwarf meant and was a little annoyed. He had Yelle to think of and did not want to be distracted by some cheap Bretonnian peepshow.

Another carriage arrived outside, and Hals and Hergard von Tasseninck were admitted. The Grand Prince had a handkerchief clapped to his forehead and was bleeding into it.

'Someone threw a rock at father,' said Hergard.

Hasselstein's goblet was empty and he decided he would like a refill. This had the makings of a very tiresome evening.

'Near...'

Rosanna felt like a tiny fish in the presence of a whale. The creature they hunted was nearby and hungry.

The contact had come out of nowhere and latched onto her brain. She wondered if the Beast had been among the crowd in Luitpoldstrasse. She could have looked into the murderer's eyes and only now be feeling the effects.

The presence was overwhelming, freezing her to the spot. Her bowels wanted to let go, but she fought to control her body.

Kleindeinst stood back, concerned.

There was violence around him too. He had killed a man this afternoon and she couldn't look at him without feeling it. Over and over in her head, Joost Rademakers's throat crunched under his fist.

Then, she was free.

Gasping, she said, 'He's near. Very near...'

'Where?'

She tried to scry a direction, turning in a circle.

'That way,' she pointed. It was the direction the crowd had taken.

'Towards the Street of a Hundred Taverns?'

'Yes.'

She imagined the Beast loping along among the crowds, unseen by them, inflamed by their savagery. He would have had a taste of blood by now.

'Captain Kleindeinst,' she said.

'Yes?'

She remembered the dark heart of the thing that had touched her mind. It had been like a concentrated cloud of blackness, with spears of silver lightning inside it.

'The Beast is getting ready to kill again.'

IX

Johann was able to arrive without too much fuss, because the Countess Emmanuelle had to make a grand entrance before any of her escorts. She had stepped out of the carriage as if expecting a cheering crowd and been disconcerted by the surly few standing by the inn, growling evilly.

Descending to the green velvet carpet, Johann could feel the hostility radiating at him. A man with a Fish insignia hawked a lump of phlegm onto the carpet and stalked away, disgusted.

Leos half-drew his sword, but thought better of it. If even the Deadly Blade was thinking twice, then something must be seriously wrong.

Elsaesser fussed nervously and tried to hurry them across the pavement. There were shouts off in the distance and they had passed the fire-fighters several times, dashing from one disaster to another.

Inside, Johann accepted de la Rougierre's greetings and took the measure of the company.

Mikael Hasselstein was as near drunk as Johann had ever seen him. He lurched towards them when they came in, but held back. Hals von Tasseninck was showing off a bandage, surrounded by serving girls, and his son was sulking about something. Dien Ch'ing, the Celestial, was sitting calmly, picking at a plateful of food. Marquess Sidonie dropped her glass when Leos walked in and looked around for a weapon, but was unable to find anything.

'Uncle Johann,' said Luitpold, 'how nice to see you.'

Johann bowed a little.

'And you too, Leos, of course.'

The viscount clicked his heels.

'I was afraid it was going to be a dull evening,' the future Emperor said, too loudly, 'but now I see we have a fine crew here tonight.'

Luitpold had had a little to drink and he wasn't used to it. Johann knew that he was honour-bound to look out for the heir. That gave him something else to worry about.

A few surprise guests showed up: Oleg Paradjanov, the Kislevite military attaché; Snorri Svedenborg, one of the legates from Norsca; Mornan Tybalt, gloomily muttering about the sense of his thumb tax bill; and Baron Stefan Todbringer, son and heir to the Graf Boris of Middenheim. That was two more major foreign powers, an important minister of the court and another electoral seat.

He exchanged conventional pleasantries with the dignitaries and tried to watch everyone.

Elsaesser was standing by the door, nibbling on a cold chicken leg, stranded somewhere between servant and guest. Kleindeinst had sent the officer to watch over Johann, but as a spy or a guard he was not sure. The sharp young copper might be useful.

Hasselstein was in a corner with the countess, talking intently, illustrating his points with firm gestures. She looked bored. That would make a change, a man boring Emmanuelle von Liebewitz. At another time, Johann might have derived some amusement from the reversal. But not just now. Where was Wolf? And the Beast?

He had begun to suspect everyone. Most of the people in the room, except obviously Luitpold, were highly likely candidates.

He remembered the scrap of green velvet he had found in the alley adjacent to this place. He was almost tempted to go through all the cloaks in the hall and look for a torn patch. But nothing was ever that easy. Except in bad melodramas.

'Baron Johann,' said the Marquess Sidonie, 'might I speak with you? I'm getting up a petition to present to the Emperor and I was wondering whether you would consider lending your seal to it. As an elector, you have a lot of influence.'

Johann asked the thin-nosed woman what her petition was against.

She sniffed and said, 'Duelling, elector. It should be banned.'

There was a clapping sound and Johann turned to face the small stage at one end of the room. De la Rougierre was standing up, laughing.

'Honoured guests,' he said, raising a goblet, 'welcome to this magnificent affair. I trust that you've all been properly fed and watered...'

Snorri, who had drunk a quite considerable amount, roared his approval.

'That is what I like to hear. Bretonnian hospitality is, as you know, legendary.'

'That's true,' muttered Hasselstein, who had turned away from the countess, 'in the sense that you can't prove it ever existed.'

The dwarf gave the Lector a nasty look and continued: 'I have selected only the best entertainment for your pleasure tonight. Permit me to introduce you to a lady whose talents are substantial...'

The lights dimmed and the curtains parted. A flautist began to play a familiar old tune.

A dancer stepped out onto the stage, but Johann was more interested in the faces of the guests.

Looking at them, as they gazed with expressions ranging from the rapt to the disgusted, he wondered.

Which, if any...?

There was fighting throughout the docklands.

Wolf couldn't understand what the fuss was about and couldn't find anyone sane enough to tell him.

He tried to keep out of the way, although he could feel his blood rising. His wet clothes had dried on him like a second skin.

He smelled blood and fire, and gripped his hook as if it were a part of him.

The Hooks and the Fish had formed a temporary, unprecedented alliance and were throwing people off one of the docks. A large crowd cheered with each splash.

Wolf saw that the victims were all in uniform or armour. Templars, militiamen, palace guards, officers of the watch.

'Death to Karl-Franz!' shouted a rabble-rouser.

The men in armour were struggling in the water, trying to cut the leather ties and let it fall off their bodies before it dragged them down. They were thrashing up a white foam.

He couldn't understand it at all. Before the fog blew up, the city had been normal. Now everyone was blood crazy.

A bully laid hands on him and he instinctively lashed out, not with a fist like a man but curved fingers like an animal.

'We've got one that scratches here, lads,' said the bully.

Wolf concentrated hard and made a fist. He broke the man's nose and stuck an elbow in his chest. The man dropped to his knees, hands clasped over his bleeding face.

Wolf ran, hoping to be well away before any of the bully's friends rallied round and decided he could do with another cold bath.

He had his hook in his hand now and would be ready for any further trouble.

He did not know the way to the Wayfarer's Rest and kept looking for an inn or a building he recognized so he could get his bearings.

He collided with a group of young men and knew he was bound for the river. He held up his hook and tensed for a struggle.

But it never came.

'It's von Mecklenberg,' a familiar voice said. 'Wolf.'

Otho Waernicke loomed out of the fog and embraced him. The party were all Leaguers.

'We thought you were done for, for sure. With what happened to Trudi, we were certain the Beast had got you.'

Trudi's name was like an arrow sinking in up to the feathers.

'Trudi? The Beast?'

Otho didn't have time, or the desire, to explain.

'The wine-drinking contest is off,' the student leader said. 'Three hundred years of tradition scuppered. It's terrible.'

'We're fighting for the Emperor,' a student declared. 'The call has gone out to all the Leagues. The forces of revolution are inside the walls and we must all stand up or fall into perdition.'

It was a fine speech and would have been finer if the deliverer hadn't slurred almost all his words, been supported by two of his fellows and breathed out Estalian sherry in its gaseous form.

'Where's Trudi?' Wolf asked Otho.

The student leader couldn't conceal anything. 'Dead, Wolf. It was the Beast. Last night...'

Wolf dropped to all fours and howled. The yell of his grief rose in his throat and escaped into the night, reverberating throughout the quarter.

Otho and the Leaguers stood back, amazed. The patriot was dumbstruck.

Wolf stood on his hind legs and tore at himself. His hook ripped his shirt and ploughed through his chest hair. He didn't feel the new pain, for his heart had already been pierced.

He turned from his friends and ran, more animal than man. He ran through fog and fire, his mind racing ahead of itself, trying not to believe what he knew must be true.

He was the monster. He had always been the monster. Even before Cicatrice.

In his mouth, his shifting teeth hurt.

X

As Milizia danced, de la Rougierre's mouth filled with spittle. The big woman was monumental, magnificent, magisterial. For her, he would usurp a kingdom, slaughter a brother, betray his honour.

And tonight he would have her all to himself, to do with as he saw fit.

Rosanna led him. His knife out, he followed her.

'This way, this way, this way,' she muttered, over and over.

She was dowsing for the Beast.

They were in the ladder of streets running parallel to the Street of a Hundred Taverns, zig-zagging closer to the main thoroughfare.

Occasionally, they passed people running one way or another, but a look at Harald's knife convinced them to keep going and leave the odd pair alone. An animal had screamed a few moments ago, but it was silent – dead? – now.

He could feel it too, now. He had never thought of himself as having a gift, but the turmoil in his stomach must mean something. The Beast was near.

Harald gripped the hilt of his Magnin and saw the fires gleam in the polished surfaces of the blade.

His guts gnawed at themselves.

When they caught the Beast, the murderer would live only long enough to confess before witnesses. Then, it would be ended. Harald's justice was neater and more final than that of the courts. No cells, no lawyers, no ropes. Just a quick, clean thrust.

Maybe then he would be able to eat again.

At the end of the street, someone stood, looking up into the sky, panting as he tried to peer through the fog.

Harald's stomach went quiet.

'Be careful,' he told the scryer.

She was still muttering, still leading him.

The man in the fog let out a cry that could not have come from a human throat.

Rosanna stopped and Harald stepped in front of her.

He had taken no chances with his weapon. When commissioning his knife, he had instructed Magnin to stir a little silver into the steel. Nothing, living or dead, would survive its sharp kiss.

The thing that had howled hunched over, its arms touching the cobbles like forelegs. A claw-thing was scraped on the stone.

It advanced, more like an animal than a human being.

Harald held up his knife for a throw...

They could see its yellow and red eyes, glowing in its dark face.

Rosanna touched his arm, holding him back.

'No,' she said, 'don't kill it yet. We have to be sure.'

Dead would have been sure enough for Harald, but the scryer had been right so far.

A fire flared up to the left of them, windows exploding from a house, and light spilled into the street.

The thing's face was human, and recognizable from Rosanna's sketch.

'Wolf,' she said, 'give yourself up.'

The Elector of Sudenland's brother crouched, tensed to leap. Harald's knife went up and his eye fixed on the madman's exposed, bloody chest. One flick and the blade would be through his heart.

'Wolf,' Rosanna said, soothing...

Von Mecklenberg stood up. His claw was nothing but a docker's hook. He was confused.

Harald knew Rosanna was doing something.

'Usually, I pick up,' she whispered, 'but sometimes I can send...'

Wolf looked panicked. He was shivering. He might have been a monster, but now he was just a frightened young man.

'What...'

'I'm sending him Trudi's death.'

Wolf howled again.

Emmanuelle von Liebewitz, Countess-Elector of Nuln, was bored, and boredom made her angry.

She had not ventured out on this hell of a night to watch some cow-like creature shake her udders all over a stage.

It was most disappointing after the magnificence of the von Tasseninck ball. Most disappointing.

And Mikael was being tedious beyond words. Lector of Sigmar or not, he would have to join Dany and the others in the doghouse.

Of course, she could always pass him on to Leos. She would like that, even if Mikael would be disgusted.

No, with this one, that would be too big a risk.

'Yelle,' he whispered to her, loudly. 'Yelle, answer me...'

She pretended to be interested in the show.

Yes, Mikael was on the Out List.

Wolf clapped his hands over his ears – his hook scraping his scalp – but could not shut out the pictures in his head.

It was the red-headed girl. She was doing it.

The tall, wide-shouldered man's knife shone.

He sensed, *saw*, Trudi dying. In his mind, he was murderer *and* victim. It was too much to bear.

Trudi!

He choked back a howl. He was a man, not an animal.

The blood gushed and the flesh tore. It was extended, painful and played over and over again. It was slow and fast at the same time, like a weirdroot rush.

With an effort, he broke away from the girl and fled.

He could hear them coming after him, but he ran on strong, swift legs. He thought he could outdistance the pursuers.

He was quarry and huntsman in one.

Luitpold had never seen anything like Milizia. He did not believe, even in his most secret dreams, that there were actually women like her.

In the palace libraries, there were various locked volumes devoted to the arts of amorousness, and he had been a skilled lockpick since his childhood. He had always assumed that the illustrations were exaggerated. Certainly, none of the women he had had contact with could have hoped to fill out their fantastic frames. Not even the Countess Emmanuelle, who had briefly taken a slightly creepy interest in him – because of what he would be rather than who he was. But Milizia was a woodcut come to life. And, with each scarf, more of her was disclosed.

Luitpold's mouth had gone dry.

He crossed his legs to prevent embarrassment.

When he was Emperor, he thought, he could have anything he wanted. He tried to keep a straight face.

A servant girl, almost as generously proportioned as Milizia, brought him some more wine and he smiled at her like an idiot.

A duel to the death in the morning and now Milizia. In his secret diary, he would mark this down as a Five Star Day.

Ulrike was heavier dead than she had been alive. Luckily, he had had the cloak to wrap her in.

He walked slowly through the crowds, as if shattered by the shock, the corpse in his hands. He let her hair trail on the ground and had exposed her pale face, with the red hole in the forehead, to the air.

As the people realized who it was he held, they fell silent. One or two devout atheists made the sign of Sigmar or some other god. Hats came off heads and were held to breasts. More than one revolutionist fell into a fit of sobbing.

At the entrance to the Street of Many Taverns, just across the way from the Old Emperor Bridge, he ran into Prince Kloszowski's brigade of student insurrectionists. They had just successfully broken through the positions of the Imperial Militia and were enthusiastically tossing soldiers into the river.

Kloszowski saw Ulrike's face and was stopped dead.

'I shall commit suicide,' he said, with feeling.

Yefimovich held the corpse up, so everyone could see who it was.

'No,' Kloszowski shouted, changing his mind, 'that would be too easy. I shall become a celibate and dedicate myself forever to the memory of the Angel of the Revolution!'

Yefimovich laid her down and opened the cloak to disclose the extent of the mutilation. There were gasps of horror.

'No,' said the Prince, 'that too is mere cowardice. I shall write an epic poem about her life. Through me, Ulrike shall live forever.'

'What happened,' asked Brustellin, 'for Sigmar's sake, Yefimovich, what happened?'

'It was the Beast,' he replied. 'He struck her down.'

The crowd hissed. 'The Beast, the Beast, the Beast!' Yefimovich could feel the emotions running through the mass of people, grief, horror, anger, hatred.

'Death to the Beast!' someone shouted.

'Yes,' cried Yefimovich, 'death to the Beast!'

He snatched at the bloody green velvet and held it up.

'I didn't see his face,' he said, 'but he wore this!'

Everyone knew what that meant.

The mob would comb the city for aristocrats, courtiers, palace servants, diplomats. Even anyone who wore green. Then, there would be a glorious bloodbath. A revolution.

'Death to the green velvet,' he shouted.

...and tomorrow, when the Emperor's people woke up, there would be reprisals. The city would be ruined by the upheaval, the great made low and the meagre raised on high.

'Death to the green velvet, death to the Beast!'

They lifted him up, taking up and amplifying his shouts. He heard the word 'death' over and over, coming as one voice from the mob's thousand mouths.

The crowd walked over Ulrike and marched up the Street of a Hundred Taverns.

Yefimovich offered up this, his concrete prayer to Tzeentch, the Changer of Ways, and knew that the Chaos Power was pleased with him.

XI

Milizia threw in every move she knew and let the music ripple through her. She might be big, but she had a lot of muscle control. She knew exactly what she was doing with her body.

Etienne was a conquest already, so she let him alone, targeting others.

As usual, stepping out into the light, she immediately picked the prospects. Young men were best, especially if they were quiet, withdrawn, a little embarrassed. Those were the ones who turned to fire most rapidly, who reached most easily into their pouches and came up with the coin.

This afternoon, the dwarf had given her quite a workout. She wondered if she was up to another session, with a more normally-sized lover. In the end, it was worthwhile. Each pfennig got her nearer to escaping from Gropius and the Flamingo Club.

There were two good prospects.

First, there was the young man sitting near the stage, barely restraining himself. She found that the music often took her near him and she took care to lean over and make her shoulders work hard. She let a scarf drip away from her big ridiculous tits and stroked herself. That always gave the customers a charge, the fools.

The Number Two possibility was a little older and a lot quieter. Sitting back a way, his face was in darkness, but she got the impression of a softly handsome man. He was feigning total lack of interest, but she could see through that. He was so elaborately not looking at her, that she knew his interest was keen.

The Front Seat Boy would be easier, but perhaps Number Two would be more rewarding. Once he was started, he might be a real swordsman.

This was a strange commission, she thought. The Bretonnian dwarf and his Celestial friend were up to something. Everybody in this room wanted something and was working hard to get it. She was no different.

She climbed the strong curtains and scissored her legs in the air. The big Norseman yelled his approval and the beautiful woman sitting in front of him looking angrier and angrier glanced death at her.

She went back to the Front Seat Boy and gave him some more interesting views. She unpeeled a scarf from around her middle, allowing the paste gem in her belly-button to catch the light, and gently flicked out with it, brushing the boy's nose. He was startled, but laughed.

Kneeling down, she looped the scarf around the boy's neck and worked away. His eyes were firmly fixed on her chest, and she noticed that he wore more jewelry than most ladies of the court. His face was familiar, but she did not know who he was.

Two men in armour were marching towards them, seriously intent on protecting their charge from strangulation.

She took back her scarf and stood up, working her hips from side to side.

Suddenly, she knew where she had seen a face like that before. In profile, it was somewhere very close to her heart. On one face of the Karl-Franz crown.

That put the Front Seat Boy out of her dicing league. She was ambitious, but she knew her limitations.

The future Emperor was disappointed, but his metal covered bodyguards obviously felt better.

Maybe in a few years, she thought, he would give the household halberdiers the slip and search her out. Even Emperors are men, in the end.

The flautist was in a frenzy now. Milizia had heard he was half-elf, or something. She moved faster, loosening the remaining scarves.

Her chest was tired of jiggling and she had an ache in one ankle. But she danced on.

Etienne was clapping in time to the music and the Norseman was singing along. At least half the audience was appreciative.

She wondered about the Celestial. Miele at the Flamingo had been with a Cathayan once and claimed it was a fantastic experience. He had supposedly been the master of some mystic art or other and it turned out to have applications beyond the obvious.

No, the Celestial was too wrapped up in his own schemes even to pay attention.

That left Number Two.

She vaulted off the stage, almost cartwheeling, and strode towards the Shy Swordsman.

He would be hard to draw out, but she had never failed yet.

'Milizia,' Miele had said, 'you could seduce the statue of Sigmar outside the Temple.'

She poked out her tongue and licked her lips.

Number Two shrank back into the darkness.

Gently, gently...

She had worked up a sweat and it was rolling like oil down her body.

It would be a struggle, but she would dance on...

Wolf ran, trying to escape, trying to escape the witch and the knifeman, but also to escape from the thing inside him.

Trudi was dead. And the witch had shown him killing her.

He was on the Street of a Hundred Taverns. A mob was surging down it, calling for blood.

He was overwhelmed by the smell of fear, of anger.

He was pushed against the wall of Bruno's Brewhouse by the press of people. His chest hurt where he had cut himself.

He tried to struggle free and heard a scream, sharp and pained, close by his head.

He realized he had dragged his hook up through a man's back.

He tried to apologise, but could only gabble. He was practically sobbing.

His hook came free and the man staggered off, blood flowing, apparently without noticing his wound.

There was a green velvet carpet down by the Matthias II. The mob snatched it up and it was torn instantly to shreds.

'Death to the green velvet.'

Wolf didn't understand.

He saw Yefimovich, the agitator, among the crowds, his arms waving.

He staggered into the alley between the two inns, making his way towards the sound of flowing water.

He was free of the crush.

His hand went through an open window and, on an impulse, he pulled himself through into the darkness.

There was darkness outside, but it was the dark in himself that made him terrified.

De la Rougierre watched Milizia trying hard with young von Liebewitz and felt sorry for the silly girl. There was no way she could know she was wasting her time on him.

Still, this was proving to be a most interesting and rewarding evening.

'Out of our way,' Harald said, 'let us through.'

Rosanna supposed there were very few men in the Empire who could make themselves be listened to in a situation like this.

The Street of a Hundred Taverns was a battleground again, but on a larger scale than before. The Hooks and the Fish were fighting side by side, following Yefimovich's revolutionaries. And the League of Karl-Franz was pitching in to back up the Knights Templar, the palace guard and what little was left of the watch.

She realized that more people were being killed within her sight at this very moment than the Beast had managed throughout his rampage.

Captain Kleindeinst shouldered his way through.

Wolf still left a trail and she could still fix on it.

The poor creature was mad with fear. This was not the predator she had imagined.

They were very near where this had all started for her, the alley where they had found Margarethe Ruttmann.

Helmut Elsaesser couldn't be less interested in Milizia. Even the Countess Emmanuelle didn't hold much attraction for him this evening.

It was in the air, like ozone. A kind of excitement that was terrible and wonderful at the same time.

The music gave him a headache.

Inside, he felt feverish, but his face and hands were cold, almost shivering.

Near the door, he could hear something of what was going on outside. A lot of people were shouting and there was great destruction.

He should do something. But he was under orders to stay with the Baron Johann.

Very well. He would follow the example of brave Sigmar and hold his position to the last.

XII

Professor Brustellin's heart was broken and so he had thrown himself into the conflict, determined to end his life and lie next to his beloved Ulrike. Without an Angel, the Revolution was doomed, but at least it could die heroically, setting an example. The flame he had lit would burn steadily for a long time. And the fuse would get steadily shorter. The Empire would explode in the end. It was a historical inevitability. Nothing ever stays the same.

He had a hook in his hand and was fighting with the watch. He saw the face of Professor Scheydt, who had had him flogged and expelled, in every watchman he dragged down and ripped.

He recognized some of his former students, fighting on both sides. The old faithful inkies were with the revolution, and the decadent League of Karl-Franz fought for the standard of the oppressors.

He never felt the swordthrust that killed him.

It was accidental, the Hook who struck the fatal blow being unused to the weapon he had taken from a fallen Templar. The man knew what he had done, but never told his comrades, simply taking to drink whenever the names of the martyr heroes of the revolution were recited.

Scythed through the neck and trampled underfoot, Brustellin left behind a book that would inspire revolutions, in the Empire and in distant lands, for centuries after his death.

Of course, that was little comfort to him.

What is this fool woman doing?

Leos von Liebewitz was outraged. If he was being insulted, then the dwarf would pay for it.

The ridiculous woman continued to flaunt herself.

Leos was disgusted.

Harald found the open window.

'He went through here?'

The scryer told him he was right.

He stabbed into the darkness, then pulled himself through. His shoulders scraped.

He flicked his tinderbox and found himself in a storeroom.

'He's not here. Come in.'

Rosanna squeezed and he helped her.

The room was neglected and there were footprints in the dust.

'An easy trail?'

'Careful,' she said.

'I know. A cornered Beast is dangerous.'

They pushed through a door. There was music coming from some where.

The Beast was straining inside the man-shell, aching for blood, for flesh.
The music excited it.

Its claws popped out.

The front doors of the Matthias II gave way like boxwood.

Yefimovich led the mob into the inn. It could not have been better. In the hallway, three very frightened footmen were clustered by an over-burdened coat rack.

There was a line of green velvet cloaks.

The crowd screamed.

What was this accursed interruption?

De la Rougierre vowed that the landlord would suffer for allowing this to happen.

Even Milizia was distracted enough to miss a few steps.

Johann stood up and signed to Elsaesser. His first duty was to protect the future Emperor.

There must be a back way out of this place.

He looked around. There were four visible doors, not counting any that might be behind the stage curtains.

That might be the safest route, through the dressing rooms. There was bound to be a performers' entrance.

The young officer stepped forwards, but tripped. There was a flood of people into the room. Countess Emmanuelle screamed. She hated being in a room with commoners.

Elsaesser was struggling.

'Highness,' Johann said, 'come with me.'

Luitpold had been in a daze, but Johann pulled him out of it. Taking his hand, he dragged him up onto the stage. The heir's bodyguards saw what he was doing and tried to block the surge of the crowd with a few prods of their halberds.

There was a backstage door.

'Highness,' he said, 'through here...'

'But–'

'No arguments. Do it. Now.'

The future Emperor went before him.

Johann had a sword in his hand. He would be turning into Leos von Liebewitz next.

There was a great deal of shouting out in the banquet room. The word 'death' was being used a lot.

Johann wrenched open the backstage door, not caring whether it was locked or not.

Someone was behind the door.

He pushed forwards, squeezing between Johann and Luitpold, as if running from his own mob of would-be executioners.

Johann felt the old phantom knife in his heart.

'Wolf!'

His brother was startled by his own name and half-turned...

There were more people coming through the door.

Harald Kleindeinst. Rosanna Ophuls.

Johann had a bad feeling about this.

'Wolf,' he said. 'Wolf...'

Then he didn't have anything more to say.

Wolf was frozen, not sure whether to turn to or away from him.

Then, the curtain fell down and everything went dark.

Yefimovich was carried away by revolutionist zeal.

He didn't care if he killed for Tzeentch or for Social Justice, just so long as he killed.

Fires were set around him and he strode through them.

'Green velvet,' he cried, looking around the room.

A woman caught his eye, trying to get through a door sideways to avoid getting her dress trapped.

Jewels sparkled on her bosom.

Daggers drawn, he went for her...

Dien Ch'ing sat quietly and let whatever would come come.

Someone tried to put a knife into his eye, but he swept it away with a simple movement.

After that, he was left alone.

This was much more amusing than the clumsy, grotesque-bodied dancer had been.

Rosanna found Johann and helped him struggle to throw off the thick red curtain.

They didn't have to talk about Wolf. A touch was enough for the exchange of views.

If Wolf was the killer, Johann wanted him caught. Not killed, but caught.

Fine. He could argue with Captain Kleindeinst later.

When they were free, the inn was a hell of tangled bodies. Everyone was shouting at the top of their voice.

She sensed a very powerful, very evil presence. Another one.

Emmanuelle lifted her skirts and ran. The horrible man was chasing her, daggers slicing through the air.

She was in a dead end. Backing down a dark passage, she had come up against a wall.

She prayed to all the gods. She asked for forgiveness. Mama, Papa, forgive me! Leos, forgive me!

The horrible man – Yefimovich the fire-breather – was coming slowly now that she was trapped, enjoying himself, making passes in the air.

'Snick-snack,' he said.

As he came into the darkness, she saw that his features weren't quite natural. Something was shining under the skin, making his face look like a luminous mask.

There was something with him, something small and horrid that scuttled along the ceiling.

She screamed.

Yefimovich laughed.

Leos had his sword out and was holding off the mob.

'Look out,' someone said, 'he's dangerous.'

The fool woman was clinging to his shoulder, using him to shield her naked body. She might get in the way if it were to come to a slash-up fight.

He prodded the air in front of several revolutionists.

Their enthusiasm for the overthrow of the aristocracy was pricked and they backed away.

Cowards! He should have expected no more from peasant rabble.

Harald sliced through the curtain with his blade and stood up, shaking the heavy folds off his shoulders.

There were a lot of dangerous people in the room. But Wolf wasn't one of them.

'Yelle,' Hasselstein shouted, charging down the corridor.

The fire-breather was standing over his mistress, cackling.

The Lector was not a man of action. He was a strategist, a tactician, a politician. Within the Cult of Sigmar, he had chosen the Order of the Anvil over the Knights of the Fiery Heart, studying the Law rather than the Arts of Combat.

But he picked up a chair and ran down the corridor, shouting.

The chair smashed into Yefimovich and came to pieces. He found himself holding a leg and bludgeoned the agitator's head with it.

Yelle was screaming at the top of her lungs.

Her hands reached out and grabbed at Yefimovich's face...

...and it came off.

It was like a burst of light in the passage.

Emmanuelle shut her eyes, but the fiery face still burned in her mind.

XIII

Elsaesser had been forced into a backroom. He looked around for something useful as a weapon and found a kegspike.

'Look,' said a hard voice, 'it's an inky!'

Two Leaguers were in the room, armed with heavy clubs.

'Let's spill his swotty brains!'

He recognized them.

They had applauded at Brustellin's expulsion, and stolen the library's copies of the professor's books to use as privy paper.

'Stay back,' he said, waving his spike.

'What have you got which could make us, quill-head?'

Elsaesser reached into his jacket.

'This,' he said, producing his copper badge.

'Now,' he said, 'up against the wall and spread your legs, ape-men!'

Yefimovich's face was gone.

The cleric of Sigmar was a trembling wreck. And the countess-elector a screaming harpy.

Respighi opened the hidden door, releasing the catch at the top.

The High Priest of Tzeentch stepped into another room.

Number Two was a wash-out, Milizia decided, and gave him the shove. She could tell he wasn't interested in girls much.

Her first mission now was to get out of this mess.

No, make that second. First, she needed some clothes.

Gallantly, the Norseman threw his fur waistcoat at her. Belted around her waist, it was like a dress.

Now, escape.

She made a run for the door.

They had Hals von Tasseninck down on the floor and were kicking the teeth out of his head.

The Grand Prince's idiot son was trying to force a window and shrieking whenever anyone tried to touch him.

Harald waded into the brawl and pulled two people away from the elector's boot party. He knocked their heads together and dropped them on the floor. The rest of the kickers backed away.

Harald picked the Grand Prince up and looked into his battered and bloody face.

'Good evening, elector,' he said. 'Remember me?'

Milizia was in the dark. She was outside the inn, in an alley. The cobbles were like ice chunks under her bare feet.

At least she was safe now.

The Beast was savage, but it could be calm when it had to be.

Its chosen prey scented, it stalked her, ignoring the other blood scents whirling around in the air like fog.

Its claw was out.

The fighting was dying down now, dwindling to mere confusion. Johann had been shielding the Prince with his body, but the young man had slipped away somewhere. He prayed to Sigmar that Luitpold was sensible enough to stay away from knives and fires.

'Yefimovich's an altered,' someone had said.

'It's true, I saw him. His head is a living flame.'

'What?'

The revolutionists were getting rapidly disillusioned with their leader. No one was sure what was going on.

Suddenly, Johann was surrounded by strangers. Harald was there, with the von Tassenincks. And so was Rosanna, over with the Norseman, the Kislevite and the blue-faced, parrot-nosed Marquess Sidonie. Mornan Tybalt was sobbing and rubbing injured hands; someone had clipped one of his thumbs for him, reducing his taxable digits by one half.

But everyone else in the de la Rougierre party had spilled out into the dark.

Milizia was almost out of the alley when she bumped into him.

'You,' she said, 'out of my way.'

The shape stood firm and then stepped forwards. She backed away.

Its eyes were shining.

She felt a scream beginning...

The claw stuck into Rosanna's mind.

'Johann,' she shouted, '*it's happening now!*'

The Beast's claw stuck into the girl's stomach and her eyes clouded.

There was no time for a proper job.

Harald and the baron collided in the door Rosanna was pointing at.

He swore and helped the elector up.

Rosanna was with them.

'Which way?' he asked her.

'The alley. The way we came.'

The passage was full of bodies. They had to struggle.

Harald realized that Rosanna was screaming.

'It's killing me!'

It was killing her!

Johann thumped someone out of the way, but it was useless. The failed revolutionists were streaming against them, pushing them backwards.

Tears were pouring from Rosanna's eyes. Her screams scratched at his mind.

It was if he could feel it too.

Elsaesser had knocked the Leaguers out with a tap apiece from his spike and was feeling quite chipper. That was a blow for the inkies, if not for the revolution.

There was an empty barrel in the room, standing up like a tub, its round lid resting against the wall.

There was a small, square door, bolted, at the rear of the room by some casks. He guessed it was for rolling in barrels.

Outside, a sharp scream rose and was then cut off.

He cursed himself for standing about feeling pleased.

The bolts were rusted, but he knocked them free with his spike and put his shoulder to the door.

It fell out of the wall and he stumbled into the alley, knocking his head on the opposite wall.

There was blood in the water again. He remembered this place. Number seven, Margarethe Ruttmann.

He saw the two figures at the mouth of the alley.

And now, number nine.

The corpse slapped the cobbles, falling like a loose-jointed dummy.

Elsaesser got a good grip on the spike and stepped forwards.

Impossibly quick, the Beast was coming for him.

He raised the spike, but the killer had his wrist in a shackle-like grip.

The Beast pushed him and they both fell back through the barrel door.

Elsaesser felt something sharp slice across his stomach and then his neck. He heard rather than felt his throat opening.

He had failed. He had failed everyone.

The Beast picked him up and swung him around. He felt his shins strike wood and then he was dropped.

The Beast had shoved him into the barrel.

He was pushed down. His front was soaked with blood and he couldn't cry out. He just made a '*gack gack*' noise as he gasped for breath.

The lid came down on the barrel and he heard the blows of the cooper's hammer.

He was forced down into a squatting position, his knees up against his chest. Blood was pooling around him.

He was seeing colours in the dark.

Mrs Bierbichler had been right. He could die.

But he would die having seen the face of the Beast.

Part Five

Bestiality

I

The Commission of Inquiry decided officially that the Great Fog Riots petered out sometime soon after sunrise. Actually, the incidents continued for several days, as stragglers from various factions set about each other with leftover weapons, and the Hooks carried out a series of opportunist robberies. The fires in the East End were finally brought under control in the late afternoon, and a lot of people returned home to find their homes weren't there any more. The Commission more or less decided that this was their own fault for getting mixed up with a riot and, upon the advice of the one-thumbed minister Mornan Tybalt, opted not to crack open the treasury to provide the newly-homeless with funds for food, shelter and refuge. Whereupon there were a few more riots and the Imperial Militia, by now a great deal better experienced, moved in and restored order with a modicum of unnecessary brutality. By the end of the week, the city's population of beggars had increased by one-third and there were nightly scuffles outside the Temples of Shallya as indigents fought over the limited number of cots made available by the Clerics of Mercy.

The riots ended mainly through confusion of purpose. Rumour and counter-rumour spread through Altdorf with a supernatural rapidity. However, it was almost immediately general knowledge that Yevgeny Yefimovich was an altered and a devotee of the Ruinous Powers, and that he was also the murderer of Ulrike Blumenschein, the Angel of the Revolution. This was a heavy blow to the radical movement and Prince Kloszowski dashed off several poems excoriating the fiend in human shape who had perverted a just cause and a good woman to his own diabolical purposes. There were a few die-hard Yefimovites, but they tended to get more involved in violent feuds with the Kloszowskists than with the authorities. Professor Brustellin's body was found in the street and buried outside the city walls, a permanent shrine erected above his remains as a reminder of his great works. The watch mainly left the radicals to their own quarrels and concentrated on sorting out the debris.

It was clear that Yefimovich had killed Ulrike in an attempt to stir up the people against the Imperial court, and the Commission ruled that it was therefore proven beyond all manner of doubt that the revolutionist monster was also the murderer known as the Beast. Popular resentment against the aristocracy dwindled to its usual level of mild seething and it was safe again to walk the streets of the docklands in a green velvet cloak.

The fog began to thin, but only slightly.

Cleric-Captain Adrian Hoven finally managed to get into a room with the relevant commanders of the city watch and the Imperial Militia, and various disputes of jurisdiction were settled to everyone's satisfaction. A joint action was mounted and any remaining disorder was speedily quelled. The last disorder was ended when a discreet bribe was passed into the hands of Willy Pick, and the Hooks ceased their campaign of outright looting and vandalism.

The Commission would abandon its attempt to list all the casualties of the Great Fog Riots and no two estimates of the damage would ever tally. The Emperor Karl-Franz was reported to be 'most upset' by the whole affair and called for all the citizens of Altdorf 'to display that old Imperial spirit and rally through just as Sigmar would have wanted us to.' Grand Prince Hergard von Tassenick lobbied for the flogging of all people suspected to have been involved in the rioting, but this suggestion was rejected on the grounds that it was 'too impractical.' In the end, Rickard Stieglitz was caught, then tried for and convicted of insurrection, and given a public ear-clipping before being imprisoned in Mundsen Keep. Nineteen other individuals were jailed for various crimes, ranging from arson to seditious libel, committed during the riots. Prince Kloszowski left the city before the watch could take him and continued to write. His epic, *The Blood of Innocents*, would become an underground classic, especially after it was banned in every city and state of the Empire.

A list was posted in the Konigsplatz of all the watchmen, Templars and militiamen killed or injured. Buried in the roll of honour was the name of Helmut Elsaesser.

The Beast, of course, was still at large.

II

The Beast had come for her. It seemed to be made of solidified fog, draped in an enveloping cloak of green velvet, complete with a hood. Evil eyes stared out of the blackness where the face should have been. She could feel its rage, its hate, its violence. It moved not like a human being, not like an animal. It had a queer grace, a delicacy of gesture, and yet it radiated strength, menace, hostility. In its clouded mind, the lust for killing burned as fiercely as the weirdroot addict's need for his dream-drug. Fixed to the spot, she could not run. The fog was as thick as cotton and she could not fight through it. She was a little girl again, far from Altdorf, somewhere in the forested mountains. Behind the Beast, she sensed her parents, making no move to save their daughter. They were thinking that it would be best if the witch cuckoo were dead. Then, they could stop blaming each other for the freak. They could be part of the village again. Father could return to the tavern and hoist tankards with his friends, mother could supervise her other daughters – her real daughters – and turn them into good little dressmakers. They urged the Beast on. Rosanna was sweating, already feeling the pain the Beast would visit upon her. Her sisters were there too, with their pinching fingers and slapping hands, like the Beast's attendants. The fog stung her eyes like woodsmoke. They were in the alleyway now, between the two inns, and the murderer's hand was around her throat, its knife slicing upwards.

Rosanna woke up, her heart kicking like a baby in her chest.

There was no Beast, except in the memories she had sampled. The memories of the killer's victims.

She had been dreaming it over again, scrambled up with her own dreams.

She was crouched against a wall in the Matthias II, with a cloak – green velvet, of course – flung over her. She could not remember going to sleep.

Baron Johann von Mecklenberg was pouring out cups of tea. Harald Kleindeinst was sitting down, carving bread with a knife less impressive than the one slung on his hip.

It would have been a cosy breakfast scene were it not for all the men-at-arms milling about and the annoyed dignitaries huddled together.

The baron had thought it wisest that everyone stay in the inn for the night, under guard. Obviously, he was as much interested in penning up potential suspects as in keeping de la Rougierre's guests safe from the rioters.

Of course, Wolf was gone. And so was Yefimovich.

The Countess Emmanuelle, still in last night's ball gown, was posed like a statue, attended by her brother and the Lector. She was looking irritated, as much because the Beast was drawing attention away from her as for the inconvenience and indignity of spending a night away from her luxurious accommodation at the palace.

Some time last night, Mikael Hasselstein had given Rosanna a gold crown and told her to stay close by. The gesture annoyed her and she was reconsidering her future at the Temple. It was becoming obvious that there might be conflicts of interest between the causes of Justice and the cult of Sigmar. And the cause of the cult was especially vague just now, overlapping unnervingly with that of the Lector. The whores whose minds Rosanna had shared all charged a lot less than a gold crown for their services, but their clients had not pretended to be buying anything other than the temporary use of their bodies. Hasselstein seemed to think he could own her outright.

The Bretonnian dwarf was up and shouting, abusing various servants and militiamen for their clumsiness. The Celestial simply sipped tea and smiled.

The function room was a mess. The guest rooms upstairs had been turned over to Luitpold and his instantly-assembled guard and so everyone else had had to spend the night downstairs. Some of them must have relished the chance not to be alone, but the countess, at least, was steeped in a cold fury.

The baron smiled and brought Rosanna some tea in a goblet. The inn was running low on cups and there was broken crockery underfoot.

'Well?' she asked.

'Wolf is gone.'

'Baron, was he the Beast?'

The baron looked pained and she read genuine confusion.

'Call me Johann,' he said.

'You don't know?'

'No. I fear, but I don't know.'

'Last night, someone was saying it was Yefimovich.'

Harald said, 'He's not human.'

Hasselstein, overhearing, stepped in. 'The fire-breather tried to kill the countess. Then he escaped, killing the dancer in the alley. He is the Beast.'

Rosanna tried to think, tried to scry. She had only seen Yefimovich briefly and had not had time to probe him. There had been the aura of an inferno about him.

'Miss Ophuls will confirm his guilt,' Hasselstein said.

Johann looked at Rosanna.

She thought carefully. Yefimovich had been an altered and, she scryed, an initiate of one of the Proscribed Cults. She fixed on the memory of his bright presence. Even trying to recall him made her eyes hurt, as fires appeared to dance in her vision. He had left a very strong impression behind him. She felt his devotion to the Dark Powers, to Tzeentch. There were countless crimes to his credit, each a flame in his body. But she could not fix him as the shadowed Beast she had scried from the dead women. Yefimovich was fire, while the Beast was darkness.

'No,' she said, 'I'm not sure… I do not think Yefimovich is the Beast.'

The Lector looked at her as if she were the Beast herself, and his lips went tight, all colour squeezed out. She felt his anger boiling. He had thought he could count on her, and now he was feeling betrayed. He was prepared to be quite self-righteous about it. He could enforce all manner of penances upon her.

'Yefimovich was the Beast,' he said.

The Lector stared at her, trying to force his will into her mind. All he wanted was for her to agree with him, to wrap up the mystery, to end the investigation. It would have been so easy, and it would have satisfied everyone. She could not be sure of her intuitions. Maybe Yefimovich was the killer. He was certainly a killer.

'Yefimovich was the Beast,' Hasselstein repeated.

Rosanna gave him back his crown and answered, 'No.'

Anger flared in the Lector's mind and he gripped his coin in a tight fist. Had Harald and Johann not been there, he would have struck out at the impudent scryer. He was not used to being defied and he did not like the taste of it. He turned and walked back to the countess – his secret mistress, Rosanna realized – trailing his wrath behind him like a kite.

'What was that about?' Johann asked.

'I think I've just been excommunicated from the Cult of Sigmar.'

For the first time since she left her village, she felt free. It was a dizzying, slightly scary feeling, like walking a rope in a carnival with no safety net. She was, she realized, homeless, masterless, unemployed…

'Don't worry,' said the elector, 'you have my protection.'

Rosanna wasn't sure about Baron Johann's sudden offer, sincerely meant though it was. Practically, it might serve some use if Hasselstein were to prove vindictive. But she had relished her taste of liberty and the prospect of serving again, under the colours of a noble house rather than a religion, was disappointing. Besides, she bristled at his casual assumption of her helplessness.

But the men were thinking of other things now. She could see the same name in each of their minds. Wolf. Johann was seeing a lost youth, confused and afraid. Harald was remembering the twisted young man, barely containing his animal heart, they had encountered last night.

'Yefimovich is not the Beast,' Rosanna said. 'The mystery is not solved.'

'You're sure?' Johann asked.

Rosanna nodded.

'A pity,' said the baron. 'It would have been simple.'

Rosanna shrugged.

'The Blumenschein woman,' said Harald, 'the so-called Angel of the Revolution?'

Rosanna concentrated. There had been blood in Yefimovich's mind. New blood. He was a strong presence. She had been able to read a lot – too much – from him during their brief contact.

'I think he killed her. But not the others.'

Harald swore and the baron looked troubled. They all knew that Rosanna's intuitions would not prevent the authorities from misidentifying the Revolutionist Monster as the Beast. That left them on their own against the real murderer.

'Baron,' said Harald, 'if the Beast is your brother, then what?'

'Then he must be stopped. That is all.'

'Is it?'

Johann was trying to do the right thing, Rosanna saw. It was something bred deep into him.

'No,' he answered the captain, 'of course it isn't. Wolf is my brother and I shall do all I can for him.'

Harald was grim. 'If it comes down to it, would you stand between us?'

'Probably. Would you go through me to catch him?'

'Probably.'

'Then we understand each other, captain.'

De la Rougierre, who had quickly forgotten his dalliance with the dead dancer, was insisting that his guests be allowed free. He called Harald 'a stupid policeman,' and then backed off.

The streets had been quiet for a few hours now. Johann had sent a Templar to the palace for carriages. The coaches the guests had come in were burned-out wrecks and the horses fled.

Finally, the coaches came and de la Rougierre's guests were ferried back to their secure walls and well-armed retainers.

The last to leave was Leos von Liebewitz. The youth seemed torn. 'Johann,' he asked, 'can I help here?'

It was difficult for him, but he felt some obligation, if not to the commoner who had died then to the aristocrats who had not.

'No, Leos,' the baron answered, 'perhaps later.'

With the guests shepherded out, they were left alone at the inn.

Rosanna, Johann, Harald.

It took them a while to work out who was missing.

III

They followed the girl as she led them out of the function room, through a short passage, and towards a store-room. The place was mainly above ground, but it had the atmosphere of a cellar. Rosanna was in a half-trance, feeling her way along a cooling trail. The baron was by her side, like a courteous gentleman helping a blind person not to bump into walls, gently steering her round obstacles. Harald's stomach was beginning to ache and he felt the recent violence as surely as the scryer did.

'He's here,' she said.

'Where?' asked the baron.

'In this room.'

They looked around. This was the way they had come into the Matthias II last night. The window was still open, as was a barrel-door. The place smelled of old beer.

'We looked here last night,' the baron said. 'Those two Leaguers were unconscious in the corner.'

Harald's stomach complained.

Rosanna went around the room, touching things, frowning.

'He's here. Very close.'

She touched a barrel that was standing on its end and leaped back as if it were a heated stove.

'What is it?' the baron asked.

Rosanna pointed at the barrel. 'Inside,' she said.

Harald held up the lantern. The barrel was split near the base and blood had poured out through the taphole. It was sticky on the flagstones.

'Merciful Shallya,' the baron swore.

Harald found a cooper's hammer and tapped the barrel-lid. It gave, and he pulled the wooden circle out whole.

Helmut Elsaesser looked up, his face white, his eyes empty.

Johann could not help but feel responsible. He had, after all, intervened to keep the young officer on the Beast case. Rosanna had flinched away at the sight of the corpse and he had instinctively embraced her. He felt her body pressed warm against him, and a charge crackled from her hair, so close to his face. She relaxed for a moment and then stepped away from him, leaving only the memory of a touch. He wondered if she had seen anything in him that made her want to break contact. She was making herself look at poor, dead Elsaesser.

'Number ten,' Kleindeinst said, respectfully.

'Get him out,' said Johann.

'No, don't,' insisted the captain. 'Not yet.'

'What is it?'

'He didn't die straight away. He bled. There may be something.'

'I don't understand.'

'A message from the grave,' suggested Rosanna. 'Here.'

She was holding the barrel lid up to the light. It was stained with blood. Something was written on it.

'He may have seen his murderer, recognized him...'

Johann looked at the scrawl. There were letters. No, numbers.

As he was dying, Elsaesser had dipped a finger in his own blood and drawn numbers on the lid of his makeshift coffin.

317 5037.

'Is it a code?' he asked. 'Why would Elsaesser use a code?'

'He was there when Dickon burned the cloak, wasn't he? He may have expected the message to be found by someone who would want to hush it up. Or even by the Beast himself.'

Rosanna suggested the simplest code. 'Perhaps the numbers are letters of the alphabet. 1 for A, 2 for B and so on. That would read CA... er, G... E...'

'Yes? What's the nothingth letter of the alphabet, scryer?' asked Harald.

'Obviously, it's not so simple. Elsaesser was just out of the University, wasn't he?'

Johann tried to solve the riddle. 'Perhaps it's a map reference. At the University, they use the grid system. Elsaesser could have been pointing us to the murderer's house...'

Harald looked doubtful. 'What's the grid reference for the palace, baron?'

'I don't know.'

'And you live there. How could a simple copper know exactly a map reference in seven digits?'

'You have a point.'

'Maybe the numbers should be in bunches. There's a gap in the middle, and a smaller one here. 317. 50. 37. It could still be an address. 317 could be a house number, and the other two a street and a district.'

'I don't swallow it,' said Kleindeinst. 'Poor Elsaesser was dying, his stomach opened, his throat cut. He must have been in terrible pain. He wouldn't have had time for numerology games. It has to be something obvious.'

'There's something about the number 317 that's familiar.'

Kleindeinst snapped, 'Of course there is, that's the code number for this district.'

'Code?' Rosanna and Johann asked, at once.

'Watch code. Every watch in the Empire has a number, like a regiment of the militia. 317 is the Luitpoldstrasse Station.'

'And do individual officers have numbers?'

'Yes but you would be hard-pressed to find any watch in the Empire, much less in a slum like this, which had over five thousand men.'

'317. 5037.'

'3. 17. 50. 37.'

'3,175,037.'

'This is silly' said Rosanna. 'Maybe he was just delirious and doing mathematical problems in his head. People die with strange things in their minds. I should know.'

They looked at her and she knew what they were thinking.

'Yes,' she said, resigned, 'of course I'll try to scry him.'

Helmut Elsaesser had died gasping for breath and thinking of his landlady. There were a lot of other things, but no coherent thought.

Rosanna was still not used to violent death. She supposed she would have to go through Milizia's death, too, and still not be able to identify the Beast.

'It's almost as if the murderer can blot himself out of his victims' consciousness.'

'Is that possible?'

'Anything is possible, Johann. It's not like opening a book. It's like trying to count heads at a ball, with all the dancers on the move. I could tell you a lot about this poor boy, but I think it's best to leave him some privacy.'

'Girl,' said Harald, 'if you ever do this professionally, you'll learn that one of the things murder victims don't have is privacy.'

The thought made her unutterably melancholic.

'It's not like the melodramas,' Johann said, 'where murderers leave clues and the clever watchman sleuths them out.'

'This number is a clue,' Rosanna said. 'I'm sure of that.'

'And that green velvet Dickon burned,' said Captain Kleindeinst.

'It's a shame you didn't get to scry that,' said Johann. 'It must have come from the Beast. I held it in my hands, but I've no gift. You know, I can see it now, in every detail...'

Rosanna felt the curtains open in her mind. It happened sometimes.

'And so can I.'

'What?' exclaimed Kleindeinst.

'The velvet, I can see it. Worn along the bottom edge.'

'Yes, that's right.'

'The bottom edge?' asked Kleindeinst.

Rosanna and Johann agreed.

'But, those cloaks are thigh-length. How could it be worn along the bottom?'

Johann made a gloved fist. 'It would be worn like that, if the Beast weren't a normal-sized man...'

In her mind, Rosanna saw a dwarf...

* * *

The Countess Emmanuelle was determined. They would be leaving for Nuln as soon as possible and remaining there until this frightful business was forgotten.

She told Leos as much in the carriage and charged her brother with making the arrangements. 'Have Dany supervise the packing of my gowns,' she said. 'He'll like that.'

She had been in this city too long, staying away from her social and political responsibilities to be close to the heart of the Empire.

Mikael had kept her here longer than she had intended. In the beginning, the intense cleric, whose desire for power was as urgent as his desire for her, had been an interesting conquest. Now, he was becoming a bore. Perhaps worse than a bore.

Mikael would be a problem. He was being too ardent. He might prove unpredictably troublesome if he were not cast loose with some tact.

In her dressing room, free from her maids, she scrubbed at her face, removing last night's fading paint. Her dress was ruined. She would never wear it again. And her tiara had been stolen while she slept.

Upright in a chair, no less! She was lucky to come away from the Bretonnian ambassador's soirée with her life.

Behind her, the door opened and a small figure slipped in.

Outraged, she turned.

'De la Rougierre!' she exclaimed. 'I hope you have some explanation for this uncountenanceable intrusion.'

The ambassador grinned and, for the first time, it seemed to Emmanuelle that he really was more dwarf than Bretonnian.

He bowed, his hat swept mockingly low, and sauntered across the room...

IV

Johann felt as if his mind had been scooped out. Rosanna was apologetic, but more taken with Kleindeinst's suggestion.

'Yes, it could be? The cloak must have trailed on the ground a lot. Don't you think so?'

Johann stammered an agreement. He felt a fool for not noticing himself.

Kleindeinst spoke deliberately. 'There was a rumour that the Beast was a dwarf. And most of the knifestrokes were upwards…'

He made an underarm stabbing motion.

'Elsaesser said that the Bretonnian ambassador was intimate with several of the victims,' said Rosanna.

Johann's mind came back to him. 'And he certainly knew the dancer last night. The murders started just after he was posted to Altdorf…'

'De la Rougierre,' said Kleindeinst, his knife out. The copper rolled the name around in his mouth.

'It's just,' Johann began, trying to pin down a doubt, 'it's just that he seems to be such a clown, you know. The absurd little creature pretending to be a man. He's like a stage Bretonnian, all perfume and silly gestures, with that exaggerated accent, those ridiculous moustaches, the endless chatter…'

'He's still a dwarf,' said Kleindeinst. 'They can be vicious bastards. I should know, I've had to kill enough of them.'

'There is more than one dwarf in Altdorf.'

'That's true enough. But only one has been cropping up throughout this investigation.'

'He's an ambassador. This will be a big scandal. Relations between the Empire and Bretonnia are always questionable. King Charles won't like us executing his envoy.'

'Then we'll let him do it. A Bretonnian headsman's axe is just as sharp as an Empire blade. Just so long as the toad is squashed.'

Rosanna cried out, a wordless gulp of noise. Johann and the captain looked at her. She had her hands knit as if in prayer. 'I'm an idiot,' she said, slowly, 'and you are too…'

Hasselstein pushed his way in without knocking and his heart shrank into stone. Yelle was not alone and the prospect of her companion replacing him in her bed made the Lector want to vomit bile.

'What are you doing here?' he said.

The dwarf turned away from Yelle, his hand going to the hilt of his ridiculously short sword.

'Both of you,' the countess said, 'get out. You are here uninvited.'

'I merely wished to apologise for last night, countess elector,' said de la Rougierre, dripping Bretonnian smarm.

Hasselstein laughed bitterly.

'I'm sure that was the extent of your motive, ambassador.'

Yelle had her face off and was snarling like a cat.

'I said "get out", if anyone's interested...'

'Lector,' said the dwarf, 'you are a cleric, but your deity is a warlike one. I am not honour-bound not to fight you. Remember that.'

Leos appeared at the door, his ready hand on his swordhilt. He looked at Hasselstein and de la Rougierre, unsure which to kill first.

Yelle screeched and flung an enamelled brush at them.

'Mikael, ambassador... *out!*'

'It's not from a cloak...'

She should have known straight away. Before the Temple came for her, she had been apprenticed to her mother, the seamstress. She had hated every minute of it, preparing ridiculously decorated outfits for the local lord and lady. Her fingers were still grooved and scarred from the rough needles.

'...it's from a dress.'

'What?'

'The stitching is completely different. The hem is higher. Even the thickness of the velvet is wrong.'

'A dress?'

'Yes, a formal dress. Maybe a ball gown.'

'Merciful...' began Kleindeinst.

'...Shallya,' completed Johann.

'Are you trying to tell us that the Beast is a woman?' asked Kleindeinst.

Rosanna reached into herself, combining the images of the murderer she had picked out of the victims' minds. It was dark, slim and a sharp edge sparkled like a jewel.

'No...' she said. 'Yes.'

'Which?'

The Beast came out into the light and Rosanna saw her face.

'Yes.'

The Beast was beautiful...

'The palace,' Rosanna said, 'now!'

...beautiful and terrible.

The man-shell shrank, the boy-shell shrivelled...

All the former selves were dead. There was only the Beast.

It takes its claw and prepares for the last of them. The last of the disgusting women. The worst of them.

It is not sure whether it is hunting, or waiting. Anyway, it will be over soon.

This is the last of the grudge kills.

The Beast pads through the palace. It is proud to walk in the light. It – no, *she* – does not need to hide any longer.

There is someone else in her mind, troubling her. A woman, a filthy woman! The Beast sees red hair, a pretty face.

There's a number, too. 317-5037. The woman presence doesn't understand. 317-5037?

The Beast is puzzled, for a moment. Then, it becomes clear. And she laughs...

There was a watch carriage outside the inn. Harald commandeered it and took the reins, while the baron helped Rosanna up onto the seat.

The scryer was almost in a trance, her open eyes twitching. She was like a human dowsing rod. She didn't speak, just sat rigid.

Harald whipped the horses and the carriage tore through the fog. He hoped that the vehicle made enough noise to warn people to keep out of the way.

He imagined the map of the city and took the shortest route to the Emperor Karl-Franz Bridge and then on to the palace.

'It's Emmanuelle,' said the baron. 'The Marquess Sidonie was with us all the time last night.'

Harald didn't say anything. Nothing was proved yet.

'There were no other women in the company.'

A horse reared up in the fog, looming. It was one of the runaways, as yet not rounded up.

Harald pulled back hard and kept his own animals on course.

The stray was panicked, but galloped out of the way, fading into the grey murk.

'But the countess? Why?'

They were over the bridge and the streets were wider. There was mercifully little traffic, what with the fog and the leftover from the riots.

'Kleindeinst,' the baron said, 'earlier, you claimed that a womanslayer was the worst kind of criminal there was.'

Harald grunted a yes.

'Well, could you become one?'

Harald thought of the Countess Emmanuelle, tried to imagine her with knives in her frail hands, tearing away at the dead women, cutting young Elsaesser's throat.

He still couldn't answer the baron's question.

Ahead of them, its massive outline clearly visible, a stone hammer raised high above the structure, was the palace.

And inside was the Beast.

'I think my sister wants you to leave,' Leos said, calmly.

De la Rougierre and Mikael Hasselstein looked at the viscount and were chilled into silence. Leos took his hand away from the hilt of his sword and everyone breathed again.

'Yes,' said Emmanuelle, 'that's right.'

His sister was frayed around the edges. Without her paint on, the delicate lines around her mouth and eyes were visible.

The dwarf and the cleric both wanted to protest, but Leos counted on their taking his swordsmanship seriously.

De la Rougierre broke first. He clapped his hat on his head and left the room, attempting to draw himself up to a dignified height.

'Yelle,' Hasselstein pleaded, 'can't we–?'

'No,' Emmanuelle said, 'we can not. Please go.'

The cleric made useless fists in the air and backed out of the room, grinding his teeth. He looked as if he would scream as soon as he got out of earshot, or take out his anger on a servant. His robes of office brushed the floor as he walked.

The door closed behind them.

Emmanuelle's face was twisted. Her hands were up in the air, sharp nails pointed like talons.

'Yelle,' Leos said, 'it is over...'

Emmanuelle screeched.

Within seconds, Viscount Leos von Liebewitz was dead. And the Beast had killed him.

V

A pair of guardsmen stood in the middle of the gateway, with their pikes crossed, barring the road.

Kleindeinst shouted a warning, but made no attempt to stop.

Johann wondered if the two men would stay and be trampled. He held his breath.

Rosanna was mumbling and painfully gripping his arm.

The guards decided on survival over honour and Kleindeinst lashed the horses. The carriage rushed through the gateway.

Someone had unlocked the portcullis chain and it rumbled down behind them, spikes spearing the stone.

A guardsman drew his sword, but Kleindeinst pushed his badge in the soldier's face.

Johann showed his face and the guardsman saluted.

'Elector,' he said.

'I'm sorry for this,' Johann said, 'but it's urgent. I'm on the Emperor's business.'

Rosanna snapped out of her trance and vaulted out of the carriage, landing well.

'Follow us,' Johann ordered the gate guards.

Rosanna led the way, as if she knew every stone of the palace, and Kleindeinst and Johann had to stride to keep up with her.

She was taking them to the guest apartments.

At the main door of the block, they ran into Mikael Hasselstein. His face was stony and his knuckles white. Rosanna pushed her former patron out of the way without seeming to recognize him and pulled open the door.

'In there,' she said. 'The Beast.'

Hasselstein took notice. 'What?'

There was no time for explanations.

The party marched through the passageway. Along the way, they picked up Mnoujkine, the guests' steward. Johann told him to have all the other servants and guests evacuated.

'We think we have a killer trapped in here.'

'Countess Emmanuelle?' Hasselstein said. 'Yelle?'

Rosanna stopped outside the door of the von Liebewitz apartments

599

as if she had walked into an invisible wall. She pointed at the door, her hand shaking.

'What is this about Yelle?'

The door was locked.

'Break it down,' Johann ordered.

Kleindeinst put his shoulder to the door, but rebounded with an oath. 'That's solid oak, with iron crossbars.'

A guard stuck his halberd into the crack, between the hinges, and tried to prise the door open. The shaft of the weapon snapped.

Beyond the door, there was feminine laughter. The sound squirted ice-water into Johann's blood.

Johann kicked the door and uselessly jarred his bones.

'Get axes,' Kleindeinst ordered.

'Yelle? Yelle!'

'Shut up, Lector,' said Johann. 'Rosanna? What's happening in there?'

Rosanna was flagging. She had made it this far, but the strain was showing.

'Dying,' she said, 'she's killing... dying... him...'

The axes came.

'This door dates back to the time of Wilhelm II,' said Mnoujkine, 'it's a valuable antique. The Emperor will be most distressed.'

'We'll buy him a new one,' said Kleindeinst, hefting the first axe.

A chunk of wood flew out of the door and the passage shook.

'Stand back,' said Johann, pulling Rosanna out of the way. She clung to him, like a child.

He was glad he was not seeing in his mind what she was in hers.

Kleindeinst smashed the wood around the lock and the door began to split.

There was still laughter.

The door came apart, falling in three pieces. Kleindeinst threw the axe away and pulled out his knife.

'After me,' he said...

Inside the von Liebewitz apartments, everything seemed ominously in order. Cloaks and coats were hung neatly in the hallway. There was an open fire in the reception room and a book was open on the dining table. *The Treachery of Oswald*, by Detlef Sierck.

'Careful,' Harald said, cautioning the others.

The laughter was coming from somewhere.

'Lector,' Harald said to Hasselstein, 'where is she?'

The cleric had to be shoved by the baron to make a reply. 'Her dressing room. It's just down the corridor.'

A woman who killed women. That was something new in his experience. There were always surprises, although few were ever pleasant.

'Countess,' he said, loudly, 'this is the watch. We would like to talk to you.'

The laughter stopped.

'Emmanuelle,' said Baron Johann, 'it's important.'

Quiet.

Harald looked at the baron and guessed that he received the elector's approval.

He stepped sideways into the corridor, pressing his back against the wall opposite the row of doors.

'Which one?' he asked, softly.

'The third,' said Hasselstein.

Harald edged down until he stood opposite the door.

Johann and the three guards cautiously came into the narrow corridor. Harald hoped that none of the company would have to die.

He touched the point of his Magnin to the door and pushed hard. The door was not latched, it swung open.

First, he saw someone lying, dead or in a faint, by a dressing table, a green velvet cloak thrown over them.

Then, he saw the Beast. The murderer came at him, her train flying behind her. She was veiled and wore a richly decorated ballgown. There were some contraptions fitted over her hands, gloves with sharp hooks. The Beast had claws.

He raised his knife to slash, but his hand was slammed out of the way.

Mikael Hasselstein had crammed himself through the door and thrown himself at Harald's arm, dragging him down. He sank his teeth into the watchman's hand.

Harald slammed the Lector with his elbow, but Hasselstein kept his grip.

The Beast stood still, poised, claws ready.

The baron tried to haul Hasselstein off Harald, but couldn't get a grip.

The wiry cleric was fighting as if possessed. Hate could do that, or love.

Incredibly, Hasselstein off-balanced Harald and pushed him back into the corridor, tumbling in a bruised bundle with Johann.

'Yelle,' Hasselstein said, dropping to his knees before the Beast, 'Yelle, I love...'

The Beast slashed him across the face, her claws sinking into his cheek and hooking onto his skull. He was lifted off his knees and hurled aside, a cloud of blood blossoming around his head.

The Beast laughed like a little girl, then howled like a wolf.

317 5037.

The number rolled in Rosanna's mind.

Johann crawled across the floor, trying to disentangle himself from Harald Kleindeinst.

She saw the number written in blood on the underside of a barrel-lid.

317 5037.

Rosanna had her hands under Johann's arms and was pulling him up.

The Beast was still laughing. Hasselstein was yelping, his hand to his bloody face.

She got her arms around Johann and got him upright. She felt his body close to hers,

317 5037.

The lid circled.

Urgently, Rosanna kissed him. He was astonished, but responded.

As their mouths met, so did their minds.

Suddenly, without any communication in words, they knew a lot more about each other. She saw Johann in the woods, firing his fatal shot, and at the top of the world, facing the monster that had been, and would be again, his brother.

He saw her as a little girl, resented by her sisters, kept at a distance by her parents, impressions flooding into her mind from everywhere.

Rosanna hoped they would both survive.

Together, they saw the numbers.

317 5037.

The lid was rolling across a floor, revolving like a wheel.

317 5037.

They had read it wrong.

The lid rolled and fell, so that they could see what Elsaesser had written rightside-up.

It was obvious now. There was no clever code. The officer had just tried to write, but been unable to finish, the name of his murderer.

Not 317 5037.

LEOS LIE...

Their minds parted. Johann and Harald were standing up again, facing the Beast. Hasselstein was not in the way.

The Beast's veil slipped.

VI

The viscount's face was painted, his lips rouged. He looked like a younger version of his sister. He had been a handsome young man, now he seemed to be a startlingly beautiful woman.

Johann, his mind still reeling from the touch of Rosanna, tried to understand. Leos was mad, and dressed as his sister. He was the Beast, a murderous she-creature with razor claws. But he was still Deadly Leos, the calculating duellist. Two murderers, the brutal and the elegant, in one body.

Leos slashed at the air, snarling.

Harald parried with his knife. The Magnin clashed with Leos's claws and there were sparks.

Not hampered by the ball gown, Leos moved fast, striking out and just missing Harald's throat.

The watchman stumbled over a carpet and sat down, his knife spinning away across the polished floorboards.

Johann had his sword drawn. He thrust in front of Leos, preventing him from bending over Harald and tearing out the man's throat.

Leos hissed and turned on Johann.

The Beast held up its claws and rattled them together, like a woman showing off her painted nails.

Johann was reminded of the man-woman altered he had duelled with at the top of the world.

For a moment, Leos was back. He stood up straight, the dress hanging absurdly on him, and beckoned with his right hand, his left reaching behind him.

Too late, Johann saw he was picking up a sword from the top of a chest. The weapon had been neatly placed on top of a pile of folded garments. Leos's clothes.

The claws didn't affect Leos's grip. His blade came up.

Finally, it had come to this.

Johann made the first strike and Leos effortlessly brushed it away. They both had the measure of the fight and joined in serious swordwork.

The dress didn't slow Leos's feet, but there was a certain awkwardness about his carriage. Johann tried to work on the weakness, but Leos defended perfectly, turning every attack with contemptuous ease.

Johann recognized the echoes of Valancourt of Nuln. He had seen the great teacher give a demonstration for the Emperor once. But Leos had improved upon his mentor's moves. There was a cruelty that undercut his elegance. He was less artful, but more dangerous.

As they fought, Johann looked into Leos's empty face, searching for an answer. Rosanna would scry one, he hoped. For now, there was only the fight.

A double thrust slipped through his guard and he felt his cheek sting. He knew the cut was deep.

He had forgotten Leos's claws. With a snarl, the Beast latched its left hand to Johann's shoulder, biting deep. Leos pulled back, trying to get the distance between them for a decisive thrust.

Johann drove his knee into Leos's stomach and swiped at his opponent's rapier, ignoring the pain in his shoulder.

The hooks came free and the duellists were apart again.

Kleindeinst was up, with his knife ready, but Leos was moving too fast to give him an opening. He was standing in front of Rosanna, protecting her.

With a flurry of moves, Leos advanced, inflicting a dozen tiny rips upon Johann's clothes, scratching the skin beneath. That was for show, but also to wear him down.

Johann had not fought seriously since the Top of the World. He had never considered it a fit amusement. But now, the instincts came back to him. What Leos had studied in gymnasia and duelling courts, he had learned in forests and battles. With each hurt, he felt stronger, faster. Technically, Leos was the greater duellist and the savagery of the Beast powered his attacks. But Johann was the skilled survivor.

Johann picked up a candelabrum with his left hand, his shoulder protesting, and jabbed at Leos with it. The flames were snuffed, but the feint distracted the murderer.

Johann saw his opportunity and took it, raising his swordarm in a muscle-stretching salute, then slicing down, chopping through the air with a whipping whistle. Leos tried to step back, but – for the first time in his career as a duellist – was caught by the end of the blade.

The point of Johann's sword slipped into Leos's flesh just below his collarbone and drew a line down across his torso, tearing cloth and skin. The cut would be too shallow to do anything more than itch, but Johann hoped the flapping dress and the blood would slow him down, make him defeatable.

Surprise flared in Leos's pale eyes. The dress tore and Johann stepped back, bringing his sword up for another thrust.

The dress gaped open, just as Johann's blade was aligned for the heart-piercing move.

Johann saw Leos's white skin and couldn't move. He willed himself to make the fatal strike, but couldn't.

He had won, but he had lost also...

* * *

There was nothing else for it.

Harald tossed the knife around, grabbing the blade firmly, and then threw it.

The Beast was caught, the knife sunk into the naked skin just below the heart.

'Sister...' Leos said and collapsed.

For the first time, Harald was unsure about killing a murderer. He felt like a womanslayer.

Rosanna slipped past him and went to the viscount.

He was still alive...

The dress was torn, from neck to waist.

Baron Johann stood still, his sword trembling, his mouth open.

'Sigmar's holy hammer,' swore Mnoujkine.

Viscount Leos von Liebewitz had been a woman.

Rosanna was holding his head, like a cleric trying to shrive a distracted sinner.

'This isn't enough,' she said. 'We have to know why.'

'No,' said the baron, 'Rosanna, don't...'

She ignored him and kissed the dying Beast. As their mouths joined, a shock ran through the scryer's body...

'Help her,' Johann said.

Harald didn't know who he meant.

VII

As they died, Rosanna lived the Beast's life...

'But I don't want a little sister,' a pretty child said, 'I want there to be only me.'

Her father protested, but mother – already a convert to the cause of her eldest daughter's position as the Empire's greatest beauty – was insistent.

'What my little Yelle wants, my little Yelle shall have.'

Their father, the old Elector of Nuln, knew what his wife and daughter wanted was wrong, but he had always been a slave to women.

In the end, he was glad to have one less in his household. And he had always wanted a son. If he had lived, he would have found an ally in the 'boy,' Leos, who grew up to hate women so much...

'Don't touch yourself there. That's disgusting!'

Then blows. Leos was taught with whippings to cover her body at all times. She came to think of herself as a boy. He suppressed the memory of his brief life as a girl. He played with wooden swords, not dressed-up dolls. He wanted to be a swordsman when he grew up and face hordes of goblins or trolls single-handed, leaving mountains of green-skinned dead wherever he adventured.

Father, Chancellor of the University, would lock himself up with his books of history, while mother supervised the children. Yelle would be rewarded, Leos would be beaten. If she transgressed, he was punished. He came to tolerate the punishment, then to yearn for it. The idea of punishment appealed to him. Later, he would approach it from another angle and become the chastiser rather than be the chastised. It was only right.

When Yelle was seventeen and Leos eight, mother died in a coach accident. Leos was properly a boy by then, but the Beast was growing inside him as he had grown inside his mother. The Beast was not the girl he would have been if raised as one, but the girl that had been imprisoned, tortured, suppressed. And she was angry.

Shortly after the death of her pet cat, Yelle stopped beating the boy. She was his mother now and could have him sent away or punished at will. She used her power over him sparingly, remembering just what she had created in her brother.

Besides, Leos was now devoted to his sister. If he ever fought with the local boys, it would turn out that his opponent had angered him by insulting Yelle. And if he ever fought, Leos would win. Emmanuelle became quite protective of Leos, mothering him far better than their real mother had.

The Beast had tasted blood already. The two men, who didn't matter, and sweet, ripe Natasha. When her claw had slipped into Natasha's peach-soft flesh, she had known what her purpose was. Women (Yelle excluded) were disgusting. Creatures of Evil. The Beast was born to kill women, to be as great a scourge to them as Sigmar had been to goblinkind.

At the University, Leos was taught swordsmanship by the great Valancourt, and soon his blade was blooded.

The Beast felt strange about the blade. She loved to lick it sometimes, gently scratching her tongue to get the taste of the blood, but it was not a claw. And the boy-shell's duelling partners were men.

The first claw was a hunting knife that had been father's. The Beast loved that claw and still cherished it. After the first kills, when the blade was still wet, the Beast would hold the knife between her thighs, feeling the hilt against her forbidden place. It made her feel complete.

Later, the Beast had fashioned more suitable claws and come out of the boy-shell more often. Yelle had so many pretty dresses, so many pretty jewels, so many pretty things... And the Beast's knife-gauntlets matched so many of her sister's dresses.

The Beast still thought women were disgusting. They were weak and foolish, not like herself. The Beast wanted to couple only with men, to feel their rough, hairy bodies. Even the boy-shell had no romantic interest in the feeble girls of the court with whom he danced at balls. He was rumoured to have broken the heart of Clothilde of Averheim through his cruelty, but actually the hurt was done by a simple lack of interest. Sometimes, the Beast would try on her sister's gowns and feel the killing lust flare in her heart.

Usually, she could hide inside Leos, coming out when she had to strike. But on her hunting expeditions, she would frequently dress up as if for a ball, selecting a green velvet gown with a matching cape.

But Leos hated himself for having the Beast's desires. Later than the Beast, he became a killer too. He killed elegantly with his sword, while the Beast ripped with her claws. They never really became one, and would fight continually.

The Altdorf victims were only the latest in an unbroken chain of corpses. Lately, the Beast had raged more, been less cautious, given Leos less time to clear up and cover the tracks.

The fight for control of the body became a constant thing.

In the end, as was inevitable, the Beast won.

VIII

The Countess Emmanuelle's dressing room was filled with people. From somewhere, more guards and servants had appeared. As an Elector, Johann was in charge of the situation.

Mnoujkine had called the palace physician and Mikael Hasselstein was lying on the countess's daybed, having his ripped face seen to. He might lose an eye, and his upper lip was so badly torn that he would have trouble talking, but he would live. Emmanuelle herself was unharmed, but she had fainted and been covered with Leos's cloak while her brother – it was still hard to think of him as a her and as the countess's sister – dressed in one of her gowns.

Johann and Harald were most concerned with Rosanna. She was in another trance state, dreaming furiously. Leos lived for a few minutes with Harald's knife through her heart and died without saying anything.

'We'll never know why,' Harald said.

Johann knew the captain was wrong. 'Rosanna will know,' she said.

'Maybe it would be best if she didn't...'

Kleindeinst gently eased his knife out of the Beast's breast, wiped it on the cast-aside velvet cloak, and slipped it into its sheath.

'Green velvet,' he said, rubbing the rich material between his fingers. 'This has been a lot of trouble for such rotten stuff.'

Johann picked up Rosanna and carried her away from Leos's body. She was mumbling and fighting the dream.

He took her out of the dressing room and into the first bedroom he could find, where he laid her out gently. The room was sparsely decorated, as untenanted and characterless as a guest chamber in an inn. It had been Leos's room.

The only objects which suggested an occupant were a row of cameos on a dresser, small and cheap portraits of handsome young men – heroes of the Empire, popular actors, the sons of distinguished families. Johann recognized an indifferent picture of himself among the collection. In a rack on the wall, there were several fine swords.

Rosanna would wake up on her own, soon. He could leave her to that.

In the reception room, the countess was surrounded by solicitous servants, her face a beautiful mask. Johann had never noticed before how closely she resembled Leos. Normally, the younger sister would have been the greater beauty. But there was very little 'normally' about this business. He wondered how much his fellow elector had known, had guessed, had suspected...

Then, he thought of Wolf. His brother was still out there, confused and hurt.

Emmanuelle was talking in a low, serious voice, giving orders to Daniel Dorrie, one of her retainers and, it was rumoured, one of her lovers. The smooth-faced young man was paying close attention.

Kleindeinst stood by the door, examining his axe-work. Emmanuelle knew he had brought Leos down and seemed to be talking with Dorrie about the officer. Killing the relatives of electors was getting to be a habit with him. Johann swore to himself that the captain wouldn't get into any more trouble for his action. Any of them would have done the same thing. In the end, Johann thought it was probably best for poor Leos. Earlier today, he had thought of the Beast as a monster. Already, the murderer had become 'poor Leos.'

There was a movement from behind him and Rosanna came out of the bedroom, a hand pressed to her head as if she were hung over. She was unsteady on her feet. He supported her, but she pushed away from him and stood on her own.

Johann and Kleindeinst both looked at the scryer, both asking the same question in their head.

Why?

Rosanna put out her hands to steady herself and knocked a small ornament from a stand. It smashed on the floor. Emmanuelle looked over and tut-tutted, then went back to Dorrie's orders.

The scryer took a deep breath and became fully awake.

'It's over,' Johann said.

Rosanna shook her head and, without saying anything, walked towards the Countess Emmanuelle.

Dorrie put his hand under his cloak, reaching for a knife, instinctively protecting his mistress. Kleindeinst's hand got to Dorrie's wrist before the favourite's hand got to the knife.

Rosanna took hold of the Countess-Elector of Nuln by the chin and tilted her head upwards. She looked at the other woman, hawked loudly and spat in her face...

EPILOGUE

Johann & Rosanna

She still couldn't bring herself to explain it all to them. The Countess Emmanuelle von Liebewitz was back in Nuln with her courtiers and her conscience, her sister buried in the family vaults with an inscription referring to her as 'beloved son and brother.' Rosanna could never forget the ten deaths she had experienced during this investigation – the nine women and Elsaesser – but the lifelong death of the girl who had never been allowed to live was the worst thing she had ever known. Leos had never even had a girl's name.

The three met in a coffee house well away from the Street of a Hundred Taverns and mainly sat without talking. Johann was not pressing her to talk, but thought she would tell him eventually. Maybe she would. Harald really didn't want to know, although there was a sore point inside him, a voice that whispered 'womanslayer.'

'Don't blame yourself,' she said.

'I don't. You misread me. I killed something that had to be killed. That's all.'

It wasn't, but she didn't contradict him.

Officially, Leos had fought one duel too many, on a matter of honour, and been bested by Harald Kleindeinst. Followers of the viscount's career were surprised that he should choose to match blades with an untitled watchman, but few were interested enough to question the story. Sam Warble, a halfling investigator hired by the Marquess Sidonie to delve into Leos's character and habits in the hope of uncovering something that would help her avenge the death of her husband, eventually returned to Marienburg, having just missed turning up some real surprises. The investigator had a few questions left, but Harald had convinced Warble not to ask them too loudly and he had proved very persuasive in the matter. The marquess, pleased enough at the end of the business, had paid the halfling his full fee in any case, and was planning on erecting a statue to her husband in the Marienburg market square.

Harald drank his coffee and, impatient with them, got up to leave.

He said his goodbyes and pulled on his coat. His copper badge was on one lapel. He unpinned it and dropped it on the table.

'I suppose I shall not be needing this any more.'

Johann picked up the badge.

'I understand,' Kleindeinst said, 'that the countess-elector has petitioned for my prosecution. Doubtless, Hals von Tasseninck has forgotten the service I did him during the riots and seconded her motion. If I'm lucky, I'll be able to get my old job back at the Reik and Talabec.'

Johann handed the officer the badge.

'I have talked with the Emperor. This time, I really have. Karl-Franz isn't so bad, you know. The countess will not be welcome at the palace for a long time. He has personally blocked her paper and I doubt that she'll press it further. I have told her that if she does, I shall tell Detlef Sierck the true story of the Beast and he will cancel that Zhiekhill and Chaida play and stage instead a spine-chiller called *The Secret Life of Leos von Liebewitz.*'

Harald nearly laughed. He pinned the badge on again.

'Back to the docks, I suppose,' he said.

'Dickon has been removed, I understand.'

'Yes.'

'You'll be the new commander in Luitpoldstrasse then?'

Harald shrugged. 'I'm not a commander, I'm a street copper. Besides, there's no station in Luitpoldstrasse, remember...'

'I'll have extra funds diverted to the watch, I promise. I'll make it my business to get the station rebuilt. But it will be different this time.'

'It will have to be.'

Harald Kleindeinst walked out of the coffee house and left them together.

Johann looked tired for a moment.

Outside, the fog had completely dispersed, but it was winter. There was already a light fall of snow and the windows were frosted over. There were still plenty of burned-out buildings in the city and whole areas of the East End were ruins. There was a tent settlement amid the cinders and ashes, and the cold was already a problem. Grand Theogonist Yorri's Riots Commission wasn't doing anything about that. Yefimovich was still at large, with a thousand crowns offered for anyone who turned him in, sought for the Beast's crimes as well as his own. The insurrections had died down, but Prince Kloszowski's latest pamphlet harped on the familiar neglects and the freezing inner-city dispossessed were repeating his verses under their steaming breaths as they stamped their feet, as much with irritation as the cold.

After Leos's death, there was a rash of singular occurrences, which Rosanna thought of as omens in reverse: Dien Ch'ing, the Cathayan ambassador, disappeared from the palace; Detlef Sierck announced a horror play which would give the rest of the city the nightmares Rosanna had already been having to cope with; Etienne de la Rougierre was recalled to Bretonnia and rebuked by King Charles Tete d'Or for his licentiousness; Ch'ing's proposed expedition to the Dark Lands, suspected as a scheme to distract the Empire from subtler evils closer to home, was abandoned; Mikael Hasselstein resigned his position as Lector and entered a secluded branch of the Cult of Sigmar, taking a vow of silence as part of a self-induced penance; by night, the network of streets between the docks and the Street of a Hundred Taverns again became thick with women soliciting; people still lived, suffered and died...

'I never found my brother,' Johann said. 'He's not returned to the University.'

'He's hurt and confused, but he'll mend. I scry him occasionally. He's still in the city. He knows he's not the Beast now. I promise you.'

Johann let his coffee cool. 'I must find him,' he said. 'He was the reason I got into this thing. I must see it through. I think he still has a trace of the warpstone in him. You must have felt that when you touched his mind.'

Rosanna agreed. 'But the warpstone isn't the only thing that can twist a person out of true, Johann...'

'You are right. There are worse ways of altering than to have a face of fire or daemon's horns or a little wolfishness.'

Rosanna thought of Leos and was angry again. The girl inside the boy-shell had been a walking knot of agony. Then, she looked at Johann and calmed herself. The baron needed a scryer and she was without a position.

She centred herself and tried to reach out with her mind...

The city teemed with hurts and resentments, with plenty and poverty, with nobility and savagery, with devotion and injustice, with Law and Chaos. She brushed hundreds of minds as they were tossed around like peas in a soup, each sealed in its own little shell of skull. She was wary of letting any of them in. The taste of Leos was still too strong with her. Over the last weeks, she had often found herself dreaming Leos's dreams, choking on her memories. No matter how much she tried to dispel, her gift still gave her a curse. Also, she had flashes of Johann's past, of Elsaesser's, even of Wolf.

She knew the feel of Wolf's mind and searched for it. Her senses swelled to encompass the whole of the city. It would be like picking out one particular pea in a lake of soup, but it could be done.

Johann noticed her distraction. 'Rosanna, what is it?'

'I can help you, Johann,' she said, laying her hand over his.

Silver Nails

Red Thirst

Eventually, Vukotich was awoken by the steady rumbling of the wheels and the clatter of the chains. It was dark inside the closed wagon, but he could tell from the bumpy ride that they weren't in Zhufbar any more. A paved road within the walls of the city wouldn't be as bumpy as this. They were being taken up into the mountains.

He smelled his travelling companions well before his eyes got used enough to the gloom to make out their shapes. There were too many of them to be comfortably confined in the space available, and, despite the mountain cool outside, it was uncomfortably hot. Nobody said anything, but the chains clanked as the wagon lurched over obstacles or swayed from side to side. Someone started wailing, but someone else cuffed him soundly and he shut up.

Vukotich could still feel the blow that had knocked him out. An acolyte of the Moral Crusade had bludgeoned him with his blessed iron during the arrest and he supposed from the pains in his chest and legs that the Guardians of Purity had taken the opportunity to kick him thoroughly when he was unconscious. Glinka's blackhood bastards might not be much when it came to knocking back the juice or groping the girls, but they were certainly unequalled champions of unnecessary violence. He only wished he'd been awake when the Company of Killjoys reached for their skullbreakers. He'd been through enough campaigns to learn a little about self-defence.

Like everyone else, Vukotich hadn't at first taken Claes Glinka seriously. He had been hearing a lot lately about this cleric who adhered to no particular god, but called himself the Guardian of Morality, and preached fiery sermons in rural town squares against lasciviousness, in favour of the sanctity of marriage and lamenting the decline of the Empire's moral values. For Glinka, all the things a man might take pleasure in were steps on the Road to Chaos and Damnation. Then, so swiftly that most people barely had time to react, Claes Glinka had won some measure of Imperial approval and was the figurehead of a sizeable movement.

His crusade swept through the Old World from town to town, from city to city. In Nuln, he had managed to get the university authorities to close down the Beloved of Verena, a brothel that had been serving the students and lecturers of the city since the days of Empress Agnetha. In the

Sudenland, he had supervised the destruction of the fabulously-stocked wine cellars of the Order of Ranald, and seen to the burning of that region's famous vineyards. His agitators worked in the councils of the rulers to change the laws, to enforce prohibitions against strong drink, public and private licentiousness, even sweetmeats and tobacco. Many resisted, but a surprising number, frequently those most known for their own personal laxity, caved in and let Glinka have his way.

Vukotich tested his shackles. His feet were chained to a bar that ran the length of the wagon, inset into the floor. His hands were in manacles, stringing him between the prisoners either side of him. He felt like a trinket on a memento bracelet. The smell got worse as the journey progressed. The wagon made no latrine stops and some of the prisoners didn't have Vukotich's self-control.

He had come to the fortress-city in search of work. His last employment had ended with the rout of Vastarien's Vanquishers by the bandits of Averland. Upon the death of Prince Vastarien, he became free to pledge his sword-arm to another employer and he had hoped to find a suitable position with one of the warrior aristocrats attending the Festival of Ulric in Zhufbar. The festival, dedicated to the God of Battle, Wolves and Winter, took place each autumn to celebrate the onset of winter, and was held in a different city every year. This was where the campaigns against the creatures of darkness were planned, where the arrangements for the defence of the Empire were made and where the disposition of Emperor Luitpold's forces was decided. It was also the best place for a masterless mercenary to come by a position.

The boards of the wagon's roof were ill-fitting, and shafts of sunlight sliced down into the dark, allowing him to see something of his companions. Everyone was in chains, their feet shackled to the central bar. Most of them had obvious bludgeon wounds. To his left, stretching the chain between their wrists to its utmost, was a fellow with the oiled ringlets of a nobleman of Kislev, dressed only in britches that had been put on back to front. He was in a silent rage and couldn't stop trembling. Vukotich guessed he would rather have remained in whoever's bed he had been hauled from. An old woman in well-worn but clean clothes wept into her hands. She was repeating something, over and over, in a steady whine. 'I've been selling herbs for years, it's not against the law.' Several others were long-term boozers, still snoring drunkenly. He wondered how they'd react when they found out they were about to take the Cure in a penal colony. All human misery was here. And the misery of several of the other higher races too. Opposite were three dwarfs, roped together and complaining. They poked at each other's eyes and grumbled in a language Vukotich didn't know.

Zhufbar had been different this time. Claes Glinka was in town, and had gained the ear of the fortress-city's Lord Marshal, Wladislaw Blasko. There were posters up all over the streets, announcing strict laws against gambling, drinking, brawling, dancing, 'immodest' music, prostitution, smoking in public and the sale of prohibited stimulants. Vukotich had laughed at the pompously-phrased edicts and assumed they were all for show. You couldn't hold a festival for the God of Battle and expect a city-load of off-duty soldiers not to spend their time dicing, getting drunk, fighting, partying, chasing whores or chewing weirdroot. It was just ridiculous. But the black-robed acolytes were everywhere. In theory, they were unarmed, but the symbol Glinka had chosen for the crusade was a two-foot length of straight iron carved with the Seven Edicts of Purity, and those were well in evidence whenever the Guardians attempted to enforce the new laws.

On his first morning in the city, Vukotich saw three hooded bully-boys set upon a street singer and batter the lad senseless with their iron bars. They trampled his mandolin to pieces and dragged him off to the newly-dedicated Temple of Purity. Where before there had been ale-holes and tap-rooms, there were now crusade-sanctioned coffee houses, with in-house preachers replacing the musicians and cold-faced charity collectors rather than welcoming women. On his last visit, Vukotich had found it impossible to walk down the city's Main Gate Road without being propositioned by five different whores, offered a chew of weird-root for five coppers, and hearing twelve different types of street singer and musician competing for his attention. Now all he found were tiresome clerics droning on about sin and Moral Crusaders rattling collection tins under his nose.

The prisoner shackled to his right hand was a woman. He could distinguish her perfume amid the viler odours of the other convicts. She sat primly, knees together, back straight, looking more fed up than desperate. She was young and dressed in immodestly thin silks. Her hair was elaborately styled, she wore a deal of cheap jewellery and her face was painted. Something about the set of her features struck him as predatory, tenacious, hungry. A whore, Vukotich supposed. At least a third of the convicts in the wagon were obvious prostitutes. Glinka's Crusade was especially hard on them.

The first day of the festival had been fine. He had attended the grand opening ceremony and listened to the speeches of the visiting dignitaries. The Emperor was represented by no less a hero than Maximilian von Konigswald, the Grand Prince of Ostland, whose young son Oswald had recently distinguished himself by vanquishing the Great Enchanter, Constant Drachenfels. After the ceremony, he had found himself at a loose end. Later in the week, he would learn which generals were hiring. But now, everyone was busy renewing old friendships and looking for some entertainment. Vukotich had fallen in with Snorri, a half-Norse cleric of Ulric he had served with during his time defending Erengrad from the trolls, and they had toured the hostelries. The first few houses they visited were deadly dull, with apologetic innkeepers explaining that they were forbidden by law to serve anything other than beer and watered-down wine and then only for an absurdly brief given period each evening. There were always hooded acolytes sitting in the corner to make sure the taverners obeyed Glinka's edicts.

As they stormed out of the third such place, a small fellow with a black feather in his cap sidled up to them and offered, for a fee, to guide them to an establishment that cared little for the crusade and its restrictions. They haggled for a while, and finally handed over the coin, whereupon Blackfeather led them through a maze of alleyways in the oldest part of the city and down into some disused defence tunnels. Zhufbar had been a dwarf city originally, and the Norseman had to bend over double to get through the labyrinth. They heard noisy music and laughter up ahead, and their hearts warmed a little. Apart from anything else, they'd be able to stand up straight. It turned out to be a 'Flying Inn,' a revelry that moved from place to place, two steps ahead of the crusade. Tonight, it was in an abandoned underground armoury. A band of elf minstrels were playing something good and loud and raucous, while their admirers chewed weirdroot to better appreciate the music. Blackfeather offered them dried lumps of the dream-drug, and Snorri shoved one into his mouth, surrendering to the vividly-coloured dreams, but Vukotich declined, preferring to sample the strong black ale of the city. Girls wearing very little were dancing upon a makeshift stage while coloured lanterns revolved and different varieties of scented smoke whirled. Huge casks were being tapped and the wine was flowing freely, dicers and card-players were staking pouches of coins and a dwarf jester was making a series of well-appreciated lewd jokes about Glinka, Blasko and various other leading lights of the Moral Crusade. Someone somewhere was making a lot of money from the 'Flying Inn'. Of course, Vukotich had barely drained his first tankard and started looking around for a spare woman when the raid started...

And here he was, in chains, bound for some convict settlement in the mountains. He knew they'd put him to work in some hell-hole of a mine or a quarry and that he'd probably be dead within five years. He cursed all Guardians of Morality and rattled his chains.

For once, he had a stroke of luck. His left manacle was bent out of shape, its rivets popped. He slipped his hand free.

Now, when the wagon stopped, he would have a chance.

Once they were out of the city, Dien Ch'ing felt free to pull off his black steeple-hood. This far to the west, the people of Cathay were uncommon enough to attract attention, and so the Order's face-covering headgear was a convenient way of walking about unquestioned. The round-eyed, big-nosed, abnormally-bearded natives of this barbarous region were superstitious savages, ignorant enough to suppose that his oriental features were marks of Chaos and toss him into the nearest bonfire. Of course, in his case, they wouldn't have been entirely unjustified. All who ascended the Pagoda of Tsien-Tsin, Lord of the Fifteen Devils, Master of the Five Elements, had more than a trace of the warpstone in their blood.

A few too many clashes with the Monkey-King's warrior monks had forced him to leave the land of his birth, and now he was a wanderer across the face of the world, a servant of Tsien-Tsin, an unaltered acolyte of Chaos, a Master of the Mystic Martial Arts. He had been shepherded through the Dark Lands by the goblins, and conveyed across the World's Edge Mountains to the shores of the Blackwater. There was an Invisible Empire in the Known World, an empire that superseded the petty earthly dominions of the Monkey-King, the Tsarina of Kislev or the Emperor Luitpold. This was the empire of the Chaos Powers, of Khorne and Nurgle in the west and north, and of Great Gojira and the Catsidhe Daemons in the east. Tsien-Tsin, the Dark Lord to whom he pledged his service, was known here as Tzeentch. The Proscribed Cults of Chaos flourished, and the warp-altered horde grew in strength with each cycle of the moons. The kingdoms of men squabbled, and the Invisible Empire grew ever more powerful.

They made slow progress up into the mountains. Ch'ing sat on his padded seat beside the driver of the second wagon. He was impatient to get this coffle to the slave-pits, and be back about his business in Zhufbar. He had made this run many times and it was becoming boring. Once they reached the secret caves where the goblins waited, the convicts would be separated into three groups. The young men would be taken off to work in the warpstone mines of the Dark Lands, the young women sold to the slave markets of Araby, and the remainder slaughtered for food. It was a simple business and it served the Powers of Chaos well. Always, he allowed the goblins to pick out a woman or two, or perhaps a comely youth, and watched them at their sport. Claes Glinka would be shocked at the ultimate fate of those whose sins he abhorred. Ch'ing laughed musically. It was most amusing.

But this was not the time for amusements. There was important business to be transacted at the Festival of Ulric. There were many high-ranking servants of Chaos in the city, and they too were plotting strategy. When Ch'ing had been visited in the Dark Lands by Yefimovich, the Kislevite High Priest of Tzeentch, he had been told that the dread one wished him to take a position within the Moral Crusade and do his best to turn Glinka's followers into an army for the advancement of Chaos. Thus far, his subtle strategies had worked well. The crusade hoods could conceal more than slanted eyes and Ch'ing knew that many an iron-carrying acolyte bore the marks of the warpstone under his mask. Glinka was a blind fanatic and easily duped. Sometimes, Ch'ing wondered whether the Guardian of Morality had not made his own dark bargain with the Invisible Empire. No one could put aside so many pleasures without a good reason. However, Glinka was just as likely sincere in his passions. All western barbarians were mad to some extent. Ch'ing wondered what it must be like to fear one's own appetites so much that one sought to suppress the pleasures of all the world. To him, thirsts existed to be slaked, lusts to be satiated, desires to be fulfilled.

The sun was full in the sky now. The coffle had been on the road all night. Most of the convicts would still be asleep or nursing their hangovers. There were three wagons in all, and although the drivers were used to the mountain roads, progress was still frustratingly snail-like.

Just now, they were on a narrow ledge cut into a steep, thickly forested incline. Tall evergreens rose beside the path, their lowest branches continually striking the sides of the wagons.

There were bandits in the mountains, and worse things: altered monstrosities, renegade dwarf bands, black orcs, skaven and beastmen. But he took comfort; there was unlikely to be anything worse out there than himself. His position on the Pagoda gave him the power to summon and bind daemons, to tumble through the air in combat, and to fight for a day and a night without breaking a sweat.

The first wagon halted and Ch'ing nudged the driver beside him to rein in the horses. The animals settled. Ch'ing waved to the third wagon, which also creaked to a stop.

'Tree down ahead, master,' shouted the acolyte on the first wagon. Ch'ing sighed with irritation. He could use a simple spell to remove the obstacle, but that would drain him, and he knew the Blessings of Tsien-Tsin would be required soon for other purposes. There was nothing for it but to use the available tools.

Holding his robes about him, he stepped down to the road. He had to be careful of his footing. It would be easy to take a fall and wind up bent around a tree hundreds of feet below. The mightiest of warrior magicians always met their deaths through such small missteps. It was the gods' way of keeping their servants humble.

He walked round to the back of the wagon and unlocked the door. The foul stench of the prisoners wafted out and he held his nose. Westerners always smelled vile, but this crew were worse than usual.

The convicts cringed away from the light. He knew some of them would be startled by his Celestial face. So be it. They were in no position to be offended.

'Attention,' he said. 'Those of you who do not assist us in the removal of the tree that blocks our path will have their ears severed. Volunteers?'

The driver yanked at the chain threaded around the central bar of the wagon and took out the keys. Guards with whips and swords clustered around the wagon. Ch'ing stood back. The central bar was raised and the convicts were hauled out, their ankle-shackles pulling off the bar like beads from a string. Their feet were free, but they would still be chained wrist to wrist.

First out was the fragile girl he had been warned against. She didn't like the strong sunlight, and covered her eyes. After her was a sturdy young man with more than a few battle scars. Vukotich, he knew. One of the mercenaries. Then, there was a pause as the half-naked Pavel Alexei hesitated on the lip of the wagon.

Something was wrong.

The whore and the mercenary were shackled together, and the man held his arm up awkwardly, as if chained to the degenerate. But the Kislevite was pressing his hand to his forehead, an empty manacle dangling from his wrist.

Two of the prisoners were loose from the chain.

The mercenary looked him in the eyes, and Ch'ing saw defiance and hatred reflected at him.

He had his hand on his scimitar-handle, but the mercenary was fast.

Vukotich embraced the girl, lifting her up into his arms and threw himself off the road. The two of them became a ball and bounced into the woods. Their cries of pain sounded out as they vanished between the trees.

Pavel Alexei, bewildered, tried to follow them, but he was still chained to the next prisoner, and he slipped, dangling from the wagon by his manacled left wrist.

Ch'ing sliced with his scimitar and the Kislevite fell at his feet, leaving his neatly-severed hand in its iron cuff at the end of the chain.

'Anyone else?' he asked mildly. 'No? Good.'

The cries had stopped. The whore and the mercenary were probably dead down there, but Ch'ing could take no risks.

'You, you and you,' he indicated three guards. 'Find them and bring them back.'

They stepped off the road and began to edge their way downwards.

'And take off those hoods,' Ch'ing added. 'You'll only slip and break your necks.'

The guards pulled their hoods back and followed the path of broken bushes and scraped trees that marked the escapees' route down the mountain. Soon, they were gone.

The Kislevite was whimpering, pressing fingers over his leaking stump.

'Perhaps next time you won't be so keen to share the bed of another man's wife, Pavel Alexei,' Ch'ing said.

The Kislevite spat at his shoes.

Ch'ing shrugged, and the driver killed Pavel Alexei with his iron bar. The goblins expected a certain wastage along the road.

Ch'ing pulled out his clay pipe and tamped in some opium from his pouch. He would travel to the Pagoda for a few moments, in search of further enlightenment.

Then, when the guards brought back the whore and the mercenary, he would make sure they were dead, and then the coffle could be on its way again.

Thank the gods, he had not broken any bones in the tumble down the mountainside. But his clothes were ragged, and great patches of skin were scraped from his back and shins. The girl didn't seem greatly hurt either. Too bad. It would have been easier if she were dead. Her silks were torn, her long hair was loose, and she had a few bruises, but she wasn't bleeding.

He hauled her to her feet, pulling on the chain between them, and dragged her through the trees, away from the flattened bush that had broken their roll. It was important to get away from any trail that could be followed. They had gained some time on the guards by their dangerous, headlong descent, but there would be acolytes after them. A brief exchange of glances with the Celestial in charge of the coffle had convinced Vukotich this was not a man to expect much from in the way of mercy.

'Keep quiet,' he told the girl. 'Do what I say. You understand?'

She didn't look as panicked as he had expected. She simply nodded her head. He thought she was even smiling slightly. She was probably a weirdroot-chewer. A lot of whores were. They sold you their body, but kept their dreams for themselves. It was much the same with swords-for-hire, he supposed.

He picked their way through the trees, taking care with his footing. It was hard to keep a balance with their wrists chained together. The girl was agile and unfussy, and kept up with him easily. She had a lot of control. She was probably very good at what she did. He wondered whether she were more than a street harlot. More than one great assassin had found a career as a courtesan an efficient way to get close to their targets.

They would be expected to keep going down, so Vukotich took them up, hoping to strike the roadledge a few miles behind the wagons. The Celestial was unlikely to send men back after them, and it would be impossible to turn the coffle round. They should be able to get away if they made it too much trouble to bring them in. Somewhere, there were slave-pits waiting for the convicts, and the Moral Guardians wouldn't want to have three wagonloads of prisoners stranded half-way up a mountain just to bring in a couple of minor carousers. Of course, you could never tell with fanatics...

The girl grabbed his wrist. Their chain rattled. She tugged.

'That way,' she said. 'There are three men coming.'

She was sharp. At first he couldn't hear anything, but then her words were confirmed by clumping feet and huffing breaths.

'They've split up,' she said. 'One will be here soon.'

She looked around.

'Can you climb that tree?' she asked, indicating a thick trunk.

Vukotich snorted. 'Of course.'

He must be staring at her.

'Now,' she said. 'Quickly.'

He snapped to and obeyed her as if she were a sergeant-at-arms. It was awkward, but there was a stout branch within reach, and he was able to chin himself one-handed. She dangled from the chain, and swung herself up like an acrobat, then hauled him onto the branch. They were both securely perched. He was breathing hard, but she kept her wind.

'Don't be amazed,' she said. 'I've done this sort of thing before. Lots of times.'

He had been staring at her again. She pulled a branch, and they were hidden behind the thick leaves.

'Now,' she said. 'Be quiet.'

They could hear the acolyte now, blundering around below. He wasn't tracking them properly, just looking at random. They must have found the bush where their tumble ended, and split up in three directions. These bullies were city boys, unused to following people through trails of broken twigs and trampled grass.

Vukotich and the girl both had their hands against the trunk, steadying themselves. He saw the chain hanging between their wrists, and noticed something odd about their shackles. His manacle was plain iron, flecked with odd lumps of some other stuff that sparkled. Hers was different, a padded ring of leather sewn around the metal. He had never seen that before. It looked as if their captors wanted to spare her the discomfort of a chafed wrist, but he couldn't believe Glinka would wish to treat a whore so lightly. More likely, the cuff was designed to prevent her slipping free by dislocating her thumb and pulling her slender hand out of the metal grip.

He guessed her age at sixteen or seventeen. She was slim, but not delicate. She was perfectly balanced on the branch, with an almost catlike ease. In the sunlight, her harlot's paint made her look like a child's doll: white face, red lips, blue-shadowed eyes. She had spoken Old Worlder with a slight accent. Bretonnian, he thought. Like him, she was far from home.

It was a shame, but he would have to get rid of her at the first opportunity. No matter how competent she seemed, chained to him as she was she was as useful to him as an anvil.

The unhooded acolyte was directly below them now, robes swishing as he looked about. He had a wicked curved sword in one hand, and his bar in the other. He didn't seem to be guarding anyone's purity. He let loose a very un-moral stream of blasphemous oaths. Vukotich could have sworn that the lumps on the acolyte's forehead were the buds of daemon horns.

Not for the first time, Vukotich wondered if there was something extremely sinister behind Glinka's crusade.

The girl laid her hand over his and nodded sharply. He was a beat behind her thinking, but caught up.

Together, they leaped from the branch and onto the acolyte. He cried out, but she got her free right hand over his mouth and stifled him. Vukotich looped their chain around his throat and they both pulled. The acolyte struggled, but he had dropped his weapons. His hand groped for Vukotich's face, but he pushed it away. All three fell to the sloping ground and the acolyte was pressed beneath them into the mulchy soil.

Vukotich's wrist hurt, but he kept up the pressure. The girl was pulling equally hard. The chain bit into the acolyte's neck and his face was red with blood. Noises gargled in his throat. The whore took her hand away from the man's mouth and Vukotich saw the teeth-bruises in the heel of her palm. She made a fist and punched the guard's face.

The acolyte's tongue had expanded to fill his mouth. Blood gushed from his nose. His eyes rolled upwards and showed only white.

The girl drew her forefinger across her throat. Vukotich nodded. The acolyte was dead.

They disentangled their chain from his throat and stood up. Vukotich gave a silent prayer to his family totem. *Let the blood I have spilled be not innocent.* He looked around and picked up the curved sword. It felt natural in his hand. He had been naked without a weapon.

As he admired the blade, he felt the tug of the manacle, and stuck out his arm, directed by the girl. The swordpoint sank into the chest of the acolyte who was rushing at them. His was the force behind the killing stroke, but she had provided the aim. He should not have been distracted in the first place. He should have been ready himself to react.

Their hands were entwined around the swordhilt now. They withdrew it from the dying acolyte and stood over the bodies. The first had latent horns, the second wolfish teeth. Under the hoods, things were not so pure.

'One more,' she said. 'No. He's sensed what's happened, and is running away, back up to the road. He'll get help.'

Vukotich had to agree with her.

'Downwards,' she said. 'If there's no pass in the crotch of this valley, there must be a stream. We can follow it.'

Vukotich had another priority. He took the sword into his left hand and looked around. There was a fallen tree. That would do for a chopping block.

He dragged her over, and laid the chain on the wood.

'That's useless,' she said. 'The chain is tempered iron. You'll just blunt the sword.'

Nevertheless, he chopped down. The blade turned aside, kinked where it had met the iron links. The chain showed a scratch of clean metal, but wasn't broken.

It was a shame, but...

He pulled her hand and slipped her sleeve away from her wrist. He looked her in her face.

'I'm a swordsman and you're a whore,' he said. 'You can practise your trade without your left hand, but I need my right...'

Red rage sparked in her eyes.

'That won't...'

He struck the blow and felt a shock that jarred his arm from wrist to elbow. The sword bounced and scraped against her padded manacle.

'...work.'

Incredulous, he looked at her wrist. There was a purple bruise where he had struck, but the skin wasn't even broken. He should have sheared her hand clean off.

She sighed, as if with impatience.

'I told you. You should have listened, fool swordsman.'

His left hand felt as if it had been struck with a stone. She took the bent sword out of it as if she were taking a toy from a child, and threw it away. She shook her left hand, trying to get the pain out of her wrist.

Vukotich noticed he had torn the leather around her shackle. The exposed metal core caught the light and shone silver.

Silver!

Her eyes were almost completely red now. She smiled, revealing sharp white teeth, needle canines delicately scraping her lower lip.

Iron for him, silver for her. Their captors had known what they were about.

The leech thing took his throat with an unbreakable grip and leaned across to kiss him.

Genevieve knew she should kill Vukotich, wrench his arm off, and have done with it.

But, vampire or not, she wasn't that sort of girl.

In six hundred and thirty-nine years of more-or-less life, she had been and done a lot of things. Including plenty she wasn't proud of. But she had never been, and wasn't now, a casual murderess.

She'd killed for sustenance, she'd assassinated several people without whom the world was a better place, and she'd killed in combat – the two dead acolytes lying back there beneath the trees bore witness to that – but she'd never just slaughtered someone because it was the easiest course to take.

Not that she hadn't been severely tempted on many occasions.

Her grip on Vukotich's neck relaxed and she pushed him away.

'Come on,' she told the startled mercenary, her eyeteeth receding into their gumsheaths. 'We have to move quickly.'

The anger subsided and her eyes cleared. She still felt the red thirst. But there was no time to bleed the fallen. Drinking from the newly dead wasn't pleasant, but she had done it before. She would have been more worried that there would be warpstone in the acolytes' blood. She was immune to most diseases, but the caress of Chaos wasn't like plague or the fevers. Her natural defences might not be enough to keep her whole with that stuff inside her.

She jerked him to his feet and led him downwards. Unlike the traditional melodrama heroine, she was highly unlikely to twist her ankle and become a nuisance for her big, brave protector. She was able to sense the root-holes and low shrubs that might trip them up.

She had been right. They came to a shallow stream that ran fast downwards. It must eventually feed into the Blackwater. If they followed it, they would find a settlement. She hoped it would be one with a blacksmith who held a very low opinion of Claes Glinka's Moral Crusade. If not, it would mean resorting to force and terror, and she was tired of that. She had come to Zhufbar to get away from her reputation for great deeds and she did not relish another brush with the makings of songs and folktales.

She tugged the chain and her padded manacle shifted. She felt a sharp sting as the exposed silver pressed against her flesh and let out a pained hiss. She twisted the manacle and the burning stopped, but the metal still gleamed white.

She took a handful of mud from the stream and gave it to Vukotich.

'Smear this on the tear,' she said. 'Please.'

He took the mud and, without questioning her, applied it to the manacle like a healer putting a poultice on a wound.

'Thank you,' she said. She took a large leaf and stuck it over the mud, tightening it around the leather. It would dry and fall off eventually, but for now it would protect her.

'Don't worry,' she told him. 'I'm not going to drain you dry at a draught. Not that I wouldn't be justified after your amateur attempt at surgery.'

She rubbed her wrist. The bruise was already fading. He had nothing to say. He wasn't even sheepish.

'Come on,' she tugged again. They jogged along the stream, feet splashing in the water. He was wearing heavy marauder's boots, while she only had dancer's slippers.

'But...' he began.

She was ahead of him. 'Yes, I know. Running water. Vampires aren't supposed to be able to cross it.'

He nodded, exerting himself to keep apace with her.

'That holds true only for the Truly Dead. They're the ones who can't stand religious symbols or garlic or direct sunlight. I'm not one of those. I never got around to dying.'

He wasn't the only one who didn't know much about vampires. Glinka's vigilante squad had come for her with wreaths of garlic around their necks, bearing enough medals of Shallya and Verena to slow them down considerably. One of her 'clients' must have informed on her. They came to her room in the East Wall Hostelry just after sun-up, when she would normally be sinking into her daytime doze, and found her with Molotov, an official from the Kislevite delegation to the Festival of Ulric, delicately tapping his throat. They had silver scythes and hawthorn switches, and soon had her bound and helpless. She had expected to feel the prick of a stake against her ribs, and for it all to be over.

Six hundred and thirty-nine years wasn't a bad run for her coin – it was more than Chandagnac, her father-in-darkness, had managed – and she had at least the feeling, since the death of Drachenfels, that she had done something worthwhile with the length of her life. But they had just chained her and kept her.

Vukotich was coughing and spluttering now, his human lungs exhausted by their pace, and she slowed down. She could not help but be amused at seeing the warrior so helpless, so easily outstripped by someone who must seem to him like a little girl. This would pay him back for her wrist, and prompt him to go less by appearances in the future. He was in his thirties, she supposed, solidly built and with a good crop of battle-scars. There was a simple strength to him. She could feel it in his aura. If there was time, she would like to bleed him, to take some of his strength.

The tsarina's man had been dissolute, his blood too sauced with stinging vodka and weirdroot juice. Molotov had been a poor lover too, a disappointment all round. She had been working the festival, paid by

Wulfric, Master of the Temple of Ulric, to go with visiting dignitaries the cult wished to sweeten up. She was being paid a little extra for any sensitive military information she might happen upon in the course of her duties, but so far the diplomats and generals from outside the Empire had been more interested in boasting of their achievements on the battlefield or in the boudoir than in talking about fortifications and siege engines. Whore-cum-spy wasn't the most noble of her many professions, but it was better than being a barmaid. Or a heroine.

The stream was rushing swift about their feet now. They would have to watch out for waterfalls. They had descended to the foothills. As far as she could tell, there were no acolytes on their track. She hoped that Dien Ch'ing had given up on them, but somehow she knew that was too much to ask the gods.

She had seen the Celestial before. At the opening ceremony of the festival, when the acolytes of the Moral Crusade doffed their hoods for the singing of the sacred songs of Ulric. She had travelled in the Orient, spending a century sailing between Great Cathay and the islands of Nippon, and knew more about the East than most of the inward-looking citizens of the Old World. Yellow faces were unusual in the Empire, and Ch'ing's must be unique among the followers of Glinka. She had planned to mention him to Wulfric when next she gave her report. She could sense powerful magics about him. Not the familiar enchantments of the Empire's wizards, but the subtler, more insidious spells she had learned to fear in the East. Master Po, with whom she had shared three decades, had taught her a little of the magic of Cathay. She barely had her foot on the Pagoda, but she could recognise one advanced many levels towards the apex. Ch'ing was a dangerous man – and he was no Moral Crusader.

Vukotich stumbled and fell. She dragged him a few yards then pulled him out of the water. He lay exhausted, breathing heavily. Impatient, she sat beside him and tried to feel her way back into the woods. No one was following them.

For the moment, they could afford to rest.

The bloodsucker told him her name. All of it. Genevieve Sandrine du Pointe du Lac Dieudonné.

'Yes,' she said at his involuntary start of recognition, 'that one.'

'The vampire in the songs of Brave Oswald?'

She nodded in irritated confirmation.

'You killed Drachenfels.'

'No. I was there, though. Unconscious. I missed the big battle.'

Vukotich couldn't understand. Being this near to the unhallowed creature appalled him, made him want to puke his guts, but he was as curious as he was disgusted.

'But what are you doing–'

'As a whore? It's nothing. I've been a pit fighter in my time, and you wouldn't want to give that as your profession to a census taker. I've swept stables. And I've been a slave... in Araby and the Dark Lands. That's one thing about living forever. You get to try everything.'

Vukotich found it difficult to reconcile this bedraggled, street-fighting little girl with the glamorous immortal in the songs. She seemed distracted, annoyed about something. She could stand him trying to chop off her hand, but she didn't like being forced to tell him who she was. She wasn't what he expected of the undead. Those he had met before had been foul-smelling monstrosities, vermin to be captured, staked, beheaded and forgotten. He mustn't let this one's almost human appearance fool him. Appealing or not, this was a woman-shaped piece of filth. In this world, there were natural things and there were monsters. Genevieve was a monster.

Biting down on the words, he asked, 'But... well, you must be a heroine of the Empire?'

She spat in the stream. Her phlegm was threaded with blood.

'Yes, but sometimes heroines are embarassing, you know? Especially if they live forever and drink blood. I got fed up with being surrounded by politely terrified officials who thought I was going to go for their throats at any moment.'

'And Prince Oswald?'

'He's not like the songs, either. No one ever is. I met Magnus the Pious once, and he tried to put his hand up my dress.'

She was distracted, thinking of her prince. He supposed the man must have used her and bested her. She was fetching, but she was a dead thing, an instrument of evil. Vukotich had killed several of her like in his campaigns.

But she could have her uses. Vampires, as he had seen, were unnaturally strong. With a crafty grin, he held up his manacled hand.

'Did you think I hadn't thought of that?' she said. 'I tried back in the wagon. Look.'

She held up her left hand. The fingertips were burned.

There was something mixed with the iron of his shackles. 'Silver,' she said. 'Not enough to weaken the links, but enough to be uncomfortable for me.'

'So,' he sneered, 'your powers haven't done us any good at all really.'

Her eyes fired again. 'Not much, they haven't. How do you suppose your other manacle, the all-iron one, got broken?'

She made a fist, and Vukotich imagined the iron cracking in her grip.

They still had shackles around their right feet, dangling the chains that had been threaded to the bar in the wagon. Fortunately, one silver cuff had been enough expense for the Guardians of Morality. She prised her own anklet apart and dropped it in the stream.

'I should just let you drag that thing, shouldn't I?'

Vukotich didn't ask for help. With a gesture of exasperation, Genevieve bent over and freed him. The crack of breaking metal was as loud as a pistol shot.

By now, the hammering inside Vukotich's chest had died down.

'Can you go on? I can carry you if you can't, although, as I'm sure you'll understand, I'd rather not...'

'I can walk,' he told her, his cheeks reddening. She pulled him upright. By the sun overhead, he judged it to be nearly noontime, and he was getting hungry. And thirsty.

With a chill, he wondered if Genevieve were feeling the same.

Although direct sunlight didn't affect her as it would one of the Truly Dead, Genevieve felt a growing lassitude. It was a clear autumn afternoon and unclouded sunlight filtered down through the tall, straight trees, and fell heavily upon her. Her eyes were watering and she wished she had the smoked glasses she usually wore by day. They were left with the rest of her things in the East Wall. Her exertions had tired her and she could no longer outstrip Vukotich with ease. The mercenary was tiring too, and they had continually to lean on each other for support. Their chain was a nuisance.

Vukotich was an intolerant man and instinctively disliked vampirekind. That was not uncommon. Master Wulfric, who was only too pleased to make use of her to further the ends of the Empire, was much the same: have her risk her life for the Greater Glory of Ulric, but don't invite her to sit at your table, don't let her go to a coffee house with your son, don't encourage her to worship at your temple. She'd had over six hundred years of wandering from place to place, leaving stake-waving, garlic-smeared, silver-scythed would-be monster killers behind her. Almost all of them were dead now, left behind by the years. But she took scant comfort from that.

The trees were thinning, and afternoon turned to evening. She could feel her senses sharpening and now she was propping up Vukotich, pulling him onwards, her full strength returning. And with the strength came the red thirst. Her teeth hurt as they shifted in her jaw and her mouth filled with blood-threaded saliva. Soon, she must feed.

She heard Vukotich's strong heartbeat and felt the steady, even circulation of his blood. His distaste for the act might add some spice to it... But she wasn't desperate enough yet to bleed an unwilling partner.

For a few miles, the woods had been different. There were treestumps bearing the marks of axe and saw, well-trampled pathways, old bones and discarded food wrappings. Above the trees, the smoke of several chimneys combined into a spectral twister which dispelled into the sky.

'There's a village up ahead,' she said.

They stopped and tried to do something about their chain. Vukotich was wearing a long-sleeved leather jerkin and was able to wrap most of the chain around his forearm then pull the sleeve down over it. They had to hold hands like young lovers, their fingers entwined.

'Now, this is going to be uncomfortable,' she said, 'but if I put my arm around your waist, under your jerkin, and you twist your arm backwards...'

Vukotich winced. Genevieve wondered if he wasn't hurt inside from the fall or the fight.

'There.'

Together, they strolled towards the village, not exactly convincing as a woodsman and his girlfriend out for an evening in the forest, but not exactly obvious as runaway convicts either.

It was a small settlement, a few peasant dwellings clustered around a hillock, upon which stood a nobleman's hunting lodge. There were fires in a few of the houses, but the lodge was dark. It must be between seasons.

Genevieve guessed they might be in luck. Where there were huntsmen, there would have to be a good ostler's and a good smithy.

It was full night now and her blood was racing. But she would have to restrain herself. They couldn't deal with a blacksmith at night. They would have to sound out the villagers first, win the smith over by stealth, and make sure that they weren't in a nest of Glinka's moralists.

'Let's find a woodshed,' Vukotich said. 'Maybe there'll be tools.'

Genevieve hadn't thought of that. Vukotich could probably swing a hammer as well as any smith.

She felt a chill. She was alerted to some danger. She put her forefinger over Vukotich's mouth.

There were people coming out of the woods. Genevieve heard armour creaking. Armed men.

They saw lanterns approach and heard people talking. The acolytes must be searching the area.

But surely they weren't important enough to warrant this much time and these many men?

The lanterns came out of the woods, and a small group of men-at-arms emerged, trudging into the village. They were being directed by a sergeant on horseback. He bore a familiar crest on his helmet, that of the Blasko family, and his breastplate was decorated with the mailed fist symbol of Zhufbar. Genevieve had seen soldiers dressed like this in the city. They were with the Lord Marshal's elite personal guard.

Escaped felons or not, Wladislaw Blasko was unlikely to be concerned about a couple of offenders against public morals.

The soldiers were conducting a house-to-house search. Doors were pulled open and the peasants quietly stood aside to let the men look around. Blasko's guards were efficient and polite. They were careful not to break anything. They didn't seem to be searching for anyone or anything in particular. From the way the soldiers and the villagers acted, she guessed that this was a familiar procedure. The sergeant even took the time to sweet-talk a middle-aged woman who brought him a goblet of wine.

The wine was a good omen. None of Claes Glinka's foul coffee for these men. The crusade had not taken hold here.

Genevieve pulled Vukotich into an alley between buildings, not too quietly. She felt his body tense, and knew he was expecting a fight.

'Relax,' she told him. 'They're not here for us.'

But they had been noticed.

'Who's over there?' shouted the sergeant. A soldier fast-walked across the roadway to investigate, his lantern jogging.

Genevieve put her free hand up to Vukotich's face and kissed him. He squirmed and tried to protest, but then realised what she was trying to do. He went limp in her embrace, not resisting, not reciprocating.

Tasting him, she felt the need for blood.

The lantern was shone at them and they looked, blinking, at the soldier.

The man-at-arms laughed, and turned away. 'It's all right, sir,' he shouted. 'Courting couple.'

'Lucky devils,' said the sergeant. 'Leave them alone. We've plenty more forest to sweep.'

The lantern was taken away. Vukotich went tense again and Genevieve put her hand on his chest, restraining him. She felt his heart beating fast, and realised her nails were growing longer, turning to claws.

She regained control and her fingerknives dwindled.

Vukotich was bleeding slightly, from the mouth. She had cut him when they kissed. A shudder of pleasure ran through her as she rolled the traces of his blood around her mouth. She swallowed and felt warm.

The mercenary wiped his mouth with the back of his hand and looked at her in disgust.

Soon, she must feed. It was more than a physical need. It was a spiritual desire. The red thirst wasn't much like the simple need men and women felt for water. It had more in common with the acute craving of the far-gone weirdroot addict, or the lusts of the libertine.

The soldiers had gone now.

'We must find somewhere for the night,' he said.

She was irritated, but saw the sense. She was off her best in the day, but could still keep moving. He needed to sleep. They would have to proceed to his advantage for the moment.

'The lodge. No one's using it.'

Slowly, their bodies pressed together, they made their way up to the hunting lodge. It wasn't especially large or luxurious, but it was better than a floor of pine needles, a roof of sky and a quilt of leaves.

They didn't even need to break in. There was an unfastened window at the rear. Inside, the lodge was one large room, carpeted with furs, with a sleeping gallery running around the ceiling. Hunting trophies hung on the walls.

Vukotich found a bottle of wine and unstoppered it, drinking deep. He offered it to her, but she declined.

With some awkwardness, they climbed the ladder to the gallery and found a corner where, under some furs, Vukotich could sleep. He finished the bottle and passed out.

Genevieve sat, her arm outstretched as Vukotich curled into a protective position, and let the night go to waste.

Vukotich dreamed of the Battle at the Top of the World. He had had these nightmares since childhood, and the strega of his village tried many times to read in them intimations of his future. In these dreams, his body was unfamiliarly heavy and hurt, not with the wounds of combat but with the weight of years. On a vast plain, where his breath turned to ice in the air, he found himself amid a conflict in which all the races of the Known World fought apparently at random. Hideously altered creatures clashed in purposeless jousts, many shades of blood darkening the ground. They were all knee-deep in the bones of the fallen. In the darkness, Vukotich fought...

Then, he was awake. The vampire was close, her hand over his mouth. Annoyed, he made fists. Did she think he was a child who cried out in the night?

There was light in the lodge, and he could hear voices.

Genevieve's face loomed over his. With her eyes, she directed his attention.

There were people in the lodge, standing around a blazing fire.

'He will be here soon?' asked a tall, completely bald man in ceremonial armour edged with purple silks and wolf's fur.

A robed and hooded figure nodded.

The bald man paced impatiently, a goblet clutched in his hand. From his bearing, Vukotich could tell that this was a man unused to being kept waiting, a man of power. Vukotich was sure he had seen the man before, perhaps at the opening ceremony of the Festival of Ulric, along with all the other generals and barons and Imperial heroes.

Genevieve mouthed a name and Vukotich caught it: *Blasko*.

Vukotich looked again. Yes, it was Wladislaw Blasko, the Lord Marshal of the fortress-city. Also, the man who had allowed Claes Glinka's crusade to take hold, who had let Zhufbar's famously riotous wine palaces be turned into glum coffee houses with religious tracts on every table and cold ashes in the hearths.

Blasko drained his goblet at a gulp and held it out for an attendant to refill. The glowing purple liquid certainly wasn't Glinka's coffee.

As Blasko paced, the robed figure stood as still as a devotional statue. He wore the hood of a Moral Crusader, but there was something strange, almost inhuman, about his bearing. Although his head was bowed, he stood a full hand's breadth taller than the Lord Marshal, and his elbows seemed to bend the wrong way. Vukotich guessed that whoever was underneath the hood had a touch of the warpstone.

Morality and mutation. These were strange partners.

Vukotich understood now why there had been soldiers in the village. The Lord Marshal was the commander of Zhufbar, and Zhufbar was a key link in the chain of fortresses that stretched from Karak Ungor in the icy north down the World's Edge Mountains to Karak Azgal in the volcano-blighted south. These were the only line of defence against the Dark Lands, where the goblin hordes still ruled, where daemons raged, where schemes were laid against humanity. Such an important man does not go anywhere without making sure no assassins lie in wait. If they survived this escapade, Vukotich would suggest that Blasko engage some new elite guards. His current crop had been easily fooled. Were he and the vampire bitch out to win favour with the Proscribed Cults, they could easily kill the Lord Marshal from their hiding place, and maybe an Empire would totter a little.

A group of newcomers arrived, bringing with them a chill blast of night air and a few traces of mist. Blasko was pleased that his wait was over.

'Hah,' he said, 'good! Comrade, some wine?'

The chief of the newcomers, robed like the tall figure, shook his head. Blasko had his own goblet refilled again.

The two robed men exchanged bows and gestures, communicating in ways Vukotich did not understand.

The newcomer, whose black robes were edged with discreet scarlet, broke off his silent conversation and turned to Blasko.

'I am Yefimovich,' he said, pulling off his hood.

Blasko spluttered his drink and stepped back. Vukotich felt a rush of terror, as Yefimovich's inner fires spread red light up into the gallery.

He was like a living statue of transparent glass, perfect in every detail, filled with fire. Eyes like black marble peered out of his infernal face and he smiled.

His robes fell away from his blazing hands and he clapped Blasko on the shoulder. Vukotich expected the Lord Marshal to burst into flames, but although he flinched he was unharmed. With fascination, he gingerly laid his hand over Yefimovich's, and suffered no hurt.

'Our dark masters demand strange sacrifices, Wladislaw,' the fiery man said.

Yefimovich spoke Old Worlder with a Kislevite rasp.

'Will I...?'

Blasko was unable to finish his question.

'Undoubtedly,' Yefimovich replied. 'Something will be required of you. You must learn to leave your preconceptions about physical form behind. This might seem quite a startling condition, but it is surprisingly pleasant. With the changes of the warpstone come certain improvements. With strange sacrifices come strange rewards. It is different for each soul, Wladislaw. Who knows what is locked within your heart?'

Blasko turned away. His goblet was empty again.

Yefimovich's still-masked lieutenant walked across the room, swaying slightly. Underneath his robes, his limbs moved the wrong way. He must have more elbows and knees than was natural. Vukotich was thankful that this horror was decorously covered.

Always, the marks of Chaos had filled him with a fear that made him detest himself. He had killed many of these warp-spawn, but he could never kill his dreams. The Battle at the Top of the World still waited for him each night.

'Things are well, I trust?' Yefimovich asked.

Blasko didn't look at the fiery man, but he replied, 'Yes. I have made the arrangements for the closing ceremony of the festival.'

'Glinka will speak?'

'He will preach. On the shores of the Blackwater, there will be a gathering of all the representatives. Glinka will call for the Emperor to embrace his Moral Crusade...'

Yefimovich laughed, nastily. 'Then he will die?'

'Yes. The man you sent me will carry out the assassination. Glinka's wizard advisers are interested only in orthodox magic. The Celestial has methods unfamiliar to them.'

'Excellent, excellent. You are well placed to succeed to the position of power within the crusade?'

Blasko gulped more wine. 'Of course, of course. My trusted aides already outnumber Glinka's people on the inner councils of the Temple of Purity. I shall be appointed in his stead.'

Yefimovich's face flared into a grin. 'And as the power of the crusade grows, so shall the influence of our Invisible Empire. There is an amusing irony, don't you think, in our taking advantage of a campaign against sin?'

Blasko didn't say anything. He was sweating. Vukotich noticed that the attendant who brought him his wine was bone-white with terror. They weren't all monsters. Yet.

Genevieve was intent on the conversation, her brows knitted. Vukotich wondered where her sympathies would lie. As a monster, she must have some affinity with Yefimovich and his like. But she had campaigned against Drachenfels, the Great Enchanter. She wasn't like the other creatures of darkness he had encountered.

Yefimovich embraced the quivering Blasko and kissed him on the mouth, obviously enjoying the Lord Marshal's discomfort. Vukotich remembered how he had felt in Genevieve's cold embrace, feeling her razor teeth against his lips.

'Tzeentch willing, we shall meet again in three days, Wladislaw,' said the monster, 'after the ceremony. I shall look forward to your elevation. As our friend from the east might say, you are to climb the Pagoda...'

With his robed comrades, Yefimovich left. Blasko turned to his attendant and wiped his lips. Vukotich remembered the sweet taste of Genevieve, the shameful moment when he had felt aroused by her, felt a desire for her to continue the dark kiss...

The attendant was crying now, almost gibbering with fear.

Blasko was in a cold fury, trying to purge himself of his rage. He looked around for something to hurt.

'Stop that whimpering, Meyyes,' he snarled.

The attendant, no more than a lad, fell to his knees, and began to pray to Shallya for forgiveness.

Blasko threw the dregs of his goblet into the fire, and looked for a long moment into the flames. The attendant kept praying, his pleas to the goddess interrupted by sobs.

The Lord Marshal turned round, a dagger in his hand, and shut Meyyes up.

He kicked the corpse, and left the lodge.

* * *

As he did each morning, Dien Ch'ing cast the yarrow sticks. Something about the configuration disturbed him. This close to the assassination, he was liable to fuss over details, to take additional precautions. He was still in an ill humour over the pair who had escaped from the coffle yesterday. They weren't important, but they were a flaw in the tapestry of his life, and if he were to neglect such things the whole fabric would come apart.

He uncrossed his legs and stood up. His cell in the Temple of Purity was bare of all decoration, but there was an exquisitely carved trunk under his cot. It was the only thing he had brought with him from Cathay, and it had been blessed by a High Priest of Tsien-Tsin with a blood sacrifice.

Reciting the words of restraint, he opened the trunk. If he were to stray by so much as a syllable from the ancient ritual, he knew his heart would burst in his chest. Tsien-Tsin demanded perfection.

From among the other magical implements, Ch'ing drew out a shallow, unpatterned bowl. He set it on the flagstone floor and filled it with water from the jug by his cot. Then he added three drops of jaguar oil from a phial he found in its slot in the trunk. He slipped a thumb into his mouth and sank his teeth into the fleshy part, piercing the skin. He squeezed out precisely three drops of his blood, and set the bowl spinning.

The oil and the blood swirled in the water, clouding it over. Ch'ing focused his mind, trying to see the Pagoda in the water, its lower levels strewn with lotus and chrysanthemum, its upper levels decorated with the bones of those who had failed Tsien-Tsin.

Music was forbidden within the temple by order of Claes Glinka, who claimed that even the most devotional air was an invitation to lewd behaviour. But Ch'ing heard the orchestra of the Fifteen Devils playing on the Pagoda. For a moment, he was melancholy for the land of his birth.

He gave the bowl another spin, and it revolved as if on an axis like a potter's wheel. The impurities in the water collected around the rim, and the bowl became a window.

Ch'ing saw a hunting lodge in the forests, first from the outside, then from within. He nodded to himself. This was where Wladislaw Blasko and High Priest Yefimovich should have met last night, to discuss the work of the Proscribed Cults. The window was high up in the lodge, and Ch'ing saw Blasko and Yefimovich talking silently below.

What was wrong with this picture?

The conspirators were not alone. Ch'ing cursed Blasko's western wizards and their lack of true vision. The Lord Marshal should not have, need not have, allowed his business to be overheard.

There were two of them, in the gallery, listening attentively to things that were not their concern.

The window sank towards the eavesdroppers, and Ch'ing recognised them. The vampire and the mercenary. He included himself in his curses. This would not have happened had he not been careless.

The bowl slowed and the window closed. He was simply staring at a bowl of water.

The Celestial thought things through. He could not admit his mistake to Blasko, lest he be replaced as assassin. It was important to Tsien-Tsin that he, and not some feeble initiate necromancer of Nurgle, deliver the Moral Crusade into the hands of the Dark Gods. If he were to step aside, his bones would adorn the Pagoda.

Genevieve and Vukotich must be found, and silenced.

He took a bamboo flute and blew a silent note, conjuring the spirit of a humble ancestor who had been buried under the tree which provided the wood for the instrument. Ancestor Xhou formed in the air, and he despatched the spirit at once to harry the pair.

Then he set out to perform his devotions for the crusade.

They had stolen an ox-cart, and were on the road to the Blackwater. It was as good a direction as any, considering that to the east were the Dark Lands, to the south the Blood River and the Badlands, and to the west the Black Mountains. What they had learned last night troubled Vukotich a little, but it was really none of his concern. Like Genevieve, he had no especial cause to wish to protect Claes Glinka from his enemies. He was not a citizen of the Empire, and he was not currently sworn to serve anyone. If the Crusade of Purity were to be infiltrated completely by the Proscribed Cults, then it could hardly inflict any more damage than it was already wreaking in its intended form. Until someone paid him, this was not his fight. And Genevieve, he suspected, stood to profit from the encroachments of Chaos. Surely, her filthy kind would be more likely to be tolerated if the likes of Yefimovich were to rule over the Old World.

Their best plan was still to find a smithy and go their separate ways. Vukotich could certainly breathe easier without the leech girl as an anchor.

They had found some rag blankets in the cart and wrapped them around themselves. Genevieve was dozing now, her head against his shoulder, the blanket tight over their shackles. He held the reins in his left hand and let the ox do the work. They were supposed to be an old peasant couple. They had met no one on the road worth lying to.

If Blasko's followers were to come to power in the fortress cities, they would be able to betray the World's Edge defences to the goblin hordes. There would be wars. Noble houses would be set against each other. The Empire's armies would clash with the forces of Chaos. Kislev, Bretonnia and Estalia would have to pitch in. Everyone would have to take sides. There would be plenty of work for a mercenary. A war would be good for business.

But still Vukotich remembered his dreams. There was little honour, glory or profit in his nightmare of battle.

Cloaked in the robes of Purity, the inhumans could get close to the Emperor himself, could all but take over the Empire. Maybe there would be no great fields of combat, only a series of treacheries, betrayals and ignoble victories.

The cart trundled across a crossroads. There was a sturdy gallows built there. A dead dwarf hung from the rope, flies swarming on his face.

They were getting near civilisation again.

Genevieve was awake, her fingers digging into his side.

'There's something dead here.'

'Just a sheep thief,' he told her.

'No. His spirit is gone. Someone else remains. A foreign spirit, from a very great distance...'

There was a miniature explosion in the air and something took shape. It was indistinct and it flew as fast as a hummingbird. It danced above the ox's head.

Genevieve threw back the blanket and made some passes in the air with her hands.

Vukotich's right hand had gone to sleep. It dangled under hers from their chain.

'I'm not very good at this. I've never been much of a spellslinger.'

The spirit settled and became a small old man in patterned golden robes, sitting cross-legged in the air over the ox. He had long fingernails and stringy moustaches like the Celestial's.

'Greetings, honoured ones,' he said, in a tiny voice. 'I bring you the multiple blessings of my most worshipful descendant, Master Dien Ch'ing, who has attained the exalted position on the Fifth Tier of the Pagoda of Tsien-Tsin. I am Xhou Ch'ing, unworthy dog of a servant, and I request your kind permission to convey to you a proposition upon which I hope you will look with merciful favour.'

Genevieve managed to get a charm to work and violet fire sprung from her nails. Xhou waved the bolts aside as if a light breeze had disarranged his moustaches, and continued.

'My descendant bears you no ill-will, and promises that he intends to do you no further harm. All he requires is that you remain within these forests for three days, and not attempt to communicate any information you may have come by at the hunting lodge last night to anyone in the city of Zhufbar. Thereafter, he will reward you with anything you desire... riches, a position, spiritual guidance, arcane knowledge. All these can be yours if you simply refrain from taking action...'

Xhou had floated nearer and was now holding steady an arm's length away from them. He kept his position in the air relative to the cart even as it moved forwards. Vukotich's reins passed through Xhou, remaining visible inside the transparent spirit.

Genevieve was working frantically, but she had very little magic. Xhou kept absorbing her blows with ease. He purred suavely, making more and more offers. Vukotich had the feeling that they were in trouble.

'It pains me to raise the possibility,' Xhou said, his face an exaggerated tragic mask, 'but were you not to give your assent to my descendant's honourable and equitable proposition, I would suspect that he intends to do you considerable injury. As a favoured associate of the Lord of the Fifteen Devils, he can summon up considerable enchantments, against which you would have no chance at all of prevailing. Indeed, I am privileged to be familiar with the exquisite torments to which you are likely to be subject if, regrettably, you do not hold your worthy tongues, and I can assure you that the pains you will experience will be extensive, varied, unmerciful and...'

Suddenly, Genevieve lashed out with her right hand, dragging Vukotich's arm away from his body. Her hand sank into Xhou's form, and she dipped her arm into the spirit to the elbow.

Xhou flew to pieces, and was gone.

Vukotich was astonished. Genevieve smiled, a little smugly. 'Vampires aren't the only things that don't like silver.'

'Of course.'

'There'll be other attacks. The Celestial won't stop at sending messengers.'

Vukotich knew she was right.

'If we change our direction, we might appease him. If we went to the Black Mountains that would show we have no intention of interfering in his business.'

The vampire looked shocked. 'You'd let them get away with it?'

Vukotich shrugged. 'Why not? I don't give a lashworm's tooth for Glinka.'

'But what of the Old World?'

'It's not my master. I have no master. If I'm paid, I'll fight. If not, then the Emperor and the Chaos cultists can tear each other to scraps for all I care.'

The vampire was quiet for a moment. Vukotich pulled the reins and halted the ox.

'Do we turn around?' he asked.

Genevieve's face was unreadable. She had scraped off her whore's paint and looked very much like a child.

'Well?'

'No,' she said. 'We'll go to Zhufbar and save that damned killjoy. We have no choice.'

'You may not, but I do.'

Genevieve smiled, teeth gleaming. She rattled the chain. 'Vukotich, where I go, you go. Remember that.'

'We should part soon. You can be about your business, and I shall follow my own course.'

The vampire was exasperated. 'You really are an Iron Man, aren't you? You've nothing but your calling.'

Vukotich almost remembered something, but it was from his long-vanished, never-again-thought-of past. It passed.

'Pay me, and I'll fight.'

'Very well. I'll become your mistress. You may not like it.'

Vukotich looked at her. 'You have nothing, bloodsucker. You have no gold to buy me.'

Genevieve laughed bitterly. 'No, but I have a little silver.'

* * *

By nightfall, they were in Chloesti, a medium-sized town. They arrived during some ceremony. There was a huge bonfire in the town square and the familiar robed figures were approaching in a procession, throwing fuel into the blaze. It was a solemn occasion, without any music or dancing. Genevieve supposed it might be some kind of funeral rite. The old practices died hard in the outlying settlements of the Empire. Once, hundreds of years ago, she'd been thrown into a fire just like this in a Black Mountain village. It had taken ten years to grow all her skin back. She was surprised that the Moral Crusade had established itself even out here in the wilds. It lent an added urgency to her sense of mission. Blasko must be stopped.

Since they made their bargain, Vukotich had been quiet. Genevieve wasn't certain how they could get past whatever barriers the Celestial was erecting to stop them, but she knew if she could get to Temple Master Wulfric, she could do something. If they were lucky, this affair would discredit Glinka as well as Blasko, and the Empire could get back to its comfortable mix of vice and virtue. It was strange how fate came around. Here she was, pretending to be a heroine again. When this was over, she would go back to being a barmaid, or perhaps seek out the Convent of the Order of Eternal Night and Solace and retreat from the messes of humankind. She was tired of great deeds, of songs and chap-books.

They found the path of the cart blocked by townsfolk, standing in silence as the Moral Crusaders marched up to the fire.

'What's going on?' Genevieve asked.

A dejected-looking young man cursed and spat. 'Glinka's Goodbodies just took over the Burgomeister's offices.'

'What's in the fire?'

A respectable-looking woman shushed them. She had a noticeable moustache.

The young man, who had obviously been drinking something not coffee, ignored her.

'Immoral books, they say, the meddling morons. They can't read and they can't write, but they know which books aren't good for you.'

Genevieve was intrigued. What could Chloesti harbour capable of outraging the crusade? Was there perhaps a secret cache in the area, containing the Proscribed Grimoires of Slaanesh, as famously illustrated by the perverse woodcutter Khuff, or Berthe Manneheim's long-forbidden *Arts of a Courtesan?*

'Immoral, hah!' the young man spat again. 'Children's picture books, and the plays of Tarradasch. Images offend the gods, they say, and words are worse. Words are the worst thing of all, because they make people think, make people want for things outside the narrow range of their experience. Things like freedom. The freedom to think, to love, to question. The freedom to breathe.'

Two acolytes struggled by with a huge painting depicting the sister goddesses Shallya and Myrmidia at play. The technique was crude, but there was a certain naive charm to the interpretation. It was tossed into the flames and consumed in an instant.

Acolytes on horseback dashed into the square, dragging broken statues behind them with ropes. Stone and plaster limbs and heads shattered against the cobbles. A head rolled under the ox's hooves. Painted marble, it looked unpleasantly realistic.

The fires burned fiercely. Firefly sparks spiralled up into the air like daemon ticks.

'It must be hard for them,' the young man said, 'to be confined to burning poems, when what they'd really like to do is burn poets.'

The complainer's hands, Genevieve noticed, were liberally stained with ink, and his hair was a fingerlength longer than customary in this region. There was a large, floppy blossom in the lapel of his waistcoat, and his sleeves were loose and embroidered. She deduced his profession.

'Barbarous fools,' the poet shouted, waving a fist. 'You'll never silence the voice of Art!'

The woman with the moustache was deeply offended now. She had a child with her, a plump boy who was looking up at the angry poet with obvious admiration. Anyone capable of so upsetting his mama must have something worth watching. Burning pages floated above the square, crumbling to black ash.

The poet had attracted the acolytes and a few of them were converging on him. Genevieve shrank against Vukotich, trying to seem like an innocent bystander.

'He's the trouble-maker,' said the woman, pointing. 'The long-haired disgrace.'

The child was pulling at her skirts. She swatted him and dragged him away.

The acolytes took hold of the poet and wrestled him out of the crowd.

The woman was fighting her son now. 'Come, come, Detlef,' she said, 'you don't want to be with these nasty people. Poets and playwrights and actors and harlots. You're to be a vegetable merchant, like your papa, and keep us comfy in our old age.'

Genevieve felt sorry for the little boy. She looked at him. He couldn't have been more than six or seven.

The acolytes had their iron bars out now and were giving the poet a pummelling. He was still shouting about Art living forever. There was blood on his face.

'And she's in it too,' the vegetable merchant's wife screeched, pointing at Genevieve. 'She's with the scribbling swine!'

The acolytes' hoods bobbed as they looked up at the cart. Vukotich shook his head. He must seem massive from below, and definitely presented a more threatening appearance than the reedy poet.

'Well,' said the woman, 'aren't you going to chastise them as sinners?'

Genevieve and little Detlef stared at each other. There was something about his chubby face. He seemed fascinated with her. That happened sometimes, especially with children. Vampires were supposed to have that power, and some she had known – certainly including her father-in-darkness Chandagnac – had indeed been possessed of it. With her, it was a random, unselective, rare thing. And it worked both ways.

The acolytes thought better of picking on Vukotich and dragged the poet away. The mercenary glowered at the vegetable merchant's wife. She was shoved forwards by the crowd and Vukotich put out a hand to fend her off. She backhanded his arm out of the way, and he fell in the seat, his hand flailing down by the woman's skirts. Genevieve wondered what he was doing. He righted himself. The woman forced her way away from the wagon, tugging on her son's arm. Little Detlef smiled at Genevieve, and was gone.

The moment was over, the *frisson* passed.

A wheelbarrowload of books went into the fire and the acolytes pitched the barrow itself after them. There were no roars of approval, just a blank silence. Someone on a raised platform was preaching a sermon against wine, sensational literature, dancing and licentiousness.

'Her,' someone shouted, pointing at a young woman standing near them, 'she makes up to all the men, leads good husbands astray...'

The woman cringed, and turned to run, her long braids falling from her headscarf.

'And Ralphus Mariposo,' shouted another voice, 'he is always singing, always dancing...'

The accusations flew. Townsfolk turned on each other, branding their neighbours as degenerates, lechers, drunkards, gluttons, slack-workers, weirdroot-chewers, inverts, daemon worshippers, adulterers, rumour-mongers, body snatchers, abusers of the livestock, lycanthropes, changelings, subversive elements, free-thinkers, hobgoblins-in-disguise, traitors to the Empire. Some were hauled out by the acolytes and beaten. Others fled, or were turned upon by the crowds.

Genevieve nudged Vukotich and tried to get him to back the cart out of the crowd, but it was impossible. The people were packed in too tight, and the animal couldn't move. It strained in its harness.

There was a near-riot now. Cobblestones had been pulled up and were flying through the air. One struck Genevieve in the head, doing no harm. The ox was down on its knees now, people fighting around it.

'...perverter of children... imbiber of foul liquors... oblater at unclean altars... strangler of young goats... sourer of cream... giver of short measures...'

'We have to get out of this,' she told Vukotich.

The ox's hide was bloody now. Someone had stabbed the animal. Two men were fighting with knives, each accusing the other of molesting a girl called Hilde Goetz. Someone was pushed into the fire, and ran screaming through the crowd. It was an immensely fat dwarf, and his oiled hair was burning like a lantern.

Vukotich put his arm around her, wrapping the chain about her back, and got a good grip. He stepped down from the cart, helping her as if she were an invalid.

'Out of my way,' he said. 'My wife is going to have a baby.'

The brawlers separated, and they were able to make their way out of the crowd. She was surprised at his presence of mind in coming up with a reasonable excuse for their behaviour.

'You,' he said to one of the knifemen. 'Where's the nearest hostelry?'

Vukotich towered over the man. His opponent stood off while he answered the mercenary.

'Th-the Easeful Rest,' he said. 'It's on the Karak Varn road, to the north.'

'Thank you, friend. My regards to Hilde Goetz.'

They walked away from the crowd, Vukotich supporting her as if her time were near. She moaned and groaned.

The brawlers got back to their fight, knives flashing in the firelight.

'We'll take refuge for the night,' he said, 'and be on our way early tomorrow.'

'We've no money, Vukotich.'

He grinned and produced a pouch of coins.

'The goodwife with the moustache won't miss it.'

The Easeful Rest was the type of hostelry where all the previous customers appear to have been couples named either Schmidt or Braun. The night man was snoring, balanced against the wall in his chair, when Vukotich and Genevieve arrived, their blanket around their shoulders as if it were raining outside. With his left hand, which he was getting used to favouring, Vukotich rang the bell, and the night man fell out of his chair.

'A room for the night,' Vukotich said.

The night man ambled over, and pulled out the great, leatherbound ledger and a quill. He opened its pages as if handling a sacred grimoire containing the secret whereabouts of Sigmar Heldenhammer, and wrote in the date.

'Your name?' he asked.

'Schmidt,' Vukotich said. 'Johann and Maria Schmidt.'

The night man's throat apple bobbed up and down.

'We've stayed here before,' Vukotich insisted.

'Yes,' the night man agreed, 'before... before was, I'm afraid, a different matter. The Moral Crusade, you understand...'

Vukotich glowered, trying to look as intimidating as possible.

'...without a certificate of marriage, I'm sorry, but we have no rooms available...'

With his left hand, Vukotich reached out and grasped a handful of the night man's shirt.

'We're good customers. Mrs Schmidt and I have always enjoyed the hospitality of the Easeful Rest.'

'Um... er... certainly. It's a pleasure to see you again, Mr Schmidt... I hope you and your lovely wife enjoy your stay with us.'

Vukotich grunted. The night man held out the quill, and Vukotich reached for it.

Genevieve grabbed his wrist and kept his right hand by his side, and took the quill herself.

'I'll sign, shall I, dear?' she said. 'Johann has hurt his hand.'

Embarrassed at having nearly made such a blunder, Vukotich kept quiet as Genevieve neatly scribbled their aliases in the register.

The night man found a candle and a key, and gave them instructions to find their room. It was off the first floor landing, with a commanding view of the pigpens and, alas, the fragrance to go with it.

'I could do with a bath,' Genevieve said.

'No chance in a filth-hole like this,' Vukotich replied, stamping on a many-legged creature that scuttled out from under the large bed. 'Besides, we'd have to cut ourselves out of our clothes.'

'You could do with a bath, too. A couple of days in that outfit hasn't perfumed you too much.'

She wandered around the room, looking in the drawers of the chests and opening the cupboards, and he, of necessity, trailed with her. Finally satisfied she had the measure of the room – a mixture of curiosity and caution, she tugged him over to the bed, sat down, and unlaced her torn and grimy slippers.

He was ready to drop on the bed and die, but Genevieve, the night creature, was more awake than ever.

Her clothes had stood up even less well than his to the exertions of the last few days. Flimsy in the first place, they were now indecent enough to give Claes Glinka apoplexy. She slipped the blanket off and dropped it on a floor, then stretched like a cat. Almost playfully, she pulled their chain, and raised her sharp nails to brush his cheek.

Vukotich would never understand women, much less vampire women.

'How old…?' he asked.

She pouted slightly. 'Very.'

They were both on the bed now, their chain curled daintily between them. Vukotich wasn't tired any more.

Genevieve unfastened her chemise, and exposed her slim white body to the light of two moons. Her chest rose and fell. She still breathed.

That was important to Vukotich, to know she was not really dead, just different. He'd been with women who were different before, and never caught a trace of the warpstone.

He rolled over and kissed her harshly. She didn't struggle, but he could tell she thought he tasted bad. With both hands, her arm and the chain in the way, he unfastened his britches.

She didn't fight him. She held him patiently and responded pleasantly, but he could tell she wasn't caught up in their love-making. A lesser whore would have counterfeited a reaction, cajoled and flattered him. The chain got caught between them and left red link-marks on their bodies.

It was over quickly.

Exhausted, sweat-damp, Vukotich pulled himself from her, and crawled under the coverlet. A chain's-length away, he lapsed into sleep.

Her touch came on his face, cool and pointed.

'Satisfied?' she asked. It was a traditional whore's question.

He breathed a 'yes,' hoping he would not dream of the Battle tonight.

'Good.' She kissed him gently, and slipped beside him, curving her body against his.

She kissed him again. Half-asleep, he could not respond.

She kissed his shoulder, and his neck.

He felt a brief prick of pain as her mouthknives parted his skin, and then drifted into a daze.

He was emptying, slowly, deliciously...

The waterbowl showed a town across the Blackwater. Chloesti. Dien Ch'ing had never been there, but he knew where it was. There was a hostelry. The Easeful Rest. A most apt name. Most apt.

Venerable Xhou had proved a disappointment, and would be bound by Tsien-Tsin in the Netherhells beneath the Pagoda for a century or so as a punishment for failure. The vampire and the mercenary would require a sterner lesson.

On the flagstones, warmed by the light of the early morning sun, Ch'ing laid out scraps from his trunk. A dried piece of bamboo from the Forbidden Fields of Wu-Fan-Xu. An empty ivory vessel from Jackal Province. A phial of soil from the Eternal Gardens of the Monkey-King. A sealed bauble of water from the Great River of Cathay. A smear of eternally-burning sulphur from the Dragon's Tongue Slopes.

Wood. Air. Earth. Water. Fire.

Ch'ing conjured up the Five Element Masters, the chief subject daemons of Tsien-Tsin.

The Masters would bar the interlopers' path.

Ch'ing pulled on his robes. He must meditate for a day and a night. For tomorrow, his magic would be needed in the service of Tsien-Tsin.

Tomorrow, Claes Glinka would die.

Vukotich woke up to an intense awareness of his hurts. He felt every wound he had ever sustained, as if they were open and bleeding again. His limbs were anvil-heavy. The sunlight was a hammerblow.

'Don't worry,' she said. 'It'll wear off.'

He sat up and lunged for her. The sudden movement triggered a series of hitherto-unnoticed pains, and, seized up, he sank gently back onto the pillow. His rage still burned.

'You bled me, you bitch!'

She was fully dressed, some of the bedclothes converted into a practical skirt and shawl.

She looked at him, unreadably.

'It was only fair. You took your pleasure of me.'

He fingered the wounds on his throat. They still itched.

'What have you done to me? The light hurts.'

She took a physician's look into his eyes.

'You'll be a little sensitive for a few days. Nothing more. You won't be my get. Not that you'd have any right to complain if you did. How many girls have you left pregnant on your campaigns, eh?'

'That's...'

'Not the same? I know. Come on, get up. We've a day and a night to get to Zhufbar.'

Vukotich remembered it all. The assassination. His bargain with the leech. He'd had some unsavoury masters and mistresses in his years as a sword-for-hire, but this one was the crowning glory of a murky career. No one was ever going to sing songs about him.

She helped him dress. It was humiliating, but his movements were slow, as if he had all the physical symptoms of drunkenness without the exhilaration, and hers were deft. They were getting used to managing the chain, and it vanished without much fuss up his sleeve and under her new shawl.

Downstairs, the night man was still on duty. At least, he was still there. And there were others waiting for them. A couple of local bully-boys with the symbols of the Moral Crusade pinned to their sleeves, a steeple-hooded acolyte of Purity, and a timid, spinsterish cleric of Verena.

The night man pointed at them. 'That's Mr and Mrs Schmidt,' he said, trembling.

Vukotich's heart slumped in his chest.

'Made quite a night of it, by the looks of them,' said the acolyte.

Vukotich wished he had thought last night to steal a weapon.

'Married, are you, then?' asked the acolyte.

'For three years, now,' replied Genevieve. 'We've two children, left with their grandmother in Zhufbar.'

The acolyte laughed nastily. 'Pull the other one, it's got Taal's ant-lers on it.'

'Marriage,' began the cleric, 'is a sacred thing. Its name should not be abused and sullied for the furtherance of base carnal lusts.'

Vukotich thought the Worshipper of Learning and Wisdom would have been truly upset to learn what had actually happened in their room last night. His blood, what little of it was left, started to race again.

'If you're married,' said the acolyte, 'then you won't mind taking a few vows before the Goddess of Truth, would you?'

The cleric pulled out a sacred text from under her cloak, and started looking through it for the marriage ceremony. There must be a con-densed version for urgent occasions.

The bullies were smirking. Vukotich knew this charade had more to do with the universal desire to poke into everybody's business than with any notion of spiritual purity. He remembered that Claes Glinka's idea of just punishment for fornication was a thorough stoning.

'Do you, Johann Schmidt, take this woman...'

Suddenly, every scrap of furniture in the room burst into splinters. The chairs, the desks, the low table loaded with religious tracts, even the beams in the ceiling. Everything made of wood. One of the bullies had false teeth, which leaped out of his mouth. The staircase beneath Vukotich and Genevieve collapsed.

Instinctively, he covered her with his body, and his back was lashed by innumerable needles.

The wooden fragments danced in the air.

The acolyte dropped to his knees, a chairleg protruding from his heart. He tore at his hood, pulling it away from an open, ordinary face. One of the bullies was bleeding and moaning on the floor, the other had been thrown out of the hostelry.

The night man made a dash for the window, but the sill and the cross-bars reached out for him. The cleric looked for the rite of exorcism.

This must be some cursed Celestial magic.

The wooden whirlwind was assembling into a manshape.

Vukotich dragged Genevieve out of the Easeful Rest through a new-made hole in the wall. She was lucky not to have suffered the acolyte's fate. A length of oak or ash through her heart would have ended her eternity.

The wood daemon erupted from the ruins of the inn, pursued by the chanting priestess. It had a face, and its face looked angry. The streets were full of panicking people.

The Moral Crusaders had come in a carriage, which stood waiting at the kerb. Vukotich hauled Genevieve, who was picking bits and pieces out of her clothes, up onto the seat, and grabbed the reins.

'Hang on tight.'

He whipped the horses and the carriage tottered away from the Easeful Rest. People got out of the way, fast. The wooden creature loped after them, but it wasn't used yet to physical form, and they outdistanced it. It was hampered by its size and the buildings in its way, but it kept steady on their trail, smashing whatever got in its way.

'What was that?' Vukotich asked as they cleared Chloesti, and followed the beaten-earth Blackwater Road. The horses had had enough of a fright to give them added speed. The carriage rattled as it jumped in and out of the wheelruts.

'A Cathayan Wood Master,' Genevieve breathed. 'I hoped I'd never see one of those things again. It's an elemental.'

'Wood? That's not an element.'

'It is in Cathay. Along with the usual ones... Air...'

A wind blew up, knocking the horses over, tilting the carriage. Two of the wheels spun backwards in mid-air. Vukotich hauled on the reins, but felt himself slipping...

'...Earth...'

The road in front of them erupted like a volcano, spewing muddy soil into the sky...

'...Water...'

A small pond rose out of the ground, shaping itself as it twisted. The carriage was on its side now, and they were sprawled, feeling the movements in the road as the elementals formed.

'...and Fire!'

There was a terrific explosion.

Genevieve tried to remember the tales Master Po had told her in Cathay. One of them had some relevance to their current situation. The Monkey-King, when he was a Monkey-Prince, had faced all five Masters, and bested them through trickery.

They were under the carriage now, with the Masters standing over them, more or less in oversize human form. The Wood Master exchanged a ferocious look with the Fire Master, and Genevieve remembered the fable.

It was ridiculous, but it was the only thing she had that might work. 'It's like the dragon swallowing its tail,' she muttered, 'or the scissors-paper-stone game.'

She crawled out from under the wrecked vehicle, dragging Vukotich on his chain.

She bowed in the Cathayan fashion, and addressed the elementals in their own language.

'Masters, I recognise that my time has come to pass beyond the gates of life. I grant you an honourable victory. However, in view of my many years I would request that my death be solely the responsibility of the mightiest of the mighty. May I enquire which of you is the most powerful, the most terrible, the most feared?'

She thought she had the Monkey-Prince's speech down to the last word.

The Tales of Master Po were evidently prohibited on the Pagoda, for the five giants looked, bewildered, at one another.

'Come now, one of you must be mightier than the others. It is to him I would offer my surrender.'

The Fire Master roared. The Air Master blew a hurricane. The Earth Master rumbled like a tremor. The Wood Master creaked like an aged tree. The Water Master showered them with rain.

'Surely, all of you cannot be the mightiest? One of you must be Lord of all Others. Each must have his place on the Pagoda.'

Vukotich was open-mouthed, unable to understand.

The Masters clamoured again, each insisting on his superiority over all the others.

'This, I do not believe,' Genevieve said. 'Five Masters, all of equal mightiness. Truly, my death will be quintuply honoured.'

The Fire Master lashed out a tentacle of flame, and Genevieve flinched. But she need not have, the Water Master had knocked the flame aside. The Fire Master shrank away from the Water Master, causing the Wood Master to take a few steps backwards to avoid the Fire Master's burning body.

The elementals argued among themselves.

Finally, arguments were not enough. The Masters turned on each other, and the area was devastated.

Vukotich and Genevieve, spared in the fight because they were the prize, stood in an island of calm amid the chaos.

'While the Monkey-Prince laughed,' Master Po had said, 'the Fire Master burned up the Wood Master, the Wood Master broke the hurricanes of the Air Master, the Air Master blew away into dust the Earth Master, the Earth Master absorbed the moisture of the Water Master, and the Water Master doused the flames of the Fire Master. Eventually, Lord Tsien-Tsin transported all the Masters back to the Pagoda, and subjected them to his wrath.'

In the fable, it sounded a lot neater and cleaner than it was. Mud rained down on them, and charred chunks of wood. The elementals merged into one body, and that body tore itself apart. They were deafened by the shrieks of the suffering daemons.

'Thank you, Master Po,' Genevieve said, bowing her head.

Finally, calm fell. The area was littered with burned wood and splatters of mud. The air was still. Boiling pools hissed.

Vukotich gave thanks to his gods in a tongue Genevieve didn't know.

'What did you say?' he asked.

'I told them a story.'

He was satisfied.

Their carriage was useless. One of the horses was lamed, the other dead.

'So,' she said. 'We walk to the Blackwater, and then to Zhufbar.'

They trudged through the mud, and left the remains of the Element Masters behind them.

They reached the shores of the Blackwater by nightfall. Vukotich felt strange as the sun set, the weakness that had nagged at him all day fading with the light. Evidently, there were compensations to being bled by a vampire. The day's journey had been hard on them both and they had abandoned all pretence of hiding their chain. If they were taken now, they could at least tell their story and pass on their responsibility. But they met no one on the road save a party of dwarfs who vanished into the forests at the first sight of them.

Genevieve had been quiet since she convinced the elementals to destroy themselves, and Vukotich had saved his lungs for walking. Something invisible hung between them, a communion of blood that linked them as surely as their chain of silver and iron. Weary under the sun, Vukotich had tasted the vampire's dreams. There was nothing coherent, just a set of impressions, of tastes, of images.

Last night, taking her into his bed, he had felt a certain shame mixed in with his desire. Although he could not deny his attraction to the girlshape, he had still felt almost a disgust at himself for so wanting the monster. Now, he had changed his opinion. Genevieve Dieudonné was a creature of the night, but she was no thing of Chaos. Her flesh might be cool, but she was more truly human than many he had known. Feelings he had never allowed himself danced just beyond his thoughts, waiting to move into his mind just as the forces of Chaos wait forever to overwhelm the world.

The Blackwater was still, two moons reflected in its dark, glassy surface. All the harbours and jetties for pleasure boats and fisherfolk were on the other side, at Zhufbar and Karak Varn. This was the further shore, where the forests stood at the edge of the inland sea and the mad wolves drank the salt water.

It would take too long to travel around the Blackwater. They must find a boat and cross.

The moons were high and Vukotich's blood was singing. He could hardly contain his energies, and found himself fidgeting with the chain.

'Stop that,' Genevieve said. 'It'll wear off in a few days. You've a trace of my blood in you. With Ulric's blessing, it will give you the strength to get us across the sea.'

Vukotich wanted her again. Here, where the dark waters lapped the stony shore, he wanted to make a bed and force himself upon her. He was dizzy with lust. But more than he wanted her, more than he needed a release for his desires, he wanted her to open the wounds on his neck, and bleed him. If she drank from him again, he felt sure that the vague impressions she had left him with would become glass-clear in his mind. Knowledge would be his. He would be stronger, better, purer. He pulled his shirt away from his bites. They were bleeding.

Delicately, like a clean-minded cat, she licked his throat. A thrill coursed through his body. He could taste the spices in the night air. His hearing was as acute as hers. He waited for the prick of her teeth.

'Come on,' she said, yanking his chain, 'we've no time for that. Stop mooning like a lovestruck poet and help me find a boat.'

Her words were like slaps across the face. She turned and pulled, and he stumbled along after her.

He thought of the silver he was being paid and he was ashamed of himself. He thought of her flat, closed, understanding face as he made love to her, and he hated himself. He thought of her sharp-furred tongue cleaning away the blood seeping from his wounds... and he made himself pick up his feet and trail after her.

They found an old rowing boat tied up at a disused quay. Genevieve thanked the gods, and Vukotich examined it closely.

'It's rotten,' he said. 'The bottom will give way. It's a miracle it hasn't sunk at its mooring.'

'But it will get us across the Blackwater,' said Genevieve, the blood-fire in her eyes. 'Because it must.'

Emerging at dawn from his trance of preparation, Dien Ch'ing pulled on his acolyte's robes. He would join the others of the Temple of Purity outside the city walls, on the shores of the Blackwater. This small inland sea, one hundred miles in length, fifty miles across, was famous for the impenetrability of its depths. A fabulous monster was rumoured to inhabit it, and the fishermen were always competing with tall tales of the creature's size, ferocity and mysteriousness. After today, there would be other stories told about the Blackwater. The story of Claes Glinka's death on its shores.

Ch'ing joined the procession as it left the temple, and bowed his hooded head. Under his robe, he carried the magical blade that could strike from afar.

Wladislaw Blasko would have his speech of vengeance rehearsed. And his confederates in the conspiracy would have an especially hideous mutant – a dog-headed retard – ready to take the blame and be promptly put to death by the militia. Then, quietly, he would be able to depart the city for Kislev, where Lord Tsien-Tsin and High Priest Yefimovich would have other missions for him. The Invisible Empire rewarded its faithful servants.

The sun shone down on the inky black waters, and the delegates to the Festival of Ulric were waiting in the especially erected stands. It had been a hard week of ceremony, secret negotiation, planning, bargaining, speech-making and decorous feasting. Glinka's coffee houses had been overflowing with officers searching in vain for entertainment.

Glinka was at the head of the procession of purity, his hood thrown back. Ch'ing was a few acolytes behind him, focusing his attention on the small of the Moral Crusader's back, where the shadowblade would strike.

Everyone was quiet. Glinka would have no music for this parade. Ch'ing had read the speech the Crusader intended to deliver and mused to himself that even the staunchest defender of the Empire would secretly bless him for cutting it short.

There was a stage put up on the beach, the shimmering black waters lapping at its foundations. Blasko stood upon it, with several of his men-at-arms, and with some heroes of the Empire. Maximilian von Konigswald looked bored and sullen. A week without strong drink or a pretty girl does that to a soldier.

Blasko was calm, collected, prepared. There would be no trouble there. He was perfectly schooled in his part.

Blasko shook Glinka's hand as the crusader took the lectern, and was brushed off. He smiled at the slight. Ch'ing kept well away from Glinka, but felt the magical buzz building up in the knife. Without removing it from his robe, he could thrust into the Moralist's vitals...

Glinka began his address, and the distinguished audience grew restless.

Ch'ing called for the strength of Tsien-Tsin to do the bidding of the Invisible Empire of Chaos.

Glinka got worked up about the sorry state of the Empire's morals, and pointedly looked from face to face as he listed the sins even the most exalted were prone to: lechery, drunkenness, dishonesty, gluttony, questioning of authority and sacrilege.

Ch'ing's fist grew hot as the magic charge grew.

Suddenly, from behind, there was a commotion. Glinka paused, and everyone turned...

There was a small boat on the water, near the stage. Two people were climbing out of it, hauling themselves up the support beams. A man and a girl, chained together at the wrist.

Ch'ing pulled out the knife and pointed. A bolt of blue flame squirted across the stage. The vampire twisted out of the way.

Maximilian's sword came into his hand and Ch'ing had to give him a jolt. He couldn't waste the magic. Glinka had to die.

The Moralist was white with terror. He turned to run, and Ch'ing discharged the killing fire in his direction.

Someone got in the way – an unlucky acolyte – and burst into flames. Robes streaming fire, he leaped into the waters.

Vukotich and Genevieve were on him now, and he was using the magical implement as a simple dagger.

The mercenary was heavy, but would be an experienced hand-to-hand fighter. The vampire seemed frail, but he knew that must be an illusion. He would not underestimate these foes.

He stabbed and slashed, but there was a coil of rope under him and he lost his footing. The gods were being unkind to him, punishing him for his arrogance. So be it.

The devil-dagger clattered across the stage. He threw off his assailants, and leaped upright, balancing perfectly. He called for the strength of Lord Tsien-Tsin.

He was alone among his enemies. Very well. It was time to demonstrate his own mastery.

It was time these big-nosed westerners learned the meaning of the Mystic Martial Arts.

The Celestial took up an unfamiliar fighting stance, standing lightly on his feet, his arms casually outstretched, his hands like chopping blades. Vukotich had heard something of the combat techniques of Cathay and Nippon. Now, he supposed, he was going to get a taste of them.

Dien Ch'ing leaped, feet out. Vukotich knew he was going to take a terrific blow on the chest, and probably lose his ribs. But Genevieve was fast, and yanked him out of the way, launching a fast blow of her own.

She punched Ch'ing in the side, and brought him down.

Blasko had a knife out and was panicking. He stabbed at the girl, ordering his men to follow suit.

Genevieve avoided the daggerthrust, and kicked Blasko's weapon from his grip. Ch'ing launched a toe-point kick at the vampire's head, and struck the empty air where it had been.

Blasko's men had their halberds up, but Maximilian put up his hand, and overruled their master. Of course, as Prince Oswald's father, he must know who she was.

'Treachery!' shouted the Grand Prince.

Blasko reached for Vukotich's neck. The mercenary grabbed the Lord Marshal's wrists and squeezed. Blasko sank to his knees, but as Vukotich bent over him, he pulled the chain, and Genevieve was off-balanced.

Ch'ing chopped at her face with his hands. Another girl would have been killed, but she was just pushed backwards. The Celestial was unbalanced and launched himself into the air. Twisting like a daemon acrobat, he sailed over the halberdiers and landed rightside-up behind Genevieve, landing a snake-swift punch on her shoulder as she turned to face him.

Someone started screaming in a loud, high-pitched voice. It was Claes Glinka, howling for help while people fought for his life.

Blasko struggled out of Vukotich's grip and made a dash for safety, careering through his own men. His nerve had gone completely. He came to the edge of the stage, and tottered over. There was a splash.

Vukotich and Genevieve stood up, their chain taut between them. Dien Ch'ing smiled at them, bowed, and launched his last attack.

His hands took on a golden glow as he passed them through the air, and his eyes shone. He muttered in his own language, calling down unholy powers. Lightning crackled around him and a wind came up from nowhere.

He levitated off the stage and floated towards them, gesturing wildly.

'Sorcery!' shouted someone. A couple of mages tried working spells of their own. Maximilian ordered everyone to stand back.

The Celestial rose slowly, wisps of white matter emerging from his mouth and taking a shadowform around him. He was floating in the middle of a phantom creature, his eyes glaring out through the horned sockets of a snarling dragon, his outstretched arms the leading edges of ragged spectre wings.

A pike was flung at his heart. It turned aside, and clattered to the stage, the force of the throw spent. A mage, the symbols of power standing out on his cloak, strode forwards, his hands up, chanting wildly. Dien Ch'ing let rip with a laugh that literally froze the blood, and the mage was struck with the full impact of it, frost sparkling on the surface of his eyeballs, white droplets of iced sweat starting out on his exposed face. He tumbled like a broken statue, and cracked against the stage.

Everybody stood back.

Vukotich looked at Genevieve, who was staring up at the Celestial, her face set, her body tense.

Ch'ing grew a foggy grey claw from his chest and it drifted out at the end of an arm, reaching for Glinka. The Moralist shrieked and sobbed, and clutched at the robes of an acolyte who was trying to flee. The ghost hand settled upon Glinka's head and closed into a fist. Glinka's screams shut off, but his twisted features were dimly discernible through the thickening murk.

The Celestial's wings were spreading, casting an expanding shadow over the crowd below. The rope of ectoplasm that linked him to Glinka pulsed and thickened. A flower opened in his chest, and bubbles of purple erupted into the ghost arm, drifting through the grey fog towards Glinka's head. Vukotich sensed that if the purple touched the man's face, he would be dead.

'Silver and iron,' said Genevieve, raising her left arm, dragging Vukotich's right up with it. 'Silver and iron.'

The links touched the spectral arm and jerked up into it, cutting like a heated wire through hardened cheese.

In their attempt to bind them, their captors had given them two of the most magical elements known to alchemy. Silver, anathema to vampires, shapeshifters and spirits. And iron, the scourge of daemonkind.

The chain emerged from the top of the ectoplasmic tube, and the spectral limb came apart, a light dew falling from the air where it had been. Glinka was screaming again and pleading with someone for help. Maximilian slapped him with the pommel of his sword and shut him up.

Vukotich and Genevieve, their chain stretched between them, looked up at the Celestial. Ch'ing beat his wings and rose into the sky.

Maximilian ordered the archers to bring him down, but their shafts snapped in two as they neared the mage. He was still protected by powerful daemons.

Before he vanished into the clouds, Dien Ch'ing waved a cloaklike wing in mocking farewell. To Genevieve, he said, 'We'll meet again, my lady,' and then he was gone. Vukotich felt a spurt of anger. Why did the Celestial see Genevieve as his chosen foe? Was he so insignificant as to be ignored? Then, a bone-deep tiredness hit him, and his head was as heavy as lead. He watched the mage blend with the grey clouds, and sank to his knees, pulling at Genevieve.

'Blasko's gone,' Maximilian said. 'All that armour has taken him to the bottom. He'll be food for the Blackwater Beastie.'

'Grand Prince,' said Genevieve, between breaths, 'there was a plot. The Lord Marshal was in league with the Proscribed Cults.'

Maximilian snorted. 'I thought as much. Never cared for the fellow. Wouldn't put an egg in his broth. No taste.'

Vukotich tried to get up, but his limbs were too much for him. His aches were beginning to tell. And he hadn't eaten for days.

'Sir,' said one of the men-at-arms to Maximilian. 'Look.'

The Grand Prince strolled over. Genevieve followed, and Vukotich had to crawl after her on his elbows like a dog.

Attendants were trying to calm down Glinka, whose robe had fallen open.

'Glinka's an altered,' said the guard.

It was true. There were spindly extra arms descending from the Moralist's armpits.

'Not so pure, after all, eh?' Maximilian was trying not to gloat. Vukotich knew this revelation would mean the end of the Moral Crusade. The Grand Prince turned to an attendant. 'Get me a drink,' he said. 'Get us all a drink. And I don't mean blood-and-damned coffee!'

A blacksmith was found, and their shackles sawn off. Genevieve was quiet, surrounded by officials asking her questions. She was polite in her answers, but distant. Vukotich rubbed his wrist. It felt strange to be free. It was amazing what you could get used to if you had to. Then, he collapsed again.

He woke up to find Maximilian von Konigswald by his bed, with a bottle of *Alte Geheerentode* rum.

He had slept for two days.

During that time, mobs had torn down the Temple of Purity, and Claes Glinka had been imprisoned for his own protection. Since his exposure as an altered, he had been a raving madman. His coffee houses closed down, and mainly reopened as the taverns they had once been. The second-hand bookstalls in the market were burdened with unsaleable tracts of moral improvement. Wladislaw Blasko's body had not been found, and a new Lord Marshal had been appointed from among the ranks of the city's best men. Dien Ch'ing had disappeared completely, spirited away by daemons. According to Celestial lore, any follower of the dread Tsien-Tsin who failed in the accomplishment of a mission could expect and long and painful afterlife in the Netherhells, and so Ch'ing was not thought to have escaped justice by his disappearance. The Courtesans' Guild had declared that its members would work one evening for free in celebration at the downfall of the Moral Crusade, and the largest city-wide festival ever to be seen in Zhufbar had taken place. And Vukotich had missed it.

'Where's...'

'The girl?' Maximilian looked puzzled. 'Gone. She slipped away before all the celebrations started. A pity. She'd have been a heroine all over again. It's her way, though. She did the same thing after she and my son... well, you know the story.'

Vukotich sat up in bed. His wounds didn't pain him so much now, although his throat was still tender.

Genevieve! Gone!

'She said something about a retreat. Some convent or other. In Kislev. You'd best leave her be, lad. Heroine or not, she's still... well... not quite like us, you know. No, not quite like us.'

Maximilian poured him a goblet of the dangerous spirit, and he scalded his throat with it.

'She left you something, though. She said you'd know what it was for.'

Vukotich took another fiery swallow. Hot tears came to his eyes. It was the strong spirit. *Alte Geheerentode* would make any man's eyes water.

The Grand Prince threw the padded ring, shining silver where it was sawn through, onto the bed.

'Genevieve said you'd understand. Do you?'

Fingering the marks on his neck, Vukotich wasn't sure. Inside him, the last sparks of her were fading. The wounds he would wear forever, but the link he had had with the vampire was shattered with their chain.

He picked up the silver, and gave it to Maximilian. 'Give it to the temple,' he said, 'for the poor.'

'Which temple?' asked the Grand Prince.

Weariness crept up Vukotich's body again. Inside him something was dying.

'Any one,' he replied. 'Any one.'

No Gold in the Grey Mountains

On the opposite crag, the seven towers of the Fortress of Drachenfels thrust skyward like the taloned fingers of a deformed hand. The sunset bloodied the castle as Constant Drachenfels, the Great Enchanter, had done in life. Joh Lamprecht had heard all the stories, all the songs. He knew of the long-lived monster's numberless crimes and of his eventual downfall and defeat. Brave Prince Oswald and Fair Genevieve, his vampire ladylove, had ended the horror, and now the castle was untenanted, all but the most earthbound ghosts flown to the beyond. However, it was still shunned. No peasant of this mountain region would dare set his boot upon the path to Drachenfels while the stories were told in whispers, the songs remembered by ill-favoured minstrels. And that was what made the place ideal for Joh's purposes.

Big, slow Freder was too lackwitted to be concerned with superstition, and dark, quiet Rotwang too wrapped up in his own skills to take any notice of the rumoured creatures in the darkness. Which left only young Yann Groeteschele to be frightened by the old legends, the shadows and the night winds. Joh could count on the young bandit's unswerving loyalty for as long as Groeteschele's fear of him outweighed his fear of the name of a dead sorcerer. That should be a considerable time.

Groeteschele had only heard the songs about Drachenfels's Poison Feast and the Sack of Gisoreux, but he had been present when Joh broke the back of Warden Fanck and led the mass escape from the penal quarrypits of the Vaults, to the south, and the fringes of Loren Forest he had held down the writhing body of Guido Czerepy, the silk merchant, while Joh tortured out of him the location of his hidden cache of gold.

In the still air, the rattle of the coach was audible from several miles away. Joh keened like a crow and Rotwang answered from his position of concealment down by the road. Joh tapped Groeteschele and indicated the youth's crossbow. The lamps of the coach became visible in the evening haze. Joh felt the old excitement in his vitals and gripped the hilt of his curved sword. He had taken the scimitar from the corpse of a slain envoy of Araby, shortly after relieving the man of the jewelled tokens of esteem he was bearing to the Imperial court, and found it a more satisfactory item of killing steel than the common straight sword of the Old World.

Groeteschele slipped a quarrel into his crossbow and steadied it against his cheek. Joh kept his eyes on the coach. As robberies went, this was simple. Three times last year, he had held up the same coach – carrying gold from the Kautner seam down from the mountains and through the Reikwald Forest to Altdorf – and the trick had been easier each time. Once the miners had paid their tax tribute to the Emperor's collectors they were hardly disposed to buy guards to escort it to Karl-Franz's coffers and so it was placed on the regular mail and passenger run.

Tonight's plunder would serve to equip Joh and his band for a more daring, more profitable exploit. Joh had a nice little Tilean princedom marked down, its vaults ripe for plundering, but he would need to hire specialists, to buy equipment that could not be stolen, and to make arrangements with a slightly dishonourable banking house to dispose of the accrued funds. A chest of Kautner gold should set the job up perfectly.

The coach was near enough for Joh to see the horses' breath frosting. The coachman sat alone on the box, draped in a cloak. He would be wearing a breastplate under his garments, but killing the coachman never stopped anything anyway.

There was a long, creaking sound and a crash. A tree fell on the road just as the coach had passed. Good. Freder had done his part well. Joh nodded and Groeteschele stood up, firing and reloading. His first quarrel took the lead horse of the four-strong team in the side of the neck and it tripped. A figure darted into the road, sword flashing. Rotwang drove his blade deep into the animal and it fell. He leaped aside, and the team continued, dragging its dying comrade a few yards.

Joh made his way down from the rocky mountainside towards the road, Groeteschele following. He had complete confidence in Rotwang's expertise with this manoeuvre. It was tricky. Many bandits were crippled or worse when they got tangled up with the horse they were trying to immobilise. But Rotwang was the best killer Joh had ever seen, trained to it from birth.

When he came out of the trees, all was well. The coach was halted, and Rotwang stood a little way away from it, red sword dripping. Freder held the still-standing horses and glowered up at the coachman. His height, broad shoulders and apish appearance helped to deter many a solid citizen from interfering in the band's business. Joh nodded to Groeteschele and the young man climbed up beside the quivering coachman and sorted through the luggage, throwing parcels and packages to the dirt road. Someone inside the coach was complaining loudly.

'It's not here,' Groeteschele said.

'What!' snapped Joh. 'Idiot, it must be. Look harder.'

It should be in a small chest with the Imperial crest and a fine Bretonnian lock. It usually was. Groeteschele rooted among the remaining cargo.

'No, nothing,' he said.

Joh signed to Rotwang, who walked towards the coach. The coachman was trembling, praying to all the gods. Groeteschele climbed down and Rotwang pulled himself up to the top of the coach. He moved like a big cat, with strong but apparently lazy gestures, and he could strike like a daemon. He sat beside the coachman, plucking and throwing away the man's whip, and then did something to the man with his hands. The coachman screamed, and Joh knew Rotwang's inexpressive face would be wearing a slight smile. Rotwang whispered, passed his hands over the coachman's body again and there were more screams.

Little knives flashed red in Rotwang's hands, and he paid some attention to the coachman's face. Finally, the bandit spat into the road and pushed the coachman off his seat. The man sprawled, dead, beside his vehicle.

Joh looked up at Rotwang.

'No gold,' the killer told him. 'The Kautner seam petered out three months ago. No more gold in the Grey Mountains.'

Joh swore, calling down the wrath of Morr on this venture. He had blundered badly, and would have to redeem himself or lose position. Groeteschele was young and Freder was a clod, but Rotwang – who had so far displayed no taste for leading the band – could easily take his place.

'What is the meaning of this?'

The coach door opened and a well-dressed man stepped out. His elegantly booted foot landed on the coachman's body and he cringed away. He looked at Joh and Groeteschele and drew a long, fine duellist's sword. He assumed a fighting stance and looked at Joh, waiting for the bandit to strike the first blow. Groeteschele shot him in the head and he staggered back, shaking from the blow. Freder pulled his purse away from his belt and threw it to Joh. It was heavy, but not heavy enough to make this job worth its while. The ill-advised hero slid down the coach and sat, dead, in the road beside the coachman, eyes staring either side of Groeteschele's bolt.

Joh went to the open door and looked into the coach.

'Hello,' said a musical female voice, 'are you a bandit?'

She had golden curls, and was dressed fit for the Imperial court in a brocaded dress with pearls worked into the bodice. She was not ostentatiously bejewelled, but her fingers and ears yielded more gold than many a small miner's claim would in a year. Her pale oval face was lovely, delicate and lightly painted.

She sat on the plush seat of the coach like a dressed-up doll, her feet not touching the floor. Joh judged her to be about twelve years old.

'Is there anything worth stealing?' Groeteschele asked.

Joh smiled at the girl, who smiled back.

'I think so.'

Her name, she told them, was Lady Melissa d'Acques, and she was distantly related to both the royal family of Bretonnia and the Imperial House of the Second Wilhelm. She had insisted the bandits bring her luggage to Drachenfels when they took her there, and from the number, quality and expense of the dresses in her travelling wardrobe, Joh knew her family would be capable of paying a substantial ransom for

her return. So far as he could make out, the girl was somewhat simple
for her age. She treated her captors as if they were servants pretending to be bandits and this whole episode a game to while away a dull
afternoon in the gardens. So far, this had worked to Joh's advantage –
she had ridden on Freder's saddle and given them no trouble – but he
dreaded the inevitable moment when she tired of play and wanted to be
taken home. Typically, she seemed to have found a soulmate in Freder,
with whom she was laughing and joking, exchanging nonsense rhymes.
If only she knew how many men and women the rough-faced giant had
killed with his hands alone.

She didn't complain at the quality of the food they gave her at their
camp, which was pitched in one of the courtyards of the fortress, and
she tried cheerfully to answer all his questions. His problem was that, in
order to convert his stroke of luck into gold crowns, he needed to know
more about Melissa's family. How he could get in touch with her father,
for instance. But Melissa, although only too willing to expound at childishly tedious length about the minutiae of her family life, was unwilling
or unable to give an address where her family could be contacted, and
only had the vaguest awareness of anything outside the cloisters of her
aristocratic circle. Joh gathered her family maintained households in Parravon, Marienburg and Altdorf, and that several of her male relations
could be found in the courts of Bretonnia and the Empire.

As Melissa spoke, Freder squatted by her, grinning, enraptured by her
stories about playthings, pets and servants. Everyone and everything
in the d'Acques circle had a nickname. She experimented with several
unflattering nicknames for Freder, and tried to extend the practice to Joh
and Groeteschele. The wolf-faced Rotwang she was – wisely – a little
afraid of, and so Joh had him see to business elsewhere, settling down
the horses. It was vital that he learn more...

'Tell me, Melissa, where is your father now? Were you travelling to
him?'

Melissa cocked her head to one side and then the other. 'That depends,
Mr Joh. Sometimes, he's in his castle, sometimes he's in his palace. Now,
he's probably in his palace.'

'And where is his palace?'

'He's a count, you know, and a baron. It gets so confusing remembering. The servants have a terrible time. In Bretonnia, he's a count, and
in the Empire, he's a baron, and there are fearful penalties for getting
them mixed up. We travel between Bretonnia and the Empire quite a bit.'

Melissa yawned, forgetting to cover her mouth, and stretched. She
didn't appear to be very comfortable in her starched and formal clothes.
That might mean she was being sent on a short journey, that she had
people nearby. She hadn't known the man in the coach at all before
setting out, and hadn't formed a good opinion of him. 'He pinched my
cheeks and patted my hair too much. He deserved to be killed.'

Lady Melissa was quite a startling little girl. The aristocracy bred its
young bloodthirsty, Joh guessed. Certainly the duke's son he had had to

kill all those years ago, after the fop had run through Joh's father from behind on a minor quarrel, had been a death-happy fool. That had been the first step on the road to outlawry. There was a song about Joh Lamprecht, telling of how he was driven to the bandit life by injustice and tyranny, but Joh knew he would never have been content to be a copper miner like his father and grandfather. He would have been a bandit even if he had been born on the estates of Benedict the Benevolent, rather than the iron-fisted Duke of Diijah-Montaigne.

'I'm tired,' she said. 'Can I go to bed now?'

Joh nodded to Freder, who took the child up in his arms like a fond father, and bore her away. Joh had had Rotwang air out one of the bedrooms in the castle, and do his best to clean the cobwebs away. They had chosen a room with a still-functioning lock and an available key. It had no exterior windows and would serve as a comparatively luxurious cell.

Freder came back, grinning, to the campfire.

'Well?' Groeteschele asked Joh.

Rotwang came out of the shadows suddenly.

'We could do very well out of the lady,' Joh said. 'But we'll have to take it slowly. She's rich. They aren't like you and me, Groeteschele. They have strange ways. I think we'll be able to find out about her family, and then we'll bargain for a ransom.'

'What if they don't want her back?' Rotwang asked. He was a foundling, sold for a pit-fighter before he could walk, and had no ideas about his real family. Joh sometimes wondered if Rotwang were entirely human.

'Of course they'll want her back, Rotwang. She's a precious package.'

Freder tried to say something. It took him a long time to get a sentence out, and usually it wasn't worth the wait. Because they were all tired, Joh, Rotwang and Groeteschele sat back and let him speak.

'Cuh-cuh-cuh-couldn't w-we cuh-cuh-cuh-keep her?'

Rotwang spat in the embers. They hissed. The shadows closed in.

In the darkness of the Fortress of Drachenfels, the Old Woman crept, her fingers curved like claws, her still-sharp mind reaching before her. She had no need of her eyes after all these centuries. As a creature of the night, the cursed stones were comfortable to her. There were intruders now, and she would have to see them off or be destroyed. Her veins were thinned and her sharp teeth slid in and out of their gumsheaths. It was too long since she had slaked her red thirst.

Drachenfels was gone, but he had left something of himself behind. She could taste the residue in the foul air. The spirits writhed deep in the shadows. But the living beings stood out like beacons. She latched onto them all, sipping their thoughts – although she would rather have been sipping their blood – and fixing them in her ancient mind.

The bandits and their prisoner. It was an interesting situation. She found human relationships endlessly fascinating. There were so many ways they could be broken down, set aside and tampered with. For her, there was pleasure in the panic and fear she could whip up in the bandits before the feeding frenzy fell upon her, just as an epicure would prepare his palate for the main course with a selection of *aperitifs* or a great amorist postpone lovemaking with extensive foreplay.

She was pleased that the strongest physically of the living men was the weakest in mind. That made things so much easier. His strength would nourish her, help her get through the long night, and deal with the more dangerous of the intruders.

Her eyes filled with blood.

Joh was startled awake, as if by a mailed fist clenching around his heart. He was sure he had cried out. Groeteschele was shaken out of sleep at the same moment. They bumped heads. Blinking in the afterlight of the fire, they looked at each other. Something was wrong, but they couldn't tell what it was. Joh had been dreaming, he knew, but the dream vanished from his head as he was jolted out of the fug of sleep. It had been a bad one and he was sweating.

Rotwang was up, daggers in both hands. He kicked something and it rolled towards the light.

Groeteschele let out an involuntary oath, his voice womanish and shrill. Freder's head lay at his feet.

'The rest of the oaf is here,' Rotwang said.

Joh stabbed a pitch-covered torch at the embers. It caught, and he held it up.

Rotwang stood over Freder's bulky body. The head had been taken off neatly and there was almost no blood. This was not a natural killing.

'It's this place,' Groeteschele said. 'It stinks of that devil Drachenfels.'

'The Great Enchanter is dead and gone,' Joh said.

'So is Fat Fool Freder,' said Rotwang.

'There's someone else here with us.' Groeteschele was shivering, but not with the cold. In his nightshirt, with his long, milky-white face, he looked himself like a cheap engraving of a ghost.

'That's obvious. It's a big place.'

'The girl?'

Joh had a moment of concern for the Lady Melissa. He did not want her dying in any manner he could not profit from.

The three bandits pulled on jackets and boots over nightclothes. Joh swore as he cut his palm open on the silver spur he had forgotten to remove from his rough riding boots. There was no time now. Weapons in their hands, they entered the wing of the castle where the captive's room was. Rotwang lead them through the dark. The sharpness of his eyes in shadow was among his most valuable attributes.

Joh knew how serious their trouble was when he noticed that Rotwang wasn't sure about the path he was taking. The fortress was legendary for its labyrinthine and contradictory byways. That was one of the reasons Joh had chosen to pitch camp in the courtyard.

After a moment of near panic, they found the room. 'Look,' said Rotwang.

The wood around the handle was deeply scored, as if a knife-fingered hand had tried the door.

It was still locked. Rotwang fumbled with the key, and opened the door.

'What are you doing?' Melissa said, sitting up in bed, her hair loose. 'Am I to be murdered in my bed?'

As soon as he saw Freder's bodiless head, Rotwang knew that Joh Lamprecht's time as a King of Banditti was over. It only remained for Rotwang to live out this night in the castle, and leave. Perhaps he would turn to the mercenary life again and enlist in one of the many armies of the Old World. There were always opportunities for people with his skills, and many employers uninterested in the legalities of his previous adventures. He was not profligate in the deployment of his abilities, and liked to see gold from each of his killings. So far, the coachman had not been worth the effort. The little girl would never bring more than her jewellery. Kidnapping was a fool's crime, and had Joh proposed it outright Rotwang would have left there and then. The business of the bungled coach hold-up had been bad enough, but the kidnapping – and now the death of one of their number – told him that the days of easy plunder were at an end.

Currently, Joh was trying to talk to the Lady Melissa, to no great purpose. The girl knew nothing. Groeteschele was sitting in a chair, hugging himself. The youth was badly scared. He had been as courageous as any in the band's previous exploits, but had only faced cold steel and human muscle. Whatever it was that walked this castle was no natural thing, Rotwang knew.

Prince Oswald should have had the place razed to the ground once the Great Enchanter was dead.

'We stay here and protect the girl,' Joh ordered.

Rotwang didn't know if his chief fully meant what he said. He had not hitherto been noted for his sense of chivalry. Still, a farmer would guard from wolves a calf he fully intended to butcher on the morrow.

Groeteschele was too deeply frightened to answer. Joh looked to Rotwang.

This was as good a position as any to defend.

He nodded.

Joh sat on the Lady Melissa's bed, and told the child to lie back and go to sleep. He stroked her hair, almost tenderly.

'Good night, Mr Joh.'

The little girl smiled, shrugged, and pulled the covers up over her head.

'Shut the door and wait, Rotwang,' Joh said. 'It'll come to us.'

'I know.'

Joh wondered if the only dangers in the castle were outside the room. Groeteschele was nearly mad with fear, and the mad can be dangerous to those who mean them no harm. The lad was gripping his sword with both hands, holding it vertical in his lap, his forehead pressed against

KIM NEWMAN

the flat of the blade. His eyes were active, looking at every corner of the room, but empty of intelligence. Joh had never bothered to find out what Groeteschele had been before Warden Fanck shackled them together in the quarries. They had shared days and nights ever since, but Joh still knew nothing of Groeteschele's antecedents, his former life, his original crime. Somehow, he knew it was too late now.

And Rotwang was slow to respond to his orders, taking a second to think things through. Obedience was no longer automatic. The killer was out for himself, and would not hesitate to leave the others to a ghastly death if he thought he could survive the better for it. After all, the man had lasted so long in his profession precisely because he was dangerous, treacherous, conscienceless. Often, Joh had wondered what the result would be if he were to duel with the killer. Rotwang would have the edge in training, experience and simple skill, but Joh thought the other man was dead inside. He killed without passion, without interest, and Joh suspected – hoped – his own brand of hot-blooded combat would prove superior to Rotwang's chilly discipline. It was a question he had never felt the need to put to a practical test.

The torch burned in its sconce, filling the room with red shadows. The Lady Melissa slept, or seemed to, the covers rising and falling as she breathed.

Joh had to turn the situation around to his advantage. He had to extort a suitable ransom from the d'Acques clan. He had to proceed to his Tilean pickings and make his name as a strategist. There would be more songs about Joh Lamprecht. More odes to his glories.

Outside, in the bulk of the castle, there were sounds. Joh knew the same winds that had blown the night before were setting shutters to rattle and old furniture to creak. But amid the thousand tiny natural sounds of night, there were silences that betokened huge and malevolent presences. Drachenfels was dead. There was no question of that. But the dead could still be dangerous. Perhaps something of the Great Enchanter remained behind in his fortress, waiting, watching, hungry...

Like Groeteschele, he clutched his weapon as a cleric does the symbol of his deity.

He could only wait.

The Old Woman was glutted with the first of her victims. Freder's blood had proved rich, and with it came a rush of the memories of his body. She felt his pains and his pleasures as she drained him lustily. She had absorbed his life, and freed his tethered, childish spirit from its cage of meat. As an afterthought, she left him for the others to find. She found it easy to pass through the castle. Locked doors, walled-up passages, and trap-laden corridors posed no problems for her. Like a mist, she could pass where she willed.

From Freder's dull memories, she learned about the others. It was easy to see how to proceed against them. So easy. People never changed, never learned. They were always easy.

In the warm darkness she made and unmade fists, extending and retracting her hard, sharp nails.

Her thirst was quenched. The rest of the night's work would be for the pleasure of it.

Considering who her prey were and their intentions towards their captive, the Old Woman believed she served the cause of Justice as surely as any Imperial man-at-arms or thrice-blessed servant of Verena.

She could still taste the blood in her mouth.

She reached out for the weakest of the minds against her, and forced herself in.

After sitting still for over an hour, Groeteschele screamed. His sword leaped slightly in his hands and blood trickled down his forehead. He stood up, the blade scraping his skin. Joh was startled out of a half-sleep by his friend's cry and pushed himself off Melissa's bed. The child miraculously stayed asleep. Rotwang took an apparently casual interest.

Groeteschele dropped his sword. He was bleeding profusely, but his self-inflicted wound looked comparatively minor. His scream died away, but he kept whimpering.

'Calm yourself,' Joh ordered.

Groeteschele didn't take any notice. He was gabbling to himself, his meaning impossible to gauge. Blood dropped from his cheeks and chin onto his nightshirt. He shook his head and wrung his hands. He could have been posing for a statue of the muse of fear.

Joh reached out to take hold of Groeteschele's shoulder, but the younger man dodged back, his terror increased by the prospect of human contact.

Rotwang stood aside, impassive.

Groeteschele began to chant something in a language Joh didn't recognise. It was the unknown tongue the bandit used when he sometimes talked in his sleep, the tongue Joh assumed was that of the never-mentioned land of his birth. As he chanted, he made signs in the air with his fingers. Droplets of blood detached from his face and fell to the floor.

Groeteschele hit the door and passed through. Joh heard him blundering down the corridor, still chanting.

The bedclothes rose in a hump, and the Lady Melissa burrowed her way sleepily to the surface.

'What's going on?' she asked.

Joh's face was wet. Groeteschele had splashed him with his own blood. 'Watch the girl,' he told Rotwang. 'I'm going after him.'

Rotwang nodded. Melissa smiled and rubbed her eyes.

Lantern in one hand, scimitar in the other, Joh stepped outside. He could still hear Groeteschele babbling.

He walked slowly, towards the noise.

Joh Lamprecht was a sentimental old fool, Rotwang thought. The boy, Groeteschele, was dead, and Joh should have left him to rot. But Joh had formed an attachment to the youthful Yann, and would not be dissuaded from plunging into the darkness to face whatever horrors lay dormant in Drachenfels, waiting for him with claws, pincers and hot coals.

He paced the bedroom, struggling with unfamiliar feelings. Hitherto, he had faced death with a cool reserve born of a knowledge that those who let their emotions take over in a crisis were those least likely to walk away whole. In combat, he was as dispassionate as a surgeon, and he still lived, while all the berserkers he had faced were wormshit.

Now, he felt fear. Not just the healthy quickening that kept you cautious in the pit, that reminded you to keep your body away from your foeman's blade, but a deep-down fear that whispered to him, incessantly compelling him to throw down his sword and run like Groeteschele, run until he was free of Drachenfels, free of the Grey Mountains...

He knew that was the way to die, but the temptation was still there.

The little girl was sitting up in bed now, playing with her long, fine hair.

Although roused in the middle of the night, her curls seemed naturally composed rather than tangled. Joh was right; the rich were different.

He had pledged his sword for the rich all his life. In the pits as a child, he had been wagered on by aristocratic sportsmen who prided themselves in picking a winner. Later, he had fought for the Elector of Middenland when his tenant farmers tried to resist a raise in the tithe. So much blood spilled, so much profit made, and so little of it, in the end, for his own benefit.

'Mr Rotwang?' the girl asked. He didn't reply, but she continued. 'Mr Rotwang, are you a really brave and ferocious bandit, like Blaque Jacques in the songs?'

He ignored her. Brave and ferocious. That is what he had been earlier in the evening, before the accursed Joh Lamprecht led him to this doom-laden castle and exposed him to the terrors of the dark.

Brave and ferocious. Now, he was not so sure about that.

He could still hear Groeteschele chanting. The monotone had changed now and the young man seemed to be singing. He was breathing badly, interrupting the song in the wrong places and Joh assumed he was near the end of his strength. Good. He didn't want to have to fight his comrade to bring him back.

He had never realised before how much the young man meant to him. Freder had been a cretin, and Rotwang was beyond conversation, which meant Groeteschele was the only person in the band Joh could talk to, could hand down the benefit of his experience to. Unconsciously, he had been training the lad to be his successor on the outlaw path. Without him, Joh's nights would be long and empty. All the passed-on wisdom would go to waste.

If Yann Groeteschele died here in Drachenfels, there would be nobody left. When Joh himself passed on, there would be nobody left alive who knew the workings of the Three Gold Crowns Scam, the mechanics of the Vault-Piercing Screw, the profit to be had from the Joh Lamprecht

Stagecoach Switch Manoeuvre. Without Groeteschele, Joh's life would be a waste.

In the back of his mind, Joh knew these thoughts weren't like him. Groeteschele was another crossbowman, no more nor less. Warden Fanck and sheer chance, not a bond of affection, had shackled them together. And yet, here in the dark of Drachenfels, something was coming out of him. He thought he was being worked on, and tried to resist.

Joh found Groeteschele backed up in a blind corridor, squeezed into a corner, still chanting. His eyes were shut tight, crusted over with his scabbing blood, and he was tracing symbols in the dust. Joh recognised a few gods' names – Shallya, Verena, Ulric – in Groeteschele's litany, and the scrawl on the floor included approximations of several sacred signs.

'Come, lad, there's nothing to fear,' Joh lied.

Groeteschele kept up his mad prayer. Joh set down his lantern and went to his comrade, and bent over, hoping to help him to his feet, to guide him back to Melissa's room to await the dawn.

Groeteschele's right hand was still tracing signs, but his left was at the belt he had drawn around his nightshirt, gripping something tightly. As he touched the young man's right upper arm, Joh realised what Groeteschele was holding.

He kept his quarrels strung on his belt.

Joh tried to pull back, but Groeteschele was fast. His eyes flicked open and his left hand shot upwards. He spat a curse, and lodged the point of the crossbow bolt between Joh's chest and shoulder.

Joh felt the the weapon scrape his upper ribs and sink through the joint. Pain flowed up and down his arm and he dropped his scimitar. Groeteschele was standing up now, working the quarrel deeper, his right hand caught in Joh's hair.

They struggled together. The lantern was knocked over under their feet and a small spill of burning oil spread in the dirt. Joh saw red shadows dancing on the walls as he wrestled with Groeteschele. He punched the young man in the belly with his left hand and knocked the wind out of him. Groeteschele broke the clinch and staggered away. He let go of the quarrel with a final yank that shot another bolt of pain into Joh's torso.

Groeteschele was going for Joh's dropped sword. Joh kicked him in the side and tipped him over. He fell into the burning pool, and his flimsy cotton nightshirt caught in an instant, flaming up to his legs.

Screeching curses, Groeteschele came at Joh, the flames spreading over his entire body.

Joh stepped back and there was a wall where one hadn't been before. He struck the stone with his wounded shoulder, and screamed out loud, nearly fainting with the agony. He held up his left arm like a shield as the fiery Groeteschele lurched forwards. The bandit's smooth face was on fire now, the features running like wax, and the enclosed space was thick with the stench of burning flesh.

Joh's scimitar was ten yards away, and Groeteschele stood between him and it. He only had one weapon available.

Clenching his teeth against what he was about to do to himself, he got a proper grip on the barbed bolt in his shoulder. He hoped to be able to pull it out as easily as one draws a dagger from a sheath, but the arrowhead tip tore muscle as he extracted the spike. He invoked the name of Khorne and held up the dripping quarrel like an offering.

A great scream was building up inside Groeteschele's chest, and emerged through an enlarged and ravaged mouth as he leaped at Joh, his flame-tipped hands reaching out to throttle.

With his left hand, Joh stabbed, aiming for the cut on Groeteschele's forehead. He struck home and, thumb over the end of the quarrel, forced the steel into his friend's brain.

Groeteschele's eyes died, and Joh pushed the dead man away from him. His left sleeve was alight. He tried to reach for it with his right hand, but as his elbow bent a crippling wave of pain made him sink to his knees. He scraped his burning sleeve against the wall, and the fires went out.

He felt like curling up and going to sleep, letting his pains fade away. But he knew that would be fatal.

At least his legs were uninjured. Unsteadily, using the wall as a brace for his back, he got to his feet.

Now, he realised how little notice he had taken of the path to this place. He had no idea how to get back to Rotwang and Melissa.

The fires died down and he was in total darkness, alone with his pain.

Trusting to instinct, he pushed himself away from the wall and followed the corridor.

The Old Woman's brain buzzed with the emotional discharge from the clash between the former friends. Their pain and fear was so much the greater for the bond between them broken by their fight. Her mouth was dry, but jolts of pleasure coursed through her human-seeming body.

Over a thousand years ago, when she was truly young, her coach had been stopped by a bandit. Not a gold-seeking thug such as these, but a wild-haired monster of the bloodline of Belada the Melancholy, an unlettered savage who could live for an eternity but who lacked the refinement to make such an existence bearable.

She was that vampire's get, his daughter-in-darkness, and she had birthed many a blood herself. The lady Genevieve, whose finest moment had come in this castle, was her granddaughter-in-darkness, the get of her get. It had been a proud, productive life...

Freder's blood flowed through her veins, mingling with her own ichor. It was time she killed again, took more sustenance.

Two bandits and their little captive. They were alone in Drachenfels. The configuration was amusing.

In the morning they would all be dead. But the Old Woman's death would be like life. The others would be gone, used-up husks thrown away to rot.

Her eyeteeth extended and grew sharper and she ran her velvety tongue over them.

* * *

The little girl smiled innocently at Rotwang. A few minutes ago, he had realised he was nervously walking up and down the carpet and resolved to calm himself. Now he stood stock still, barely breathing, swordhilt in his hand. He didn't have too tight a grip – that made you too inflexible when it came to responding to an attack – and he was visualising a stylised wolf's head in his mind. It was the symbol he had worn as a pit fighter, and it always helped him relax before a battle to dwell upon its shape. Maybe the wolf was his personal talisman. He had always favoured Ulric, God of Battle, Wolves and Winter, over the more obvious Khaine, Lord of Murder, as the protector of his profession.

Sometimes, he dreamed that he *was* a wolf. He had been thickly-pelted as a child, although he was not abnormally hairy now, and he wondered if his unknown parents had lycanthrope blood in them. He had never shapeshifted, but he was not like other men in many ways.

The girl was singing to herself, a Bretonnian lullaby he didn't recognise.

'Mr Rotwang?'

'Yes, my lady?' He hated himself suddenly, for lapsing into the servile form of address. But it was only natural to him. 'What is it?'

'Tomorrow, when the sun comes up, will we be here?'

He had no answer.

Melissa scrambled out of bed. She wore a long, gold-embroidered nightdress that could almost pass for a ball gown. Her bare white feet were silent on the thick carpet. She danced around the room to her lullaby, holding her skirts out and curtseying to an imagined courtly admirer.

When Rotwang was her age, he had been killing for seven years. He resented the Lady Melissa for her family, her wealth, her childhood. All these things had been denied him. He hated his possibly wolfish parents for abandoning him among men. He should have been suckled on the steppes, raised with the pack, and taught the trick, the trick of shaking aside human form.

The door was hanging open now. Since Groeteschele and Joh had pushed through it, he hadn't bothered to pull it shut. Anything that could so neatly decapitate Freder wouldn't be bothered by a lock. Rotwang preferred to see what was coming at him.

Outside in the gloom, he could make out a bare stone wall, interrupted by niches containing long-unlit lamps. Constant Drachenfels was rumoured to favour human oil in his lamps. It would not have been out of character for the Great Enchanter, whose reign stretched back to the time of Sigmar and beyond.

'Mr Rotwang,' asked the child, 'when are you going to try and kill me?'

Rotwang turned and looked at the open face of the child, feeling her words like the slap of an armoured gauntlet across his cheek. He held up his sword, out in the open. He hoped she could see it was no immediate threat to her.

But again, he had no answer for her. Something foul-smelling came out of the darkness behind him, and a claw-gripped hand fastened on his shoulder...

* * *

The Old Woman fastened on Rotwang's mind, and burrowed deep. She found the wolf, and she turned it loose.

Rotwang was raising his sword to the Lady Melissa. Joh assumed he had gone mad, and laid a hand on the bandit's shoulder, spinning him around.

Rotwang's eyes were yellow, and his nose was reassembling as a snout. The creature opened its mouth and disclosed pointed, discoloured teeth. It was still Rotwang – his front tooth was still chipped – but a beast was rising inside him.

The little girl backed away and climbed up onto her canopied bed. She held onto a bedpost and watched.

Joh leaned against the doorjamb, a dreadful numbness seeping from his swollen shoulder through his entire body.

Rotwang lashed out and he ducked aside. Still, the creature's claws brushed his head, tearing lines in his scalp.

The Rotwang-thing had thrown its sword away. The bandit didn't need the knives sheathed on his belt. He had knives in his fingers.

It was strange that you could ride with someone for five years and never know certain things about them.

Joh's knees felt weak. His arm was useless. He was going to die soon, and he thought the easiest thing to do would be to offer his throat to Rotwang's teeth and nails. But he had been surviving too long to take the easy way out.

His scimitar was gone, and his knives. But he still had his boots. And his silver spurs.

Silver. If Rotwang were a true werewolf, he would be averse to silver.

Rotwang lunged at him, coming on all fours. Joh reached up with his left hand for the top of the door and got a grip, hauling himself into the air. His left shoulder felt lanced, but he managed to get himself aloft.

Rotwang, his charge started, passed under him. He jabbed down with his heels, and dug in as deep as he could.

The creature howled like a wounded wolf and reared up. Joh was pushed against the lintel and lost his grip. His head smashed against the stone and he felt something break inside.

He was falling, and he was face-down on the floor. The howling thing was on his back. He kicked upwards, hoping to slice with his spurs.

The weight was gone and he tried to roll over.

Melissa was still watching, as she might do a puppetshow at court. She was giggling and clapping. There was something seriously wrong with the way the little girl had been brought up.

He reached for his heel and twisted one of his spurs off. The spiked star spun as he sliced the air with it.

Rotwang was suffering. His clothes were torn, and his thickly-furred body was bleeding.

Man and monster got shakily to their feet.

Rotwang breathed noisily, blood and saliva dripping from his twisted snout. His shoulders were huge, and his claws extended.

Joh held up the spur.

Rotwang rushed at him, and he chopped into the monster's face, drawing the spur through his eye into his snout.

Claws sunk into the meat of his belly, and he broke away, leaving his weapon lodged in the werewolf's face.

He pressed the flaps of skin on his stomach, holding his insides in. He could feel almost nothing.

That was bad.

Rotwang was leaning against the bed, shaking and twitching as he changed back into human form. Blood streamed from his wounded head.

Melissa reached out and patted his shoulder, smoothing the thinning fur. She could have been looking after a family pet.

The rich. They were barely human.

Melissa's expression changed. She looked almost sad as Rotwang's wolfish growls faded into the human sounds of painful sobs. The spur was still stuck into his head. She opened her pretty little mouth, and Joh saw the unnaturally sharp teeth flash as she fastened on Rotwang's neck, tearing through to the vein.

A gusher of blood came out of the bandit, and Melissa suckled greedily.

The Old Woman drank the bandit's wolf-spiced blood, feeling his spirit depart as she stole his life from him.

He had killed others. Many times, he had killed without mercy. She did only what was right.

When it was done, when Rotwang was empty, she wrestled his head off and turned her attention to the wounded man in the corner.

'Hello Mr Joh,' she said, 'does that hurt?'

Melissa, the old woman who seemed to be a child, knelt by him and watched as he died.

'You were my favourite bandit, you know,' she said.

He couldn't feel pain any more, but from the writhing wetness he couldn't contain in his gutwound, he knew it was bad.

'How... old...?'

Melissa daintily pushed her hair aside. Her eyes were remarkable. Joh should have noticed them before. Eyes of experience in a face of innocence.

'Very old,' she said. 'Over eleven hundred years. I never grew up.'

The cold was settling in now. Joh felt it travelling up his body.

'Your... family...?'

She was wistful, almost melancholy. 'Dead and dust, I'm afraid. My human family, at least. I have sons-in-darkness, but none who would have paid you a ransom.'

He was shivering now. Seconds lasted for an age. The final grains of sand of his life took an eternity to drip through the glass waist. Was this death? A slowing curve that forever dragged out the pain, but never really ended. Or was that life for Lady Melissa d'Acques?

He had one last chance. Silver. Vampires like the stuff no more than werewolves. He scrabbled for his other heel, but his fingers seemed swollen, awkward, and wouldn't respond. He cut himself. Melissa took one of Rotwang's dropped knives and deftly cut away the spur, flipping it to the other side of the room without touching it. She smiled at him, the sympathy of a victor. There was nothing more to do but die.

She took a dainty kerchief and dabbed the smears away from her bee-stung lips. At once a child and an ancient, she was beautiful but beyond his understanding.

'Kiss me,' he said.

She tipped his head away from his throat, and granted him his wish.

The next morning, the sun rose over the Fortress of Drachenfels, and a small human figure made its way down the mountain towards the road.

Lady Melissa left the bodies were they were. Those she had drained were decapitated. The bandits would not be her get. She was more responsible than some undead fools who let loose a plague of thoughtless offspring.

She hauled her bulky but light trunks down to the road and made a canopied chair of them.

Sunlight hurt her eyes a little, but she was not one of the Truly Dead bloodsuckers who burst into flames after cock's crow.

As the sun climbed, she settled down to wait. The road below Drachenfels was ill-travelled, but someone would come along eventually.

Under her makeshift sunshade, she closed her eyes and slept.

The Ignorant Armies

And we are here as on a darkling plain
Swept with confused alarms of struggle and flight,
Where ignorant armies clash by night.

– Matthew Arnold, 'Dover Beach'

Settling Tsarina down, he saw the frozen blood around her hooves. The last blacksmith's nails had gone too deep. The horse's ankles weren't good, and the last three weeks' ride had been hard on her. She'd barely been worth the price they'd paid for her when she was fresh. Now, she was a dependent. And they couldn't use dependents.

'There, Tsarina, there,' he said, smoothing the horse's mane, feeling her fragile warmth through thick hair. Her flesh wouldn't be warm much longer. Not through another snow, another skirmish, or another day's ride.

As always, Vukotich had been right. When they had bargained successfully with the trader months ago, Johann had suggested calling the pair Tsar and Tsarina in honour of the ruling house of Kislev. The Iron Man, face unreadable under his scars, had snorted and said, 'Johann, you don't give a name to something you may have to *eat*.'

Vukotich had been in the northern forests of Kislev before, as a mercenary in the service of Tsar Radii Bokha, subduing an insubordinate boyar, fending off minor incursions from the Wastes. He had known what he was talking about. This wasn't the Old World, this was a cruel country. You could see it in the faces of the people, in the iron-hard ground and the slate-coloured sky. In the forests, you could see it in the gallows-trees and the looted graves. Everything had been hacked and scarred into misery. In the hostelries, the songs had been brutal or gloomy, the food was like spiced leather, and all the jokes referred to filthy practices involving the livestock.

In the dusk, Johann saw Vukotich, a spiky shadow in furs, emerging from the trees with an armload of firewood. Stripped of the ice-threaded bark, the wood would burn smokily, but it would burn the night through. Vukotich dumped his load in the centre of the dark brown circle from which he had cleared the snow. What little light was left in the sky had to fight its way down through four-hundred foot trees. They should have made camp an hour ago to be relatively secure by nightfall, but they had been pushing on, Tsarina had been limping, and – just maybe, without consciously working at it – they had wanted to be a temptation to Cicatrice's tail-draggers. Sigmar knows, Johann thought, it would be sweet to be done with this business.

The horse whinnied, and Johann felt her hot breath on his wrist. He loosened a drawstring and pulled off his glove, making a fist against the cold. Then he stroked the horse again, twining his fingers in her mane. The beast knew, he could tell. He could see the panic in her clouded eye, but she was too tired, too resigned, to fight back. Tsarina would welcome death. Vukotich stood over man and horse, his hand on his knifehilt.

'Do you want me to do it?'

'No,' said Johann, drawing one of his own knives – a hunter's pride, one edge honed to razor sharpness, the other serrated like a joiner's saw. 'I named her, I'll finish her...'

He breathed into Tsarina's nostrils, soothing the horse with his naked left hand, his gauntleted right bringing up the knife. He looked into her eyes, and felt – imagined he felt – the animal willing him to be swift. He got a good grip, and drove into Tsarina's neck, puncturing the major artery. He sawed through muscle and gristle to make sure the job was well done, and then shuffled back on his knees to avoid the spray. He felt the frozen earth through his padded knee-protectors. His britches would be speckled with Tsarina's red tomorrow. The horse kicked and emptied fast, the spirit flown forever. Johann made silent prayer to Taal, the God of Nature and Wild Places, one of the few gods he bothered to appease these days. He stood up and brushed bloody snow from his clothes.

Vukotich knelt and put his hand in the flow of blood as one might put one's hand in a mountain stream. Johann had seen him do the like before. It was some superstition of his native land. He knew what the man would say now, 'innocent blood'. It was like a little prayer. One of Vukotich's sayings was 'never underestimate the power of innocent blood.' If pressed, the old soldier would invoke the blessed name of Sigmar, and trace the sign of the hammer in the dust. Johann shied away from magic – he had had some bad experiences – but all knew of Sigmar's harsh benevolence. If there were miracles to be had, only he could be even half-counted upon. But Sigmar's mercy, Sigmar's hammer and Sigmar's muttered name had done nothing for the horse. She was still now. Tsarina was gone, and they had meat for two weeks' journey in this forest.

Vukotich wiped his hand clean, flexed the fingers as if invigorated, and produced his flint. Johann turned, and saw his companion had constructed a simple pyramid fire, building a tent of logs over a nest of twigs. Dry grass was hard to come by here, but Vukotich could root out mosses and combustible fungi to start a blaze. Vukotich struck his flint, the fire took, and Johann smelled the fresh smell of woodsmoke. His eyes watered as a cloud of smoke wrapped his head, but he kept his place. Best to ignore the discomfort. The smoke column passed, twisting around to reach for the other man. It was an infallible rule of the fire, that it would have to smoke in someone's face.

'So it's horse tonight?' asked Vukotich.

'Yes, we'll have to cure the meat tomorrow if we're to carry on.'

'Is there any question of that?'

'No,' Johann said, as he always had.

'You wouldn't lose any honour if you were to return to your estates. They must have gone to ruin since we left. I'll continue the tracking. I'm too old to change. But you needn't keep up with it. You could make a life for yourself. You're the baron now.'

He had heard the speech before and many variations on it, almost from the beginning. Never had he seriously considered returning to his ruined home, and never – Johann thought – had Vukotich expected him to. It was part of the game they played, master and servant, pupil and tutor, man of iron and man of meat. In some circumstances, Johann knew, meat breaks less easily than iron.

'Very well.'

Johann set to butchering the horse. It was one of the many skills he wouldn't have acquired had he been a better shot at sixteen. If his shaft hadn't missed the deer and pierced Wolf's shoulder... If Cicatrice's band hadn't chosen to lay waste the von Mecklenberg estate... If the old baron had employed more men like Vukotich, and less like Schunzel, his then-steward... If...

But young Johann had been fumble-fingered with a longbow, Cicatrice had realised too well the weakness of the Empire's outlying fiefdoms, and Schunzel had fussed more over wall-hangings and Bretonnian chefs than battlements and men-at-arms. And now, when he would ordinarily have been currying favour for his family at Karl-Franz's court in Altdorf, Baron Johann von Mecklenberg was gutting a nag in a clearing dangerously near the frozen top of the world. *The Arts of a Nobleman.* If he were ever to write a book, that's the title he would want to use.

Together, they pulled strips off the carcass and hung them on a longsword supported over the fire by two cleft branches. It was black from many previous services, stained by dried-in grease, and could never be used in a polite engagement. Throughout his education, Johann had been taught that weapons were the jewels of a nobleman, and should be treated as a master musician would his instrument, a sorcerer his spells and spices, or a courtesan her face and figure. Now, he knew a sword was a tool for keeping you alive, and that meant filling your insides far more often than it did exposing someone else's.

'You saw the tracks today?' asked Vukotich.

'Four, more-or-less human, travelling slowly, left behind for us.'

Vukotich nodded. Johann sensed his teacher's rough pride in him, but knew the old man would never admit it. The schooling was over, this was life...

'They'll turn soon. If not tonight, then the next night. Two of them are weak. They've been on foot from three days into the forest. The skaven is lamed. Pus in his bootprints. If he lives, he'll lose a foot to the gangrene. They'll all be tired. They'll want to get it over with while they still have an advantage.'

'We're on foot too, now.'

'Yes, but they don't know that.' In the firelight, Vukotich's face was a dancing mass of red and black shadows. 'Two of them will be broken, given this duty because Cicatrice wants to get rid of them. But since the Middle Mountains, he will have stopped underestimating us. He lost enough raiders in that pass to make him think us more than a nuisance. So, two of them will be good. One of them will be a champion, or something very like. It'll be altered. Twisted, but not crippled. It's something big, something enhanced. Something they think will take care of us.'

His eyes shone with flame. 'I'll watch first.'

Johann was aware of the aching in his back, his legs, the cold that had settled into his bones when they crossed the snowline and would never – he dreaded – depart. How much more would Vukotich, with his many past wounds, with the increasing weight of his years, feel the aches and the chills? The Iron Man never complained, never flagged, but that didn't mean he had no feeling, no pain. Johann had seen him when he felt unobserved, seen him sag in his saddle, or massage his much-broken left arm. After all, the man couldn't go on forever. Then what?

What of Cicatrice? What of Wolf?

They ate, chewing the tough meat slowly, and Vukotich mulled some spiced wine. Warm inside at least, Johann climbed into his bedroll in his clothes, pulling the furs about him. He slept with his knife in his hand, and dreamed...

The Baron of Sudenland had two sons, Johann and Wolf. They were fine boys and would be fine young men. Johann, the older by three years, would be baron after his father, and an elector of the Empire. He would be a warrior, a diplomat and a scholar. Wolf, who would be his regent when the business of the Empire took him to Altdorf, would be Johann's strong right hand. He would be a jurist, a master huntsman and an engineer. Joachim, the old baron, was proud to have two such sons, who would, upon his death, preserve his lands and bear his responsibilities. And the people of the barony were pleased they would not have to live under the whims and woes of petty tyrants, as did so many others throughout the Empire. The old baron was much loved, and his sons would do him honour. New words were made up for old songs, celebrating each achievement of the growing boys.

The old baron engaged many tutors for his sons; tutors in history and geography, in the sciences, in the ways of the gods, in etiquette and the finer accomplishments, in music and literature, in the skills of war and the demands of peace, even in the rudiments of magic. Among these was a warrior who had served throughout the Old World and beyond. The survivor of numberless campaigns, he never talked of his origins, his upbringing, even of his native land, and he had but one name: Vukotich. The baron had first met Vukotich on the field of combat, during a border dispute with an unruly neighbour, and had personally captured the mercenary. Neither man spoke of it, but after the battle, Vukotich put aside his profession and swore allegiance only to the House of von Mecklenberg.

The baron had many homes, many estates, many castles. One summer, he and his retinue chose to spend time in an isolated stronghold at the edge of the barony. There, in the greenwood, his sons would learn how to hunt game, and win their trophies. This Joachim had done when he was a youth, and this his sons would now do. With pride, the old baron watched from the towers of his castle as Vukotich took his sons off into the woods, accompanied by Corin the Fletcher, his arms master. Whatever Johann and Wolf killed would grace the baron's table that evening.

Wolf was a born huntsman and was blooded his first day in the woods, bringing down a quail with a single quarrel. He soon became proficient with the longbow, the crossbow, the throwing lance, and all manner of traps and snares. Wolf, it was said partly in jest, was well-named, for he could stalk any beast of the forest. From birds, he progressed to boar and elk. He was equal to them all, and it was said that Wolf might be the first von Mecklenberg in generations to bring home a unicorn, a jabberwock or a manticore as trophies of his prowess in the woods. Corin had discovered that Andreas, one of the stable boys, had once been apprenticed to a taxidermist, and soon had the boy assigned to the preparing and mounting of Wolf's trophies. Within a month, there were more than enough to fill his corner of the great hall of the von Mecklenbergs.

But Johann found the chase not to his taste. Early, he had developed an interest in the animals of the wood, but he couldn't see them through a hunter's eyes. Shooting at straw targets, he could best his brother with any weapon; but with a living, breathing creature before him, his hand faltered and his eye was off. He was too moved by the magnificence of a full-grown stag to want to see it dead, beheaded and stuffed, with glass eyes and dusty antlers. Everyone understood, which made it much worse for Johann, who was foolish enough to think compassion a womanish weakness. The old baron, seeing in Wolf his younger self, nevertheless recognised in Johann the makings of a better man than either of the huntsmen could be. To Vukotich, he confided 'Wolf's delight in the hunt will make him a good regent, but Johann's instinctive turning-away from killing will make him a *great* elector.' But Johann tried to overcome his quirk of the mind. He would not give up eating meat, and he believed he could not honourably eat if he could not hunt in good conscience, so he applied himself.

Still, one day, while out with Wolf, Corin and Vukotich, Johann missed a deer he had a clear shot at, and his arrow slipped through the trees, lodging in his brother's shoulder. It was a clean, shallow wound and Corin dressed it quickly, but Vukotich was sufficiently cautious to send the boy back to the castle. Johann had felt bad enough then, but later this incident would come to haunt his nights. If his life had a turning point, that careless shaft was it. Afterwards, nothing was as it was supposed to be.

There had always been outlaws, of course. Always been evil men, always been the altered ones. Especially in the forests. There had been raids and battles and bloodshed. There were many areas of the Empire where the servants of the Law dared not venture. And there had been many campaigns against the dark. But there had never been a Champion of evil like Cicatrice. So named for the livid red weal scratched across his face by the claw of a daemon in the service of Khorne, Lord of Blood, Cicatrice had come out of the Wastes transformed beyond humanity. With his so-called Chaos Knights, Cicatrice had terrorised the Southlands, unfettered in his bloodlust in victory, eluding capture even in defeat. Emperor Karl-Franz himself had placed 50,000 gold crowns upon his head, but – though many had tried, and failed to survive the attempt – none had claimed the reward. The songs of his crimes were dark and dramatic, full of blood and fire, and just barely tainted with fascination. For the people of the Empire, used now to the comforts and pettiness of civilisation, Cicatrice was an important figure. He was the outcast, a monster to remind them of the things waiting beyond the circle of light.

Cicatrice had seen a weakness in the summer home of the von Mecklenbergs and mounted a raid that had shocked the Empire. An elector murdered, his household put to the sword, his castle razed to the ground, his child – and the children of his retinue – stolen away. Never had there been such an atrocity, and rarely since did the other electors travel anywhere remote without a force of men capable of besting a small army. Hitherto, stealth, poison and treachery had been the favoured weapons of the night. Cicatrice had changed that. Truly, he was a Chaos Champion, and even the warlords of the Empire credited him as a brilliant strategist. If only because he was still alive and at the head of his Knights twenty years after his first raids, Cicatrice was unique among the servants of evil.

In his dreams, Johann kept being pulled back to that burning castle. He saw his father again, hanging in pieces from trees twenty feet apart. He saw poor, fat, silly Schunzel, the fires in his face and belly still alight. He saw Vukotich, in a rage he had never shown before or since, hacking at a wounded beastman, screaming questions for which there would be no answers. Then there were the slaughtered horses, the violated servant girls, the unidentifiable corpses. Absurdly, he remembered the tennis lawns – not a scrap of green among the red – with its pile of eyeless heads. A skaven had been left behind, a rat-faced mutant he found among the carcasses of his tutors, sawing off fingers for rings. For the first time, Johann had killed without effort. He had never since hesitated to kill, higher race or beast. He had learned his last lesson.

There was another elector now, a cousin who called himself baron, and claimed that Johann had given up his rights to the title by deserting the remnants of the House of von Mecklenberg and setting off on his travels. Johann would not have argued with him. The business of Empire had to continue, and he had other business.

Even with his shoulder wounded, Wolf would have fought. But he was not among the dead. He was among the missing. At thirteen years of age, he would have interested Cicatrice.

That had been ten years, and inconceivable miles, ago. They had followed Cicatrice's band in ragged circles around the Empire; up through the Grey Mountains to the borders of Bretonnia, surviving ambushes on the waterfront of Marienburg, then through the Wasteland into the Drak Wald Forest – where Johann and Vukotich had been enslaved for a spell by a mad dwarf with a magic mine – and up through the Middle Mountains – where they had fought off a concerted attack, and lost Corin the Fletcher to a goat-headed monstrosity – into the Forest of Shadows. Then, down into the Great Forest and east through Stirland towards the World's Edge Mountains where the powers of darkness are paramount, and where they struggled against phantoms that were sent against their minds by powerful enchanters.

The seasons came and went, and the slow progress continued. Johann knew they had been close more times than he could count, but always something had intervened. He had forgotten how many ravaged settlements they had passed through, seeing themselves mirrored in the numb rage of the survivors. Cicatrice's band was unstable, and they had met deserters, cast-offs or defeated would-be champions. Vukotich had more scars now, and Johann wasn't the youth he had been.

Back and forth, up and down, the wandering had progressed across the land, constantly at the edges of the Old World, constantly at the extremes of experience. Johann had seen horrors beyond the imagining of his tutors, had learned not to concern himself with the caprices of the gods, and had survived so far. He had given up expecting to see each day's dawn, he had almost given up expecting to see Wolf at the end of it.

But still, even to the top of the world, they kept on Cicatrice's tracks. By day, Johann tried not to think about the past, or the future; by night, he could think of nothing else. He had long since become used to sleeping badly.

The hand on his shoulder shook him awake. He opened his eyes, but didn't say anything.

'They've turned,' said Vukotich, his voice low and urgent, 'their stink is in the air.'

Johann slipped out of his bedding and stood up. The forests were quiet, save for the drip of snow, and the laboured breathing of Vukotich's horse. The fire had burned to ash, but was still casting a glow. The chill had not left his bones. Ice daggers hung like lanterns from the lower branches of the trees, mysteriously lit from within.

They rolled furs into man-sized humps, covered them with bedding and arranged them near the fire. In the dark, they would pass. Vukotich took his crossbow from his saddle and selected a quarrel. He checked the sleeping horse Johann couldn't help but think of as Would-Have-Been-Tsar. Then, they withdrew into the forest.

The wait wasn't long. Johann's sense of smell wasn't as acute as Vukotich's, but he eventually heard them. His tutor had been right: there were four, and one was limping. The noises stopped. Johann pressed close to a treetrunk, shrouding himself in its shadow.

There was a sound like the tearing of silk, and the bedding rolls shuddered. Each was pierced with a crossbow bolt where the head would be. They glowed green, and emitted little puffs of fire and smoke. Johann held his lungs. He didn't want to breathe even a trace of whatever poison that was.

The flares died and nothing moved in the clearing. Johann gripped the hilt of his sword, while Vukotich brought up his crossbow. He didn't favour poison, but with his eye he didn't need to.

Johann heard his heart beating too loud, and fought against all the imagined sounds in his head. Finally, the real sounds came.

A human shape detached itself from the darkness and ventured into the clearing. It limped badly, and its head was elongated, with shining eyes and sharp little teeth. It was the skaven. Piebald, with tatters of clothing over oddments of armour, the ratman was distorted in the ember-light. It stood over the murdered bedrolls, its back to them. It wore the eye-in-the-point-down-pyramid symbol of the Clan Eshin on its ripped blackhide jacket, and the stylised scarface worn by all the followers of Cicatrice. Vukotich put his bolt through its eye. The skaven breathed in sharply, and half-turned. Vukotich's arrowhead stuck out bloody a few inches from its chest. The ratman went down.

Johann and Vukotich circled away from their spot, until they faced the direction from which the thing had come. There were eyes in the darkness. Vukotich held up three fingers, then two. Three against two. It had been worse before.

Fire exploded above them, as arrows pinned balls of burning rag to trees. The balls exploded and rained streamers of flame around them. Three figures came into the clearing, tall but shambling. Johann could smell them now. One of them wasn't alive.

Vukotich put a quarrel through the throat of the creature in the centre, but it still kept walking. It walked to the fire, and Johann saw a rotted ruin of a face. It was leaking dust from its split neck. It had been female, once. Now, it wasn't a person, it was a puppet. One of the others must have raised it, or been given the reins by the magician who had. Like many of Cicatrice's Knights, it had a line of red warpaint across its face, echoing its leader's scar. It moved awkwardly because of its mortal wounds, but that wouldn't stop it from being deadly.

'We'd better do something about that,' said Vukotich, 'before it gives us the Tomb Rot.'

Together, Johann and Vukotich ran forward and counted coup on the undead woman, whipping it with their swords, taking care not to touch the diseased thing. Johann felt brittle bones breaking inside it. The thing staggered from side to side as it was struck, and stepped onto the embers of the fire. Its tattered shroud caught light and so did its desiccated shins. When the flame reached its pockets of rancid flesh, they cooked through with a foul hiss. With an awful keening, the creature became a writhing mass of fire. Johann and Vukotich stepped back, prodding it with swordpoints, staying out of its burning reach.

Its companions came forward now, faces flickering in its dying light.

Johann parried a blow and felt its force ringing throughout his entire body. His opponent was taller by a head, and heavily armoured, but its reactions were slower, and its helmet was distorted by a head that seemed to have expanded inside it. It was an altered of some sort, a human being under the influence of the warpstone, that unclassifiable substance so many Servants of the Night had about them, turning into the physical image of whatever dark desires or fears it had harboured. The changes were part of the bargain made with whatever forces they owed allegiance, Johann knew. He had seen too many barely human things left in Cicatrice's wake. This thing was plainly in the throes of some fresh alteration. Under its helm, it would be some new monstrosity.

Johann stepped back and slashed across the creature's chest, denting its breastplate, caving in the scarface symbol etched into the metal. Suddenly, he felt arms around him and pain at his back. The burning thing had hugged him. He shook free, smelling his scorched clothing, ignoring the pain, and ducked away from a blow that could have sheared his head from his shoulders. The undead got in the way again, and the Knight reached out with a huge hand. The giant got a grip on its flame-haloed head and with a grunt crushed it to dust. It fell, useless now, and the Knight returned its attentions to Johann.

Vukotich was grappling close with a toad-faced altered with too many limbs and green ichor was sizzling in the snow around them as his knife went in and out of the thing's bloated stomach. It didn't seem slowed by its many wounds. Vukotich had an arm around its neck, pressing down its inflating ruff.

Johann faced the Knight and made a few tentative passes at its legs. It was already slow; a few bone-deep cuts would make it slower. He realised that the thing was roaring. Johann wasn't sure, but it sounded unpleasantly like the laughter of the heroically insane. The altered's dented breastplate sprung outwards, spiked from within by hard eruptions springing from its mutating body. Whoever it had once been, it was under the warpstone now, progressing far beyond humanity. The Knight screamed its poison mirth, and tugged at its armour. The breastplate came free and Johann saw the growing spines and plates on its skin. Cicatrice's face was tattooed on its chest. The helmet stretched outward, cracks appearing in the beaten steel, horns pushing through above the eyeholes like bulbshoots emerging from fertile soil. Johann thrust at the altered's chest, but his sword was turned aside by the creature's armoured hide. The Knight wasn't even bothering to fight back. Johann struck at its neck and his sword lodged deep. It still laughed at him and his sword wouldn't come free. He pulled two knives from his belt and sunk them into the altered's body, aiming for the kidneys. The laughter continued and the Knight began to peel away the ruined sections of his helmet.

Eyes peered at Johann from bone-ridged cavities. There were seven of them, arranged across the Knight's forehead. Two were real, five were polished glass set in living flesh. Johann prayed to the gods he'd ignored for years. The Knight dislodged Johann's sword from its neck and threw it away.

'Hello, Master Johann,' it said, its voice piping and childish, almost charming. 'How you've grown.'

It was – it had been – Andreas, the von Mecklenberg stable boy, the mounter of trophies. He had found other tutors since Johann had seen him last.

The great hands reached for him, and Johann felt weights on his shoulders. The fingers gripped like blacksmith's tongs. There was no longer ground under his feet. Johann smelled Andreas's foul breath, and looked up into his former servant's mask of expanded flesh. He pulled the knives from the altered's sides and sawed away at its stomach and groin with them. He merely cut through altered flesh that grew back as he ravaged it. Andreas pushed him and he flew twenty feet through the air. He hit a tree, for a moment dreading that his back was broken, then fell. The earth was hard and he took the fall badly.

Vukotich's opponent was downed, and the tutor strode towards the Knight, two-handed sword raised. Andreas put out an arm to stop him and brushed aside the swinging blow. He grabbed Vukotich's wrists with one hand and forced the Iron Man to his knees. The altered was still laughing. Daemons screeched in his laughter and murdered children wailed. Andreas pushed Vukotich back, bending him double, shoving his head towards the still-burning remains of the undead, forcing his own sword towards his face. Vukotich struggled back, and Andreas's huge shoulders heaved as he exerted pressure on the dwarfed human. The sword was fixed between their faces, shuddering as they threw their full strength at each other. The Knight shrugged off his back armour, which fell from him, and Johann saw a streak of white down the creature's mottled and encrusted back.

Ignoring the pain, he ran across the clearing, stepping in the mess Vukotich had made of his toadman, and hurled himself onto Andreas's back. There, the alterations were not quite complete. He drove his knives in between the Knight's horny shoulderblades, where a patch of boyish skin remained between the bony plates, and sawed down the line of his spine, going as deep as he could, cutting through ribs. Blood gushed into his face, and at last he felt his thrusts sink into the real, unaltered Andreas, doing some damage.

The laughter stopped and the altered stood up, trying to shake Johann from his back. Johann gripped Andreas's waist with his knees, and continued his sawing. His hands were inside now, and he was hacking at random, hoping to puncture what left of the heart. Something big in Andreas' torso burst and he fell writhing to the ground. Johann kept riding him, his hands free now, stabbing where he could. Andreas rolled over, and Johann disengaged himself from the dying Knight. He stood up and wiped blood out of his eyes.

Andreas lay face-up, red froth on his lips, the light fast going from his face. Johann knelt and took his head in his hands.

'Andreas,' he said, trying to reach through the Knight of Darkness to the stable lad, 'what of Wolf?'

The Knight gathered phlegm in his throat, but let it drip bloodily from his mouth. In the two living eyes, Johann saw something still human. He plucked the glass eyes from the face and threw them away.

'Andreas, we were friends once. This wasn't your fault. Wolf. Where's Wolf? Is he still alive? Where is Cicatrice taking him?'

The dying man smiled crooked. 'North,' he gasped, broken bones kniving inside his flesh as he spoke, 'to the Wastes, to the Battle. Not far now. The Battle.'

'What battle? Andreas, it's important. What battle?'

The ghost of the laughter came again. 'Baron,' Andreas said, 'we were never friends.'

The stable boy was dead.

Vukotich was hurt. The toadman had lost his dagger early in their struggle and his barbed hands hadn't proved a threat. But, when cut, he bled poison. The green stuff ate through clothing, discoloured skin, and seeped dangerously into the body. Vukotich had spilled a lot of it on himself. When the morning light penetrated to the clearing, Johann saw the irregular holes in Vukotich's leggings, and realised his tutor was having trouble standing. He tottered and fell.

'Leave me,' Vukotich said through clenched teeth. 'I'll slow you down.'

That was what Johann had been taught to do, but he had never been a model pupil. With handfuls of snow, he rubbed at Vukotich's wounds, working away until most of the poison was gone. He had no idea how deep the blight had sunk into his flesh, and also didn't know anything about the properties of the toadman's blood. But if it were fatal, Vukotich would have told him so, in an attempt to get Johann to leave him. He tore a spare shirt into rags, and bandaged where he could. Vukotich was quiet, but winced throughout. Johann didn't ask him if he were in pain.

With branches, and strips of leather from their fallen enemies' clothes, Johann made a stretcher which he fixed to Would-Have-Been-Tsar's halter. It was rough, but padded with furs it sufficed. He helped the unprotesting Vukotich onto the stretcher and wrapped him warmly. The old soldier lay still, gripping a sword as a child grips a favoured toy, his face still stained green in patches.

'We're going north,' Johann said. 'We'll be out of this forest by night. There'll be some settlement before the steppes.'

That was true, but didn't necessarily imply a welcome, a healer and a warm bed. There was a saying: 'In the forests, there is no law; on the steppe, there are no gods.' This was still Kislev, but no tsar reigned here. Beyond the steppes were the Wastes, where the warpstone was the only rule, changing men's minds and bodies, distorting souls, working its evil on all. It was Cicatrice's spiritual homeland, and the only surprise was that his trail hadn't brought them there earlier.

They travelled slowly, and Johann was proved wrong. By nightfall, they were still in the forest. Vukotich slept fitfully as he was dragged, voicing the pains he would never admit to when awake. Would-Have-Been-Tsar plodded on like a machine, but Johann knew the horse wouldn't out-live the moon. They'd need fresh horses on the steppes if they were to keep up with Cicatrice, and Vukotich would need healing.

The next day, after an undisturbed night's camp, the trees began thin-ning and the gloom lifted. There was even a trace of sun in the dead sky. Johann had seen tracks, had found the spot where Cicatrice had camped – the gutted corpse hanging by its feet from a tree was an obvi-ous signpost – and knew they continued on the right trail. Beneath the corpse, someone had scrawled TURN BACK NOW in the snow in fresh blood. Johann spat at the message.

It took a while to realise how strange this country was. There was no birdsong, and he had long since ceased to notice any animals. At first, he was so relieved not to be constantly on guard against wolf and bear – he had three rakemarks on his back to remind him of an old encounter – that it didn't occur to him quite how ominous the lack of life was.

The forest finally died. Johann passed through a thick stretch where tree corpses leaned against each other, or rotted where they lay, and emerged onto the barren steppe. It was like passing from night into day. Looking back, he saw the edge of the forest like a wall extending to the horizon on either side. The trees were packed together like the fortifica-tions of a castle, and didn't seem to fall outward.

If the forest was dead, the steppe was deader. There were scraggy clumps of grass and areas of naked, frozen earth. The snows had been thin, but still remained here and there. In a hundred years, this would be desert.

In the distance, a trail of grey smoke spiralled up into the empty sky, and something large and ungainly with wings flapped slowly through the air.

'There's a village ahead, Vukotich.'

They rested a while, and Johann dripped some water – they had been reduced to melting snow – into his tutor's mouth, then fed the horse. It had been over a month since they'd seen another creature who'd not tried to kill them. Perhaps, by some miracle, there would be some hospi-tality to be bought at the village. Johann wasn't too hopeful, but hadn't developed Vukotich's automatic distrust. Men still had to earn his enmity.

Vukotich wasn't speaking, conserving his strength, but Johann could tell his tutor was mending. In him, life was like a seed that lives through the arctic winter to sprout when spring brings a trace of warmth. Twice, Johann had thought him dead and been proved wrong. Cicatrice's ban-dits had given him the name Iron Man.

Johann chewed a long strip of Tsarina as he rode towards the smoke, and tried not to think about Andreas, not to think about Wolf. He remem-bered the stable lad as a cheerful youth, and could not see in him the beginnings of the Chaos Knight. But they had been there. Perhaps it had always rankled with Andreas that he was born to serve, while Johann and Wolf were born to the barony. The ways of the warpstone were subtle. They could steal into a man's heart – a child's heart – and find the resentments, the petty injuries, the flaws, then work on them until the heart was rotten as a worm-holed apple. Then, the outer changes began. In Andreas, in the toad-thing, in the many others they had seen over the years. The goat-headed altered that had killed Corin the Fletcher had once been a simple cleric of Verena, Goddess of Learning and Justice, lured into evil by a desire to glance at the Forbidden Books. Cicatrice himself had been a distant relative of the Prince-Elector of Ostland, posted to the Wastes by a jealous rival during a family feud, changed now beyond recognition.

What could warpstone have done to Wolf? Would his brother remember the unlucky arrow in his shoulder, and greet his rescuers with a murderous attack? Would he even recognise Johann? With each year, the likelihood of his putting up any resistance diminished. Now, most probably, he would have to be rescued against his will. And even then, he might prove too far gone in the ways of darkness to help.

Johann and Vukotich had not discussed the end of their search. It had always been assumed between them that Wolf would be rescued. But just lately, Johann had begun to wonder. He knew that he could never bring himself to raise an arm against his brother, but what of Vukotich? Did the Iron Man feel it would be his duty, if Wolf could not be saved, to put an end to him by the sword? Vukotich had mercy-killed before, in his wars, even along their trail. Would it be so different? And would Johann try to stop him? He suspected that, even wounded, Vukotich was the better duellist.

Something crunched under Would-Have-Been-Tsar's hooves, jolting Johann out of his unhappy reverie. He looked down. The animal was standing on a clean skeleton, his right foreleg buried in a ribcage that gripped his ankle like a trap. Johann dismounted, and pulled the old bones away. The skeleton was nearly human, but for the horns on the skull and the extra rows of teeth.

They were in the middle of a sea of bones, stretching as far as the horizon. This must be the site of some ancient plague, or some calamitous conflict...

Andreas had spoken of a battle.

Johann got up on the horse, and continued, proceeding slowly. The stretcher dragged through long-undisturbed bones. Some of the skeletons were barely recognizable. Johann shuddered and kept his eyes on the smoke. He could see now that it was coming from a group of low buildings, more an outpost than a village. But there would be people. What kind of people would live among the detritus of massacre?

When Vukotich awoke, Johann would ask him about the battle. He would know who had fought here, and why. As if it mattered. Some of the skeletons were hundreds of years old, he thought. Their armour and weapons long since stolen away, only their useless bones remained.

Then the smell hit him. The smell he'd become used to. The smell of the zombie that had been with Andreas, the smell of all recently-dead things. The stench of decay.

The quality of the dead had changed. These skeletons were clothed with rags of flesh. They were more recently dead, or else preserved by the cold. They didn't crumble under the horse's hooves or the trailing edge of Vukotich's stretcher.

It was a bumpy ride. Johann half-turned in the saddle, and saw Vukotich waking up. The stretcher rose over a huddled corpse, dragging it a few feet before leaving it behind. Empty eye sockets looked up, and a second mouth gaped in its throat. One of its arms was a man-length clump of tentacles, now withered like dry seaweed. It had been stripped naked.

'The Battlefield,' said Vukotich.

'What is this place?'

'Evil. We're close to Cicatrice. This is what he's come for.'

Vukotich was in pain again. Talking hurt him, Johann knew. The tutor slumped back on his stretcher, breathing hard.

The dead were around them in heaps. Some were obviously fresh-killed. There were birds now. Unclean carrion-pickers, tearing at exposed flesh, pecking out eyes, fighting over scraps. Johann hated the carrion birds. There was nothing worse than living off the slaughtered.

Armies had passed this way, less than a day ago by the looks of some of their leavings. And yet they had been following a band of raiders, not an army. Cicatrice could command only a hundred Knights at his best, and his band was well below strength since their exploits in the Troll Country.

'The gathering,' Vukotich got out, 'is here. Cicatrice will be one among many.'

A pack of rats, close together like a writhing carpet, swarmed over a skeleton horse, and swept towards the stretcher. They skittered up over the branches and fastened on Vukotich's legs. He waved his sword and sent them flying away. The cutting edge was red. Johann could see his tutor had been bitten.

'Damn. The plague'll get me yet.'

'Easy. We're nearly at the village.'

Vukotich coughed, and shook on his stretcher. He spat pink froth. 'By nightfall,' he gasped. 'We must be there by nightfall.'

The skies were reddening when they reached the village. It consisted of a scattering of shacks around a central long, low hall. The buildings were all sunken, little more than roofed cellars with slit windows and fortifications. Johann was reminded of the shelters he had seen in lands afflicted by tornadoes and hurricanes.

There were no dead among the buildings. Indeed, the corpses seemed to have been cleared away from a rough circle around the village. There was a hitching rail by the hall. Johann dismounted and tied Would-Have-Been-Tsar to it.

'Yo,' he shouted, 'is anyone here?'

Vukotich was awake again, shivering in his wrappings.

Johann shouted again, and a door opened. There was a depression in the earth beside the hall, and the entrance was in it, surrounded by bags of dirt. Two men came out of the hall. Johann touched his swordhilt until they were in full view. Neither was significantly altered. One, who stayed back near the door, was a beefy, middle-aged man with a leather apron and a gleaming bald pate. The other, who came forward, was scarecrow thin, a wild-haired individual with a tatty mitre perched on his head. He was weighed down with amulets, badges, medals and tokens.

Johann recognised the icons of Ulric, Manann, Myrmidia, Taal, Verena and Ranald. Also, of the Chaos Powers, including the dreaded Khorne; the Gods of Law, Alluminas, Solkan; Grungni, Dwarf God of Mining; Liadriel, Elven God of Song and Wine. The hammer of Sigmar Helden-hammer, Patron Deity of the Empire, was there. No priest could truly bear the talismans of so many disparate, mutually hostile gods. This was a madman, not a cleric.

Still, it is best to treat the mad with courtesy.

'Johann,' he said, extending his empty hand, 'Baron von Mecklenberg.'

The man approached sideways, his gods tinkling as he did, smiling the smile of an imbecile.

'I'm Mischa, the priest.'

They shook hands. Mischa darted away, cautious. Johann noticed he wore the dagger of Khaine, Lord of Murder, as well as the dove of Shal-lya, Goddess of Healing and Mercy.

'We mean no harm. My friend has been injured.'

'Bring them inside,' barked the bald man. 'Now, before nightfall.'

Vukotich had mentioned nightfall. Johann had a bad feeling about that. He had had an unrelishable experience with a certain vampire family in the Black Mountains.

'Come, come,' said Mischa, gesturing to Johann to come inside the hall. He danced a little on one foot and waved a loose-wristed hand in the air. Johann saw the blood in his eyes, and held back.

He turned to Vukotich, who was struggling to sit up, and helped his friend. The Iron Man was unsteady on his feet, but could stumble towards the hall. Johann supported him. The bald man came out of his hole in the ground and lifted Vukotich's other shoulder. Johann sensed strength in him. Between them, while Mischa darted around uselessly, they got Vukotich through the door.

When Mischa was in, the bald man slammed the door behind him and slid fast a series of heavy bolts. It took Johann a few moments to get used to the semi-darkness inside the hall, but he gathered immediately that there were others inside.

'Darvi,' asked someone, 'who are they?'

The bald man let Vukotich sag against Johann, and stepped forward to reply. The interrogator was a dwarf who held himself oddly.

'This one calls himself a baron. Johann von Mecklenberg. The other hasn't spoken...'

'Vukotich,' said the Iron Man.

'Vukotich,' said the dwarf, 'a good name. And von Mecklenberg. An elector unless I miss my guess, and I never miss my guess.'

'I've abdicated that responsibility, sir,' said Johann. 'Who might I be addressing?'

The dwarf came out of the shadows, and Johann saw why his movements were strange.

'Who might you be addressing?' The dwarf chortled, and bowed very carefully, the hilt of the sword shoved through his chest scraping the beaten earth floor. 'Why, the mayor of this nameless township. I'm Kleinzack... the Giant.'

Kleinzack's sword was held in place by a complicated arrangement of leather straps and buckles. It stuck out a full foot from his back, and seemed honed to razor sharpness. Johann was reminded of the apparatus used by actors to simulate death, two pieces fixed to a body to look like one speared through it.

'I know just what you're thinking, your excellency. No, this isn't a trick. It goes all the way through. A miracle I wasn't killed, of course. The blade passed through without puncturing anything vital, and now I daren't have it removed for fear the miracle won't be repeated. You can learn to live with anything, you know.'

'I can believe it, Mr Mayor.'

'You've met Mischa, our spiritual adviser. And Darvi, who is the keeper of this inn. Come share our meagre fare, and be introduced to the rest of us. Dirt, take his cloak.'

A hunched young man with limbs that bent the wrong way shuffled out of the shadow at Kleinzack's order, and took Johann's cloak from his shoulders, carefully wrapping it as he crept away.

A madman, a cripple, a dwarf... This was truly a peculiar community.

Kleinzack took a lantern and twisted up the flame. The interior of the hall became visible now. There was a long table, with benches either side.

A young woman in the remnants of a dress that mightn't have been out of place at one of the tsar's famous balls passed by the diners, doling out a stew into their bowls. They were as tattered a collection of outcasts as Johann had ever broken bread with.

Kleinzack climbed a throne-shaped chair at the end of the table, and settled his sword into a well-worn notch in the back.

'Sit by me, your excellency. Eat with us.'

Johann took his place, and found himself looking across the table at an incredibly ancient creature – perhaps a woman – who was enthusiastically sawing at a hunk of raw meat with a large knife.

'Katinka doesn't favour civilised cuisine,' said Kleinzack. 'She's a native of this region, and only eats her meat raw. At least it's helped her keep her teeth.'

The crone grinned, and Johann saw teeth filed to nasty points. She raised a chunk of flesh to her mouth, and tore into it. Her cheeks were tattooed, the designs crumpled by her wrinkles.

'She's a healer,' said the dwarf, 'later, she will tend to your friend. She can do all manner of things with herbs and the insides of small animals.'

The young woman splashed stew into Johann's bowl. He smelled spices, and saw vegetables floating in the gravy.

'This is Anna,' the woman curtsied with surprising daintiness, balancing the pot of stew on her generous hip. 'She was travelling with a fine gentleman of Praag when he tired of her, and left her for our village as repayment for our hospitality.'

Anna's eyes shone dully. She had red hair, and would have been quite pretty cleaned up. Of course, Johann realised, he wasn't himself much used to baths and scents and etiquette. That part of his life was long gone.

'Naturally,' laughed Kleinzack, 'we don't expect such gratitude from all our guests.'

Various diners joined in, and banged their fists on the table as they guffawed. Johann didn't find the hilarity pleasant, although the stew was excellent. The food was the best he'd tasted in some months, certainly better than smoked horse.

The meal passed without incident. No one asked Johann what his business was, and he refrained from asking anyone how this village came to be in the middle of a battlefield. The villagers were too busy eating, and Mischa the priest made the most conversation, invoking the blessings of a grab-bag of gods upon the night. Again, Johann felt uneasy about that.

Katinka took a look at Vukotich, and produced some herb balms which, when applied, soothed his wounds a little. The Iron Man was asleep again, now, and didn't seem to be suffering much.

The hall was sub-divided into sleeping chambers. Several of the villagers scuttled off to them when the eating was done, and Johann heard bolts being drawn. Kleinzack produced some foul roots and proceeded to smoke them. Johann refused his kind offer of a pipe. Anna – who didn't speak – fussed with the dishes and cutlery, while Darvi drew ale from casks. Dirt shuffled around, keeping out of the way.

'You're far from home, Baron von Mecklenberg,' announced Kleinzack, puffing a cloud of vile smoke.

'Yes. I'm searching for my brother.'

'A-ha,' mused the dwarf, sucking at his pipe, 'run away from home, has he?'

'Kidnapped by bandits.'

'I see. Bad things, bandits.' He found something funny, and laughed at it. Dirt joined in, but was silenced by a cuff around the head. 'How long have you been after these bandits?'

'A long time.'

'Long, eh? That's bad. You have my sympathy. All the troubled peoples of the world have my sympathy.'

He stroked Dirt's tangled hair, and the bent boy huddled close to him like a dog to his master.

Something fell out of Dirt's clothing, and glinted on the floor. Kleinzack's face clouded, and Johann noticed how quiet everyone else was.

With elaborate off-handedness, Kleinzack downed his pipe and picked up his goblet. He drank. 'Dirt,' he said, suavely, 'you've dropped a bauble. Pick it up and bring it to me.'

The boy froze for a moment, then scuttled to the object. His fingers wouldn't work, but he finally managed to squeeze the thing between

thumb and forefinger. He laid it on the table in front of Kleinzack. It
was a ring with a red stone.

'Hmmn. A nice piece. Silver, I do believe. And a ruby, carved into a
skull. Very nice.'

He tossed it to Johann.

'What do you think?'

Johann could hardly bear to handle the thing. It was somehow
unpleasant to the touch. Perhaps he had been seeing too many skulls
lately. This one was slashed diagonally. It was a familiar scar. Cicatrice was nearby.

'Crude workmanship, but it has a certain vitality, eh? Your excellency
doubtless has many finer jewels than this.'

Johann put it down on the table. Kleinzack snapped his fingers, and
Anna brought the ring to him. He gazed into its jewel.

'Dirt.' The boy looked up. 'Dirt, you evidently want this trinket for
your own.' The boy was doubtful. A rope of spittle dangled from his
lips. 'Very well, you shall have it. Come here.'

Dirt shambled forwards on his knees and elbows, advancing like an
insect. He held out his hand, and Kleinzack took it.

'Which finger, I wonder...'

The dwarf jammed the ring onto Dirt's little finger, then bent it sav-
agely back. Johann heard the snap as the bone went. Dirt looked at his
hand, with its finger sticking out at an unfamiliar angle. There was blood
on the ruby. He smiled.

Then the din started outside.

Johann had been in enough battles to recognise the noise. The clash of
steel on steel, the cries and screams of men in the heat of combat, the
unforgettable sound of rent flesh. Outside the village hall, a full-scale war
was being fought. It was as if armies had appeared out of the air, and
set at each other with the ferocity of wild animals. Johann heard horses
neighing in agony, arrows thudding home in wood or meat, shouted
commands, oaths. The hall shuddered, as heavy bodies slammed into
it. A little dust was dislodged from the beams.

Kleinzack was unperturbed, and continued to drink and smoke with
an elaborate pretence of casualness. Anna kept efficiently refilling the
dwarf's goblet, but was white under her filth, shaking with barely suppressed terror. Dirt tried to cram himself under a chair, hands pressed
over his ears, eyes screwed shut as clams. Darvi glumly stood by his bar,
eyes down, peering into his pint-pot. Katinka bared her teeth, apparently
giggling, but Johann couldn't hear her over the cacophony of war. Mischa was in his corner, kneeling before a composite altar to all his gods,
begging at random for his own skin.

Outside, one faction charged another. Hooves thundered, cannons
boomed, men went down in the mud and died. Johann's ears hurt.

He noticed that Darvi, Katinka and a few of the others had padded
wads of rag into their ears. Kleinzack, however, did without; evidently,

he was far gone enough to last a night of this.

They were all mad, Johann realised, maddened by this ghost of battle. Could it be like this every night?

He went to Vukotich, and found his friend awake but rigid, staring in the dark. The Iron Man took his hand and held it tight.

Eventually, incredibly, Johann slept.

He awoke to silence. Rather, to the absence of clamour. His head still rung with the memory of the battle sounds, but outside the hall it was quiet. He felt hung-over, and unrested by his sleep. His teeth were furred and his muscles ached from sleeping sitting up.

He was alone in the hall with Vukotich. Light streamed in through slit windows. His tutor was still in deep sleep, and Johann had to work hard to slip his hand out of the Iron Man's grip. His fingers were white, bloodless, and tingled as his circulation crept back.

Puzzled, he went to the door, and found it hanging open. He put a head round it and saw nothing threatening. Hand on sword, he went outside, and climbed up the steps cut into the earth. The air was still and smelled of death.

The village stood in the middle of a field of the dead and dying. There were fires burning, carrying on the wind the stink of scorching flesh, and weak voices cried out in unknown tongues. Their meaning was clear, though. Johann had heard the like after many a combat. The wounded, calling for succour, or for a merciful blade.

At the hitching post, he found what was left of Would-Have-Been-Tsar. An intact head still in its bridle, hanging loose from the wood. The rest of the horse was a blasted, blackened and trampled mess, frosted with icy dew. It was mixed in with the limbless remnant of something small. A dwarf or a goblin. It was hard to tell, the head being mashed to a paste in the hardened mud. From now on, Johann would walk.

Ghosts or not, the armies of night left corpses behind. He scanned the flat landscape, finding nothing but the remains of war. Where did they come from? Where did they go? All the dead bore the marks of the warpstone. He could sense no pattern to the battle, as if a multitude of individuals had fought each other for no reason, each striving to kill as many of the others as possible.

That made as much sense as many of the wars he had seen on his travels.

Dirt came from the other side of the hall, his body strapped into the semblance of straightness by leather and metal appliances. He was still a puppet with too many broken strings, but he was upright, even if his head did loll like a hanged man's, and he was walking as normally as he ever would. Johann noticed his broken finger splinted and bandaged, and wondered if he'd come by his other twisted bones in the same manner. He was carrying a double armful of swords, wrapped in bloody cloth. He smiled, revealing surprisingly white and even teeth, and dropped his burden onto the earth by the hall. The cloth came apart, and Johann saw red on the blades. He had learned about weapons – formally and by experience – and recognised a diversity of killing tools: Tilean duelling *epees*, Cathay dragon swords, two-handed Norse battle blades, curved scimitars of Araby. Dirt grinned again, proud of his findings, and fussed with the swords, arranging them on the ground, wiping the blood off, bringing out the shine.

Johann left him to his business and went among the dead.

The villagers were on them like carrion birds, stripping armour and weapons, throwing their booty into large wheelbarrows. He examined one catch, and found rings, a silver flask of some sweet liqueur, an unbloodied silk shirt, a bag of gold crowns, a jewel-pommelled axe, a leather breastplate of Elven manufacture, a good pair of Bretonnian boots. Anna was filling this barrow. She worked delicately with the corpses, robbing them as if she were a nurse applying a poultice. As he watched, she slipped the rings from the stiff fingers of a dandified altered, then progressed to his filigreed armour. Without pausing to appreciate the workmanship, she loosed the leather ties on his arm-plates, and pulled them free. His skin was rotten beneath, and had been even before the battle. She eased his dragon-masked helmet from his head, and a knotted rope of silky hair came loose with it. His features were powdered and rouged, but had decaying holes in them. His eyes opened, and his limbs spasmed. With a small, ladylike move, Anna passed a knife under his chin, and he slipped back, blood trickling onto his chest. He sighed away his life, and Anna worked his body armour loose.

Sickened, he turned away, and saw Kleinzack. The dwarf was bundled up in furs and wore a ridiculous hat. In daylight, the sword through him looked more bizarre than ever.

'Good morning, excellency. I trust you slept well.'

He didn't reply.

'Ah, but it's fine to be alive on such a morning.'

Mischa appeared, laden down with more religious tokens – some still wet – and bent low to whisper in Kleinzack's ear. The mayor laughed nastily, and slapped the mad priest. Mischa scurried off yelping.

'The gods have made him mad,' said Kleinzack, 'that's why they tolerate his sacrileges.'

Johann shrugged, and the dwarf laughed again. The mirth was beginning to grate on him. He was unpleasantly reminded of Andreas's deathly laughter. Truly, he had fallen among madmen.

Darvi and another man were building corpse fires. They couldn't hope to burn all the dead, but they were managing to clear the area nearest the hall. Those too big to be carried whole to the blaze were cut up and thrown on like logs. Katinka came to Kleinzack and offered him a bracelet she had found.

'Pretty-pretty,' he cooed, holding the bracelet up so its jewels caught the light. He slipped it over his wrist and admired it. Katinka hovered, bowed down, waiting for an indulgence. Kleinzack reached up and stroked her ratty hair. She hummed to herself in idiot contentment, and he sharply tweaked her ear. She cried out and he pushed her away.

'Back to work, hag. The days are short, and the nights are long.' Then, to Johann, 'Our work is never done, you see, excellency. Each night there are more. It never ends.'

A hand fell on Johann's shoulder, and squeezed. He turned. Vukotich was up, a broken lance serving as a staff. His face had kept its green-ish look, the scars standing out white and hard, and there was pain behind his eyes. But his grip was still strong. Even hobbling, he radi-ated strength. He was still the Iron Man who inspired terror even in Cicatrice's worst.

'This is a Battlefield of Chaos, Johann. This is what Cicatrice has been heading for all along. It's nearly over. He'll be close by here, sleeping, with his creatures about him.'

Kleinzack bowed to Vukotich, shifting his sword slightly. 'You know about the battle, then?'

'I've heard of it,' said Vukotich. 'I was near here once when I was younger. I saw the Knights coming here.'

'For over a thousand years, they've been fighting among themselves, proving themselves. All the Champions come here sooner or later to see if they've got what they say they have. And most of them haven't. Most of them end up like these poor dead fools.'

'And that's how you live, dwarf,' spat Johann. 'Robbing the dead, sell-ing their leavings?'

Kleinzack didn't seem offended. 'Of course. Someone has to. Bodies rot, other things don't. If it weren't for us, and for our forebears, this plain would be a mountain of rusting armour by now.'

'They sleep in great underground halls nearby,' said Vukotich, 'sleep like the dead. This is an important stage in their development, in their alteration. They lie comatose by day on warpstone slabs, changing form, ridding themselves of the last traces of humanity. And by night, they fight. In small groups, in single combat, at random, they fight. For a full lunar month, they fight. And if they survive, they go back into the world to spread their evil again.'

'And Cicatrice?'

'He'll be here. Asleep now, as befits a general. We'll find him, and Wolf with him.'

Vukotich looked tired. From his eyes, Johann could tell it would be over soon, one way or another.

'You,' Vukotich addressed Kleinzack, 'carrion crow. Have you found anything bearing this symbol?' He produced a cloak-clasp with the emblem of Cicatrice's band, the stylised human face deformed by a red lightning bolt in imitation of their leader's daemon-claw scar.

The dwarf held up a hand, and rubbed his thumb against his fingers. Vukotich tossed him the clasp, and he made a great show of examining it as if appraising the workmanship.

'I can perhaps recall some similar item...'

Vukotich produced a coin and cast it at Kleinzack's feet. The dwarf looked exaggeratedly insulted, and shrugged helplessly.

Johann dropped a purse of coins to join the single crown and Klein-zack smiled.

'It all comes back to me. The scar.' He passed a finger diagonally across his face, kinking a little over his nose. 'Very distinctive. Very unusual.'

'It's an unusual man we're after.'

'The man whose followers bear this design?'

'Yes. Cicatrice, the bandit.'

Kleinzack laughed again. 'I can do better than show you a man who bears the image of this scar...'

The dwarf spun the clasp in the air and caught it.

'I can show you the man who bears the scar itself.'

A claw grasped Johann's heart, and squeezed.

'Cicatrice?'

The dwarf nodded, smiling, and held out his open hand. Johann gave him money. Kleinzack made a great pretence of examining his payment, biting into one gold crown, leaving shallow marks across the Emper-or's face. He looked at Johann and Vukotich, savouring his momentary power over them.

'Come,' he said, at length, 'follow me.'

Vukotich was still slowed by his wounds, but managed to hobble along with the dwarf. Johann felt frustrated by their measured pace as they went their way through the heaps of the dead, out onto the bloody steppe. For ten years, he had been waiting to confront Cica-trice. That scarred face – which he had never seen, but which eternally recurred on his men's emblem – had haunted his nights. He had never exchanged a blow or a word with the bandit, but Johann knew his history as well as he knew his own, and felt that by following in Cicatrice's tracks, he had become as close to him as to a brother. A hated brother. Now, he remembered their separate battles. He meas-ured his bested foes against Cicatrice's, wondering whether he was truly the Chaos Champion's equal in battle. He supposed he would find out soon enough.

Johann was impatient. Ten years was too long. It was well past time to get this over with.

No. He slowed himself, keeping in step with Vukotich and Kleinzack, helping his tutor over the rougher patches of ground, reining in his unruly imaginings. He would not hasten now. He had stayed alive for this day, kept himself going beyond all human endurance. He would not fumble at the last and chance Wolf's life. He found a calm in the centre of his heart, and let it seep through his being. The tightness in his chest eased. He began to see with a deadly clarity.

Almost unconsciously, he checked his weapons. His knives were in their greased sheaths, his sword hung easily from his belt. The blades could be in his hands faster than a human eye could register. After ten years on the trail, he could kill sometimes faster than he could think. It was a habit of which he looked forward to purging himself.

He remembered the initial arrow, brushing the deer's hide, proceeding with what had seemed like supernatural slowness towards his brother's shoulder. Johann hadn't used a longbow since, preferring to concentrate on hand-to-hand iron and steel.

'It's not much further,' wheezed Kleinzack. The dwarf was out of breath, and his sword shivered each time he filled his lungs. 'Just over this ridge.'

The ridge was not a geographical feature, it was an arrangement of dead horsemen and their steeds, cut down by a row of cannons. The third or fourth charge had broken through, but the casualties had been appalling. Johann tried not to think of the ranks upon ranks of flesh underfoot as he helped Vukotich up over the obstacle. Kleinzack swarmed with surprising agility over the cavalry corpses, pulling himself along using belts and saddles as hand-holds.

Darvi and a group of rangy, dead-faced men were hard at work, cutting valuables loose from the bodies with saws and shears. They were working on a pile of felled knights. One man was tugging at a plumed helmet whose owner was still feebly resisting, despite the depth and number of his mortal wounds. This one was in the latter stages of the changes, limbs barely recognisable as human, leathery batwings torn and crumpled beneath him, torso swollen up by a breastbone that was thrusting through papery skin like a knifeblade. The tatterdemalion's head twisted this way and that with the helmet, but finally his robber got a good enough grip and with one determined tug pulled his prize away.

The altered was old, his cheeks sunken and serrated, all his teeth gone save for two yellow tusks that had worn grooves in his lips. His hair was white and sparse, knotted in rat-tails on one side where he had once been partially scalped. And a red scar ran diagonally across his face, kinking a little over the nose.

Their search was over.

But this was not the Cicatrice Johann had pictured. This was a dying misfit, altered beyond practicality, lost even to himself.

'I want to talk to him,' Johann told Kleinzack.

'That's of no mind to me, your excellency...'

The dwarf wandered off, signalling Darvi and his men to follow. There were still pickings to be had. Something was screaming a few hundred yards away. Kleinzack's crew ambled towards it, their killing tools ready for use.

Johann and Vukotich stood over the man they had followed for so long. He hardly seemed aware of their presence, being absorbed in the business of dying. Cicatrice was still vaguely trying to stand up, but ankles broken and swollen to the thickness of a normal man's waist wouldn't support him. Uncomprehending eyes opened and blinked on his bare shoulders, purposeless tendrils waved languidly in the flow of blood from the rib-deep wound over his heart.

'Cicatrice,' said Johann, feeling the syllables of the name on his tongue, 'listen to me...'

The old altered looked up with fast-dimming eyes, and managed a smile. Red treacle oozed from his mouth.

'Cicatrice, I am the Baron von Mecklenberg.'

Cicatrice coughed, somewhere between a sob and a laugh, and turned his head to Johann. For the first time, the hunter and the hunted looked upon each other. Johann saw recognition in Cicatrice's eyes. The dying monster knew who he was. And he would know what he had come for.

'Wolf. Where's Wolf?'

Cicatrice raised a six-taloned hand, and pointed down at the earth, then made a general gesture, indicating the whole area.

'Here?' Cicatrice nodded.

'What have you done to him?'

'What... have... I... done to... *him!*' Cicatrice gathered his voice, and forced the words out. 'What have I done to him? Why, my dear baron, surely you should ask... what has he done to me?'

He held a claw to his opened breast, and dipped it in the blood.

'Wolf fought you? Wounded you?'

The laugh came again – the laugh Johann had been hearing from too many throats since this began – and Cicatrice's smile became cruel and indignant. Johann could see the shadow of the fearsome warrior chieftain's face over the shrunken and abused features of this poor creature.

'Wolf has killed me.'

With a certain pride, Johann turned to Vukotich. The Iron Man was an iron statue, his face unreadable. 'You see, Vukotich,' he said, 'Wolf resisted all these years. Here, in the heart of darkness, Wolf has turned on his captors and escaped.'

'No,' said Cicatrice, barely able to control his spasming now. These were his last minutes, last seconds... 'No, he has not escaped. Wolf now leads my army. For two years now, he has ridden at the head of our columns, planned our raids. I'm an old man. I've been tolerated. Until now. Now the Scar is dead, and the Young Wolf will have his time.'

Cicatrice reached into his wound, and pulled at his beating heart, holding it up.

'At least your brother chose to kill me face to face. His blade didn't come from the back.'

Blood ran through Cicatrice's talons. His heart puffed up like a toad and then collapsed. With his last strength, the bandit squeezed out his own life.

On the way back to the village, it was Vukotich who supported Johann, guiding him as an enchanter might one of the raised dead. Suddenly, the thousands of miles he had travelled in the past ten years weighed heavy upon him, as if each were a measure of time, not distance.

He had been concentrating so hard upon his search, his quest, that he had failed to perceive the shifting circumstances that now rendered the whole endeavour all but meaningless.

Wolf was in no need of rescue. A few days ago, Wolf had sent four creatures to kill his brother. In the last two years, how many traps and schemes had he created? How he must wish him dead!

'It's not Wolf,' Vukotich said. 'Whatever he has become, it's not Wolf. Your brother died a long time ago, in the woods, in Sudenland. He spilled his innocent blood. What we must find – find and *destroy* – is like the thing we burned in the forest, a monstrosity using what's left of his body.'

Johann had no argument.

By the time they were back in the village, the sky was already darkening. Days really were short this far north. Johann heard distant thunder, in the ground, and imagined the hordes stirring from their sleep, examining themselves for new alterations, new improvements.

Would he even recognise Wolf?

Kleinzack was standing before his hall, surrounded by his people. Mischa was chanting, and dancing epileptically, invoking long-dead deities, calling for protection from all manner of perils. The villagers had stowed their day's prizes, and were preparing for another night of cowering.

Johann would have to stay outside this night, and search through the carnage for his brother, seek to challenge him to mortal combat. He had no doubt that he could survive in the thick of a melee, but he wondered if he could come so close to the creatures of the warpstone, with their roiling auras of evil, without himself beginning the long, slow metamorphosis into monstrosity. If he were to start altering, he thought he could trust Vukotich to stick a spear through him.

A circle noosed around his left ankle, biting into the leather of his boot, and he was pulled off balance. He saw the wire rising out of the earth as it was reeled in. Kleinzack jumped aside as the whirring machine behind him pulled the steel thread in yard by yard. Darvi was working a handle. Johann fell badly, jarring his back, and was dragged too fast across the ground to sit up and free himself. His clothes were abraded, and his sword-hilt dug into the ground like a plough. A net was thrown over him, and he felt a metal-tipped boot impact with his ribs. His arms were tangled in the net, and he felt heavy weights on them. Anna and Katinka were kneeling, pressing him to the ground as they hammered pegs down, pinning the net, limiting his movement.

Twisting his head, he saw Vukotich spinning his broken lance, surrounded by six or seven of Darvi's brawny corpse-strippers. He gored one through, but his weapon was tugged out of his grip and the circle closed. He went down under it. Later, when they'd avenged their friend with a severe pummelling, they dragged him to the hall and pinned him out beside Johann.

Approaching carefully, Kleinzack and Darvi extracted the weapons from Johann's sheaths. He tried to resist, but only got another kick for his pains. The dwarf made a great play of examining the sword, appreciating the workmanship, and then taking it away.

All the while, Mischa danced, sprinkling foul-smelling liquid on Johann, daubing arcane symbols on the earth, and reciting from various scrolls of manuscript he kept about his person.

Johann gathered he and Vukotich were being laid out to appease the gods. At least, that was what Mischa was telling the villagers.

Eventually, the mad priest stopped, and went inside with the rest of the villagers.

Above the net, the sky was nearly black. The subterranean sounds were louder now and Johann could feel the earth under him shaking. He tensed all his muscles and exerted as much pull as he could. One of the pegs popped out of the ground, and his right hand was free. He strained again. The pegs were loosening, but it would take time to fight his way out of the net.

Then a shadow fell over him, and he heard the now familiar laugh. It was Kleinzack.

'Happy now, excellency? You'll soon see your brother. I'm only sorry I shan't be here to witness your touching reunion, to see your first embrace after so many years...'

The dwarf's hands were on him, patting pockets for coins.

'Of course, your brother has already paid me well for arranging this little get-together, but I don't see why I shouldn't also extract some tribute from you. It's only fair.'

Kleinzack took the pouches from Johann's belt, and the amulet with the family crest from his neck. Then he tried to work off the signet ring from his right hand.

Johann grabbed the dwarf's hand and held tight. Kleinzack thumped him, hard, but was still held. He spat in the dwarf's face and, summoning all his strength, sat up. Pegs burst free – those driven by Anna seemed a shade less well-rooted than those Katinka had seen to – and the net gathered in Johann's lap as he fought loose of it.

Kleinzack's gloating smarm had bubbled away, and his face was a mask of terror. He started blubbering, begging for mercy.

The ground was trembling constantly now, and he could hear hooves, the clanking of armour, shouts of defiance and other, barely human, sounds. A great many creatures were coming this way.

He held Kleinzack at arms' length. The stubby legs kicked, but the mayor couldn't reach Johann's torso. He had adjusted his grip now, and held the dwarf by a fistful of jerkin, just under the protruding hilt of the sword.

'You've left me here, unarmed, to die, dwarf.'

Kleinzack didn't say anything, just drooled. His bowels had let go, and he was dripping.

'You took away my sword. Up here, that's as much murder as taking away my life.'

There were creatures around them in the darkness, human and otherwise.

'You owe me a sword, Kleinzack. I'll take yours.'

He threw Kleinzack upwards. The dwarf seemed to hang in the air for a moment, eyes wide with disbelief. Johann reached out and grasped the hilt of the sword in the mayor. The dwarf's weight dragged it down. Kleinzack screamed as the sharp blade shifted in his chest. The point of the sword dug a few inches into the ground. He put a boot on Klein-zack's belly, and pushed the dwarf's body down the length of the sword. The straps and belts came free, and Kleinzack flailed, the long-ago kill-ing stroke finally accomplishing its purpose.

Johann drew his new sword from its scabbard of flesh, and kicked the dead dwarf away.

The fighting had begun, and the dark was pierced by bright flashes. Fires were started, and creatures hurled themselves against each other. An altered head rolled past Johann's feet as he cut Vukotich loose from his net. A cannonade exploded close by and Vukotich took a peppering of shot in one leg. Johann felt blood pouring down his face, from a chip lodged in his forehead, and tried to smear it away.

Nobody was paying particular attention to them, although Johann killed anything that came within a few yards of them, just to make sure. Vukotich took a two-bladed, dagger-topped waraxe from a fallen troll, and split the face of a bear-faced Norse warrior who was hefting a sword at him. As the bearman fell, Johann saw the scarface design on his belt-buckle. He had been one of Cicatrice's.

No, one of Wolf's.

Johann and Vukotich fell back against the hall, leaning on the roof. It was a defensible position. Before them, the warriors hacked and slashed at each other, not caring who they wounded. Ribbons of blood flew through the air. The killing continued.

They didn't have to wait long.

Among the frighteningly random conflict there walked one group who seemed cooler, murderous but purposefully so. They fought their way through the throng towards the hall, towards Johann and Vukotich. There were less than they might have expected – Wolf must have taken bad losses during the last week of fighting by night – but they were death-hardened. Each wore, somewhere about him, the scar.

And one luxuriously-maned, red-eyed, fang-snouted giant wore it as a blood-coloured tattoo across his face.

Wolf.

Wolf growled, low and feral in the back of his throat. Then the growl rose to a snarl, and spittle flew from his lupine snout. Then the snarl ended with a gulped intake of air, and Wolf's chest swelled. He howled like the animal he had become, baying at the skies. He clutched and unclutched his great, furred fists.

He carried no weapons but the three-inch, razor-edged claws that ended his fingers and toes, and the rows of teeth in his face. Johann guessed that with those natural assets he wouldn't need to.

Again, Vukotich had been right. There was nothing, that he could see, left of his little brother.

Then the wolf smiled at him, and passed a claw through the air, bidding him come forward.

Wolf's bandits held back, keeping the rest of the battle away from the area now marked out for the fight to the death.

'Forgive me,' Johann said, as he lashed out with Kleinzack's sword. Wolf threw up an arm, tendons shifting beneath his pelt, and the sword-blow was deflected. The altered Wolf must have iron in his muscle and bone. Johann's strike had left a graze, which trickled blood, but no more. It should have sheared through, severing the arm.

Wolf moved fast and Johann had to stumble backwards, losing his foot-ing, to avoid the snipping of the claws. Wolf kicked out with a barbed, bootless foot, and a claw-toe raked across Johann's stomach, cutting through his layered-leather armour. He pushed upwards as he stood, grabbing Wolf's ankle with both hands and turning it, off-balancing the creature that had been his brother. Almost immediately, he lost his grip and Wolf was righting himself. He stood like a man, ready to wrestle with the arts they had been taught as boys, but he fought like a beast, who had to use tooth and claw or go hungry tonight.

Vukotich was still leaning against the sloping roof of the hall, breathing heavily. He was watching his pupils, but also wary of Wolf's comrades, ready to pitch in with an axe if the strangely altered rules of fair combat were breached. Otherwise, he was leaving Johann and Wolf to their struggle.

Johann saw that Wolf had indeed grown with his alterations, finding a shape to fit his name, yet retaining every spark of his intelligence. His eyes were cruel but gleamed with sharpness of mind. The clawstroke across his face marked him as a leader. He would never have been baron, but he had proved that he could rise to power by his own designs.

Had Johann not missed his deer, what would Wolf have made of him-self? How would his strength, now perverted into monstrosity, have been made manifest? Truly, the division between Hero and Hellspawn is fine, no thicker than a slender arrow...

The cut at his belly had gone deeper than he thought, and he felt his own blood soaking the inside of his clothes. Knots of pain were forming, too, and he tried not to think of the depth of his wounds. He had seen men vainly trying to coil their insides back in, and knew how perma-nent damage to the vitals was. Wolf showed no sign of hurt, although he had struck him again and again with the edge of Kleinzack's sword. His brother's hide was thicker than any armour.

They circled each other, like wrestlers looking for a good hold. He remembered that he had always bested his brother when they were boys. The three years between them gave him the advantage, and Wolf had been shamed only when Johann, hoping to give his brother a taste of victory, had held back and allowed himself to be beaten. Had that experience festered in the captive boy's mind while the powers of the warpstone were exerted on him? Was that the secret anger that had fuelled his alteration?

Johann bled from the shoulder now, almost the exact spot where he had wounded Wolf so many years ago, and wondered whether that claw-thrust had been a deliberate reminder.

Wolf wore a metal shoulderpiece with the mark of Cicatrice picked out in jewels, covering the site of his long-healed wound. It was one of several for-show scraps of armour adorning his body.

Wolf jabbed again, with a blade-tipped forefinger, and again gored his shoulder. Now, he was sure it was deliberate. Wolf was drawing the fight out, reminding him of the long-ago error that had brought them to this...

He heard a clash and a scream, and glimpsed a tableau behind Wolf. One of the bandits had gone for Vukotich and was on its knees in front of the Iron Man, axe embedded between its eyes. The axe came free and Vukotich whirled to take on another attacker. Things were coming to an end and Wolf's men were clearing up the side issues.

Wolf dropped to all fours and charged like an animal, his long, still-golden hair streaming behind him. His back arched, and Johann saw the points of his vertebrae thrust against his skin. With a two-handed grip, he sliced into Wolf's humped back, aiming for the spinal column. Hide peeled and the sword jarred in his hands. Wolf roared, apparently feeling pain for the first time in the fight. He twisted away, rolling in a ball, and then stood like a man again, and closed with his brother.

Johann's swordpoint touched his breast, and he froze. Wolf looked at Johann, the sword held between them. Johann had a good grip and Wolf leaned forward into it. His hairy skin dimpled around the sharp end of the blade, and Johann felt the hilt pushed against his stomach. He could let go of the sword and it would stay between them, held by their bodies. For an instant, the brothers locked eyes, and he knew he was lost. Wolf snarled, strings of saliva hanging from his snout, and coals glowed deep in his blood-filled eyes.

Wolf held his shoulders and pulled his brother towards him in a killing embrace. The sword should have burst through the skin, and pierced his heart neatly...

Instead, the sword bent. First, it simply strained and Johann felt the pommel driving painfully into his wounded gut. Then, with an agonising creak, a natural weakness in the iron was worked on, and the weapon bent as easily as a green branch. Wolf's snarl continued and the sword was pulled out of Johann's hand. It fell away, useless.

Vukotich was still fighting. Three of Wolf's men were out, but the last two had him pinned to the roof, and were cutting him. The Iron Man was bleeding badly and his blood had an unhealthy, greenish tinge.

Wolf and Johann grappled with each other, wrestling again. He felt the claws going into his wounded shoulder, digging deep in the flesh. He brought his knee up, and slammed into Wolf's rock-hard belly. The blow had no effect. He took a handful of Wolf's hair, and tugged it sharply. A patch came away bloody, but Wolf didn't flinch. Wolf made a fist, and aimed for Johann's face. He took the blow on his chin, and reeled back, his head ringing, his vision shaking.

His shoulder was a fiery mass of pain now. And his left knee wasn't working properly. And he had no weapons save for his hands. And his mind.

Wolf howled, with a note of triumph, and came after him. He was tempted to turn and run. But he wouldn't get ten feet in the battle anyway. He might as well die by Wolf's hand as by that of an unknown minion of the night.

He made a hard-edge of his hand, as the monks of Nippon were known to do, and chopped at Wolf's neck. Wolf moved before the blow could land, and he skinned the leading edge of his hand on the jewelled armour plate.

Wolf screamed, and lashed out clumsily, claws closing in the air a foot to the left of Johann's face.

That was the reminder he needed. That was the message what was left of his brother had been giving him. He felt the pain in his own shoulder, but ignored it, and took hold of the scarface-marked armour piece.

He wrenched it off, and looked at the patch of untreated, rotted wound beneath. Worms writhed in it, a flash of bone could be seen in the mangled meat. The fur around was grey.

Wolf looked at Johann with the eyes of the boy he had been, and silently begged for it to be over.

Johann found a sword on the ground, bloodied but unbroken. Wolf was down on one knee, as if waiting to be knighted. Johann calculated that he could drive the blade through the old wound, past the shoulderbones, and into his brother's heart.

The flow of blood from his temple had halted, but there were tears on his face, salt stinging a cut on his cheek.

Johann hefted the sword aloft, and held it point-down above Wolf, ready to thrust deep, ready to finish his quest...

But things changed, and Vukotich was under him, between the brothers, mortally wounded but still moving. Johann had already begun to bring the blade down. It slipped into the Iron Man just below the v of his throat and slid through flesh and bone.

Incredibly, he stood up. Johann backed off. Wolf was curled up behind Vukotich, cheated of his death. Vukotich turned and pulled the sword from his neck. He held the weapon against him, point lodged beneath his chin, and then drew it across his body.

He opened himself and his blood fell upon Wolf. Innocent blood.

There was a coppery smell and Vukotich glowed with a violet light. He was mumbling at the last, reciting some charm or spell of his homeland, bleeding all over the thing he had once nurtured, taught and loved as a son.

Then he fell sideways, dead.

Johann went to Wolf, reaching for the sword in Vukotich's already-stiffening hands and found the source of the violet light. Wolf was glowing, surrounded by a man-shaped cloud of insubstantial mist. The glow pulsated, and the mist grew thicker. Johann couldn't see his brother through it.

Innocent blood. Never underestimate the power of innocent blood,

Vukotich had said.

He tried to touch his brother, but his gloved hand couldn't penetrate the mist. It was yielding, but refused to break.

An enormous male altered with four-foot antlers charged them, and Johann brought his sword up, scraping the velvet from a tine. The stag-man howled and his face was engorged purple with rushing blood. Johann cut him down expertly, and took on the two twin goblins who followed, tricking them into spearing each other. Then came an octo-poid monstrosity with the eyes of a beautiful woman, and a tiny-headed giant with four mace-handed arms. And others, and others.

As if possessed, Johann fought them all. He stood over his cocooned brother, and held off the hordes until morning.

At first light, the battle stopped. It was like a combat sport. An unheard referee had ended the match and everyone could go home. Johann had been trading blows with an androgynous popinjay who wielded a thin, deadly rapier. When the sun first tainted the sky, the creature sheathed its sword and bowed elaborately to Johann, swishing a ruffled sleeve through the air. All around them, combatants had left off trying to kill each other and were breathing hard. The sudden quiet was unnerving.

Johann looked at his enemy of the moment. There was a disturb-ing touch of invitation, of frightful promise, in its womanish smile. Its beauty was almost elven, although its neutered but well-muscled form was human.

'Until tonight?' it said, gesturing in the air.

Johann was too exhausted to reply. He simply shook his head, con-scious of the blood and sweat falling from his face.

'A pity,' it said. It kissed two fingers, and pressed them to Johann's lips, then turned and walked away, gorgeously embroidered cloak swing-ing from side to side, the buds of horns poking through its girlish hair. Johann wiped the scented blood taste from his mouth. It joined the others, and they trudged wearily away, leaving behind the losers of the night's conflict. They were tonight's losers, or the next night's, or a hundred nights from now and far from this place's. When you fight for Chaos, you fight with Chaos. And you can't fight with Chaos and win.

Johann fell to his knees beside Wolf. Vukotich's corpse was stiff as a statue now, and had suffered much abuse during the course of the night. But his normally hard face had softened. Johann realised just how little he really knew about the man he had lived with, fought along-side, travelled with and eaten with for ten years. At the end, though, Sigmar was with him. And magic had been in his blood. He traced a hammer in the earth.

Wolf's cocoon had stopped glowing, and was dry and papery now, with thick veins. Johann touched it, and it broke. Wolf was stirring. The unidentifiable matter fell away in dusty scales. Johann tore it away from his brother's head.

A thirteen-year-old face appeared.

There were people about now: Anna, Darvi, Dirt, Mischa. The mad priest gave thanks to another dawn. With a single glance, Johann convinced Darvi not to fight him. Dirt bent down by the brothers and grinned.

'You're the mayor now,' Johann told him. 'Get Katinka. My brother's been hurt and needs a poultice.'

There was an arrow wound in Wolf's shoulder, fresh and clean and bleeding.

The Warhawk

The Blackgull

I

The ground was his enemy, his prison. All his life, Warhawk had tried to escape its dreary pull. He was more comfortable up here on the roof-tops than down below on the grimy cobbles, but his aim was higher still, in the freedom of the skies. On his wrist, Belle shifted slightly, hooded head bobbing. He envied her her wings, her flight. But soon, when the Device was complete, he would share her life, would truly be able to take her for his mistress and mate.

When, as the Device decreed, thirteen had died, he too would be able to soar above the dirt, plunge through the clouds, battle the cross-currents of the winds. Nine were dead already. And Number Ten was down below, an insectile speck crawling through cramped streets, never raising eyes from their boots, never dreaming of the wonders above. He did not know him or her yet, but they were already marked for death.

Warhawk had been capricious so far, choosing some of the sacrifices carefully, but picking others entirely at random. One of the most distinguished he had come upon by chance. It had never been explained satisfactorily why a cleric of Solkan, supposedly engaged in important archaeological work in the Grey Mountains, should be disguised as a ragged beggar in the streets of Altdorf, importuning the crowds outside the Vargr Breughel Memorial Playhouse. But that was precisely the activity in which Professor Bernabe Scheydt had been engaged when Belle took him. Warhawk knew all men led iceberg lives, four-fifths submerged in the dark. Death sometimes brought submerged things to the surface.

Balancing carefully, leaning to one side to counter Belle's weight, he walked along the knife-point roof-prow of the Temple of Shallya. He strode without fear across the gap between the temple and the Imperial Bank, scaled the gabled cone of the bank's upper cupola, and finally reached his chosen perch for the night – the service platform just below the great clock. Inside the cupola, machinery ground together, time relentlessly marching forward with the hands on the clockface. In a world slowly eaten away by Chaos, time was a certainty, and the bank clock was a byword for reliability. It was accurate to a quarter-hour, probably the most sophisticated timepiece in the Empire.

Down below, as the night people emerged, the Konigplatz became busy, crowded. It was chilly, but Warhawk, wrapped in his padded leather armour, felt nothing. His body bruised by too many falls, he had been careful in stitching together his black protective suit. A close-fitting hood covered his face, stylised hawk's beak picked out on the leather, feathery swirls around the eyeholes. The few who had seen him swore he was a ghost, or a bird-headed altered.

He looked across the Konigplatz, the Place of Kings, at the cluster of Imperial statues forming a crowd of their own, jostling around the great form of hammer-wielding Sigmar, the earliest emperors faceless lumps of stone, the most recent vulgar caricatures, each vying for a better position. It was the tradition for a new-elected emperor to commission his own statue to add to those of his predecessors. After two and a half thousand years, it proved politic to let the oldest statues crumble away to make room. Still, another period like the Year of the Seven Emperors, which followed the death of the Emperor Carolus twelve hundred years ago, would require the demolition of one of the buildings abutting the Konigplatz to make space for the figures.

Belle's talons were tight on his wrist, razored extensions snug in the grooves of his thick, reinforced glove. She was a good bird, the best he had ever trained – schooled almost from the egg to be a huntress, a weapon – and she would be the greatest of her age. His father would have been proud of Belle. She was easily the equal of the famous Sebastian or Boris the Ferocious, and, in time, she might be as fearsome as Minya, the huge she-hawk who had turned the Battle of Axe-Bite Pass, taking out the eye of Cervello the Traitor, and dying to save his father on the upper slopes of the Fastness of Jagrandhra Dane.

He looked down, scanning the crowds for a sign. From a full five storeys above, they were all tiny, insignificant creatures. His sacrifice was down there somewhere, waiting for a death that was the next movement of the Device. Some gesture, some colour, some sound drifting up. Something would call out. It always did. Meanwhile, Belle was patient. With Belle, the Warhawk had no need of jesses to restrain her ankles or hood to cover her eyes. She would not take to the air until he signalled.

The watchman, Kleindeinst, reminded Warhawk of his father. They had the same hard eyes, the same scarred determination. He had seen Harald Kleindeinst in public several times, even attended a citizens' meeting where angry questions had been directed ceaselessly at the captain. Kleindeinst swore he would clip Warhawk's wings, but had accomplished nothing. At first, the Warhawk thought Kleindeinst might prove a worthy adversary. The copper had brought down the Beast Yefimovich last year, ending the series of murders that had shaken the city during the fog riots. The palace itself had requested the watchman be given charge of the current investigation. Warhawk had sat with the broadsheet writers and concerned businessman, and watched Kleindeinst reel as he was angrily denounced by speaker after speaker. The people of Altdorf wanted decisive action, and couldn't see how powerless the watchman truly was. Kleindeinst would never understand the Device, much less impede its workings. Before the meeting's scheduled end, Captain Kleindeinst had left the room and stalked out alone, renewing his vow, striding from the watch station ahead of the crowd's jeers.

Down below, small knots of people were assembling around the empty bases of the oldest statues. In the evenings, speakers would take advantage of these ready-made platforms to address the crowds, preaching the worship of a lesser god, advocating the institution of an unheard-of political system, spreading gossip and sedition, or making public some commercial venture. In the past, Warhawk had himself spoken in that manner, declaring his intention to conquer the skies, ignoring the laughter of the unwashed mob and the sneers of the wizards. A Brustellinite revolutionist occupied his old pedestal. He was calling for a general uprising against the Emperor, and his audience, loyalists to a man, were getting restless. A strolling watchman, club already out, was moving in on the speaker, doubtless ready to make an arrest, and give the revolutionist a chance to get acquainted with the worthies he decreed should be free by spending a few nights in a straw-and-dung-floored cell with pick-pockets, beggars and cutpurses.

Harald Kleindeinst had been a disappointment. Warhawk was almost sorry for the copper. With each sacrifice, Kleindeinst's position became more dangerous. By the time the Device was complete, the captain would be lucky to escape the wrath of the people he served. His body would hang on the docks for the river-birds. While he was rotting, Warhawk would be learning the ways of the air, striving ever higher, released at last from the tyranny of mud and stone. Still, Kleindeinst was as much a part of the Device as he was himself. He remembered his father saying that you should choose your enemies as carefully as you pick your friends.

It was his father who first told him of the Device, who had explained its workings. It was not magic, but alchemy, a true science. Magic only worked for wizards, but alchemy was for all who followed the steps. Wizards were arrogant, conjuring fire from the phlogiston in the air and sneering at ordinary men with their sulphur-sticks. But eventually magic would be swept away, and the Warhawk would fly, not through clouds of mystery and superstition, but upon solid principles of logic and balance. In the mean time, blood sacrifice must be made.

The watchman shouldered through the crowd and laid a hand on the revolutionist's leg. Everyone was shouting. The unkempt Brustellinite jumped upwards, making a grab for the outstretched arm of the statue of the Empress Magritta, and swung like an ape. The copper scrambled up after the fire-breather, egged on by the crowd.

Warhawk knew.

He pointed leisurely, shrugging with his wrist. Belle's wings spread elegantly and flapped. The bird rose from her perch, and swayed into the air, almost floating, beating her wings only when absolutely necessary. That was one of his father's tricks: teaching the bird to glide silently towards the victim.

The empress's arm broke at the shoulder and the revolutionist fell into the hostile crowd, who set about pummelling and kicking him. The watchman, sweating from his exertions, looked down. He removed his cap and used it to wipe his forehead.

Belle brought her feet down like a diver executing a back-flip and settled, claws-first, around the copper's head, her beak digging into the back of his neck, her knife-ended claws rending his cheeks and throat. The crowd were too busy with the Brustellinite to notice the sacrifice. Warhawk felt the thrill of his kill, knowing the Device was one death closer to completion. He already heard the clouds calling to him and could feel the magnetic pull of the stars.

Belle let the watchman fall and his body tumbled into the crowd. Shrieks and screams rose into the night and his bird spiralled up away from the sacrifice.

He heard his name, repeated over and over, and stretched out his wrist for his faithful servant.

People were pointing up at him. He took care to be silhouetted against the clockface. He was not like the Beast, skulking in shadows and fogs. He was a clean predator of the skies and his daring was a message. A message to the ground-crawlers he despised, to the watchman who could never catch him, to the spirit of his departed father.

He was the Warhawk!

Belle landed on his wrist and he brought her close to his leather-covered mouth. He kissed her bloodied beak, feeling the warm wetness through his mask.

Climbers were already attempting to scale the bank. But by the time they reached his perch, he would have long since flown. With the song of the air in his heart, his devoted bird on his wrist, he disappeared from the clock platform. A touch of disappointment leapt inside him – disappointment that this was not the thirteenth sacrifice, that feet and hands not wings were the instruments of his escape... He began to make his pre-planned way down to the hated ground.

II

Every time this happened, more people found an excuse to loiter around the abused corpse and get in the way. All of them had shit they wanted to dump on Harald, but none of them were prepared to get in an orderly queue and take their turn. Standing by the dead watchman – undisturbed since the killing – was like being in the middle of a group of squawking vultures. They all shouted at him at once, protesting, abusing, questioning.

Captain Harald Kleindeinst – 'Filthy Harald' to some – tried to block out the noise and concentrate on the job. This time, his job was Klaus-Ulric Stahlman, forty-three, constable of the watch, Altdorf-born, wife and three children, dead in the Konigplatz gutter. A twenty-year flatfoot, his life had been spent walking the streets, clubbing trouble-makers, warming his swelling guts in defiance of regulations with peach schnapps, hauling in the more obvious drunks and whores, chasing fleetfoot pick-pockets and hanging around bored in the drizzle waiting for his shift to end. His record showed no promotions, no commendations, no complaints, nothing. The station captain, Katz, could barely remember him.

Stahlman had to be identified from his badge number. The bird had lifted the scalp and skin off his skull as if removing a hood. The collar of his uniform and the front of his tabard were stained with his blood, and there were vertical slashes where scrabbling claws – augmented by sharpened metal attachments – had torn. Harald was long past losing his lunch over such things, but these mutilations were becoming monotonously familiar. The Warhawk was a great leveller; grand duchess or scrubwoman, great general or fat old copper: all were equal with their faces off.

Ignoring the ghoulish sensation-seekers, the crowd consisted of six ordinary watchmen, four from the Konigplatz district and two from Harald's own Atrocities Commission: Captain Katz of the Konigplatz, greatcoat over his nightshirt; three pests from competing broadsheets, scratching nasty details on little tablets; a pale-looking physician from the Temple of Shallya, who had been passing and was drafted in to give the gory details; Ehrich Viereck, former commandant of the Commission, still gnawing away at the edges of the case; and Rasselas, supposedly an official of the Imperial Bank, actually a spy in the pay of Chancellor Mornan

Tybalt. Within minutes of the murder, the news was all over the city, and the vultures were gathering in the place where the hawk had been.

Harald nodded and one of his watchmen draped a canvas sheet over Stahlman. That made the bloodthirsters lose interest and drift away. Katz and Viereck were muttering together, hatching a scheme to haul Harald off the case. After nine – no, ten – corpses, Harald would not ordinarily have minded. Only he couldn't live with the idea of the Warhawk walking, or flapping, away free. These killings were a personal affront now, each corpse another bleeding wound. Harald would end them or be ended himself.

Rasselas was concerned that the men Harald had sent up to the cupola be careful not to disturb the delicate machine. He was being explicit on the point. Harald wondered whether the Warhawk had selected his perch on purpose, to involve Tybalt and the Imperial counting house in the investigation. Few things were as guaranteed to hinder the path of a watchman as the helpful hand of that olive-eyed, sallow-skinned, one-thumbed schemer. Harald had met Tybalt briefly during the Great Fog Riots, while in pursuit of the Beast, the last pattern-killer to plague the city.

'Well,' Viereck snapped, chewing at the wounds, 'this is what your "softly, softly" methods achieved, Kleindeinst. A watchman dead and the whole city laughing at us.'

'Feel free to apprehend and execute the Warhawk again, Ehrich,' Harald said, calmly, shutting Viereck up.

When the Warhawk had first struck, no one had believed there was a human agency involved in the killings, and the militia had gone around with crossbows skewering every pigeon and duck in the skies. Someone took it into his head to slaughter the ravens that traditionally flocked around the west tower of the Emperor's palace. Street-dwellers and hovel-huddlers who hadn't tasted meat in their lives were suddenly able to eat fowl every night. Then, when the black-hooded Warhawk had been seen with his bird, Viereck had taken over. His investigative methods were simple, brutal and grossly ineffective.

After each killing, he found a vaguely likely suspect – a commercial falconer, an unliked ornithologist, a rat-catcher who used a hawk – and made an arrest, announcing that he would put them to the torture until the case was solved. After a few days in Mundsen Keep with Viereck and some expensive equipment, the suspect would confess and be hanged, whereupon there would be jubilation in the street, Viereck would be declared the hero of the day, and the Warhawk would strike again, leaving another clawed corpse in the street and an Atrocities Commission in search of a new suspect.

'At least the investigation was making progress when I was in charge, Kleindeinst,' Viereck blustered.

Harald looked at the man, fixing him with his eyes, and Viereck looked away, sweating.

After three hangings, Viereck had been removed from his position – it was rumoured at the insistence of the Emperor himself – and Harald Kleindeinst had been seconded from the Dock Watch to head the investigation of the killings. Now, three months and four victims later, he knew no more than the day he had first heard of the murders.

'This cannot go on,' Rasselas insisted, stating the obvious, 'business is suffering. People are withdrawing funds from the bank and leaving the city. There'll be a crisis.'

The first to leave the city – as usual, Harald reflected – had been the Imperial family. Officially, they were spending the summer on the Ostland estates of the Grand Prince Hals von Tasseninck, another green velvet-set jewel among mankind, so the young Prince Luitpold could gain some experience of life in the provinces. Harald guessed the House of the Second Wilhelm was actually scared of the caress of claws that held no respect for lineage and breeding.

These were not like the Beast's killings, when only street drabs had suffered. Thus far, clerics, militiamen, titled ladies, greengrocers and street urchins had fallen alike under the talons. Everyone was in danger, and those who could afford it were removing themselves.

'The shipping lines are taking all their business to Marienburg,' Rasselas prattled on. 'It's beyond reason.'

Baron Joachim von Unheimlich, patron of the ultra-aristocratic League of Karl-Franz, was advocating Altdorf be placed under martial law, and that troops quell the uprising obviously being fomented by the Warhawk. It was the Beast scenario all over again, the killings were being used by every faction to their own ends. It was Harald's job to set all these distractions aside and to home in on the killer himself. Or herself. In all probability, these were not political crimes, crimes for gain, or even crimes for sport. These were pattern killings, the work of a clever madman who made his own rules and stuck to them. If he could understand the Warhawk's rules, then he had a chance of catching him.

'The Konigplatz Watch Widows and Orphans Society will place an additional reward,' Katz of the 'platz announced to the scribblers, 'of one hundred crowns. Our fallen brother, Schlieman, will be avenged.'

'Stahlman?' asked an ink-fingered writer, only to be ignored.

Another broadsheet character had bribed a copper to lift the canvas and was sketching the dead man's red-covered skull.

Harald realised he was in danger of losing control of the investigation. The Atrocities Commission was not what he was used to. It had too many men, too many ledgers, too many conventions.

The resources should have helped, but he was hobbled by them. He missed the days when he was a lone hunter, just him and the quarry, stalking the streets until the chase was over.

Viereck knelt by the corpse, and began praying loudly to Ulric and Sigmar, calling their wrath down upon the foul murderer, then turning his profile so the sketch artist could include him in his picture. Noticing this, Katz too bent over, thrusting his studiedly grim face into the area the man was sketching, trying to look resolute. The two watchmen seemed more than ever like ghouls, lunching on the dead man's entrails.

'Captain Kleindeinst,' asked another of the reporters, 'how do you react to suggestions that your lax approach to wrong-doers has proved an encouragement to the Warhawk murderer?'

Years ago, when he had killed an elector's nephew who was on the point of raping and murdering a servant, this reporter's sheet had branded him a monstrous thug whose excesses should be curbed with the lash.

'I react by feeding the suggester his own boots and kicking him off the docks.'

The reporter made a great show of writing that down.

A fly coach trundled into the 'platz, and Harald felt almost relieved. With her around, things might start moving again. One of his watchmen opened the carriage door and a slim young woman with red hair stepped out. She didn't look like much, but she was the best hope Harald had of snaring the Warhawk.

'Let me through,' Rosanna Ophuls told the crowds, 'I'm a scryer.'

III

Scrying the 'platz for a trace of the bird was like trying to catch a butterfly one-handed. It was what Rosanna had expected, she had been through it before at the scenes of the other Warhawk murders. It was a futile task, but it had to be done.

Someone hissed 'witch', and was shut up. The stab of anonymous hate and fear from the crowd still hurt her. It was hard to make people understand what she was. All her life, she had been called a witch, a freak, a monster. Only when she was needed did she become an angel of mercy, a saviour. And she hadn't saved anyone recently.

Harald kept them all back, and – through a heroic effort she could sense as if it were a blazing bonfire – kept them quiet, while she tried her best.

'It's mixed up with the residue of the dead man,' she explained, eyes tight shut, as she brushed the bloodied pedestal with her fingertips, shivering as the left-behind emotions of Klaus-Ulric Stahlman shot into her.

He had died in panic, like the others, unable to understand what was happening. Spurs had gouged his eyes, so he had seen nothing. As he screamed, talons raking away his cheeks and lips, he had heard the beating of wings, hard edges of bone cracking his skull. There had been no final prayer, no thought for his wife and children, no sense even of surprise. It had been quick, but agonising.

'There was another man on the pedestal,' she said, seeing him through the dead watchman's memory, 'an agitator, a revolutionist.'

'Liebenstein,' interrupted Katz, distracting her, 'We have him, a Brustellinite sewer rat.'

Rosanna opened her eyes and blinked, her contact with the past lost completely. The morning sights and smells flooded in, blotting out her scrying. Harald told the other captain to be quiet.

There were still sticky patches of gore everywhere, bright in the sunlight.

She shut her eyes, and was back in the night. It was hard to make people understand that scrying wasn't like scanning a page in a book, going straight to the sentence you needed and absorbing it instantly. It was like a children's game, reaching into a barrel of sawdust, not knowing whether you'd come up with a ripe apple or a cat's skull.

She heard the revolutionist ranting with all the fervour of a fanatical preacher espousing the worship of his god, holding up the martyred Professor Brustellin – dead in the fog riots – as the idol of a new kind of society, one without privilege or injustice, without hunger or crime.

Then Stahlman had intervened, and the Brustellinite – Liebenstein – was gone, lost in the darkness, and her focus was on the watchman. The bird speared into her consciousness and Stahlman was dying again. Rosanna tried to ignore the watchman, to latch onto the tiny mind-presence of the bird.

'It is a hawk,' she said, 'female, I think. A name beginning with B. Beate. Bella? No, Belle.'

'The hawk's master?' Harald prompted.

She concentrated hard. Animals were difficult, and birds – apart from fish – the most difficult of all. Their minds were focused on food and procreation to the exclusion of all else. They ignored so much, there was little impression worth reading.

'A black hood,' she said, seeing a distorted image she realised was the bird's field of vision, 'a kind hand...'

A chunk of red meat came near the bird's face, juicy and oozing, pinched between two gloved fingers. Rosanna gulped and swallowed nothing, echoing the bird's movements.

'He feeds her,' she said. 'He loves her, nurtures her.'

There was nothing more.

Rosanna opened her eyes. 'That's it,' she said, 'I'm sorry.'

She didn't need her scrying to sense their disappointment. Hope seeped out of them like air from a pin-pricked pig's bladder. She was cold and shaking. Harald wrapped her cloak around her shoulders.

Viereck, Katz from the 'platz and Rasselas were unimpressed, but Harald was solicitous.

'Thank you,' he said.

'I was no help.'

'We have a name. Belle.'

'A bird's name. Not a man's.'

Like Harald, she had been on this case since last year, paid a small salary by the Atrocities Commission. Like Harald, she was frustrated. All they had learned was negative.

There was no connection between the victims. There was no political, financial or personal motive. Before these killings, there had been no previous crimes of a similar nature. There was nothing to suggest the Warhawk was a member of any Proscribed Cult, although the killings might conceivably be sacrifices of some kind. The murders had taken place all over the city, with no pattern as to the locations.

Killings had taken place at all hours of the day and night, although mostly under the cover of darkness. A masked falconer had been seen, but he – or she – was of average height and build, face completely covered. The murderer left no calling cards, no signature clues, no indication at all as to who he might be or what his motive was.

Harald turned to Rasselas. 'Is the way up to the clock cleared?'

The bank official was about to protest, but Harald's hand unconsciously drifted to the prominent hilt of his Magnin throwing knife, and his ice-chip blue eyes narrowed. Rosanna felt the force of his personality narrowed like sunbeams by a magnifying glass, and saw Rasselas twitch under the glare.

'It's been arranged,' he said.

Harald nodded. 'Rosanna,' he said, 'the Warhawk set his bird on the watchman from above, as usual. He was seen on the platform below the clock.'

Rosanna looked up at the Imperial Bank. She had seen the clock practically every day since she came to the city – it was one of Altdorf's landmarks – but had never before noticed the small platform, bounded by low rails, beneath it. There was a watchman up there now, waiting.

'Let's go,' she said, swallowing spit.

'You're not afraid of heights, are you?' Harald asked.

'No,' she said, the bottoms of her feet curling with anticipated fear, 'not at all.'

'Good,' he nodded.

Rasselas led the way.

IV

He had nothing to fear from the witch woman. With Belle asleep on her perch back in his attic and his leather suit hung in the closet alongside his father's old clothes, he was no longer Warhawk. He was just himself, one of the crawling crowd. He didn't even look up at the skies with longing. Only with Belle on his wrist and leather on his face was he the man the witch was seeking, the beneficiary of the Device.

The witch woman was not much more than a girl, a pretty reed of a creature in a pale red dress, walking as if on eggshells, hands held out slightly to ward others away. She wasn't comfortable with people, he realised. She must see into their hearts, into their secret lives. He had been careful not to get near her.

At first, he had stayed away from the scenes of the sacrifices. It had been enough to take Belle home and to read in the broadsheets of Captain Viereck's foolish attempts to scare him off course. But when he realised how safe he was, how impossible it would be for anyone to connect him with Warhawk, he had ventured out.

Kleindeinst led Rosanna away, towards the bank. Watchmen told the crowd to disperse, and most did. But he stayed where he was, sucking on his pipe, for all the world like an ordinary idler, mildly interested but no more. His tobacco tasted sweet, and his gaze rose with the smoke from his pipe-bowl. The smoke was pulled apart by the winds and dispersed into the sky.

When Kleindeinst had taken over, he had got into the habit of returning to observe the watchmen. Outside the Vargr Breughel, while the torn and broken Scheydt was being carted off, he had seen Detlef Sierck, the great actor, and Genevieve Dieudonné, his famous vampire paramour, and he had been most impressed.

Some people were born important, were born to be stars. It was nothing to do with breeding or position, but with a capability to affect the world, to change things, to get things done, to fulfil ambitions. His father and Prince Vastarien, Detlef and Genevieve, Imperial ministers and electors, even Kleindeinst and Rosanna. These were important people, stars. Detlef and Genevieve had defeated the Great Enchanter, Kleindeinst and Rosanna had tracked down the Beast. These were achievements. He had never been important, as his father had been, but he was becoming so.

When the Device was complete, he would be the most important of all, the most outstanding. Everyone would know who he was, but no one would be able to lay a hand on him. He would fly higher than the strongest archer could shoot an arrow. His father had soared, but his wings would take him above his father. His wings would take him among the stars. He would be a star.

One interesting thing was that he was not the only face who showed up at each of the Warhawk sites. There were a couple of reporters from the broadsheets who always arrived within minutes, and interrogated the crowds. He had described himself – the black-suited, leather-cloaked Warhawk – to them several times, but he was so ordinary they did not even realise he was the same person. Others were just sensation-seekers or bizarre obsessives. He realised they were his admirers, just as the women who waited outside the Vargr Breughel for a glimpse of Detlef Sierck were the great actor's admirers. Their tight-lipped, hungry faces made him feel like a star.

He had seen his symbol, a bright-eyed hawk, chalked up on walls, and slogans encouraging his purpose. On the pedestal of the old Emperor Luitpold statue was written 'Fear the Warhawk'. That made him smile inside, made him feel the itching lines on his back where his wings would sprout.

Kleindeinst and Rosanna were climbing the bank, ascending to his perch.

'You,' said a burly watchman, 'move on.'

He smiled at the officer and bowed, then sauntered off, hands in his pockets, jauntily whistling 'Come Ye Back to Bilbali, Estalian Mariner'. It was time he went to his birds. Belle would need feeding, petting and rewarding.

His step was so light he could barely feel the hated cobbles beneath the soles of his boots. He was almost flying already.

V

There was not enough room on the platform for all interested parties, so Harald took a delight in banning everyone but Rosanna and himself. The others stood and watched from inside the cupola, the vast and incomprehensible wheels and works of the clock hanging above, holding their hands over their ears to shut out the ticking, ringing, rending, wrestling sounds of the mechanism. Rasselas proudly began to explain the mechanism to anyone interested, whereupon his audience jammed fingers further into ears.

Rosanna leant lightly on the rail, hair whipped by the wind, eyes shut, searching inside herself for whatever it was she had that made her what she was. Harald had used her on other cases, ever since their brush with the Beast, but he still didn't really understand how scrying worked. He knew it wasn't simple, knew it did things to her he could never appreciate.

He noticed the girl's knuckles were white. She was gripping the rail as if it were life itself.

There were bird droppings on the platform, some fresh. And boot-prints – no special makers' marks or distinctive treads to serve as clues, like in one of Ferring the Balladeer's mysteries – in the dust. Without Rosanna's abilities, Harald could reconstruct the killer's movements. The Warhawk had stood here a while, picking his target. He had stood still – the prints were clear, not overlapped – and unmoving, patiently waiting. Handprints showed the holds he had used when escaping. Harald's stomach roiled, as it often did when he caught a scent of crime.

Stahlman regularly patrolled the 'platz, so the Warhawk could have picked him as a victim well in advance and turned up in order to get him. But it was more likely that he chose his perch first, and then selected the man who was to die. Still, killing a watchman was an obvious taunt. He wondered whether the Warhawk was trying to speak directly to him, taking a copper as a demonstration that he could defy Filthy Harald and live.

The first watchman up here had found a feather. After ten killings, the Atrocities Commission had enough feathers to stuff an eiderdown for that luxury-loving slut, Countess Emmanuelle of Nuln. Like the others, this specimen was undistinctive. All the second-best ornithologist in the city could tell was that it came from an ordinary hawk, and that the bird was in good health and probably well-groomed. Of course, the man had hardly been disposed to cooperate with the watch after the way Viereck had treated the best ornithologist in the city.

'I feel him,' Rosanna said, in a matter-of-fact way. 'It is a he, a man. He's dark inside, not much there. Like an empty suit of armour. An empty suit of leather armour.'

Harald paid attention, taking care not to get too near the girl. She could be confused that way. The wind was changing, blowing her hair across her face. If she were not so haunted, Rosanna would have reminded him of his wife.

His dead wife.

She was shaking now, her body jarring the rail, her chin bobbing, her head making strange – birdlike? – little movements.

'I am him,' she said, 'I am the Warhawk.'

'What's he thinking of?'

She hesitated. 'He has no real mind. And yet, he remembers his father. A taller, bigger man. Of course, in his memory he's a child and his father towers over him. But there's something. He constantly matches himself against his father, trying to outdo him, trying to fill his shadow...'

That was common enough among pattern-killers. There was always something in their childhood, their family background. Then again, considering the number of wretched parents around, it was a miracle the world wasn't overrun by pattern killers.

'His father... is... was...'

'Yes?'

Rosanna was shaking violently now, as if in the early stages of a seizure. He was worried for her and stepped nearer.

'His father was the Warhawk.'

'The Warhawk.'

She nodded, her hair whipping. She was turned away from him, but he knew her eyes were shut. Beyond her, he could see the statues of all the emperors since the time of Sigmar. Pigeons – a rarity in Altdorf these days – roosted in Sigmar's helmet and flocked on his dropping-encrusted hammer.

There was a wrenching sound, like a sword being pulled out of a stone wall and Rosanna lurched forwards, a scream starting from her mouth. Harald reached forward, grabbing her shoulders, holding hard. The clock's bells began chiming, impossibly, torturously loud.

The rail had come out of the masonry and Rosanna was toppling from the platform. Her weight pulled at him and one of her feet slipped over the edge.

'In his mind,' she shouted over the din of the chimes, 'he's flying, he's with the hawk!'

Her legs were over the lip of the platform now and she was gripping his arm. For an awful moment, he thought they would fall. He grabbed the end of the rail still embedded in the wall and pulled, hauling her away from the edge. She got both feet back on the platform. The others were crowding around the door, concerned. Katz reached out, feet well braced, and held his arm. Rosanna clung tight to him. She had very nearly gone off the front of the building.

They stood up and leaned away from the edge. Rosanna whistled out a breath and shook her head, smiling shakily. She gripped him hard. Then her hold relaxed and she pushed herself away, slipping into the cupola. The others got out of her way.

What had she read? What had she read from him?

He was shaking himself, as if fear had bled out of her mind into his. He stopped his trembling, stilling his own heart with an iron fist inside his chest.

Harald followed Rosanna inside. The chimes finished.

VI

In the attic, his birds were mostly asleep. He had trained them to be night flyers.

He prowled between the coops and perches, checking on his favourites. Belle was resting, head tucked under one wing. The barbs attached to her feet weren't chafing her. A good attack bird should have weapons as grown-in as a never-removed wedding ring.

His back, where the wings would grow, was itching constantly, two invisible rashes on his shoulderblades. Candlewax dripped on his hand, stinging.

He remembered his father, a statue on the hillside, mind soaring up in the body of his Minya. The Warhawk, the first Warhawk, had left his son in early childhood. Each of the boy's memories of the man was a polished perfect cameo that would stay with him forever.

Some of the birds shifted. It was comfortably hot up here in the windowless dark, only occasional shafts of light beamed in through the slats around the hatchways. The natural smells were strong, comforting, constant.

In his memory, his father was always still, a shell, his true self absent. He remembered looking from his father's impassive mask of a face to the dancing shape in the sky, and feeling the beginnings of understanding.

He lined the birds' coops with broadsheets that contained stories about the latest sacrifice.

The next movement of the Device must be bold.

In a corner of the attic, he contemplated the detritus of his earlier paths. Here were the remains of his first machines, bent metal and torn canvas, broken-toothed clockwheels and tangles of snapped wire. He had wasted years. He had always known that the answer was in science, not magic. But it was only recently that he had remembered his father's talk of the Device.

A clever man might fly. A man with no magic, but with the love of the sky in his heart.

Once, he had consulted a wizard about the Device, and the man had laughed at him, concealing his terror and envy with scorn. Wizards were all afraid of being caught out, of being shown up as frauds. They all pretended that Devices were nonsense, jealously guarding their own exclusive powers.

When he could fly, he would take a delight in tormenting wizards.

He must sacrifice again, soon. This time the sacrifice must be deliberately chosen. As it neared its completion, the Device had to be tended carefully, each move provoking its successor.

He thought of Kleindeinst and his witch woman, wondering if they were ready for what they must do next.

It would be a gamble, but it was his only possible move. Would his father have approved? He didn't know. It didn't matter. When the Device was complete, there would only be one Warhawk.

He went downstairs, and put on his hood.

VII

The offices of the Atrocities Commission were in the watch station on Luit-poldstrasse, the largest in the city. Harald had a desk there, and notional control over a small army of clerks and record-keepers, but Rosanna knew he spent as little time as possible surrounded by quill-pushers and ink-wells. A street copper, he had no patience with ledgers.

But now they were forced to fall back on dusty books. Every sur-face in the room was piled high with yellowing paper. Viereck was a poor organiser and the files from his period of command were chaotic. Anything of an earlier vintage – and there'd been a watch station on Luitpoldstrasse for centuries – was as likely to have been used as a taper for lighting cigars as to have been preserved. By the inexorable law of bureaucracy, the chances of a document's survival could be reckoned in inverse proportion to its usefulness, which meant that anything with a possible bearing on the case was liable to be ashes on the wind, while badly-spelled grocery lists or Imperially-decreed alterations to the watch uniform were preserved for posterity.

'I should have made the connection before,' Harald was fretting. 'War-hawk isn't exactly a commonplace name.'

Rosanna was less sure of this. Now it had come up she knew she'd heard the name before these killings, but not in any context that could possibly apply to the current crimes.

'Surely, the first Warhawk wasn't a murderer? He was some kind of hero, wasn't he?'

She dimly recalled a ballad recounting great victories and a noble death.

'Good question. But you get to be a hero by doing the same thing murderers do.'

'Killing?'

'There's nothing wrong with killing,' he snarled, 'just so long as the right people get killed.'

As Harald flicked furiously through forty- and fifty-year old gazetteers, Rosanna's eyes watered from the raised dust. It was late afternoon and the lantern in the office was smoking badly. One bad sputter from lan-tern to papers and this place would burn like a Mondstille bonfire. She had already been hauled out of one burning watch station by Harald

Kleindeinst, and had no intention of repeating the experience. She opened the lantern and trimmed the wick.

'After all,' Harald continued, 'who killed most often, the Beast or Sigmar? Killing for a cause may be all well and good, but there are some for whom the killing is more important than the cause.'

'When did our murderer start being called Warhawk?'

'Another good question, and one our friend Viereck should have troubled himself to answer.'

'I've seen it chalked up on walls.'

'Usually, the names of pattern-killers – the Beast, the Slasher, the Ripper – start in the broadsheets, but this time I think it just appeared out of the air, like our quarry's bird.'

Rosanna thought back to her scrying of the Warhawk. She could pick up names sometimes. It depended on how people, in the supposed secrecy of their skull, thought of themselves. One of the fundamentals of magic was the true naming of things and individuals, Once you knew a person's true name, you had a measure of power over him or her. In this business, that was literally the case. If they knew the Warhawk's true name, he could be tracked down and stopped.

Harald coughed as another cloud of dust rose from an unrolled scroll.

In his private self, the killer thought of himself as Warhawk, but behind him was a greater shadow, the Warhawk. Unmistakably, the Warhawk was the murderer's father. Rosanna had sampled his childhood, his memories of punishments and favours.

A clerk, cheek permanently stained by the ink-dribble from the feather-pen lodged above his ear, staggered in, and deposited another armful of documents on an already overburdened table.

'Found it,' Harald said, quietly.

Rosanna crossed the room and looked over the captain's shoulder.

The scroll was an old indictment, dated nearly thirty years ago. It bore the seal of the Emperor Luitpold, and it was a list of charges laid against Prince Vastarien, beginning with disloyalty to the Empire and concluding with the raising of a private army to pursue the prince's own military ends.

'Vastarien's Vanquishers,' Harald said, through gritted teeth.

'Who were they?' she asked.

'I keep forgetting you're young,' he said. 'Prince Vastarien was before you were born.'

'I know the name.'

'Mention it to anyone my age and you'll get an interesting reaction one way or the other, an eternal curse or a prayer to Sigmar. Whatever the prince was, he was extreme about it.'

'Was he a hero?'

'A lot of people thought so. A lot of other people – obviously including the old Emperor and most of the court – disagreed violently. No one really knows what happened to him in the end, up in the Fastness of Jagrandhra Dane, but if he'd come back he would as likely have spent the remainder of his life in Mundsen Keep as have been weighed down with honours and glory.'

Rosanna read the charges against the prince. They were lengthy and detailed, alleging all manner of moral turpitude, unseemly conduct and dangerous behaviour. It appeared that a raid against river pirates on the Urskoy had almost caused a tiny war between the Empire and Kislev, rattling Tsar Radii Bokha's cage enough to prompt a strong diplomatic complaint. However, scrawled in a different hand from the rest of the document was an instruction that the indictment not be proceeded with, over the personal signature of Maximilian von Konigswald, one of the old Emperor's closest advisors. Evidently, Prince Vastarien had been let off, the tsar appeased some other way.

'Who are the heroes of the day, Rosanna?' Harald asked. 'That mysterious fellow who's said to be the scourge of goblins and beastmen? Detlef Sierck, genius and defier of Drachenfels? Hagedorn, the wrestler who could put anyone on the mat three out of three falls? Graf Rudiger von Unheimlich, the foremost huntsman of the Empire? Your intrepid swordsman friend, the Baron Johann von Mecklenberg?'

Rosanna blushed at the mention of Johann. He was with his brother, back on their estates in the Sudenland.

'Well, when I was a lad, Prince Vastarien was one of those names. The traitor Oswald von Konigswald was another, so that goes to show how seriously you should place your trust in heroes. If Vastarien did a tenth of the things the ballads and chap-books claim he did, he was the greatest citizen of the Empire since Sigmar. He was also probably the most completely insane fool that ever lived. He raised his own cadre of fellow heroes, and fought his campaigns, ignoring Imperial edicts, smiting whoever he decided was the enemy of his cause.'

'Vastarien's Vanquishers?'

'That's what they called themselves. Next time you see the Baron Johann, ask him about a man called Vukotich. Iron Man Vukotich.'

'I am not likely to be seeing…'

'I'm sorry,' he said, in a rare moment of solicitousness, 'I shouldn't tease like that. We all have our scars. Anyway, our Warhawk – the first Warhawk – was one of the prince's heroes.'

He turned the scroll over, and tapped a list of names, written in a watery ink that had faded to pale blue.

'Here,' he said, 'see…'

Rosanna's eyes ran down the list. The Vukotich Harald had mentioned was there. And, near the bottom, the single word, 'Warhawk'.

VIII

Harald didn't get out to Mundsen Keep very often. Too many old acquaintances were permanent guests here. This black, slit-windowed pile beyond the city walls was where Altdorf dumped its human refuse. Debtors and murderers, revolutionists and thieves, out-of-favour courtiers and long-forgotten scapegoats. All ended up in the depths of the Keep. Even here, in the governor's airy and well-lit apartments, the aura of misery was strong.

Rosanna had never visited the prison, and he could tell she was appalled by the place. The Keep was outside the city walls because no one could stand to live too close to the human stench that hung around it. No amount of lye and water could dispel the stink.

She didn't say anything, but Harald knew she was thinking of the criminals she'd helped send here. Since Baron Johann left for the Sudenland, Rosanna had been very helpful to the watch. Without her, there would be a few more felons loose in the streets and sewers. And without the watch – now she was no longer welcome at the Temple of Sigmar – Rosanna would have no means of income.

Governor Gerd van Zandt received them in his office, and listened patiently to Harald's request.

'Out of the question,' Van Zandt said, fluttering a heavily-scented handkerchief under his large nose.

'The prisoner Stieglitz is in solitary confinement and is to have no contact with the outside world. There are revolutionists everywhere, they constantly try to smuggle messages in or out...'

'Are you suggesting that I'm a Brustellinite?'

Harald glared at the governor, who quivered and looked away.

'No, er, not at all, Captain Kleindeinst. It's just that... rules and regulations, you know... we must have discipline.'

'Rickard Stieglitz is still alive?'

'Um, yes,' Van Zandt sputtered.

'Fine, then it is imperative we speak with him.'

'As I said, that is, um, not possible.'

Harald leaned over, and took hold of Van Zandt's ruffled shirt-front, getting a good grip, hoping some of his flabby flesh was caught in the folds. He hauled the man out of his padded chair and lifted him into the air, letting his skinny legs dangle.

732

'Nothing is impossible in Mundsen Keep, governor. Prisoners can get extra food, ale enough to drown a halfling, a supply of weirdroot, jars of olla milk, even the occasional woman or pretty-boy. All it takes is influence, money, a favour. We both know that. And we both know no money changes hands in the Keep without a tithe slipping your way.'

'This is outrageous... these charges... ridiculous...'

'I don't care, Van Zandt. I send them here and that's an end of it. What you do then is up to you. And the Imperial Prison Reform Committee. I have friends on that committee. Maybe I should see my old friends more often. Talk things through. I'm well-known for my strict views on penal conditions. I could be called in to give testimony. And that testimony could go either way.'

'Ah... ah... ah...'

'I hate criminals. They make my stomach churn. And do you know how my stomach feels now? Like a storm at sea, Van Zandt. As if there were a criminal very close by. Almost as close as the end of my arm.'

Van Zandt's shirt was tearing and blood had drained out of his face.

'You understand me?' Harald said, dropping the governor back into his chair.

Van Zandt nodded. 'Yes, I understand.'

'Good, now arrange for my associate and I to see the prisoner, Stieglitz.'

'Yes, of course, right away, captain...'

Van Zandt hurried out of his office. Harald turned to Rosanna, and shrugged.

'What else could I do?'

The scryer must disapprove of him, of his methods. But they worked well together. She would accept anything that bore fruit. Before, he had not been the kind of watchman who did well with a partner – he'd buried too many good men – but Rosanna Ophuls was different. Her expertise was in a different area, and complemented his. His stomach and her conscience had given many criminals cause to regret their sins.

'I still don't understand,' she said. 'This revolutionist, what does he have to do with the Warhawk?'

Harald patted the scroll, rolled up in his belt.

'One of the habits of heroes is that they die young. Plain men like me live to an old age, but heroes tend to go down fighting. Do you think that Konrad fellow intends to die in bed of the gout? So, it follows that a thirty-year-old list of Vastarien's Vanquishers isn't likely to have many still-warm bodies on it.'

'Stieglitz is one of them?'

'That's right. Lucky for us. In his youth, before he fell in with Brustellin and Kloszowski and the rest of the firebrands, Rickard Stieglitz was one of Vastarien's muscle-flexers. An axe-hefting mountain of meat and bone.'

'How did someone like that wind up dedicated to the overthrow of the aristocracy?'

'Someone with a title took his wife, killed his children and cut off his arm.'

'That would do it.'

'When he was captured after the fog riots, he had his ears clipped. I understand there's not much of him left.'

Harald had never been with the special corps who rousted the ten brands of revolutionist who preached sedition against the Emperor. That was a militia job. Sometimes the palace guard or the Knights Templars of Sigmar helped out. A simple copper had no politics.

'You hope he'll be sane enough to remember the Warhawk's real name, if he ever knew it, and well-disposed enough towards the watch, who penned him up here, to share the knowledge with us?'

Harald's stomach was eating away at him again.

'He has no reason not to, Rosanna. Our murderer is no champion of the oppressed. The Warhawk is just a scummy killer. If Stieglitz is still enough of an idealist to want justice for all, he'll help.'

'Sometimes you sound like a Brustellinite yourself.'

Harald spat. 'Revolutionists? I hate 'em. Dreamers and bullies and trouble-makers.'

The door opened, and a prisoner was dragged in by two trusties. The man was weighed down with chains, his head hung. His ears were scabbed over, his face a ruin of scars and his left arm missing. Those were the injuries Harald had been expecting. Also, one of his eyes was gone, one bare foot was inflated with pus to the size of a football, only the little finger and thumb remained on his right hand, and through his rags there were obvious burn-marks on his back and chest. The mountain of meat and bone had been worn down to a pathetic hump.

Rosanna shuddered and stifled a cry. The trusties dropped the prisoner on the floor and the scryer went to him, helping him huddle into a sitting position.

Harald looked at the governor, accusing him.

'Revolutionists are not popular with the other prisoners,' Van Zandt explained. 'Murderers and rapists resent being walled in with filth who advocate disloyalty to Karl-Franz. He was in the hole for his own protection.'

'I'm sure.'

'Harald,' Rosanna said, 'how can we question this man?'

'What do you mean?'

'He has no ears to hear what we ask, and no tongue to give answer.'

'No tongue?'

Stieglitz's mouth gaped open and Harald saw the scryer was right. Beyond his few remaining teeth was a black hole. Harald looked again at the governor.

'He kept shouting Brustellinite slogans from his hole, slanders against the Imperial family and the electors. "Throw off your chains, kill your betters, seize the land," things like that. I thought it best he be silenced.'

'If you acted this way within the city walls, Van Zandt, you'd answer to me. It'd be interesting to see the kind of treatment you would get from your fellow convicts if, through some malfeasance, you were yourself sentenced to serve time in Mundsen Keep.'

Van Zandt turned a sickly colour. It must be his greatest nightmare, to wake up one morning chained on filthy straw, as an inmate rather than the master of this place.

'Can he read?' he asked.

'I don't know. I doubt it.'

Rosanna held up a paper from Van Zandt's desk, and ran her finger along a line of writing, a question in her eyes. Stieglitz nodded. He could read.

Harald gave the scryer the scroll. She showed the prisoner the list, pointing out his own name, then indicating the Warhawk's.

Stieglitz's single eye narrowed. He was trying to understand. In his cage of abused flesh, he was still a thinking man.

Harald gave Rosanna a pencil, and she wrote on the scroll.

What was the Warhawk's true name?

A ghastly keening came from the back of the prisoner's throat as he tried to give an answer. For some reason, he did want to help. Maybe he had no cause to love his old comrade in the Vanquishers? Maybe he was completely broken and pliable?

'The stink in here,' complained Van Zandt, waving his handkerchief. 'These people have no concept of personal cleanliness. Myself, I bathe once or twice a month.'

Van Zandt signalled to a trusty, who opened one of the casements, letting in a waft of forest-scented air. From the window, it was a hundred-foot sheer drop. The trusty, as much a prisoner as the ruin on the floor, looked out at the city walls, the trees and the road below, with a yearning that was like a knife in Harald's gut.

Stieglitz stopped gurgling and Rosanna handed him a pencil and the scroll. His remaining fingers couldn't hold the pencil properly and he dropped it. Rosanna picked it up and slipped it back into his hand, keeping it there with her own fingers.

'He was left-handed,' Van Zandt explained, 'that was why the duke, um, er... you know...'

Harald knew.

Between them, Stieglitz and Rosanna made a mark on the parchment. It was useless. The first letter might have been an M, or an A, or an E, or a dwarfish rune, or a meaningless squiggle – or anything.

They gave up. Stieglitz sagged, dejected.

Harald wanted to break Van Zandt's neck. In taking away Stieglitz's tongue, he was as responsible for the next death – and the one after that, and the one after that, and all the others – as the Warhawk himself.

Rosanna sighed.

'I'll have to scry him,' she said, reluctantly. 'The name must be uppermost in his mind. He's been trying to write it.'

Harald knew why she was unhappy. Sharing what was in Stieglitz's skull – the pain, the suffering, the hatred – would be a filthy business, like fishing for a jewel in a cesspit.

Rosanna took the prisoner's hand, and shut her eyes.

From the window, the trusty screamed, and fell out of the way. Harald turned, his Magnin suddenly in his hand.

The bird came into the office, its huge wings beating, and moved as fast as water on an incline. Van Zandt covered his head and dived behind a desk.

A beak sliced down, across the trusty's chest, loosing a bright red trail of blood. Then, the creature went for Rosanna.

Harald slashed, but missed. A heavy wing struck his wrist, stunning him, and his knife thumped against carpeted stone.

Rosanna's hands were over her face, her contact with Stieglitz broken. With the hand that still had feeling, Harald grabbed at the bird. He felt feathers come free, but it dodged him.

Then it struck at Stieglitz's neck, the force of the beak-blow breaching his artery. A fountain of blood splashed over the hawk, spattering its wings, masking its face. It attacked silently, not a squawking terror but a resolute instrument of murder as conscienceless and perfect as an arrow.

Harald had his knife again, and threw. It sliced cleanly through the distance.

The bird was out of the way, and the knife jammed to the hilt into a wooden panel by Stieglitz's hanging head, vibrating fiercely.

The mercenary revolutionist was dead, what was left of his life ripped from him, his blood soaking the rags on his chest and pooling around him. The flow of his own blood washed part of him clean, revealing white skin beneath the grime of the Keep.

Harald tried to catch the bird, but it was gone through the window in an instant, flapping back towards the city. It circled a tall tree a quarter of a mile off, and landed in the branches as if finding a nest. He could see a tiny figure, all in black, receiving his murderous pet.

He made huge fists and slammed them against the windowsill, imagining laughter on the wind.

IX

He slithered down the tree like a monkey, gripping with his knees, Belle on his shoulder. Number Eleven had been the trickiest yet, but it was a clean kill, a clever kill. The Device was functioning perfectly.

Kleindeinst had been there, as he had expected – known – he would be. He had almost guided the watchman himself, directing him as he would one of his birds.

He let Belle go, and leaped from tree to tree, relishing the moments he was in open air with nothing beneath him. When he began to plummet, he would put out a hand and catch a branch. Over the years, his body had become creaky through disuse. But, with the Device in motion, he had been training himself as rigorously as he trained his birds. When he had wings, he would need to be agile, to bend himself to the ways of the sky.

With an inevitable disappointment, he finally came to ground, thumping against the softly-grassed forest floor. The jolt shot through his entire skeleton, making him bite his tongue, and he stumbled against the bole of a tree, gripping until his balance returned.

On the ground, he was clumsy.

He held out his wrist and Belle settled.

'Two to go,' he said. 'And we'll be together always.'

X

Captain Viereck was back in the office at the Atrocities Commission by the time they returned from Mundsen Keep. He must have spies everywhere. Rosanna was not surprised.

She had been too close to Stieglitz at his death, and the tongueless scream that poured from his broken mind still echoed inside her. In the carriage, Harald had been slumped and brooding. He felt his defeat keenly. Sometimes Rosanna was surprised at the depths of fellow-feeling 'Filthy Harald' was capable of. She wondered about his wife. The dead one he didn't talk about. Ever.

By the end of the day, it was official. Harald Kleindeinst was back on the Dock Watch, and the Warhawk investigation was Viereck's responsibility. By the end of the evening, the case was back on its original course, with an acrobat – who had been accused in an anonymous letter – under arrest and on his way to Van Zandt's pet torturers. Harald disappeared while Rosanna was being seen to by the Luitpoldstrasse station physician, getting salve pasted on her superficial cuts.

Of course, she was off the case too.

She had tried. She went to Viereck, and found him with Rasselas, toasting their capture of the Warhawk. She explained their line of inquiry to them, laying out all she knew about Vastarien's Vanquishers, the first Warhawk, and Stieglitz.

They thanked her for her concern and had her escorted out into the streets.

It was a cold evening, with the first traces of an Altdorf fog. She looked up at the night skies and imagined a bird passing across the face of the visible moon. A bird of prey, alone and hungry, impersonally cruel and casually deadly.

As so often happened since she left the Order of Sigmar, where she had been cloistered since girlhood, Rosanna felt alone and uncertain. She could see so many things – random and useless information poured from the heads of passersby, from the cobblestones under her shoes – but if she turned her scrying in upon herself, there was just a blank space, a vacuum in the centre of a whirlpool.

She supposed she should go back to her lodgings. And sleep.

XI

Until his captaincy could be reviewed by a board which – including, as it did, Rasselas of the Imperial Bank and a colonel of the watch he knew to be in the pay of Hals von Tasseninck – would recommend either his demotion to beat-pounding serf or dismissal (again) from the watch, Harald still had his copper badge. And he would always have his Magnin.

The heaviest throwing knife in the world, the Magnin had been his friend through innumerable bloody nights. He noticed Rosanna shrank away from it as if it were a red-hot poker, and assumed she must be able to flash visions of the knife's past experiences.

With his Magnin in its sheath on his hip, and his badge pinned on the breast of his tunic, he strolled into the Sullen Knight, a hostelry that fully deserved its reputation as the rowdiest, most dangerous, most violent on the Street of a Hundred Taverns. Normally, watchmen only ventured into the Sullen Knight in groups of four or more, with swords drawn and pistols primed. But tonight, he was alone.

He elbowed his way between two young men who were attempting to strangle each other and glanced around. Several brawlers looked up from their fights, alerted by the flash of copper.

A broad-shouldered Kislevite, beaded braids hanging from the unshaved half of his scalp, roared and charged Harald, seeing only the badge. It was Bolakov, a perennial visitor to the cells in Luitpoldstrasse when there were enough watchmen available to subdue him. By the time the foreigner got to him, Harald had a fist out ready for the thug's face.

Bolakov crumpled and fell. He must be too drunk to recognise Filthy Harald. No one else made his mistake. Still feeling acid in his guts from his bad day, Harald sunk his boot into Bolakov's side, denting his ribs. A few grinding broken bones would take the Kislevite bully boy out of the brawling business for a few days.

Harald ordered a bottle of schnapps from Sam the barman and looked around, wondering if there were any other heads he should bother to thump. He saw a thin man in a black leather jacket trying to slip out the back way and knew he was in luck.

'Stop, Ruger,' he shouted, 'or find out if I can throw this knife faster than you can get through that door!'

Mack Ruger froze, hands well away from the docker's hook on his belt, and turned.

'Good choice,' Harald told the weirdroot vendor.

Ruger looked guilty, wondering which of his crimes was coming back to haunt him. Harald knew there was quite a list.

'Drink with me,' Harald ordered.

'I… uh… no thank you, sir, I was just leaving…'

'That was not an invitation, Ruger.'

'No, of course.'

Ruger, a Hook – a member of one of the waterfront gangs – sat down, and Harald pulled a chair up to his table, setting the schnapps down between them. Someone thought that Harald turning his back gave them an opening – evidently not noticing the useful full-length mirror behind the bar – and reached for a leadweight at his belt. Harald tossed a heavy pint-pot over his shoulder, and smashed the cosh-man's wrist without even turning to look.

'Still in business?' he asked Ruger.

'This and that, you know,' the Hook replied.

'You usually set up shop at the Breasts of Myrmidia so you can sell your foul stuff to the students from the University, don't you?'

Ruger didn't bother to deny it. He could probably lay his hands on more arcane herbs and potions than one of the university's tame wizards or a palace physician.

'Of course, what with the Fish taking over the Breasts, you must have had to find a new territory.'

Ruger tried a shrug. The Fish were the Hooks' deadliest rivals, and the two factions had been feuding for generations. Harald had personally ended the last Waterfront War, and his reputation was etched into the gangs' consciousnesses as if by acid.

'Nothing is certain in this life, Ruger. Are you carrying?'

Ruger began to say no, but gave up.

'I need something,' Harald said. 'Something in your line.'

A crack of a knowing smile started, but Harald slapped it off the degenerate's face. 'Don't think you know anything about me, Ruger. Don't ever make that mistake.'

'No, captain.'

The angry mark on the vendor's cheek was like a birthmark.

'The berserkers of Norsca snort a herbal powder before they go into battle,' Harald said. 'It takes away their pain, makes them feel stronger, almost invincible.'

'Daemon dust.'

'That's the stuff. Give me some.'

Ruger was about to protest, but Harald took the Magnin out and laid it on the table.

'Look at the beautiful line of the blade,' Harald commented, 'a work of art.'

The vendor sorted through his pouch, and came up with three bundles, dried leaves twisted into balls.

'This is expensive,' Ruger said.

'I get a watchman's discount.'

That meant he was stealing the daemon dust. Ruger knew there was nothing he could do about it.

Harald took the first leaf and crumbled it. A blue powder spilled into his palm. He pinched it like snuff, and shoved it up one nostril, inhaling sharply.

Turning to the barman, he said, 'Sam, find the four biggest, meanest, hardest, toughest bruisers in the place and tell them from me that their mothers enjoyed sexual congress with farm animals.'

The daemon dust exploded in his brain as he swallowed half the schnapps. This was dangerous, but he needed something to make him not care how hurt he got in the next few hours. Liquid fire ran through his veins, and he held his breath to keep himself from exploding.

Being a detective hadn't helped him catch the Warhawk. Now, he would try being a berserker.

By the time he was ready, Sam had more than four roughs for him. It took him nearly a minute to disable them all. He broke a stool over Ruger's head as a thank you for the dust and hurled his empty bottle at Sam's head, then tossed a table at the long mirror, enjoying the tinkling of the broken fragments as they showered onto the floorboards. This shut everyone up, and got the attention of even those so absorbed in their own fights that they had ignored his devastation of the bruisers. Then, he made an announcement he intended to repeat in every tavern on the street.

'My name is Harald Kleindeinst, captain of the Dock Watch, late of the Atrocities Commission. Filthy Harald. I'm declaring my own war on the crime on this street. Every whore, every weirdroot vendor, every cutpurse, every Hook, every Fish, every non-aligned thug, every pimp, every fortune teller, every assassin, every cudgel artist, every knifeman, every burglar, every mountebank, every swindler, every dwarf-molesting mother's ruin of you, take notice. My war will continue until someone gives me the name I want, or the name of someone who knows the name I want. Then things will be back to business as usual. All of you, listen, and remember. My war will go on, until I have the true name of the man they call the Warhawk.'

Harald stepped over Bolakov on his way out of the Sullen Knight. The dust put off any pain he should have been feeling. His face must be bruised badly, and he felt himself bleeding into his shirt. He didn't want to think about what would happen when the daemon dust wore off...

XII

He was on the Street of a Hundred Taverns, buying a paper of roast chestnuts from a stall by the Drunken Bastard, when Kleindeinst exploded out of the Sullen Knight, spilling bodies all around him.

Even though the watchman was off the case, he knew Kleindeinst would not stop searching for him. Kleindeinst stumped across the road as if wearing a heavy suit of armour and pushed into the Drunken Bastard, an establishment that catered exclusively to miserable, solitary drinkers and the nimble-fingered pickpockets who preyed on their depleted coin-pouches.

Chewing on a nut, he wandered near the door, and listened to the speech Kleindeinst made to the surprised sots. It gave him a thrill, and he was pleased.

The Device was moving smoothly.

Kleindeinst strode out of the Drunken Bastard and pushed through the queue by the chestnut stall.

'You have your Imperial permit?' he asked the trader.

The man fumbled in a satchel, not for the permit but for a bribe. Kleindeinst grinned down at the pathetic coins in his hand and flung them to the ground, whereupon a pack of urchins appeared from the alleyways and descended on the pickings like hungry wolves, fighting and tearing.

Kleindeinst took the chestnut trader's brazier and poured it over his stall, spreading hot coals.

'You're closed, criminal,' he spat.

The watchman stalked away from the mess he left – other stall-holders in his path shutting up their belongings and retreating – and shoved his way into the next tavern, the Beard of Ulric.

Warhawk chewed his chestnuts, and waited.

A body came flying out of the Beard of Ulric and skidded into the gutter.

Warhawk tittered.

XIII

By the time the sun came up, Harald had covered the entire Street of a Hundred Taverns, and spread his message throughout Altdorf. He broke the neck of a Fish who tried to knife him outside Bruno's Brewhouse and he stopped the heart of a poison-clawed Hook with the heavy wedge of his Magnin in the tap room of the Wayfarer's Rest. In the Holy Hammer of Sigmar, the gathering place of professional murderers, he beat Ettore Fulci, the noted Tilean strangler, to a bloody pulp. Then he had impressed the cultivated Quex – acknowledged fashion leader of the city's assassins – with the need to find some way of ending the career of the amateur Warhawk if he wanted to be able to ply his trade without extraordinary difficulty. Quex was reluctant, so Harald broke three of his fingers and shredded his best cloak. Venturing into the Crescent Moon, haunt of the unquiet dead, Harald slipped his Magnin into the dry throat of a thousand-year-old hag, letting air whistle into her skull as he told the assembly of the thirsty dead what his conditions were for letting them remain in this world. In the rooms above the Crown and Two Chairmen, he used open hands on the girls, not hurting them overmuch but bruising their faces enough to dent their trade for a few nights.

Having recently learned that the nervous landlord of the Staff of Verena was paying the highest rate of protection money on the street to both the Hooks and Fish, as well as a retainer to the regulars of the Holy Hammer of Sigmar, all to ensure the safety of his business and patrons, Harald paid the Staff a visit and did as much damage as possible. He left the place a ruin, and the landlord howling at how little protection his illicit outlay had actually purchased. Finding a couple of officers from the Dock Watch standing guard outside an illegal dice tourney in the basement of the Von Neuwald Arms, he slammed their skulls together and tossed their badges into the sewers. Then he stormed into the tourney, breaking heads, hands and legs with a stout oak chair. He took the gamblers' coins from the grid and threw them into the gutter for the beggars.

It was a watchman's maxim that the solution to every crime in the Empire could be discovered on the Street of a Hundred Taverns. Still, there were other places, and so in the small hours, Harald ventured off the thoroughfare. The Fish had a place on the docks, a warehouse where they stored all the goods that 'slipped overboard during unloading', and

Harald broke in while the guards were snoring drunkenly. He emptied a cask of Estalian brandy over a dozen bolts of Bretonnian silk, and then carelessly dropped a flaming torch onto the soaked material, leaping through a trapdoor to escape the resulting explosion.

The daemon dust in his mind prevented the cold of the river from biting through his flesh and he didn't come out of the Reik until he was past the Three Toll Bridge. He found 'Count' Bernhard Brillhauser scraping the pavement with his feathered cap on Temple Street, offering to take any provincials who were new in town on a tour of the 'exciting' underworld of the city. It was said that you hadn't really visited the capital city of the Empire unless you'd been fleeced by the 'Count'. Along with the changing of the Imperial Guard, a visit to the Konigplatz and the latest presentation at the Vargr Breughel Memorial Playhouse, it was one of the experiences of Altdorf.

Leaving the 'Count' with his hat in the back of his throat, Harald barged into the Temple Street Gymnasium, where a trial of strength was on between Hagedorn, the famous wrestler, and Arne the Body, the gym's proprietor. Arne was known for his perfectly-developed limbs, and, from time to time, for his availability to any of his wealthy clientele who might require some discreet pain-infliction.

Harald pulled Arne out of the ring, just as the contestants were bending iron bars with much bicep-flexing and neck-straining, and tossed him against a climbing frame, the dust-strength in his body giving him an edge over the perfect physical specimen. As far as he knew, Hagedorn had never broken the law, so he left the bewildered hayseed – a blinking column of muscle surrounded by fawning women – alone. With the second pinch of daemon dust up his nose, he felt he could probably have tangled with the master of the mats and won. He took Arne's half-bent iron and wrapped it around his neck, fixing him to the frame. Then he punched the trainer's rock-hard gut muscles a few times. The Body swore he knew nothing about the Warhawk, and Harald told him he'd be coming back if Arne were lying.

He didn't need sleep. In fact, he felt stronger by the moment and jogged through the early morning streets, bursting with energy he needed to burn off. A dozen or so people had come to him with spurious help, trying to frame their enemies for the Warhawk crimes, others sincerely dumping information on him, or just flapping their lips. Nothing usable had come to light.

He made his way across the city to the University, where he wanted to throw a scare into the cut-ups of the League of Karl-Franz, and shake the cobwebs of the revolutionist movement. The Imperial loyalists – all of whom, he suspected, were supported by that shadowy kingmaker, Graf Rudiger von Unheimlich – and the revolutionists – split into Brustellinite, Kloszowskist and Yefimovite factions, but still tied together by hatred for the aristocracy – were closely linked with the rest of the city's human vermin, and he didn't see why, if he was coming down so hard on pimps and killers, he should let them off lightly.

In one of the coffee houses near the university, he found Detlef Sierck, the actor, drinking off a hangover and moaning to anyone who would listen about the fickleness of women, all the while handing out flyers for his latest production, *She Served Him Ill*.

One of the early murders had taken place outside Sierck's theatre on Temple Street, and Harald had questioned the man – and his now-vanished vampire mistress – closely. Sierck was still too drunk to remember him and, since he was completely ruled out of the investigation, Harald left him to his headache.

In the university square, he encountered Brand, a soberly-dressed cleric of Ranald he remembered from a series of assaults on priestesses of Shallya. None of the victims had been willing to identify the cleric as the degenerate, but Harald had known the man was guilty. Judging that this was as good a time as any to make up for the deficiencies of the justice system, Harald dragged Brand to the gates of the Ueli von Tasseninck School of Religious Studies, and beat a confession out of him, continuing the beating long after the culprit had yielded up all his sins, then draping his battered but breathing body over the statue of that invert Ueli von Tasseninck that his uncle, Grand Duke Hals, had sponsored. The statue reminded Harald of the time he had first been expelled from the watch, for foolishly assuming the laws against rape and murder applied even to people whose uncles were electors of the Empire, so he prised an iron bar out of a fence and returned to chip away Ueli's sainted face. Quite a crowd gathered – students, harlots, lecturers, guilty bystanders – and he made his speech to them.

It got better every time.

'My name is Harald Kleindeinst, captain of the Dock Watch,' he began. 'Filthy Harald. I'm declaring my own war…'

Suddenly, like a towel falling from his eyes, the daemon dust wore off. All the pain of the world flooded into his body.

He didn't even scream, he just collapsed.

XIV

Even two days after Harald's rampage, the Street of a Hundred Taverns looked as if a raiding party of Chaos Knights had laid waste to the thoroughfare. And then a wave of goblin scavengers had gone through, mistreating the wounded and breaking whatever had been left whole by the first assault. It was hard to believe one man – even Harald Kleindeinst – had done this much damage.

As usual, beggar children tugged at Rosanna's shawl. As usual, she gave them more than she should. Every loiterer on the street seemed injured in some way, superficially or seriously. Workmen were everywhere, repairing windows, carting away broken furniture, re-hanging smashed signs, painting over bloodstained walls. The gutters glittered with shards of broken mirror glass.

A couple of patrolling watchmen were exchanging jokes, where usually they would be venturing carefully, hands on clubs. The ordinary run of street crime had dropped almost to nothing in the last two days. Pickpockets had broken fingers, whores bore unsightly facial bruises, and cudgel-artists wouldn't be hefting a weapon until broken elbows set. But none of this had stopped the Warhawk.

Twelve dead – one since Harald's rampage. Rosanna felt a Harald-like need to put an end to the killing spree. With every death, the whole case changed, turned about-face. She wondered how Harald would feel when he heard about the latest atrocity.

'Miss Ophuls,' a voice called.

She turned. A nondescript man, in early middle age, leaned against a lamp-post, painfully eating an apple. His lip was split and bruised. She had a presentiment that the Warhawk case was about to crack open down the middle.

'Rosanna Ophuls?'

She couldn't scry much from him. He was a typical non-entity, nothing strong enough inside him to count as an identity.

'You work with Kleindeinst?'

Rosanna nodded.

'Mack Ruger,' he said, introducing himself with a thumb to his chest. 'Your friend paid me a visit two nights back.'

'So I see.'

He rubbed his face. 'I got off easy compared to some.'

'Pimp, right?'

'Your reputation is exaggerated. Weirdroot.'

'A thriving trade, I suppose.'

'I do bearably. Everyone has a right to dream.'

'If they've money.'

'I'm a businessman.'

Rosanna would have laughed, but there was an image in Ruger's mind he could not keep shielded. A swooping bird.

'You know the name?' she said, suddenly intuiting.

He shook his head. 'No, but Stieglitz wasn't the last of Vastarien's Vanquishers. There are other survivors. One can be found on this street.'

'How much?'

He shook his head. 'This is a gift. Just be sure you tell Kleindeinst this came from me. He already owes me for the face. I'll want concessions.'

Rosanna almost felt as if she were Harald, the rage boiling inside until it had to volcano through the top of her skull.

'Give me the name,' she said, 'or I'll be sure to tell Captain Kleindeinst you withheld it.'

Ruger paled behind his bruise.

'Gurnisson,' he said. 'Gotrek Gurnisson.'

'A dwarf?'

Ruger nodded. 'He's at the Crooked Spear, with a human tagalong, Felix Jaeger.'

Rosanna thought she might have heard of Gurnisson. Dwarfs were long-lived and had good memories. If he had served with the first Warhawk, Gurnisson would know his true name.

'Tell Kleindeinst to be careful with the dwarf. Gurnisson won't appreciate his usual rough treatment. He's a trollslayer.'

'That won't matter,' Rosanna said.

'I warned you,' Ruger said. 'That's all I could do.'

Without thanking the man, Rosanna left, looking for a vacant carriage.

XV

In his dreams, Eleni had been alive again. There was no crime in the city. Pattern killers were mythical creatures. His stomach didn't play up. And the Emperor was concerned with the welfare of his subjects.

When he woke up, the world was a festering wound and he was a squashed maggot writhing inside it.

The daemon dust was flushed from his body, and his first urge was to reach to his belt for the third leaf-twist. Everything ached, hurt, screamed or burned.

He was out of his clothes, in a bed, under blankets. The dust was gone.

'Easy,' a voice said. A cool, feminine voice. An angel's.

Sitting up, he felt hammerblows to his head. He was strong. He told the pain to go away. It was stronger.

Gripping the edge of the bed, he stayed upright.

'You're in the Luitpoldstrasse Station,' the voice said. 'You've been asleep for two days.'

'Eleni?'

His eyes focused, and he saw Rosanna. She looked surprised.

'Eleni?' she asked.

'Never mind.'

Rosanna was by his bedside. There were others in the room. Rasselas was there, bowed low beside his master, Mornan Tybalt. And Graf Rudiger von Unheimlich, sneering with distaste at the commoners.

'What happened?'

'You're back on the case,' Rosanna told him.

Harald looked at Tybalt and von Unheimlich. They both nodded, brief acknowledgements that this was true.

'Viereck?'

'The twelfth victim.'

Harald clutched the blankets and started forwards, a wave of agony convulsing him.

'What?'

'He was on execution dock,' Rasselas explained, 'supervising the hanging of the acrobat. The bird came from nowhere and took his head almost off.'

'The hawk left a message, like a carrier pigeon. It was for you.'

Rosanna gave him a slip of paper. He managed to hold it with his banana-clumsy fingers, and focused on the few words.

'COME AND GET ME, KLEINDEINST.'

It bore a seal with the imprint of a hawk's clawfoot.

Rosanna, while close to him, whispered, 'I have a name. Another of Vastarien's Vanquishers.'

She didn't want the others to hear. He understood immediately. In this case, no one could be trusted.

'Get me some clothes,' Harald shouted at the dignitaries, 'and a pot of strong coffee.'

He thought Rasselas might be smiling, but the Imperial Chancellor and the Patron of the League of Karl-Franz remained grim and set in their expressions.

'By the way,' said the chancellor, 'that business of you brutalising every criminal in the city?'

'Yes.'

'Disgraceful. Consider yourself reprimanded.'

'Got to keep the customers satisfied, eh?'

Tybalt looked as if he had mistaken an onion for an apple and taken a big bite.

Praying for the pain to go away, Harald got out of bed.

XVI

His back was on fire now, only the leathered weight of the cloak, so like wings, could cool him. Venturing out without his Warhawk suit had been torture today. From now on, until the Device was complete, he would wear the leather constantly. He adjusted the hood, until it settled like a new skin.

One more sacrifice, and the air would be his realm.

The watch captain had died pitifully, screaming and fouling himself. Viereck was a poor specimen next to Kleindeinst.

He thought back to the night of Kleindeinst's rampage. The watchman had mistaken him for a panderer, and roughed him up a little. Warhawk had been almost amused and unable to stifle his laughter. The watchman must have thought him mad, or one of those inverts who gain pleasure from pain. Kleindeinst had pushed him into the gutter outside the Beard of Ulric, and left him giggling.

'We have chosen our instrument well, Belle,' he told his bird. 'He shall be the last component of the Device.'

The hatch in the roof was open, and beyond was the sky.

XVII

In the saloon of the Crooked Spear, it was impossible to miss the dwarf. He had climbed a stool and was hunched over the long bar, an axe half his size set down amid a small forest of foam-smeared empties. To Harald, the trollslayer looked like what you'd get if you sawed off Arne the Body's legs at the knees. He was still drinking, despite the occasional complaints of a reedy-looking young man at his elbow. Harald knew Gurnisson had a reputation as a brawler, and it was said the last time he'd been drunk enough to be penned in a cell he'd got out by chewing through the bars.

There was a piper in the corner, half-way through an assault on a popular sea-shanty. Rosanna was the only woman in the place. The other drinkers were heavily muscled warrior-types, proud of their fighting scars, prouder of their barrel-shaped limbs. Doubtless, they all exercised daily at Arne's gymnasium, and nightly in the back-alleys of the Street of a Hundred Taverns, exchanging blows with each other. The Sullen Knight was the inn for amateur bruisers and brawlers. The Crooked Spear was where the seriously violent misfits came.

And Gurnisson was the most seriously violent misfit in the place.

Well, maybe the second...

'Gurnisson,' he announced, loud enough to shut up the piper.

The dwarf didn't turn from his drink, but his shoulders heaved enormously, straining the stitching of the back of his jerkin.

'Couldn't you try just asking him politely?' Rosanna suggested. 'Maybe he'll want to help.'

'Gotrek Gurnisson,' he said, louder.

The trollslayer looked over his shoulder, a bleary eye casting around for the man who'd spoken his name.

'Who wants to know?' he asked, hand tightening on the shaft of his axe.

'Captain Harald Kleindeinst of the Dock Watch.'

Gurnisson's companion, who'd obviously heard about Filthy Harald, rolled his eyes upwards and prayed silently for deliverance. The inn was thick with the scent of impending combat.

'Bastard,' someone shouted behind him, 'you broke my brother's arm!'

An enormous young man who didn't look familiar lunged at Harald.

He stepped out of the way, and made a simple move with his elbow, listening for the crack of bones giving way in the hulk's forearm.

'There,' he said, 'now you're twins.'

Screaming in a high-pitched yelp, the would-be avenger retreated. Gurnisson grinned.

'Nicely done, copper.'

'It was nothing,' Harald said, pulling up a stool next to the trollslayer.

'We don't serve her kind here,' the ear-, nose- and lip-ringed barman said, nodding with distaste at Rosanna, who was being given a chair by Gurnisson's companion.

'Witches,' the barman said, and spat.

'You just changed your policy,' Harald told him.

The barman considered it a moment, and went along with Harald's suggestion.

'Schnapps for me, sherry for the lady, and whatever these gentlemen are drinking.'

The drinks came.

'You made a noise on the street a few nights gone, copper,' Gurnisson said.

Harald agreed.

'A good thing you didn't run into me.'

'Good for you, or good for me?'

The dwarf showed his sharp yellow teeth, and his face flared in an angry-looking grin.

'Let's say it was good for the city,' Gurnisson's companion suggested as a compromise.

'Felix Jaeger,' he said, shaking Harald's hand and kissing Rosanna's.

'Why do you seek me out, copper? Have there been complaints?'

'No more than usual. I just want a name from you. The name of a criminal.'

'I be no snitch.'

'This be no ordinary criminal. I'm talking about the Warhawk.'

Gurnisson looked puzzled. 'The murderer? Why should I know his name?'

'You knew his father.'

'Knew a lot of people's fathers, and grandfathers, and great-grandfathers.'

'You were with Prince Vastarien?'

Gurnisson's thick features twisted into an expression approximating the wistful. 'A long time ago. We were fools then. All of us.'

'There was another Warhawk.'

Gurnisson looked as if he'd just bitten into a rancid rat. He tried to wash the taste out of his mouth with a swig of ale.

'A bad one, he was. Some like soldiering too much. It lets them do things they couldn't do as civilians without being chased by people like you.'

Harald wondered what it must have been like in the Vanquishers. Had they been heroes or monsters? Or a mixture of both?

'Kept to himself, did Warhawk. Always with his precious birdies. Minya, Sebastian. Cheep cheep cheep. They were his childlings. The only things he cared for, the only things real to him.'

'He had a name?'

Gurnisson paused, took another swig.

'Robida,' he said. 'Andrzej Robida, curse his dead and rotten-to-Khorne guts.'

Now it had come, it was a disappointment. Sometimes, the answer to a mystery was like a daemon dust rush, a sudden influx of understanding and vision.

The name Andrzej Robida meant nothing to him.

XVIII

He took out his father's falconer's clothes, and laid them on the floor. With the lamp behind him, his shadow filled the suit. Old Andrzej had been a bigger man than his son. But Warhawk would outgrow the dead man's stature.

Belle flexed her wings on the stand, as Warhawk took a knife to the old clothes, ripping the rotten material apart, scratching the floor.

The birds reacted to the noise, and began calling to each other, screeching, squawking, scratching.

Warhawk stabbed the shadow, gouging the wood of the floorboards.

Soon...

XIX

Rosanna waited until they were out on the street to tell him. Since meeting Ruger, she had become cautious. She had scried something from the weirdroot dealer that made her trust only Harald. Treachery was a part of this thing.

'I know of an Andrzej Robida,' she said.

Harald stopped in his tracks, and turned to her. In the lamplight, his face seemed set as a statue's.

'He was well known a few years ago, especially at the Temple of Sigmar. He was a patron of the sciences. He knew the old lector, Mikael Hasselstein. They used to debate the possibilities of human invention.'

'Tell me, quickly,' Harald said.

'Robida was the sponsor of the inventors' contest. You remember, he offered one hundred thousand crowns to anyone who devised a machine which could fly under its own power. A machine, not a magic trick. All those rickety winged creations plunging from the walls of the city, into the Reik, into the trees. The crowds assembled to laugh at each new failure. Wax wings, inflated silk bladders, man-lifting kites.'

'Wings,' Harald said. 'All through this, I've been hearing the cursed flutter of wings.'

There was a watchman coming down the street, on his rounds. And an unoccupied carriage trundling, idling, looking for trade.

'Robida is a rich man. He has a big house near the palace.'

'He must be the Warhawk.'

'Yes,' she said, thinking, 'he must.'

Shockingly, suddenly, Harald embraced her, kissed her. Then, he was hailing the carriage.

'Get to the Luitpoldstrasse and send the watchmen after me,' he said, climbing in. 'Klove,' he shouted to the watchman, flashing his copper, 'look after this woman.'

Her mind was racing. During their brief contact, Harald had poured images from his mind into hers. She knew he was going after Robida alone, leaving her behind to protect her.

There was something else nagging her.

She watched the carriage rattle off down the street.

'Miss?' the watchman, Klove, asked.

Rosanna was about to say something, but a drunk was expelled from Bruno's Brewhouse, and staggered against them.

Klove clouted the man, and sent him reeling into the gutter.

'Be off with you, Ruger,' he shouted at the drunk. 'And keep quiet, or I'll confiscate your pouch.'

Wheels were whirring inside her head.

'Is that Mack Ruger?' she asked the copper.

'Yes,' he spat, 'the pest. Not worth the trouble of hauling him in.'

Ruger twisted in the gutter and looked up, grinning. He was not just drunk. Weirdjuice dribbled down his chin, and his eyeballs were swimming.

Rosanna had never seen him before.

XX

A big house near the palace.

That wasn't much of an address, but it would have to do. Harald had ordered the carriage-man to take him to the palace district. Former Lector Hasselstein – whom Harald had no cause to remember fondly – had retired from public life and entered a secluded order, but Harald hoped he could scare up someone at the Temple of Sigmar who could tell him where Andrzej Robida lived.

It felt right in his guts. Robida was the Warhawk.

This all had something to do with wings.

'Faster,' he ordered the intimidated carriage-man. 'This is life or death.'

He would find Robida's address within the hour, even if he failed at the temple. If necessary, he would break into the palace itself and find some toady who knew the patron of the sciences.

It would be over soon.

XXI

Belle was too good a bird to be impatient.

Warhawk stroked her wings.

The blood of twelve was on her beak. Soon, it would be the blood of thirteen.

The Device was almost complete.

The blood of just one more sacrifice was needed.

He regretted the time he had wasted on the mechanical sciences. All those strange flapping, churning, straining machines plummeting from the walls. He should have thought of magic first.

It was all so simple.

Thirteen sacrifices, and the freedom of the skies would be his.

Kleindeinst must be out there already, on his way. Warhawk had been spacing out the sacrifices, waiting until he knew Gotrek Gurnisson was in the city.

Gurnisson was a part of the Device too. Just as they all were, all the dead, all the flies buzzing around the sacrifices. The witch-woman, Kleindeinst, the criminal he had impersonated, the poor dupes Viereck had hanged...

It was as his father had told him, so many years ago. Thirteen must die by one bird, and that bird's master would be free of the ground.

But there were other rules.

The first sacrifice must be a child.

The fifth a woman of the aristocracy.

The tenth a man of authority.

The twelfth a slayer of innocent men.

And the thirteenth...

Belle's head rubbed against his black leather glove. Kleindeinst was out there, coming closer...

The thirteenth must come to the sacrifice of their own accord.

XXII

Magister Spielbrunner did not relish being hauled out of his bed by a scryer and quizzed intently about alchemical spells. But he was coming around to accepting it.

'Flight,' the wizard said, 'that's an old one.'

Spielbrunner was young for a wizard, almost boyish. Rosanna had met him briefly when she was with the temple, and remembered his obvious interest in her. He was still interested, and that meant he was putting up with this intrusion into his home.

'After lead-into-gold, rejuvenation, invincibility, sexual potency and foretelling the future, flight is the most popular lunatic fancy. People always come to wizards begging for wings. As if we could work miracles...'

They were in Spielbrunner's study, a modern and uncluttered room, with a no nonsense air about it. His books were dusted regularly and well-kept, and his equipment was stored precisely and in order.

'There are many methods for attempting the power of flight,' he continued, flattening his hair with one hand, and pulling his night-robe tight about his thin body. 'None of them work, of course,' he added. 'Not really. Not for long. Although temporary power of flight – to get you out of a tight situation, say – is comparatively easy for the trained magician. Ten years of study and contemplation, a strict spiritual discipline and a few of the right incantations, and... whoosh!'

'Our man isn't interested in a temporary power of flight. He wants actual wings.'

'Some altereds of Chaos sprout wings. And other things.'

Spielbrunner was picking through books, looking for something.

'This would have to involve murders,' she prompted. 'A number of them.'

'Oh, you mean a Device,' he said, with disgust. 'Superstitious rubbish, like all short-cuts. Popular for a while with unlettered idiots trying to poach some of the benefits of wizardry – meagre though they are, I assure you – without going through the irksome business of actually acquiring magical skills. Everybody wants to be a magician...'

Not everybody, she thought.

'But nobody wants to give up their entire life to becoming one. And that, I am sorry to say, is the only way to get there. As for Devices – nasty, barbarous things – nobody bothers with them any more.'

'Someone still bothers,' she said, unpleasant pictures in her mind.

'Oh dear.'

XXIII

It was nearly dawn, and he had wasted time at the temple, going through the former lector's neglected papers while a dim-witted novice held the candle and shivered. Finally, a couple of Templars turned up and he had to dissuade them from throwing him out. But, as it happened, he had found nothing. In the end, Harald got the address the way he should have done in the first place, by asking a watchman.

On this side of the river, the watchmen weren't what he was used to on the docks. Patrolling the palace, the embassies and the temple districts – all well equipped with their own armed guards – these coppers spent more time making sure their uniforms were smart than chasing cutpurses or roughing up Hooks and Fish.

Still, a flash of the badge got him cooperation from an officer in the Templeplatz Station, and precise directions to the Robida Estate. Harald had looked around at the languid night staff of the station and decided he would do best to go alone.

Knife in hand, he stood before the nondescript but elegant house. Above the door, the name 'Robida' was picked out in elaborate scrollwork, a soaring hawk bas-relief above it.

It was as if Warhawk were announcing himself.

The door was open. Inside, he fancied he heard the flutter of wings.

The first light was in the sky as Harald walked up to the house, and pushed the door open with his boot.

'Don't,' a familiar voice shouted from across the street, 'you're expected!'

XXIV

Rosanna had tracked Harald from the temple to the watch station, pushing Spielbrunner's carriage-man to speed at each turn. The wizard had explained the Device to her and let her have the use of his coach. She now owed him favours, and that was sunk into her like a fish-hook. It was not generally a good thing to be in a wizard's debt.

'He's been pulling you here all along,' she explained.

Harald stepped over the threshold, into the gloomy hallway. Dawn-light streamed in through a dull window at the far end.

'It's part of the Device.'

She kept up with Harald, but he ignored her explanations.

The house was filthy, its floor matted with dry birdlime and trodden-in feathers. The wall-hangings had been rent apart by beaks and claws. There were chewed bones everywhere.

They went upstairs, following the point of Harald's knife.

'If he kills one more, he believes he'll be able to fly.'

Harald snorted a laugh. 'That's madness.'

'Yes, madness.'

They looked around the landing. There were paths on the floor, but wherever the master of this house chose not to venture was abandoned, cobweb-ridden rubbish.

The smell was worse than Mundsen Keep.

They followed the largest path, where a track had been worn through the bird droppings almost to the faded carpet.

At the end of the corridor was a ladder, which led up through an open trapdoor in the ceiling. Above, she heard the small sounds of birds.

She scried danger.

Carefully, Magnin out, Harald pulled himself up one-handed. Birds squawked, but no attack came.

She followed him. There was a hatch in the attic, a gable leading to the roof. A slight wind blew in. Rosanna saw the sun rising over the roofs of the city.

'He's out there,' she said. 'Waiting.'

XXV

It was perfect.

They came through the hatch and stood on his roof.

'He's brought you here,' the witch-woman was saying, unsteady on her feet, 'for the Device. You're to be the last sacrifice.'

Warhawk laughed silently inside his hood, and stood up. Belle's wings spread. 'No, my dove,' he said, 'not him, you.'

Belle glided in silence, beak aimed at the scryer's heart.

Warhawk saw the mask of fear on her face. He had known earlier, when they met in the Street of a Hundred Taverns, that Kleindeinst was the string which would pull her to this site.

'You came of your own accord, remember.'

Belle's arched wings flattened out, and she began to dive. The witch-woman's feet slipped, and she fell away from Kleindeinst. Warhawk realised she was terrified up here, afraid of heights.

He was almost there. In an instant, the Device would be complete and he could fly from this rooftop.

Kleindeinst's hand moved, and something shiny flew from it, turning over and over, scything the air.

Belle tumbled from the sky, and Warhawk felt a beak in his own heart. His bird, his twelve-times-blooded bird, thumped against the slates.

Screeching himself, he attacked, leaping across the gap between the roofs, his boots steady on the shifting tile, and scooped up Belle in his arms.

She was still living.

It could still be done.

XXVI

The hooded figure charged them, waving his bird like a shield, and leaped from a ledge a man's height from their level, landing hard on Rosanna. He set about lashing her with the bird.

She couldn't see anything, but she could feel what he was doing. The bird's beak bit into her.

'Die, die, die,' he grunted through his mask.

She imagined the face of the man who had represented himself to her as Mack Ruger, contorted behind the black leather.

The beak tore at her clothes. The bird was still alive, spitted with the knife, but clinging on until the Device was complete.

'Die, die, die...'

The Warhawk – Andrzej Robida – sounded like a bird himself, a pecking, gouging bird.

'Die, die, die...'

Gods, she thought, what if Speilbrunner was wrong? What if the last thing she were to see in this life was the Warhawk taking to the skies, proud wings spread, blood dripping from his talons?

Fear had enveloped her as soon as she had emerged from the attic hatch and realised how far above the cobbles of the city street she was. Now, the fear was threaded through with pain and panic.

The force of Warhawk's rage, of his need, pummelled her as much as his blows. She scrabbled with her hands, biting back her screams, praying...

'Die, die, die...'

XXVII

Harald's stomach churned and tore itself apart.

The Warhawk was on Rosanna, battering her with his dying bird. He made bird sounds as he assaulted the scryer. Again, Harald had sought a monster and found only a madman.

He strode across the roof, his hands out. The Magnin had taken care of the damned bird, and now it was down to him to deal with the bird's master.

He took Warhawk by the back of the neck, gripping the collar of his leather cloak, and pulled him away.

The murderer was no stronger than the average man, but he was frenzied and determined. He scratched at Harald's arms, twisting in the copper's grip.

Rosanna, sobbing and bleeding, crawled away and clung to a chimney. She was scratched, but she would live.

The Warhawk kicked backwards at Harald's shins. He couldn't hurt him any more than he was already hurting. The murderer could not stop him. It was all over.

Harald turned the Warhawk around, and looked into the mad eyes that stared out through his mask.

He lifted the man off his feet.

'So you want to fly, do you?'

Warhawk squawked.

He heaved the murderer above his head, and tossed him as far as possible out over the street. For the briefest of moments, the black leather silhouette hung in the air, cloak spread behind him.

'Try flapping your arms,' Harald suggested.

The Ibby the Fish Factor

I

It was the worst kind of sunset. The sky, red to the west, churned with cloud the angry colour of fresh-spilled blood. Even squat statues cast shadows as long as temple steeples. Passersby were fringed incarnadine in the dying sun. At the eastern end of Konigplatz was the colossal building that housed Altdorf's law courts and the headsman's offices: its thousand leaded windows caught the last light and flashed vivid, painful orange into her sensitive eyes.

As the dark crept across the 'platz, her vampire senses quickened. Mites and motes dancing in the summer evening caught her attention. Genevieve could distinguish each and every speck – dust or insect – and chart its random course. The background chatter of city noise rose like an orchestra tuning up, and she could make out words spoken in anger or affection across the square. The calls of birds pecking each other over scraps of food and the cries of competing proclaimers became an assault on her ears. Despite her need to pass as ordinary, nightfall brought her to full life, pricking the red thirst she must not slake. Sharpening nails cramped inside her too-tight velvet gloves, curling in on themselves like hooks. She ground her teeth, trying to keep her lips demurely clamped over swelling, razor-edged fangs.

Her eyes hurt most. She saw too many ghosts in the last light of day.

This season, with Clause 17 proclaimed all over the capital of the Empire, it wasn't a good idea to wear smoked glasses on the streets. Let alone affect a red-lined black cloak, sleep in a coffin, neglect to cast a reflection, shapeshift into a bat or wolf, flinch from an icon, or ask for six hundred and seventy-six candles on her birthday cake.

Or smile too sharply.

Genevieve had never been a cloaks-and-coffins sort of vampire. She couldn't transform into anything except an angrier, sharper-toothed and clawed version of her regular self. She could bear garlic, a useful trait in a person forced occasionally to subsist on the blood of Tileans who bathe their food in the stuff. Her conscience was clear enough that holy emblems held no horror for her.

But sunlight made her eyes ache. Enough of it would start her skin peeling.

And she needed to drink warm human blood quite often. That was

never going to make her popular. This summer, with Antiochus Bland's
Sanitation Bill posted all over this part of the Empire, it was also an invitation to be guest of honour at a corpse-burning party.

At the city gates this afternoon, Genevieve had pointedly been asked to
kiss a blessed amulet by a bored watchman who didn't take the trouble
to clean the baubles between uses. Symbols of Shallya, Verena, Ulric and
Sigmar were available. Just ahead of her in the queue, a fastidious merchant cringed at being handed a Sigmarite hammer still glistening with
the slobber of a sickly farmer's boy. The silk-seller, unfortunate enough
to have eyebrows that met suspiciously over his nose, was hauled out of
the line by a couple of black-robed clerics of Morr and put to the Question. She gave thanks that Bland's Boyos were too intent on the merchant
to pay attention to her insignificant person, and chastely pressed closed
lips to a pewter Dove of Verena. She slipped through the gate, trying to
ignore the yelps of indignation and worse emanating from the hut-like
shrine of Morr set up beside the watch-point. Now she knew how strin-
gently Clause 17 was being enforced. She had chosen one of the market
gates, because word was that the daily stream of dodgy characters that
flowed in and out of the Imperial city dissuaded the Cult of Morr from
using silver icons – several sets had gone missing – in the kiss-the-god
test. A clean conscience wouldn't have helped her with silver.

Since then, she had dawdled in the Konigplatz like a first-time visitor
from the sticks, pretending to count the jostling statues of past emperors, not talking to strangers like her mama had told her, hoping to see
someone famous in the flesh. She pointedly bought half a dozen apples,
eating them pips and all. Anyone who cared to pay attention would know
she was the sort of girl whose diet didn't extend far beyond fruit, bread,
cheese and the occasional turnip pasty.

She had made sure to get green apples, not red.

Yum yum. Human food. Wouldn't eat anything else, no sirrah.

Never eat anything red. Or drink it either.

The red thirst was starting to bite. Her fang-teeth ached and tore the
inside of her mouth. The taste of her own blood made it worse.

She had not fed in weeks. That made her crotchety.

Apart from other inconveniences, she felt stuffed inside. Well-chewed
apples filled her like mud. Her stomach and bowels weren't used to
stubborn solids. It was an effort to keep the food down. How horribly
ironic it would be: to pass all the other tests and be given away by
undigested fruit-pulp.

Under the great statue of Sigmar, cloaked in the cool dark of its swelling shadow, she held her body still. Sudden movements would betray
her as not human. She deliberately lifted the last apple to her mouth,
arm slower than the human eye, imagining the air as thick as water. She
overdid it to the point where she might be mistaken for one of those
strange street performers who do things as if living only half as fast as
everyone else.

The moons came out, shiny as new pfennigs.

She was reminded of feeding and her fangs became needle-keen.

She bit into the big apple, jaw-hinges dislocating momentarily, and took the whole core out. Her mouth was full, cheeks bulging like a hamster's, and she had to push with her fingers to get it all in. The trick of distension didn't work for her gullet, and she had to thump her throat to keep from choking.

'Gone down the wrong hole, eh?' said a loiterer.

She couldn't speak, but tried to swallow. A cannonball was lodged somewhere between her voice box and her stomach.

The loiterer got close enough for a lot of little details to come in focus. His doublet had been tailored for someone else but invisibly mended to fit him, and was embroidered with mock cloth-of-gold. His boots were cheap too, tricked up with shiny buckles to look expensive. She scented a wrong 'un, but mostly saw the tiny throb of the pulse in his throat, between the ruff of his shirt and the sharply defined line of his beard. Under pink skin, she saw red and blue.

She heard his heartbeat and perceived the flow of blood under his skin.

He patted her on the back with one hand, dislodging the last of the cannonball and reached for her purse with the other.

She swallowed gratefully and pinched his wrist instinctively, halting his grab.

'You misunderstand,' he tried to wheedle. 'I am merely pointing out the vulnerability of your poke. The 'platz is full of thieves at this hour. And you must protect yourself.'

'Quite so,' she said.

She exerted pressure with her thumb and forefinger, digging into the loiterer's wrist. A shiny sliver dropped from his fingers to the cobbles – an edge rather than a blade, but keen enough to do the job.

'You're a cutpurse,' she said.

His face was screwed up with pain. Nails had forced through the finger-seams of her glove and were stuck into his wrist. Bright blood welled up like a soap bubble and fell, tumbling over itself, to splash on cobbles.

The blood shone with colours only she could see.

She had to force herself not to throw herself on the ground and lick up the spillage.

She looked into the cutpurse's eyes. And saw no reflection of her face.

He was terrified. Then cunning, growing too confident.

'And you're a leech,' he sneered. 'Unhand me, monster!'

A small crowd was gathering. Fellow pickpockets, she guessed, come to admire or critique the sham swell's technique. The professionals must have noticed her quickness at fending off his expert poke-grab. No one now thought she was an innocent girl on her first visit to the big city.

A watchman was coming this way. By his helmet, with its feather and shiny badge, she knew him for one of the ceremonial toy soldiers who policed the more public and official districts.

She let go of the thief's wrist, but he took hold of hers.

'We've got one of them!' he shouted. 'Officer, send for Bland's Boyos.

This foul inhuman creature must be turned over to the Cult of Morr. We've a leech for the burning!'

A cobblestone bounced off her forehead. Insults and excoriations were called out. Several of the crowd held up flaming torches on long sticks. The lamplighters, of course. As the hisses and mutters spread, the effect was uncomfortably close to mobs she remembered of old. Yokels with firebrands and farm implements, swarming over the countryside. Ranting clerics and pompous rural burgermeisters, leading from behind. Execution without trial, and the shrill cry of 'Death to the dead!'

Five hundred years ago, well before Antiochus Bland ascended to the Temple Fathership of the Cult of Morr, the Undead Wars – fomented by the von Carstein clan, those Sylvanian lunatics who claimed to speak for all vampirekind – had set off the worst of the persecutions. The average Count von Carstein proved enormously keen on leading armies of rotting mindless strigoi against the higher races and dreaming of an eternal feast of blood. However, those master tacticians tended not to be about when vampires you could actually hold a conversation with were picked off in ones and twos by those doughty bands of scythe-waving, fire-building, stake-brandishing clods every village had sitting around the inn waiting to impale, incinerate or quarter anyone to whom they took a dislike.

'Off with her head,' shouted some silly woman.

'Beheading's too good for the likes of her!'

The rake Chandagnac, her own father-in-darkness, had been among many comparatively blameless purge victims, hunted down and destroyed by clerics of Ulric. Since Chandagnac had also gifted the ill-remembered Tsarina Kattarin with the Dark Kiss, Genevieve supposed he was indirectly responsible for as much bother as the von Carsteins. Just as the Undead Wars were dying down, Kattarin overwhelmed her addle-headed mortal husband to become absolute ruler of Kislev, exerting a bloody grip that lasted centuries. She'd be on the throne still if her great-great-great grandchildren hadn't got fed up with an immortal ice queen blocking succession and conspired to transfix her like a butterfly. The body, preserved by the cold of Kislev's Frost Palace, was still on display as an Awful Warning.

'Put silver needles in her eyes,' shouted a thin girl with more imagination than most. Genevieve had not heard that one before.

'That's a good idea, Hanna,' said a friend of the cleverclogs. 'Silver needles!'

She found herself backed up against the base of the statue of Sigmar.

The torch-flames got closer. The watchman forced his way to the front of the crowd.

'What's all this, then?' said the copper. 'Move along smartly, you lot.'

The watchman, tabard let out over his comfortable stomach, caught sight of the cutpurse and reached for his cudgel.

'Oh, it's you, Donowitz. Still dunking for pokes? And picking on the young ones again. It'll be Mundsen Keep this time. No more warnings.'

Genevieve noticed that Donowitz wore his cap aslant to conceal a wax ear. He'd been clipped at least once.

'I am entirely innocent, your worship,' said the cutpurse. 'I found this daughter of darkness preying on decent living folks. She's a ghastly monster of the night. An undead hag in a girlish shape. Look at the red in her eyes. See how she shows her fangs and claws.'

Genevieve became acutely aware that her mouth was open and her gloves shredded. Her red thirst was up, she was coiled to spring. If it was to end tonight, she'd take some human bastards to true death with her. They might have her head off, but she'd go out with the taste of Altdorf blood in her throat.

'We're going to do what Temple Father Bland says, and treat her properly,' said Donowitz, instantly self-elected mob-leader. 'Strip her for the Question, lay silver lashes on her skin, then despatch her with stake, fire and sickle.'

'Oh aye,' said rather too many enthusiasts.

'Hold on,' said one fellow. 'I must rush home and fetch me old dad. He wouldn't want to miss this.'

'Sell tickets, why don't you?' Genevieve shouted at the dutiful son as he scurried off.

'None of your lip, monster,' said the watchman.

'Officer,' she said to him. 'It's a fair cop. My name is Genevieve Dieudonné. I am indeed a vampire… ghastly monster, undead hag and so forth. I freely surrender myself to the Konigplatz Watch. Kindly escort me to a cell to await the laying of actual criminal or spiritual charges against me. I should like to stand on my right as a citizen of the Empire in good standing to send one written message, to my friend the Emperor Karl-Franz, whose life I happened to save from the infernal designs of the traitor Oswald von Konigswald and the Great Enchanter Constant Drachenfels.'

She hated bringing it up all the time, but the situation seemed to demand it.

The copper scratched his chin. Someone poked her leg with a stick and she involuntarily snarled.

'Well, um, miss, I, er…'

'Don't be blinded by her vampire powers of fascination,' said Donowitz. 'And don't hark to all this legal nonsense. She's a dreaded leech and we've caught her in bloodsuckery. She's no more rights than any other abomination.'

'Didn't you people hear what I said?' Genevieve shouted, annoyed. 'Thirteen years ago, I saved the whole Empire!'

'That's as may be,' said Silver Needles Hanna, 'but what have you done for us lately?'

She was prodded again. A mean-eyed dwarf in short lederhosen had got between everyone's legs and was close to her. He had a special prodding-stick.

'Death to the dead!'

The cry was taken up.

She was prodded again, through her skirt. The gnarled stick was a bit sharp.

'Shove it in her heart, Shorty,' said Hanna. Genevieve had expected more from Silver Needles, but people always turned out to be disappointments.

With that in mind, she still tried to look imploring to the watchman.

Someone tipped his helmet from behind and the peak slid over his eyes.

'I have your watch-number officer,' she said. 'I'll remember it if you let this unruly mob run riot.'

She had misjudged the copper. He looked stricken at being singled out.

'See, she's divined this poor fellow's watch-number with her magic powers,' said the vendor who'd been happy to sell her unripe apples all afternoon. 'She's a witch as well as a vampire.'

'It's written on his helmet, goathead,' said Hanna helpfully.

'I can't be doing with all this,' said the watchman. 'My shift ended at nightfall. Just be sure you do a decent job of it.'

He turned and walked away.

The prodding dwarf was closer, gurning up at her with yellowed teeth and eyes.

'You think that once they've done for all the vampires they won't turn on dwarfs next?'

Another mistake. Shorty lifted her skirt with his stick and leered at her knees. Half the crowd laughed. The other half complained this wasn't in the dignified spirit of a proper vampire-slaying.

'Oh, let Shorty have his fun. It's not as if she were human.'

The dwarf put his face to her skirts and drew in a huge breath, sucking at her scent.

This was just disgusting!

'Hang this lark for a game of tin soldiers,' said Genevieve.

She braced herself against Sigmar's plinth and stamped on Shorty's face, jabbing her heel against his squash nose. Her kick propelled Shorty off the cobbles. He cannoned through the crowd and splashed down satisfyingly in a puddle.

'What a bully,' said Silver Needles Hanna. 'Vampires are all the same.'

Genevieve had inherited the dwarf's prodding stick, which seemed a lot shorter in her grip than it had in Shorty's stubby fingers. She held it up like a duelling blade. People pulled out the knives and swords kept out of sight when the watch was around. Someone even started powdering a pistol.

'Before we proceed further,' she said, 'there's one thing I'd like to get perfectly clear. You're all criminals. Cutpurses, ponces, jack-up artists, hugger-muggers, layabouts, bawds and the like. And you're about to *murder* me. But you feel pretty good about it. You've had a hard day stealing, fleecing, whoring and cheating, but you think killing me is, as it were, your *good deed for the week*. Doesn't that strike any of you as *insane*? Have I ever hurt any of you? Except "Dunkin" Donowitz and the prod-happy pervert, both of whom started any trouble they got. So far as you know, have I ever hurt anyone you've ever met?'

'It's not what you've *done*,' said Hanna, 'it's what you *are!*'

'I thought as much.'

Genevieve flung the stick away. She invoked whichever Gods of Law were left over to care about justice for the undead. Tensing her thighs and calves in a semi-crouch, she fixed her mind on a point thirty feet above her head and sprang up into the air. With a run-up, she might have made it to the raised warhammer. As it was, she slammed against the statue's broad belt, face scraping weathered stone belly-muscles. Her clumsy hands found no hold, and she slid down between Sigmar's mighty thews. She scrabbled for something – anything! – to grab.

'Sacrilege!' shouted too many people.

Genevieve had cause to thank the sculptor who defied conventional morality by insisting that the greatest memorial to the founding hero of Empire be anatomically correct and heroically proportioned enough to get a grip on. When Altdorfers swore by Sigmar's holy hammer, they didn't just mean the one he held up ready to smash goblin skulls.

She found rests in the muscles of Sigmar's knees for her boot-toes, drew in a breath, and climbed the statue monkey-fashion, swarming up over the hero's waist and chest. Perching on his shoulder like a gargoyle, she leant against the flaring wings of his helm. Up close, she realised that the white texture of his beard came from centuries of incontinent pigeons.

'That's what we have in common, my lord,' she breathed. 'One minute, you're a hero of the Empire. The next, they're crapping all over you.'

Just about now, being able to shapeshift into bat-form would have been a useful attribute.

Something burning spanged against Sigmar's helm. A lamplighter's torch, thrown as a makeshift spear. Someone down there in the swelling crowd would probably have a crossbow.

It was time to make a dignified exit.

'Death to the dead!'

There was a flash, a sizzle and some screaming. The pistolier had fumbled his loading and set fire to himself. They couldn't blame her for... who was she fooling? In their current mood, the crowd was likely to blame her for sour milk and clogged drains.

A couple of bold would-be vampire-slayers were trying to scale Sigmar's plinth. One fell off and was caught by the crowd, then tossed up to try again.

Genevieve took a run along Sigmar's heroic arm, got her hands around the shaft of his more conventional hammer and swung a couple of times, trying to remember the tumbling moves she had learned in Cathay from Master Po. She launched herself into space and reached forward like an acrobat, aiming herself at the huge flat green scowl of the Empress Magritta.

The tradition was that every new emperor and empress was supposed to commemorate their investiture by commissioning their own statue and adding it to the crowd in Konigplatz. After two and a half millennia, space was at a premium. Most of early post-Sigmar emperors were worn down to little more than stubs. City planners still dreaded another upheaval like the Year of Seven Emperors, which had forced them to demolish the beautiful little shrine of Repanse de Lyonesse to make way for a spectacularly ugly and undignified jostle of poisoned, stabbed, hot-collared and defenestrated one-week wonders.

Even that was less of a disaster than the statue of the Empress Magritta. After the Bronze Lady browbeat the electors into giving her the throne, she decreed her statue should reflect her stature and be twice the height of Sigmar's. When she was eventually succeeded, after a deft bit of backstabbery, the often-forgotten Emperor Johann the Grey was acutely embarrassed by the colossa frowning down disapproval on the whole city, and wondered how to go about breaking tradition by getting rid of the thing.

The problem was half-solved when the statue proved so heavy that it plunged through its shoddy sandstone plinth and lost three-quarters of its height by sinking long legs and most of its body into the sewers and tarns under Altdorf. A story went that on the night of the Big Plunge, the stern stone face of the Sigmar statue was seen to smile broadly. Die-hards who spent centuries whining that things were never right again after the Bronze Lady was booted out perpetually sought to raise public subscriptions for the re-elevation of the statue to its former glory.

As it was, Magritta's spiked crown was in just the right place.

Genevieve caught the spikes and vaulted over them, concealing herself neatly inside the sculpted crown.

Most of the Konigplatz emperors were solid stone, but Magritta was hollow metal. Before the big plunge, it had been possible to climb up inside the statue and peer out over the city from the crown. There must be a hatch somewhere. Rooting through the clogged detritus inside the crown – the contents of which she didn't want to think about – she found a ring. At the first pull, it came off in her hand.

Trying to ignore the shouting from below and the flaming arrows striking Magritta's solid hair, she felt out the edges of the hatch.

An arrow arced down into the crown, narrowly missing her leg. The fire blotted her vision with dazzling squiggles, but after the flare the light was useful. She was in a large bird's nest, surrounded by fragments of eggshell and hundreds of animal bones. Since there were few twigs in the city, the nest was woven of whatever came to beak: stolen items of clothing, at least six parasols and umbrellas, entire potted shrubs and a lot of simple garbage. A still-living weirdroot sported healthy bulbs, presumably enabling the dweller in this nest to fly higher than any other bird in the city.

She pulled the stoutest umbrella skeleton out of the nest and slid it into the hatch-crack, lifting the heavy metal flap enough to get her hand under its lip.

As well as shouting from below, she heard angry squawking from above.

A city legend had it that after 'Filthy' Harald Kleindeinst ended the career of the pattern killer Warhawk, the murderous trainer's birds escaped and took to the high perches of Altdorf. The hardy, vicious, overlarge sky pirates stole babies and dogs to feed their young.

She didn't need to find out if that was true or not.

Hauling up the hatch, she slid into the comforting if odorous gloom and let herself fall a dozen feet. The hatch clanged shut above her. Light filtered through the green lenses in Magritta's eyes. The crowd sound was muffled.

Now she just had to work her way down to the base of the statue and leave through the door in the empress's heel. Which was a thousand feet below her, and underwater.

It was a good thing she didn't need to breathe.

II

'Detlef, I'm deeply disappointed that you of all people should take this unproductive attitude. I can't understand why you'd wish to display such an unbalanced – indeed, unnatural – view of the undead in such an influential space as the theatre. Young people – indeed, children – patronise this place, they have unformed and easily-influenced minds. Surely, you concede that you have a duty by everything holy to present all arguments before coming down firmly on the side of the living?'

Detlef Sierck, actor/manager/playwright-in-residence of the Vargr Breughel Memorial Theatre, considered his visitor. The wheedling, smiling, Antiochus Bland was not physically impressive. Detlef had inches on the man and outweighed him by half, but the Temple Father of the Cult of Morr acted as if this snug room was his office, not Detlef's. Usually, the broad desk gave Detlef a sense of power over supplicants and auditionees, but now he felt trapped, wedged in by furniture that pressed on his substantial belly, pinned back by Bland's fixed eyes.

Elsie, the angelic foundling Poppa Fritz had taken on to sell programs and interval sweetmeats, brought in a tray with a pot of fresh beef tea and a couple of goblets. Bland looked at the reddish liquid suspiciously, but the twelve-year-old's open face won him over. There had been some backstage talk of dosing Bland's tea with weirdroot, but Detlef hoped nothing had come of it. The Temple Father could hardly become *more* dream-haunted, deranged and obsessive.

'Thank you most kindly, missy,' said Bland, turning his smile on the girl. He fished a pfennig from his tummy-pouch and gave it to her. 'It must be very sad – indeed, tragic – to be an orphan. I often worry about what might happen to my own three lovely children if their dear mama should be snatched away by fiendish creatures of darkness. There's nothing more important – indeed, prudent – than a good solid savings account with a respectable house of bankers. If you invest this tiny chap wisely, it might grow up to be a great big schilling.'

Little Orphan Elsie, an expert judge of character and coinage, raised the pfennig to the corner of her mouth, eye-teeth bared for a healthy bite. Detlef caught her eye with a quick head-shake, dissuading her from treating the Temple Father like a palmer-off of snide coins.

Elsie thanked Bland for the pfennig and left. Detlef hoped the child was sensible – indeed, human – enough to squander the coin on a hair-ribbon or an almond biscuit. To the gallows with good solid savings accounts and respectable houses of bankers. Ulric knows he hadn't saved anything as dull as money at her age; or at any age since then, come to that. It all went back into the theatre. He was only one flop away from his old debtor's cell at Mundsen Keep.

He drank his own beef tea, the closest he'd get to meat this week, and didn't cringe when Bland's shark-smile was turned back on him.

It was too easy to think that, with a new production in rehearsal, he had better things to do than debate Clause 17. Actually, this little chat with the Temple Father was the most important meeting he had had all year. If he didn't play this scene as masterfully as any he'd ever enacted, there wouldn't be a new production and, in all probability, wouldn't even be a theatre.

He was holding back mention of the fact that he had once saved the Empire.

That and half-a-pfennig was enough to get buy a bun from Elsie's tray these days.

Understandably, Karl-Franz chose not to patronise the theatre. The last time the Emperor showed up for a Detlef Sierck premiere, the traitor Oswald had tried to kill him and the Great Enchanter Drachenfels nearly came back from the dead to take over the Known World – which at least prevented him from falling asleep in his chair and having to rely on an advisor to tell him how much he liked the show. But his son Prince Luitpold, the eager teenager of the old days grown into a straight young blade, had never missed a Vargr Breughel opening (or closing). According to the scurrilous newsheet *Boulevardpresse*, the heir presumptive had the largest private collection of immodest paintings of the company's leading lady, Eva Savinien, in the city. There were flower-growing smallholders in far-off Upper Gris Mere whose entire business depended on the prince's habit of sending Eva a dozen bouquets of rare blooms every night she appeared on the stage. However, this morning the palace had returned the complimentary tickets to the Imperial box with a curt note from a steward stating that Prince Luitpold would be unavoidably detained on the night the theatre was holding the gala debut of Detlef's new play, *Genevieve and Vukotich; or: A Celestial Plot in Zhufbar*. This afternoon, messengers from all over the city – all over the Empire, it seems – returned half a house's worth of invitations. Most of them couldn't even be bothered to think up a half-decent prior engagement.

The current situation didn't make it advisable to support *Genevieve and Vukotich.*

'The cultural industry has a vital – indeed, crucial – part to play in maintaining the moral health of the Empire, Detlef,' purred Bland. 'Look to the Imperial Tarradasch Players and *Death to the Dead!* Educational and instructive stuff. And a sound investment. Folk too often forget the Undead Wars, you know. I'm insisting that they be in the core curriculum of all schools of history. And what of those mummers who put on Wilhelm Konig's verse drama *Vampireslayer* for the children? Could that fine work not be adapted for the legitimate stage? You would be perfectly – indeed, superbly – cast as stouthearted Gotrek, scourge of the undead.'

Gotrek was a dwarf! Detlef didn't play parts which required him to wear boots on his knees.

'There are so many fine subjects. The evil of the Vlad von Carstein and his whole rotten dynasty. The depredations of Bloody Kattarin. The murders of the vampire Wietzak. With so much wonderful – indeed, inspirational – material to choose from, I can't quite see your problem. Why do you have to bring up this Zhufbar business?'

'It happened, Temple Father.'

'Many things happened. That doesn't mean they should be raked up on stage at every opportunity. With so much wholesome – indeed, life-enhancing – matter to write about, why must you dwell on the undead? On the filthy, stinking, bloodlusting, crawled-up-from-the-unhallowed-grave monsters who so threaten the fabric of our unparalleled Imperial society? Of course that's only my opinion. You are free to hold another. This city isn't ruled by a tyrannical absolutist like Kattarin the Great. She used to kill poets, you know. Slowly. If you wrote something she didn't like, you wouldn't be reasoned with. Indeed, you'd be exsanguinated and tossed to the wolves.'

'Genevieve isn't Kattarin.'

'They are sisters, though. Sisters-in-darkness. Who's to know when the smile will turn pointy?'

Temple Father Bland was potty about vampires.

Detlef had assumed his entire family was killed in an undead clan raid, but it wasn't so simple. Though no vampire had ever actually done anything to hurt Bland, the very idea of them crawled under his skin and festered. Most people didn't feel anything either way about leeches. If something was tearing open their necks, they were agin; if something was saving the Emperor from Drachenfels, they were for. Otherwise, live and let live – or unlive, or whatever. There were orc hordes and daemons to worry about, so what was a little nip here and there? And, really, weren't most vampires just human beings with longer lives and differing dietary habits? To Detlef's mind, actresses were a lot creepier – you never knew what they were thinking or whose throat they'd go for next. And all the worst villains Detlef had met were full humans, even counting drama critics.

But Bland was a fanatic on the subject and there was no talking to him about it.

If he were just a ranter, no one would have noticed, but the cleric was far cannier than that. He had bided his time, smiling and working energetically, climbing his way up within the Cult of Morr, god of the dead. Now, he was the youngest Temple Father anyone could remember. Detlef, at forty-five, had a good half decade on Tio Bland. The only lines on the cleric's face were the stretches around his perpetual smile.

Traditionally, the Cult of Morr wasn't even one of the major faiths; it was chiefly concerned with burial rites and grounds and respect for those who had the decency to lie down when they died. But in the last ten years, a succession of scandals had rocked the traditional allies of Imperial power. The rot had started with Oswald von Konigswald – if you couldn't trust an elector not to conspire with ancient evil, anyone was liable to turn out to be crooked as a corkscrew.

As demonstrated by the satirical revues Detlef mounted late at night after the main show to bring in the inky student and grumbling would-be revolutionist audience, holders of high office could no longer automatically expect undiluted respect. With the likes of Temple Father Mikael Hasselstein of the Cult of Sigmar, Graf Rudiger von Unheimlich of the League of Karl-Franz or one-thumbed chancellor Mornan Tybalt – rogues and schemers, all – retired, dead or out of favour, even minor court players saw their chances to make moves.

Bland's opportunity came with a minor septicaemic plague scare. With bodies lying where they fell and watchmen and the militia terrified to touch them, the Cult of Morr stepped forward and offered to take over the collection and disposal of the dead. It was no more than a traditional sacred duty. Bland, then in his first months of office, worked so tirelessly, personally supervising the corpse-harvest, and the outbreak was quelled before it could fully blossom. A few tiresome relatives complained of undue haste in hefting departed uncles into the cremation pits, but that was a small price to pay.

Then, somehow, the cult's remit in dealing with bodies had expanded. In the satirical revue *Altdorf After Dark,* Detlef had pinned his face into an approximation of the Bland smile and played the part of 'Antoninius Blamed' and explained reasonably – indeed, sincerely – that the clerics of Morr correctly judged that everyone walking round was a potential body. Thus, the cult felt they more or less had the right – indeed, responsibility – to bury or burn people on the assumption that they'd become corpses eventually. It was as well to get the funerary arrangements over with while the pre-deceased could still appreciate them.

Bland made a point of seeing the show and laughing very loudly.

He wasn't laughing now. Up close, Detlef realised Bland didn't even smile properly. It was only his lips and teeth. His eyes were frozen and scary, never blinking, all pupil.

'Maybe you're too close to the subject matter, Detlef…'

Detlef bristled. He knew where this was leading.

'You draw too much from one person's account of the kerfuffle in Zhufbar all those years ago. Current – indeed, dominant – thought holds that the situation was by no means as clear-cut as interested parties have made out. History may look more kindly on Claes Glinka's well-intentioned moral crusade than you do in your work…'

Detlef did not know how Bland had got hold of a manuscript copy of his as-yet unperformed play. When he found out, someone was going to be fired, without references but with bruises.

'Who knows, maybe Wladislaw Blasko may emerge in the corrected historical accounts as a much-maligned figure? As an artist – indeed, as an honest recorder – can you afford to stake your reputation on the word of… of a dead-alive thing in woman-shape, a bloodlusting nosferatu who'd drink the world if we let her. Indeed, a bitch vampire!'

'Hold it there, Bland,' said Detlef, making fists under his desk. 'You're talking about the woman I love.'

Bland sniffed. 'There are laws against interfering with corpses,' he said, darkly.

'There are many laws.'

Bland had bored everyone he spoke to on the subject of vampires for years, but learned his lesson. His Sanitation Bill had not, on the face of it, seemed to have anything to do with his hobby-horse. The Cult of Morr, after the plague crisis, formed a commission with city-planners, watch commanders and officials of the court, then drafted a program of suggestions to prevent further outbreaks. It seemed like a good idea. Detlef himself signed a petition asking that the findings of the report be ratified as the law of the city. The Emperor graciously acceded, extending the shield of the Sanitation Bill to all the Empire. Into the bill, Bland had smuggled the legal grounds for his personal crusade, Clause 17: 'Any body unclaimed by a family member within three days of death is to be turned over to the Cult of Morr for burial or burning.' The dead should be ashes or under the ground and that was the end of it.

Of course, the sting came in the definition of 'dead'.

'Temple Father, how's this for a compromise? I shall retitle the work *Vukotich and Genevieve.*'

Bland's smile stretched still further as, behind his eyes, he thought it through. It took long seconds for the pfennig to drop. He rumbled that he was being spoofed again. His eyebrows pointed up in the middle and honest-to-Verena moist droplets started from his knotty pink tear-ducts.

'I'm going out of my way to accommodate you, Detlef, with regards to your status as a pre-eminent – indeed, paramount – artist of the Empire. I know how many crowns the theatre contributes to the city treasury. It wounds me that you should treat this business with such undue levity. If you only knew the work – indeed, thought – that has gone into all this. I've carted plague-ridden corpses to the burning-pits when everyone else has fled, Detlef. My dear wife and three lovely children begged me – indeed, pleaded heart-rendingly – to stay home safe from infection, but I saw my duty and shrank not from it. I was willing to get my hands dirty to do the right thing. Can you say the same?'

Now might be the time to mention saving the Empire.

Bland stood up. The silver sword he wore over his robes got caught up in the trailing hem. He affected a bandolier of wooden knives and squeeze-bulbs of garlic (one of which was leaking). As far as Detlef knew, Bland had never slain so much as a tick. It was possible that he had never actually been in a room with a vampire – the undead weren't that common in Altdorf.

Not for the first time, Detlef wondered what was eating the Temple Father.

Poppa Fritz, eternally-aged stage-manager and general factotum of the Vargr Breughel, popped into the office just in time to show Bland the way to the street, where a couple of pike-toting clerics awaited their master. From the window, Detlef saw the Temple Father shake hands with various members of the crowd of permanent protest, hugging old ladies and kissing held-up babies, before heading for his black hearse-like carriage. As Bland passed, the scowling crowd cheered up momentarily. When he was gone, they went back to their dignified 'Death to the Dead' chants and harassment of anyone coming and going.

Detlef's back hurt from sitting and listening to rot for so long. He could have demolished a seven-course meal, but was on one of his periodic beef-tea diets, to get his weight down so he could offer a reasonable simulation of the lean, hard 'Iron Man' Vukotich opposite Eva Savinien's lithe impersonation of She-Who-Must-Not-Be-Mentioned-Except-on-Stage.

It was a long time since maidens collected portraits of Detlef Sierck. The drama critic of the Altdorf *Spieler* had pointed out that in his last two productions, Detlef had taken the roles of kings, Magnus the Pious and Boris the Incompetent, and had managed to get through the runs of both plays without getting off his throne except to make a curtain speech or fall down dead. Detlef considered challenging the upstart scribbler to a duel, but realised it was true – which was why *Genevieve and Vukotich* was full of fight scenes, active lovemaking, general dashing about and hanging from the rafters. He was spending his mornings at the Temple Street gymnasium where Arne the Body was either trying to get him in shape or murder him in the most humiliating manner imaginable. Strangely, all the theatre cats seemed to have gone on a diet too – Poppa Fritz reported that they were losing weight mysteriously, one more thing to worry about.

Maybe Bland had something. It was nearly ten years since Genevieve had left the city. Time to let the memory go.

His neck-bites, long-healed and invisible to everyone else, itched.

Would it be easier if he knew she was dead? Bland's Clause 17 could scoop her up as easily as any other poor leech. No, she'd survived this long. She'd outlive the persecutions, outlive Detlef.

There was a smell in the office. Not garlic.

A tapping came.

The Vargr Breughel was shot through with secret passageways, sliding panels and hidden hollows. The theatre had once been haunted by the creature they had called the Trapdoor Daemon, who moved behind the walls and spied through one-way dressing room mirrors. That was also a painful memory, yet another Genevieve anecdote saved for a later play – one with a last act he still didn't feel ready to write. Besides, audiences didn't like it when the girl left the boy at the end. *Downbeat* closed on the second week of previews. Bruno Malvoisin, the Trapdoor Daemon, had been a shapeless squid-human mutant hidden under a huge cloak and hat – a role Detlef could play without fasting or exercise.

Detlef went to the case where bound folios of his scripts were kept. The tapping came from behind it. And the smell.

Water was seeping under the panel. Had the Trapdoor Daemon returned? Surely, poor Malvoisin was dead.

Trembling, Detlef tripped the hidden catch. A small creature, hair in wet rat-tails, filth all over her, tumbled out.

Instantly recognisable green eyes opened in her mask of dirt.

'You came back,' he said.

Not one of his better speeches.

'I had to,' Genevieve replied.

Detlef had a moment of might-have-been panic. If she'd tapped only a few minutes earlier, she would have come out of the wall while the Empire's premier vampire-hater was in the room, with expert pikemen within his call and a beltful of sharpened stakes. He swore he'd have fought for her, but the outcome would not have been in doubt.

Under the ground or in ashes.

Genevieve wiped off her face with a muddy sleeve. She still looked like a lass of sixteen summers.

She touched him. His knees wouldn't support him.

They held each other.

III

The office was the same, but Detlef looked older. Not just bigger, but softer, greyer. However, the fire in him was the same. Genius still flickered like a half-crazy light behind his eyes. She had not expected her thirst for him to rush back in such a flood, as if she'd tasted his blood last night, not ten years ago.

The room smelled of blood. And of her.

She'd been in the tunnels under the Vargr Breughel Memorial Playhouse before, but never had to swim out of a filth-clogged bronze empress and wade through the vile main sewers of Altdorf to make her entrance. She was a stinking ruin.

Detlef took a speaking-tube from a hook and whistled into it.

'Poppa Fritz…'

'Is Poppa Fritz still here? Still alive? He must be older than I am. It's wonderful that someone else doesn't change.'

Detlef waved her quiet.

'Poppa, I've, um, spilled something all over myself… Yes, yes, I should try to keep my temper, but you know Tio Bland… Could you send up Renastic with a tub of warm water and some soap? And towels.'

Genevieve stood in the middle of the room, trying not to drip on anything precious. The hideous embroidered elf carpet, which Detlef had said would be the first thing to go when he took over the theatre, was still here.

'You get used to it,' Detlef said to her, hand briefly over the tube. 'It's not so bad.'

He still had the trick of reading her oddest thoughts.

'Just coughing, Poppa… Oh, and could you get Elsie to look in Kerreth's workshop and fetch the Genevieve costumes, if they're finished.'

'Genevieve costumes?'

He waved her quiet again.

'Splendid… No, there's no rush. Thanks, Poppa.'

Detlef hung up the hook.

'The one thing you could say that would make him suspicious, darling, was "there's no rush". With you, with this place, there's always a rush.'

'I suppose you're right. I wasn't thinking.'

Detlef was overwhelmed and not just by the sewer smell. She should have expected that. He had smears on his face and chest from hugging her. He wore a big, unbelted smock and even that was over-filled.

'You haven't changed,' he said. 'You could be my grand-daughter.'

'You haven't changed either. Not where it counts.'

He shrugged sadly, not believing her. She took his hands and gripped. 'Your eyes are the same.'

'I need lenses to con my own scripts.'

'That's not what I mean.'

The taste of blood was in the air. Her tongue slithered over the razor-points of her teeth.

On the desk stood a big pot of beef tea. Her eyes darted to it.

'You haven't... eaten?' he ventured.

She shook her head. He let her hands go and picked up the pot.

'Do you mind using my goblet? I can get a fresh one if you'd rather?'

She took the pot from him and tipped the spout to her mouth. She opened wide and poured. It took half a minute to drain the tea. She set it down and wiped her lips on the back of her hand.

'Better?'

'Takes the edge off,' she said. 'It's not blood, but what is?'

His hands crept up, involuntarily, to his collar, as if the room were too hot and he was buttoned up too tight.

She'd drunk a lot of blood, in passion and anger, since she was last here, but she'd never let herself be touched by the living men and women whose veins she tapped. She had known friends, victims, hosts, servants, pick-ups, enemies, meals, sacrifices. While he lived, Detlef was her only lover.

But she could not ask him to let her batten on him.

It would not be fair to bleed him and leave.

'I've missed you,' she admitted.

He sighed, in agony. 'I've not missed you, Gené. Because in my mind you were never gone.'

She noticed a playscript on the desk and picked it up.

'*Genevieve and Vukotich*. What can this be about?'

She flipped over the pages. She remembered telling Detlef about the bad business in Zhufbar, when she had been shackled to the mercenary Vukotich and nagged him into thwarting a scheme of the Chaos champions Dien Ch'ing and Yevgeny Yefimovich. When sharing with him the whole story, tactfully omitting full details of a bedroom scene she realised was represented with uncanny accuracy in this play-script, she had realised that in the middle of it came their first meeting, when he was just a little boy and she a runaway from Claes Glinka's moral crusade.

'It's a good story,' he said, a little sheepish. 'It'll be very popular. I wonder how that warm water's coming.'

She looked at more scenes. She wondered how Detlef intended to pull off the confrontation with the five Celestial elementals. He usually resisted big special effects, claiming the most important magic in the theatre was in the verse and the acting and that giant gasp-inducing daemon apparitions transformations were just a sideshow. If audiences left the play talking about the monsters, then they had been distracted from the true import of the drama.

It occurred to her that a play with a vampire heroine might not be kindly met in this season of Clause 17.

'Detlef,' she said, 'you're too brave. This could be the ruin of you, but it's so sweet. Though I feel your "Genevieve" is a little nicer than the original. Back then, I was basically earning a living as a dancing slut, remember? You shouldn't make me out to be some priestess of Shallya.'

'It's just an entertainment.'

'You don't write anything that's "just an entertainment".'

'How would you know? You've missed ten years. I've downslid. I do jokes and murdered kings and write myself parts which involve a great deal of sitting down. It's a while since I did anything really fine. You can't be a child prodigy at my age. A lot of things I've not even been able to finish.'

He was acting, out of habit.

'Rot and rubbish, Detlef. I've not been here to see you act, but I can still read. Your folios are available even in the savage outlands where I've spent most of my time.'

'Pirated editions from which I've not seen a pfennig.'

'And there are the sonnets.'

He blushed red. All his poems were about her.

'You've read them?'

'Not all the run of *To My Unchanging Lady* were destroyed. Students pass copies around, some hand-written and bound inside misleading boards to throw off the book-burners. Do you know how much you have to pay to get hold of a suppressed work?'

'Yes. I bribe the provincial censors to ban my best material so I can charge outrageously. Makes up for what I lose on those damned unauthorised folios. Being illegal is always good for cash businesses. Weirdroot tubers cost a lot more than potatoes.'

She giggled and he laughed.

'This is somewhere between uncomfortable and wonderful,' he said.

'Wasn't it always?'

Poppa Fritz came upstairs with Renastic, a new scene-shifter Detlef claimed was surprisingly strong for one so thin and sallow-looking, carrying a hip-bath full of warm water between them. Detlef had her hide behind the door. She was sorry for the deception: she liked Poppa Fritz and looked forward to cuddling with the old man. But Detlef was right: it wouldn't do just yet to let too many people know the vampire Genevieve was back in town. Renastic, a Sylvanian with a widow's peak, had potent breath and she was surprised to recognise him. She knew she would have to pass on the odd little scene she had witnessed from the secret passageway.

Stripped of her vile clothes, she slid luxuriously into the water, sighing with pleasure. In an ever-changing world, some delights were eternal – like a warm bath after a long dirty spell.

'One thing about that Renastic fellow,' she said. 'He has an odd little friend.'

'What do you mean?'

'As I was making my way through the old Trapdoor Daemon tunnels, I saw through one of the mirrors into a dressing room. There was only one candle lit, so it was dark, and the mirror is almost entirely crusted over with muck so I couldn't make much out. But your friend Renastic was there, in full evening dress with black cloak and all, dandling something on his lap that I couldn't quite see. Someone, rather. Someone child- or goblin-sized. Not a child, though. And not a goblin either, I think. He was playing with it, like a pet or a familiar. But the talk was heated. They were having quite a lively discussion, an argument.'

'I've no idea who this small person might be.'

'I had one of my weird feelings about him. Like there was no one there, at least no one with a soul. There was a certain amount of "yes, master"-ing. They were talking about someone or something called "Gottle".'

'Sounds dwarfish.'

'That's what I thought. "Gottle of Glood". I heard another name, one which doesn't have very pleasant associations: "Vlad".'

'So Alvdnov's little friend is named after Vlad von Carstein? No wonder he doesn't show his face much. He isn't liable to be very popular in the current climate.'

'"Alvdnov Renastic"? There's something strange going on there.'

'There's something strange going on everywhere. Tell me something I don't know, Gené.'

'That'll have to wait until after I'm clean.'

She sank under the water, letting it close over her face. Her knees rose from the seas like mythical islands, her hair floated like catchweed and trapped the toy ships Poppa Fritz had put into the bath.

IV

The corpse with the gaping hole under his chin lay face-up in the gutter of the Street of a Hundred Taverns, ringed by clerics and coppers.

'His worries are over,' said Johannes Munch. 'This could have waited.'

Bland turned furiously on the watchman, struck speechless by such rank stupidity. Surely the Sergeant with Special Responsibility for Unlawful Killing must heed the undead menace. With each passing minute, the dead man became more dangerous.

'I think, sergeant,' interpreted Liesel von Sutin, Bland's scribe-proclaimer, 'that the Temple Father feels it is exactly that unhelpful attitude which has brought us to this dreadful pass.'

Munch looked wearily at Bland and Liesel.

'I lament for the old days, when the clerics of Morr stood decently back and let a copper do his job, then quietly came in and dragged the stiff off to the Temple for disposal.'

Bland wondered if there was anything suspect about the reddish glint in the sergeant's eyes. It mightn't just be a devotion to cheap Estalian wine. A question would have to be asked about Sergeant Johannes Munch.

A Clause 17 sympathiser in the Old Town Watch had sent a runner to the Temple of Morr with word of the suspect slaying. Bland had known straight away that this marked the start in earnest of the campaign. Everything else had just been preliminary. With a quivering sense of purpose, Bland had rallied his core team – Liesel, undeadslayers Preiss and Bruin – and held a brief prayer circle, then hastened over to the site of the homicide. The Temple Father had taken resolute charge of the situation, ordering Dibble, the cloddish watchman who had first tripped over the dead man, to fetch the Sergeant with Special Responsibility. The pockmarked Munch was initially hard to locate because he was 'at choir practice' – an accepted euphemism for getting blind drunk while telling lies about old cases down at The Blue Lantern, the coppers' tavern.

Munch didn't seem to feel this particular man-slaying worth interrupting a good Filthy Harald anecdote over. Bland, expecting as much, had gone over the watchman's head and summoned a specialist from private practice. Her carriage had just arrived and she was crossing the street.

'Now we shall see some progress,' Bland announced.

Rosanna Ophuls, scryer-for-hire, slid between Munch and Liesel, then took a casual glance at the dead man.

'Throat torn out with a docker's hook,' she said. 'Gang killing. Fifteen crowns please, Temple Father.'

Bland knew Ophuls was wrong.

This was the Street of a Hundred Taverns. And among those hundred was the Crescent Moon, notorious haunt of the vermin undead. It was a problem to determine exactly where the establishment was, though Bland didn't believe the rumours that the Crescent Moon shifted its physical building nightly. Just as soon as the place hung up a sign visible to proper human eyes, he would have the damned haunt of noxious evil closed down and put to the torch.

If you let the leeches run loose, this was what happened.

The dead man's wound was ragged and dry, black rather than red. His eyes were open, frozen in terror.

The scryer stood with her arms folded, tapping her foot. Bland judged her for an irritating person, a woman who would never show the commitment necessary for the campaign. It was time for another proclamation from the Cult of Morr, against the 'nay-saying ninnies' who heeded not 'the dangers of the dark'. He made a mental note to have Liesel work something up. With the campaign in full boom, the cult's scribe-proclaimer was busier and busier.

'With respect to your professional abilities, Miss Ophuls, might not a second glance – indeed, a proper scrying – reveal that this is merely *supposed* to look like a gang killing?'

The woman looked down at the dead person.

'Surely, the bloodlusting fiend, consumed by the madness of his or her red thirst, fell on this poor – indeed, innocent – soul and drained him dry, then used a hook or some other such implement to cover up the crime, to cast suspicion elsewhere.'

Ophuls wasn't convinced. She was not doing the job she expected to be paid for.

'You haven't even touched him,' Bland said.

'She doesn't really need to, Temple Father,' said Munch. 'That "poor – indeed, innocent – soul" is Ibrahim Fleuchtweig, war chief of the Fish. Last week, three Hooks were trussed up and thrown in the Reik. On his orders. This is an escalation of the feud. If a Fish is hooked, or a Hook drowned, it doesn't take a divining witch – no offence, Rosie – to tell you who's responsible.'

'The sergeant is right, sir,' said Dibble. 'We all know Ibby the Fish in the Tavern Watch. A warrant was out for him in connection with the murders of Nosy the Cripple, Josten the Grabber and Dirk the Dirk.'

'Don't think I'm convinced by all these ridiculous names,' said Bland. 'You make them up to suggest your squalid calling is glamorous.'

Ophuls shrugged and made a *pfui* sound.

'You're being paid – indeed, well-paid – to do a job,' Bland insisted. 'Now get down in the gutter and scry.'

She looked at Bland as if she were exceeding her brief and trying to divine something about *him*. Then, she made a decision.

'Very well. Stand back, lads. I don't want your sins crowding in.'

Everyone except Bland moved away sharply, giving Ophuls a clear circle around the dead man to work in.

'You too, Temple Father.'

He naturally hadn't assumed she included him.

Arranging a muffler on the cobbles so she could kneel, Ophuls took off her mittens and rubbed her hands together.

'Cold night,' she said. 'Have to get some feeling in.'

She flexed her fingers and waved her hands hocus-pocus fashion over the corpse. She touched him, patting his jacket first and working towards the mess around his neck. Closing her eyes, she put her hands on the wound.

Bland's skin crawled. There was something not human about scryers. The undead had a knack for *knowing*, too. This woman might not drink blood, but she'd bear watching. Better to be safe than sorry, and one could always apologise afterwards.

'I sense a lot of drinking.'

Munch snickered. Bland gave him a nasty look that shut him up. There was no room for levity when a vampire attack was being detected.

'A *lot* of drinking. Bugman's Six-X. Enough to float a river-barge and addle a thaumaturgy professor. An enormously full bladder. A stagger into the alleyway behind Bruno's Brewhouse. A flash in the dark. Something sharp?'

'Fangs?'

She shook her head and let the corpse alone. 'A docker's hook, as used by the Hooks, the dockyard gang notoriously at war with the Fish, the dockyard gang to which the deceased was affiliated.'

He didn't like her tone of voice. She was pulling her mittens back on.

'You can't be certain.'

'No one can be *certain*, Temple Father, but you hired a scryer so you could get closer to certain than you were. You have had my professional opinion. If you want some free advice on top of that, you should take my word as being as near certain as you're likely to get.'

'Why is the corpse so pale? Indeed, bloodless?'

She looked up at the moons and down at the dead face. For a moment she was quiet, seeing something.

'This is the way the dead look,' she said, closing the corpse's eyes with her fingertips. 'Empty and abandoned.'

'At the Temple of Morr, we are quite familiar with the dead,' said Liesel. 'It is our duty to reverence the broken vessel to ease the path of the departing spirit. And to dispose of the vessel lest it be refilled by something unholy and unclean.'

Ophuls stood up and wrapped her muffler around her neck.

'If that's settled, Temple Father,' said Munch, 'you can do the job you're supposed to and cart Ibby away now. His gang-buddies have already forgotten him and won't claim the body, so it's up to you to get it off the cobbles.'

Thanks to the Sanitation Bill, the temple had to be alerted about any sudden death. Bland had been keeping an eye out for suspect reports like this one. He knew how the body should be served.

Bland wasn't ready to let go yet.

'What did you see?' he asked Ophuls.

'I beg your pardon, Temple Father?'

'Just then. You scried something.'

'Nothing important. Just the scrap of a life. It's odd what people think about when they're dying.'

'Their families?'

Bland thought of his dear wife and three lovely children.

'Sometimes. Mostly it's stuff you can't understand. Personal things they couldn't explain even if you could ask them. And sometimes it's random, as if they wanted to be distracted from the business of dying. Ibby thought it had turned cold all of a sudden. How's that for a way to spend your final seconds? Grumbling about the weather?'

Bland shook his head and raised a finger. 'You scry but you don't *see*. Think on what she said the dead man thought. "It had turned cold *all of a sudden*." Unnatural cold. They travel about inside their own evil clouds sometimes. They can become black fog or white mist and creep up on their victims. The undead. This proves – indeed, conclusively proves – what I've been saying all along. This was a vampire killing.'

Ophuls began to say something, but he continued, silencing her.

'They've been biding their time, waiting for a chance to strike at me. Ever since I showed my colours. They know I'm their enemy – indeed, their destroyer. This is the beginning of a war, a war between the living and the dead. It's the von Carstein days all over again. You'll all have to decide which side you're on and Morr help you if you go against the live and holy.'

Dibble scratched his head under his helmet.

Ophuls was frightened now, shrinking away from him. Good. What did she see? That he was right, of course.

'The dead are dangerous. The Cult of Morr will take over now. Preiss, you know the procedure.'

The tall cleric muscled through and stood over the dead man.

'Don't think you'll be rising again to bedevil the living,' vowed Preiss.

The cleric raised his staff and sank the sharpened end into the rib-cage. Bland heard the point scrape cobbles. It was important to transfix the dead thing to the ground. Most people got it wrong and thought it was enough to sink a stake into the heart or spear the undead standing up. Impalement was merely a preliminary binding, fixing the monster – potential monster, in this case – to the holy earth. Preiss leant on his staff with all his weight, digging between the cobbles. It wasn't easy, which is why the cult had acolytes like Preiss, a former pupil of Hage-dorn the wrestler, on hand.

'That's disgusting,' whined Munch.

'Disgusting,' snapped Bland. 'I'll tell you what's disgusting. A grave-rotted thirsty monster glutting itself fat on the blood of your lovely children or dear old grandma. That's what's disgusting.'

'Leave it alone,' said Ophuls, quietly.

'Not until the job's done.'

'But it's an old wives' tale that all those killed by vampires rise as vampires themselves. Sire vampires turn their get by the Dark Kiss. That means they give their own altered blood to favoured victims as they drink from them.'

'So you admit that this was a vampire killing?'

Ophuls threw her hands up.

'You can go now,' said Bland. 'Your part in this is over.'

Liesel took Ophuls by the elbow and steered her away. 'Present your chit at the Temple of Morr after one o'clock tomorrow,' said the scribe-proclaimer, 'and your price will be met in full, less Imperial tax.'

Preiss had Ibrahim Fleuchtweig fully skewered. He gave the nod to Braun, who came in with his silver-bladed axe and hacked off the corpse's head. It took a few blows and some sawing.

'You might have ruined a good evening's wine-bibbing,' said Munch, 'but I can't complain that the clerics of Morr don't lay on any entertainment. Ibby has been more thoroughly killed than any other corpse I've seen this month.'

'It's not done yet,' Liesel told him. 'The Temple Father must perform a final rite.'

Bland pulled on thick leather gauntlets. He picked up the startled-looking head, then stuffed its mouth with garlic taken from a pouch on his belt.

'Unclean undead spirit, I cast thee out.'

Liesel made a lightning sketch, preserving the moment of triumph.

'Could you hold the head up higher, Temple Father? Get the light from the streetlamp. And could Brother Preiss step out of the way? There, that's perfect.'

By tomorrow, Liesel's sketch would be copied and posted all over the city. Woodcuts would be sent to all the broadsheets, and this time they would have to run the pictures. Until now, the campaign had consisted only of speeches and dull legal matters. This was news, and news was what the vulgar masses craved above all else.

Everyone in the Empire would soon know that Antiochus Bland had personally prevented Ibrahim Fleuchtweig's rising from the dead as an unhallowed thing intent upon stalking the innocent. The Temple Father didn't care a jot for the glory of the deed, but he knew every holy campaign needed its leaders, its heroes. The people needed his example.

When Liesel was done, he dropped the head and left final disposal – hauling the thing away in the cart and its immolation in the eternally-burning corpse fires of the temple – to Preiss and Braun.

'That's another leech up the chimney, Temple Father,' said Liesel.

Bland was proud of himself, proud of his cult, proud of his purpose.

V

Now she was cleaned up and dressed, Detlef thought the vampire looked even younger. Eva Savinien was tall: her 'Genevieve' costume made the real woman seem like Little Orphan Elsie dressed in a grown-up's gown. Genevieve fussed with the belt and raised the hemline above her ankles.

'That's better,' she said. 'Now I don't have to wade.'

Detlef knew he was scratching his bites.

The fact that Genevieve was back was enormous. It could change anything, or mean nothing. He was tantalised, which was doubtless the point. In vampire terms, a ten-year absence might be the equivalent of him nipping out for a pouch of ready-rubbed from the tobacco merchant on Luitpoldstrasse and dawdling a bit in a café on the way back. Genevieve might move back in here for good and give in and marry him, but she might also disappear before the 'platz clock struck midnight and never think of him again.

That wasn't fair. She thought of him, obviously.

She was here.

She moved swiftly about the room, doing that vampire act of shifting at speed between languid poses so that she seemed to vanish and appear all over the place. It was a habit of hers when she was excited. Or just-fed. She kept asking questions about mutual friends and acquaintances.

'And young Prince Luitpold, how is he?'

'Otherwise engaged for our first night, it seems. Tio Bland is listened to at the palace.'

'That's their loss. I'd thought better of the boy.'

'Not a boy any more. He looks like a juvenile lead.'

'I hope they let him have some fun before marrying him off to Clothilde of Averheim.'

'He's rather taken with Eva.'

Genevieve laughed, like music. Detlef recalled she had never warmed to Eva Savinien. It was understandable: while possessed by something left behind by the Great Enchanter, Eva had tried to kill them both.

'Eva plays me, I gather.'

'She's very good. Got over that whole brouhaha with the animus and the Trapdoor Daemon. She's undoubtedly the best you since, well, since you.'

'I am retired from the stage. I had a very limited range. I could only play myself.'

'That's the story with half the great stars of the theatre.'

She settled in the chair that had been warmed by Temple Father Bland.

Reality crept back. He had been dazzled a while by the delight of having her here. Now he remembered the danger.

'Gené, you know it's not safe in the city for, ah, people like you.'

'Bretonnian girls? That's not news. Our governesses tell us from infancy about the perils awaiting in Altdorf for innocent mademoiselles fresh off the barge.'

'Vampires, Gené. This Clause 17 business...'

'Whose bloody silly idea was that? I tell you, if I'd signed a petition in favour of it I'd be utterly ashamed and prostrate with apology.'

She peeped out at him from under a curtain of drying hair.

'You're teasing.'

'You're scowling. Wind'll change and your face'll set.'

'Not my face. I'm a master of disguise. You're the one who can't change her looks.'

She made a vampire mask, flared eyebrows and fangs.

'See, I'm a monster. Fit only to be ashes or under the ground.'

Then she poked her tongue out.

'You could have stayed in the forests, or gone back to that convent at the other end of the world. All this would have passed and you'd be safe again.'

Suddenly, she was serious.

'Detlef, I've had enough of hiding, of being safe. What if Glinka's moral crusade came back and all theatrical performances were prohibited? Do you think you'd be happy in a monastery waiting for it to pass? You know you'd organise plays in the back-rooms of inns and woodland clearings and anywhere you could gather an audience. If they sent you to the headsman for being an actor, you'd deliver a soliloquy from the block and wouldn't shut up for a full fifteen minutes after the axe had fallen. It's like that with me. I can't pretend I'm what I'm not.'

'You weren't always a vampire.'

'Like you weren't always an actor. I was a child once. Most of us were. Now I'm... well... I'm...'

'Genevieve Sandrine de Pointe du Lac Dieudonné.'

'You remember all of it. Darling, you're the only one who does.'

She was over the desk and in his lap. His mouth was on hers, carefully. He remembered how to kiss her without getting cut open.

'You're still thirsty,' he whispered, 'not for beef tea.'

'I can't ask you for that,' she said, suddenly sounding old.

'You can't ask me to let you starve.'

Her forehead wrinkled as he pulled his collar away from his neck.

'Gené, bite me. You won't really have come back until you do.'

She pulled away from him, wiped her hair out of her face and looked close into his eyes, running her fingernails across the furrows around his temples and into his hair. Her face was in shadow, but her eyes shone green as the southern sea.

'You haven't changed,' she said.

She pounced like a cat and her teeth slipped into his neck.

He held her tight as his blood pulsed into her mouth, feeling her ribs with his elbows, his hands knotted in her hair.

He told her he loved her. She murmured and he knew what she meant.

VI

Detlef's office wasn't a boudoir. Genevieve knew he wouldn't have a divan in there, he was fed up with jokes about eager young actresses and the casting couch. They would have to make do with his padded chair and the broad top of the desk.

Without detaching her mouth from his rich throat, she slid out of her loose dress and helped him with his clothes. There was more of him than she remembered, and he complained about his back when she dragged him out of the chair, but nothing had changed between them.

She couldn't keep her hands off him, though she had to be careful about her talons. It was too easy to get carried away.

'This is the second most impressive organ of maleness I've got a hold on this evening,' she said.

He looked at her oddly.

'Wrong time for that story,' she admitted.

'You can't expect me to let it lie at a time like this,' he said. 'Look at it from my position.'

'I'm not naked flat on my back on a desk with a vampire nuzzling my throat.'

Surprisingly, with the agility of his old stage heroes, Detlef heaved her off him and reversed their positions, pinning her like a wrestler. He carefully lowered himself onto her and started tickling the hollow of her own throat with his beard.

'This torture continues until you talk, vampire wench.'

She laughed and gave in. 'I had to climb the statue of Sigmar in the 'platz.'

'Oh no, not the one with the enormous–'

'Oh yes. That one.'

'Holy hammer of Sigmar!'

'Absolutely.'

Then, with an ease that comes from practice, his own hammer struck her anvil.

With his blood in her, she was stronger, faster, better. But it was his life that infused her, the peppery tang of everything that he was. When younger, he used to introduce himself as 'Detlef Sierck, genius'. Then, it had been a defence against criticism. Now, when he mostly passed himself off as a hack, it was true. She tasted the poetry he hadn't yet written.

Most of the night passed. Detlef dozed between exertions, but she became more awake as moonlight shone in through the office window.

'You've not said why you're here,' he murmured.

'In Altdorf? In the Vargr Breughel?'

'Both. Either.'

'Don't be upset, but I came to see someone who isn't you.'

He was fully awake again. She'd known that would sting.

'There's someone *else*?'

'Not like that. Believe me, there's no one else like you. Strange as it seems, you come along only once in even a lifetime like mine. I've come to see another vampire. A very important one.'

'Here?'

He looked around, shivering.

'Uh-huh,' she said. 'Under your own roof, passing for alive.'

'Impossible!'

He got off the desk and began pulling on his trews. She whipped into the dress. Vampire swiftness took the drudgery out of all those dozens of little hooks and buttons. She was dressed before he could get to his smock, and helped him into it like a mother with a baby.

'It's that Sylvanian scene-shifter, isn't it?' blurted Detlef.

'No, no, Renastic isn't the vampire who sent for me.'

They weren't alone in the room. Genevieve wasn't sure when the other had crept in. For modesty's sake, she hoped it had only been within the last few minutes.

'It's about time, granddaughter-in-darkness,' said the high, familiar voice.

Genevieve looked at a shadowed corner and there she was. Her little face was silvered in the moonlight.

'Elsie?' blurted Detlef, aghast. 'Little Orphan Elsie?'

'I'd best make an introduction,' said Genevieve. 'This is the sire of my sire, the Lady Melissa d'Acques. She's an elder, one of the senior vampires of the Known World.'

'You're t-t-twelve,' sputtered Detlef. 'That's what you said. And you lost your parents in a coach accident.'

'I'm well over eleven hundred, actually. And I did lose my parents in a coach accident, only it happened a very long time ago. I've quite got over it. Most important things happened long enough ago for me to get over them. But I'm fed up with all the fetching and carrying you and that goat Fritz have had me do these last weeks, while I was waiting for my dear grand-get to arrive. It's sheer exploitation of child labour, that's what it is.'

Detlef lay back down on the desk and covered his eyes.

'I don't know why he's so upset,' said Lady Melissa. 'I let you love-bats have enough canoodling-time together before pushing in so we can get on with the matter for which I summoned you.'

'I'm dreaming,' he said. 'This isn't happening.'

'Don't mind him,' Genevieve told Lady Melissa. 'He's a genius. You have to make allowances.'

'We didn't have geniuses in my day.'

Detlef groaned.

Genevieve swept the very old lady up in her arms and danced her around the room like a real little girl. Lady Melissa was all right if you could get her to smile and be playful for a while. When she was serious, people tended to die.

'I've missed you too, grand-mama,' she said, kissing Lady Melissa's cold cheek.

VII

'We missed you at the last gathering,' the Lady Melissa told her grand-get. 'Elder vampires from all over the Known World were represented at the Convent of Eternal Night and Solace.'

The girl had the decency to look a touch guilty. Her fat human pet was merely puzzled. Melissa knew it was rarely much use explaining anything to shortlivers. In this case, she would probably have to spell it out letter by letter: a daywalking serf was sadly going to be a necessity.

'I was travelling, grand-mama. I didn't receive my invitation until it was too late.'

She knew better than to credit that, but didn't mind.

'I can't blame you, child. There's nothing more *boring* than a gathering of elder vampires. Believe me, I've suffered enough of them in my centuries. All those long grey faces and ragged black cloaks. The stag-at-rut jousts as two old fools get in a squabble about some mortal morsel. You hear the same stories over and over. Mostly, yarns about how we didn't really lose the Undead Wars blah blah blah and are just biding our time before we emerge from our mountain fastnesses and take up rightful positions as rulers of humanity blah blah blah fountains of virgin blood as our right delivered up by the unworthy blah blah blah enough to make you stuff your ears with wax and spend a century sulking in a tomb hoping the prattle will end.'

Sierck was still looking strangely at her. She bugged her eyes out back at him and he flinched.

'Pity the poor little orphan, sirrah,' she said in her squeaky, whiny Elsie voice. All these supposed theatre folk around and no one had seen through her. 'I've had to chase rats, you know. This hasn't been easy for me.'

'I'm terribly sorry, ah, my lady.'

'And well you might be, shortlife. But you're just a blood-cow. You'll be gone in a few years.'

'Grand-mama!' Genevieve was shocked.

'Don't chide your elders, child. It's very unbecoming. I'm sorry to have to hurt your feelings, Herr Genius, but there's no point pretending, is there? Then again, I suppose pretending is what you mostly do. Oh, I can't be bothered with this being-polite-to-the-food business. Genevieve, we'll have to deal with this Tio Bland fellow ourselves. The cattle won't be any help at all. And you never know when they'll turn on you. They're your devoted slaves one moment and chasing you with sharp sticks the next. Did I ever tell you about that witch-hunter in Quenelles in the time of the Red Pox? Of course I did. No need to be kind about it. I tell the same stories too many times, just like all the other cobwebbed elder vampire bores.'

'Is she always like this?' Sierck asked.

Genevieve nodded. 'Isn't she adorable?'

'Less of that cheek, child,' Melissa snapped. 'Where was I? Ah, yes. The gathering. This Clause 17 nonsense was much debated. Elder Honorio is concerned, and you know how unflappable he is. Baron Wietzak of Karak Varn chewed through a stone table. He actually did it. I saw the bite he took out of the thing. Ugly table, actually. dwarf manufacture. Have you noticed how they deliberately make the legs too short for humans? Just right for me, though. So hard cheese to their nasty little schemes. I'm babbling, am I not? That's what comes of being Little Orphan Elsie for weeks and weeks.'

Sierck's mouth was an O of astonishment.

'I take it back,' said Genevieve. 'She's not usually this bad.'

'I'm not usually trying to save vampirekind from extinction.'

Melissa sensed a rat behind the books on one of the shelves, little heart beating at ramming speed, warm blood pulsing through its thready veins.

'Excuse me,' she said. 'Some of us have to make do.'

She was across the room and back in a beat, having ferreted the furry creature out and even rearranged the books in order. She sensed the animal's panic and looked into its glittering eyes, ordering its tiny brain to go to sleep and not mind what was going to happen next.

She popped the rat into her mouth and ate it whole.

Then she dabbed her lips with a kerchief, looking to Genevieve for approval. Without mirrors, vampires had to rely on each other when it came to presenting a face to the human world.

'A scrap on the upper lip.'

Melissa dabbed.

'There,' said Genevieve. 'Got it. You look pretty as a picture again.'

Genevieve chucked Sierck's chin and finally shut his mouth.

'The starving cats,' he said. 'You're the reason why they haven't been eating well.'

'Kitty-kitties are overrated,' she said. 'Your ratters were fat and lazy. I'll have to start on them once the rats run out. So be warned. Unless, Herr Kind Genius, you'd care to open a vein for a poor little orphan without a friend in the world.'

'Now now, grand-mama, none of that.'

Melissa stuck out her lower lip.

'You were talking about saving vampirekind from extinction.'

'So I was, child. Very conscientious of you to remind me.'

'Who are all these people she's talking about?' asked Sierck. 'It's as if I've come in on the fifth act.'

'I've told you about the Convent of Eternal Night and Solace,' Genevieve told the human. 'The retreat for vampires in the World's Edge Mountains. Elder Honorio is the master there.'

'A very old-womanish sort of master,' sniped Melissa.

'You are hardly one to throw that accusation at anyone.'

'What's a gathering?'

'Just what it sounds like,' Genevieve explained. 'Elder vampires *gathering* together for a set period. It's not that different from the drinking, hunting and yarning festivals the League of Karl-Franz or any other fraternal organisation throws at any opportunity.'

'Drinking and hunting?' Sierck looked stricken.

'You've upset him, child.'

'Shush, grand-mama. Detlef knows what vampires are like. Just because Tio Bland is an idiot doesn't mean that some, and I mean *some*, of us aren't bloodthirsty barbarians. Sadly, Kattarin wasn't that atypical of vampirekind.'

Melissa remembered the tsarina well. She had been fond of bathing in the blood of her courtiers' children. Anyone could see that was excessive and would lead to trouble.

'I told your sire not to make get of that Kislevite princess, child. Kattarin had a daemon in her before she was turned. But would Chandagnac listen? None of you fledgling vampires heeds your sire. That's something I agree with Honorio about. If you had respect for tradition none of this would have happened. Now, about this assassination plot against Tio Bland...'

Sierck gasped again, tiresomely.

'The pair of you are here to assassinate Tio Bland?'

Trust a human to get the wrong end of the stake.

'Merciful Shallya no,' said Melissa. 'We're here to *stop* him being assassinated.'

The rat-tail twisted in her stomach and she burped.

'I do beg your pardon,' she said. The back of her throat clogged and she began to cough. 'It all comes from the wrong diet.'

She hacked and spat a hairball out on the back of her hand. She was ready to scrape it off on the wall, but Genevieve hemmed and pointed at the waste-paper basket. Exaggeratedly, Melissa tidied the ball up and disposed of it properly.

'Happy now?'

'That's better, grand-mama. No need to make a mess.'

Unlike Genevieve, Melissa d'Acques had sired prodigiously. Over the centuries, she'd made over a hundred sons-in-darkness. They had given her grand-get without count. But they'd mostly drifted, finding their own paths through life and death, barely remembering that she still lived. Too many of her bloodline had listened to the Counts von Carstein and wound up destroyed in the Undead Wars or the persecutions.

Genevieve wasn't the sole survivor of Melissa's line, that of the great Lahmia, but she was the nearest thing the old woman had to family in the human sense. She thought that without Genevieve she would no longer take an interest in the affairs of the world, and for that connection she was grateful.

It was all very well to retreat into contemplation like Elder Honorio or lose oneself in the red thirst like Kattarin, but it wasn't living. And being undead meant you still lived, no matter what the vampire-haters might say.

She looked at Genevieve and Sierck.

'It was Wietzak's fool idea,' Melissa said. 'He actually wants another Undead War. He is claiming kinship to that Sylvanian rabble. He went to his keep at Karak Varn, to terrorise the peasants and raise up bands of strigoi warriors. You know what strigoi vampires are like, my dear. No finesse at all. Just mindless mouths on legs, purpose-made footsoldiers. The von Carsteins relied too much on them, and we all know where that led. Baron Wietzak has decreed that all enemies of vampirekind should be smitten down blah blah blah terrible vengeance against the human upstart who dares bibbledy-babbledy-boo sure and certain swift angel of painful death and so forth.'

'Wietzak is here?' asked Genevieve. 'Stalking Tio Bland?'

'He's not that mad. No, he's sent assassins. Or hired some local leech to do the job for him. He's not short of a golden hoard or two.'

'You won't find me grieving for Bland,' said Sierck. 'Death will shut the little stoat up, if nothing else will.'

That had occurred to Melissa. Only a few hours ago, when the Temple Father gave her a pfennig and some blather about investment it had been all she could do not to sink her fangs into the soft pouch of flab beneath his chin and tear into a major artery. Still, she had to be reasonable about these things.

'You know that's not true, Detlef,' said Genevieve. 'If a vampire kills Bland, it will prove everything he's been saying about us. He might be dead, but his cause will be taken seriously. Others will fill his place, and they'll be a lot less clownlike. Have you ever heard of the Tsarevich Pavel Society?'

'Pavel was the one who did for Kattarin?' he asked.

'Eventually, yes. There's been a Kislevite society in his name ever since. Die-hard vampire haters in high positions. They'll be watching Bland, seeing how popular his message becomes. I was nearly impaled by a mob this evening. Imagine those same mobs with watchmen and men-at-arms and witchfinders in their midst, backed by the force of Imperial decree. It won't matter if a vampire is guilty, innocent or a monster, we'll all be ashes or under the ground. And I personally will probably be killed, against which I happen strongly to be.'

'Ah, me too,' agreed the overwhelmed human.

'Now that's settled,' said Melissa, 'how are you two going to go about saving this Bland person's miserable neck?'

VIII

A huge poster outside the Temple of Morr showed fearless vampire-slayer Tio Bland holding up an annoyed-looking, enormously-fanged and red-eyed severed head in triumph. A banner-line read 'Death to the dead!' and an engraving which was supposed to look like spontaneous graffiti declared 'Ashes or under the ground!'

A stuffed black bat child's plaything with big red eyes and comical teeth, was impaled against a board with a wooden spike, red paint splashed around the heart-wound, with dribbles artfully swirled to spell out 'Rule one: no leeches!' In the bright light of early afternoon, Genevieve thought yet again that she was never going to get away with this.

A pair of black-robed acolytes, just like the thugs who had roughed up the silk-merchant yesterday, guarded the temple door. They seemed to be comparing the length of their weapons.

'I tell you, Willy, if a vampire attacked here and now, I would bring my silver-headed pike to bear and have its heart out in a trice.'

'Very impressive, Walther, but I'd have shoved my silver-bladed knife through the selfsame heart in half-a-trice.'

'That's as might be, but within the merest quarter-trice, I'd have...'

She could foresee where this conversation was going.

'Begging your leave, worshipful sirs,' she began, putting on an accent, 'be this the Temple of Morr?'

The temple-shaped building was jet-black, had a statue of the God of Death on the roof, was covered in symbols of Morr and had 'TEMPLE OF MORR' engraved in gold over the doorway.

'It might be,' said Willy the Knife. 'It depends on who's asking?

'I be Jenny Godgift, come from far Wissenland.'

She did a little giggle thing in the back of her throat and rolled her eyes.

'That's a long journey for such a pretty little thing,' said Walther the Pike. 'You must have a good pair of legs under you.'

Genevieve brayed like an Estalian donkey, laughing through her nose.

'You be makin' me blush, illustrious personages. That be not kindly nor clever neither.'

Her cheeks were rouged to simulate blushing. Vampires couldn't redden with embarrassment, which was why dabs of rosiness here and there made such a useful disguise. Anyone might take her for a living human if they didn't look too closely. Detlef, master of all the theatrical arts, had been meticulous in applying a thin, subtle coat of face-paint. Her vampire pallor was covered, and she looked like a girl who had spent a lot of time outdoors in the sun. The strangest part of it had been sitting still in front of a dressing room mirror, seeing her long-lost face re-appear in ghost-form as Detlef layered make-up over her unreflecting skin. Did she really look like that? With a wig and lipstick, her reflection seemed complete – except for the socket-like eyeholes. She wouldn't pass a real looking-glass inspection, but if she happened to walk past a mirror – there were bound to be many in the temple – she'd at least not appear as a walking empty dress.

'Be this where the brave vampire-slayers work?' she asked.

She was sure she was overdoing it, but Detlef said an actor should never be afraid of the obvious. Most real people weren't. Witness: Willy and Walther, the comedy relief guards.

The clerics smiled indulgently at her. Genevieve let her lashes flutter. Thanks to facepaint on the eyelid, one of her eyes stuck shut. She got it open again before anyone noticed.

'Mistress Godgift,' said Willy, 'you need not fear the undead in this district.'

She made the signs of as many gods as she could remember, which came perilously close to an arm-dance.

'Gods be thanked,' she said. 'I've a powerful loathing for the undead in all their evil forms. I've come to join up.'

'Acolytes of Morr have to be apprenticed in childhood,' said Walther. 'Then work in a mortuary for two full years, pass exams in funerary rites, then…'

'But I wish only to slay the vampire creatures. Temple Father Bland must be endangered all the hours of the day and night, from bloodsucking fiends out to silence his holy pure words of justice. I am minded that one such as he needs a personal bodyguard.'

'I'm sure you mean well, mistress. But it takes more than a good heart.'

'I be practiced. I be very adept in all the latest techniques of vampire-slaying.'

Willy and Walther, a bit bored with her eager country girl act, shrugged at each other.

'I know how to put silver needles in their eyes.'

Willy looked a bit queasy at the thought.

'Leave your name with the mother superior's assistant,' said Walther, 'and a place where you can be reached by messenger. I'm sure we'll be in touch.'

'Be you brushing me off?'

Willy laughed uncomfortably. 'Not at all, Mistress Godgift.'

'Be you giving me the once-around-the-hayricks-and-left-in-the-spinney treatment?'

Walther was more to the point. 'We're on duty. We're much too important to deal with the likes of you.'

'Do you really think you be bravos enough to protect Antiochus Bland?'

She was worried that her country girl accent had turned abruptly piratical.

The guards were too annoyed to care. Willy tapped his knife-hilt, only it wasn't there. Genevieve held it up, careful not to touch the silver blade. She had lifted it from him with a swift grasp.

'Looking for this?'

Willy's face was dark. Walther's pike arced down. When its point scraped cobbles, Genevieve was out of its way. She had stood to one side, and had her foot poised to stamp down. She neatly snapped the pikeshaft.

'What if a vampire did that, sirs? What then?'

A few passersby stopped to pay attention. Willy and Walther liked that even less than having their toys taken away.

This was where she could use all those Celestial fighting arts she had studied under Master Po. A few passes of mantis style *gungfu*, and she'd be inside the temple and secure in her new job of bodyguard-in-chief to the Empire's most notorious vampire-hater. She reminded herself not to use teeth or claws. That would be a dead giveaway.

'Two schillings on the foreign wench,' said a gambler.

Genevieve would have bet on herself. Then someone barged out of the temple. He had to bend down to get under the lintel of the main door.

'Your two and raise you two,' said another gambler. 'That's Lupo Preiss, the wrestler.'

Oh wonderful. Genevieve gave up a silent lament for the days when clerics were reedy fellows with candlewax on their cuffs and weak eyes from too much reading. Back then, she could have trounced a whole temple-load of them without resorting to mantis-style. Sloth-style would have done.

'A crown on Brother Preiss,' went up the cry.

Genevieve's original champion muttered, 'Too rich for me.'

'What is this racket?' declared Brother Preiss.

'Mistress Nuisance is trying to force her way in,' said Willy No Knife.

'She says her name is Jenny Godgift,' said Walther the Half-Pike.

'I just feel Temple Father Bland should be properly protected,' she insisted.

Brother Preiss hefted up his sleeves and cracked his knuckles. He had the sort of hands that suggested he crushed rocks to powder to keep in trim.

'She damaged temple property,' whined Walther, holding up his broken pike.

'And stole some too,' moaned Willy.

Genevieve gave Willy his knife back. He made a play of cleaning its blade on his sleeve.

'Do you still want to fight, girl?' asked Preiss.

'I be a humble supplicant from far-off Wissen–'

Preiss took her by the shoulders and lifted her off the ground. Some of the crowd gasped. Genevieve wished she were back in Konigplatz with the vampire-killing mob. At least they were amateurs.

She turned in Preiss's grip, shrugging out of his fingers, and dropped to the ground. Taking her best shot first, she pivoted in her sprawl like a gypsy dancer, getting her shoulder and elbows against the cobbles so she could concentrate all the strength of her body into the tensed muscles of her right leg. She propelled a kick into Preiss's stomach.

Her boot-toe took him low, doubling him over.

She had to be fast to get out of the way as the ex-wrestler fell to his knees. Some bets started changing again. She made axe-blades of her fingers, a Nipponese trick Master Po had been fond of, and chopped down on Preiss's neck. His cowl protected him, but he must have felt the blow. She had to hop to avoid his grasping hand. If he got his fingers around any part of her, he wouldn't lose his grip a second time.

Honourably, she stood back and let Brother Preiss stand up.

An evil vampire would have kicked him in the head while he was down. She gave herself a gold star for being good, and hoped someone remembered her Shallya-like mercy at her funeral.

Preiss didn't show any sign of being hurt, though she must have given him at least a tummy-bruise with her first kick. She still felt the jarring of her foot against his packed-in meat, as if her leg-bones were jellied by the impact. The cleric was a trained fighter, which meant he didn't make the mistake of getting angry.

'Why are we wasting energy scrapping?' she asked. 'Surely, we all hate vampires. Nasty dead-alive things spewn from the grave to bedevil good folk such as we.'

Preiss made fists and came at her with a left-right-left hook-jab-jab combination. She leaned out of the first blows, but the third caught her on the forehead – she was sure he was aiming at her chin – and she staggered back.

Her first panicked thought was that her face-paint would have come off on his knuckles, but luckily her well-fixed wig had a fringe appropriate for her country girl disguise.

There were at least thirty-eight points on the male human body where a simple pass with her vampire talons or fangs would tap into wells of blood, leading within seconds to the loss of any capability of fighting back or even of life itself. Preiss left nine, or possibly ten, points totally unguarded. A vampire could easily take down the wrestling cleric and win herself supper into the bargain.

But she couldn't afford to fight like a vampire.

Remembering Master Po, she hooked her arms up and advanced, mantis style.

'She's a loony,' sneered Willy.

Preiss shook his head, knowing better. He assumed the correct defensive stance, right forearm out horizontally in front like a bar, left hand fisted and close to the stomach.

At the last moment, she switched to dragonclaw-style.

That got past his guard. She thumped him just above the ear, then again in the larynx. And her knee got to his side. She felt the impact again, but heard Preiss grunt as he took a blow to the kidney.

Judging at high-speed, she knew where to put her feet as she got her shoulder into Preiss's side where she had just kneed him. Then, with a strain on her own neck and spine, she lifted him off the ground. This was his own trick – wrestling, Hagedorn-style. She tossed him up and slammed him down.

Then she got a knee on his throat and her elbow poised over the bridge of his nose.

He said nothing but patted the ground three times.

She sprang away from him and bowed. There was some applause, but she kept her eyes on the ground. Preiss took his time about getting up, careful of his bruises. Willy and Walther busied themselves dispersing the crowd. Genevieve heard the clinking of coins passed from losers to winners. She regretted not having a slice of her own action.

'Brother Preiss,' she said. 'My humble apologies. I came here not to do any soul harm, but rather to prevent a great man – Temple Father Bland – from coming to harm.'

'She said she wanted to be Temple Father's bodyguard,' said Willy.

Preiss looked her up and down. Genevieve assumed the wrestler would not be disposed to like her. Then he smiled and she was horrified to realise that, contrary to expectation, Preiss liked her *quite a lot*. She gathered no woman had ever served him as she had. He found the novelty stimulating in all sorts of ways she didn't want to think about.

'Get Mistress Godgift a proper habit for a Temple Sister,' said Preiss. 'And tell mother superior to find her a place to lay her head. Not too far from the centre cloister. I want her always close by, and Temple Father Bland will agree with me. Since last night, we are at war with the undead. This woman will be first among our warriors.'

Genevieve saluted.

IX

With *Genevieve and Vukotich* in rehearsal, the Vargr Breughel Theatre would have been dark but for Detlef's 'open-stage nights' policy. The programme of an evening was set aside for all those who fancied themselves entertainers – jesters and jugglers mostly – to come up, be introduced to the paying throng – other jesters and jugglers, mostly – and try out their acts. Most hopefuls only lasted a minute or so before a volley of last week's vegetables silenced their venerable jokes or croaked songs. They would slink off into the wings, covered in rotten cabbage, vowing to go back to the counting-house or the tannery and forget any notions they had nurtured about a life of wealth, fame and unlimited beautiful lovers on the stage. The theatre only charged a modest admission fee and let in those who chanced performing free of charge, but the canny business manager Guglielmo Pentangeli had struck an agreement with the farmers' market to take away all the unsaleable fruit and veg at the end of the day. This was then sold to amateur critics who got far more enjoyment from pelting the acts than watching them. After each open-stage night, produce was gathered from the backdrop and sold again, as fodder for the carriage-company stables in Hasselhoff Street.

This evening, Detlef was preoccupied. He performed his usual duties as Master of Ceremonies, setting up each poor and trembling act with a few brief and witty introductory remarks, but his thoughts were with Genevieve in the Temple of Morr. He tried to comfort himself by believing that Bland would assume no vampire would be insane enough voluntarily to walk into the one building in the city where they were most likely to be impaled, beheaded and consigned to the furnace. It wasn't much help.

Tonight's losers were even more pathetic than usual.

First up was a longshanks scholar from the University who did impressions of notable Imperial personages. He barely got into his satirical depiction of Konrad the Hero when an entire vegetable marrow burst against his face, hammering him against the backdrop. As the glowering Renastic dragged the insensible scholar offstage, Detlef supposed he should have mentioned that Konrad's Oath of Devotion Society was in the house tonight. Then came an Estalian guitarist with an enormous wave of oiled hair cockatoo-combed up over his forehead. He actually managed to finish his number without so much as a tomato, perhaps because the sweetness of his plucking was matched by the extreme obscenity of his lyrics. A magic act wasn't so lucky, and Renastic – whom Detlef still thought bore close-watching – had to rush out with a bucket of sand to smother the flames that had leaped from the wizard's brazier to his robes at the climax of his first and only trick.

The Three Little Clots, dwarfs in loud check jerkins and baggy trousers, came on and abused each other with eye-pokes, beard-tugs and mallet-blows to the skull for five minutes. They did each other more harm than any flung fruit and had the wit to work the audience attack into their routine – the bald-pated one with the knock-knees kept snatching thrown edibles out of the air and stuffing them into his mouth while the bespectacled one with an explosion of lightning-struck hair quipped that this was the best meal they could expect all month.

After that, Detlef sacrificed a string of stuttering jokesters, an old woman who tied inflated pig-bladders into strange shapes she claimed were animals, a temperance lecturer who mistakenly thought this was a fine opportunity to take his message to the masses, an elf who dressed as a human woman and propositioned sailors, another conjurer who made himself disappear and never came back and a dock-labourer who took off his shirt and did peculiar things with his stomach tattoos.

It was always a good idea to wind up with a sure winner, so he brought on Antonia Marsillach, who danced athletically, and sans much in the way of costuming, behind strategically-placed roc-feather fans. The Three Little Clots came back, to popular acclaim, and snatched away Antonia's fans, which they used to batter each other as the unblushing dancer outdid the stomach-writher in assuming unlikely positions and the audience expressed their appreciation with a hail of flowers.

'Good show tonight,' said Guglielmo as Detlef rushed past him backstage.

'Sign the Clots to a long-term contract, extend Antonia for another two weeks and ask the greasy guitarist to come in next week for a proper audition. I never want to see any of the others in here again.'

'It shall be done, *maestro*.'

Genius was all very well, but Detlef knew he'd be back in debtors' prison if it weren't for Guglielmo's knack of arranging matters to keep a flow of money coming in and a trickle of money going out.

He found Lady Melissa in his dressing room, sat in his favourite chair, feet dangling over the edge, sharpening her teeth against a bit of old bone.

'I hope you're proud of that, Herr Genius. Very edifying and educational, I'm sure.'

'We don't admit children on open-stage nights, Missy.'

'I don't see why not. There's precious little to engage the grown-up intellect or the finer sensitivities. Captain Tattoo was tasty, though.'

Detlef noticed a red smear on the old girl's lips. He was momentarily horror-struck.

'Don't worry,' she said. 'He was knocked unconscious by a turnip. I just tapped him a little. He'll wake up with such a throbbing head that he won't notice the healed-over wound. And don't call me "Missy".'

'What if the Illustrated Churl runs into one of Bland's Boyos? They check up on suspect neck-bites, *Missy*.'

'I doubt they bother with big toes, though.'

'There's a vein in the big toe?'

She held her thumb and forefinger almost together. 'Just a titchy one. Useful for supping on the sleeping. You just have to lift the far edge of the quilt and take a nuzzle.'

'I could cheerfully have lived the rest of my life without knowing that.'

'What about your own neck, Herr Genius? It bears the unmistakable seal of Mademoiselle Dieudonné.'

Detlef was changing into street-clothes. He picked a shirt with a dandyish ruff, and arranged it over his bites. Then, he buttoned a waistcoat up over his stomach and looked to the vampire for approval.

'It'll pass for humans. But another vampire will spot you for cattle from across the room.'

Detlef was alarmed.

'Don't worry,' she said. 'It's an advantage where we're going. You're marked as the property of a vampire lady. Young bloods will steer well clear of your veins.'

'*Property?*'

'Don't get huffy. It's no worse than the way you shortlivers talk about your mistresses or pets. And I'm sure Gené is as fond of you as you are of any stray dog or passing trollop.'

Detlef couldn't decide whether Melissa was a nasty old lady or a horrid little girl. She was either too old or too young to care for anyone's feelings but her own. She was very unlike her granddaughter-in-darkness. He realised that he had only ever known one vampire, and he had made the mistake of thinking the nightbreed were all like Genevieve. It was much the same as Tio Bland thinking vampires were all like the Counts von Carstein.

'And don't look so hurt,' Melissa sniped. 'You had me skivvying and scurrying without a thought for putting me in school or seeking out my family. It's all about masters and servants, bleeders and bled.'

'How long is it since you received a good spanking?'

Melissa swallowed shock and put on her orphan face.

'You wouldn't…'

'If we can't be civil to each other, then we won't find out, will we, my lady? Now, have we had word from Genevieve?'

Melissa took a tied scroll from her sleeve.

'A messenger came while you were on stage. She has risen rapidly within the Cult of Morr and gained employment as a bodyguard to that Bland fellow. Very enterprising.'

This was better than they had hoped. But Detlef still had an image of Genevieve surrounded by flaming torches, stakes, mirror and silver scythes.

'So, one of us is close to the target,' said Detlef. 'It's up to us to go out and scare up the assassin.'

Melissa slid off the chair. She was dressed up in another stage costume, from Tarradasch's tear-jerker *The Little Princess Sonja in Exile*. It
was the fur-trimmed hooded cloak from the cast-into-the-cold-cold-snows
scene. She had the little red foxfur boots as well.

She stuck out her grey-gloved hand, as if wanting to be escorted across
a busy street. He took her paw and led her up through the thronging
backstage corridors and out of the theatre. A crowd at the stage door
were petitioning the Three Little Clots for autographs on scraps of paper,
not caring that none of them could write. Detlef recognised the two disguised aristocrats who were competing for the affections of la Marsillach,
eyeing each other from behind domino masks and enormous bouquets
of Gris Mere blossoms.

'Old Detlef's taking them younger and younger,' jeered someone.

Detlef reddened. That was not an item he looked forward to appearing in the *Boulevardpresse*.

Melissa kicked the jeerer in the shin.

'How dare you be rude about my dear old uncle!'

'Sorry,' yelped the hopping man.

She kicked him in the other shin.

'So you should be.'

The jeerer fell over and the Three Little Clots laughed at him.

Detlef felt more much kindly towards his 'niece'.

X

So long as she kept quiet, Genevieve found it easy to seem like part of the traditional funereal statuary of the Temple of Morr. All around were reminders of the grave she had never found time to lie in: wreaths of black flowers, refectory tables shaped like tombs, marble urn soup tureens, chairs with gravestone backs and seats, mausoleum dormitories with cots like coffins, skullfaced-doorknobs, ossuary skirting boards. She had never seen a place so desperately in need of the cheery touch of an elf interior designer with a passion for bright orange and turquoise cushions and sweet little paintings of happy kittens and fat babies.

Brother Preiss had ordered her to stay always a few arms' lengths from the Temple Father and watch him like the proverbial Warhawk.

Within the Temple of Morr, acolytes were expected to show due deference and not speak unless a superior addressed them directly. She was relieved not to have to keep up the Jenny Godgift voice.

Antiochus Bland, all eyes and smile, had put out his warm, wet hand to be kissed when Preiss presented her to him. Ever since, he had paid her no attention.

Now, after the evening rituals, Bland was in conference. Genevieve had to stand still in an itchy black robe, stacked against the wall of the temple inner sanctum like a mummified grandparent. She was one of several sisters in attendance on Bland and his cadre of cronies. Preiss had told her to act like an ordinary attendant, unless provoked. She was getting lost inside her impostures: she was a Bretonnian vampire pretending to be a live country lass dressed in the robes of Morr to seem like a serving wench while acting as a body-guard. She would have liked to see Eva Savinien pull that little lot off.

With Bland was Sister Liesel, the visionary behind the holding-up-a-severed-vampire-head poster and the skewered-bat-toy arrangement. She was working her way down a long list of petty matters, mostly to do with news items placed with the venerable *Spieler* or the scandalous *Boulevardpresse*.

'As you remember, Temple Father,' said Sister Liesel, 'some concern was expressed that by putting so much weight on the broadsheets we were neglecting the vital illiterate segment of the citizenry. It is still a sad fact that barely three in ten Altdorf households contain someone who can read and write. Our vital message must be delivered to the whole of the city.'

'The masses will follow the elite,' said the freckle-faced but venerable Father Knock, who had a habit of passing his thin fingers through his thinner red hair, constantly trying to rearrange it over his orange-ish expanse of scalp. He had been Temple Father before Bland and seemed to think all this vampire-slaying a distraction from the proper business of the Cult of Morr. 'It has always been that way, and that way it always shall be.'

'Actually, father, it's a misconception that the most influential people are literate,' said Liesel. 'Many aristocratic families actively discourage their sons from learning to read. The finer houses retain a pet scholar to read aloud any letters or papers that might be necessary. In the von Sutin household, my brothers were schooled only in hunting, duelling and wenching. My father graciously permitted my useless female head to be filled with letters so I could perform minor tasks. Reading out the results of wrestling matches upon which he had placed unwise wagers, for instance. As above, so below – only inkies like me can read or care to.'

Genevieve had known straight off that Sister Liesel was the real danger in the temple. She had set Bland down as one of those people who were obsessed with vampires but (literally) wouldn't recognise one if it kissed his hand, but the scribe-proclaimer was cooler and more calculating. Sister Liesel's fingers were permanently ink-stained from all her ledgers and scrolls, but the eyes behind her thick spectacles were clear and clever. It was her job not to miss much, and Genevieve had hung back to avoid coming to her notice.

'How shall we reach these unfortunate – indeed, unenlightened – souls, high and low?' asked Bland.

'I have taken care of that,' said Sister Liesel. 'I have hired criers to proclaim stories of the campaign in the streets, simplified versions of the material we have supplied to the broadsheets. The story of your swift action of last night has been heard in every square and market-place. This direct manner serves us well, but I have given some thought to subtler methods. I understand, Temple Father, that you found Detlef Sierck unsympathetic to our good works?'

Genevieve bit her lip. Detlef had told her about Bland's visit.

Bland shook his head sadly. 'He will come round, sister, but for the moment he is insensible – indeed, blinded – to the danger. A sad, sad case. A man of such talent, burdened by such old-fashioned notions.'

'If the theatre will not serve the temple, then we must have our own theatre.'

'Sister Liesel,' blurted Father Knock, 'The expense, the expense! Our coffers are already depleted, what with the night-patrols and the purchase of extra equipment. Why, our debts to the silversmiths alone run into…'

The sister waited for Bland to dismiss Knock's protest, then continued: 'I agree that the establishment of a conventional theatre is beyond us for the moment, but our grant to the mummers has yielded excellent results.

Vampireslayer is very popular with the young. It is my proposal that we extend this policy and sponsor a number of puppet-theatre booths. It is a long-established tradition among the masses to leave their children in front of the puppets as they busy themselves drinking or buying groceries. Why should we not take advantage of that neglect, to offer instruction as well as entertainment?'

Liesel produced a very inky bundle of manuscript.

'I might not be Jacopo Tarradasch, but I am in my own small way a playwright. This is my rewritten version of the popular history *Kattarin and Pavel*. Temple Father, you will be pleased to learn that I have given the vampire-slaying Tsarevich several choice speeches extracted from your own recent public pronouncements. Of course, I've told the carver to make the puppet of Pavel an endearing likeness of yourself. You are our public face in this campaign, our sharpest weapon against the night.'

Genevieve remembered the real Pavel as tall, fork-bearded and (thanks to the tsarina's temper) one-armed. She occasionally wondered how he had managed to do the deed, but supposed he got someone to hold the stake against the old monster's heart while he wielded the mallet.

'This is all very encouraging, sister. What do the people think?'

Genevieve understood another of Liesel's innovations was a miniature census, whereby she sent her apprentices into the streets in secular dress and had them ask passersby pointed questions about the Temple of Morr and Antiochus Bland, and vampires and what should be done about them.

'This afternoon's poll is a significant advance on yesterday's. Fully two-thirds of those we approached were of the "ashes or under the ground" persuasion, which means a switch of many from the "mildly troubled by vampires" to the "strongly hate and fear" category. Almost all the "indifferent to vampires" have gone over to "mildly troubled", and all the "nothing against vampires" fools have switched their tune to "indifferent". I venture to think that by next week, the "indifferents" will have vanished like dew in the morning. Our census-takers are calling this the "Ibby the Fish factor".'

'Hardly in keeping with the dignity of the campaign,' said Bland.

'Their enthusiasm is strengthened by occasional levity, Temple Father. And people remember the name "Ibby the Fish" better than... what was it?'

'Ibrabod Furtwingle? Iblochal Fonebonio?'

'I rest my case, Temple Father. In point of fact, it was Ibrahim Fleuchtweig.'

'There, I would have got it eventually.'

'Without a doubt. But most people have not your gifts. Last night, Ibby the Fish was a dead dockyard bully. Then he was a martyr to humankind, preyed upon by the undead. Now, he is a destroyed potential vampire, the first vanquished foe in the campaign.'

'Surely, not everyone who suffers a vampire bite rises from the dead?' said Knock. 'We'd be overrun.'

'The alchemists are still debating the matter,' said Liesel.

'That's something else we must change,' said Bland, eyes alight. 'Wasting – indeed, squandering – treasury funds on trying to *understand* the undead. What we need from alchemists are better, surer ways of killing – indeed, exterminating – the fiends, not airy-fairy theories of how they came to be. Evil is beyond understanding. It should just be burned out or cut away.'

Liesel clapped, and glanced around the room. The other sisters clapped too, and Genevieve joined in. With others carrying the applause, Liesel pulled out a tablet and stylus and wrote down what Bland had said.

'I'll have that in the *Spieler* tomorrow, Temple Father,' she said, scribbling furiously. '"Wasting trees... funds... trying to *understand*... we need from alchies... better, surer ways of exterminating... not airy-fairy theories... evil beyond understanding... should be burned out or cut away." Very well said.'

Genevieve hoped the meeting was over. She was sure her face-paint needed a touch up.

'The other matter,' said Brother Preiss, who hadn't spoken throughout Liesel's report.

'Ah yes,' said Sister Liesel. 'We need to be careful.'

Preiss clapped his hands once and the sisters began to file out of the sanctum. Genevieve wasn't sure whether she should join them, but Preiss caught her eye and kept her back. When the others were gone, Liesel and Knock swivelled in their chairs to look at her.

'Mistress Godgift is our new secret armament,' said Preiss, proudly. 'She has rare qualities.'

Liesel lowered her spectacles to assess Genevieve.

'I suppose a bodyguard who looks like a bodyguard is too much to ask for.'

'They're easy to find, sister,' said Preiss. 'Too easy. Our enemies can smell them streets away. They'll overlook Sister Jenny.'

Liesel didn't seem convinced, but let it drop.

'Do we know more of the plot?' Bland asked. 'I confess I'm almost excited to know that the vampires of the World's Edge have vowed to put an end to me. It shows we're doing the right thing, rattling the proper cages.'

'Some cages should be left alone,' muttered Knock.

Preiss put his big hands on the table.

'A vampire assassin is stalking you, Temple Father,' he said. 'That much we knew, but our spies now tell us she is already in Altdorf. She has been seen.'

'*She?*' Bland's smile stretched almost to his eyes. 'A bitch vampire?'

'And a practiced murderer. By her hand died Wladislaw Blasko, Lord Marshal of the city of Zhufbar, and Graf Rudiger von Unheimlich, Master of the League of Karl-Franz.'

It was all Genevieve could do not to goggle her eyes like an idiot.

'We are up against a cunning and deadly creature, Temple Father,' said Preiss. 'None other than the vampire Genevieve Dieudonné!'

XI

Melissa led Genevieve's pet down the Street of a Hundred Taverns, weaving him carefully in and out of the late-evening crowds. It was late summer (which all vampires hated because of the long light evenings) and the last of the pink still streaked the sky. A lot of convivial drinkers were on the street, outside their chosen hostelries. Only the sotten patrons of the Drunken Bastard preferred to skulk in shadow as they got miserably soused. She happened, from merest chance, to peek into Slut Alley, where Altdorf's cheapest harlots plied their trade standing up with skirts tucked into their belts. Sierck clapped his big hand over her eyes and hurried her on, scolding like a proper responsible adult.

She didn't want to admit it, but she was starting to become fond of the bearish Detlef Sierck – not in a liquid lunch sort of way, since she respected her grand-get's grazing rights, but in the way she had felt about the very best of her foster parents down through the centuries since her 'coach accident'. Not many shortlivers could make her laugh, but Sierck could. She had a shrewd idea that was why Genevieve was so drawn to him, not for his genius or the quality of his blood or the stoutness of his heart. A sense of humour was rare in the higher races, as demonstrated by the Three Little Clots, and Sierck had the knack of being funny in that way which meant she wasn't sure whether he was trying or not. And she was even starting to like being called 'Missy'.

'Disgraceful,' said a thin-nosed cleric of Ulric. 'Look at that old reprobate dragging a poor child into a district like this. Obviously, his devotion to the daemon drink exceeds any responsibility he ought to feel for the moral welfare of the young.'

Melissa noticed the man was standing outside the Crooked Spear, sipping a thin tube of something green.

'And what are you doing in a whoreboy's haunt, father,' she snapped. 'Missionary work?'

The cleric sniffed with dignity, 'Precisely.'

'Pull the other one, Doris,' said a painted halfling lad. 'It's got antlers on.'

Sierck tugged her away.

'Are you getting into trouble again, Missy?'

'Defending your honour, uncle.'

'That can take care of itself.'

In the street outside the Sullen Knight, half a dozen separate brawls were coalescing into one big fight. A watchman blustered and waved his cudgel, but none of the bruisers noticed.

'Evening, Dibble,' said Sierck to the copper.

Dibble saluted with his cudgel.

'Quiet night…?' Sierck commented.

A bitten-off ear was spat into the gutter.

'Seen worse, Mr Sierck,' said Dibble. 'Did you hear about Ibby the Fish? That Tio Bland is an ass's arse, if you ask me. And Sergeant Munch isn't so polite about him. Ibby was no more a vampire than your little girl there. What's your name, missy?'

'Lady Melissa d'Acques,' she said.

'"Missy" will do,' said Sierck, slipping a hand into her hood and ruffling her curls.

'Would you like a candied pear?' asked Dibble.

'I'm not to take sweets from strange men,' she said.

'Very wise.'

A scatter of teeth spread over the cobbles. Melissa felt her own fangs sliding from their gumsheaths.

'Can we go, uncle, all the blood is making me…'

'Sick? Yes, of course. Come along, Missy. Evening, Dibble.'

'Evening, Mr Sierck.'

Sierck steered her around the brawl, shielding her with his body when some unfortunate came flying across the street. At the centre of the fight was a one-eyed sailor with anchor tattoos on his muscle-swollen forearms. Green juice slobbered over his chin, marking him as an addict to some vegetable drug.

Shortlivers had so many bad habits.

'Now where is this place? The Crescent Moon?'

Sierck had been looking up at inn-signs. That wouldn't help him.

'The sign is painted above the door, in black on a blackboard. You have to have sharp eyes like mine to see it.'

'Very clever.'

'In the circumstances, if you ran a tavern for vampires would you want to advertise with letters of green flame?'

'You have a point, Missy.'

'So I do. Several, in fact, uncle. And here we are.'

The door was in a wall across an alley between the Seven Stars and the Crown and Two Chairmen. Anyone not in the know would take it for a blocked-off shortcut to the next street.

Melissa knocked in a complex rhythm on the door. A peephole opened. Red eyes stared out at Sierck, narrowed and hostile. Sierck pointed down at Melissa's head. She smiled up and saw approval.

'Long live the dead,' she recited.

The door was open in a flash. Melissa and Sierck were pulled inside, and the door closed as if it had never been open.

This was the Crescent Moon, Altdorf's famous vampire tavern.

XII

When the meeting was concluded, Genevieve almost gave herself away. With Detlef's blood still coursing through her and hours until cockcrow, she was at her most awake. It took moments to realise she was now expected to go to bed. She'd been given her own cell, off the temple's central cloister, near enough the Temple Father's apartments to be on call in case of an emergency.

This alone earned her the enmity of Mother Superior Debora, who believed all novices should sleep in a dormitory and put in months of silent sweeping and prayer before being allowed to light an incense taper, let alone given her own private cell and entrusted with special duties. Debora was an old crony of Father Knock's, part of a grumbling faction within the Cult of Morr dismissively referred to as 'Old Temple'. Genevieve had picked up, from close observation, that a good two-thirds of ordinary clerics were of the Old Temple persuasion. But Bland's Boyos ran the cult: those who expressed no enthusiasm for his vampire-slaying campaign were relegated to menial duties, those who climbed aboard his band-wagon (like the sham Jenny Godgift) were advanced double-time to the inner circle.

Alone in her tiny room, she considered the latest surprise.

So, Genevieve Dieudonné was expected, to come as an assassin. Admittedly, she'd once been blackmailed by former chancellor Mornan Tybalt, now in retirement-cum-exile beyond the Middle Mountains, to assassinate the odious Graf Rudiger von Unheimlich. As things had turned out, she had found cause to kill the graf, but she hadn't done it for Tybalt and she hadn't collected blood-coin on von Unheimlich. As for Wladislaw Blasko, he'd fallen into the Black Water without so much as a push from her. In that messy little business, so tidied up in Detlef's play, she had been trying to *prevent* an assassination.

She'd stopped Oswald killing the Emperor, too.

She did not murder people. Especially not for money.

But the Cult of Morr had serious intelligence that suggested otherwise. Could it even be true? Had Lady Melissa clouded her mind with her elder's powers of fascination, leaving orders in the back of her brain which would catch light when she heard a particular bell and drive her to fetch off Antiochus Bland's head with a single blow?

It wasn't likely.

Brother Preiss and Sister Liesel had spoken of 'deep cover' agents within the camp of the enemy. They knew that Genevieve had been summoned to the city, and had a fair idea that she was the vampire who escaped the mob in the Konigplatz two days ago. Surely, no vampire would collaborate with Bland's Boyos, but many of the undead had living serfs, lovers and human cattle. Those who shunned the light of day needed tombs and coffins guarded. Many of those full humans must seethe with resentment against their ever-thirsty masters.

According to the insurrectionist poet Prince Kloszowski, whom she had met in Tilea, Professor Brustellin – father of the revolutionist movement – likened all aristocrats to the titled vampires of Sylvania, metaphorically draining the blood of their inferiors. It stood to reason that, come the revolution, the undead oppressors would be hunted down in their own lairs by their own minions. If she had to spend her days hauling away bloodless peasant corpses left to rot by Baron Wietzak of Karak Varn, with only the occasional whipping in the way of thanks, she'd sign up with Bland's campaign too.

She started wondering whether another Undead War might not be the answer. It'd thin out the ranks of the truly atrocious, and teach the survivors to mind their manners. Then, she realised she had been swayed by Bland, had started to think like him. She wondered if he had his own power of fascination, an inbuilt knack like scrying or firestarting. That would explain his rapid ascendance, and the sudden appearance of his fanatical following.

Sitting on her cot, she listened out. She could hear clerics washing, using the jakes, undressing, going to bed, snoring. When the temple was silent, she ventured from her cell.

Bland's apartments were guarded by hand-picked men, closer in ability to Brother Preiss than Willy and Walther. The general defences of the building were good: nothing that would keep out a creature who could transform into a silent mist but generally up to the job. A system of bell-alarms was set to trip the unwary intruder: it took some care to get around without setting the things off. She was glad of the opportunity to practise her night-skills.

She took the opportunity to snoop.

Across the cloister quadrangle, a single candle-flame burned. Many dramatic situations began with a single candle-flame burning.

Genevieve crept close and saw into a small chapel.

Beneath the spreading wings of a huge stuffed raven – sacred bird of Morr, of course – a cleric was bowed over an altar. No, that wasn't it at all. The cleric was Liesel von Sutin. She was not at her devotions but bent over a desk, scratching at a scroll with a long black quill. She hummed tunelessly and almost beneath the range of human hearing, her mouth set in determined concentration. She had taken off her spectacles and perched them irreverently on the raven's glassy beak.

Genevieve relaxed. The scribe-proclaimer wasn't likely to notice her.

The story the cleric had half-told at the meeting struck a chord of sympathy with Genevieve. Her own father, dead for centuries, had no sons to favour over his daughters, but he had distinct ideas on what was becoming for a dutiful girl of good family. Even Chandagnac had given her the Dark Kiss expecting a devoted servant for eternity, something between a mistress and a mother. Before becoming a vampire, Genevieve had considered a clerical life – it was a traditional path for the daughters of minor aristocracy 'with too much character' (which was to say, too obnoxious) to be eased out of the mansion by an arranged marriage.

Liesel von Sutin was the cleverest person in the temple, yet she was trapped again – working like a slave, awake when everyone else was comfortably in bed. All to fulfil the cracked dreams of a man who wasn't even a father or husband to her.

Did Liesel love Tio Bland? The Temple Father's 'dear wife and three lovely children' were staying in the country at the moment, and he could easily satisfy a passing interest in the worshipful scribe-proclaimer. Genevieve was surprised to find herself believing he was committed enough to his image of self not to take advantage of any female opportunity that came his way in the course of his campaign. Maybe that made it worse: to love someone for their faithfulness to another. That must be a nasty burr under anyone's chemise.

Liesel turned and held up her candle.

'Who's there?' she whispered. Genevieve saw she had reached for an icon – not a raven of Morr, but a dove of Shallya.

'Sister Jenny,' Genevieve said. 'I couldn't sleep.'

Liesel was relieved and dropped the dove.

'I know how you feel,' she said. 'I don't sleep. Haven't for years, except in cat-naps. I work through the night. There's so much to do.'

Genevieve stepped into the chapel.

Sister Liesel unhooked her spectacles from the raven and put them on. They made her eyes seem enormous and watery.

'You're Preiss's pit-fighter?'

'I do what I have to,' Genevieve said.

'You've lost your accent, I hear.'

Genevieve's nails sharpened. She kept her hands in the sleeves of her robe.

'Never let the mask slip around men,' said Liesel. 'Never let them know you're not a foolish girl. Take my example.'

'Everyone knows you're not a fool.'

'Exactly, and look where it's got me. What do you think of this?'

Liesel held up a sketch. A fanged she-creature bearing down on a resolute, scythe-wielding Tio Bland. The sister had used red ink for bloodied eyes and fangs.

'That's our enemy,' she said. 'This Dieudonné creature.'

Genevieve wondered if there was a resemblance.

'I wish she would come and it would be over,' said Liesel.

'She won't get near the Temple Father,' Genevieve said. 'Not on my watch.'

'Commendable spirit, sister. But I've a piece of advice for you. It might shock you. Do you care to hear it?'

Genevieve nodded.

'When the vampire attacks, and she *will* attack... if it comes down to a choice between saving Temple Father Bland or yourself...'

Genevieve tried to peer behind the shield of Liesel von Sutin's spectacles.

'Save yourself.'

XIII

Detlef found himself pressed against the wall by Heinrich and Helga, two creatures with the same face. Heinrich wore his hair long for a man, Helga wore hers short for a girl. They dressed in identical costumes: pale blue hose and doublets embroidered with dozens of tiny skulls. The vampires had not started out as twins, but had been together for so long that they had bled into each other, coming to look and think alike, an old married couple with centuries to manage convergence.

As one sniffed around his neck bites and the other stroked his hair with long, lacquered nails, Detlef saw a red flicker in their eyes.

'He's got the marks on him...'

The flicker passed from one to the other.

'He's been bled within the last day.'

'He is the property...'

'...of a lady elder.'

The Crescent Moon wasn't crowded, but Helga and Heinrich were vampires enough to be getting on with. Detlef realised his feet were off the floor, and he was mounted on the wall like a trophy. The vampire couple continued to examine him, as he might assess a horse he was thinking of buying.

'A strong heart...'

'...but past his prime.'

The tavern was a low-ceilinged room, a vaulted space with too few lanterns for human comfort. Behind the bar – where Genevieve had once worked – thin-faced, sharp-fanged women bustled. Above them were arrangements of leather-straps and glass tubes. With business off thanks to Clause 17, only three of these contraptions were filled with warm bodies, spigot-taps stuck into major veins so the blood could be decanted in measures for the customers. Two of the 'barrels' were fat pigs, but one was an ailing youth trussed and hung upside-down, floppy hair dangling, wriggling a little in discomfort.

Detlef understood that in less jittery times, the Crescent Moon had a surplus of applicants for the position of barrel. Some were would-be vampires hoping to meet a patron who would bestow the Dark Kiss upon them, others derived a species of perhaps-unhealthy pleasure from the binding and draining.

According to Genevieve, the latter had to be watched carefully – they would try to come back too many times and let themselves be bled empty. This barrel did not look as if he was in anything like ecstasy, and no one was drinking from him anyway.

'There are kisses enough…'

'…for us all.'

'Helga, Heinrich,' snapped Lady Melissa. 'You have shown off enough. Now let Mr Sierck go, apologise profoundly and get back to playing with yourselves. No one finds your antics charming any more. If you can't treat guests properly, you can go to your crypt and think upon your shortcomings for, oh, eighteen months.'

Gently, the vampires let him down. They brushed off his coat where it had pressed against the slightly-damp brickwork. One pinched his bottom, but he let it pass.

'We respect the lady elder…'

'…and accord you courtesy.'

'That sounds awfully grudging, you two. Do I have to remind you of the circumstances of our last meeting? You were seeking shelter from witchfinders. A certain gracious lady elder obliged you with a carriage. One or other of you would have suffered a nasty beheading. And we all know how long the survivor would have lasted.'

The vampires bowed to Melissa.

'You are an honoured guest, living man…'

'…and you are welcome in the Crescent Moon.'

'That's better. Now, leave us alone.'

Helga and Heinrich faded backwards into the shadows. Their pale, slightly-glowing faces seemed to linger a moment, then went out like candles. Detlef heard them creeping away.

'Some of us regret the loss of the looking glass, and will go to great lengths to provide themselves with reflections.'

'There's a story there, Missy.'

'Oh, I hope not. Couldn't you write something amusing for a change? I always liked *A Farce in the Fog*. Whatever happened to your early, funny plays?'

'The world stopped making me laugh.'

'Gené has a lot to answer for, if you ask me. It is my considered opinion, and I've had a long time to form it, that no work of narrative art can be truly great unless it contains at least one good laugh. All Tarradasch's tragedies have clowns in them.'

Melissa looked comically serious, lecturing him in this mausoleum.

'There, you're smiling again. Let's just blend in with the crowd, and you let me do the talking.'

They made their way past empty tables to the bar.

At the far end, a scarecrow creature wrapped in a tattered black shroud looked down at a bowl of spiced pig-blood. It opened a hole in the cerements around its face and unrolled a long, tubelike tongue into the blood, then proceeded noisily to drain its dinner.

'You don't want to know about the Mosquito Man,' said Melissa.

Detlef silently agreed with her.

Melissa rapped her tiny knuckles on the bar.

'Katya, some service, if you please.'

One of the barmaids came over. Her flat, pretty face was covered with soft, silky hair. She had slit pupils and permanent fangs.

'Lady Melissa, what is your pleasure?'

'Who's the "special"?'

Melissa thumbed at the human barrel.

'A student of the Dark Arts. Making good on a wager he lost. We've had better, but at least he's free of disease. With business down, we take what we can get. The girls have been nipping from him all night and none have dropped dead.'

'Very well, I shall have a glass of the special.'

'Coming right up,' said Katya, holding a goblet under the student's neck and opening the spigot. The barrel shook as the flow filled the goblet to the brim. Detlef saw the straps around his head included a leather-ball gag in his mouth, doubtless to keep him quiet so as not to upset the delicate sensibilities of the customers.

'We've a barrel-place saved for Tio Bland if he ever finds the doorway,' said Katya. When she mentioned the Temple Father's name, her cat-face contorted into a jungle snarl. 'There'd be a queue out onto the street if we could chalk his name up on the bill of fare.'

Detlef nudged Melissa.

'I was forgetting myself,' she said. 'Do you have anything for living people? What is it they drink? Tea, wine, milk?'

Katya looked as if an indecent suggestion had been made.

'We don't usually serve *his kind* in here,' she said, pointedly not looking at Detlef, 'but since you're such a favoured customer, I'll see if we can't scare something up.'

The barmaid called to a junior, a girl-faced woman with snow-white hair and blue bat tattoos on her swanny neck. Katya addressed her in a language Detlef didn't know, which seemed to have miaows in it. The other barmaid replied, without much enthusiasm, but scurried off in little steps. She wore a skirt that was almost immodestly tight (and limiting) from thigh to ankle, but spread out like octopus tentacles around her feet.

'Gela thinks she saw some wine about. We keep a little in the cellar, to top up the barrels.'

Melissa looked at her own goblet.

'It's been a long, dry spell,' she said, then lifted the drink and sucked it down at a single draught, her movement a blur. With red on her lips, Melissa's eyes burned like flares and Detlef thought he saw a jewel-faceted skull under suddenly-transparent flesh. Then, the elder vampire shook her head, setting her curls bouncing, and swallowed. She looked like a little girl again.

'Here,' said Katya, grudging.

A dusty mug of weak wine was shoved across the bar towards him. It sloshed a bit. Melissa ordered another measure of the special.

'Two is my limit,' she said. 'Must keep a clear head.'

Detlef took a swig of the wine and decided to leave the rest. It had gone to vinegar years ago.

'Someone in here will know something,' said Melissa. 'It's just a question of knowing who to ask.'

'A brilliant observation, Missy.'

'Think you could have found this place on your own, Herr Genius? Or that you'd have fought off the Necksuck Twins?'

'I concede that you are far more fearsome than me.'

'So you should.'

Melissa's second drink came, and she sipped this one, casting her eyes around the room.

'Anyone unusual been in lately?' she asked Katya.

The cat-vampire shrugged. 'Most of the unusuals have been staying away. A lot of the regulars have left the city. Some have gone underground.'

'She means that those with crypts and graves are lying in them, bloated on their last meals, hoping to sleep for seventy-five years or so and wake up in a world without Bland's Boyos. It's not a stupid thing to do. I myself snoozed through the Undead Wars, surrounded by pressed and dried flowers. I woke up to find a shrine thrown up around me and a group of outcast dwarf miners worshipping me as some sort of sleeping martyr princess. They'd somehow got hold of a handsome prince whose kiss was supposed to bring me back to life.'

Melissa sipped.

'Does this story have a happy ending?' he asked.

'Oh yes. Well, sort of. I drained the prince and raised him as my get. He had to be put down, though. The red thirst made him blood simple. He killed those dear little dwarfs. And all their animal companions. And quite a few other people, actually. These things happen. A lot of vampires can't hold their drink like me. I have learned much in my many, many years.'

She had finished her second special.

'Just one more, I think, Katya. Since it comes after a long fast. And make it a double.'

'Glad to oblige, my lady.'

Melissa was beginning to glow. She was sat cross-legged on a tall stool. She was still wrapped in her furs, which made her face all the tinier.

'Ask the girl if she knows about Ibby the Fish?' Detlef suggested.

'I was getting to it, Mr Genius. Who's in charge of this investigation, eh? Don't hurry me. Shortlivers always hurry too much. Katya, you heard him. Any word on the late Ibrahim Fleuchtweig?'

'He was a Fish,' said Katya. 'Hooks got him. End of story.'

'I thought as much.'

'Vampires don't bother Fish. Or Hooks, come to that. It's one thing to have a cult on a campaign to wipe you out, but it's a lot more serious if one of the dock gangs gets a down on you. Sleeping a century won't be much use then. Those bravos tell their children and their children's children to keep up a feud. Look at the Hooks and Fish, themselves. Been at each other's throats since the time of Sigmar.'

'So all this business with the posters and the proclamations, making out that Tio Bland prevented Ibby from rising as a vampire? That's just...'

'Wormshit,' said Katya. 'Now, if you'll excuse me, I have to drain the pig again. Mosquito Man has finished his appetiser.'

The barmaid moved away. She had a certain lithe, catlike grace, and the back of her dress bustled out suggesting a tail. Detlef wondered how one would manage her without getting seriously clawed.

'You have to stroke the fur the right way.'

He was shocked to be so transparent. 'Missy,' he said, haughtily, 'I don't know what you mean.'

'Liar.'

'Well, yes.'

'I won't tell Gené, but only if you promise to write something about me. Something light and charming. No orphans in the snow, no deaths at the dead of night. Just delights.'

'I shall try.'

Looking across the bar to the entrance archway, Detlef saw a pair of black boots on the stairs. A newcomer had been admitted. A black cloak followed the boots, and then a sallow face.

'Ah-hah,' said Detlef. 'I thought as much.'

He knew the new patron at once. The fellow had the decency to look shifty at being caught out.

'If it isn't the Sylvanian scene-shifter, "Alvdnov Renastic". Or should I say, anagrammatically... Vlad von Carstein!'

The exposed von Carstein raised his cloak to ward off the truth.

'Don't be silly, Mr Genius,' said Melissa. 'He's not a vampire.'

'Then what's he doing here?'

She scrunched up her face, like a very drunk person trying to seem sober, and thought about his question.

'I've no idea. Let's ask him. Avldovn Rascinet, whatever your name is, come here and be grilled severely. Hop to it, scene-shifter.'

She started hiccoughing, which was something he didn't think vampires did.

Renastic, not denying anything, slunk over at them. His long cloak was bulked out, making the scene-shifter look like a hunchback.

Melissa pounded her fists against the bar. She had no breath to hold, but she banished the hiccoughs somehow.

'Must be something in that student,' she said. 'He's probably a secret weirdroot-chewer. I'm tired, Mr Genius. Give me a cuddle.'

She lurched, almost falling from her stool, tumbling into his arms. Gingerly, he held her to him like a baby, patting her back. She laid her head on his shoulder and mumbled about wanting to sleep.

Renastic didn't know how to take this.

Helga and Heinrich, noticing Melissa was *hors de combat*, had crept back, and were paying keen attention.

'So you're not a vampire?' Detlef asked.

'I never said I was,' said the Sylvanian.

'But your name?'

'It's what you said it was. Vlad von Carstein. Count Vlad von Carstein, actually. The fifteenth to hold the title. I prefer not to use it.'

Detlef pointed with his freer hand, shifting Melissa up closer in his grip.

'And you expect us not to suspect you!' she said.

'How would you feel having the same name as a notorious villain? Being a direct descendent of one of the most evil creatures ever to walk the Known World? Who nearly destroyed this city and the Empire? If you were called "Constant Drachenfels" at birth, wouldn't you think up something else as soon as you could?'

That sounded reasonable.

'But you're in a vampire tavern?'

'Family obligations. Nothing I'm happy about. The problem with being the current Count von Carstein isn't just persecution from the likes of Tio Bland, it's all the vampires wanting you to turn into one of them and lead a holy war against the living. That's why I left Sylvania in the first place. I'm here, among the undead of Altdorf, to renounce any claim people might think I have to be considered leader of vampire-kind. I just want to get on with my life. I like working in the theatre. I've been practising my own turn, and am hoping you'll give me a spot at the next open-stage night.'

Only now did Detlef notice Renastic lacked fangs.

'What kind of turn?' he asked.

Renastic dramatically threw back his cloak to reveal a miniature version of himself attached to his arm like a parasitic twin, a smiling wooden head with a widow's peak and a sharp goatee, atop a trailing body in a child-sized evening outfit complete with cloak and shiny leather shoes.

'Gentriloquism,' said the dummy, mouth flapping.

'This is Vlad,' said Renastic, from his own mouth.

'Yes, I'm Glad,' said the dummy, with an exaggerated Sylvanian accent, 'the gloodthirsty gampire. Why did the gampire cross the road? Gecause it was suckeeng the glood of the cheecken? Hah hah hah. I got a meel-lion of 'em. Egeryone a weenner!'

Renastic made a grinning end-of-the-act grimace.

'What do you think, Mr Sierck?' he asked, eagerly.

'It needs work, Renastic.'

'Get me a gottle of glood,' shouted Vlad.

Detlef understood what Genevieve had seen in the darkened dressing room. Renastic practising his act. She would laugh when she heard.

Melissa mumbled into his shoulder, saying the act was terrible, but the stagestruck scene-shifter didn't hear.

'What does he mean, "needs work"?' said Vlad the Dummy, angrily.

'We should practise more. Think of better jokes.'

'Gullshit! What does he know? I theenk I'll suck his glood!'

'Oh don't do that, Vlad,' said Renastic, shaking the dummy angrily. 'I really must apologise, Mr Sierck...'

'Gug off, human!'

'...he gets carried away sometimes. Very temperamental. Like all vampires.'

Renastic put his hand over the dummy's mouth, stifling further protests. Vlad's head shook in fury.

It was a reverse of Helga and Heinrich. Two people in one body, rather than one person in two.

Weird.

He set Melissa on her stool, and shook her. She came awake, showing red eyes and fangs.

'I've got the beginnings of a very bad headache,' she said.

'I know the feeling.'

Helga and Heinrich had slid down the bar. They were standing either side of Renastic, hands slipping in and out of his pockets, tongues darting at his face.

'Fresh blood...'

'...noble blood.'

'He's a von Carstein,' Melissa said. 'You'd best leave him alone. His relatives might not take kindly to you tapping him.'

The twins huffed.

'Does every live cow who comes in here...'

'...have a patron and protector?'

'It's most vexing...'

'...and a true frustration.'

'You can bite the little one,' said Melissa.

Detlef didn't understand, until Helga – or Heinrich, it was hard to tell – darted at Vlad, and bit into wood.

'Watch my wrist,' said Renastic.

Spitting – the face of the twin who hadn't bit as contorted as that of the one who had – Helga and Heinrich withdrew again.

Renastic shrugged his hand out of Vlad and looked at his white cuff. The skin wasn't broken.

'So you aren't even an interested party in all this?' Detlef asked.

'I wouldn't say that. I don't want to be a vampire, but I'm still a Count von Carstein. I know Bland's Boyos won't make any fine distinctions when they're avenging their Temple Father's murder. I'll be just as likely to get hoisted on a stake as Baron Wietzak himself.'

'You know about the assassination plot?' said Melissa, aghast.

'Oh yes. It's all anyone talks about backstage. Kerreth had it from Antonia, who heard it from Eva's dresser, who...'

Detlef felt that Melissa had got her wish and he was back playing farce again.

'And, of course,' said Renastic, 'tonight's the night. She'll be at the temple, by now. Let's hope for all our sakes that she's not as good an assassin as she is everything else.'

'You know who Wietzak's hired killer is?' asked Detlef.
Renastic nodded.
'Doesn't everyone?'

XIV

'What was that?' said Genevieve.

'I didn't hear anything,' said Liesel von Sutin, a little too quickly.

She had forgotten she wasn't supposed to have sensitive-as-a-bat's vampire ears. It hadn't been an obvious disturbance, just a faint clanking – perhaps a stifled groan. Suggestive enough.

'I think I should check on the Temple Father.'

'He has night-guards.'

Sister Liesel held her sleeve. The woman was apprehensive, close to scared.

Genevieve's night-senses were pricking. She stretched her upper lip to cover her sharpening teeth.

'No harm in checking.'

Reluctantly, it seemed, the scribe-proclaimer let her go. Genevieve padded across the quadrangle, towards Bland's apartments. Liesel hesitated a moment, then followed. The sister's footfalls sounded very loud. Genevieve signed to her to be quieter.

Genevieve ducked under a hanging, and knew something was wrong.

The first guards were sprawled at their posts.

Fresh-spilled blood hit Genevieve's nostrils like a snort of daemon dust. Her night-vision grew more acute. She saw the blood on the guards' throats as a vivid scarlet, pooling in the folds of their vestments, pulsing from twin neck-wounds. Something had crept up on these two and struck serpent-fast.

Vampire-swift.

They had been attacked as they took a snack break. Bread and cheese was spread around, soaked in blood – so much *blood!* Broken mugs spilled strong milky tea. With so many smells making her eyes sting, she had to concentrate. Blood, tea, milk, cheese. And something else, something herbal and repulsive.

'Merciful Shallya,' swore Liesel, almost falling over the bodies. 'Are they…'

'No, but they will be if their wounds aren't treated.'

Genevieve, suppressing the red thirst screaming from the savage stem of her brain, checked the wounded guards, feeling for heartbeats.

'Is this a vampire attack?' Liesel asked.

'It looks like it, doesn't it?'

Sister Liesel was suffering from shock, quivering with potential panic. She was demanding attention when Genevieve ought to be following the trail.

'Stay here and see to these men,' Genevieve ordered. 'Press something over the bites. Anything to stop the bleeding.'

'Don't go,' Liesel said. 'Jenny, please.'

'I have to.'

She pushed through the door. Bland's apartments were reachable only by doors at the end of this corridor. There should be two more guards.

The doors were open and the guards lay bleeding on the floor.

The herbal smell was more noticeable. Genevieve almost staggered.

She sprinted silently down the corridor.

Inside Bland's quarters, a small fire burned on a carpet, a dropped lamp in the middle of it. Flames cast shadows on the low ceiling, where a painted Morr presided over the torments and rewards of the beyond.

Genevieve caught the assassin at her work.

The blonde woman held Temple Father Bland in a vampire embrace, bending him over backwards at the knees. The cleric was in his nightshirt and cap, awake but frozen with terror, open eyes twitching, perpetual smile a rictus grin.

Blood on his neck.

'Stop,' said Genevieve.

The assassin raised her bloodied face and looked at her.

It was as if the gift of a reflection had returned. Genevieve was looking into her own face. Rather, at the nightmarish worst she had ever looked – a mask lit by wavering flame, eyes red bursts, finger-length fangs bloodied, streaks of gore in her hair.

'Who dares disturb the feeding of the vampire Genevieve?'

The voice was her own but different, coming from outside her skull.

Dazzled by the firelight and befuddled by all the spilled blood, Genevieve wondered what this creature was. Had her vampire self detached from her own body and set out on its own to kill?

Then, she saw through it.

'Do I really look like that?'

The assassin recognised her.

'You!' she said, startled.

'How inconvenient for you,' said Genevieve.

The assassin dropped Bland, whose head fell dangerously near the fire. He was twitching, still alive.

'Not inconvenient at all,' said the assassin, whom Genevieve saw was taller than her, with a longer reach. 'The vampire Genevieve murders Tio Bland, and is then captured and destroyed at the scene of the crime. It's better than the original plan.'

'Do you really think you can be me, Eva?'

'I've been playing you for years,' said Eva Savinien. 'The critics say

I'm much better at it than you were. In the Genevieve Dieudonné business, you're an amateur.'

Genevieve faced herself. The fangs and claws were functional fakes. The hair was a wig.

Only the blood was real.

'How much is Wietzak paying you? Surely you could do better as a royal mistress?'

'Wietzak? He's not the half of it, sister.'

'You're not my sister.'

Genevieve leaped at Eva, but tripped over Bland, whose bulk wrinkled the carpet on the slick stone floor. Eva darted out of the way with something close to vampire swiftness. The actress had been possessed once, by something called the animus – it had emerged from the ruins of the fortress of Drachenfels for revenge. When it quit this host, the animus had left something of itself behind.

The blow came out of the dark, and caught the back of her head as if landed by a mace.

This was not like fighting a living woman.

Genevieve, lifted off the floor, sailed across the room. She hammered against a case of old books, which tumbled around her as the shelves collapsed. A heavy wooden board struck her head like a hammer. She put out her hands to steady herself and her sharpened fingers sank into book-pages. They were all blank, impressive bindings with nothing inside. That said something about their owner.

Still, she was doing her best to save the man's life.

'He won't be grateful,' purred Eva, suddenly close to her face. 'Tio Bland will still hate you. I've just opened his throat a little. You must be *thirsty*. All this blood spilled and none to drink. You must hate him, Genevieve. I'm not a vampire, and I hate him. I'll help you get away. You can have the credit. You'll be a heroine to your kind. You'll be another Kattarin...'

'One was enough, play-actress.'

Genevieve jabbed out with the heel of her hand, smartly clipping Eva's chin. One of the assassin's fangs was jarred loose. Her eyes widened as she nearly choked on it. She spat the thing out, a carved chicken bone.

Eva's clawfingers – steel-and-silver sheaths with curved barbs – came for Genevieve's face. The tips just raked skin, and dreadful black pain slashed across her cheek, eating to the bone.

She was out of the way of the second strike.

From behind, she got a hold on Eva's neck, and wrenched off her wig.

Eva's hands came up and tore off Genevieve's own wig. It had been securely attached and a lot of hair came with it.

They stood with each other's hair in their hands.

The fire spread to the fallen volumes. Flamelight rose. Bland was trying to get up on his hands and knees but kept falling. Blood trickled from his mock-bites.

Eva shredded Genevieve's wig and let the segments fall. She was skilled with her sharp killing-talons. And she'd had the foresight to use silver.

'I can take out your heart, lady leech.'

'You have to find it first.'

Mantis-style would leave her sides open. Too easy to get to the heart under the arms. Genevieve knew she'd have to fight like the bare-knuckles bruisers in Arne's gymnasium, elbows close to her ribs, punching with jabs, concentrating on the head and belly.

She damned Eva for her extra height, her extra inches of reach.

She slammed at Eva's head, with the same left-right-left, hook-jab-jab combination Preiss had tried on her. Eva ducked the hook, but took both the jabs. Her left eye was bruised and bloodied, then her cheek-bone broken. Genevieve stood back and pivoted, arching out her leg, knee loose, foot stretched. She landed her boot-toe in the big eye-cheek wound.

Eva gave out a satisfying yelp.

'Time for a final bow, understudy,' suggested Genevieve.

Eva recovered, faster than Genevieve had expected, and reached, taking a grip on Genevieve's side, on the soft part below the rib-cage.

Four needles of agony cut through her robe and lanced into her body. She opened her mouth in a scream that wouldn't come.

Eva took another hold, on Genevieve's shoulder. A thumb-thorn stuck into her neck. Hot hurt spread, covering her from upper arm to upper ear. Half her vision was fuzzy. Eva's face was half-blur, half-mask-of-hate. Eva held Genevieve pinned, squeezing her side. But the thorn in her neck was the killing tool – it probed, parting veins and stringmeat, and scraped her jaw-bone.

It was agonising.

'The first time I played you,' Eva said, conversationally, 'in the *Treachery of Oswald* revival, I slept with Detlef. When this is over, I'll go back to him. I'll gut him and let you take the blame. You'll be remembered as a monster.'

Genevieve took a firm hold on the talon stuck into her neck. The silver sheath seared her palm, but one more pain among so many could be ignored. She extracted the thorn from her flesh, twisting brutally. With a snap, she broke Eva's thumb.

Then, she hammered her forehead against the bridge of Eva's nose.

Cartilage gave way and a cloud of blood exploded all around.

Some of it went into Genevieve's mouth and she tasted Eva. There was almost nothing there.

Eva's hands went to her face.

Genevieve was free, though two of the fake fingers were still stuck in her side like white-hot arrowheads. With fast fingers and gritted teeth, Genevieve plucked the claws and threw them away.

Eva, horror-struck at the assault on her good looks, held her hands over her squashed nose. Blood poured between her fingers.

The room was on fire now.

Genevieve slung Bland over her shoulder and stepped into the corridor.

That herbal smell hit her again.

Liesel had dragged the two inner guards away. She was surrounded by four bleeding, unconscious men at the end of the corridor.

'Wake up, Brother Preiss,' shouted Genevieve.

Liesel still seemed too horrorstruck to move.

Genevieve set Bland down with the guards. His wounds were shallow, though his nightshirt was on fire. Almost absent-mindedly, Liesel patted out the flames.

'Get Preiss,' Genevieve insisted.

That smell! She knew what it was. Ground sleeprose petal, usually taken in tea. Before Eva came along, the guards had been drugged. The assassin had an ally within the Temple of Morr.

'Liesel,' Genevieve said, 'it's important. The danger isn't over. Snap out of it.'

'This isn't how it was supposed to be,' Liesel muttered. 'I told you to save yourself.'

'I'm fine. So will he be. But we must act fast...'

There was an explosion within Bland's apartments, and a crack shot through the walls. Genevieve half-turned and saw a creature of flame exploding through the doorway. Eva, burning all over, charged down the corridor, screeching, claws reaching.

Genevieve punched her in the heart, knocking her down.

She tried to smother Eva's flames – apart from other considerations, she wanted the actress-assassin alive to explain herself – but the fire kept bursting back wherever it was slapped out. Eva's face was black but for her eyes and teeth. She struggled, scratching at Genevieve though her claws were gone.

Genevieve's own clothes were smouldering.

Fire was less bad for vampires than silver. But enough flame would kill her.

A beam split above and the ceiling fell in. A broken spar plunged, jagged end like a stake, and speared into Eva's heart, stopping her writhing.

The actress died like a vampire.

Genevieve made it out of the collapsing corridor in time.

Liesel was doing her best trying to heave five heavy, insensible men away from danger.

There was other activity in the temple now.

Brother Preiss and Father Knock were here. And other brothers and sisters, half in robes, half in nightwear. The collapse of the corridor had limited the fire to Bland's apartments.

She heard Preiss order Willy and Walther to organise a bucket-passing line from the stables-pump to quell the blaze. Knock had some of his Old Temple cronies see to certain sacred items he wanted removed to a place of safety. Thoughtfully, someone tossed a pail of water over Genevieve, drenching her robes and drowning fire she hadn't noticed.

A chaplain-healer was looking at the guards and the Temple Father.

'They've been bitten,' he said.

Everyone was looking at Genevieve. Her hands, swelling and insensible from silver poisoning, went to her hair. Some of the wig-pins were still there. The last of her healthy country lass's make-up was washed away.

'Sister Jenny,' said Preiss. 'You have fangs.'

XV

'Ladies, gentlemen, excuse me,' he declared. 'I am Detlef Sierck, genius.'

Certainly, his announcement attracted attention. As a good entrance line should. Melissa gave him a little round of applause.

The central quadrangle of the Temple of Morr was smoky and crowded. A row of bleeding, insensible bodies were being seen to by a chaplain-healer and several sister-nurses. A wrestler-sized cleric – Detlef recognised Lupo Preiss from his epic bouts with Hagedorn a decade ago – had Genevieve, who seemed to be in a sorry state again, pinned to the ground. Several guards held down her arms and legs.

'That lady is Genevieve Dieudonné, my fiancée. She is under the protection of my sword. I call upon you in the name of the Empire and common decency to let her up at once. If you do not comply, I shall be forced to cut you to ribbons.'

He bowed slightly and held up his sword, blade catching the lantern-light.

A brother rushed onto the scene, holding a wooden mallet and a short sharp stake. He caught sight of Detlef's blade and skidded to a halt. He didn't hand the vampire-slaying apparatus to Preiss.

'What is this intrusion?' asked the sister with spectacles.

Detlef spotted her instantly as the one in charge. He recalled her name: Sister Liesel von Sutin.

'A rescue,' Detlef declared.

'And you've brought a *child* with you?'

Melissa smiled, showing fangs.

'Oh,' said the sister. 'That sort of child.'

In the carriage on the way over from the Street of a Hundred Taverns to the Temple of Morr, Detlef had tried to persuade Lady Melissa that it would be best if she didn't accompany him as he forced his way into a nest of vampire-slayers. She'd said she had no intention of missing out on any of the fun and had, at her age, learned to walk into and out of far worse places. When that hadn't impressed him, she just started repeating everything he said word for word in a high-pitched child-voice that scraped his nerves. Finally, he had just given in and told her not to look smug about it.

'The assassin must be destroyed,' said Preiss.

'Genevieve isn't the assassin,' said Detlef. 'She has been defamed by a woman named Eva Savinien, who came here in disguise.'

'This thing came here in disguise.'

Genevieve tried to sit up. She was bleeding from several places, had been set on fire and put out, and her white skin was blotchy with what looked like swollen insect-bites. The last of her make-up was washed away.

'You are not to call my grand-get a "thing",' said Melissa.

The child-shaped vampire walked across the quad and stood over the brothers pinning down Genevieve. Melissa tapped her foot and looked cross.

'Let her go, you bullies.'

Force of personality persuaded the clerics to slink back.

'Genevieve is a heroine,' said Melissa. 'She has saved your horrid Temple Father. I hope you'll learn a lesson about the undead from this. A living woman came to kill Tio Bland but a soulless vampire saved his life.'

Genevieve flung her long arms around Melissa's tiny neck, exhausted and grateful.

'Ugh, child,' said Melissa, 'you'll ruin the furs. How did you get so bedraggled?'

'Lady elder,' Genevieve gasped, 'my apologies.'

Genevieve still hugged her grandmother-in-darkness, face lost in voluminous fur.

Preiss looked to the injured, soliciting further orders from Bland. The Temple Father was alive but unconscious, bandages wrapped around his neck, face pale. Then, the wrestler looked to the woman in charge.

'Sister Liesel?'

The sister was thinking.

'Vampires have come among us,' she said, at last. 'And their human slaves. They must be put to the stake.'

Genevieve's face reappeared. She looked at Liesel, eyes burning.

'But, *Liesel…*'

Detlef recognised a complicated flow of emotions. The set-up within this temple was beyond instant understanding.

'Impostor, betrayer, assassin,' said Liesel, pointing at Genevieve.

Genevieve stood up, setting Melissa aside.

'No,' said Genevieve. 'I'm not the betrayer here. The assassin had help inside the temple, but not from me. Liesel, you swear by Shallya, not Morr. You are a very clever woman in a world that too rarely rewards you. I don't think you're dim enough to subscribe to Tio Bland's vampire prejudice. But you do see opportunities for advancement. After the assassination, what were you to become? The guardian of Bland's memory? Would you relay his wishes from the beyond and take control here? Make up a title like "Temple Mother" or "High Priestess? Everyone is already looking to you for orders. They've got used to it in the last months. Will you have us all killed and get back into your huddle with Baron Wietzak? Cooking up another Undead War so you can both make names for yourself?'

A lot of eyes were on the sister.

'Jenny,' she said, 'I hoped great things for you.'

'There is no Jenny. She was just pretend. Just as there was really no Liesel.'

'Brother Preiss, kill this leech. Now.'

The wrestler looked at Sister Liesel and shrugged. He made no move.

'With the Temple Father injured, I assume command here,' said Knock the elderly priest. 'A sister cannot decree the policy of the temple. Even the lowest novice brother comes in the precedence before the mother superior.'

An elderly woman in robes beamed approval. Sister Liesel fumed.

'To kill, even to kill a vampire, is to usurp the domain of Great Morr,' continued the Father, making devout signs. 'He alone decides when to take a soul. There must be no more blasphemy.'

'Aye, Father Knock,' assented Preiss.

Sister Liesel, frustrated, was still thinking. She knelt by Bland and began to shake him.

'Wake up, Temple Father, the vampires are here!'

'Leave him be,' said Father Knock.

'He's dying,' said the healer. Nothing can be done.'

'You see,' said Liesel. 'They're monsters.'

Detlef had not put away his sword. He thought he still might have to fight for Genevieve.

The brother with the stake and mallet held them up, ready for use.

Bland's eyes fluttered open. He was still smiling. His face must just be in the habit. He looked ghastly.

Father Knock muttered last rites and sprinkled incense over the Temple Father, with what Detlef intuited was a certain grim satisfaction.

'They've killed you,' Liesel told Bland.

'I was always prepared,' gasped the Temple Father, 'ready to fall first – indeed, to die – in the conflict, so long as my ending was a greater beginning. Here starts the Last Undead War, which must end with the eradication – indeed, obliteration – of the vampire taint from the world...'

To come so far and fail! Detlef would have killed Bland himself, only that seemed to be what the martyr wanted. The eager vampire-slayer tapped mallet to stake, and looked at Genevieve's chest.

'This is silly,' said Melissa. 'You, sawbones, out of my way.'

The chaplain-healer stepped back. Liesel looked electric hatred at Melissa. 'Don't let her near.'

Brother Preiss had a firm hold on Sister Liesel's shoulders.

Melissa got on her knees and crawled to Bland. She nestled into his lap, and stroked his bandaged neck. He smiled indulgently, until she showed her adorable little fang-teeth, then he cringed, eyes rolling upwards.

'Leech,' he gasped.

'Hush, silly man,' said the vampire.

Melissa raised her wrist to her mouth and bit as if into an apple, pricking her own vein.

Scarlet blood welled. She jammed the spouting wound into Bland's mouth. The Temple Father's eyes widened, and went red with the infusion. Melissa chewed away his bandages and sank her fangs into the red scratches on his neck.

Her whole body bucked as she drank deeply, sucking Bland's blood as he swallowed hers. This was how little leeches were made.

It lasted a while.

When the mutual feeding was over, Melissa dropped Bland and stood up. She was shaky on her feet, having lost as much blood as she'd drunk. Genevieve steadied her.

'He's dead,' said the chaplain-healer, hand on Bland's heart.

'Not for long,' said Melissa. 'Lay him out, and have a goat or something close by. When he wakes up, he's going to be very *thirsty*.'

'And he might want to reconsider his policy on vampires,' suggested Genevieve.

XVI

She had tried to find out what was to become of Liesel von Sutin. According to Temple Father Knock, the sister was on a retreat in the Northern Wastes, devoting herself to the simple duties of cleaning and cooking for an order of ascetic monks who had vowed never to look a woman in the eyes much less talk to one. Genevieve still wasn't sure what she thought of Liesel. She kept hearing Knock's proud statement that 'even the lowest novice brother comes in the precedence before the mother superior'. The only comfort she could take was that, as a vampire, she should live to see that change, in the Cult of Morr and throughout the human world. It would be a long while coming, though. Even Brustellinite anarchists like Prince Kloszowski, who wanted to bring down kings and lords and set peasants on an equal footing with their former masters, treated women like strange combinations of slave, slut and long-suffering mother.

The Temple of Morr wasn't issuing much news about her newest brother-in-darkness – perhaps because the responsibility for issuing any news had formerly laid with the now-closed scribe-proclaimer's office. The *Boulevardpresse* alleged that the cult's goat consumption had risen tenfold and that novices wore silver collars when attending late-night services. Tio Bland's 'dear wife and three lovely children', on an extended tour of the provinces, were not expected to return to the city this season.

The whole vampire campaign had blown over completely. Under Knock and his 'Old Temple' faction, the Cult of Morr announced a 'Back to basics' campaign, and clerics were busying themselves with their former good works and funereal duties. Clause 17 was, by quiet agreement, struck from the Sanitation Act.

Happy hour in the Crescent Moon had lasted a week. Lady Melissa would never have to pay for the special ever again.

The Vargr Breughel was looking for a new leading lady. The surprise success of Renastic and Vlad, the comedy ventriloquist and his vampire dummy, meant that the theatre could play variety to full houses while auditions were held for *Genevieve and Vukotich*. She had sensed that Detlef was working up to asking her to play herself again, and had deftly reasserted her permanent retirement from the stage.

No one had been arrested for the murder of Ibby the Fish, but Watch

Sergeant Munch announced that progress was being made on the case. The monthly number of Hooks found floating off the docks was roughly equal to the number of Fish found hooked in back-alleys.

Munch was more concerned with the 'mosquito murders', a series of gruesome deaths among well-connected criminals who had recently bought themselves out of Mundsen Keep but ran into a strange instrument of justice that sucked all the flesh out of their skins through a single puncture-wound over the heart. It was rumoured that 'Filthy Harald' Kleindeinst and his sometime partner Rosanna the Scryer were on the case, which involved a conspiracy reaching from the lowest stews of Wharf Vermin Way to the perfumed palaces of Imperial Row.

Baron Wietzak was truly dead – transfixed with hawthorn, beheaded with silver, burned in a holy fire, ashes scattered in the sunshine. Someone had told the Tsarevich Pavel Society how to penetrate his castle crypts via secret passageways unknown to anyone under a thousand years old. Melissa claimed not to know anything about that.

It turned out that Eva Savinien had been profitably moonlighting as an assassin for years, committing murders for hire during the times when she was 'resting' – though she earned far less as a killer than she did as a star actress, suggesting some compulsion lingering from her old encounter with the animus. The story of her Zhiekhill-and-Chaida life came out in the *Boulevardpresse*. The body recovered from the fire at the temple was impossible to identify and so many of her admirers hoped she was merely missing.

And Genevieve was still here. In the theatre, in the city.

She couldn't remember precisely how it had happened, but she and Detlef seemed to be engaged. Obviously, the traditional silver ring was out of the question but gold was a fair substitute.

Waking at nightfall from a day's lassitude in the divan she had insisted be installed in the office, she saw Detlef at his desk, scratching quill to parchment, a fresh candle burning. He was working on a second sonnet cycle. He was losing weight and the character lines in his face were firming up. When he was writing, he had the concentration of a dedicated schoolboy.

She watched him for several minutes before he noticed her. When he did, he smiled, set aside his pen and blotted the page.

'Tonight,' he said, 'you can read it.'

She had been waiting for that.

At once, she was across the room. She slipped into Detlef's lap, and greedily snatched up the paper. For an instant, she was disappointed to find he had not been working on a poem. He was drafting an announcement to go into the *Spieler*, of their wedding.

The ceremony would be held on stage, with the Arch-Lector of the Cult of Sigmar solemnising the vows of nuptial devotion and Honorio of the Convent of Eternal Night and Solace reading the invocations of fortune and long life. Melissa was monopolising Kerreth the costumier with many refinements of the pattern for the gown she was to wear as maid of honour. Prince Luitpold, heartbroken by the disappearance of Eva Savinien but cheered by a sudden interest in the dance stylings of Antonia Marsillach, had consented to represent the Imperial court at the wedding. He was to become official patron of the Vargr Breughel Memorial Theatre, which ought to make future censorship of Detlef Sierck productions unlikely and was 'one in the eye for the fogeys of the Imperial Tarradasch Players'. The wedding reception was to be at the Crescent Moon, which would consent to admit living people equally with the undead for the occasion and had been instructed to import vintages of quality for the cellar. Rumour had it that virgin lads from the mountains, raised on only fresh beef and purest springwater, were being brought to the city to be on offer as the special for that evening. Genevieve had issued strict instructions to Poppa Fritz and Guglielmo Pentangeli that the Three Little Clots were on no account to be allowed to organise Detlef's stag night – but had few illusions that her wishes would be acceded to in the matter.

Genevieve hummed over the announcement, then approved.

'Missy says I make up too many tragic endings,' Detlef told her. 'Just for a change, let's live happily ever after.'

'It's worth a try,' she said.

Detlef bared his neck to be kissed.

ABOUT THE AUTHOR

Kim Newman is an award-winning author, film critic and broadcaster. As 'Jack Yeovil', he wrote the popular Vampire Genevieve and Dark Future novels for Black Library. He has a vast array of further fiction credits to his name, and his passion for film has led him to write several books on the subject. He has also written for television, radio and theatre, and has directed a small film. He lives in Islington, North London.

YOUR
NEXT READ

WARHAMMER™ HORROR

THE HARROWED PATHS
by various authors

Ancient evils, dark secrets and hidden dangers abound in this collection of short horror stories from the grim worlds of Warhammer.